The Treasury of American Short Stories

The Treasury of American Short Stories

Selected and with an Introduction by

Nancy Sullivan

DOUBLEDAY & COMPANY, INC.
Garden City, New York

ISBN: 0-385-17139-0
Library of Congress Catalog Card Number 80–2438
First Edition

Printed in the United States of America

Design by Jeanette Portelli

ACKNOWLEDGMENTS

Grateful acknowledgment is made to the following for permission to reprint their copyrighted material:

"Life Isn't a Short Story," by Conrad Aiken. Copyright 1934 by North American Review Corp. Copyright renewed © 1962 by Conrad Aiken. Reprinted by permission of Brandt & Brandt Literary Agents, Inc.

"The Kugelmass Episode," copyright © 1977 by Woody Allen. Reprinted from SIDE EFFECTS by Woody Allen, by permission of Random House, Inc. Originally appeared in *The New Yorker*.

"The Egg," by Sherwood Anderson. Copyright 1921 by B. W. Huebsch, Inc. Renewed 1948 by Eleanor Copenhaver Anderson. Reprinted by permission of Harold Ober Associates, Inc.

"Sonny's Blues," from GOING TO MEET THE MAN, copyright © 1957 by James Baldwin. Reprinted by permission of The Dial Press.

"Lost in the Funhouse," copyright © 1967 by The Atlantic Monthly Company, from the book LOST IN THE FUNHOUSE by John Barth. Reprinted by permission of Doubleday & Company, Inc.

"Concerning the Bodyguard," from GREAT DAYS by Donald Barthelme. Copyright © 1978, 1979 by Donald Barthelme. Reprinted by permission of Farrar, Straus and Giroux, Inc.

"A Reasonable Man," copyright © 1976 by Ann Beattie. Reprinted from SECRETS AND SURPRISES by Ann Beattie, by permission of Random House, Inc.

"A Silver Dish," copyright © 1978 by Saul Bellow. First appeared in *The New Yorker*. Reprinted by permission Russell & Volkening, Inc. as agents for the author.

"Nothing Ever Breaks Except the Heart," copyright 1941 by *The New Yorker Magazine, Inc.*, from the book NOTHING EVER BREAKS EXCEPT THE HEART by Kay Boyle. Reprinted by permission of Doubleday & Company, Inc.

"The Night Club in the Woods" from THE COLLECTED STORIES OF HORTENSE CALISHER (Arbor House). Reprinted by permission of Candida Donadio & Associates, Inc. Copyright © 1955 by Hortense Calisher.

"Children on Their Birthdays," copyright 1948 by Truman Capote. Reprinted from SELECTED WRITINGS OF TRUMAN CAPOTE, by permission of Random House, Inc.

"Neighbour Rosicky," copyright 1932 by Willa Cather, renewed © 1960 by Executors of the Estate of Willa Cather. Reprinted from OBSCURE DESTINIES by Willa Cather, by permission of Alfred A. Knopf, Inc.

"Torch Song," copyright 1947 by John Cheever. Reprinted from THE STORIES OF JOHN CHEEVER, by permission of Alfred A. Knopf, Inc.

"Parker's Back," from EVERYTHING THAT RISES MUST CONVERGE by Flannery O'Connor. Copyright © 1965 by the Estate of Mary Flannery O'Connor. Reprinted by permission of Farrar, Straus and Giroux, Inc.

"One for the Road," copyright 1946 by John O'Hara. Reprinted from THE TIME ELEMENT AND OTHER STORIES by John O'Hara, by permission of Random House, Inc.

"A Conversation With My Father," from ENORMOUS CHANGES AT THE LAST MINUTE by Grace Paley. Copyright © 1972, 1974 by Grace Paley. Reprinted by permission of Farrar, Straus and Giroux, Inc.

"You Were Perfectly Fine," from THE PORTABLE DOROTHY PARKER. Copyright 1929, © renewed 1957 by Dorothy Parker. Originally appeared in *The New Yorker*. Reprinted by permission of Viking Penguin, Inc.

"The Grave," by Katherine Anne Porter from THE LEANING TOWER AND OTHER STORIES, copyright 1944, 1972 by Katherine Anne Porter. Reprinted by permission of Harcourt Brace Jovanovich, Inc.

"Light Timber," by Nancy Potter, copyright © 1981 by Nancy Potter. Reprinted by permission of the author.

"The Valiant Woman," from the book PRINCE OF DARKNESS AND OTHER STORIES by J. F. Powers. Copyright 1947, renewed © 1972 by J. F. Powers. Reprinted by permission of the author.

"I Always Wanted You to Admire My Fasting," from READING MYSELF AND OTHERS by Philip Roth. Copyright © 1973 by Philip Roth. Reprinted by permission of Farrar, Straus and Giroux, Inc.

"The Daring Young Man on the Flying Trapeze," by William Saroyan from AFTER THIRTY YEARS: THE DARING YOUNG MAN ON THE FLYING TRAPEZE. Copyright 1934, © 1964 by William Saroyan. Reprinted by permission of the author.

"In Dreams Begin Responsibilities," by Delmore Schwartz from IN DREAMS BEGIN RESPONSIBILITIES AND OTHER STORIES. Copyright 1937 by New Directions; copyright 1948 by Delmore Schwartz; © 1966 by Kenneth Schwartz. Reprinted by permission of New Directions.

"Three Heroines," copyright © 1975 by Peter Taylor. Reprinted from IN THE MIRO DISTRICT AND OTHER STORIES by Peter Taylor, by permission of Alfred A. Knopf, Inc.

"The Secret Life of Walter Mitty," copyright 1942 by James Thurber. Copyright © 1970 by Helen Thurber. From MY WORLD—AND WELCOME TO IT published by Harcourt Brace Jovanovich, Inc. Originally printed in *The New Yorker*.

"The Bulgarian Poetess," copyright © 1965 by John Updike. Reprinted from THE MUSIC SCHOOL by John Updike, by permission of Alfred A. Knopf, Inc. First appeared in *The New Yorker*.

"Welcome to the Monkey House," from WELCOME TO THE MONKEY HOUSE by Kurt Vonnegut, Jr. Copyright © 1967 by Kurt Vonnegut, Jr. Originally published in *Playboy*. Reprinted by permission of Delacourt Press/Seymour Lawrence.

"A Worn Path," by Eudora Welty. Copyright 1941, © 1969 by Eudora Welty. Reprinted from her volume A CURTAIN OF GREEN AND OTHER STORIES by permission of Harcourt Brace Jovanovich, Inc.

"After Holbein," by Edith Wharton from ROMAN FEVER AND OTHER STORIES. Copyright 1928 Curtis Publishing; copyright renewed. Reprinted by permission of Charles Scribner's Sons.

"The Farm," by Joy Williams, copyright © 1979 by *Antaeus*. Reprinted by permission of the author.

In Memory of Daniel F. Sullivan, Jr.

Contents

Introduction

As a distinct literary form, the short story has existed for only about a century and a half, although stories, tales, parables, and other short narratives have been spoken or written since men and women first began to communicate. A conglomeration of literary forces such as the witty eighteenth-century essay, a renewed interest in narrative "sketches" of local scenes and characters, and a revival of enthusiasm for traditional short tales and ballads stirred American writers from the very first until, by the early nineteenth century, many had already become masters of the short story's intricate, sophisticated, and challenging possibilities.

During the seventeenth and eighteenth centuries most American prose writing was utilitarian: accounts of travel and exploration, histories, biographies and autobiographies, sermons and other religious writings, and political tracts. Although some novels and plays were published earlier, long works of fiction did not gain either significant critical attention or wide readership until the 1820s with the appearance of the novels of James Fenimore Cooper. Similarly, a smattering of short fiction such as gothic narratives and character sketches had appeared late in the eighteenth century, but it was not until Washington Irving's *The Sketch Book of Geoffrey Crayon, Gent.* was published in 1820 that the short story or tale assumed a separate role in American letters. Even though Irving was less interested in the plot or characters than in the way the story was written, he did introduce in *The Sketch Book* one of the most famous characters and legends in American literature, that of the lazy, likable Rip Van Winkle. For this creation, among others, Irving deserves recognition as the American godfather of the form we know today as the short story. But if he is the godfather, Nathaniel Hawthorne, Edgar Allan Poe, and Herman Melville share in the genre's true paternity.

Definitions of the short story sometimes begin negatively. It is not a mini-novel; it is not a simple tale or the account of a simple incident; nor is it merely an anecdote or a sketch. What then is it?

William Faulkner once observed that it was easier to write a novel than a short story. "Yes, sir. You can be more careless, you can put more trash in it and be excused for it. In a short story that's next to the poem, almost every word has got to be almost exactly right. In the novel you can be careless but in the short story you can't." That statement differentiates the short story from the novel, but still does not define it. For Flannery O'Connor's definition brings us, perhaps, a little closer. For her, the short story was *not* a joke, *not* an anecdote, *not* a lyric rhapsody in prose, *not* a case history, and *not* a reported incident. For her the short story "is none of these things because it has an extra dimension and I think this extra dimension comes about when the writer puts us in the middle of some human action and shows it as it is illuminated and outlined by mystery." Certainly this is true of the "human action" in "Parker's Back," the O'Connor story included in this anthology. If O'Connor's theory about the short story sounds vague and mysterious, that's as it should be. And perhaps it is as close as we can get—or need to get—to a final definition. O'Connor and Faulkner wrote marvelous short stories that escape definition. This is also true of those major nineteenth-century American writers Hawthorne, Poe, and Melville. These early practitioners of what was still an uncertain and somewhat ambiguous genre had a great impact on its development and on its subsequent direction. They wrote prefaces and reviews that helped to define the short story as a unique literary form, one that soon achieved fame as being particularly American. Of these critical statements the most famous and influential was Poe's definition of the short tale in his review of Hawthorne's *Twice-Told Tales* (1842).

Poe initially points out the similarities between the "sketches" in that volume and those of Washington Irving, although he finds Hawthorne's superior. It is in his consideration of Hawthorne's "imaginative tales" that his central ideas about the aesthetic of the "tale" (his own included) are clarified:

Were we called upon, however, to designate that class of composition which, next to such a poem as we have suggested, should best fulfill the demands of high genius—should offer it the most advantageous field of exertion—we should unhesitatingly speak of the prose tale, as Mr. Hawthorne has here exemplified it. We allude to the short prose narrative, requiring from a half-hour to one or two hours in its perusal. . . . In the brief tale . . . the author is enabled to carry out the fullness of his intention, be it what it may. During the hour of perusal the soul of the reader is at the writer's control. There are no external or extrinsic influences resulting from weariness or interruption.

A skillful literary artist has constructed a tale. If wise, he has not fashioned his thoughts to accommodate his incidents; but having conceived, with deliberate care, a certain unique or single *effect* to be wrought out, he then invents such incidents—he then combines such events as may best aid him in establishing this preconceived effect. . . . In the whole composition there should be no word written, on which the tendency, direct or indirect, is not to the one pre-established design.

Poe's concern with literary technique provoked these stern views on what would come to be known as the short story; they have remained valid for American writers in other respects. The short story writer Ruth Suckow, has pointed out that "short stories were a way of making America intelligible to itself." Valid reasons for this phenomenon were the fragmentation, "the chaos, the unevenness, the diversity of American life that made short stories such a natural artistic expression in the first place." In ways Poe could never have predicted, an eager, hasty, impatient country could respond instantly to a short story "requiring from a half-hour to one or two hours in its perusal."

Melville, on the other hand, was fascinated by "this great power of blackness" in Hawthorne's fiction that "fixes and fascinates." Melville recognized in Hawthorne qualities in his own nature that he had described compellingly: the alienation and tragedy rumbling beneath the placid, optimistic surface of nineteenth-century America, a legacy of the strained preoccupation with evil that had formed a perplexing element in the American experience from the Puritan beginnings. Both Hawthorne and Melville turned inward to explore what motivated characters and influenced their conduct. Setting, plot, and technique were subordinated, although not abandoned, in the attempt to deal with the psychological complexities of characters driven by fear, the taint of unidentified evils, and their subsequent scars. This fascination with the warped psyche and ensuing alienation would continue to absorb the authors of American fiction into the twentieth century. For example, in a letter to John Hawkes, Flannery O'Connor wrote, "Hawthorne interests me considerably. I feel more of a kinship with him than with any other American." The persisting impact of Hawthorne and Melville is apparent in the work of numerous and diverse contemporary American writers. Certain dark perspectives on the human condition found in the stories of Saul Bellow, John Cheever, Shirley Jackson, John Hawkes, and Joyce Carol Oates, for instance, link them securely to those earlier writers' concepts of evil, terror, and the vagaries of the human heart. At the same time, Poe's influence is apparent in the works of some of those writers already mentioned as well as others such as Donald Barthelme and Kurt Vonnegut. While the stories in this anthology where not chosen to illustrate their authors' particular legacies, the linking is inevitable.

Any discussion of literary influences must be cautious. Writers frequently absorb their style and technique by osmosis and are not even consciously aware of their models or their borrowing. The writer's unique perspective in creating a world is the combined result of his or her special talents, special interests, and the circumstances of childhood as well as education or the lack of it. So many factors are involved in the creation of a work of fiction that any superimposed pattern must be viewed as artificial. What follows is merely a *suggestion* of the obvious forces rumbling between the pages.

Mark Twain left a profound impact on American prose fiction, and Hemingway celebrated this legacy when he declared that all modern American literature came out of *Huckleberry Finn.* What Hemingway was implying was his own debt to Twain who taught him the power of the particular and the impact of the local translated into the universal. Huck Finn is not just Huck Finn; he's every American boy confronting the reality of his own particular surroundings. This becomes true of Hemingway's male characters as well. Nick Adams is a good example as, to a lesser degree, is Tom in "The Light of the World." F. Scott Fitzgerald, also affected by Twain's sense of place and mores, explored a more mannered and limited world since both he and Hemingway, like Henry James, appreciated a European atmosphere that would have made Twain itchy and cantankerous. Perhaps Fitzgerald learned this sense of the particular from Hemingway rather than from Twain himself, as did the numerous other American writers later affected by Hemingway's style and sense of isolation and by Fitzgerald's alienated heroes. But it was Twain who prepared the way.

Although Mark Twain remarked that he would rather be condemned to John Bunyan's heaven than read Henry James's *The Bostonians*, generally considered the least popular of James's novels, the subtle influence of James on fiction writers appears in many stories that examine the mores, manners, and social milieu of America: stories by writers such as Edith Wharton, John Cheever, F. Scott Fitzgerald, John O'Hara, and Peter Taylor.

In addition to literary influences, vital as they are to most writers, personal geography, with all of its attendant customs, dialects and idiosyncrasies, is an equally important consideration. Once at home in America and willing to accept and even exploit the areas they knew best, rather than to pretend that differences did not exist, America's fiction writers curried their own regions and neighborhoods to produce a literature rich in variety and nuance. They would not settle for a homogenized America.

Individual writers have chronicled the customs, language, and sense of place for every section of the country. Among the southerners, William Faulkner, represented here by "That Evening Sun," caught the impact of the geography as well as the South's acute cultural differences. Eudora Welty, Truman Capote, and Flannery O'Connor constructed their stories out of similar local materials but with surprisingly different results. Willa Cather, on the other hand, looked to the Nebraska prairies of her own youth as the affirmative setting for "Neighbour Rosicky" while writers such as Sarah Orne Jewett, John Cheever, and Shirley Jackson relied on the East to convey their comprehensive themes in particularized settings. Racial and ethnic awareness, often in an urban setting, characterizes many stories by Saul Bellow, James Baldwin, Bernard Malamud, James Alan McPherson, and Philip Roth. Baldwin's "Sonny's Blues," set in New York City, achieves a particularly forceful interpretation of racial tension with universal overtones partially through its use of an electric urban setting.

The short story is a demanding literary form. Its brevity and intensity can win general readers who have little time or patience for longer works. Its most skillful writers must, however, exercise the greatest selectivity and precision. It is a curious paradox that the United States, a large and diverse nation, has sometimes been better expressed in the particular scene and individual personality revealed by a short story than in the sprawling abundance of landscape and the crowded scenes presented in a novel. It is in this celebration of the particular that American short stories achieve universality. Whatever their style, perspective, theme, or intention, the most successful stories of the past and present introduce us to our countrymen and allow us to share their central experiences.

During its relatively brief history, the American short story has demonstrated impressive variety and innovation. Its writers have not only celebrated particular regions and ethnic strains but, finally, the entire national personality. They have created entertaining characters with common and diverse temperaments. They have investigated the major struggles and dilemmas of their times. The continuing vitality of the American short story is assured by an abundance of brilliant young writers, a number of whom are represented in this collection.

NANCY SULLIVAN

The Treasury of American Short Stories

The Legend of Sleepy Hollow

WASHINGTON IRVING

(1783–1859)

(Found among the Papers of the late Diedrich Knickerbocker)

> A pleasing land of drowsy head it was,
> Of dreams that wave before the half-shut eye;
> And of gay castles in the clouds that pass,
> Forever flushing round a summer sky.
>
> CASTLE OF INDOLENCE.

In the bosom of one of those spacious coves which indent the eastern shore of the Hudson, at that broad expansion of the river denominated by the ancient Dutch navigators the Tappaan Zee, and where they always prudently shortened sail, and implored the protection of St. Nicholas when they crossed, there lies a small market town or rural port, which by some is called Greensburgh, but which is more generally and properly known by the name of Tarry Town. This name was given, we are told, in former days, by the good housewives of the adjacent country, from the inveterate propensity of their husbands to linger about the village tavern on market days. Be that as it may, I do not vouch for the fact, but merely advert to it, for the sake of being precise and authentic. Not far from this village, perhaps about two miles, there is a little valley, or rather lap of land among high hills, which is one of the quietest places in the whole world. A small brook glides through it, with just murmur enough to lull one to repose, and the occasional whistle of a quail, or tapping of a woodpecker, is almost the only sound that ever breaks in upon the uniform tranquillity.

I recollect that when a stripling, my first exploit in squirrel shooting was in a grove of tall walnut trees that shades one side of the valley. I had wandered into it at noon time, when all nature is peculiarly quiet, and was startled by the roar of my own gun, as it broke the sabbath stillness around, and was prolonged and reverberated by the angry echoes. If ever I should wish for a retreat, whither I might steal from the world and its distractions, and dream quietly away the remnant of a troubled life, I know of none more promising than this little valley.

From the listless repose of the place, and the peculiar character of its inhabitants, who are descendants from the original Dutch settlers, this sequestered glen has long been known by the name of SLEEPY HOLLOW, and its rustic lads are called the Sleepy Hollow Boys throughout all the neighbouring country. A drowsy, dreamy influence seems to hang over the land, and to pervade the very atmosphere. Some say that the place was bewitched by a high German doctor during the early days of the settlement; others, that an old Indian chief, the prophet or wizard of his tribe, held his powwows there before the country was discovered by Master Hendrick Hudson. Certain it is, the place still continues under the sway of some witching power, that holds a spell over the minds of the good people, causing them to walk in a continual reverie. They are given to all kinds of marvellous beliefs; are subject to trances and visions, and frequently see strange sights, and hear music and voices in the air. The whole neighbourhood abounds with local tales, haunted spots, and twilight superstitions; stars shoot and meteors glare oftener across the valley than in any other part of the country, and the night mare, with her whole nine fold, seems to make it the favourite scene of her gambols.

The dominant spirit, however, that haunts this enchanted region, and seems to be commander in chief of all the powers of the air, is the apparition of a figure on horseback without a head. It is said by some to be the ghost of a Hessian trooper, whose head had been carried away by a cannon ball, in some nameless battle during the revolutionary war, and who is ever and anon seen by the country folk, hurrying along in the gloom of night, as if on the wings of the wind. His haunts are not confined to the valley, but extend at times to the adjacent roads, and especially to the vicinity of a church at no great distance. Indeed, certain of the most authentic historians of those parts, who have been careful in collecting and collating the floating facts concerning this spectre, allege, that the body of the trooper having been buried in the church yard, the ghost rides forth to the scene of battle in nightly quest of his head, and that the rushing speed with which he sometimes passes along the hollow, like a midnight blast, is owing to his being belated, and in a hurry to get back to the church yard before day break.

Such is the general purport of this legendary superstition, which has furnished materials for many a wild story in that region of shadows; and the spectre is known, at all the country firesides, by the name of The Headless Horseman of Sleepy Hollow.

It is remarkable, that the visionary propensity I have mentioned is not confined to the native inhabitants of the valley, but is unconsciously imbibed by every one who resides there for a time. However wide awake they may have been before they entered that sleepy region, they are sure, in a little time, to inhale the witching influence of the air, and begin to grow imaginative—to dream dreams, and see apparitions.

I mention this peaceful spot with all possible laud; for it is in such little retired Dutch valleys, found here and there embosomed in the great state of New York, that population, manners, and customs, remain fixed, while the great torrent of migration and improvement, which is making such incessant changes in other parts of this restless country, sweeps by them unobserved. They are like those little nooks of still water, which border a rapid stream, where we may see the straw and bubble riding quietly at anchor, or slowly revolving in their mimic harbour, undisturbed by the rush of the passing current. Though many years have elapsed since I trod the drowsy shades of Sleepy Hollow, yet I question whether I should not still find the same trees and the same families vegetating in its sheltered bosom.

In this by place of nature there abode, in a remote period of American history, that is to say, some thirty years since, a worthy wight of the name of Ichabod Crane, who sojourned, or, as he expressed it, "tarried," in Sleepy Hollow, for the purpose of instructing the children of the vicinity. He was a native of Connecticut, a state which supplies the Union with pioneers for the mind as well as for the forest, and sends forth yearly its legions of frontier woodmen and country schoolmasters. The cognomen of Crane was not inapplicable to his person. He was tall, but exceedingly lank, with narrow shoulders, long arms and legs, hands that dangled a mile out of his sleeves, feet that might have served for shovels, and his whole frame most loosely hung together. His head was small, and flat at top, with huge ears, large green glassy eyes, and a long snipe nose, so that it looked like a weathercock perched upon his spindle neck, to tell which way the wind blew. To see him striding along the profile of a hill on a windy day, with his clothes bagging and fluttering about him, one might have mistaken him for the genius of famine descending upon the earth, or some scarecrow eloped from a cornfield.

His school house was a low building of one large room, rudely constructed of logs; the windows partly glazed, and partly patched with leaves of old copy books. It was most ingeniously secured at vacant hours, by a withe twisted in the handle of the door, and stakes set against the window shutters; so that though a thief might get in with perfect ease, he would find some embarrassment in getting out; an idea most probably borrowed by the architect, Yost Van Houten, from the mystery of an eelpot.

The school house stood in a rather lonely but pleasant situation, just at the foot of a woody hill, with a brook running close by, and a formidable birch tree growing at one end of it. From hence the low murmur of his pupils' voices conning over their lessons, might be heard of a drowsy summer's day, like the hum of a bee hive; interrupted now and then by the authoritative voice of the master, in the tone of menace or command, or peradventure, by the appalling sound of the birch, as he urged some tardy loiterer along the flowery path of knowledge. Truth to say, he was a conscientious man, and ever bore in mind the golden maxim, "spare the rod and spoil the child."—Ichabod Crane's scholars certainly were not spoiled.

I would not have it imagined, however, that he was one of those cruel potentates of the school, who joy in the smart of their subjects; on the contrary, he administered justice with discrimination rather than severity; taking the burthen off the backs of the weak, and laying it on those of the strong. Your mere puny stripling, that winced at the least flourish of the rod, was passed by with indulgence; but the claims of justice were satisfied, by inflicting a double portion on some little, tough, wrong headed, broad skirted Dutch urchin, who sulked and swelled and grew dogged and sullen beneath the birch. All this he called "doing his duty by their parents"; and he never inflicted a chastisement without following it by the assurance, so consolatory to the smarting urchin, that "he would remember it and thank him for it the longest day he had to live."

When school hours were over, he was even the companion and playmate of the larger boys; and on holyday afternoons would convoy some of the smaller ones home, who happened to have pretty sisters, or good housewives for mothers, noted for the comforts of the cupboard. Indeed, it behooved him to keep on good terms with his pupils. The revenue arising from his school was small, and would have been scarcely sufficient to furnish him with daily bread, for he was a huge feeder, and though lank, had the dilating powers of an Anaconda; but to help out his maintenance, he was, according to country custom in those parts, boarded and lodged at the houses of the farmers, whose children he instructed. With these he lived successively a week at a time, thus going the rounds of the neighbourhood, with all his worldly effects tied up in a cotton handkerchief.

That all this might not be too onerous on the purses of his rustic patrons, who are apt to consider the costs of schooling a grievous burthen, and schoolmasters as mere drones, he had various ways of rendering himself both useful and agreeable. He assisted the farmers occasionally in the lighter labours of their farms, helped to make hay, mended the fences, took the horses to water, drove the cows from pasture, and cut wood for the winter fire. He laid aside, too, all the dominant dignity and absolute sway, with which he lorded it in his little empire, the school, and became wonderfully gentle and ingratiating. He found favour in the eyes of the mothers, by petting the children, particularly the youngest, and like the lion bold, which whilom so magnanimously the lamb did hold, he would sit with a child on one knee, and rock a cradle with his foot, for whole hours together.

In addition to his other vocations, he was the singing master of the neighbourhood, and picked up many bright shillings by instructing the young folks in psalmody. It was a matter of no little vanity to him on Sundays, to take his station in front of the church gallery, with a band of chosen singers; where, in his own mind, he completely carried away the palm from the parson. Certain it is, his voice resounded far above all the rest of the congregation, and there are peculiar quavers still to be heard in that church, and which may even be heard half a mile off, quite to the opposite side of the mill pond, of a still Sunday morning, which are said to be legitimately descended from the nose of Ichabod Crane. Thus, by diverse little make shifts, in that ingenious way which is commonly denominated "by hook and by crook," the worthy pedagogue got on tolerably enough, and was thought, by all who understood nothing of the labour of headwork, to have a wonderfully easy life of it.

The schoolmaster is generally a man of some importance in the female circle of a rural neighbourhood, being considered a kind of idle gentleman like personage, of vastly superior taste and accomplishments to the rough country swains, and, indeed, inferior in learning only to the parson. His appearance, therefore, is apt to occasion some little stir at the tea table of a farm house, and the addition of a supernumerary dish of cakes or sweetmeats, or, peradventure, the parade of a silver tea pot. Our man of letters, therefore, was peculiarly happy in the smiles of all the country damsels. How he would figure among them in the church yard, between services on Sundays; gathering grapes for them from the wild vines that overrun the surrounding trees; reciting for their amusement all the epitaphs on the tombstones, or sauntering, with a whole bevy of them, along the banks of the adjacent mill pond; while the more bashful country bumpkins hung sheepishly back, envying his superior elegance and address.

From his half itinerant life, also, he was a kind of travelling gazette, carrying the whole budget of local gossip from house to house; so that his appearance was always greeted with satisfaction. He was, moreover, esteemed by the women as a man of great erudition, for he had read several books quite through, and was a perfect master of Cotton Mather's History of New England Witchcraft, in which, by the way, he most firmly and potently believed.

He was, in fact, an odd mixture of small shrewdness and simple credulity. His appetite for the marvellous, and his powers of digesting it, were equally extraordinary; and both had been increased by his residence in this spell bound region. No tale was too gross or monstrous for his capacious swallow. It was often his delight, after his school was dismissed of an afternoon, to stretch himself on the rich bed of clover, bordering the little brook that whimpered by his school house, and there con over old Mather's direful tales, until the gathering dusk of evening made the printed page a mere mist before his eyes. Then, as he wended his way, by swamp and stream and awful woodland, to the farm house where he happened to be quartered, every sound of nature, at that witching hour, fluttered his excited imagination: the moan of the whip-poor-will from the hill side; the boding cry of the tree toad, that harbinger of storm; the dreary hooting of the screech owl; or the sudden rustling in the thicket, of birds frightened from their roost. The fire flies, too, which sparkled most vividly in the darkest places, now and then startled him, as one of uncommon brightness would stream across his path; and if, by chance, a huge blockhead of a beetle came winging his blundering flight against him, the poor varlet was ready to give up the ghost, with the idea that he was struck with a witch's token. His only resource on such occasions, either to drown thought, or drive away evil spirits, was to sing psalm tunes;—and the good people of Sleepy Hollow, as they sat by their doors of an evening, were often filled with awe, at hearing his nasal melody, "in linked sweetness long drawn out," floating from the distant hill, or along the dusky road.

Another of his sources of fearful pleasure was, to pass long winter evenings with the old Dutch wives, as they sat spinning by the fire, with a row of apples roasting and sputtering along the hearth, and listen to their marvellous tales of ghosts and goblins, and haunted fields and haunted brooks, and haunted bridges and haunted houses, and particularly of the headless horseman, or galloping Hessian of the Hollow, as they sometimes called him. He would delight them equally by his anecdotes of witchcraft, and of the direful omens and portentous sights and sounds in the air, which prevailed in the earlier times of Connecticut; and would frighten them wofully with speculations upon comets and shooting stars, and with the alarming fact that the world did absolutely turn round, and that they were half the time topsy-turvy!

But if there was a pleasure in all this, while snugly cuddling in the chimney corner of a chamber that was all of a ruddy glow from the crackling wood fire, and where, of course, no spectre dared to show its face, it was dearly purchased by the terrors of his subsequent walk homewards. What fearful shapes and shadows beset his path, amidst the dim and ghastly glare of a snowy night!—With what wistful look did he eye every trembling ray of light streaming across the waste fields from some distant window!—How often was he appalled by some shrub covered with snow, which like a sheeted spectre beset his very path!—How often did he shrink with curdling awe at the sound of his own steps on the frosty crust beneath his feet; and dread to look over his shoulder, lest he should behold some uncouth being tramping close behind him!—and how often was he thrown into complete dismay by some rushing blast, howling among the trees, in the idea that it was the gallopping Hessian on one of his nightly scourings.

All these, however, were mere terrors of the night, phantoms of the mind, that walk in darkness; and though he had seen many spectres in his time, and been more than once beset by Satan in diverse shapes, in his lonely perambulations, yet daylight put an end to all these evils; and he would have passed a pleasant life of it, in despite of the Devil and all his works, if his path had not been crossed by a being that causes more perplexity to mortal man, than ghosts, goblins, and the whole race of witches put together, and that was—a woman.

Among the musical disciples who assembled, one evening in each week, to receive his instructions in psalmody, was Katrina Van Tassel, the daughter and only child of a substantial Dutch farmer. She was a blooming lass of fresh eighteen; plump as a partridge; ripe and melting and rosy cheeked as one of her father's peaches, and universally famed, not merely for her beauty, but her vast expectations. She was withal a little of a coquette, as might be perceived even in her dress, which was a mixture of ancient and modern fashions, as most suited to set off her charms. She wore the ornaments of pure yellow gold, which her great great grandmother had brought over from Saardam; the tempting stomacher of the olden time, and withal a provokingly short petticoat, to display the prettiest foot and ankle in the country round.

Ichabod Crane had a soft and foolish heart toward the sex; and it is not to be wondered at, that so tempting a morsel soon found favour in his eyes, more especially after he had visited her in her paternal mansion. Old Baltus Van Tassel was a perfect picture of a thriving, contented, liberal hearted farmer. He seldom, it is true, sent either his eyes or his thoughts beyond the boundaries of his own farm; but within those every thing was snug, happy, and well conditioned. He was satisfied with his wealth, but not proud of it, and piqued himself upon the hearty abundance, rather than the style in which he lived. His strong hold was situated on the banks of the Hudson, in one of those green, sheltered, fertile nooks, in which the Dutch farmers are so fond of nestling. A great elm tree spread its broad branches over it, at the foot of which bubbled up a spring of the softest and sweetest water, in a little well, formed of a barrel, and then stole sparkling away through the grass, to a neighbouring brook, that babbled along among elders and dwarf willows. Hard by the farm house was a vast barn, that might have served for a church; every window and crevice of which seemed bursting forth with the treasures of the farm; the flail was busily resounding within it from morning to night; swallows and martins skimmed twittering about the eaves, and rows of pigeons, some with one eye turned up, as if watching the weather, some with their heads under their wings, or buried in their bosoms, and others, swelling, and cooing, and bowing about their dames, were enjoying the sunshine on the roof. Sleek unwieldy porkers were grunting in the repose and abundance of their pens, from whence sallied forth, now and then, troops of sucking pigs, as if to snuff the air. A stately squadron of snowy geese were riding in an adjoining pond, convoying whole fleets of ducks; regiments of turkeys were gobbling through the farm yard, and guinea fowls fretting about it like ill tempered housewives, with their peevish discontented cry. Before the barn door strutted the gallant cock, that pattern of a husband, a warrior, and a fine gentleman, clapping his burnished wings, and crowing in the pride and gladness of his heart—sometimes tearing up the earth with his feet, and then generously calling his ever hungry family of wives and children to enjoy the rich morsel which he had discovered.

The pedagogue's mouth watered, as he looked upon this sumptuous promise of luxurious winter fare. In his devouring mind's eye, he pictured to himself every roasting pig running about with a pudding in his belly, and an apple in his mouth; the pigeons were snugly put to bed in a comfortable pie, and tucked in with a coverlet of crust; the geese were swimming in their own gravy; and the ducks pairing cosily in dishes, like snug married couples, with a decent competency of onion sauce; in the porkers he saw carved out the future sleek side of bacon, and juicy relishing ham; not a turkey, but he beheld daintily trussed up, with its gizzard under its wing, and, peradventure, a necklace of savoury sausages; and even bright chanticleer himself lay sprawling on his back, in a side dish, with uplifted claws, as if craving that quarter, which his chivalrous spirit disdained to ask while living.

As the enraptured Ichabod fancied all this, and as he rolled his great green eyes over the fat meadow lands, the rich fields of wheat, of rye, of buckwheat, and Indian corn, and the orchards burthened with ruddy fruit, which surrounded the warm tenement of Van Tassel, his heart yearned after the damsel who was to inherit these domains, and his imagination expanded with the idea, how they might be readily turned into cash, and the money invested in immense tracts of wild land, and shingle palaces in the wilderness. Nay, his busy fancy already realized his hopes, and presented to him the blooming Katrina, with a whole family of children, mounted on the top of a waggon loaded with household trumpery, with pots and kettles dangling beneath; and he beheld himself bestriding a pacing mare, with a colt at her heels, setting out for Kentucky, Tennessee, or the Lord knows where!

When he entered the house, the conquest of his heart was complete. It was one of those spacious farm houses, with high ridged, but lowly sloping roofs, built in the style handed down from the first Dutch settlers. The low, projecting eaves formed a piazza along the front, capable of being closed up in bad weather. Under this were hung flails, harness, various utensils of husbandry, and nets for fishing in the neighbouring river. Benches were built along the sides for summer use; and a great spinning wheel at one end, and a churn at the other, showed the various uses to which this important porch might be devoted. From this piazza the wondering Ichabod entered the hall, which formed the centre of the mansion, and the place of usual residence. Here, rows of resplendent pewter, ranged on a long dresser, dazzled his eyes. In one corner stood a huge bag of wool ready to be spun; in another a quantity of linsey-woolsey just from the loom; ears of Indian corn, and strings of dried apples and peaches, hung in gay festoons along the walls, mingled with the gaud of red peppers; and a door left ajar, gave him a peep into the best parlour, where the claw footed chairs, and dark mahogany tables, shone like mirrors; andirons, with their accompanying shovel and tongs, glistened from their covert of asparagus tops; mock oranges and conch shells decorated the mantelpiece; strings of various coloured birds' eggs were suspended above it; a great ostrich egg was hung from the centre of the room, and a corner cupboard, knowingly left open, displayed immense treasures of old silver and well mended china.

From the moment Ichabod laid his eyes upon these regions of delight, the peace of his mind was at an end, and his only study was how to gain the affections of the peerless daughter of Van Tassel. In this enterprize, however, he had more real difficulties than generally fell to the lot of a knight errant of yore, who seldom had any thing but giants, enchanters, fiery dragons, and such like easily conquered adversaries, to contend with; and had to make his way merely through gates of iron and brass, and walls of adamant, to the castle keep, where the lady of his heart was confined; all which he achieved as easily as a man would carve his way to the centre of a Christmas pie, and then the lady gave him her hand as a matter of course. Ichabod, on the contrary, had to win his way to the heart of a country coquette, beset with a labyrinth of whims and caprices, which were for ever presenting new difficulties and impediments, and he had to encounter a host of fearful adversaries of real flesh and blood, the numerous rustic admirers, who beset every portal to her heart, keeping a watchful and angry eye upon each other, but ready to fly out in the common cause against any new competitor.

Among these, the most formidable, was a burly, roaring, roystering blade, of the name of Abraham, or, according to the Dutch abbreviation, Brom Van Brunt, the hero of the country round, which rung with his feats of strength and hardihood. He was broad shouldered and double jointed, with short curly black hair, and a bluff, but not unpleasant countenance, having a mingled air of fun and arrogance. From his Herculean frame and great powers of limb, he had received the nick name of Brom Bones, by which he was universally known. He was famed for great knowledge and skill in horsemanship, being as dexterous on horseback as a Tartar. He was foremost at all races and cock fights, and with the ascendancy which bodily strength acquires in rustic life, was the umpire in all disputes, setting his hat on one side, and giving his decisions with an air and tone admitting of no gainsay or appeal. He was always ready for either a fight or a frolick: but had more mischief than ill will in his composition; and with all his overbearing roughness, there was a strong dash of waggish good humour at bottom. He had three or four boon companions, who regarded him as their model, and at the head of whom he scoured the country, attending every scene of feud or merriment for miles round. In cold weather he was distinguished by a fur cap, surmounted with a flaunting fox's tail, and when the folks at a country gathering descried this well known crest at a distance, whisking about among a squad of hard riders, they always stood by for a squall. Sometimes his crew would be heard dashing along past the farm houses at midnight, with whoop and halloo, like a troop of Don Cossacks, and the old dames, startled out of their sleep, would listen for a moment till the hurry scurry had clattered by, and then exclaim, "aye, there goes Brom Bones and his gang!" The neighbours looked upon him with a mixture of awe, admiration, and good will; and when any mad cap prank, or rustic brawl, occurred in the vicinity, always shook their heads, and warranted Brom Bones was at the bottom of it.

This rantipole hero had for some time singled out the blooming Katrina for the object of his uncouth gallantries, and though his amorous toyings were something like the gentle caresses and endearments of a bear, yet it was whispered that she did not altogether discourage his hopes. Certain it is, his advances were signals for rival candidates to retire, who felt no inclination to cross a lion in his amours; insomuch, that when his horse was seen tied to Van Tassel's paling, of a Sunday night, (a sure sign that his master was courting, or, as it is termed, "sparking," within,) all other suitors passed by in despair, and carried the war into other quarters.

Such was the formidable rival with whom Ichabod Crane had to contend, and, considering all things, a stouter man than he would have shrunk from the competition, and a wiser man would have despaired. He had, however, a happy mixture of pliability and perseverance in his nature; he was in form and spirit like a supple jack—yielding, but tough; though he bent, he never broke; and though he bowed beneath the slightest pressure, yet, the moment it was away—jerk!—he was as erect, and carried his head as high as ever.

To have taken the field openly against his rival, would have been madness; for he was not a man to be thwarted in his amours, any more than that stormy lover, Achilles. Ichabod, therefore, made his advances in a quiet and gently insinuating manner. Under cover of his character of singing master, he made frequent visits at the farm house; not that he had any thing to apprehend from the meddlesome interference of parents, which is so often a stumbling block in the path of lovers. Balt Van Tassel was an easy indulgent soul; he loved his daughter better even than his pipe, and like a reasonable man, and an excellent father, let her have her way in every thing. His notable little wife too, had enough to do to attend to her housekeeping and manage her poultry, for, as she sagely observed, ducks and geese are foolish things, and must be looked after, but girls can take care of themselves. Thus while the busy dame bustled about the house, or plied her spinning wheel at one end of the piazza, honest Balt would sit smoking his evening pipe at the other, watching the achievements of a little wooden warrior, who, armed with a sword in each hand, was most valiantly fighting the wind on the pinnacle of the barn. In the mean time, Ichabod would carry on his suit with the daughter by the side of the spring under the great elm, or sauntering along in the twilight, that hour so favourable to the lover's eloquence.

I profess not to know how women's hearts are wooed and won. To me they have always been matters of riddle and admiration. Some seem to have but one vulnerable point, or door of access; while others have a thousand avenues, and may be captured in a thousand different ways. It is a great triumph of skill to gain the former, but a still greater proof of generalship to maintain possession of the latter, for a man must battle for his fortress at every door and window. He who wins a thousand common hearts, is therefore entitled to some renown; but he who keeps undisputed sway over the heart of a coquette, is indeed a hero. Certain it is, this was not the case with the redoutable Brom Bones; and from the moment Ichabod Crane made his advances, the interests of the former evidently declined; his horse was no longer seen tied at the palings on Sunday nights, and a deadly feud gradually arose between him and the preceptor of Sleepy Hollow.

Brom, who had a degree of rough chivalry in his nature, would fain have carried matters to open warfare, and have settled their pretensions to the lady, according to the mode of those most concise and simple reasoners, the knights errant of yore—by single combat; but Ichabod was too conscious of the superior might of his adversary to enter the lists against him; he had overheard a boast of Bones, that he would "double the schoolmaster up, and lay him on a shelf of his own school house"; and he was too wary to give him an opportunity. There was something extremely provoking in this obstinately pacific system; it left Brom no alternative but to draw upon the funds of rustic waggery in his disposition, and to play off boorish practical jokes upon his rival. Ichabod became the object of whimsical persecution to Bones, and his gang of rough riders. They harried his hitherto peaceful domains; smoked out his singing school, by stopping up the chimney; broke into the school house at night, in spite of its formidable fastenings of withe and window stakes, and turned every thing topsy-turvy, so that the poor schoolmaster began to think all the witches in the country held their meetings there. But what was still more annoying, Brom took all opportunities of turning him into ridicule in presence of his mistress, and had a scoundrel dog, whom he taught to whine in the most ludicrous manner, and introduced as a rival of Ichabod's, to instruct her in psalmody.

In this way, matters went on for some time, without producing any material effect on the relative situations of the contending powers. On a fine autumnal afternoon, Ichabod, in pensive mood, sat enthroned on the lofty stool from whence he usually watched all the concerns of his little literary realm. In his hand he swayed a ferule, that sceptre of despotic power; the birch of justice reposed on three nails, behind the throne, a constant terror to evil doers; while on the desk before him might be seen sundry contraband articles and prohibited weapons, detected upon the persons of idle urchins, such as half munched apples, popguns, whirligigs, fly cages, and whole legions of rampant little paper game cocks. Apparently there had been some appalling act of justice recently inflicted, for his scholars were all busily intent upon their books, or slyly whispering behind them with one eye kept upon the master; and a kind of buzzing stillness reigned throughout the school room. It was suddenly interrupted by the appearance of a negro in tow cloth jacket and trowsers, a round crowned fragment of a hat, like the cap of Mercury, and mounted on the back of a ragged, wild, half broken colt, which he managed with a rope by way of halter. He came clattering up to the school door with an invitation to Ichabod to attend a merry making, or "quilting frolick," to be held that evening at Mynheer Van Tassel's, and having delivered his message with that air of importance, and effort at fine language, which a negro is apt to display on petty embassies of the kind, he dashed over the brook, and was seen scampering away up the hollow, full of the importance and hurry of his mission.

All was now bustle and hubbub in the late quiet school room. The scholars were hurried through their lessons, without stopping at trifles; those who were nimble, skipped over half with impunity, and those who were tardy, had a smart application now and then in the rear, to quicken their speed, or help them over a tall word. Books were flung aside, without being put away on the shelves; inkstands were overturned, benches thrown down, and the whole school was turned loose an hour before the usual time; bursting forth like a legion of young imps, yelping and racketing about the green, in joy at their early emancipation.

The gallant Ichabod now spent at least an extra half hour at his toilet, brushing and furbishing up his best, and indeed only suit of rusty black, and arranging his looks by a bit of broken looking glass, that hung up in the school house. That he might make his appearance before his mistress in the true style of a cavalier, he borrowed a horse from the farmer with whom he was domiciliated, a choleric old Dutchman, of the name of Hans Van Ripper, and thus gallantly mounted, issued forth like a knight errant in quest of adventures. But it is meet I should, in the true spirit of romantic story, give some account of the looks and equipments of my hero and his steed. The animal he bestrode was a broken down plough horse, that had outlived almost every thing but his viciousness. He was gaunt and shagged, with a ewe neck and a head like a hammer; his rusty mane and tail were tangled and knotted with burrs; one eye had lost its pupil, and was glaring and spectral, but the other had the gleam of a genuine devil in it. Still he must have had fire and mettle in his day, if we may judge from the name he bore of Gunpowder. He had, in fact, been a favourite steed of his master's, the cholerick Van Ripper, who was a furious rider, and had infused, very probably, some of his own spirit into the animal, for, old and broken down as he looked, there was more of the lurking devil in him than in any young filly in the country.

Ichabod was a suitable figure for such a steed. He rode with short stirrups, which brought his knees nearly up to the pommel of the saddle; his sharp elbows stuck out like grasshoppers'; he carried his whip perpendicularly in his hand, like a sceptre, and as his horse jogged on, the motion of his arms was not unlike the flapping of a pair of wings. A small wool hat rested on the top of his nose, for so his scanty strip of forehead might be called, and the skirts of his black coat fluttered out almost to the horse's tail. Such was the appearance of Ichabod and his steed, as they shambled out of the gate of Hans Van Ripper, and it was altogether such an apparition as is seldom to be met with in broad day light.

It was, as I have said, a fine autumnal day, the sky was clear and serene, and nature wore that rich and golden livery which we always associate with the idea of abundance. The forests had put on their sober brown and yellow, while some trees of the tenderer kind had been nipped by the frosts into brilliant dyes of orange, purple, and scarlet. Streaming files of wild ducks began to make their appearance high in the air; the bark of the squirrel might be heard from the groves of beech and hickory nuts, and the pensive whistle of the quail at intervals from the neighbouring stubble field.

The small birds were taking their farewell banquets. In the fullness of their revelry, they fluttered, chirping and frolicking, from bush to bush, and tree to tree, capricious from the very profusion and variety around them. There was the honest cock robin, the favourite game of stripling sportsmen, with its loud querulous note; and the twittering blackbirds flying in sable clouds; and the golden winged woodpecker, with his crimson crest, his broad black gorget, and splendid plumage; and the cedar bird, with its red tipt wings and yellow tipt tail, and its little monteiro cap of feathers; and the blue jay, that noisy coxcomb, in his gay light blue coat and white under clothes, screaming and chattering, nodding, and bobbing, and bowing, and pretending to be on good terms with every songster of the grove.

As Ichabod jogged slowly on his way, his eye, ever open to every symptom of culinary abundance, ranged with delight over the treasures of jolly autumn. On all sides he beheld vast store of apples, some hanging in oppressive opulence on the trees, some gathered into baskets and barrels for the market, others heaped up in rich piles for the cider press. Further on he beheld great fields of Indian corn, with its golden ears peeping from their leafy coverts, and holding out the promise of cakes and hasty pudding; and the yellow pumpkins lying beneath them, turning up their fair round bellies to the sun, and giving ample prospects of the most luxurious of pies; and anon he passed the fragrant buckwheat fields, breathing the odour of the bee hive, and as he beheld them, soft anticipations stole over his mind of dainty slap jacks, well buttered, and garnished with honey or treacle, by the delicate little dimpled hand of Katrina Van Tassel.

Thus feeding his mind with many sweet thoughts and "sugared suppositions," he journeyed along the sides of a range of hills which look out upon some of the goodliest scenes of the mighty Hudson. The sun gradually wheeled his broad disk down into the west. The wide bosom of the Tappaan Zee lay motionless and glassy, excepting that here and there a gentle undulation waved and prolonged the blue shadow of the distant mountain: a few amber clouds floated in the sky, without a breath of air to move them. The horizon was of a fine golden tint, changing gradually into a pure apple green, and from that into the deep blue of the mid-heaven. A slanting ray lingered on the woody crests of the precipices that overhung some parts of the river, giving greater depth to the dark grey and purple of their rocky sides. A sloop was loitering in the distance, dropping slowly down with the tide, her sail hanging uselessly against the mast, and as the reflection of the sky gleamed along the still water, it seemed as if the vessel was suspended in the air.

It was toward evening that Ichabod arrived at the castle of the Heer Van Tassel, which he found thronged with the pride and flower of the adjacent country. Old farmers, a spare, leathern faced race, in homespun coats and breeches, blue stockings, huge shoes and magnificent pewter buckles. Their brisk withered little dames in close crimped caps, long waisted short gowns, homespun petticoats, with scissors and pincushions, and gay calico pockets, hanging on the outside. Buxom lasses, almost as antiquated as their mothers, excepting where a straw hat, a fine ribband, or perhaps a white frock, gave symptoms of city innovation. The sons, in short square skirted coats with rows of stupendous brass buttons, and their hair generally queued in the fashion of the times, especially if they could procure an eel skin for the purpose, it being esteemed throughout the country as a potent nourisher and strengthener of the hair.

Brom Bones, however, was the hero of the scene, having come to the gathering on his favourite steed Daredevil, a creature, like himself, full of mettle and mischief, and which no one but himself could manage. He was in fact noted for preferring vicious animals, given to all kinds of tricks, which kept the rider in constant risk of his neck, for he held a tractable well broken horse as unworthy of a lad of spirit.

Fain would I pause to dwell upon the world of charms that burst upon the enraptured gaze of my hero, as he entered the state parlour of Van Tassel's mansion. Not those of the bevy of buxom lasses, with their luxurious display of red and white: but the ample charms of a genuine Dutch country tea table, in the sumptuous time of autumn. Such heaped up platters of cakes of various and almost indescribable kinds, known only to experienced Dutch housewives. There was the doughty dough nut, the tenderer oly koek, and the crisp and crumbling cruller; sweet cakes and short cakes, ginger cakes and honey cakes, and the whole family of cakes. And then there were apple pies and peach pies and pumpkin pies; besides slices of ham and smoked beef; and moreover delectable dishes of preserved plums, and peaches, and pears, and quinces; not to mention broiled shad and roasted chickens; together with bowls of milk and cream, all mingled higgledy-piggledy, pretty much as I have enumerated them, with the motherly tea pot sending up its clouds of vapour from the midst —Heaven bless the mark! I want breath and time to discuss this banquet as its deserves, and am too eager to get on with my story. Happily, Ichabod Crane was not in so great a hurry as his historian, but did ample justice to every dainty.

He was a kind and thankful creature, whose heart dilated in proportion as his skin was filled with good cheer, and whose spirits rose with eating, as some men's do with drink. He could not help, too, rolling his large eyes round him as he ate, and chuckling with the possibility that he might one day be lord of all this scene of almost unimaginable luxury and splendour. Then, he thought, how soon he'd turn his back upon the old school house; snap his fingers in the face of Hans Van Ripper, and every other niggardly patron, and kick any itinerant pedagogue out of doors that should dare to call him comrade!

Old Baltus Van Tassel moved about among his guests with a face dilated with content and good humour, round and jolly as the harvest moon. His hospitable attentions were brief, but expressive, being confined to a shake of the hand, a slap on the shoulder, a loud laugh, and a pressing invitation to "fall to, and help themselves."

And now the sound of the music from the common room or hall, summoned to the dance. The musician was an old grey headed negro, who had been the itinerant orchestra of the neighbourhood for more than half a century. His instrument was as old and battered as himself. The greater part of the time he scraped away on two or three strings, accompanying every movement of the bow with a motion of the head; bowing almost to the ground, and stamping with his foot whenever a fresh couple were to start.

Ichabod prided himself upon his dancing as much as upon his vocal powers. Not a limb, not a fibre about him was idle, and to have seen his loosely hung frame in full motion, and clattering about the room, you would have thought Saint Vitus himself, that blessed patron of the dance, was figuring before you in person. He was the admiration of all the negroes, who, having gathered, of all ages and sizes, from the farm and the neighbourhood, stood forming a pyramid of shining black faces at every door and window, gazing with delight at the scene, rolling their white eye balls, and showing grinning rows of ivory from ear to ear. How could the flogger of urchins be otherwise than animated and joyous; the lady of his heart was his partner in the dance; and smiling graciously in reply to all his amorous oglings, while Brom Bones, sorely smitten with love and jealousy, sat brooding by himself in one corner.

When the dance was at an end, Ichabod was attracted to a knot of the sager folks, who, with old Van Tassel, sat smoking at one end of the piazza, gossipping over former times, and drawling out long stories about the war.

This neighbourhood, at the time of which I am speaking, was one of those highly favoured places which abound with chronicle and great men. The British and American line had run near it during the war; it had, therefore, been the scene of marauding, and been infested with refugees, cow boys, and all kinds of border chivalry. Just sufficient time had elapsed to enable each story teller to dress up his tale with a little becoming fiction, and in the indistinctness of his recollection, to make himself the hero of every exploit.

There was the story of Doffue Martling, a large, blue bearded Dutchman, who had nearly taken a British frigate with an old iron nine pounder from a mud breastwork, only that his gun burst at the sixth discharge. And there was an old gentleman who shall be nameless, being too rich a mynheer to be lightly mentioned, who in the battle of Whiteplains, being an excellent master of defence, parried a musket ball with a small sword, insomuch that he absolutely felt it whiz round the blade, and glance off at the hilt: in proof of which, he was ready at any time to show the sword, with the hilt a little bent. There were several more who had been equally great in the field, not one of whom but was persuaded that he had a considerable hand in bringing the war to a happy termination.

But all these were nothing to the tales of ghosts and apparitions that succeeded. The neighbourhood is rich in legendary treasures of the kind. Local tales and superstitions thrive best in these sheltered, long settled retreats; but are trampled under foot, by the shifting throng that forms the population of most of our country places. Besides, there is no encouragement for ghosts in most of our villages, for they have scarce had time to finish their first nap, and turn themselves in their graves, before their surviving friends have travelled away from the neighbourhood, so that when they turn out of a night to walk the rounds, they have no acquaintance left to call upon. This is perhaps the reason why we so seldom hear of ghosts except in our long established Dutch communities.

The immediate cause, however, of the prevalence of supernatural stories in these parts, was doubtless owing to the vicinity of Sleepy Hollow. There was a contagion in the very air that blew from that haunted region; it breathed forth an atmosphere of dreams and fancies infecting all the land. Several of the Sleepy Hollow people were present at Van Tassel's, and, as usual, were doling out their wild and wonderful legends. Many dismal tales were told about funeral trains, and mournful cries and wailings heard and seen about the great tree where the unfortunate Major André was taken, and which stood in the neighbourhood. Some mention was made also of the woman in white, that haunted the dark glen at Raven Rock, and was often heard to shriek on winter nights before a storm, having perished there in the snow. The chief part of the stories, however, turned upon the favourite spectre of Sleepy Hollow, the headless horseman, who had been heard several times of late, patroling the country; and it was said, tethered his horse nightly among the graves in the church yard.

The sequestered situation of this church seems always to have made it a favourite haunt of troubled spirits. It stands on a knoll, surrounded by locust trees and lofty elms, from among which its decent, whitewashed walls shine modestly forth, like Christian purity, beaming through the shades of retirement. A gentle slope descends from it to a silver sheet of water, bordered by high trees, between which, peeps may be caught at the blue hills of the Hudson. To look upon its grass grown yard, where the sunbeams seem to sleep so quietly, one would think that there at least the dead might rest in peace. On one side of the church extends a wide woody dell, along which raves a large brook among broken rocks and trunks of fallen trees. Over a deep black part of the stream, not far from the church, was formerly thrown a wooden bridge; the road that led to it, and the bridge itself, were thickly shaded by overhanging trees, which cast a gloom about it, even in the day time; but occasioned a fearful darkness at night. Such was one of the favourite haunts of the headless horseman, and the place where he was most frequently encountered. The tale was told of old Brouwer, a most heretical disbeliever in ghosts, how he met the horseman returning from his foray into Sleepy Hollow, and was obliged to get up behind him; how they gallopped over bush and brake, over hill and swamp, until they reached the bridge, when the horseman suddenly turned into a skeleton, threw old Brouwer into the brook, and sprang away over the tree tops with a clap of thunder.

This story was immediately matched by a thrice marvellous adventure of Brom Bones, who made light of the gallopping Hessian as an arrant jockey. He affirmed, that on returning one night from the neighbouring village of Sing-Sing, he had been overtaken by this midnight trooper; that he had offered to race with him for a bowl of punch, and should have won it too, for Daredevil beat the goblin horse all hollow, but just as they came to the church bridge, the Hessian bolted, and vanished in a flash of fire.

All these tales, told in that drowsy under tone with which men talk in the dark, the countenances of the listeners only now and then receiving a casual gleam from the glare of a pipe, sunk deep in the mind of Ichabod. He repaid them in kind with large extracts from his invaluable author, Cotton Mather, and added many very marvellous events that had taken place in his native state of Connecticut, and fearful sights which he had seen in his nightly walks about Sleepy Hollow.

The revel now gradually broke up. The old farmers gathered together their families in their wagons, and were heard for some time rattling along the hollow roads, and over the distant hills. Some of the damsels, mounted on pillions behind their favourite swains, and their light hearted laughter mingling with the clatter of hoofs, echoed along the silent woodlands, sounding fainter and fainter until they gradually died away—and the late scene of noise and frolick was all silent and deserted. Ichabod only lingered behind, according to the custom of country lovers, to have a tête-a-tête with the heiress; fully convinced that he was now on the high road to success. What passed at this interview I will not pretend to say, for in fact I do not know. Something, however, I fear me, must have gone wrong, for he certainly sallied forth, after no very great interval, with an air quite desolate and chopfallen—Oh these women! these women! Could that girl have been playing off any of her coquettish tricks?—Was her encouragement of the poor pedagogue all a mere sham to secure her conquest of his rival?—Heaven only knows, not I!—Let it suffice to say, Ichabod stole forth with the air of one who had been sacking a hen roost, rather than a fair lady's heart. Without looking to the right or left to notice the scene of rural wealth, on which he had so often gloated, he went straight to the stable, and with several hearty cuffs and kicks, roused his steed most uncourteously from the comfortable quarters in which he was soundly sleeping, dreaming of mountains of corn and oats, and whole valleys of timothy and clover.

It was the very witching time of night that Ichabod, heavy hearted and crest fallen, pursued his travel homewards, along the sides of the lofty hills which rise above Tarry Town, and which he had traversed so cheerily in the afternoon. The hour was as dismal as himself. Far below him the Tappaan Zee spread its dusky and indistinct waste of waters, with here and there the tall mast of a sloop, riding quietly at anchor under the land. In the dead hush of midnight, he could even hear the barking of the watch dog from the opposite shore of the Hudson; but it was so vague and faint as only to give an idea of his distance from this faithful companion of man. Now and then, too, the long drawn crowing of a cock, accidentally awakened, would sound far, far off, from some farm house away among the hills—but it was like a dreaming sound in his ear. No signs of life occurred near him, but occasionally the melancholy chirp of a cricket, or perhaps the guttural twang of a bull frog, from a neighbouring marsh, as if sleeping uncomfortably, and turning suddenly in his bed.

All the stories of ghosts and goblins that he had heard in the afternoon, now came crowding upon his recollection. The night grew darker and darker; the stars seemed to sink deeper in the sky, and driving clouds occasionally hid them from his sight. He had never felt so lonely and dismal. He was, moreover, approaching the very place where many of the scenes of the ghost stories had been laid. In the centre of the road stood an enormous tulip tree, which towered like a giant above all the other trees of the neighbourhood, and formed a kind of land mark. Its limbs were gnarled, and fantastic, large enough to form trunks for ordinary trees, twisting down almost to the earth, and rising again into the air. It was connected with the tragical story of the unfortunate André, who had been taken prisoner hard by; and was universally known by the name of Major André's tree. The common people regarded it with a mixture of respect and superstition, partly out of sympathy for the fate of its ill starred namesake, and partly from the tales of strange sights, and doleful lamentations, told concerning it.

As Ichabod approached this fearful tree, he began to whistle; he thought his whistle was answered: it was but a blast sweeping sharply through the dry branches. As he approached a little nearer, he thought he saw something white, hanging in the midst of the tree: he paused and ceased whistling; but on looking more narrowly, perceived that it was a place where the tree had been scathed by lightning, and the white wood laid bare. Suddenly he heard a groan—his teeth chattered, and his knees smote against the saddle: it was but the rubbing of one huge bough upon another, as they were swayed about by the breeze. He passed the tree in safety, but new perils lay before him.

About two hundred yards from the tree, a small brook crossed the road, and ran into a marshy and thickly wooded glen, known by the name of Wiley's Swamp. A few rough logs, laid side by side, served for a bridge over this stream. On that side of the road where the brook entered the wood, a group of oaks and chestnuts, matted thick with wild grape vines, threw a cavernous gloom over it. To pass this bridge, was the severest trial. It was at this identical spot that the unfortunate André was captured, and under the covert of those chestnuts and vines were the sturdy yeomen concealed who surprised him. This has ever since been considered a haunted stream, and fearful are the feelings of the schoolboy who has to pass it alone after dark.

As he approached the stream, his heart began to thump; he, however, summoned up all his resolution, gave his horse half a score of kicks in the ribs, and attempted to dash briskly across the bridge; but instead of starting forward, the perverse old animal made a lateral movement, and ran broadside against the fence. Ichabod, whose fears increased with the delay, jerked the reins on the other side, and kicked lustily with the contrary foot: it was all in vain; his steed started, it is true, but it was only to plunge to the opposite side of the road into a thicket of brambles and alder bushes. The schoolmaster now bestowed both whip and heel upon the starvelling ribs of old Gunpowder, who dashed forward, snuffling and snorting, but came to a stand just by the bridge with a suddenness that had nearly sent his rider sprawling over his head. Just at this moment a plashy tramp by the side of the bridge caught the sensitive ear of Ichabod. In the dark shadow of the grove, on the margin of the brook, he beheld something huge, misshapen, black and towering. It stirred not, but seemed gathered up in the gloom, like some gigantic monster ready to spring upon the traveller.

The hair of the affrighted pedagogue rose upon his head with terror. What was to be done? To turn and fly was now too late; and besides, what chance was there of escaping ghost or goblin, if such it was, which could ride upon the wings of the wind? Summoning up, therefore, a show of courage, he demanded in stammering accents—"who are you?" He received no reply. He repeated his demand in a still more agitated voice.—Still there was no answer. Once more he cudgelled the sides of the inflexible Gunpowder, and shutting his eyes, broke forth with involuntary fervour into a psalm tune. Just then the shadowy object of alarm put itself in motion, and with a scramble and a bound, stood at once in the middle of the road. Though the night was dark and dismal, yet the form of the unknown might now in some degree be ascertained. He appeared to be a horseman of large dimensions, and mounted on a black horse of powerful frame. He made no offer of molestation or sociability, but kept aloof on one side of the road, jogging along on the blind side of old Gunpowder, who had now got over his fright and waywardness.

Ichabod, who had no relish for this strange midnight companion, and bethought himself of the adventure of Brom Bones with the gallopping Hessian, now quickened his steed, in hopes of leaving him behind. The stranger, however, quickened his horse to an equal pace; Ichabod pulled up, and fell into a walk, thinking to lag behind—the other did the same. His heart began to sink within him; he endeavoured to resume his psalm tune, but his parched tongue clove to the roof of his mouth, and he could not utter a stave. There was something in the moody and dogged silence of this pertinacious companion, that was mysterious and appalling. It was soon fearfully accounted for. On mounting a rising ground, which brought the figure of his fellow traveller in relief against the sky, gigantic in height, and muffled in a cloak, Ichabod was horror struck, on perceiving that he was headless! but his horror was still more increased, on observing, that the head, which should have rested on his shoulders, was carried before him on the pommel of the saddle! His terror rose to desperation; he rained a shower of kicks and blows upon Gunpowder, hoping, by a sudden movement, to give his companion the slip—but the spectre started full jump with him. Away, then, they dashed, through thick and thin; stones flying, and sparks flashing, at every bound. Ichabod's flimsy garments fluttered in the air, as he stretched his long lank body away over his horse's head, in the eagerness of his flight.

They had now reached the road which turns off to Sleepy Hollow; but Gunpowder, who seemed possessed with a demon, instead of keeping up it, made an opposite turn, and plunged headlong-down hill to the left. This road leads through a sandy hollow shaded by trees for about a quarter of a mile, where it crosses the bridge famous in goblin story, and just beyond swells the green knoll on which stands the whitewashed church.

As yet the panic of the steed had given his unskilful rider an apparent advantage in the chase, but just as he had got half way through the hollow, the girths of the saddle gave way, and he felt it slipping from under him; he seized it by the pommel, and endeavoured to hold it firm, but in vain; and had just time to save himself by clasping old Gunpowder round the neck, when the saddle fell to the earth, and he heard it trampled under foot by his pursuer. For a moment the terror of Hans Van Ripper's wrath passed across his mind—for it was his Sunday saddle; but this was no time for petty fears: the goblin was hard on his haunches; and (unskilful rider that he was!) he had much ado to maintain his seat; sometimes slipping on one side, sometimes on another, and sometimes jolted on the high ridge of his horse's back bone, with a violence that he verily feared would cleve him asunder.

An opening in the trees now cheered him with the hopes that the Church Bridge was at hand. The wavering reflection of a silver star in the bosom of the brook told him that he was not mistaken. He saw the walls of the church dimly glaring under the trees beyond. He recollected the place where Brom Bones' ghostly competitor had disappeared. "If I can but reach that bridge," thought Ichabod, "I am safe." Just then he heard the black steed panting and blowing close behind him; he even fancied that he felt his hot breath. Another convulsive kick in the ribs, and old Gunpowder sprung upon the bridge; he thundered over the resounding planks; he gained the opposite side, and now Ichabod cast a look behind to see if his pursuer should vanish, according to rule, in a flash of fire and brimstone. Just then he saw the goblin rising in his stirrups, and in the very act of hurling his head at him. Ichabod endeavoured to dodge the horrible missile, but too late. It encountered his cranium with a tremendous crash—he was tumbled headlong into the dust, and Gunpowder, the black steed, and the goblin rider, passed by like a whirlwind.

The next morning the old horse was found without his saddle, and with the bridle under his feet, soberly cropping the grass at his master's gate. Ichabod did not make his appearance at breakfast—dinner hour came, but no Ichabod. The boys assembled at the schoolhouse, and strolled idly about the banks of the brook; but no schoolmaster. Hans Van Ripper now began to feel some uneasiness about the fate of poor Ichabod, and his saddle. An inquiry was set on foot, and after diligent investigation they came upon his traces. In one part of the road leading to the church, was found the saddle trampled in the dirt; the tracks of horses' hoofs deeply dented in the road, and evidently at furious speed, were traced to the bridge, beyond which, on the bank of a broad part of the brook, where the water ran deep and black, was found the hat of the unfortunate Ichabod, and close beside it a shattered pumpkin.

The brook was searched, but the body of the schoolmaster was not to be discovered. Hans Van Ripper, as executor of his estate, examined the bundle which contained all his worldy effects. They consisted of two shirts and a half; two stocks for the neck; a pair or two of worsted stockings; an old pair of corduroy small clothes; a rusty razor; a book of psalm tunes, full of dog's ears; and a broken pitch pipe. As to the books and furniture of the schoolhouse, they belonged to the community, excepting Cotton Mather's History of Witchcraft, a New England Almanack, and a book of dreams and fortune telling, in which last was a sheet of foolscap much scribbled and blotted, in several fruitless attempts to make a copy of verses in honour of the heiress of Van Tassel. These magic books and the poetic scrawl were forthwith consigned to the flames by Hans Van Ripper, who from that time forward determined to send his children no more to school, observing, that he never knew any good come of this same reading and writing. Whatever money the schoolmaster possessed, and he had received his quarter's pay but a day or two before, he must have had about his person at the time of his disappearance.

The mysterious event caused much speculation at the Church on the following Sunday. Knots of gazers and gossips were collected in the church yard, at the bridge, and at the spot where the hat and pumpkin had been found. The stories of Brouwer, of Bones, and a whole budget of others, were called to mind; and when they had diligently considered them all, and compared them with the symptoms of the present case, they shook their heads, and came to the conclusion, that Ichabod had been carried off by the gallopping Hessian. As he was a bachelor, and in nobody's debt, nobody troubled his head any more about him, the school was removed to a different quarter of the hollow, and another pedagogue reigned in his stead.

It is true, an old farmer, who had been down to New York on a visit several years after, and from whom this account of the ghostly adventure was received, brought home the intelligence that Ichabod Crane was still alive; that he had left the neighbourhood partly through fear of the goblin and Hans Van Ripper, and partly in mortification at having been suddenly dismissed by the heiress; that he had changed his quarters to a distant part of the country; had kept school and studied law at the same time; had been admitted to the bar, turned politician, electioneered, written for the newspapers, and finally had been made a Justice of the Ten Pound Court. Brom Bones too, who, shortly after his rival's disappearance, conducted the blooming Katrina in triumph to the altar, was observed to look exceedingly knowing whenever the story of Ichabod was related, and always burst into a hearty laugh at the mention of the pumpkin; which led some to suspect that he knew more about the matter than he chose to tell.

The old country wives, however, who are the best judges of these matters, maintain to this day, that Ichabod was spirited away by supernatural means; and it is a favourite story often told about the neighbourhood round the winter evening fire. The bridge became more than ever an object of superstitious awe, and that may be the reason why the road has been altered of late years, so as to approach the church by the border of the millpond. The schoolhouse being deserted, soon fell to decay, and was reported to be haunted by the ghost of the unfortunate pedagogue; and the plough boy, loitering homeward of a still summer evening, has often fancied his voice at a distance, chanting a melancholy psalm tune among the tranquil solitudes of Sleepy Hollow.

POSTSCRIPT

Found in the Handwriting of Mr. Knickerbocker

The preceding Tale is given, almost in the precise words in which I heard it related at a corporation meeting of the ancient city of Manhattoes, at which were present many of its sagest and most illustrious burghers. The narrator was a pleasant, shabby, gentlemanly old fellow, in pepper and salt clothes, with a sadly humorous face, and one whom I strongly suspected of being poor, he made such efforts to be entertaining. When his story was concluded, there was much laughter and approbation, particularly from two or three deputy aldermen, who had been asleep the greater part of the time. There was, however, one tall, dry looking old gentleman, with beetling eye brows, who maintained a grave and rather severe face throughout; now and then folding his arms, inclining his head, and looking down upon the floor, as if turning a doubt over in his mind. He was one of your wary men, who never laugh but upon good grounds—when they have reason and the law on their side. When the mirth of the rest of the company had subsided, and silence was restored, he leaned one arm on the elbow of his chair, and sticking the other akimbo, demanded, with a slight, but exceedingly sage motion of the head, and contraction of the brow, what was the moral of the story, and what it went to prove.

The story teller, who was just putting a glass of wine to his lips, as a refreshment after his toils, paused for a moment, looked at his inquirer with an air of infinite deference, and lowering the glass slowly to the table, observed, that the story was intended most logically to prove,

"That there is no situation in life but has its advantages and pleasures, provided we will but take a joke as we find it:

"That, therefore, he that runs races with goblin troopers, is likely to have rough riding of it:

"Ergo, for a country schoolmaster to be refused the hand of a Dutch heiress, is a certain step to high preferment in the state."

The cautious old gentleman knit his brows tenfold closer after this explanation, being sorely puzzled by the ratiocination of the syllogism; while methought the one in pepper and salt eyed him with something of a triumphant leer. At length he observed, that all this was very well, but still he thought the story a little on the extravagant—there were one or two points on which he had his doubts.

"Faith, sir," replied the story teller, "as to that matter, I don't believe one half of it myself."

D.K.

Rappaccini's Daughter

NATHANIEL HAWTHORNE

(1804–1864)

A young man, named Giovanni Guasconti, came, very long ago, from the more southern region of Italy, to pursue his studies at the University of Padua. Giovanni, who had but a scanty supply of gold ducats in his pocket, took lodgings in a high and gloomy chamber of an old edifice which looked not unworthy to have been the palace of a Paduan noble, and which, in fact, exhibited over its entrance the armorial bearings of a family long since extinct. The young stranger, who was not unstudied in the great poem of his country, recollected that one of the ancestors of this family, and perhaps an occupant of this very mansion, had been pictured by Dante as a partaker of the immortal agonies of his Inferno. These reminiscences and associations, together with the tendency to heartbreak natural to a young man for the first time out of his native sphere, caused Giovanni to sigh heavily as he looked around the desolate and ill-furnished apartment.

"Holy Virgin, signor!" cried old Dame Lisabetta, who, won by the youth's remarkable beauty of person, was kindly endeavoring to give the chamber a habitable air, "what a sigh was that to come out of a young man's heart! Do you find this old mansion gloomy? For the love of Heaven, then, put your head out of the window, and you will see as bright sunshine as you have left in Naples."

Guasconti mechanically did as the old woman advised, but could not quite agree with her that the Paduan sunshine was as cheerful as that of southern Italy. Such as it was, however, it fell upon a garden beneath the window and expended its fostering influences on a variety of plants, which seemed to have been cultivated with exceeding care.

"Does this garden belong to the house?" asked Giovanni.

"Heaven forbid, signor, unless it were fruitful of better pot herbs than any that grow there now," answered old Lisabetta. "No; that garden is cultivated by the own hands of Signor Giacomo Rappaccini, the famous doctor, who, I warrant him, has been heard of as far as Naples. It is said that he distils these plants into medicines that are as potent as a charm. Oftentimes you may see the signor doctor at work, and perchance the signora, his daughter, too, gathering the strange flowers that grow in the garden."

The old woman had now done what she could for the aspect of the chamber; and, commending the young man to the protection of the saints, took her departure.

Giovanni still found no better occupation than to look down into the garden beneath his window. From its appearance, he judged it to be one of those botanic gardens which were of earlier date in Padua than elsewhere in Italy or in the world. Or, not improbably, it might once have been the pleasure-place of an opulent family; for there was the ruin of a marble fountain in the centre, sculptured with rare art, but so wofully shattered that it was impossible to trace the original design from the chaos of remaining fragments. The water, however, continued to gush and sparkle into the sunbeams as cheerfully as ever. A little gurgling sound ascended to the young man's window, and made him feel as if the fountain were an immortal spirit that sung its song unceasingly and without heeding the vicissitudes around it, while one century imbodied it in marble and another scattered the perishable garniture on the soil. All about the pool into which the water subsided grew various plants, that seemed to require a plentiful supply of moisture for the nourishment of gigantic leaves, and, in some instances, flowers gorgeously magnificent. There was one shrub in particular, set in a marble vase in the midst of the pool, that bore a profusion of purple blossoms, each of which had the lustre and richness of a gem; and the whole together made a show so resplendent that it seemed enough to illuminate the garden, even had there been no sunshine. Every portion of the soil was peopled with plants and herbs, which, if less beautiful, still bore tokens of assiduous care, as if all had their individual virtues, known to the scientific mind that fostered them. Some were placed in urns, rich with old carving, and others in common garden pots; some crept serpentlike along the ground or climbed on high, using whatever means of ascent was offered them. One plant had wreathed itself round a statue of Vertumnus, which was thus quite veiled and shrouded in a drapery of hanging foliage, so happily arranged that it might have served a sculptor for study.

While Giovanni stood at the window he heard a rustling behind a screen of leaves, and became aware that a person was at work in the garden. His figure soon emerged into view, and showed itself to be that of no common laborer, but a tall, emaciated, sallow, and sickly-looking man, dressed in a scholar's garb of black. He was beyond the middle term of life, with gray hair, a thin, gray beard, and a face singularly marked with intellect and cultivation, but which could never, even in his more youthful days, have expressed much warmth of heart.

Nothing could exceed the intentness with which this scientific gardener examined every shrub which grew in his path: it seemed as if he was looking into their inmost nature, making observations in regard to their creative essence, and discovering why one leaf grew in this shape and another in that, and wherefore such and such flowers differed among themselves in hue and perfume. Nevertheless, in spite of this deep intelligence on his part, there was no approach to intimacy between himself and these vegetable existences. On the contrary, he avoided their actual touch or the direct inhaling of their odors with a caution that impressed Giovanni most disagreeably; for the man's demeanor was that of one walking among malignant influences, such as savage beasts, or deadly snakes, or evil spirits, which, should he allow them one moment of license, would wreak upon him some terrible fatality. It was strangely frightful to the young man's imagination to see this air of insecurity in a person cultivating a garden, that most simple and innocent of human toils, and which had been alike the joy and labor of the unfallen parents of the race. Was this garden, then, the Eden of the present world? And this man, with such a perception of harm in what his own hands caused to grow—was he the Adam?

The distrustful gardener, while plucking away the dead leaves or pruning the too luxuriant growth of the shrubs, defended his hands with a pair of thick gloves. Nor were these his only armor. When, in his walk through the garden, he came to the magnificent plant that hung its purple gems beside the marble fountain, he placed a kind of mask over his mouth and nostrils, as if all this beauty did but conceal a deadlier malice; but, finding his task still too dangerous, he drew back, removed the mask, and called loudly, but in the infirm voice of a person affected with inward disease—

"Beatrice! Beatrice!"

"Here am I, my father. What would you?" cried a rich and youthful voice from the window of the opposite house—a voice as rich as a tropical sunset, and which made Giovanni, though he knew not why, think of deep hues of purple or crimson and of perfumes heavily delectable. "Are you in the garden?"

"Yes, Beatrice," answered the gardener, "and I need your help."

Soon there emerged from under a sculptured portal the figure of a young girl, arrayed with as much richness of taste as the most splendid of the flowers, beautiful as the day, and with a bloom so deep and vivid that one shade more would have been too much. She looked redundant with life, health, and energy; all of which attributes were bound down and compressed, as it were, and girdled tensely, in their luxuriance, by her virgin zone. Yet Giovanni's fancy must have grown morbid while he looked down into the garden; for the impression which the fair stranger made upon him was as if here were another flower, the human sister of those vegetable ones, as beautiful as they, more beautiful than the richest of them, but still to be touched only with a glove, nor to be approached without a mask. As Beatrice came down the garden path, it was observable that she handled and inhaled the odor of several of the plants which her father had most sedulously avoided.

"Here, Beatrice," said the latter, "see how many needful offices require to be done to our chief treasure. Yet, shattered as I am, my life might pay the penalty of approaching it so closely as circumstances demand. Henceforth, I fear, this plant must be consigned to your sole charge."

"And gladly will I undertake it," cried again the rich tones of the young lady, as she bent towards the magnificent plant and opened her arms as if to embrace it. "Yes, my sister, my splendor, it shall be Beatrice's task to nurse and serve thee; and thou shalt reward her with thy kisses and perfumed breath, which to her is as the breath of life."

Then, with all the tenderness in her manner that was so strikingly expressed in her words, she busied herself with such attentions as the plant seemed to require; and Giovanni, at his lofty window, rubbed his eyes and almost doubted whether it were a girl tending her favorite flower, or one sister performing the duties of affection to another. The scene soon terminated. Whether Dr. Rappaccini had finished his labors in the garden, or that his watchful eye had caught the stranger's face, he now took his daughter's arm and retired. Night was already closing in; oppressive exhalations seemed to proceed from the plants and steal upward past the open window; and Giovanni, closing the lattice, went to his couch and dreamed of a rich flower and beautiful girl. Flower and maiden were different, and yet the same, and fraught with some strange peril in either shape.

But there is an influence in the light of morning that tends to rectify whatever errors of fancy, or even of judgment, we may have incurred during the sun's decline, or among the shadows of the night, or in the less wholesome glow of moonshine. Giovanni's first movement, on starting from sleep, was to throw open the window and gaze down into the garden which his dreams had made so fertile of mysteries. He was surprised and a little ashamed to find how real and matter-of-fact an affair it proved to be, in the first rays of the sun which gilded the dew-drops that hung upon leaf and blossom, and, while giving a brighter beauty to each rare flower, brought everything within the limits of ordinary experience. The young man rejoiced that, in the heart of the barren city, he had the privilege of overlooking this spot of lovely and luxuriant vegetation. It would serve, he said to himself, as a symbolic language to keep him in communion with Nature. Neither the sickly and thoughtworn Dr. Giacomo Rappaccini, it is true, nor his brilliant daughter, were now visible; so that Giovanni could not determine how much of the singularity which he attributed to both was due to their own qualities and how much to his wonder-working fancy; but he was inclined to take a most rational view of the whole matter.

In the course of the day he paid his respects to Signor Pietro Baglioni, professor of medicine in the university, a physician of eminent repute, to whom Giovanni had brought a letter of introduction. The professor was an elderly personage, apparently of genial nature and habits that might almost be called jovial. He kept the young man to dinner, and made himself very agreeable by the freedom and liveliness of his conversation, especially when warmed by a flask or two of Tuscan wine. Giovanni, conceiving that men of science, inhabitants of the same city, must needs be on familiar terms with one another, took an opportunity to mention the name of Dr. Rappaccini. But the professor did not respond with so much cordiality as he had anticipated.

"Ill would it become a teacher of the divine art of medicine," said Professor Pietro Baglioni, in answer to a question of Giovanni, "to withhold due and well-considered praise of a physician so eminently skilled as Rappaccini; but, on the other hand, I should answer it but scantily to my conscience were I to permit a worthy youth like yourself, Signor Giovanni, the son of an ancient friend, to imbibe erroneous ideas respecting a man who might hereafter chance to hold your life and death in his hands. The truth is, our worshipful Dr. Rappaccini has as much science as any member of the faculty—with perhaps one single exception—in Padua, or all Italy; but there are certain grave objections to his professional character."

"And what are they?" asked the young man.

"Has my friend Giovanni any disease of body or heart, that he is so inquisitive about physicians?" said the professor, with a smile. "But as for Rappaccini, it is said of him—and I, who know the man well, can answer for its truth—that he cares infinitely more for science than for mankind. His patients are interesting to him only as subjects for some new experiment. He would sacrifice human life, his own among the rest, or whatever else was dearest to him, for the sake of adding so much as a grain of mustard seed to the great heap of his accumulated knowledge."

"Methinks he is an awful man indeed," remarked Guasconti, mentally recalling the cold and purely intellectual aspect of Rappaccini. "And yet, worshipful professor, is it not a noble spirit? Are there many men capable of so spiritual a love of science?"

"God forbid," answered the professor, somewhat testily; "at least, unless they take sounder views of the healing art than those adopted by Rappaccini. It is his theory that all medicinal virtues are comprised within those substances which we term vegetable poisons. These he cultivates with his own hands, and is said even to have produced new varieties of poison, more horribly deleterious than Nature, without the assistance of this learned person, would ever have plagued the world withal. That the signor doctor does less mischief than might be expected with such dangerous substances is undeniable. Now and then, it must be owned, he has effected, or seemed to effect, a marvellous cure; but, to tell you my private mind, Signor Giovanni, he should receive little credit for such instances of success—they being probably the work of chance—but should be held strictly accountable for his failures, which may justly be considered his own work."

The youth might have taken Baglioni's opinions with many grains of allowance had he known that there was a professional warfare of long continuance between him and Dr. Rappaccini, in which the latter was generally thought to have gained the advantage. If the reader be inclined to judge for himself, we refer him to certain black-letter tracts on both sides, preserved in the medical department of the University of Padua.

"I know not, most learned professor," returned Giovanni, after musing on what had been said of Rappaccini's exclusive zeal for science—"I know not how dearly this physician may love his art; but surely there is one object more dear to him. He has a daughter."

"Aha!" cried the professor, with a laugh. "So now our friend Giovanni's secret is out. You have heard of this daughter, whom all the young men in Padua are wild about, though not half a dozen have ever had the good hap to see her face. I know little of the Signora Beatrice save that Rappaccini is said to have instructed her deeply in his science, and that, young and beautiful as fame reports her, she is already qualified to fill a professor's chair. Perchance her father destines her for mine! Other absurd rumors there be, not worth talking about or listening to. So now, Signor Giovanni, drink off your glass of lachryma."

Guasconti returned to his lodgings somewhat heated with the wine he had quaffed, and which caused his brain to swim with strange fantasies in reference to Dr. Rappaccini and the beautiful Beatrice. On his way, happening to pass by a florist's, he bought a fresh bouquet of flowers.

Ascending to his chamber, he seated himself near the window, but within the shadow thrown by the depth of the wall, so that he could look down into the garden with little risk of being discovered. All beneath his eye was a solitude. The strange plants were basking in the sunshine, and now and then nodding gently to one another, as if in acknowledgment of sympathy and kindred. In the midst, by the shattered fountain, grew the magnificent shrub, with its purple gems clustering all over it; they glowed in the air, and gleamed back again out of the depths of the pool, which thus seemed to overflow with colored radiance from the rich reflection that was steeped in it. At first, as we have said, the garden was a solitude. Soon, however—as Giovanni had half hoped, half feared, would be the case—a figure appeared beneath the antique sculptured portal, and came down between the rows of plants, inhaling their various perfumes as if she were one of those beings of old classic fable that lived upon sweet odors. On again beholding Beatrice, the young man was even startled to perceive how much her beauty exceeded his recollection of it; so brilliant, so vivid, was its character, that she glowed amid the sunlight, and, as Giovanni whispered to himself, positively illuminated the more shadowy intervals of the garden path. Her face being now more revealed than on the former occasion, he was struck by its expression of simplicity and sweetness—qualities that had not entered into his idea of her character, and which made him ask anew what manner of mortal she might be. Nor did he fail again to observe, or imagine, an analogy between the beautiful girl and the gorgeous shrub that hung its gemlike flowers over the fountain—a resemblance which Beatrice seemed to have indulged a fantastic humor in heightening, both by the arrangement of her dress and the selection of its hues.

Approaching the shrub, she threw open her arms, as with a passionate ardor, and drew its branches into an intimate embrace—so intimate that her features were hidden in its leafy bosom and her glistening ringlets all intermingled with the flowers.

"Give me thy breath, my sister," exclaimed Beatrice; "for I am faint with common air. And give me this flower of thine, which I separate with gentlest fingers from the stem and place it close beside my heart."

With these words the beautiful daughter of Rappaccini plucked one of the richest blossoms of the shrub, and was about to fasten it in her bosom. But now, unless Giovanni's draughts of wine had bewildered his senses, a singular incident occurred. A small orange-colored reptile, of the lizard or chameleon species, chanced to be creeping along the path, just at the feet of Beatrice. It appeared to Giovanni—but, at the distance from which he gazed, he could scarcely have seen anything so minute—it appeared to him, however, that a drop or two of moisture from the broken stem of the flower descended upon the lizard's head. For an instant the reptile contorted itself violently, and then lay motionless in the sunshine. Beatrice observed this remarkable phenomenon, and crossed herself, sadly, but without surprise; nor did she therefore hesitate to arrange the fatal flower in her bosom. There it blushed, and almost glimmered with the dazzling effect of a precious stone, adding to her dress and aspect the one appropriate charm which nothing else in the world could have supplied. But Giovanni, out of the shadow of his window, bent forward and shrank back, and murmured and trembled.

"Am I awake? Have I my senses?" said he to himself. "What is this being? Beautiful shall I call her, or inexpressibly terrible?"

Beatrice now strayed carelessly through the garden, approaching closer beneath Giovanni's window, so that he was compelled to thrust his head quite out of its concealment in order to gratify the intense and painful curiosity which she excited. At this moment there came a beautiful insect over the garden wall; it had, perhaps, wandered through the city, and found no flowers or verdure among those antique haunts of men until the heavy perfumes of Dr. Rappaccini's shrubs had lured it from afar. Without alighting on the flowers, this winged brightness seemed to be attracted by Beatrice, and lingered in the air and fluttered about her head. Now, here it could not be but that Giovanni Guasconti's eyes deceived him. Be that as it might, he fancied that, while Beatrice was gazing at the insect with childish delight, it grew faint and fell at her feet; its bright wings shivered; it was dead—from no cause that he could discern, unless it were the atmosphere of her breath. Again Beatrice crossed herself and sighed heavily as she bent over the dead insect.

An impulsive movement of Giovanni drew her eyes to the window. There she beheld the beautiful head of the young man—rather a Grecian than an Italian head, with fair, regular features, and a glistening of gold among his ringlets—gazing down upon her like a being that hovered in mid air. Scarcely knowing what he did, Giovanni threw down the bouquet which he had hitherto held in his hand.

"Signora," said he, "there are pure and healthful flowers. Wear them for the sake of Giovanni Guasconti."

"Thanks, signor," replied Beatrice, with her rich voice, that came forth as it were like a gush of music, and with a mirthful expression half childish and half woman-like. "I accept your gift, and would fain recompense it with this precious purple flower; but if I toss it into the air it will not reach you. So Signor Guasconti must even content himself with my thanks."

She lifted the bouquet from the ground, and then, as if inwardly ashamed at having stepped aside from her maidenly reserve to respond to a stranger's greeting, passed swiftly homeward through the garden. But few as the moments were, it seemed to Giovanni, when she was on the point of vanishing beneath the sculptured portal, that his beautiful bouquet was already beginning to wither in her grasp. It was an idle thought; there could be no possibility of distinguishing a faded flower from a fresh one at so great a distance.

For many days after this incident the young man avoided the window that looked into Dr. Rappaccini's garden, as if something ugly and monstrous would have blasted his eyesight had he been betrayed into a glance. He felt conscious of having put himself, to a certain extent, within the influence of an unintelligible power by the communication which he had opened with Beatrice. The wisest course would have been, if his heart were in any real danger, to quit his lodgings and Padua itself at once; the next wiser, to have accustomed himself, as far as possible, to the familiar and daylight view of Beatrice—thus bringing her rigidly and systematically within the limits of ordinary experience. Least of all, while avoiding her sight, ought Giovanni to have remained so near this extraordinary being that the proximity and possibility even of intercourse should give a kind of substance and reality to the wild vagaries which his imagination ran riot continually in producing. Guasconti had not a deep heart—or, at all events, its depths were not sounded now; but he had a quick fancy, and an ardent southern temperament, which rose every instant to a higher fever pitch. Whether or no Beatrice possessed those terrible attributes, that fatal breath, the affinity with those so beautiful and deadly flowers which were indicated by what Giovanni had witnessed, she had at least instilled a fierce and subtle poison into his system. It was not love, although her rich beauty was a madness to him; nor horror, even while he fancied her spirit to be imbued with the same baneful essence that seemed to pervade her physical frame; but a wild offspring of both love and horror that had each parent in it, and burned like one and shivered like the other. Giovanni knew not what to dread; still less did he know what to hope; yet hope and dread kept a continual warfare in his breast, alternately vanquishing one another and starting up afresh to renew the contest. Blessed are all simple emotions, be they dark or bright! It is the lurid intermixture of the two that produces the illuminating blaze of the infernal regions.

Sometimes he endeavored to assuage the fever of his spirit by a rapid walk through the streets of Padua or beyond its gates: his footsteps kept time with the throbbings of his brain, so that the walk was apt to accelerate itself to a race. One day he found himself arrested; his arm was seized by a portly personage, who had turned back on recognizing the young man and expended much breath in overtaking him.

"Signor Giovanni! Stay, my young friend!" cried he. "Have you forgotten me? That might well be the case if I were as much altered as yourself."

It was Baglioni, whom Giovanni had avoided ever since their first meeting, from a doubt that the professor's sagacity would look too deeply into his secrets. Endeavoring to recover himself, he stared forth wildly from his inner world into the outer one and spoke like a man in a dream.

"Yes; I am Giovanni Guasconti. You are Professor Pietro Baglioni. Now let me pass!"

"Not yet, not yet, Signor Giovanni Guasconti," said the professor, smiling, but at the same time scrutinizing the youth with an earnest glance. "What! did I grow up side by side with your father? and shall his son pass me like a stranger in these old streets of Padua? Stand still, Signor Giovanni; for we must have a word or two before we part."

"Speedily, then, most worshipful professor, speedily," said Giovanni, with feverish impatience. "Does not your worship see that I am in haste?"

Now, while he was speaking there came a man in black along the street, stooping and moving feebly like a person in inferior health. His face was all overspread with a most sickly and sallow hue, but yet so pervaded with an expression of piercing and active intellect that an observer might easily have overlooked the merely physical attributes and have seen only this wonderful energy. As he passed, this person exchanged a cold and distant salutation with Baglioni, but fixed his eyes upon Giovanni with an intentness that seemed to bring out whatever was within him worthy of notice. Nevertheless, there was a peculiar quietness in the look, as if taking merely a speculative, not a human, interest in the young man.

"It is Dr. Rappaccini!" whispered the professor when the stranger had passed. "Has he ever seen your face before?"

"Not that I know," answered Giovanni, starting at the name.

"He *has* seen you! he must have seen you!" said Baglioni, hastily. "For some purpose or other, this man of science is making a study of you. I know that look of his! It is the same that coldly illuminates his face as he bends over a bird, a mouse, or a butterfly, which, in pursuance of some experiment, he has killed by the perfume of a flower; a look as deep as Nature itself, but without Nature's warmth of love. Signor Giovanni, I will stake my life upon it, you are the subject of one of Rappaccini's experiments!"

"Will you make a fool of me?" cried Giovanni, passionately. "*That,* signor professor, were an untoward experiment."

"Patience! patience!" replied the imperturbable professor. "I tell thee, my poor Giovanni, that Rappaccini has a scientific interest in thee. Thou hast fallen into fearful hands! And the Signora Beatrice—what part does she act in this mystery?"

But Guasconti, finding Baglioni's pertinacity intolerable, here broke away, and was gone before the professor could again seize his arm. He looked after the young man intently and shook his head.

"This must not be," said Baglioni to himself. "The youth is the son of my old friend, and shall not come to any harm from which the arcana of medical science can preserve him. Besides, it is too insufferable an impertinence in Rappaccini, thus to snatch the lad out of my own hands, as I may say, and make use of him for his infernal experiments. This daughter of his! It shall be looked to. Perchance, most learned Rappaccini, I may foil you where you little dream of it!"

Meanwhile Giovanni had pursued a circuitous route, and at length found himself at the door of his lodgings. As he crossed the threshold he was met by old Lisabetta, who smirked and smiled, and was evidently desirous to attract his attention; vainly, however, as the ebullition of his feelings had momentarily subsided into a cold and dull vacuity. He turned his eyes full upon the withered face that was puckering itself into a smile, but seemed to behold it not. The old dame, therefore, laid her grasp upon his cloak.

"Signor! signor!" whispered she, still with a smile over the whole breath of her visage, so that it looked not unlike a grotesque carving in wood, darkened by centuries. "Listen, signor! There is a private entrance into the garden!"

"What do you say?" exclaimed Giovanni, turning quickly about, as if an inanimate thing should start into feverish life. "A private entrance into Dr. Rappaccini's garden?"

"Hush! hush! not so loud!" whispered Lisabetta, putting her hand over his mouth. "Yes; into the worshipful doctor's garden, where you may see all his fine shrubbery. Many a young man in Padua would give gold to be admitted among those flowers."

Giovanni put a piece of gold into her hand.

"Show me the way," said he.

A surmise, probably excited by his conversation with Baglioni, crossed his mind, that this interposition of old Lisabetta might perchance be connected with the intrigue, whatever were its nature, in which the professor seemed to suppose that Dr. Rappaccini was involving him. But such a suspicion, though it disturbed Giovanni, was inadequate to restrain him. The instant that he was aware of the possibility of approaching Beatrice, it seemed an absolute necessity of his existence to do so. It mattered not whether she were angel or demon; he was irrevocably within her sphere, and must obey the law that whirled him onward, in ever-lessening circles, towards a result which he did not attempt to foreshadow; and yet, strange to say, there came across him a sudden doubt whether this intense interest on his part were not delusory; whether it were really of so deep and positive a nature as to justify him in now thrusting himself into an incalculable position; whether it were not merely the fantasy of a young man's brain, only slightly or not at all connected with his heart.

He paused, hesitated, turned half about, but again went on. His withered guide led him along several obscure passages, and finally undid a door, through which, as it was opened, there came the sight and sound of rustling leaves, with the broken sunshine glimmering among them. Giovanni stepped forth, and, forcing himself through the entanglement of a shrub that wreathed its tendrils over the hidden entrance, stood beneath his own window in the open area of Dr. Rappaccini's garden.

How often is it the case that, when impossibilities have come to pass and dreams have condensed their misty substance into tangible realities, we find ourselves calm, and even coldly self-possessed, amid circumstances which it would have been a delirium of joy or agony to anticipate! Fate delights to thwart us thus. Passion will choose his own time to rush upon the scene, and lingers sluggishly behind when an appropriate adjustment of events would seem to summon his appearance. So was it now with Giovanni. Day after day his pulses had throbbed with feverish blood at the improbable idea of an interview with Beatrice, and of standing with her, face to face, in this very garden, basking in the Oriental sunshine of her beauty, and snatching from her full gaze the mystery which he deemed the riddle of his own existence. But now there was a singular and untimely equanimity within his breast. He threw a glance around the garden to discover if Beatrice or her father were present, and, perceiving that he was alone, began a critical observation of the plants.

The aspect of one and all of them dissatisfied him; their gorgeousness seemed fierce, passionate, and even unnatural. There was hardly an individual shrub which a wanderer, straying by himself through a forest, would not have been startled to find growing wild, as if an unearthly face had glared at him out of the thicket. Several also would have shocked a delicate instinct by an appearance of artificialness indicating that there had been such commixture, and, as it were, adultery, of various vegetable species, that the production was no longer of God's making, but the monstrous offspring of man's depraved fancy, glowing with only an evil mockery of beauty. They were probably the result of experiment, which in one or two cases had succeeded in mingling plants individually lovely into a compound possessing the questionable and ominous character that distinguished the whole growth of the garden. In fine, Giovanni recognized but two or three plants in the collection, and those of a kind that he well knew to be poisonous. While busy with these contemplations he heard the rustling of a silken garment, and, turning, beheld Beatrice emerging from beneath the sculptured portal.

Giovanni had not considered with himself what should be his deportment; whether he should apologize for his intrusion into the garden, or assume that he was there with the privity at least, if not by the desire, of Dr. Rappaccini or his daughter; but Beatrice's manner placed him at his ease, though leaving him still in doubt by what agency he had gained admittance. She came lightly along the path and met him near the broken fountain. There was surprise in her face, but brightened by a simple and kind expression of pleasure.

"You are a connoisseur in flowers, signor," said Beatrice, with a smile, alluding to the bouquet which he had flung her from the window. "It is no marvel, therefore, if the sight of my father's rare collection has tempted you to take a nearer view. If he were here, he could tell you many strange and interesting facts as to the nature and habits of these shrubs; for he has spent a lifetime in such studies, and this garden is his world."

"And yourself, lady," observed Giovanni, "if fame says true—you likewise are deeply skilled in the virtues indicated by these rich blossoms and these spicy perfumes. Would you deign to be my instructress, I should prove an apter scholar than if taught by Signor Rappaccini himself."

"Are there such idle rumors?" asked Beatrice, with the music of a pleasant laugh. "Do people say that I am skilled in my father's science of plants? What a jest is there! No; though I have grown up among these flowers, I know no more of them than their hues and perfume; and sometimes methinks I would fain rid myself of even that small knowledge. There are many flowers here, and those not the least brilliant, that shock and offend me when they meet my eye. But pray, signor, do not believe these stories about my science. Believe nothing of me save what you see with your own eyes."

"And must I believe all that I have seen with my own eyes?" asked Giovanni, pointedly, while the recollection of former scenes made him shrink. "No, signora; you demand too little of me. Bid me believe nothing save what comes from your own lips."

It would appear that Beatrice understood him. There came a deep flush to her cheek; but she looked full into Giovanni's eyes, and responded to his gaze of uneasy suspicion with a queenlike haughtiness.

"I do so bid you, signor," she replied. "Forget whatever you may have fancied in regard to me. If true to the outward senses, still it may be false in its essence; but the words of Beatrice Rappaccini's lips are true from the depths of the heart outward. Those you may believe."

A fervor glowed in her whole aspect and beamed upon Giovanni's consciousness like the light of truth itself; but while she spoke there was a fragrance in the atmosphere around her, rich and delightful, though evanescent, yet which the young man, from an indefinable reluctance, scarcely dared to draw into his lungs. It might be the odor of the flowers. Could it be Beatrice's breath which thus embalmed her words with a strange richness, as if by steeping them in her heart? A faintness passed like a shadow over Giovanni and flitted away; he seemed to gaze through the beautiful girl's eyes into her transparent soul, and felt no more doubt or fear.

The tinge of passion that had colored Beatrice's manner vanished; she became gay, and appeared to derive a pure delight from her communion with the youth not unlike what the maiden of a lonely island might have felt conversing with a voyager from the civilized world. Evidently her experience of life had been confined within the limits of that garden. She talked now about matters as simple as the daylight or summer clouds, and now asked questions in reference to the city, or Giovanni's distant home, his friends, his mother, and his sisters—questions indicating such seclusion, and such lack of familiarity with modes and forms, that Giovanni responded as if to an infant. Her spirit gushed out before him like a fresh rill that was just catching its first glimpse of the sunlight and wondering at the reflections of earth and sky which were flung into its bosom. There came thoughts, too, from a deep source, and fantasies of a gemlike brilliancy, as if diamonds and rubies sparkled upward among the bubbles of the fountain. Ever and anon there gleamed across the young man's mind a sense of wonder that he should be walking side by side with the being who had so wrought upon his imagination, whom he had idealized in such hues of terror, in whom he had positively witnessed such manifestations of dreadful attributes—that he should be conversing with Beatrice like a brother, and should find her so human and so maidenlike. But such reflections were only momentary; the effect of her character was too real not to make itself familiar at once.

In this free intercourse they had strayed through the garden, and now, after many turns among its avenues, were come to the shattered fountain, beside which grew the magnificent shrub, with its treasury of glowing blossoms. A fragrance was diffused from it which Giovanni recognized as identical with that which he had attributed to Beatrice's breath, but incomparably more powerful. As her eyes fell upon it, Giovanni beheld her press her hand to her bosom as if her heart were throbbing suddenly and painfully.

"For the first time in my life," murmured she, addressing the shrub, "I had forgotten thee."

"I remember, signora," said Giovanni, "that you once promised to reward me with one of these living gems for the bouquet which I had the happy boldness to fling to your feet. Permit me now to pluck it as a memorial of this interview."

He made a step towards the shrub with extended hand; but Beatrice darted forward, uttering a shriek that went through his heart like a dagger. She caught his hand and drew it back with the whole force of her slender figure. Giovanni felt her touch thrilling through his fibres.

"Touch it not!" exclaimed she, in a voice of agony. "Not for thy life! It is fatal!"

Then, hiding her face, she fled from him and vanished beneath the sculptured portal. As Giovanni followed her with his eyes, he beheld the emaciated figure and pale intelligence of Dr. Rappaccini, who had been watching the scene, he knew not how long, within the shadow of the entrance.

No sooner was Guasconti alone in his chamber than the image of Beatrice came back to his passionate musings, invested with all the witchery that had been gathering around it ever since his first glimpse of her, and now likewise imbued with a tender warmth of girlish womanhood. She was human; her nature was endowed with all gentle and feminine qualities; she was worthiest to be worshipped; she was capable, surely, on her part, of the height and heroism of love. Those tokens which he had hitherto considered as proofs of a frightful peculiarity in her physical and moral system were now either forgotten, or, by the subtle sophistry of passion transmitted into a golden crown of enchantment, rendering Beatrice the more admirable by so much as she was the more unique. Whatever had looked ugly was now beautiful; or, if incapable of such a change, it stole away, and hid itself among those shapeless half ideas which throng the dim region beyond the daylight of our perfect consciousness. Thus did he spend the night, nor fell asleep until the dawn had begun to awake the slumbering flowers in Dr. Rappaccini's garden, whither Giovanni's dreams doubtless led him. Up rose the sun in his due season, and, flinging his beams upon the young man's eyelids, awoke him to a sense of pain. When thoroughly aroused, he became sensible of a burning and tingling agony in his hand—in his right hand—the very hand which Beatrice had grasped in her own when he was on the point of plucking one of the gemlike flowers. On the back of that hand there was now a purple print like that of four small fingers, and the likeness of a slender thumb upon his wrist.

Oh, how stubbornly does love—or even that cunning semblance of love which flourishes in the imagination, but strikes no depth of root into the heart—how stubbornly does it hold its faith until the moment comes when it is doomed to vanish into thin mist! Giovanni wrapped a handkerchief about his hand and wondered what evil thing had stung him, and soon forgot his pain in a reverie of Beatrice.

After the first interview, a second was in the inevitable course of what we call fate. A third; a fourth; and a meeting with Beatrice in the garden was no longer an incident in Giovanni's daily life, but the whole space in which he might be said to live; for the anticipation and memory of that ecstatic hour made up the remainder. Nor was it otherwise with the daughter of Rappaccini. She watched for the youth's appearance, and flew to his side with confidence as unreserved as if they had been playmates from early infancy—as if they were such playmates still. If, by any unwonted chance, he failed to come at the appointed moment, she stood beneath the window and sent up the rich sweetness of her tones to float around him in his chamber and echo and reverberate throughout his heart: "Giovanni! Giovanni! Why tarriest thou? Come down!" And down he hastened into that Eden of poisonous flowers.

But, with all this intimate familiarity, there was still a reserve in Beatrice's demeanor, so rigidly and invariably sustained that the idea of infringing it scarcely occurred to his imagination. By all appreciable signs, they loved; they had looked love with eyes that conveyed the holy secret from the depths of one soul into the depths of the other, as if it were too sacred to be whispered by the way; they had even spoken love in those gushes of passion when their spirits darted forth in articulated breath like tongues of long-hidden flame; and yet there had been no seal of lips, no clasp of hands, nor any slightest caress such as love claims and hallows.

He had never touched one of the gleaming ringlets of her hair; her garment—so marked was the physical barrier between them—had never been waved against him by a breeze. On the few occasions when Giovanni had seemed tempted to overstep the limit, Beatrice grew so sad, so stern, and withal wore such a look of desolate separation, shuddering at itself, that not a spoken word was requisite to repel him. At such times he was started at the horrible suspicions that rose, monster-like, out of the caverns of his heart and stared him in the face; his love grew thin and faint as the morning mist, his doubts alone had substance. But, when Beatrice's face brightened again after the momentary shadow, she was transformed at once from the mysterious, questionable being whom he had watched with so much awe and horror; she was now the beautiful and unsophisticated girl whom he felt that his spirit knew with a certainty beyond all other knowledge.

A considerable time had now passed since Giovanni's last meeting with Baglioni. One morning, however, he was disagreeably surprised by a visit from the professor, whom he had scarcely thought of for whole weeks, and would willingly have forgotten still longer. Given up as he had long been to a pervading excitement, he could tolerate no companions except upon condition of their perfect sympathy with his present state of feeling. Such sympathy was not to be expected from Professor Baglioni.

The visitor chatted carelessly for a few moments about the gossip of the city and the university, and then took up another topic.

"I have been reading an old classic author lately," said he, "and met with a story that strangely interested me. Possibly you may remember it. It is of an Indian prince, who sent a beautiful woman as a present to Alexander the Great. She was as lovely as the dawn and gorgeous as the sunset; but what especially distinguished her was a certain rich perfume in her breath—richer than a garden of Persian roses. Alexander, as was natural to a youthful conqueror, fell in love at first sight with this magnificent stranger; but a certain sage physician, happening to be present, discovered a terrible secret in regard to her."

"And what was that?" asked Giovanni, turning his eyes downward to avoid those of the professor.

"That this lovely woman," continued Baglioni, with emphasis, "had been nourished with poisons from her birth upward, until her whole nature was so imbued with them that she herself had become the deadliest poison in existence. Poison was her element of life. With that rich perfume of her breath she blasted the very air. Her love would have been poison—her embrace death. Is not this a marvellous tale?"

"A childish fable," answered Giovanni, nervously starting from his chair. "I marvel how your worship finds time to read such nonsense among your graver studies."

"By the by," said the professor, looking uneasily about him, "what singular fragrance is this in your apartment? Is it the perfume of your gloves? It is faint, but delicious; and yet, after all, by no means agreeable. Were I to breathe it long, methinks it would make me ill. It is like the breath of a flower; but I see no flowers in the chamber."

"Nor are there any," replied Giovanni, who had turned pale as the professor spoke; "nor, I think, is there any fragrance except in your worship's imagination. Odors, being a sort of element combined of the sensual and the spiritual, are apt to deceive us in this manner. The recollection of a perfume, the bare idea of it, may easily be mistaken for a present reality."

"Ay; but my sober imagination does not often play such tricks," said Baglioni; "and, were I to fancy any kind of odor, it would be that of some vile apothecary drug, wherewith my fingers are likely enough to be imbued. Our worshipful friend Rappaccini, as I have heard, tinctures his medicaments with odors richer than those of Araby. Doubtless, likewise, the fair and learned Signora Beatrice would minister to her patients with draughts as sweet as a maiden's breath; but woe to him that sips them!"

Giovanni's face evinced many contending emotions. The tone in which the professor alluded to the pure and lovely daughter of Rappaccini was a torture to his soul; and yet the intimation of a view of her character, opposite to his own, gave instantaneous distinctness to a thousand dim suspicions, which now grinned at him like so many demons. But he strove hard to quell them and to respond to Baglioni with a true lover's perfect faith.

"Signor professor," said he, "you were my father's friend; perchance, too, it is your purpose to act a friendly part towards his son. I would fain feel nothing towards you save respect and deference; but I pray you to observe, signor, that there is one subject on which we must not speak. You know not the Signora Beatrice. You cannot, therefore, estimate the wrong—the blasphemy, I may even say—that is offered to her character by a light or injurious word."

"Giovanni! my poor Giovanni!" answered the professor, with a calm expression of pity, "I know this wretched girl far better than yourself. You shall hear the truth in respect to the poisoner Rappaccini and his poisonous daughter; yes, poisonous as she is beautiful. Listen; for, even should you do violence to my gray hairs, it shall not silence me. That old fable of the Indian woman has become a truth by the deep and deadly science of Rappaccini and in the person of the lovely Beatrice."

Giovanni groaned and hid his face.

"Her father," continued Baglioni, "was not restrained by natural affection from offering up his child in this horrible manner as the victim of his insane zeal for science; for, let us do him justice, he is as true a man of science as ever distilled his own heart in an alembic. What, then, will be your fate? Beyond a doubt you are selected as the material of some new experiment. Perhaps the result is to be death; perhaps a fate more awful still. Rappaccini, with what he calls the interest of science before his eyes, will hesitate at nothing."

"It is a dream," muttered Giovanni to himself; "surely it is a dream."

"But," resumed the professor, "be of good cheer, son of my friend. It is not yet too late for the rescue. Possibly we may even succeed in bringing back this miserable child within the limits of ordinary nature, from which her father's madness has estranged her. Behold this little silver vase! It was wrought by the hands of the renowned Benvenuto Cellini, and is well worthy to be a love gift to the fairest dame in Italy. But its contents are invaluable. One little sip of this antidote would have rendered the most virulent poisons of the Borgias innocuous. Doubt not that it will be as efficacious against those of Rappaccini. Bestow the vase, and the precious liquid within it, on your Beatrice, and hopefully await the result."

Baglioni laid a small, exquisitely wrought silver vial on the table and withdrew, leaving what he had said to produce its effect upon the young man's mind.

"We will thwart Rappaccini yet," thought he, chuckling to himself, as he descended the stairs; "but, let us confess the truth of him, he is a wonderful man—a wonderful man indeed; a vile empiric, however, in his practice, and therefore not to be tolerated by those who respect the good old rules of the medical profession."

Throughout Giovanni's whole acquaintance with Beatrice, he had occasionally, as we have said, been haunted by dark surmises as to her character; yet so thoroughly had she made herself felt by him as a simple, natural, most affectionate, and guileless creature, that the image now held up by Professor Baglioni looked as strange and incredible as if it were not in accordance with his own original conception. True, there were ugly recollections connected with his first glimpses of the beautiful girl: he could not quite forget the bouquet that withered in her grasp, and the insect that perished amid the sunny air, by no ostensible agency save the fragrance of her breath. These incidents, however, dissolving in the pure light of her character, had no longer the efficacy of facts, but were acknowledged as mistaken fantasies, by whatever testimony of the senses they might appear to be substantiated. There is something truer and more real than what we can see with the eyes and touch with the finger. On such better evidence had Giovanni founded his confidence in Beatrice, though rather by the necessary force of her high attributes than by any deep and generous faith on his part. But now his spirit was incapable of sustaining itself at the height to which the early enthusiasm of passion had exalted it; he fell down, grovelling among earthly doubts, and defiled therewith the pure whiteness of Beatrice's image. Not that he gave her up; he did but distrust. He resolved to institute some decisive test that should satisfy him, once for all, whether there were those dreadful peculiarities in her physical nature which could not be supposed to exist without some corresponding monstrosity of soul. His eyes, gazing down afar, might have deceived him as to the lizard, the insect, and the flowers; but if he could witness, at the distance of a few paces, the sudden blight of one fresh and healthful flower in Beatrice's hand, there would be room for no further question. With this idea he hastened to the florist's and purchased a bouquet that was still gemmed with the morning dew-drops.

It was now the customary hour of his daily interview with Beatrice. Before descending into the garden, Giovanni failed not to look at his figure in the mirror—a vanity to be expected in a beautiful young man, yet, as displaying itself at that troubled and feverish moment, the token of a certain shallowness of feeling and insincerity of character. He did gaze, however, and said to himself that his features had never before possessed so rich a grace, nor his eyes such vivacity, nor his cheeks so warm a hue of superabundant life.

"At least," thought he, "her poison has not yet insinuated itself into my system. I am no flower to perish in her grasp."

With that thought he turned his eyes on the bouquet, which he had never once laid aside from his hand. A thrill of indefinable horror shot through his frame on perceiving that those dewy flowers were already beginning to droop; they wore the aspect of things that had been fresh and lovely yesterday. Giovanni grew white as marble, and stood motionless before the mirror, staring at his own reflection there as at the likeness of something frightful. He remembered Baglioni's remark about the fragrance that seemed to pervade the chamber. It must have been the poison in his breath! Then he shuddered—shuddered at himself. Recovering from his stupor, he began to watch with curious eye a spider that was busily at work hanging its web from the antique cornice of the apartment, crossing and recrossing the artful system of interwoven lines—as vigorous and active a spider as ever dangled from an old ceiling. Giovanni bent towards the insect, and emitted a deep, long breath. The spider suddenly ceased its toil; the web vibrated with a tremor originating in the body of the small artisan. Again Giovanni sent forth a breath, deeper, longer, and imbued with a venomous feeling out of his heart: he knew not whether he were wicked, or only desperate. The spider made a convulsive grip with his limbs and hung dead across the window.

"Accursed! accursed!" muttered Giovanni, addressing himself. "Hast thou grown so poisonous that this deadly insect perishes by thy breath?"

At that moment a rich, sweet voice came floating up from the garden.

"Giovanni! Giovanni! It is past the hour! Why tarriest thou? Come down!"

"Yes," muttered Giovanni again. "She is the only being whom by breath may not slay! Would that it might!"

He rushed down, and in an instant was standing before the bright and loving eyes of Beatrice. A moment ago his wrath and despair had been so fierce that he could have desired nothing so much as to wither her by a glance; but with her actual presence there came influences which had too real an existence to be at once shaken off: recollections of the delicate and benign power of her feminine nature, which had so often enveloped him in a religious calm; recollections of many a holy and passionate outgush of her heart, when the pure fountain had been unsealed from its depths and made visible in its transparency to his mental eye; recollections which, had Giovanni known how to estimate them, would have assured him that all this ugly mystery was but an earthly illusion, and that, whatever mist of evil might seem to have gathered over her, the real Beatrice was a heavenly angel. Incapable as he was of such high faith, still her presence had not utterly lost its magic. Giovanni's rage was quelled into an aspect of sullen insensibility. Beatrice, with a quick spiritual sense, immediately felt that there was a gulf of blackness beween them which neither he nor she could pass. They walked on together, sad and silent, and came thus to the marble fountain and to its pool of water on the ground, in the midst of which grew the shrub that bore gemlike blossoms. Giovanni was affrighted at the eager enjoyment—the appetite, as it were—with which he found himself inhaling the fragrance of the flowers.

"Beatrice," asked he, abruptly, "whence came this shrub?"

"My father created it," answered she, with simplicity.

"Created it! created it!" repeated Giovanni. "What mean you, Beatrice?"

"He is a man fearfully acquainted with the secrets of Nature," replied Beatrice; "and, at the hour when I first drew breath, this plant sprang from the soil, the offspring of his science, of his intellect, while I was but his earthly child. Approach it not!" continued she, observing with terror that Giovanni was drawing nearer to the shrub. "It has qualities that you little dream of. But I, dearest Giovanni—I grew up and blossomed with the plant and was nourished with its breath. It was my sister, and I loved it with a human affection; for, alas!—hast thou not suspected it?—there was an awful doom."

Here Giovanni frowned so darkly upon her that Beatrice paused and trembled. But her faith in his tenderness reassured her, and made her blush that she had doubted for an instant.

"There was an awful doom," she continued, "the effect of my father's fatal love of science, which estranged me from all society of my kind. Until Heaven sent thee, dearest Giovanni, oh, how lonely was thy poor Beatrice!"

"Was it a hard doom?" asked Giovanni, fixing his eyes upon her.

"Only of late have I known how hard it was," answered she, tenderly. "Oh, yes; but my heart was torpid, and therefore quiet."

Giovanni's rage broke forth from his sullen gloom like a lightning flash out of a dark cloud.

"Accursed one!" cried he, with venomous scorn and anger. "And, finding thy solitude wearisome, thou hast severed me likewise from all the warmth of life and enticed me into thy region of unspeakable horror!"

"Giovanni!" exclaimed Beatrice, turning her large bright eyes upon his face. The force of his words had not found its way into her mind; she was merely thunderstruck.

"Yes, poisonous thing!" repeated Giovanni, beside himself with passion. "Thou hast done it! Thou hast blasted me! Thou hast filled my veins with poison! Thou hast made me as hateful, as ugly, as loathsome and deadly a creature as thyself—a world's wonder of hideous monstrosity! Now, if our breath be happily as fatal to ourselves as to all others, let us join our lips in one kiss of unutterable hatred, and so die!"

"What has befallen me?" murmured Beatrice, with a low moan out of her heart. "Holy Virgin, pity me, a poor heart-broken child!"

"Thou—dost thou pray?" cried Giovanni, still with the same fiendish scorn. "Thy very prayers, as they come from thy lips, taint the atmosphere with death. Yes, yes; let us pray! Let us go to church and dip our fingers in the holy water at the portal! They that come after us will perish as by a pestilence! Let us sign crosses in the air! It will be scattering curses abroad in the likeness of holy symbols!"

"Giovanni," said Beatrice, calmly, for her grief was beyond passion, "why dost thou join thyself with me thus in those terrible words? I, it is true, am the horrible thing thou namest me. But thou—what hast thou to do, save with one other shudder at my hideous misery to go forth out of the garden and mingle with thy race, and forget that there ever crawled on earth such a monster as poor Beatrice?"

"Dost thou pretend ignorance?" asked Giovanni, scowling upon her. "Behold! this power have I gained from the pure daughter of Rappaccini."

There was a swarm of summer insects flitting through the air in search of the food promised by the flower odors of the fatal garden. They circled round Giovanni's head, and were evidently attracted towards him by the same influence which had drawn them for an instant within the sphere of several of the shrubs. He sent forth a breath among them, and smiled bitterly at Beatrice as at least a score of the insects fell dead upon the ground.

"I see it! I see it!" shrieked Beatrice. "It is my father's fatal science! No, no, Giovanni; it was not I! Never! never! I dreamed only to love thee and be with thee a little time, and so to let thee pass away, leaving but thine image in mine heart; for, Giovanni, believe it, though my body be nourished with poison, my spirit is God's creature, and craves love as its daily food. But my father—he has united us in this fearful sympathy. Yes; spurn me, tread upon me, kill me! Oh, what is death after such words as thine? But it was not I. Not for a world of bliss would I have done it."

Giovanni's passion had exhausted itself in its outburst from his lips. There now came across him a sense, mournful, and not without tenderness, of the intimate and peculiar relationship between Beatrice and himself. They stood, as it were, in an utter solitude, which would be made none the less solitary by the densest throng of human life. Ought not, then, the desert of humanity around them to press this insulated pair closer together? If they should be cruel to one another, who was there to be kind to them? Besides, thought Giovanni, might there not still be a hope of his returning within the limits of ordinary nature, and leading Beatrice, the redeemed Beatrice, by the hand? O, weak, and selfish, and unworthy spirit, that could dream of an earthly union and earthly happiness as possible, after such deep love had been so bitterly wronged as was Beatrice's love by Giovanni's blighting words! No, no; there could be no such hope. She must pass heavily, with that broken heart, across the borders of Time—she must bathe her hurts in some fount of paradise, and forget her grief in the light of immortality, and *there* be well.

But Giovanni did not know it.

"Dear Beatrice," said he, approaching her, while she shrank away as always at his approach, but now with a different impulse, "dearest Beatrice, our fate is not yet so desperate. Behold! there is a medicine, potent, as a wise physician has assured me, and almost divine in its efficacy. It is composed of ingredients the most opposite to those by which thy awful father has brought this calamity upon thee and me. It is distilled of blessed herbs. Shall we not quaff it together, and thus be purified from evil?"

"Give it me!" said Beatrice, extending her hand to receive the little silver vial which Giovanni took from his bosom. She added, with a peculiar emphasis, "I will drink; but do thou await the result."

She put Baglioni's antidote to her lips; and, at the same moment, the figure of Rappaccini emerged from the portal and came slowly towards the marble fountain. As he drew near, the pale man of science seemed to gaze with a triumphant expression at the beautiful youth and maiden, as might an artist who should spend his life in achieving a picture or a group of statuary and finally be satisfied with his success. He paused; his bent form grew erect with conscious power; he spread out his hands over them in the attitude of a father imploring a blessing upon his children; but those were the same hands that had thrown poison into the stream of their lives. Giovanni trembled. Beatrice shuddered nervously, and pressed her hand upon her heart.

"My daughter," said Rappaccini, "thou art no longer lonely in the world. Pluck one of those precious gems from thy sister shrub and bid thy bridegroom wear it in his bosom. It will not harm him now. My science and the sympathy between thee and him have so wrought within his system that he now stands apart from common men, as thou dost, daughter of my pride and triumph, from ordinary women. Pass on, then, through the world, most dear to one another and dreadful to all besides!"

"My father," said Beatrice, feebly—and still as she spoke she kept her hand upon her heart—"wherefore didst thou inflict this miserable doom upon thy child?"

"Miserable!" exclaimed Rappaccini. "What mean you, foolish girl? Dost thou deem it misery to be endowed with marvellous gifts against which no power nor strength could avail an enemy—misery, to be able to quell the mightiest with a breath—misery, to be as terrible as thou art beautiful? Wouldst thou, then, have preferred the condition of a weak woman, exposed to all evil and capable of none?"

"I would fain have been loved, not feared," murmured Beatrice, sinking down upon the ground. "But now it matters not. I am going, father, where the evil which thou hast striven to mingle with my being will pass away like a dream—like the fragrance of these poisonous flowers, which will no longer taint my breath among the flowers of Eden. Farewell, Giovanni! Thy words of hatred are like lead within my heart; but they, too, will fall away as I ascend. Oh, was there not, from the first, more poison in thy nature than in mine?"

To Beatrice—so radically had her earthly part been wrought upon by Rappaccini's skill—as poison had been life, so the powerful antidote was death; and thus the poor victim of man's ingenuity and of thwarted nature, and of the fatality that attends all such efforts of perverted wisdom, perished there, at the feet of her father and Giovanni. Just at that moment Professor Pietro Baglioni looked forth from the window, and called loudly, in a tone of triumph mixed with horror, to the thunderstricken man of science—

"Rappaccini! Rappaccini! and is *this* the upshot of your experiment!"

Ligeia

EDGAR ALLAN POE

(1809–1849)

And the will therein lieth, which dieth not. Who knoweth the mysteries of the will, with its vigor? For God is but a great will pervading all things by nature of its intentness. Man doth not yield himself to the angels, nor unto death utterly, save only through the weakness of his feeble will.—JOSEPH GLANVILL

I cannot, for my soul, remember how, when, or even precisely where, I first became acquainted with the lady Ligeia. Long years have since elapsed, and my memory is feeble through much suffering. Or, perhaps, I cannot *now* bring these points to mind, because, in truth, the character of my beloved, her rare learning, her singular yet placid cast of beauty, and the thrilling and enthralling eloquence of her low musical language, made their way into my heart by paces so steadily and stealthily progressive that they have been unnoticed and unknown. Yet I believe that I met her first and most frequently in some large, old, decaying city near the Rhine. Of her family—I have surely heard her speak. That it is of a remotely ancient date cannot be doubted. Ligeia! Ligeia! Buried in studies of a nature more than all else adapted to deaden impressions of the outward world, it is by that sweet word alone—by Ligeia—that I bring before mine eyes in fancy the image of her who is no more. And now, while I write, a recollection flashes upon me that I have *never known* the paternal name of her who was my friend and my betrothed, and who became the partner of my studies, and finally the wife of my bosom. Was it a playful charge on the part of my Ligeia? or was it a test of my strength of affection, that I should institute no inquiries upon this point? or was it rather a caprice of my own—a wildly romantic offering on the shrine of the most passionate devotion? I but indistinctly recall the fact itself—what wonder that I have utterly forgotten the circumstances which originated or attended it? And, indeed, if ever that spirit which is entitled *Romance*—if ever she, the wan and the misty-winged *Ashtophet* of idolatrous Egypt, presided, as they tell, over marriages ill-omened, then most surely she presided over mine.

There is one dear topic, however, on which my memory fails me not. It is the *person* of Ligeia. In stature she was tall, somewhat slender, and, in her latter days, even emaciated. I would in vain attempt to portray the majesty, the quiet ease of her demeanor, or the incomprehensible lightness and elasticity of her footfall. She came and departed as a shadow. I was never made aware of her entrance into my closed study save by the dear music of her low sweet voice, as she placed her marble hand upon my shoulder. In beauty of face no maiden ever equalled her. It was the radiance of an opium-dream—an airy and spirit-lifting vision more wildly divine than the phantasies which hovered about the slumbering souls of the daughters of Delos. Yet her features were not of that regular mould which we have been falsely taught to worship in the classical labors of the heathen. "There is no exquisite beauty," says Bacon, Lord Verulam, speaking truly of all the forms and *genera* of beauty, "without some *strangeness* in the proportion." Yet, although I saw that the features of Ligeia were not of a classic regularity—although I perceived that her loveliness was indeed "exquisite," and felt that there was much of "strangeness" pervading it, yet I have tried in vain to detect the irregularity and to trace home my own perception of "the strange." I examined the contour of the lofty and pale forehead—it was faultless—how cold indeed that word when applied to a majesty so divine!—the skin rivalling the purest ivory, the commanding extent and repose, the gentle prominence of the regions above the temples; and then the raven-black, the glossy, the luxuriant and naturally-curling tresses, setting forth the full force of the Homeric epithet, "hyacinthine!" I looked at the delicate outlines of the nose—and nowhere but in the graceful medallions of the Hebrews had I beheld a similar perfection. There were the same luxurious smoothness of surface, the same scarcely perceptible tendency to the aquiline, the same harmoniously curved nostrils speaking the free spirit. I regarded the sweet mouth. Here was indeed the triumph of all things heavenly—the magnificent turn of the short upper lip—the soft, voluptuous slumber of the under—the dimples which sported, and the color which spoke—the teeth glancing back, with a brilliancy almost startling, every ray of the holy light which fell upon them in her serene and placid yet most exultingly radiant of all smiles. I scrutinized the formation of the chin—and, here too, I found the gentleness of breadth, the softness and the majesty, the fullness and the spirituality, of the Greek—the contour which the god Apollo revealed but in a dream, to Cleomenes, the son of the Athenian. And then I peered into the large eyes of Ligeia.

For eyes we have no models in the remotely antique. It might have been, too, that in these eyes of my beloved lay the secret to which Lord Verulam alludes. They were, I must believe, far larger than the ordinary eyes of our own race. They were even fuller than the fullest of the gazelle eyes of the tribe of the valley of Nourjahad. Yet it was only at intervals—in moments of intense excitement—that this peculiarity became more than slightly noticeable in Ligeia. And at such moments was her beauty—in my heated fancy thus it appeared perhaps—the beauty of beings either above or apart from the earth—the beauty of the fabulous Houri of the Turk. The hue of the orbs was the most brilliant of black, and, far over them, hung jetty lashes of great length. The brows, slightly irregular in outline, had the same tint. The "strangeness," however, which I found in the eyes, was of a nature distinct from the formation, or the color, or the brilliancy of the features, and must, after all, be referred to the *expression*. Ah, word of no meaning! behind whose vast latitude of mere sound we intrench our ignorance of so much of the spiritual. The expression of the eyes of Ligeia! How for long hours have I pondered upon it! How have I, through the whole of a midsummer night, struggled to fathom it! What was it—that something more profound than the well of Democritus—which lay far within the pupils of my beloved? What *was* it? I was possessed with a passion to discover. Those eyes! those large, those shining, those divine orbs! they became to me twin stars of Leda, and I to them devoutest of astrologers.

There is no point, among the many incomprehensible anomalies of the science of mind, more thrillingly exciting than the fact—never, I believe, noticed in the schools—that in our endeavors to recall to memory something long forgotten, we often find ourselves *upon the very verge* of remembrance, without being able, in the end, to remember. And thus how frequently, in my intense scrutiny of Ligeia's eyes, have I felt approaching the full knowledge of their expression—felt it approaching—yet not quite be mine—and so at length entirely depart! And (strange, oh strangest mystery of all!) I found, in the commonest objects of the universe, a circle of analogies to that expression. I mean to say that, subsequently to the period when Ligeia's beauty passed into my spirit, there dwelling as in a shrine, I derived, from many existences in the material world, a sentiment such as I felt always aroused, within me, by her large and luminous orbs. Yet not the more could I define that sentiment, or analyze, or even steadily view it. I recognized it, let me repeat, sometimes in the survey of a rapidly growing vine—in the contemplation of a moth, a butterfly, a chrysalis, a stream of running water. I have felt it in the ocean; in the falling of a meteor. I have felt it in the glances of unusually aged people. And there are one or two stars in heaven—(one especially, a star of the sixth magnitude, double and changeable, to be found near the large star in Lyra) in a telescopic scrutiny of which I have been made aware of the feeling. I have been filled with it by certain sounds from stringed instruments, and not unfrequently by passages from books. Among innumerable other instances, I well remember something in a volume of Joseph Glanvill, which (perhaps from its quaintness—who shall say?) never failed to inspire me with the sentiment;—"And the will therein lieth, which dieth not. Who knoweth the mysteries of the will, with its vigor? For God is but a great will pervading all things by nature of its intentness. Man doth not yield him to the angels, nor unto death utterly, save only through the weakness of his feeble will."

Length of years and subsequent reflection, have enabled me to trace, indeed, some remote connection between this passage in the English moralist and a portion of the character of Ligeia. An *intensity* in thought, action, or speech, was possibly, in her, a result, or at least an index, of that gigantic volition which, during our long intercourse, failed to give other and more immediate evidence of its existence. Of all the women whom I have even known, she, the outwardly calm, the ever-placid Ligeia, was the most violently a prey to the tumultuous vultures of stern passion. And of such passion I could form no estimate, save by the miraculous expansion of those eyes which at once so delighted and appalled me—by the almost magical melody, modulation, distinctness, and placidity of her very low voice—and by the fierce energy (rendered doubly effective by contrast with her manner of utterance) of the wild words which she habitually uttered.

I have spoken of the learning of Ligeia; it was immense—such as I have never known in woman. In the classical tongues was she deeply proficient, and as far as my own acquaintance extended in regard to the modern dialects of Europe, I have never known her at fault. Indeed upon any theme of the most admired, because simply the most abstruse of the boasted erudition of the academy, have I *ever* found Ligeia at fault? How singularly—how thrillingly, this one point in the nature of my wife has forced itself, at this late period only, upon my attention! I said her knowledge was such as I have never known in woman—but where breathes the man who has traversed, and successfully, *all* the wide areas of moral, physical, and mathematical science? I saw not then what I now clearly perceive, that the acquisitions of Ligeia were gigantic, were astounding; yet I was sufficiently aware of her infinite supremacy to resign myself, with a child-like confidence, to her guidance through the chaotic world of metaphysical investigation at which I was most busily occupied during the earlier years of our marriage. With how vast a triumph—with how vivid a delight—with how much of all that is ethereal in hope—did I *feel,* as she bent over me in studies but little sought—but less known—that delicious vista by slow degrees expanding before me, down whose long, gorgeous, and all untrodden path, I might at length pass onward to the goal of a wisdom too divinely precious not to be forbidden!

How poignant, then, must have been the grief with which, after some years, I beheld my well-grounded expectations take wings to themselves and fly away! Without Ligeia I was but as a child groping benighted. Her presence, her readings alone, rendered vividly luminous the many mysteries of the transcendentalism in which we were immersed. Wanting the radiant lustre of her eyes, letters, lambent and golden, grew duller than Saturnian lead. And now those eyes shone less and less frequently upon the pages over which I pored. Ligeia grew ill. The wild eyes blazed with a too—too glorious effulgence; the pale fingers became of the transparent waxen hue of the grave; and the blue veins upon the lofty forehead swelled and sank impetuously with the tides of the most gentle emotion. I saw that she must die—and I struggled desperately in spirit with the grim Azrael. And the struggles of the passionate wife were, to my astonishment, even more energetic than my own. There had been much in her stern nature to impress me with the belief that, to her, death would have come without its terrors; but not so. Words are impotent to convey any just idea of the fierceness of resistance with which she wrestled with the Shadow. I groaned in anguish at the pitiable spectacle. I would have soothed—I would have reasoned; but, in the intensity of her wild desire for life,—for life—*but* for life—solace and reason were alike the uttermost folly. Yet not until the last instance, amid the most convulsive writhings of her fierce spirit, was shaken the external placidity of her demeanor. Her voice grew more gentle—grew more low—yet I would not wish to dwell upon the wild meaning of the quietly uttered words. My brain reeled as I hearkened entranced, to a melody more than mortal—to assumptions and aspirations which mortality had never before known.

That she loved me I should not have doubted; and I might have been easily aware that, in a bosom such as hers, love would have reigned no ordinary passion. But in death only was I fully impressed with the strength of her affection. For long hours, detaining my hand, would she pour out before me the overflowing of a heart whose more than passionate devotion amounted to idolatry. How had I deserved to be so blessed by such confessions?—how had I deserved to be so cursed with the removal of my beloved in the hour of her making them? But upon this subject I cannot bear to dilate. Let me say only, that in Ligeia's more than womanly abandonment to a love, alas! all unmerited, all unworthily bestowed, I at length recognized the principle of her longing with so wildly earnest a desire for the life which was now fleeing so rapidly away. It is this wild longing—it is this eager vehemence of desire for life—*but* for life—that I have no power to portray—no utterance capable of expressing.

At high noon of the night in which she departed, beckoning me, peremptorily, to her side, she bade me repeat certain verses composed by herself not many days before. I obeyed her.—They were these:

Lo! 'tis a gala night
    Within the lonesome latter years!
An angel throng, bewinged, bedight
    In veils, and drowned in tears,
Sit in a theatre, to see
    A play of hopes and fears,
While the orchestra breathes fitfully
    The music of the spheres.

Mimes, in the form of God on high,
    Mutter and mumble low,
And hither and thither fly—
    Mere puppets they, who come and go
At bidding of vast formless things
    That shift the scenery to and fro,
Flapping from out their Condor wings
    Invisible Woe!

That motley drama!—oh, be sure
    It shall not be forgot!
With its Phantom chased forever more,
    By a crowd that seize it not,
Through a circle that ever returneth in
    To the self-same spot,
And much of Madness and more of Sin
    And Horror the soul of the plot.

But see, amid the mimic rout,
    A crawling shape intrude!
A blood-red thing that writhes from out
    The scenic solitude!
It writhes!—it writhes!—with mortal pangs
    The mimes become its food,
And the seraphs sob at vermin fangs
    In human gore imbued.

Out—out are the lights—out all!
And over each quivering form,
The curtain, a funeral pall,
Comes down with the rush of a storm,
And the angels, all pallid and wan,
Uprising, unveiling, affirm
That the play is the tragedy, "Man,"
And its hero the Conqueror Worm.

"O God!" half shrieked Ligeia, leaping to her feet and extending her arms aloft with a spasmodic movement, as I made an end of these lines—"O God! O Divine Father!—shall these things be undeviatingly so?—shall this Conqueror be not once conquered? Are we not part and parcel in Thee? Who—who knoweth the mysteries of the will with its vigor? Man doth not yield him to the angels, *nor unto death utterly,* save only through the weakness of his feeble will."

And now, as if exhausted with emotion, she suffered her white arms to fall, and returned solemnly to her bed of death. And as she breathed her last sighs, there came mingled with them a low murmur from her lips. I bent to them my ear, and distinguished, again, the concluding words of the passage in Glanvill—*"Man doth not yield him to the angels, nor unto death utterly, save only through the weakness of his feeble will."*

She died;—and I, crushed into the very dust with sorrow, could no longer endure the lonely desolation of my dwelling in the dim and decaying city by the Rhine. I had no lack of what the world calls wealth. Ligeia had brought me far more, very far more than ordinarily falls to the lot of mortals. After a few months, therefore, of weary and aimless wandering, I purchased, and put in some repair, an abbey, which I shall not name, in one of the wildest and least frequented portions of fair England. The gloomy and dreary grandeur of the building, the almost savage aspect of the domain, the many melancholy and time-honored memories connected with both, had much in unison with the feelings of utter abandonment which had driven me into that remote and unsocial region of the country. Yet although the external abbey, with its verdant decay hanging about it, suffered but little alteration, I gave way, with a child-like perversity, and perchance with a faint hope of alleviating my sorrows, to a display of more than regal magnificence within.—For such follies, even in childhood, I had imbibed a taste, and now they came back to me as if in the dotage of grief. Alas, I feel how much even of incipient madness might have been discovered in the gorgeous and fantastic draperies, in the solemn carvings of Egypt, in the wild cornices and furniture, in the Bedlam patterns of the carpets of tufted gold! I had become a bounden slave in the trammels of opium, and my labors and orders had taken a coloring from my dreams. But these absurdities I must not pause to detail. Let me speak only of that one chamber, ever accursed, whither, in a moment of mental alienation, I led from the altar as my bride—as the successor of the unforgotten Ligeia—the fair-haired and blue-eyed Lady Rowena Trevanion, of Tremaine.

There is no individual portion of the architecture and decoration of that bridal chamber which is not now visibly before me. Where were the souls of the haughty family of the bride, when, through thirst of gold, they permitted to pass the threshold of an apartment so bedecked, a maiden and a daughter so beloved? I have said that I minutely remember the details of the chamber—yet I am sadly forgetful on topics of deep moment—and here there was no system, no keeping, in the fantastic display, to take hold upon the memory. The room lay in a high turret of the castellated abbey, was pentagonal in shape, and of capacious size. Occupying the whole southern face of the pentagon was the sole window—an immense sheet of broken glass from Venice—a single pane, and tinted of a leaden hue, so that the rays of either the sun or moon, passing through it, fell with a ghastly lustre on the objects within. Over the upper portion of this huge window, extended the trellis-work of an aged vine, which clambered up the massy walls of the turret. The ceiling, of gloomy-looking oak, was excessively lofty, vaulted, and elaborately fretted with the wildest and most grotesque specimens of a semi-Gothic, semi-Druidical device. From out the most central recess of this melancholy vaulting, depended, by a single chain of gold with long links, a huge censer of the same metal, Saracenic in pattern, and with many perforations so contrived that there writhed in and out of them, as if endued with a serpent vitality, a continual succession of parti-colored fires.

Some few ottomans and golden candelabra, of Eastern figure, were in various stations about—and there was the couch, too—the bridal couch—of an Indian model, and low, and sculptured of solid ebony, with a pall-like canopy above. In each of the angles of the chamber stood on end a gigantic sarcophagus of black granite, from the tombs of the kings over against Luxor, with their aged lids full of immemorial sculpture. But in the draping of the apartment lay, alas! the chief phantasy of all. The lofty walls, gigantic in height—even unproportionably so—were hung from summit to foot, in vast folds, with a heavy and massive-looking tapestry—tapestry of a material which was found alike as a carpet on the floor, as a covering for the ottomans and the ebony bed, as a canopy for the bed and as the gorgeous volutes of the curtains which partially shaded the window. The material was the richest cloth of gold. It was spotted all over, at irregular intervals, with arabesque figures, about a foot in diameter, and wrought upon the cloth in patterns of the most jetty black. But these figures partook of the true character of the arabesque only when regarded from a single point of view. By a contrivance now common, and indeed traceable to a very remote period of antiquity, they were made changeable in aspect. To one entering the room, they bore the appearance of simple monstrosities; but upon a farther advance, this appearance gradually departed; and step by step, as the visiter moved his station in the chamber, he saw himself surrounded by an endless succession of the ghastly forms which belong to the superstition of the Norman, or arise in the guilty slumbers of the monk. The phantasmagoric effect was vastly heightened by the artificial introduction of a strong continual current of wind behind the draperies—giving a hideous and uneasy animation to the whole.

In halls such as these—in a bridal chamber such as this—I passed, with the Lady of Tremaine, the unhallowed hours of the first month of our marriage—passed them with but little disquietude. That my wife dreaded the fierce moodiness of my temper—that she shunned me and loved me but little—I could not help perceiving; but it gave me rather pleasure than otherwise. I loathed her with a hatred belonging more to demon than to man. My memory flew back, (oh, with what intensity of regret!) to Ligeia, the beloved, the august, the beautiful, the entombed. I revelled in recollections of her purity, of her wisdom, of her lofty, her ethereal nature, of her passionate, her idolatrous love. Now, then, did my spirit fully and freely burn with more than all the fires of her own. In the excitement of my opium dreams (for I was habitually fettered in the shackles of the drug) I would call aloud upon her name, during the silence of the night, or among the sheltered recesses of the glens by day, as if, through the wild eagerness, the solemn passion, the consuming ardor of my longing for the departed, I could restore her to the pathways she had abandoned —ah, *could* it be forever?—upon the earth.

About the commencement of the second month of the marriage, the Lady Rowena was attacked with sudden illness, from which her recovery was slow. The fever which consumed her rendered her nights uneasy; and in her perturbed state of half-slumber, she spoke of sounds, and of motions, in and above the chamber of the turret, which I concluded had no origin save in the distemper of her fancy, or perhaps in the phantasmagoric influences of the chamber itself. She became at length convalescent—finally well. Yet but a brief period elapsed, ere a second more violent disorder again threw her upon a bed of suffering; and from this attack her frame, at all times feeble, never altogether recovered. Her illnesses were, after this epoch, of alarming character, and of more alarming recurrence, defying alike the knowledge and the great exertions of her physicians. With the increase of the chronic disease which had thus, apparently, taken too sure hold upon her constitution to be eradicated by human means, I could not fail to observe a similar increase in the nervous irritation of her temperament, and in her excitability by trivial causes of fear. She spoke again, and now more frequently and pertinaciously, of the sounds—of the slight sounds—and of the unusual motions among the tapestries, to which she had formerly alluded.

One night, near the closing in of September, she pressed this distressing subject with more than usual emphasis upon my attention. She had just awakened from an unquiet slumber, and I had been watching, with feelings half of anxiety, half of vague terror, the workings of her emaciated countenance. I sat by the side of her ebony bed, upon one of the ottomans of India. She partly arose, and spoke, in an earnest low whisper, of sounds which she *then* heard, but which I could not hear—of motions which she *then* saw, but which I could not perceive. The wind was rushing hurriedly behind the tapestries, and I wished to show her (what, let me confess it, I could not *all* believe) that those almost inarticulate breathings, and those very gentle variations of the figures upon the wall, were but the natural effects of that customary rushing of the wind. But a deadly pallor, overspreading her face, had proved to me that my exertions to reassure her would be fruitless. She appeared to be fainting, and no attendants were within call. I remembered where was deposited a decanter of light wine which had been ordered by her physicians, and hastened across the chamber to procure it. But, as I stepped beneath the light of the censer, two circumstances of a startling nature attracted my attention. I had felt that some palpable although invisible object had passed lightly by my person; and I saw that there lay upon the golden carpet, in the very middle of the rich lustre thrown from the censer, a shadow—a faint, indefinite shadow of angelic aspect—such as might be fancied for the shadow of a shade. But I was wild with the excitement of an immoderate dose of opium, and heeded these things but little, nor spoke of them to Rowena. Having found the wine, I recrossed the chamber, and poured out a gobletful, which I held to the lips of the fainting lady. She had now partially recovered, however, and took the vessel herself, while I sank upon an ottoman near me, with my eyes fastened upon her person. It was then that I became distinctly aware of a gentle foot-fall upon the carpet, and near the couch; and in a second thereafter, as Rowena was in the act of raising the wine to her lips, I saw, or may have dreamed that I saw, fall within the goblet, as if from some invisible spring in the atmosphere of the room, three or four large drops of a brilliant and ruby colored fluid. If this I saw—not so Rowena. She swallowed the wine unhesitatingly, and I forbore to speak to her of a circumstance which must, after all, I considered, have been but the suggestion of a vivid imagination, rendered morbidly active by the terror of the lady, by the opium, and by the hour.

Yet I cannot conceal it from my own perception that, immediately subsequent to the fall of the ruby-drops, a rapid change for the worse took place in the disorder of my wife; so that, on the third subsequent night, the hands of her menials prepared her for the tomb, and on the fourth, I sat alone, with her shrouded body, in that fantastic chamber which had received her as my bride.—Wild visions, opium-engendered, flitted, shadowlike, before me. I gazed with unquiet eye upon the sarcophagi in the angles of the room, upon the varying figures of the drapery, and upon the writhing of the parti-colored fires in the censer overhead. My eyes then fell, as I called to mind the circumstances of a former night, to the spot beneath the glare of the censer where I had seen the faint traces of the shadow. It was there, however, no longer; and breathing with greater freedom, I turned my glances to the pallid and rigid figure upon the bed. Then rushed upon me a thousand memories of Ligeia—and then came back upon my heart, with the turbulent violence of a flood, the whole of that unutterable woe with which I had regarded her thus enshrouded. The night waned; and still, with a bosom full of bitter thoughts of the one only and supremely beloved, I remained gazing upon the body of Rowena.

It might have been midnight, or perhaps earlier, or later, for I had taken no note of time, when a sob, low, gentle, but very distinct, startled me from my revery.—I felt that it came from the bed of ebony—the bed of death. I listened in an agony of superstitious terror—but there was no repetition of the sound. I strained my vision to detect any motion in the corpse—but there was not the slightest perceptible. Yet I could not have been deceived. I *had* heard the noise, however faint, and my soul was awakened within me. I resolutely and perseveringly kept my attention riveted upon the body. Many minutes elapsed before any circumstance occurred tending to throw light upon the mystery. At length it became evident that a slight, a very feeble, and barely noticeable tinge of color had flushed up within the cheeks, and along the sunken small veins of the eyelids. Through a species of unutterable horror and awe, for which the language of mortality has no sufficiently energetic expression, I felt my heart cease to beat, my limbs grow rigid where I sat. Yet a sense of duty finally operated to restore my self-possession. I could no longer doubt that we had been precipitate in our preparations—that Rowena still lived. It was necessary that some immediate exertion be made; yet the turret was altogether apart from the portion of the abbey tenanted by the servants—there were none within call—I had no means of summoning them to my aid without leaving the room for many minutes—and this I could not venture to do. I therefore struggled alone in my endeavors to call back the spirit still hovering. In a short period it was certain, however, that a relapse had taken place; the color disappeared from both eyelid and cheek, leaving a wanness even more than that of marble; the lips became doubly shrivelled and pinched up in the ghastly expression of death; a repulsive clamminess and coldness overspread rapidly the surface of the body; and all the usual rigorous stiffness immediately supervened. I fell back with a shudder upon the couch from which I had been so startlingly aroused, and again gave myself up to passionate waking visions of Ligeia.

An hour thus elapsed when (could it be possible?) I was a second time aware of some vague sound issuing from the region of the bed. I listened —in extremity of horror. The sound came again—it was a sigh. Rushing to the corpse, I saw—distinctly saw—a tremor upon the lips. In a minute afterward they relaxed, disclosing a bright line of the pearly teeth. Amazement now struggled in my bosom with the profound awe which had hitherto reigned there alone. I felt that my vision grew dim, that my reason wandered; and it was only by a violent effort that I at length succeeded in nerving myself to the task which duty thus once more had pointed out. There was now a partial glow upon the forehead and upon the cheek and throat; a perceptible warmth pervaded the whole frame; there was even a slight pulsation at the heart. The lady *lived;* and with redoubled ardor I betook myself to the task of restoration. I chafed and bathed the temples and the hands, and used every exertion with experience, and no little medical reading, could suggest. But in vain. Suddenly, the color fled, the pulsation ceased, the lips resumed the expression of the dead, and, in an instant afterward, the whole body took upon itself the icy chilliness, the livid hue, the intense rigidity, the sunken outline, and all the loathsome peculiarities of that which has been, for many days, a tenant of the tomb.

And again I sunk into visions of Ligeia—and again, (what marvel that I shudder while I write?) *again* there reached my ears a low sob from the region of the ebony bed. But why shall I minutely detail the unspeakable horrors of that night? Why shall I pause to relate how, time after time, until near the period of the gray dawn, this hideous drama of revivification was repeated; how each terrific relapse was only into a sterner and apparently more irredeemable death; how each agony wore the aspect of a struggle with some invisible foe; and how each struggle was succeeded by I know not what of wild change in the personal appearance of the corpse? Let me hurry to a conclusion.

The greater part of the fearful night had worn away, and she who had been dead once again stirred—and now more vigorously than hitherto, although arousing from a dissolution more appalling in its utter hopelessness than any. I had long ceased to struggle or to move, and remained sitting rigidly upon the ottoman, a helpless prey to a whirl of violent emotions, of which extreme awe was perhaps the least terrible, the least consuming. The corpse, I repeat, stirred, and now more vigorously than before. The hues of life flushed up with unwonted energy into the countenance—the limbs relaxed—and, save that the eyelids were yet pressed heavily together, and that the bandages and draperies of the grave still imparted their charnel character to the figure, I might have dreamed that Rowena had indeed shaken off, utterly, the fetters of Death. But if this idea was not, even then, altogether adopted, I could at least doubt no longer, when arising from the bed, tottering, with feeble steps, with closed eyes, and with the manner of one bewildered in a dream, the thing that was enshrouded advanced boldly and palpably into the middle of the apartment.

I trembled not—I stirred not—for a crowd of unutterable fancies connected with the air, the stature, the demeanor of the figure, rushing hurriedly through my brain, had paralyzed—had chilled me into stone. I stirred not—but gazed upon the apparition. There was a mad disorder in my thoughts—a tumult unappeasable. Could it, indeed, be the living Rowena who confronted me? Could it, indeed, be Rowena at all—the fair-haired, the blue-eyed Lady Rowena Trevanion of Tremaine? Why, why should I doubt it? The bandage lay heavily about the mouth—but then might it not be the mouth of the breathing Lady of Tremaine? And the cheeks—there were the roses as in her noon of life—yes, these might indeed be the fair cheeks of the living Lady of Tremaine. And the chin, with its dimples, as in health, might it not be hers?—but had she then grown taller since her malady? What inexpressible madness seized me with that thought? One bound, and I had reached her feet! Shrinking from my touch, she let fall from her head, unloosened, the ghastly cerements which had confined it, and there streamed forth into the rushing atmosphere of the chamber huge masses of long and dishevelled hair; *it was blacker than the raven wings of midnight!* And now slowly opened the eyes of the figure which stood before me. "Here then, at least," I shrieked aloud, "can I never—can I never be mistaken—these are the full, and the black, and the wild eyes—of my lost love—of the Lady —of the LADY LIGEIA."

Bartleby the Scrivener

A Story of Wall Street

HERMAN MELVILLE
(1819–1891)

I am a rather elderly man. The nature of my avocations, for the last thirty years, has brought me into more than ordinary contact with what would seem an interesting and somewhat singular set of men, of whom, as yet, nothing, that I know of, has ever been written—I mean, the law-copyists, or scriveners. I have known very many of them, professionally and privately, and, if I pleased, could relate divers histories, at which good-natured gentlemen might smile, and sentimental souls might weep. But I waive the biographies of all other scriveners, for a few passages in the life of Bartleby, who was a scrivener, the strangest I ever saw, or heard of. While, of other law-copyists, I might write the complete life, of Bartleby nothing of that sort can be done. I believe that no materials exist for a full and satisfactory biography of this man. It is an irreparable loss to literature. Bartleby was one of those beings of whom nothing is ascertainable, except from the original sources, and, in his case, those are very small. What my own astonished eyes saw of Bartleby, *that* is all I know of him, except, indeed, one vague report, which will appear in the sequel.

Ere introducing the scrivener, as he first appeared to me, it is fit I make some mention of myself, my employees, my business, my chambers, and general surroundings; because some such description is indispensable to an adequate understanding of the chief character about to be presented. Imprimis: I am a man who, from his youth upwards, has been filled with a profound conviction that the easiest way of life is the best. Hence, though I belong to a profession proverbially energetic and nervous, even to turbulence, at times, yet nothing of that sort have I ever suffered to invade my peace. I am one of those unambitious lawyers who never addresses a jury, or in any way draws down public applause; but, in the cool tranquillity of a snug retreat, do a snug business among rich men's bonds, and mortgages, and title-deeds. All who know me, consider me an eminently *safe* man. The late John Jacob Astor, a personage little given to poetic enthusiasm, had no hesitation in pronouncing my first grand point to be prudence; my next, method. I do not speak it in vanity, but simply record the fact, that I was not unemployed in my profession by the late John Jacob Astor; a name which, I admit, I love to repeat; for it hath a rounded and orbicular sound to it, and rings like unto bullion. I will freely add, that I was not insensible to the late John Jacob Astor's good opinion.

Some time prior to the period at which this little history begins, my avocations had been largely increased. The good old office, now extinct in the State of New York, of a Master in Chancery, had been conferred upon me. It was not a very arduous office, but very pleasantly remunerative. I seldom lose my temper; much more seldom indulge in dangerous indignation at wrongs and outrages; but, I must be permitted to be rash here, and declare that I consider the sudden and violent abrogation of the office of Master in Chancery, by the new Constitution, as a—premature act; inasmuch as I had counted upon a life-lease of the profits, whereas I only received those of a few short years. But this is by the way.

My chambers were up stairs, at No.—— Wall Street. At one end, they looked upon the white wall of the interior of a spacious skylight shaft, penetrating the building from top to bottom.

This view might have been considered rather tame than otherwise, deficient in what landscape painters call "life." But, if so, the view from the other end of my chambers offered, at least, a contrast, if nothing more. In that direction, my windows commanded an unobstructed view of a lofty brick wall, black by age and everlasting shade; which wall required no spyglass to bring out its lurking beauties, but, for the benefit of all near-sighted spectators, was pushed up to within ten feet of my window panes. Owing to the great height of the surrounding buildings, and my chambers being on the second floor, the interval between this wall and mine not a little resembled a huge square cistern.

At the period just preceding the advent of Bartleby, I had two persons as copyists in my employment, and a promising lad as an office-boy. First, Turkey; second, Nippers; third, Ginger Nut. These may seem names, the like of which are not usually found in the Directory. In truth, they were nicknames, mutually conferred upon each other by my three clerks, and were deemed expressive of their respective persons or characters. Turkey was a short, pursy Englishman, of about my own age—that is, somewhere not far from sixty. In the morning, one might say, his face was of a fine florid hue, but after twelve o'clock, meridian—his dinner hour—it blazed like a grate full of Christmas coals; and continued blazing—but, as it were, with a gradual wane—till six o'clock P.M., of thereabouts; after which, I saw no more of the proprietor of the face, which, gaining its meridian with the sun, seemed to set with it, to rise, culminate, and decline the following day, with the like regularity and undiminished glory. There are many singular coincidences I have known in the course of my life, not the least among which was the fact, that, exactly when Turkey displayed his fullest beams from his red and radiant countenance, just then, too, at that critical moment, began the daily period when I considered his business capacities as seriously disturbed for the remainder of the twenty-four hours. Not that he was absolutely idle, or averse to business, then; far from it. The difficulty was, he was apt to be altogether too energetic. There was a strange, inflamed, flurried, flighty recklessness of activity about him. He would be incautious in dipping his pen into his inkstand. All his blots upon my documents were dropped there after twelve o'clock meridian. Indeed, not only would he be reckless, and sadly given to making blots in the afternoon, but, some days, he went further, and was rather noisy. At such times, too, his face flamed with augmented blazonry, as if cannel coal had been heaped on anthracite. He made an unpleasant racket with his chair; spilled his sand-box; in mending his pens, impatiently split them all to pieces, and threw them on the floor in a sudden passion; stood up, and leaned over his table, boxing his papers about in a most indecorous manner, very sad to behold in an elderly man like him. Nevertheless, as he was in many ways a most valuable person to me, and all the time before twelve o'clock meridian, was the quickest, steadiest creature, too, accomplishing a great deal of work in a style not easily to be matched—for these reasons, I was willing to overlook his eccentricities, though, indeed, occasionally, I remonstrated with him. I did this very gently, however, because, though the civilest, nay, the blandest and most reverential of men in the morning, yet, in the afternoon, he was disposed, upon provocation, to be slightly rash with his tongue—in fact, insolent. Now, valuing his morning services as I did, and resolved not to lose them—yet, at the same time, made uncomfortable by his inflamed ways after twelve o'clock—and being a man of peace, unwilling by my admonitions to call forth unseemly retorts from him, I took upon me, one Saturday noon (he was always worse on Saturdays) to hint to him, very kindly, that, perhaps, now that he was growing old, it might be well to abridge his labors; in short, he need not come to my chambers after twelve o'clock, but, dinner over, had best go home to his lodgings, and rest himself till tea-time. But no; he insisted upon his afternoon devotions. His countenance became intolerably fervid, as he oratorically assured me—gesticulating with a long ruler at the other end of the room—that if his services in the morning were useful, how indispensable, then, in the afternoon?

"With submission, sir," said Turkey, on this occasion, "I consider myself your right-hand man. In the morning I but marshal and deploy my columns; but in the afternoon I put myself at their head, and gallantly charge the foe, thus"—and he made a violent thrust with the ruler.

"But the blots, Turkey," intimated I.

"True; but, with submission, sir, behold these hairs! I am getting old. Surely, sir, a blot or two of a warm afternoon is not to be severely urged against gray hairs. Old age—even if it blot the page—is honorable. With submission, sir, we *both* are getting old."

This appeal to my fellow-feeling was hardly to be resisted. At all events, I saw that go he would not. So, I made up my mind to let him stay, resolving, nevertheless, to see to it that, during the afternoon, he had to do with my less important papers.

Nippers, the second on my list, was a whiskered, sallow, and upon the whole, rather piratical-looking young man, of about five and twenty. I always deemed him the victim of two evil powers—ambition and indigestion. The ambition was evinced by a certain impatience of the duties of a mere copyist, an unwarrantable usurpation of strictly professional affairs, such as the original drawing up of legal documents. The indigestion seemed betokened in an occasional nervous testiness and grinning irritability, causing the teeth to audibly grind together over mistakes committed in copying; unnecessary maledictions, hissed, rather than spoken, in the heat of business; and especially by a continual discontent with the height of the table where he worked. Though of a very ingenious, mechanical turn, Nippers could never get this table to suit him. He put chips under it, blocks of various sorts, bits of pasteboard, and at last went so far as to attempt an exquisite adjustment, by final pieces of folded blotting-paper. But no invention would answer. If, for the sake of easing his back, he brought the table lid at a sharp angle well up towards his chin, and wrote there like a man using the steep roof of a Dutch house for his desk, then he declared that it stopped the circulation in his arms. If now he lowered the table to his waistbands, and stooped over it in writing, then there was a sore aching in his back. In short, the truth of the matter was, Nippers knew not what he wanted. Or, if he wanted anything, it was to be rid of a scrivener's table altogether. Among the manifestations of his diseased ambition was a fondness he had for receiving visits from certain ambiguous-looking fellows in seedy coats, whom he called his clients. Indeed, I was aware that not only was he, at times, considerable of a ward-politician, but he occasionally did a little business at the Justices' courts, and was not unknown on the steps of the Tombs. I have good reason to believe, however, that one individual who called upon him at my chambers, and who, with a grand air, he insisted was his client, was no other than a dun, and the alleged title-deed, a bill. But, with all his failings, and the annoyances he caused me, Nippers, like his compatriot Turkey, was a very useful man to me; wrote a neat, swift hand; and, when he chose, was not deficient in a gentlemanly sort of deportment. Added to this, he always dressed in a gentlemanly sort of way; and so, incidentally, reflected credit upon my chambers. Whereas, with respect to Turkey, I had much ado to keep him from being a reproach to me. His clothes were apt to look oily, and smell of eating-houses. He wore his pantaloons very loose and baggy in summer. His coats were execrable; his hat not to be handled. But while the hat was a thing of indifference to me, inasmuch as his natural civility and deference, as a dependent Englishman, always led him to doff it the moment he entered the room, yet his coat was another matter. Concerning his coats, I reasoned with him; but with no effect. The truth was, I suppose, that a man with so small an income could not afford to sport such a lustrous face and a lustrous coat at one and the same time. As Nippers once observed, Turkey's money went chiefly for red ink. One winter day, I presented Turkey with a highly respectable-looking coat of my own—a padded gray coat, of a most comfortable warmth, and which buttoned straight up from the knee to the neck. I thought Turkey would appreciate the favor, and abate his rashness and obstreperousness of afternoons. But no; I verily believe that buttoning himself up in so downy and blanket-like a coat had a pernicious effect upon him—upon the same principle that too much oats are bad for horses. In fact, precisely as a rash, restive horse is said to feel his oats, so Turkey felt his coat. It made him insolent. He was a man whom prosperity harmed.

Though, concerning the self-indulgent habits of Turkey, I had my own private surmises, yet, touching Nippers, I was well persuaded that, whatever might be his faults in other respects, he was, at least, a temperate young man. But, indeed, nature herself seemed to have been his vintner, and, at his birth, charged him so thoroughly with an irritable, brandy-like disposition, that all subsequent potations were needless. When I consider how, amid the stillness of my chambers, Nippers would sometimes impatiently rise from his seat, and stooping over his table, spread his arms wide apart, seize the whole desk, and move it, and jerk it, with a grim, grinding motion on the floor, as if the table were a perverse voluntary agent and vexing him, I plainly perceive that, for Nippers, brandy-and-water were altogether superfluous.

It was fortunate for me that, owing to its peculiar cause—indigestion—the irritability and consequent nervousness of Nippers were mainly observable in the morning, while in the afternoon he was comparatively mild. So that, Turkey's paroxysms only coming on about twelve o'clock, I never had to do with their eccentricities at one time. Their fits relieved each other, like guards. When Nipper's was on, Turkey's was off; and *vice versa.* This was a good natural arrangement, under the circumstances.

Ginger Nut, the third on my list, was a lad, some twelve years old. His father was a car-man, ambitious of seeing his son on the bench instead of a cart, before he died. So he sent him to my office, as student at law, errand-boy, cleaner and sweeper, at the rate of one dollar a week. He had a little desk to himself; but he did not use it much. Upon inspection, the drawer exhibited a great array of the shells of various sorts of nuts. Indeed, to this quick-witted youth, the whole noble science of the law was contained in a nutshell. Not the least among the employments of Ginger Nut, as well as one which he discharged with the most alacrity, was his duty as cake and apple purveyor for Turkey and Nippers. Copying law-papers being proverbially a dry, husky sort of business, my two scriveners were fain to moisten their mouths very often with Spitzenbergs, to be had at the numerous stalls nigh the Custom House and Post Office. Also, they sent Ginger Nut very frequently for that peculiar cake—small, flat, round, and very spicy—after which he had been named by them. Of a cold morning, when business was but dull, Turkey would gobble up scores of these cakes, as if they were mere wafers—indeed, they sell them at the rate of six or eight for a penny—the scrape of his pen blending with the crunching of the crisp particles in his mouth. Rashest of all the fiery afternoon blunders and flurried rashnesses of Turkey, was his once moistening a ginger-cake between his lips, and clapping it on to a mortgage, for a seal. I came within an ace of dismissing him then. But he mollified me by making an oriental bow, and saying—

"With submission, sir, it was generous of me to find you in stationery on my own account."

Now my original business—that of a conveyancer and title hunter, and drawer-up of recondite documents of all sorts—was considerably increased by receiving the master's office. There was now great work for scriveners. Not only must I push the clerks already with me, but I must have additional help.

In answer to my advertisement, a motionless young man one morning stood upon my office threshold, the door being open, for it was summer. I can see that figure now—pallidly neat, pitiably respectable, incurably forlorn! It was Bartleby.

After a few words touching his qualifications, I engaged him, glad to have among my corps of copyists a man of so singularly sedate an aspect, which I thought might operate beneficially upon the flighty temper of Turkey, and the fiery one of Nippers.

I should have stated before that ground glass folding-doors divided my premises into two parts, one of which was occupied by my scriveners, the other by myself. According to my humor, I threw open these doors, or closed them. I resolved to assign Bartleby a corner by the folding-doors, but on my side of them, so as to have this quiet man within easy call, in case any trifling thing was to be done. I placed his desk close up to a small side-window in that part of the room, a window which originally had afforded a lateral view of certain grimy backyards and bricks, but which, owing to subsequent erections, commanded at present no view at all, though it gave some light. Within three feet of the panes was a wall, and the light came down from far above, between two lofty buildings, as from a very small opening in a dome. Still further to a satisfactory arrangement, I procured a high green folding screen, which might entirely isolate Bartleby from my sight, though not remove him from my voice. And thus, in a manner, privacy and society were conjoined.

At first, Bartleby did an extraordinary quantity of writing. As if long famishing for something to copy, he seemed to gorge himself on my documents. There was no pause for digestion. He ran a day and night line, copying by sun-light and by candle-light. I should have been quite delighted with his application, had he been cheerfully industrious. But he wrote on silently, palely, mechanically.

It is, of course, an indispensable part of a scrivener's business to verify the accuracy of his copy, word by word. Where there are two or more scriveners in an office, they assist each other in this examination, one reading from the copy, the other holding the original. It is a very dull, wearisome, and lethargic affair. I can readily imagine that, to some sanguine temperaments, it would be altogether intolerable. For example, I cannot credit that the mettlesome poet, Byron, would have contentedly sat down with Bartleby to examine a law document of, say five hundred pages, closely written in a crimpy hand.

Now and then, in the haste of business, it had been my habit to assist in comparing some brief document myself, calling Turkey or Nippers for this purpose. One object I had, in placing Bartleby so handy to me behind the screen, was to avail myself of his services on such trivial occasions. It was on the third day, I think, of his being with me, and before any necessity had arisen for having his own writing examined, that, being much hurried to complete a small affair I had in hand, I abruptly called to Bartleby. In my haste and natural expectancy of instant compliance, I sat with my head bent over the original on my desk, and my right hand sideways, and somewhat nervously extended with the copy, so that, immediately upon emerging from his retreat, Bartleby might snatch it and proceed to business without the least delay.

In this very attitude did I sit when I called to him, rapidly stating what it was I wanted him to do—namely, to examine a small paper with me.

Imagine my surprise, nay, my consternation, when, without moving from his privacy, Bartleby, in a singularly mild, firm voice, replied, "I would prefer not to."

I sat awhile in perfect silence, rallying my stunned faculties. Immediately it occurred to me that my ears had deceived me, or Bartleby had entirely misunderstood my meaning. I repeated my request in the clearest tone I could assume; but in quite as clear a one came the previous reply, "I would prefer not to."

"Prefer not to," echoed I, rising in high excitement, and crossing the room with a stride. "What do you mean? Are you moon-struck? I want you to help me compare this sheet here—take it," and I thrust it towards him.

"I would prefer not to," said he.

I looked at him steadfastly. His face was leanly composed; his gray eye dimly calm. Not a wrinkle of agitation rippled him. Had there been the least uneasiness, anger, impatience, or impertinence in his manner; in other words, had there been any thing ordinarily human about him, doubtless I should have violently dismissed him from the premises. But as it was, I should have as soon thought of turning my pale plaster-of-paris bust of Cicero out of doors. I stood gazing at him awhile, as he went on with his own writing, and then reseated myself at my desk. This is very strange, thought I. What had one best do? But my business hurried me. I concluded to forget the matter for the present, reserving it for my future leisure. So calling Nippers from the other room, the paper was speedily examined.

A few days after this, Bartleby concluded four lengthy documents, being quadruplicates of a week's testimony taken before me in my High Court of Chancery. It became necessary to examine them. It was an important suit, and great accuracy was imperative. Having all things arranged, I called Turkey, Nippers, and Ginger Nut from the next room, meaning to place the four copies in the hands of my four clerks, while I should read from the original. Accordingly, Turkey, Nippers, and Ginger Nut had taken their seats in a row, each with his document in his hand, when I called to Bartleby to join this interesting group.

"Bartleby! quick, I am waiting."

I heard a slow scrape of his chair legs on the uncarpeted floor, and soon he appeared standing at the entrance of his hermitage.

"What is wanted?" said he, mildly.

"The copies, the copies," said I, hurriedly. "We are going to examine them. There—" and I held towards him the fourth quadruplicate.

"I would prefer not to," he said, and gently disappeared behind the screen.

For a few moments I was turned into a pillar of salt, standing at the head of my seated column of clerks. Recovering myself, I advanced towards the screen, and demanded the reason for such extraordinary conduct.

"*Why* do you refuse?"

"I would prefer not to."

With any other man I should have flown outright into a dreadful passion, scorned all further words, and thrust him ignominiously from my presence. But there was something about Bartleby that not only strangely disarmed me, but in a wonderful manner, touched and disconcerted me. I began to reason with him.

"These are your own copies we are about to examine. It is labor saving to you, because one examination will answer for your four papers. It is common usage. Every copyist is bound to help examine his copy. Is it not so? Will you not speak? Answer!"

"I prefer not to," he replied in a flutelike tone. It seemed to me that, while I had been addressing him, he carefully revolved every statement that I made; fully comprehended the meaning; could not gainsay the irresistible conclusion; but, at the same time, some paramount consideration prevailed with him to reply as he did.

"You are decided, then, not to comply with my request—a request made according to common usage and common sense?"

He briefly gave me to understand, that on that point my judgment was sound. Yes: his decision was irreversible.

It is not seldom the case that, when a man is browbeaten in some unprecedented and violently unreasonable way, he begins to stagger in his own plainest faith. He begins, as it were, vaguely to surmise that, wonderful as it may be, all the justice and all the reason is on the other side. Accordingly, if any disinterested persons are present, he turns to them for some reinforcement of his own faltering mind.

"Turkey," said I, "what do you think of this? Am I not right?"

"With submission, sir," said Turkey, in his blandest tone, "I think that you are."

"Nippers," said I, "what do *you* think of it?"

"I think I should kick him out of the office."

(The reader, of nice perceptions, will here perceive that, it being morning, Turkey's answer is couched in polite and tranquil terms, but Nippers replies in ill-tempered ones. Or, to repeat a previous sentence, Nippers's ugly mood was on duty, and Turkey's off.)

"Ginger Nut," said I, willing to enlist the smallest suffrage in my behalf, "what do *you* think of it?"

"I think, sir, he's a little *luny*," replied Ginger Nut, with a grin.

"You hear what they say," said I, turning towards the screen, "come forth and do you duty."

But he vouchsafed no reply. I pondered a moment in sore perplexity. But once more business hurried me. I determined again to postpone the consideration of this dilemma to my future leisure. With a little trouble we made out to examine the papers without Bartleby, though at every page or two Turkey deferentially dropped his opinion, that this proceeding was quite out of the common; while Nippers, twitching in his chair with a dyspeptic nervousness, ground out, between his set teeth, occasional hissing maledictions against the stubborn oaf behind the screen. And for his (Nippers's) part, this was the first and the last time he would do another man's business without pay.

Meanwhile Bartleby sat in his hermitage, oblivious to everything but his own peculiar business there.

Some days passed, the scrivener being employed upon another lengthy work. His late remarkable conduct led me to regard his ways narrowly. I observed that he never went to dinner; indeed, that he never went anywhere. As yet I had never, of my personal knowledge, known him to be outside of my office. He was a perpetual sentry in the corner. At about eleven o'clock though, in the morning, I noticed that Ginger Nut would advance toward the opening in Bartleby's screen, as if silently beckoned thither by a gesture invisible to me where I sat. The boy would then leave the office, jingling a few pence, and reappear with a handful of ginger-nuts, which he delivered in the hermitage, receiving two of the cakes for his trouble.

He lives, then, on ginger-nuts, thought I; never eats a dinner, properly speaking; he must be a vegetarian, then; but no; he never eats even vegetables; he eats nothing but ginger-nuts. My mind then ran on in reveries concerning the probable effects upon the human constitution of living entirely on ginger-nuts. Ginger-nuts are so called, because they contain ginger as one of their peculiar constituents, and the final flavoring one. Now, what was ginger? A hot, spicy thing. Was Bartleby hot and spicy? Not at all. Ginger, then, had no effect upon Bartleby. Probably he preferred it should have none.

Nothing so aggravates an earnest person as a passive resistance. If the individual so resisted be of a not inhumane temper, and the resisting one perfectly harmless in his passivity, then, in the better moods of the former, he will endeavor charitably to construe to his imagination what proves impossible to be solved by his judgment. Even so, for the most part, I regarded Bartleby and his ways. Poor fellow! thought I, he means no mischief; it is plain he intends no insolence; his aspect sufficiently evinces that his eccentricities are involuntary. He is useful to me. I can get along with him. If I turn him away, the chances are he will fall in with some less-indulgent employer, and then he will be rudely treated, and perhaps driven forth miserably to starve. Yes. Here I can cheaply purchase a delicious self-approval. To befriend Bartleby; to humor him in his strange willfulness, will cost me little or nothing, while I lay up in my soul what will eventually prove a sweet morsel for my conscience. But this mood was not invariable with me. The passiveness of Bartleby sometimes irritated me. I felt strangely goaded on to encounter him in new opposition—to elicit some angry spark from him answerable to my own. But, indeed, I might as well have essayed to strike fire with my knuckles against a bit of Windsor soap. But one afternoon the evil impulse in me mastered me, and the following little scene ensued:

"Bartleby," said I, "when those papers are all copied, I will compare them with you."

"I would prefer not to."

"How? Surely you do not mean to persist in that mulish vagary?"

No answer.

I threw open the folding-doors near by, and, turning upon Turkey and Nippers, exclaimed:

"Bartleby a second time says, he won't examine his papers. What do you think of it, Turkey?"

It was afternoon, be it remembered. Turkey sat glowing like a brass boiler; his bald head steaming; his hands reeling among his blotted papers.

"Think of it?" roared Turkey; "I think I'll just step behind his screen, and black his eyes for him!"

So saying, Turkey rose to his feet and threw his arms into a pugilistic position. He was hurrying away to make good his promise, when I detained him, alarmed at the effect of incautiously rousing Turkey's combativeness after dinner.

"Sit down, Turkey," said I, "and hear what Nippers has to say. What do you think of it, Nippers? Would I not be justified in immediately dismissing Bartleby?"

"Excuse me, that is for you to decide, sir. I think his conduct quite unusual, and, indeed, unjust, as regards Turkey and myself. But it may only be a passing whim."

"Ah," exclaimed I, "you have strangely changed your mind, then—you speak very gently of him now."

"All beer," cried Turkey; "gentleness is effects of beer—Nippers and I dined together to-day. You see how gentle *I* am, sir. Shall I go and black his eyes?"

"You refer to Bartleby, I suppose. No, not to-day, Turkey," I replied; "pray, put up your fists."

I closed the doors, and again advanced towards Bartleby. I felt additional incentives tempting me to my fate. I burned to be rebelled against again. I remembered that Bartleby never left the office.

"Bartleby," said I, "Ginger Nut is away; just step around to the Post Office, won't you? (it was but a three minutes' walk), and see if there is anything for me."

"I would prefer not to."

"You *will* not?"

"I *prefer* not."

I staggered to my desk, and sat there in a deep study. My blind inveteracy returned. Was there any other thing in which I could procure myself to be ignominiously repulsed by this lean, penniless wight?—my hired clerk? What added thing is there, perfectly reasonable, that he will be sure to refuse to do? "Bartleby!"

No answer.

"Bartleby," in a louder tone.

No answer.

"Bartleby," I roared.

Like a very ghost, agreeably to the laws of magical invocation, at the third summons, he appeared at the entrance of his hermitage.

"Go to the next room, and tell Nippers to come to me."

"I prefer not to," he respectfully and slowly said and mildly disappeared.

"Very good, Bartleby," said I, in a quiet sort of serenely-severe, self-possessed tone, intimating the unalterable purpose of some terrible retribution very close at hand. At the moment I half intended something of the kind. But upon the whole, as it was drawing towards my dinner-hour, I thought it best to put on my hat and walk home for the day, suffering much from perplexity and distress of mind.

Shall I acknowledge it? The conclusion of this whole business was, that it soon became a fixed fact of my chambers, that a pale young scrivener, by the name of Bartleby, had a desk there; that he copied for me at the usual rate of four cents a folio (one hundred words); but he was permanently exempt from examining the work done by him, that duty being transferred to Turkey and Nippers, out of compliment, doubtless, to their superior acuteness; moreover, said Bartleby was never, on any account, to be dispatched on the most trivial errand of any sort; and that even if entreated to take upon him such a matter, it was generally understood that he would "prefer not to"—in other words, that he would refuse point-blank.

As days passed on, I became considerably reconciled to Bartleby. His steadiness, his freedom from all dissipation, his incessant industry (except when he chose to throw himself into a standing revery behind his screen), his great stillness, his unalterableness of demeanor under all circumstances, made him a valuable acquisition. One prime thing was this—*he was always there*—first in the morning, continually through the day, and the last at night. I had a singular confidence in his honesty. I felt my most precious papers perfectly safe in his hands. Sometimes, to be sure, I could not, for the very soul of me, avoid falling into sudden spasmodic passions with him. For it was exceeding difficult to bear in mind all the time those strange peculiarities, privileges, and unheard of exemptions, forming the tacit stipulations on Bartleby's part under which he remained in my office. Now and then, in the eagerness of dispatching pressing business, I would inadvertently summon Bartleby, in a short, rapid tone, to put his finger, say, on the incipient tie of a bit of red tape with which I was about compressing some papers. Of course, from behind the screen the usual answer, "I prefer not to," was sure to come; and then, how could a human creature, with the common infirmities of our nature, refrain from bitterly exclaiming upon such perverseness—such unreasonableness. However, every added repulse of this sort which I received only tended to lessen the probability of my repeating the inadvertence.

Here it must be said, that according to the custom of most legal gentlemen occupying chambers in densely-populated law buildings, there were several keys to my door. One was kept by a woman residing in the attic, which person weekly scrubbed and daily swept and dusted my apartments. Another was kept by Turkey for convenience sake. The third I sometimes carried in my own pocket. The fourth I knew not who had.

Now, one Sunday morning I happened to go to Trinity Church, to hear a celebrated preacher, and finding myself rather early on the ground I thought I would walk around to my chambers for a while. Luckily I had my key with me; but upon applying it to the lock, I found it resisted by something inserted from the inside. Quite surprised, I called out; when to my consternation a key was turned from within; and thrusting his lean visage at me, and holding the door ajar, the apparition of Bartleby appeared, in his shirt sleeves, and otherwise in a strangely tattered *déshabillé,* saying quietly that he was sorry, but he was deeply engaged just then, and—preferred not admitting me at present. In a brief word or two, he moreover added, that perhaps I had better walk around the block two or three times, and by that time he would probably have concluded his affairs.

Now, the utterly unsurmised appearance of Bartleby, tenanting my law-chambers of a Sunday morning, with his cadaverously gentlemanly *nonchalance*, yet withal firm and self-possessed, had such a strange effect upon me, that incontinently I slunk away from my own door, and did as desired. But not without sundry twinges of impotent rebellion against the mild effrontery of this unaccountable scrivener. Indeed, it was his wonderful mildness chiefly, which not only disarmed me, but unmanned me as it were. For I consider that one, for the time, is somehow unmanned when he tranquilly permits his hired clerk to dictate to him, and order him away from his own premises. Furthermore, I was full of uneasiness as to what Bartleby could possibly be doing in my office in his shirt sleeves, and in an otherwise dismantled condition of a Sunday morning. Was anything amiss going on? Nay, that was out of the question. It was not to be thought of for a moment that Bartleby was an immoral person. But what could he be doing there?—copying? Nay again, whatever might be his eccentricities, Bartleby was an eminently decorous person. He would be the last man to sit down to his desk in any state approaching to nudity. Besides, it was Sunday; and there was something about Bartleby that forbade the supposition that he would by any secular occupation violate the proprieties of the day.

Nevertheless, my mind was not pacified; and full of a restless curiosity, at last I returned to the door. Without hindrance I inserted my key, opened it, and entered. Bartleby was not to be seen. I looked round anxiously, peeped behind his screen; but it was very plain that he was gone. Upon more closely examining the place, I surmised that for an indefinite period Bartleby must have eaten, dressed, and slept in my office, and that, too, without plate, mirror, or bed. The cushioned seat of a rickety old sofa in one corner bore the faint impress of a lean, reclining form. Rolled away under his desk, I found a blanket; under the empty grate, a blacking box and brush; on a chair, a tin basin, with soap and a ragged towel; in a newspaper a few crumbs of ginger-nuts and a morsel of cheese. Yes, thought I, it is evident enough that Bartleby has been making his home here, keeping bachelor's hall all by himself. Immediately then the thought came sweeping across me, what miserable friendlessness and loneliness are here revealed! His poverty is great; but his solitude, how horrible! Think of it. Of a Sunday, Wall Street is deserted as Petra, and every night of every day it is an emptiness. This building, too, which of week-days hums with industry and life, at nightfall echoes with sheer vacancy, and all through Sunday is forlorn. And here Bartleby makes his home; sole spectator of a solitude which he has seen all populous—a sort of innocent and transformed Marius brooding among the ruins of Carthage!

For the first time in my life a feeling of over-powering stinging melancholy seized me. Before, I had never experienced aught but a not unpleasing sadness. The bond of a common humanity now drew me irresistibly to gloom. A fraternal melancholy! For both I and Bartleby were sons of Adam. I remembered the bright silks and sparkling faces I had seen that day, in gala trim, swan-like sailing down the Mississippi of Broadway; and I contrasted them with the pallid copyist, and thought to myself, Ah, happiness courts the light, so we deem the world is gay; but misery hides aloof, so we deem that misery there is none. These sad fancyings—chimeras, doubtless, of a sick and silly brain—led on to other and more special thoughts, concerning the eccentricities of Bartleby. Presentiments of strange discoveries hovered round me. The scrivener's pale form appeared to me laid out, among uncaring strangers, in its shivering winding sheet.

Suddenly I was attracted by Bartleby's closed desk, the key in open sight left in the lock.

I mean no mischief, seek the gratification of no heartless curiosity, thought I; besides, the desk is mine, and its contents, too, so I will make bold to look within. Everything was methodically arranged, the papers smoothly placed. The pigeon holes were deep, and removing the files of documents, I groped into their recesses. Presently I felt something there, and dragged it out. It was an old bandanna handkerchief, heavy and knotted. I opened it, and saw it was a savings bank.

I now recalled all the quiet mysteries which I had noted in the man. I remembered that he never spoke but to answer; that, though at intervals he had considerable time to himself, yet I had never seen him reading—no, not even a newspaper; that for long periods he would stand looking out, at his pale window behind the screen, upon the dead brick wall; I was quite sure he never visited any refectory or eating house; while his pale face clearly indicated that he never drank beer like Turkey, or tea and coffee even, like other men; that he never went anywhere in particular that I could learn; never went out for a walk, unless, indeed, that was the case at present; that he had declined telling who he was, or whence he came, or whether he had any relatives in the world; that though so thin and pale, he never complained of ill health. And more than all, I remembered a certain unconscious air of pallid—how shall I call it?—of pallid haughtiness, say, or rather an austere reserve about him, which had positively awed me into my tame compliance with his eccentricities, when I had feared to ask him to do the slightest incidental thing for me, even though I might know, from his long-continued motionlessness, that behind his screen he must be standing in one of those dead-wall reveries of his.

Revolving all these things, and coupling them with the recently discovered fact, that he made my office his constant abiding place and home, and not forgetful of his morbid moodiness; revolving all these things, a prudential feeling began to steal over me. My first emotions had been those of pure melancholy and sincerest pity; but just in proportion as the forlornness of Bartleby grew and grew to my imagination, did that same melancholy merge into fear, that pity into repulsion. So true it is, and so terrible, too, that up to a certain point the thought or sight of misery enlists our best affections; but, in certain special cases, beyond that point it does not. They err who would assert that invariably this is owing to the inherent selfishness of the human heart. It rather proceeds from a certain hopelessness of remedying excessive and organic ill. To a sensitive being, pity is not seldom pain. And when at last it is perceived that such pity cannot lead to effectual succor, common sense bids the soul be rid of it. What I saw that morning persuaded me that the scrivener was the victim of innate and incurable disorder. I might give alms to his body; but his body did not pain him: it was his soul that suffered, and his soul I could not reach.

I did not accomplish the purpose of going to Trinity Church that morning. Somehow, the things I had seen disqualified me for the time from churchgoing. I walked homeward, thinking what I would do with Bartleby. Finally, I resolved upon this—I would put certain calm questions to him the next morning, touching his history, etc., and if he declined to answer them openly and unreservedly (and I supposed he would prefer not), then to give him a twenty dollar bill over and above whatever I might owe him, and tell him his services were no longer required; but that if in any other way I could assist him, I would be happy to do so, especially if he desired to return to his native place, wherever that might be, I would willingly help to defray the expenses. Moreover, if, after reaching home, he found himself at any time in want of aid, a letter from him would be sure of a reply.

The next morning came.

"Bartleby," said I, gently calling to him behind his screen.

No reply.

"Bartleby," said I, in a still gentler tone, "come here; I am not going to ask you to do anything you would prefer not to do—I simply wish to speak to you."

Upon this he noiselessly slid into view.

"Will you tell me, Bartleby, where you were born?"

"I would prefer not to."

"Will you tell me *anything* about yourself?"

"I would prefer not to."

"But what reasonable objection can you have to speak to me? I feel friendly towards you."

He did not look at me while I spoke, but kept his glance fixed upon my bust of Cicero, which, as I then sat, was directly behind me, some six inches above my head.

"What is your answer, Bartleby," said I, after waiting a considerable time for a reply, during which his countenance remained immovable, only there was the faintest conceivable tremor of the white attenuated mouth.

"At present I prefer to give no answer," he said, and retired into his hermitage.

It was rather weak in me I confess, but his manner, on this occasion, nettled me. Not only did there seem to lurk in it a certain calm disdain, but his perverseness seemed ungrateful, considering the undeniable good usage and indulgence he had received from me.

Again I sat ruminating what I should do. Mortified as I was at his behavior, and resolved as I had been to dismiss him when I entered my office, nevertheless I strangely felt something superstitious knocking at my heart, and forbidding me to carry out my purpose, and denouncing me for a villain if I dared to breathe one bitter word against this forlornest of mankind. At last, familiarly drawing my chair behind his screen, I sat down and said: "Bartleby, never mind, then, about revealing your history; but let me entreat you, as a friend, to comply as far as may be with the usages of this office. Say now, you will help to examine papers to-morrow or next day: in short, say now, that in a day or two you will begin to be a little reasonable:—say so, Bartleby."

"At present I would prefer not to be a little reasonable," was his mildly cadaverous reply.

Just then the folding-doors opened, and Nippers approached. He seemed suffering from an unusually bad night's rest, induced by severer indigestion than common. He overheard those final words of Bartleby.

"*Prefer not,* eh?" gritted Nippers—"I'd *prefer* him, if I were you, sir," addressing me—"I'd *prefer* him; I'd give him preferences, the stubborn mule! What is it, sir, pray, that he *prefers* not to do now?"

Bartleby moved not a limb.

"Mr. Nippers," said I, "I'd prefer that you would withdraw for the present."

Somehow, of late, I had got into the way of involuntarily using this world "prefer" upon all sorts of not exactly suitable occasions. And I trembled to think that my contact with the scrivener had already and seriously affected me in a mental way. And what further and deeper aberration might it not yet produce? This apprehension had not been without efficacy in determining me to summary measures.

As Nippers, looking very sour and sulky, was departing, Turkey blandly and deferentially approached.

"With submission, sir," said he, "yesterday I was thinking about Bartleby here, and I think that if he would but prefer to take a quart of good ale every day, it would do much towards mending him, and enabling him to assist in examining his papers."

"So you have got the word, too," said I, slightly excited.

"With submission, what word, sir," asked Turkey, respectfully crowding himself into the contracted space behind the screen, and by so doing, making me jostle the scrivener. "What word, sir?"

"I would prefer to be left alone here," said Bartleby, as if offended at being mobbed in his privacy.

"*That's* the word, Turkey," said I—"*That's* it."

"Oh, *prefer*? oh yes—queer word. I never use it myself. But, sir, as I was saying, if he would but prefer—"

"Turkey," interrupted I, "you will please withdraw."

"Oh certainly, sir, if you prefer that I should."

As he opened the folding-door to retire, Nippers at his desk caught a glimpse of me, and asked whether I would prefer to have a certain paper copied on blue paper or white. He did not in the least roguishly accent the word prefer. It was plain that it involuntarily rolled from his tongue. I thought to myself, surely I must get rid of a demented man, who already has in some degree turned the tongues, if not the heads of myself and clerks. But I thought it prudent not to break the dismission at once.

The next day I noticed that Bartleby did nothing but stand at his window in his dead-wall revery. Upon asking him why he did not write, he said that he had decided upon doing no more writing.

"Why, how now? what next?" exclaimed I, "do no more writing?"

"No more."

"And what is the reason?"

"Do you not see the reason for yourself," he indifferently replied.

I looked steadfastly at him, and perceived that his eyes looked dull and glazed. Instantly it occurred to me, that his unexampled diligence in copying by his dim window for the first few weeks of his stay with me might have temporarily impaired his vision.

I was touched. I said something in condolence with him. I hinted that of course he did wisely in abstaining from writing for a while; and urged him to embrace that opportunity of taking wholesome exercise in the open air. This, however, he did not do. A few days after this, my other clerks being absent, and being in a great hurry to dispatch certain letters by the mail, I thought that, having nothing else earthly to do, Bartleby would surely be less inflexible than usual, and carry these letters to the post-office. But he blankly declined. So, much to my inconvenience, I went myself.

Still added days went by. Whether Bartleby's eyes improved or not, I could not say. To all appearance I thought they did. But when I asked him if they did, he vouchsafed no answer. At all events, he would do no copying. At last, in reply to my urgings, he informed me that he had permanently given up copying.

"What!" exclaimed I; "suppose your eyes should get entirely well—better than ever before—would you not copy then?"

"I have given up copying," he answered, and slid aside.

He remained as ever, a fixture in my chamber. Nay—if that were possible—he became still more of a fixture than before. What was to be done? He would do nothing in the office; why should he stay there? In plain fact, he had now become a millstone to me, not only useless as a necklace, but afflictive to bear. Yet I was sorry for him. I speak less than truth when I say that, on his own account, he occasioned me uneasiness. If he would but have named a single relative or friend, I would instantly have written, and urged their taking the poor fellow away to some convenient retreat. But he seemed alone, absolutely alone in the universe. A bit of wreck in the mid Atlantic. At length, necessities connected with my business tyrannized over all other considerations. Decently as I could, I told Bartleby that in six days time he must unconditionally leave the office. I warned him to take measures, in the interval, for procuring some other abode. I offered to assist him in his endeavor, if he himself would but take the first step towards a removal. "And when you finally quit me, Bartleby," added I, "I shall see that you go not away entirely unprovided. Six days from this hour, remember."

At the expiration of that period, I peeped behind the screen, and lo! Bartleby was there.

I buttoned up my coat, balanced myself; advanced slowly towards him, touched his shoulder, and said, "The time has come; you must quit this place; I am sorry for you; here is money; but you must go."

"I would prefer not," he replied, with his back still towards me.

"You *must*."

He remained silent.

Now I had an unbounded confidence in this man's common honesty. He had frequently restored to me sixpences and shillings carelessly dropped upon the floor, for I am apt to be very reckless in such shirt-button affairs. The proceeding then, which followed will not be deemed extraordinary.

"Bartleby," said I, "I owe you twelve dollars on account; here are thirty-two; the odd twenty are yours—Will you take it?" and I handed the bills towards him.

But he made no motion.

"I will leave them here, then," putting them under a weight on the table. Then taking my hat and cane and going to the door, I tranquilly turned and added—"After you have removed your things from these offices, Bartleby, you will of course lock the door—since every one is now gone for the day but you—and if you please, slip your key underneath the mat, so that I may have it in the morning. I shall not see you again; so good-by to you. If, hereafter, in your new place of abode, I can be of any service to you, do not fail to advise me by letter. Good-by, Bartleby, and fare you well."

But he answered not a word; like the last column of some ruined temple, he remained standing mute and solitary in the middle of the otherwise deserted room.

As I walked home in a pensive mood, my vanity got the better of my pity. I could not but highly plume myself on my masterly management in getting rid of Bartleby. Masterly I call it, and such it must appear to any dispassionate thinker. The beauty of my procedure seemed to consist in its perfect quietness. There was no vulgar bullying, no bravado of any sort, no choleric hectoring, and striding to and fro across the apartment, jerking out vehement commands for Bartleby to bundle himself off with his beggarly traps. Nothing of the kind. Without loudly bidding Bartleby depart—as an inferior genius might have done—I *assumed* the ground that depart he must; and upon that assumption built all I had to say. The more I thought over my procedure, the more I was charmed with it. Nevertheless, next morning, upon awakening, I had my doubts—I had somehow slept off the fumes of vanity. One of the coolest and wisest hours a man has, is just after he awakes in the morning. My procedure seemed as sagacious as ever—but only in theory. How it would prove in practice—there was the rub. It was truly a beautiful thought to have assumed Bartleby's departure; but, after all, that assumption was simply my own, and none of Bartleby's. The great point was, not whether I had assumed that he would quit me, but whether he would prefer so to do. He was more a man of preferences than assumptions.

After breakfast, I walked down town, arguing the probabilities *pro* and *con.* One moment I thought it would prove a miserable failure, and Bartleby would be found all alive at my office as usual; the next moment it seemed certain that I should find his chair empty. And so I kept veering about. At the corner of Broadway and Canal Street, I saw quite an excited group of people standing in earnest conversation.

"I'll take odds he doesn't," said a voice as I passed.

"Doesn't go—done!" said I; "put up your money."

I was instinctively putting my hand in my pocket to produce my own, when I remembered that this was an election day. The words I had overheard bore no reference to Bartleby, but to the success or non-success of some candidate for the mayoralty. In my intent frame of mine, I had, as it were, imagined that all Broadway shared in my excitement, and were debating the same question with me. I passed on, very thankful that the uproar of the street screened my momentary absent-mindedness.

As I had intended, I was earlier than usual at my office door. I stood listening for a moment. All was still. He must be gone. I tried the knob. The door was locked. Yes, my procedure had worked to a charm; he indeed must be vanished. Yet a certain melancholy mixed with this: I was almost sorry for my brilliant success. I was fumbling under the door mat for the key, which Bartleby was to have left there for me, when accidentally my knee knocked against a panel, producing a summoning sound, and in response a voice came to me from within—"Not yet; I am occupied."

It was Bartleby.

I was thunderstruck. For an instant I stood like the man who, pipe in mouth, was killed one cloudless afternoon long ago in Virginia, by summer lightning; at his own warm open window he was killed, and remained leaning out there upon the dreamy afternoon, till some one touched him, when he fell.

"Not gone!" I murmured at last. But again obeying that wondrous ascendancy which the inscrutable scrivener had over me, and from which ascendancy, for all my chafing, I could not completely escape, I slowly went down stairs and out into the street, and while walking round the block, considered what I should next do in this unheard-of perplexity. Turn the man out by an actual thrusting I could not; to drive him away by calling him hard names would not do; calling in the police was an unpleasant idea; and yet, permit him to enjoy his cadaverous triumph over me—this, too, I could not think of. What was to be done? or, if nothing could be done, was there anything further that I could *assume* in the matter? Yes, as before I had prospectively assumed that Bartleby would depart, so now I might retrospectively assume that departed he was. In the legitimate carrying out of this assumption, I might enter my office in a great hurry, and pretending not to see Bartleby at all, walk straight against him as if he were air. Such a proceeding would in a singular degree have the appearance of a home-thrust. It was hardly possible that Bartleby could withstand such an application of the doctrine of assumptions. But upon second thoughts the success of the plan seemed rather dubious. I resolved to argue the matter over with him again.

"Bartleby," said I, entering the office, with a quietly severe expression, "I am seriously displeased. I am pained, Bartleby. I had thought better of you. I had imagined you of such a gentlemanly organization, that in any delicate dilemma a slight hint would suffice—in short, an assumption. But it appears I am deceived. Why," I added, unaffectedly starting, "you have not even touched that money yet," pointing to it, just where I had left it the evening previous.

He answered nothing.

"Will you, or will you not, quit me?" I now demanded in a sudden passion, advancing close to him.

"I would prefer *not* to quit you," he replied, gently emphasizing the *not*.

"What earthly right have you to stay here? Do you pay any rent? Do you pay my taxes? Or is this property yours?"

He answered nothing.

"Are you ready to go on and write now? Are your eyes recovered? Could you copy a small paper for me this morning? or help examine a few lines? or step round to the post-office? In a word, will you do anything at all, to give a coloring to your refusal to depart the premises?"

He silently retired into his hermitage.

I was now in such a state of nervous resentment that I thought it but prudent to check myself at present from further demonstrations. Bartleby and I were alone. I remembered the tragedy of the unfortunate Adams and the still more unfortunate Colt in the solitary office of the latter; and how poor Colt, being dreadfully incensed by Adams, and imprudently permitting himself to get wildly excited, was at unawares hurried into his fatal act—an act which certainly no man could possibly deplore more than the actor himself. Often it had occurred to me in my ponderings upon the subject, that had that altercation taken place in the public street, or at a private residence, it would not have terminated as it did. It was the circumstance of being alone in a solitary office, up stairs, of a building entirely unhallowed by humanizing domestic associations—an uncarpeted office, doubtless, of a dusty, haggard sort of appearance—this it must have been, which greatly helped to enhance the irritable desperation of the hapless Colt.

But when this old Adam of resentment rose in me and tempted me concerning Bartleby, I grappled him and threw him. How? Why, simply by recalling the divine injunction: "A new commandment give I unto you, that ye love one another." Yes, this it was that saved me. Aside from higher considerations, charity often operates as a vastly wise and prudent principle—a great safeguard to its possessor. Men have committed murder for jealousy's sake, and anger's sake, and hatred's sake, and selfishness' sake, and spiritual pride's sake; but no man, that ever I heard of, ever committed a diabolical murder for sweet charity's sake. Mere self-interest, then, if no better motive can be enlisted, should, especially with high-tempered men, prompt all beings to charity and philanthropy. At any rate, upon the occasion in question, I strove to drown my exasperated feelings towards the scrivener by benevolently construing his conduct. Poor fellow, poor fellow! thought I, he don't mean anything; and besides, he has seen hard times, and ought to be indulged.

I endeavored, also, immediately to occupy myself, and at the same time to comfort my despondency. I tried to fancy, that in the course of the morning, at such time as might prove agreeable to him, Bartleby, of his own free accord, would emerge from his hermitage and take up some decided line of march in the direction of the door. But no. Half-past twelve o'clock came; Turkey began to glow in the face, overturn his inkstand, and become generally obstreperous; Nippers abated down into quietude and courtesy; Ginger Nut munched his noon apple; and Bartleby remained standing at his window in one of his profoundest dead-wall reveries. Will it be credited? Ought I to acknowledge it? That afternoon I left the office without saying one further word to him.

Some days now passed, during which, at leisure intervals I looked a little into "Edwards on the Will," and "Priestley on Necessity." Under the circumstances, those books induced a salutary feeling. Gradually I slid into the persuasion that these troubles of mine, touching the scrivener, had been all predestinated from eternity, and Bartleby was billeted upon me for some mysterious purpose of an all-wise Providence, which it was not for a mere mortal like me to fathom. Yes, Bartleby, stay there behind your screen, thought I; I shall persecute you no more; you are harmless and noiseless as any of these old chairs; in short, I never feel so private as when I know you are here. At last I see it, I feel it; I penetrate to the predestinated purpose of my life. I am content. Others may have loftier parts to enact; but my mission in this world, Bartleby, is to furnish you with office-room for such period as you may see fit to remain.

I believe that this wise and blessed frame of mind would have continued with me, had it not been for the unsolicited and uncharitable remarks obtruded upon me by my professional friends who visited the rooms. But thus it often is, that the constant friction of illiberal minds wears out at last the best resolves of the more generous. Though to be sure, when I reflected upon it, it was not strange that people entering my office should be struck by the peculiar aspect of the unaccountable Bartleby, and so be tempted to throw out some sinister observations concerning him. Sometimes an attorney, having business with me, and calling at my office, and finding no one but the scrivener there, would undertake to obtain some sort of precise information from him touching my whereabouts; but without heeding his idle talk, Bartleby would remain standing immovable in the middle of the room. So after contemplating him in that position for a time, the attorney would depart, no wiser than he came.

Also, when a reference was going on, and the room full of lawyers and witnesses, and business driving fast, some deeply-occupied legal gentleman present, seeing Bartleby wholly unemployed, would request him to run round to his (the legal gentleman's) office and fetch some papers for him. Thereupon, Bartleby would tranquilly decline, and yet remain idle as before. Then the lawyer would give a great stare, and turn to me. And what could I say? At last I was made aware that all through the circle of my professional acquaintance, a whisper of wonder was running round, having reference to the strange creature I kept at my office. This worried me very much. And as the idea came upon me of his possibly turning out a long-lived man, and keep occupying my chambers, and denying my authority; and perplexing my visitors; and scandalizing my professional reputation; and casting a general gloom over the premises; keeping soul and body together to the last upon his savings (for doubtless he spent but half a dime a day), and in the end perhaps outlive me, and claim possession of my office by right of his perpetual occupancy: as all these dark anticipations crowded upon me more and more, and my friends continually intruded their relentless remarks upon the apparition in my room; a great change was wrought in me. I resolved to gather all my faculties together, and forever rid me of this intolerable incubus.

Ere revolving any complicated project, however, adapted to this end, I first simply suggested to Bartleby the propriety of his permanent departure. In a calm and serious tone, I commended the idea to his careful and mature consideration. But, having taken three days to meditate upon it, he apprised me, that his original determination remained the same; in short, that he still preferred to abide with me.

What shall I do? I now said to myself, buttoning up my coat to the last button. What shall I do? what ought I to do? what does conscience say I *should* do with this man, or, rather, ghost. Rid myself of him, I must; go, he shall. But how? You will not thrust him, the poor, pale, passive mortal —you will not thrust such a helpless creature out of your door? you will not dishonor yourself by such cruelty? No, I will not, I cannot do that. Rather would I let him live and die here, and then mason up his remains in the wall. What, then, will you do? For all your coaxing, he will not budge. Bribes he leaves under your own paper-weight on your table; in short, it is quite plain that he prefers to cling to you.

Then something severe, something unusual must be done. What! surely you will not have him collared by a constable, and commit his innocent pallor to the common jail? And upon what ground could you procure such a thing to be done?—a vagrant, is he? What! he a vagrant, a wanderer, who refuses to budge? It is because he will *not* be a vagrant, then, that you seek to count him *as* a vagrant. This is too absurd. No visible means of support: there I have him. Wrong again: for indubitably he *does* support himself, and that is the only unanswerable proof that any man can show of his possessing the means so to do. No more, then. Since he will not quit me, I must quit him. I will change my offices; I will move elsewhere, and give him fair notice, that if I find him on my new premises I will then proceed against him as a common trespasser.

Acting accordingly, next day I thus addressed him: "I find these chambers too far from the City Hall; the air is unwholesome. In a word, I propose to remove my offices next week, and shall no longer require your services. I tell you this now, in order that you may seek another place."

He made no reply; and nothing more was said.

On the appointed day I engaged carts and men, proceeded to my chambers, and, having but little furniture, everything was removed in a few hours. Throughout, the scrivener remained standing behind the screen, which I directed to be removed the last thing. It was withdrawn; and, being folded up like a huge folio, left him the motionless occupant of a naked room. I stood in the entry watching him a moment, while something from within me upbraided me.

I re-entered, with my hand in my pocket—and—and my heart in my mouth.

"Good-by, Bartleby; I am going—good-by, and God some way bless you; and take that," slipping something in his hand. But it dropped upon the floor, and then—strange to say—I tore myself from him whom I had so longed to be rid of.

Established in my new quarters, for a day or two I kept the door locked, and started at every footfall in the passages. When I returned to my rooms, after any little absence, I would pause at the threshold for an instant, and attentively listen, ere applying my key. But these fears were needless. Bartleby never came nigh me.

I thought all was going well, when a perturbed-looking stranger visited me, inquiring whether I was the person who had recently occupied rooms at No.—— Wall Street.

Full of forebodings, I replied that I was.

"Then, sir," said the stranger, who proved a lawyer, "you are responsible for the man you left there. He refuses to do any copying; he refuses to do anything; he says he prefers not to; and he refuses to quit the premises."

"I am very sorry, sir," said I, with assumed tranquillity, but an inward tremor, "but, really, the man you allude to is nothing to me—he is no relation or apprentice of mine, that you should hold me responsible for him."

"In mercy's name, who is he?"

"I certainly cannot inform you. I know nothing about him. Formerly

I employed him as a copyist; but he has done nothing for me now for some time past."

"I shall settle him, then—good morning, sir."

Several days passed, and I heard nothing more; and, though I often felt a charitable prompting to call at the place and see poor Bartleby, yet a certain squeamishness, of I know not what, withheld me.

All is over with him, by this time, thought I, at last, when, through another week, no further intelligence reached me. But, coming to my room the day after, I found several persons waiting at my door in a high state of nervous excitement.

"That's the man—here he comes," cried the foremost one, whom I recognized as the lawyer who had previously called upon me alone.

"You must take him away, sir, at once," cried a portly person among them, advancing upon me, and whom I knew to be the landlord of No. —— Wall Street. "These gentlemen, my tenants, cannot stand it any longer; Mr. B—," pointing to the lawyer, "has turned him out of his room, and he now persists in haunting the building generally, sitting upon the banisters of the stairs by day, and sleeping in the entry by night. Everybody is concerned; clients are leaving the offices; some fears are entertained of a mob; something you must do, and that without delay."

Aghast at this torrent, I fell back before it, and would fain have locked myself in my new quarters. In vain I persisted that Bartleby was nothing to me—no more than to anyone else. In vain—I was the last person known to have anything to do with him, and they held me to the terrible account. Fearful, then, of being exposed in the papers (as one person present obscurely threatened), I considered the matter, and, at length, said, that if the lawyer would give me a confidential interview with the scrivener, in his (the lawyer's) own room, I would, that afternoon, strive my best to rid them of the nuisance they complained of.

Going up stairs to my old haunt, there was Bartleby silently sitting upon the banister at the landing.

"What are you doing here, Bartleby?" said I.

"Sitting upon the banister," he mildly replied.

I motioned him into the lawyer's room, who then left us.

"Bartleby," said I, "are you aware that you are the cause of great tribulation to me, by persisting in occupying the entry after being dismissed from the office?"

No answer.

"Now one of two things must take place. Either you must do something, or something must be done to you. Now what sort of business would you like to engage in? Would you like to re-engage in copying for some one?"

"No; I would prefer not to make any change."

"Would you like a clerkship in a dry-goods store?"

"There is too much confinement about that. No, I would not like a clerkship; but I am not particular."

"Too much confinement," I cried, "Why you keep yourself confined all the time!"

"I would prefer not to take a clerkship," he rejoined, as if to settle that little item at once.

"How would a bar-tender's business suit you? There is no trying of the eye-sight in that."

"I would not like it at all; though, as I said before, I am not particular."

His unwonted wordiness inspirited me. I returned to the charge.

"Well, then, would you like to travel through the country collecting bills for the merchants? That would improve your health."

"No, I would prefer to be doing something else."

"How, then, would going as a companion to Europe, to entertain some young gentleman with your conversation—how would that suit you?"

"Not at all. It does not strike me that there is anything definite about that. I like to be stationary. But I am not particular."

"Stationary you shall be, then," I cried, now losing all patience, and, for the first time in all my exasperating connection with him, fairly flying into a passion. "If you do not go away from these premises before night, I shall feel bound—indeed, I *am* bound—to—to—to quit the premises myself!" I rather absurdly concluded, knowing not with what possible threat to try to frighten his immobility into compliance. Despairing of all further efforts, I was precipitately leaving him, when a final thought occurred to me—one which had not been wholly unindulged before.

"Bartleby," said I, in the kindest tone I could assume under such exciting circumstances, "will you go home with me now—not to my office, but my dwelling—and remain there till we can conclude upon some convenient arrangement for you at our leisure? Come, let us start now, right away."

"No: at present I would prefer not to make any change at all."

I answered nothing; but, effectually dodging every one by the suddenness and rapidity of my flight, rushed from the building, ran up Wall Street towards Broadway, and, jumping into the first omnibus, was soon removed from pursuit. As soon as tranquillity returned, I distinctly perceived that I had now done all that I possibly could, both in respect to the demands of the landlord and his tenants, and with regard to my own desire and sense of duty, to benefit Bartleby, and shield him from rude persecution. I now strove to be entirely care-free and quiescent; and my conscience justified me in the attempt; though, indeed, it was not so successful as I could have wished. So fearful was I of being again hunted out by the incensed landlord and his exasperated tenants, that, surrendering my business to Nippers, for a few days, I drove about the upper part of the town and through the suburbs, in my rockaway; crossed over to Jersey City and Hoboken, and paid fugitive visits to Manhattanville and Astoria. In fact, I almost lived in my rockaway for the time.

When again I entered my office, lo, a note from the landlord lay upon the desk. I opened it with trembling hands. It informed me that the writer had sent to the police, and had Bartleby removed to the Tombs as a vagrant. Moreover, since I knew more about him than any one else, he wished me to appear at that place, and make a suitable statement of the facts. These tidings had a conflicting effect upon me. At first I was indignant; but, at last, almost approved. The landlord's energetic, summary disposition, had led him to adopt a procedure which I do not think I would have decided upon myself; and yet, as a last resort, under such peculiar circumstances, it seemed the only plan.

As I afterwards learned, the poor scrivener, when told that he must be conducted to the Tombs, offered not the slightest obstacle, but, in his pale, unmoving way, silently acquiesced.

Some of the compassionate and curious bystanders joined the party; and headed by one of the constables arm in arm with Bartleby, the silent procession filed its way through all the noise, and heat, and joy of the roaring thoroughfares at noon.

The same day I received the note, I went to the Tombs, or, to speak more properly, the Halls of Justice. Seeking the right officer, I stated the purpose of my call, and was informed that the individual I described was, indeed, within. I then assured the functionary that Bartleby was a perfectly honest man, and greatly to be compassionated, however unaccountably eccentric. I narrated all I knew, and closed by suggesting the idea of letting him remain in as indulgent confinement as possible, till something less harsh might be done—though, indeed, I hardly knew what. At all events, if nothing else could be decided upon, the alms-house must receive him. I then begged to have an interview.

Being under no disgraceful charge, and quite serene and harmless in all his ways, they had permitted him freely to wander about the prison, and, especially, in the inclosed grass-platted yards thereof. And so I found him there, standing all alone in the quietest of the yards, his face towards a high wall, while all around, from the narrow slits of the jail windows, I thought I saw peering out upon him the eyes of murderers and thieves.

"Bartleby!"

"I know you," he said, without looking round—"and I want nothing to say to you."

"It was not I that brought you here, Bartleby," said I, keenly pained at his implied suspicion. "And to you, this should not be so vile a place. Nothing reproachful attaches to you by being here. And see, it is not so sad a place as one might think. Look, there is the sky, and here is the grass."

"I know where I am," he replied, but would say nothing more, and so I left him.

As I entered the corridor again, a broad meat-like man, in an apron, accosted me, and jerking his thumb over his shoulder, said—"Is that your friend?"

"Yes."

"Does he want to starve? If he does, let him live on the prison fare, that's all."

"Who are you?" asked I, not knowing what to make of such an unofficially speaking person in such a place.

"I am the grub-man. Such gentlemen as have friends here, hire me to provide them with something good to eat."

"Is this so?" said I, turning to the turnkey.

He said it was.

"Well, then," said I, slipping some silver into the grub-man's hands (for so they called him), "I want you to give particular attention to my friend there; let him have the best dinner you can get. And you must be as polite to him as possible."

"Introduce me, will you?" said the grub-man, looking at me with an expression which seemed to say he was all impatience for an opportunity to give a specimen of his breeding.

Thinking it would prove of benefit to the scrivener, I acquiesced; and, asking the grub-man his name, went up with him to Bartleby.

"Bartleby, this is a friend; you will find him very useful to you."

"Your sarvant, sir, your sarvant," said the grub-man, making a low salutation behind his apron. "Hope you find it pleasant here, sir; nice grounds —cool apartments—hope you'll stay with us sometime—try to make it agreeable. What will you have for dinner to-day?"

"I prefer not to dine to-day," said Bartleby, turning away. "It would disagree with me; I am unused to dinners." So saying, he slowly moved to the other side of the inclosure, and took up a position fronting the dead-wall.

"How's this?" said the grub-man, addressing me with a stare of astonishment. "He's odd, ain't he?"

"I think he is a little deranged," said I, sadly.

"Deranged? deranged is it? Well, now, upon my word, I thought that friend of yourn was a gentleman forger; they are always pale and genteel-like, them forgers. I can't help pity 'em—can't help it, sir. Did you know Monroe Edwards?" he added, touchingly, and paused. Then, laying his hand piteously on my shoulder, sighed, "He died of consumption at Sing-Sing. So you weren't acquainted with Monroe?"

"No, I was never socially acquainted with any forgers. But I cannot stop longer. Look to my friend yonder. You will not lose by it. I will see you again."

Some few days after this, I again obtained admission to the Tombs, and went through the corridors in quest of Bartleby; but without finding him.

"I saw him coming from his cell not long ago," said a turnkey, "may be he's gone to loiter in the yards."

So I went in that direction.

"Are you looking for the silent man?" said another turnkey, passing me. "Yonder he lies—sleeping in the yard there. 'Tis not twenty minutes since I saw him lie down."

The yard was entirely quiet. It was not accessible to the common prisoners. The surrounding walls of amazing thickness, kept off all sounds behind them. The Egyptian character of the masonry weighed upon me with its gloom. But a soft imprisoned turf grew under foot. The heart of the eternal pyramids, it seemed, wherein, by some strange magic, through the clefts, grass-seed, dropped by birds, had sprung.

Strangely huddled at the base of the wall, his knees drawn up, and lying on his side, his head touching the cold stones, I saw the wasted Bartleby. But nothing stirred. I paused; then went close up to him; stooped over, and saw that his dim eyes were open; otherwise he seemed profoundly sleeping. Something prompted me to touch him. I felt his hand, when a tingling shiver ran up my arm and down my spine to my feet.

The round face of the grub-man peered upon me now. "His dinner is ready. Won't he dine to-day, either? Or does he live without dining?"

"Lives without dining," said I, and closed the eyes.

"Eh!—He's asleep, ain't he?"

"With kings and counselors," murmured I.

There would seem little need for proceeding further in this history. Imagination will readily supply the meagre recital of poor Bartleby's interment. But, ere parting with the reader, let me say, that if this little narrative has sufficiently interested him, to awaken curiosity as to who Bartleby was, and what manner of life he led prior to the present narrator's making his acquaintance, I can only reply, that in such curiosity I fully share, but am wholly unable to gratify it. Yet here I hardly know whether I should divulge one little item of rumor, which came to my ear a few months after the scrivener's decease. Upon what basis it rested, I could never ascertain; and hence, how true it is I cannot now tell. But, inasmuch as this vague report has not been without a certain suggestive interest to me, however said, it may prove the same with some others; and so I will briefly mention it. The report was this: that Bartleby had been a subordinate clerk in the Dead Letter Office at Washington, from which he had been suddenly removed by a change in the administration. When I think over this rumor, hardly can I express the emotions which seize me. Dead letters? does it not sound like dead men? Conceive a man by nature and misfortune prone to a pallid hopelessness, can any business seem more fitted to heighten it than that of continually handling these dead letters, and assorting them for the flames? For by the cart-load they are annually burned. Some times from out the folded paper the pale clerk takes a ring —the finger it was meant for, perhaps, moulders in the grave; a bank-note sent in swiftest charity—he whom it would relieve, nor eats nor hungers any more; pardon for those who died despairing; hope for those who died unhoping; good tidings for those who died stifled by unrelieved calamities. On errands of life, these letters speed to death.

Ah, Bartleby! Ah, humanity!

The £1,000,000 Bank-Note

MARK TWAIN

(1835–1910)

When I was twenty-seven years old, I was a mining-broker's clerk in San Francisco, and an expert in all the details of stock traffic. I was alone in the world, and had nothing to depend upon but my wits and a clean reputation; but these were setting my feet in the road to eventual fortune, and I was content with the prospect.

My time was my own after the afternoon board, Saturdays, and I was accustomed to put it in on a little sail-boat on the bay. One day I ventured too far, and was carried out to sea. Just at nightfall, when hope was about gone, I was picked up by a small brig which was bound for London. It was a long and stormy voyage, and they made me work my passage without pay, as a common sailor. When I stepped ashore in London my clothes were ragged and shabby, and I had only a dollar in my pocket. This money fed and sheltered me twenty-four hours. During the next twenty-four I went without food and shelter.

About ten o'clock on the following morning, seedy and hungry, I was dragging myself along Portland Place, when a child that was passing, towed by a nurse-maid, tossed a luscious big pear—minus one bite—into the gutter. I stopped, of course, and fastened my desiring eye on that muddy treasure. My mouth watered for it, my stomach craved it, my whole being begged for it. But every time I made a move to get it some passing eye detected my purpose, and of course I straightened up then, and looked indifferent, and pretended that I hadn't been thinking about the pear at all. This same thing kept happening and happening, and I couldn't get the pear. I was just getting desperate enough to brave all the shame, and to seize it, when a window behind me was raised, and a gentleman spoke out of it, saying:

"Step in here, please."

I was admitted by a gorgeous flunkey, and shown into a sumptuous room where a couple of elderly gentlemen were sitting. They sent away the servant, and made me sit down. They had just finished their breakfast, and the sight of the remains of it almost overpowered me. I could hardly keep my wits together in the presence of that food, but as I was not asked to sample it, I had to bear my trouble as best I could.

Now, something had been happening there a little before, which I did not know anything about until a good many days afterwards, but I will tell you about it now. Those two old brothers had been having a pretty hot argument a couple of days before, and had ended by agreeing to decide it by a bet, which is the English way of settling everything.

You will remember that the Bank of England once issued two notes of a million pounds each, to be used for a special purpose connected with some public transaction with a foreign country. For some reason or other only one of these had been used and canceled; the other still lay in the vaults of the Bank. Well, the brothers, chatting along, happened to get to wondering what might be the fate of a perfectly honest and intelligent stranger who should be turned adrift in London without a friend, and with no money but that million-pound bank-note, and no way to account for his being in possession of it. Brother A said he would starve to death; Brother B said he wouldn't. Brother A said he couldn't offer it at a bank or anywhere else, because he would be arrested on the spot. So they went on disputing till Brother B said he would bet twenty thousand pounds that the man would live thirty days, *anyway,* on that million, and keep out of jail, too. Brother A took him up. Brother B went down to the Bank and bought that note. Just like an Englishman, you see; pluck to the backbone. Then he dictated a letter, which one of his clerks wrote out in a beautiful round hand, and then the two brothers sat at the window a whole day watching for the right man to give it to.

They saw many honest faces go by that were not intelligent enough; many that were intelligent, but not honest enough; many that were both, but the possessors were not poor enough, or, if poor enough, were not strangers. There was always a defect, until I came along; but they agreed that I filled the bill all around; so they elected me unanimously, and there I was now waiting to know why I was called in. They began to ask me questions about myself, and pretty soon they had my story. Finally they told me I would answer their purpose. I said I was sincerely glad, and asked what it was. Then one of them handed me an envelope, and said I would find the explanation inside. I was going to open it, but he said no; take it to my lodgings, and look it over carefully, and not be hasty or rash. I was puzzled, and wanted to discuss the matter a little further, but they didn't; so I took my leave, feeling hurt and insulted to be made the butt of what was apparently some kind of a practical joke, and yet obliged to put up with it, not being in circumstances to resent affronts from rich and strong folk.

I would have picked up the pear now and eaten it before all the world, but it was gone; so I had lost that by this unlucky business, and the thought of it did not soften my feeling towards those men. As soon as I was out of sight of that house I opened my envelope, and saw that it contained money! My opinion of those people changed, I can tell you! I lost not a moment, but shoved note and money into my vest pocket, and broke for the nearest cheap eating house. Well, how I did eat! When at last I couldn't hold any more, I took out my money and unfolded it, took one glimpse and nearly fainted. Five millions of dollars! Why, it made my head swim.

I must have sat there stunned and blinking at the note as much as a minute before I came rightly to myself again. The first thing I noticed, then, was the landlord. His eye was on the note, and he was petrified. He was worshiping, with all his body and soul, but he looked as if he couldn't stir hand or foot. I took my cue in a moment, and did the only rational thing there was to do. I reached the note towards him, and said, carelessly:

"Give me the change, please."

Then he was restored to his normal condition, and made a thousand apologies for not being able to break the bill, and I couldn't get him to touch it. He wanted to look at it, and keep on looking at it; he couldn't seem to get enough of it to quench the thirst of his eye, but he shrank from touching it as if it had been something too sacred for poor common clay to handle. I said:

"I am sorry if it is an inconvenience, but I must insist. Please change it; I haven't anything else."

But he said that wasn't any matter; he was quite willing to let the trifle stand over till another time. I said I might not be in his neighborhood again for a good while; but he said it was of no consequence, he could wait, and, moreover, I could have anything I wanted, any time I chose, and let the account run as long as I pleased. He said he hoped he wasn't afraid to trust as rich a gentleman as I was, merely because I was of a merry disposition, and chose to play larks on the public in the matter of dress. By this time another customer was entering, and the landlord hinted to me to put the monster out of sight; then he bowed me all the way to the door, and I started straight for that house and those brothers, to correct the mistake which had been made before the police should hunt me up, and help me do it. I was pretty nervous; in fact, pretty badly frightened, though, of course, I was no way in fault; but I knew men well enough to know that when they find they've given a tramp a million-pound bill when they thought it was a one-pounder, they are in a frantic rage against *him* instead of quarreling with their own near-sightedness, as they ought. As I approached the house my excitement began to abate, for all was quiet there, which made me feel pretty sure the blunder was not discovered yet. I rang. The same servant appeared. I asked for those gentlemen.

"They are gone." This in the lofty, cold way of that fellow's tribe.

"Gone? Gone where?"

"On a journey."

"But whereabouts?"

"To the Continent, I think."

"The Continent?"

"Yes, sir."

"Which way—by what route?"

"I can't say, sir."

"When will they be back?"

"In a month, they said."

"A month! Oh, this is awful! Give me *some* sort of idea of how to get a word to them. It's of the last importance."

"I can't, indeed. I've no idea where they've gone, sir."

"Then I must see some member of the family."

"Family's away, too; been abroad months—in Egypt and India, I think."

"Man, there's been an immense mistake made. They'll be back before night. Will you tell them I've been here, and that I will keep coming till it's all made right, and they needn't be afraid?"

"I'll tell them, if they come back, but I am not expecting them. They said you would be here in an hour to make inquiries, but I must tell you it's all right, they'll be here on time and expect you."

So I had to give it up and go away. What a riddle it all was! I was like to lose my mind. They would be here "on time." What could that mean? Oh, the letter would explain, maybe. I had forgotten the letter; I got it out and read it. This is what it said:

"You are an intelligent and honest man, as one may see by your face. We conceive you to be poor and a stranger. Enclosed you will find a sum of money. It is lent to you for thirty days, without interest. Report at this house at the end of that time. I have a bet on you. If I win it you shall have any situation that is in my gift—any, that is, that you shall be able to prove yourself familiar with and competent to fill."

No signature, no address, no date.

Well, here was a coil to be in! You are posted on what had preceded all this, but I was not. It was just a deep, dark puzzle to me. I hadn't the least idea what the game was, nor whether harm was meant me or a kindness. I went into a park, and sat down to try to think it out, and to consider what I had best do.

At the end of an hour my reasonings had crystallized into this verdict.

Maybe those men mean me well, maybe they mean me ill; no way to decide that—let it go. They've got a game, or a scheme, or an experiment, of some kind on hand; no way to determine what it is—let it go. There's a bet on me; no way to find out what it is—let it go. That disposes of the indeterminable quantities; the remainder of the matter is tangible, solid, and may be classed and labeled with certainty. If I ask the Bank of England to place this bill to the credit of the man it belongs to, they'll do it, for they know him, although I don't; but they will ask me how I came in possession of it, and if I tell the truth, they'll put me in the asylum, naturally, and a lie will land me in jail. The same result would follow if I tried to bank the bill anywhere or to borrow money on it. I have got to carry this immense burden around until those men come back, whether I want to or not. It is useless to me, as useless as a handful of ashes, and yet I must take care of it, and watch over it, while I beg my living. I couldn't *give* it away, if I should try, for neither honest citizen nor highwayman would accept it or meddle with it for anything. Those brothers are safe. Even if I lose their bill, or burn it, they are still safe, because they can stop payment, and the Bank will make them whole; but meantime I've got to do a month's suffering without wages or profit—unless I help win that bet, whatever it may be, and get that situation that I am promised. I *should* like to get that; men of their sort have situations in their gift that are worth having.

I got to thinking a good deal about that situation. My hopes began to rise high. Without doubt the salary would be large. It would begin in a month; after that I should be all right. Pretty soon I was feeling first-rate. By this time I was tramping the streets again. The sight of a tailor-shop gave me a sharp longing to shed my rags, and to clothe myself decently once more. Could I afford it? No; I had nothing in the world but a million pounds. So I forced myself to go on by. But soon I was drifting back again. The temptation persecuted me cruelly. I must have passed that shop back and forth six times during that manful struggle. At last I gave in; I had to. I asked if they had a misfit suit that had been thrown on their hands. The fellow I spoke to nodded his head towards another fellow, and gave me no answer. I went to the indicated fellow, and he indicated another fellow with *his* head, and no words. I went to him, and he said:

"'Tend to you presently."

I waited till he was done with what he was at, then he took me into a back room, and overhauled a pile of rejected suits, and selected the rattiest one for me. I put it on. It didn't fit, and wasn't in any way attractive, but it was new, and I was anxious to have it; so I didn't find any fault, but said, with some diffidence:

"It would be an accommodation to me if you could wait some days for the money. I haven't any small change about me."

The fellow worked up a most sarcastic expression of countenance, and said:

"Oh, you haven't? Well, of course, I didn't expect it. I'd only expect gentlemen like you to carry large change."

I was nettled, and said:

"My friend, you shouldn't judge a stranger always by the clothes he wears. I am quite able to pay for this suit; I simply didn't wish to put you to the trouble of changing a large note."

He modified his style a little at that, and said, though still with something of an air:

"I didn't mean any particular harm, but as long as rebukes are going, I might say it wasn't quite your affair to jump to the conclusion that we couldn't change any note that you might happen to be carrying around. On the contrary, we *can*."

I handed the note to him, and said:

"Oh, very well; I apologize."

He received it with a smile, one of those large smiles which goes all around over, and has folds in it, and wrinkles, and spirals, and looks like the place where you have thrown a brick in a pond; and then in the act of his taking a glimpse of the bill this smile froze solid, and turned yellow, and looked like those wavy, wormy spreads of lava which you find hardened on little levels on the side of Vesuvius. I never before saw a smile caught like that, and perpetuated. The man stood there holding the bill, and looking like that, and the proprietor hustled up to see what was the matter, and said, briskly:

"Well, what's up? what's the trouble? what's wanting?"

I said: "There isn't any trouble. I'm waiting for my change."

"Come, come; get him his change, Tod; get him his change."

Tod retorted: "Get him his change! It's easy to say, sir; but look at the bill yourself."

The proprietor took a look, gave a low, eloquent whistle, then made a dive for the pile of rejected clothing, and began to snatch it this way and that, talking all the time excitedly, and as if to himself:

"Sell an eccentric millionaire such an unspeakable suit as that! Tod's a fool—a born fool. Always doing something like this. Drives every millionaire away from this place, because he can't tell a millionaire from a tramp, and never could. Ah, here's the thing I am after. Please get those things off, sir, and throw them in the fire. Do me the favor to put on this shirt and this suit; it's just the thing, the very thing—plain, rich, modest, and just ducally nobby; made to order for a foreign prince—you may know him, sir, his Serene Highness the Hospodar of Halifax; had to leave it with us and take a mourning-suit because his mother was going to die—which she didn't. But that's all right; we can't always have things the way we—that is, the way they—there! trousers all right, they fit you to a charm, sir; now the waistcoat; aha, right again! now the coat—lord! look at that, now! Perfect—the whole thing! I never saw such a triumph in all my experience."

I expressed my satisfaction.

"Quite right, sir, quite right; it'll do for a makeshift, I'm bound to say. But wait till you see what we'll get up for you on your own measure. Come, Tod, book and pen; get at it. Length of leg, 32"—and so on. Before I could get in a word he had measured me, and was giving orders for dress-suits, morning suits, shirts, and all sorts of things. When I got a chance I said:

"But, my dear sir, I *can't* give these orders, unless you can wait indefinitely, or change the bill."

"Indefinitely! It's a weak word, sir, a weak word. Eternally—*that's* the word, sir. Tod, rush these things through, and send them to the gentleman's address without any waste of time. Let the minor customers wait. Set down the gentleman's address and—"

"I'm changing my quarters. I will drop in and leave the new address."

"Quite right, sir, quite right. One moment—let me show you out, sir. There—good day, sir, good day."

Well, don't you see what was bound to happen? I drifted naturally into buying whatever I wanted, and asking for change. Within a week I was sumptuously equipped with all needful comforts and luxuries, and was housed in an expensive private hotel in Hanover Square. I took my dinners there, but for breakfast I stuck by Harris's humble feeding house, where I had got my first meal on my million-pound bill. I was the making of Harris. The fact had gone all abroad that the foreign crank who carried million-pound bills in his vest pocket was the patron saint of the place. That was enough. From being a poor, struggling, little hand-to-mouth enterprise, it had become celebrated, and overcrowded with customers. Harris was so grateful that he forced loans upon me, and would not be denied; and so, pauper as I was, I had money to spend, and was living like the rich and the great. I judged that there was going to be a crash by and by, but I was in now and must swim across or drown. You see there was just that element of impending disaster to give a serious side, a sober side, yes, a tragic side, to a state of things which would otherwise have been purely ridiculous. In the night, in the dark, the tragedy part was always to the front, and always warning, always threatening; and so I moaned and tossed, and sleep was hard to find. But in the cheerful daylight the tragedy element faded out and disappeared, and I walked on air, and was happy to giddiness, to intoxication, you may say.

And it was natural; for I had become one of the notorieties of the metropolis of the world, and it turned my head, not just a little, but a good deal. You could not take up a newspaper, English, Scotch, or Irish, without finding in it one or more references to the "vest-pocket million-pounder" and his latest doings and sayings. At first, in these mentions, I was at the bottom of the personal-gossip column; next, I was listed above the knights, next above the baronets, next above the barons, and so on, and so on, climbing steadily, as my notoriety augmented, until I reached the highest altitude possible, and there I remained, taking precedence of all dukes not royal, and of all ecclesiastics except the primate of all England. But mind, this was not fame; as yet I had achieved only notoriety. Then came the climaxing stroke—the accolade, so to speak—which in a single instant transmuted the perishable dross of notoriety into the enduring gold of fame: *Punch* caricatured me! Yes, I was a made man now; my place was established. I might be joked about still, but reverently, not hilariously, not rudely; I could be smiled at, but not laughed at. The time for that had gone by. *Punch* pictured me all a-flutter with rags, dickering with a beef-eater for the Tower of London. Well, you can imagine how it was with a young fellow who had never been taken notice of before, and now all of a sudden couldn't say a thing that wasn't taken up and repeated everywhere; couldn't stir abroad without constantly overhearing the remark flying from lip to lip, "There he goes; that's him!" couldn't take his breakfast without a crowd to look on; couldn't appear in an opera-box without concentrating there the fire of a thousand lorgnettes. Why, I just swam in glory all day long—that is the amount of it.

You know, I even kept my old suit of rags, and every now and then appeared in them, so as to have the old pleasure of buying trifles, and being insulted, and then shooting the scoffer dead with the million-pound bill. But I couldn't keep that up. The illustrated papers made the outfit so familiar that when I went out in it I was at once recognized and followed by a crowd, and if I attempted a purchase the man would offer me his whole shop on credit before I could pull my note on him.

About the tenth day of my fame I went to fulfil my duty to my flag by paying my respects to the American minister. He received me with the enthusiasm proper in my case, upbraided me for being so tardy in my duty, and said that there was only one way to get his forgiveness, and that was to take the seat at his dinner-party that night made vacant by the illness of one of his guests. I said I would, and we got to talking. It turned out that he and my father had been schoolmates in boyhood, Yale students together later, and always warm friends up to my father's death. So then he required me to put in at his house all the odd time I might have to spare, and I was very willing, of course.

In fact, I was more than willing; I was glad. When the crash should come, he might somehow be able to save me from total destruction; I didn't know how, but he might think of a way, maybe. I couldn't venture to unbosom myself to him at this late date, a thing which I would have been quick to do in the beginning of this awful career of mine in London. No, I couldn't venture it now; I was in too deep; that is, too deep for me to be risking revelations to so new a friend, though not clear beyond my depth, as *I* looked at it. Because, you see, with all my borrowing, I was carefully keeping within my means—I mean within my salary. Of course, I couldn't *know* what my salary was going to be, but I had a good enough basis for an estimate in the fact, that if I won the bet I was to have *choice* of any situation in that rich old gentleman's gift provided I was competent—and I should certainly prove competent; I hadn't any doubt about that. And as to the bet, I wasn't worrying about that; I had always been lucky. Now my estimate of the salary was six hundred to a thousand a year; say, six hundred for the first year, and so on up year by year, till I struck the upper figure by proved merit. At present I was only in debt for my first year's salary. Everybody had been trying to lend me money, but I had fought off the most of them on one pretext or another; so this indebtedness represented only £300 borrowed money, the other £300 represented my keep and my purchases. I believed my second year's salary would carry me through the rest of the month if I went on being cautious and economical, and I intended to look sharply out for that. My month ended, my employer back from his journey, I should be all right once more, for I should at once divide the two years' salary among my creditors by assignment, and get right down to my work.

It was a lovely dinner-party of fourteen. The Duke and Duchess of Shoreditch, and their daughter the Lady Anne-Grace-Eleanor-Celeste-and-so-forth-and-so-forth-de-Bohun, the Earl and Countess of Newgate, Viscount Cheapside, Lord and Lady Blatherskite, some untitled people of both sexes, the minister and his wife and daughter, and his daughter's visiting friend, an English girl of twenty-two, named Portia Langham, whom I fell in love with in two minutes, and she with me—I could see it without glasses. There was still another guest, an American—but I am a little ahead of my story. While the people were still in the drawing-room, whetting up for dinner, and coldly inspecting the late comers, the servant announced:

"Mr. Lloyd Hastings."

The moment the usual civilities were over, Hastings caught sight of me, and came straight with cordially outstretched hand; then stopped short when about to shake, and said, with an embarrassed look:

"I beg your pardon, sir, I thought I knew you."

"Why, you do know me, old fellow."

"No. Are *you* the—the—"

"Vest-pocket monster? I am, indeed. Don't be afraid to call me by my nickname; I'm used to it."

"Well, well, well, this is a surprise. Once or twice I've seen your own name coupled with the nickname, but it never occurred to me that *you* could be the Henry Adams referred to. Why, it isn't six months since you were clerking away for Blake Hopkins in Frisco on a salary, and sitting up nights on an extra allowance, helping me arrange and verify the Gould and Curry Extension papers and statistics. The idea of your being in London, and a vast millionaire, and a colossal celebrity! Why, it's the Arabian Nights come again. Man, I can't take it in at all; can't realize it; give me time to settle the whirl in my head."

"The fact is, Lloyd, you are no worse off than I am. I can't realize it myself."

"Dear me, it *is* stunning, now isn't it? Why, it's just three months to-day since we went to the Miners' restaurant—"

"No; the What Cheer."

"Right, it *was* the What Cheer; went there at two in the morning, and had a chop and coffee after a hard six-hours grind over those Extension papers, and I tried to persuade you to come to London with me, and offered to get leave of absence for you and pay all your expenses, and give you something over if I succeeded in making the sale; and you would not listen to me, said I wouldn't succeed, and you couldn't afford to lose the run of business and be no end of time getting the hang of things again when you got back home. And yet here you are. How odd it all is! How did you happen to come, and whatever *did* give you this incredible start?"

"Oh, just an accident. It's a long story—a romance, a body may say. I'll tell you all about it, but not now."

"When?"

"The end of this month."

"That's more than a fortnight yet. It's too much of a strain on a person's curiosity. Make it a week."

"I can't. You'll know why, by and by. But how's the trade getting along?"

His cheerfulness vanished like a breath, and he said with a sigh:

"You were a true prophet, Hal, a true prophet. I wish I hadn't come. I don't want to talk about it."

"But you must. You must come and stop with me to-night, when we leave here, and tell me all about it."

"Oh, may I? Are you in earnest?" and the water showed in his eyes.

"Yes; I want to hear the whole story, every word."

"I'm so grateful! Just to find a human interest once more, in some voice and in some eye, in me and affairs of mine, after what I've been through here—lord! I could go down on my knees for it!"

He gripped my hand hard, and braced up, and was all right and lively after that for the dinner—which didn't come off. No; the usual thing happened, the thing that is always happening under that vicious and aggravating English system—the matter of precedence couldn't be settled, and so there was no dinner. Englishmen always eat dinner before they go out to dinner, because *they* know the risks they are running; but nobody ever warns the stranger, and so he walks placidly into the trap. Of course, nobody was hurt this time, because we had all been to dinner, none of us being novices excepting Hastings, and he having been informed by the minister at the time that he invited him that in deference to the English custom he had not provided any dinner. Everybody took a lady and processioned down to the dining-room, because it is usual to go through the motions; but there the dispute began. The Duke of Shoreditch wanted to take precedence, and sit at the head of the table, holding that he outranked a minister who represented merely a nation and not a monarch; but I stood for my rights, and refused to yield. In the gossip column I ranked all dukes not royal, and said so, and claimed precedence of this one. It couldn't be settled, of course, struggle as we might and did, he finally (and injudiciously) trying to play birth and antiquity, and I "seeing" his Conqueror and "raising" him with Adam, whose direct posterity I was, as shown by my name, while *he* was of a collateral branch, as shown by *his,* and by his recent Norman origin; so we all processioned back to the drawing-room again and had a perpendicular lunch—plate of sardines and a strawberry, and you group yourself and stand up and eat it. Here the religion of precedence is not so strenuous; the two persons of highest rank chuck up a shilling, the one that wins has first go at his strawberry, and the loser gets the shilling. The next two chuck up, then the next two, and so on. After refreshment, tables were brought, and we all played cribbage, sixpence a game. The English never play any game for amusement. If they can't make something or lose something—they don't care which—they won't play.

We had a lovely time; certainly two of us had, Miss Langham and I. I was so bewitched with her that I couldn't count my hands if they went above a double sequence; and when I struck home I never discovered it, and started up the outside row again, and would have lost the game every time, only the girl did the same, she being in just my condition, you see; and consequently neither of us ever got out, or cared to wonder why we didn't; we only just knew we were happy, and didn't wish to know anything else, and didn't want to be interrupted. And I *told* her—I did, indeed—told her I loved her; and she—well, she blushed till her hair turned red, but she liked it; she *said* she did. Oh, there was never such an evening! Every time I pegged I put on a postscript; every time she pegged she acknowledged receipt of it, counting the hands the same. Why, I couldn't even say "Two for his heels" without adding, "*My,* how sweet you do look!" and she would say, "Fifteen two, fifteen four, fifteen six, and a pair are eight, and eight are sixteen—*do* you think so?"—peeping out aslant from under her lashes, you know, so sweet and cunning. Oh, it was just *too*-too!

Well, I was perfectly honest and square with her; told her I hadn't a cent in the world but just the million-pound note she'd heard so much talk about, and *it* didn't belong to me, and that started her curiosity; and then I talked low, and told her the whole history right from the start, and it nearly killed her laughing. What in the nation she could find to laugh about *I* couldn't see, but there it was; every half-minute some new detail would fetch her, and I would have to stop as much as a minute and a half to give her a chance to settle down again. Why, she laughed herself lame —she did, indeed; I never saw anything like it. I mean I never saw a painful story—a story of a person's troubles and worries and fears—produce just *that* kind of effect before. So I loved her all the more, seeing she could be so cheerful when there wasn't anything to be cheerful about; for I might soon need that kind of wife, you know, the way things looked. Of course, I told her we should have to wait a couple of years, till I could catch up on my salary; but she didn't mind that, only she hoped I would be as careful as possible in the matter of expenses, and not let them run the least risk of trenching on our third year's pay. Then she began to get a little worried, and wondered if we were making any mistake, and starting the salary on a higher figure for the first year than I would get. This was good sense, and it made me feel a little less confident than I had been feeling before; but it gave me a good business idea, and I brought it frankly out.

"Portia, dear, would you mind going with me that day, when I confront those old gentlemen?"

She shrank a little, but said:

"N-o; if my being with you would help hearten you. But—would it be quite proper, do you think?"

"No, I don't know that it would—in fact, I'm afraid it wouldn't; but, you see, there's so *much* dependent upon it that—"

"Then I'll go anyway, proper or improper," she said, with a beautiful and generous enthusiasm. "Oh, I shall be so happy to think I'm helping!"

"Helping, dear? Why, you'll be doing it all. You're so beautiful and so lovely and so winning, that with you there I can pile our salary up till I break those good old fellows, and they'll never have the heart to struggle."

Sho! you should have seen the rich blood mount, and her happy eyes shine!

"You wicked flatterer! There isn't a word of truth in what you say, but still I'll go with you. Maybe it will teach you not to expect other people to look with your eyes."

Were my doubts dissipated? Was my confidence restored? You may judge by this fact: privately I raised my salary to twelve hundred the first year on the spot. But I didn't tell her; I saved it for a surprise.

All the way home I was in the clouds, Hastings talking, I not hearing a word. When he and I entered my parlor, he brought me to myself with his fervent appreciations of my manifold comforts and luxuries.

"Let me just stand here a little and look my fill. Dear me! it's a palace —it's just a palace! And in it everything a body *could* desire, including cosey coal fire and supper standing ready. Henry, it doesn't merely make me realize how rich you are; it makes me realize, to the bone, to the marrow, how poor I am—how poor I am, and how miserable, how defeated, routed, annihilated!"

Plague take it! this language gave me the cold shudders. It scared me broad awake, and made me comprehend that I was standing on a half-inch crust, with a crater underneath. *I* didn't know I had been dreaming—that is, I hadn't been allowing myself to know it for a while back; but *now*—oh, dear! Deep in debt, not a cent in the world, a lovely girl's happiness or woe in my hands, and nothing in front of me but a salary which might never—oh, *would* never—materialize! Oh, oh, oh! I am ruined past hope! nothing can save me!

"Henry, the mere unconsidered rippings of your daily income would—"

"Oh, my daily income! Here, down with this hot Scotch, and cheer up your soul. Here's with you! Or, no—you're hungry; sit down and—"

"Not a bite for me; I'm past it. I can't eat, these days; but I'll drink with you till I drop. Come!"

"Barrel for barrel, I'm with you! Ready? Here we go! Now, then, Lloyd, unreel your story while I brew."

"Unreel it? What, again?"

"Again? What do you mean by that?"

"Why, I mean do you want to hear it *over* again?"

"Do I want to hear it *over* again? This *is* a puzzler. Wait; don't take any more of that liquid. You don't need it."

"Look here, Henry, you alarm me. Didn't I tell you the whole story on the way here?"

"You?"

"Yes, I."

"I'll be hanged if I heard a word of it."

"Henry, this is a serious thing. It troubles me. What did you take up yonder at the minister's?"

Then it all flashed on me, and I owned up like a man.

"I took the dearest girl in this world—prisoner!"

So then he came with a rush, and we shook, and shook, and shook till our hands ached; and he didn't blame me for not having heard a word of a story which had lasted while we walked three miles. He just sat down then, like the patient, good fellow he was, and told it all over again. Synopsized, it amounted to this: He had come to England with what he thought was a grand opportunity; he had an "option" to sell the Gould and Curry Extension for the "locators" of it, and keep all he could get over a million dollars. He had worked hard, had pulled every wire he knew of, had left no honest expedient untried, had spent nearly all the money he had in the world, had not been able to get a solitary capitalist to listen to him, and his option would run out at the end of the month. In a word, he was ruined. Then he jumped up and cried out:

"Henry, you can save me! You can save me, and you're the only man in the universe that can. Will you do it? *Won't* you do it?"

"Tell me how. Speak out, my boy."

"Give me a million and my passage home for my 'option'! Don't, *don't* refuse!"

I was in a kind of agony. I was right on the point of coming out with the words, "Lloyd, I'm a pauper myself—absolutely penniless, and in *debt!*" But a white-hot idea came flaming through my head, and I gripped my jaws together, and calmed myself down till I was as cold as a capitalist. Then I said, in a commercial and self-possessed way:

"I will save you, Lloyd—"

"Then I'm already saved! God be merciful to you forever! If ever I—"

"Let me finish, Lloyd. I will save you, but not in that way; for that would not be fair to you, after your hard work, and the risks you've run. I don't need to buy mines; I can keep my capital moving, in a commercial center like London, without that; it's what I'm at, all the time; but here is what I'll do. I know all about that mine, of course; I know its immense value, and can swear to it if anybody wishes it. You shall sell out inside of the fortnight for three millions cash, using my name freely, and we'll divide, share and share alike."

Do you know, he would have danced the furniture to kindling-wood in his insane joy, and broken everything on the place, if I hadn't tripped him up and tied him.

Then he lay there, perfectly happy, saying:

"I may use your name! Your name—think of it! Man, they'll flock in droves, these rich Londoners; they'll *fight* for that stock! I'm a made man, I'm a made man forever, and I'll never forget you as long as I live!"

In less than twenty-four hours London was abuzz! I hadn't anything to do, day after day, but sit at home, and say to all comers:

"Yes; I told him to refer to me. I know the man, and I know the mine. His character is above reproach, and the mine is worth far more than he asks for it."

Meantime I spent all my evenings at the minister's with Portia. I didn't say a word to her about the mine; I saved it for a surprise. We talked salary; never anything but salary and love; sometimes love, sometimes salary, sometimes love and salary together. And my! the interest the minister's wife and daughter took in our little affair, and the endless ingenuities they invented to save us from interruption, and to keep the minister in the dark and unsuspicious—well, it was just lovely of them!

When the month was up at last, I had a million dollars to my credit in the London and County Bank, and Hastings was fixed in the same way. Dressed at my level best, I drove by the house in Portland Place, judged by the look of things that my birds were home again, went on towards the minister's and got my precious, and we started back, talking salary with all our might. She was so excited and anxious that it made her just intolerably beautiful. I said:

"Dearie, the way you're looking it's a crime to strike for a salary a single penny under three thousand a year."

"Henry, Henry, you'll ruin us!"

"Don't you be afraid. Just keep up those looks, and trust to me. It'll all come out right."

So, as it turned out, I had to keep bolstering up *her* courage all the way. She kept pleading with me, and saying:

"Oh, please remember that if we ask for too much we may get no salary at all; and then what will become of us, with no way in the world to earn our living?"

We were ushered in by that same servant, and there they were, the two old gentlemen. Of course, they were surprised to see that wonderful creature with me, but I said:

"It's all right, gentlemen; she is my future stay and helpmate."

And I introduced them to her, and called them by name. It didn't surprise them; they knew I would know enough to consult the directory. They seated us, and were very polite to me, and very solicitous to relieve her from embarrassment, and put her as much at her ease as they could. Then I said:

"Gentlemen, I am ready to report."

"We are glad to hear it," said *my* man, "for now we can decide the bet which my brother Abel and I made. If you have won for me, you shall have any situation in my gift. Have you the million-pound note?"

"Here it is, sir," and I handed it to him.

"I've won!" he shouted, and slapped Abel on the back. "*Now* what do you say, brother?"

"I say he *did* survive, and I've lost twenty thousand pounds. I never would have believed it."

"I've a further report to make," I said, "and a pretty long one. I want you to let me come soon, and detail my whole month's history; and I promise you it's worth hearing. Meantime, take a look at that."

"What, man! Certificate of deposit for £200,000. Is it yours?"

"Mine. I earned it by thirty days' judicious use of that little loan you let me have. And the only use I made of it was to buy trifles and offer the bill in change."

"Come, this is astonishing! It's incredible, man!"

"Never mind, I'll prove it. Don't take my word unsupported."

But now Portia's turn was come to be surprised. Her eyes were spread wide, and she said:

"Henry, is that really your money? Have you been fibbing to me?"

"I have, indeed, dearie. But you'll forgive me, *I* know."

She put up an arch pout, and said:

"Don't you be so sure. You are a naughty thing to deceive me so!"

"Oh, you'll get over it, sweetheart, you'll get over it; it was only fun, you know. Come, let's be going."

"But wait, wait! The situation, you know. I want to give you the situation," said my man.

"Well," I said, "I'm just as grateful as I can be, but really I don't want one."

"But you can have the very choicest one in my gift."

"Thanks again, with all my heart; but I don't even want *that* one."

"Henry, I'm ashamed of you. You don't half thank the good gentleman. May I do it for you?"

"Indeed, you shall, dear, if you can improve it. Let us see you try."

She walked to my man, got up in his lap, put her arm round his neck, and kissed him right on the mouth. Then the two old gentlemen shouted with laughter, but I was dumfounded, just petrified, as you may say. Portia said:

"Papa, he has said you haven't a situation in your gift that he'd take; and I feel just as hurt as—"

"My darling, is that your papa?"

"Yes; he's my step-papa, and the dearest one that ever was. You understand now, don't you, why I was able to laugh when you told me at the minister's, not knowing my relationships, what trouble and worry papa's and Uncle Abel's scheme was giving you?"

Of course, I spoke right up now, without any fooling, and went straight to the point.

"Oh, my dearest dear sir, I want to take back what I said. You *have* got a situation open that I want."

"Name it."

"Son-in-law."

"Well, well, well! But you know, if you haven't ever served in that capacity, you, of course, can't furnish recommendations of a sort to satisfy the conditions of the contract, and so—"

"Try me—oh, do, I beg of you! Only just try me thirty or forty years, and if—"

"Oh, well, all right; it's but a little thing to ask, take her along."

Happy, we two? There are not words enough in the unabridged to describe it. And when London got the whole history, a day or two later, of my month's adventures with that bank-note, and how they ended, did London talk, and have a good time? Yes.

My Portia's papa took that friendly and hospitable bill back to the Bank of England and cashed it; then the Bank canceled it and made him a present of it, and he gave it to us at our wedding, and it has always hung in its frame in the sacredest place in our home ever since. For it gave me my Portia. But for it I could not have remained in London, would not have appeared at the minister's, never should have met her. And so I always say, "Yes, it's a million-pounder, as you see; but it never made but one purchase in its life, and *then* got the article for only about a tenth part of its value."

The Gentleman of La Porte

BRET HARTE

(1836–1902)

He was also a Pioneer. A party who broke through the snows of the winter of '51, and came upon the triangular little valley afterwards known as La Porte, found him the sole inhabitant. He had subsisted for three months on two biscuits a day and a few inches of bacon, in a hut made of bark and brushwood. Yet, when the explorers found him, he was quite alert, hopeful, and gentlemanly. But I cheerfully make way here for the terser narrative of Captain Henry Symes, commanding the prospecting party:—

"We kem upon him, gentlemen, suddent-like, jest abreast of a rock like this"—demonstrating the distance—"ez near ez you be. He sees us, and he dives into his cabin and comes out ag'in with a *tall hat,*—a stovepipe, gentlemen,—and, blank me! gloves! He was a tall, thin feller, holler in the cheek,—ez might be,—and off color in his face, ez was nat'ral, takin' in account his starvation grub. But he lifts his hat to us, so, and sez he, 'Happy to make your acquaintance, gentlemen! I'm afraid you experienced some difficulty in getting here. Take a cigyar.' And he pulls out a fancy cigar-case with two real Havanas in it. 'I wish there was more,' sez he.

"'Ye don't smoke yourself?' sez I.

"'Seldom,' sez he; which was a lie, for that very arternoon I seed him hangin' ontu a short pipe like a suckin' baby ontu a bottle. 'I kept these cigyars for any gentleman that might drop in.'

"'I reckon ye see a great deal o' the best society yer,' sez Bill Parker, starin' at the hat and gloves and winkin' at the boys.

"'A few Ind-i-ans occasionally,' sez he.

"'Injins!' sez we.

"'Yes. Very quiet good fellows in their way. They have once or twice brought me game, which I refused, as the poor fellows have had a pretty hard time of it themselves.'

"Now, gentlemen, we was, ez you know, rather quiet men—rather peaceable men; but—hevin' been shot at three times by these yar 'good' Injins, and Parker hisself havin' a matter o' three inches of his own skelp lying loose in their hands and he walkin' round wearin' green leaves on his head like a Roman statoo—it *did* kinder seem ez if this yer stranger was playin' it rather low down on the boys. Bill Parker gets up and takes a survey o' him, and sez he, peaceful-like—

"'Ye say these yer Injins—these yer *quiet* Injins—offered yer game?'

"'They did!' sez he.

"'And you refoosed?'

"'I did,' sez he.

"'Must hev made 'em feel kinder bad—sorter tortered their sensitiv' naters?' sez Bill.

"'They really seemed quite disappointed.'

"'In course,' sez Bill. 'And now mout I ask who you be?'

"'Excuse me,' says the stranger; and, darn my skin! If he doesn't hist out a keerd-case, and, handin' it over to Bill, sez, 'Here's my kyard.'

"Bill took it and read out aloud, 'J. Trott, Kentucky.'

"'It's a pooty keerd,' sez Bill.

"'I'm glad you like it,' says the stranger.

"'I reckon the other fifty-one of the deck ez as pooty—all of 'em Jacks and left bowers,' sez Bill.

"The stranger sez nothin', but kinder draws back from Bill; but Bill ups and sez—

"'Wot is your little game, Mister J. Trott, of Kentucky?'

"'I don't think I quite understand you,' sez the stranger, a holler fire comin' intu his cheeks like ez if they was the bowl of a pipe.

"'Wot's this yer kid-glove business?—this yer tall hat paradin'?—this yer circus foolin'? Wot's it all about? *Who* are ye, anyway?'

"The stranger stands up, and sez he, 'Ez I don't quarrel with guests on my own land,' sez he, 'I think you'll allow I'm—a gentleman!' sez he.

"With that he takes off his tall hat and makes a low bow, so, and turns away—like this; but Bill lites out of a suddent with his right foot and drives his No. 10 boot clean through the crown of that tall hat like one o' them circus hoops.

"That's about ez fur ez I remember. Gentlemen! thar wa'n't but *one* man o' that hull crowd ez could actooally swear what happened next, and that man never told. For a kind o' whirlwind jest then took place in that valley. I disremember anythin' but dust and bustlin'. Thar wasn't no yellin', thar wasn't no shootin'. It was one o' them suddent things that left even a six-shooter out in the cold. When I kem to in the *chapparel*—bein' oncomfortable like from hevin' only half a shirt on—I found nigh on three pounds o' gravel and stones in my pockets and a stiffness in my ha'r. I looks up and sees Bill hangin' in the forks of a hickory saplin' twenty feet above me.

" 'Cap,' sez he, in an inquirin' way, 'hez the tornado passed?'

" 'Which?' sez I.

" 'This yer elemental disturbance—is it over?'

" 'I reckon,' sez I.

" 'Because,' sez he, 'afore this yer electrical phenomenon took place I hed a slight misunderstanding with a stranger, and I'd like to apologize!'

"And with that he climbs down, peaceful-like, and goes into the shanty, and comes out, hand in hand with that stranger, smilin' like an infant. And that's the first time, I reckon, we know'd anythin' about the gentleman of La Porte."

It is by no means improbable that the above incidents are slightly exaggerated in narration, and the cautious reader will do well to accept with some reservation the particular phenomenon alluded to by the Captain. But the fact remains that the Gentleman of La Porte was allowed an eccentricity and enjoyed an immunity from contemporaneous criticism only to be attributed to his personal prowess. Indeed, this was once publicly expressed. "It 'pears to me," said a meek newcomer,—who, on the strength of his having received news of the death of a distant relative in the "States," had mounted an exceedingly large crape mourning-band on his white felt hat, and was consequently obliged to "treat" the crowd in the barroom of Parker's Hotel,—"it 'pears to me, gentlemen, that this yer taxin' the nat'ral expression of grief, and allowin' such festive exhibitions as yaller kid gloves, on the gentleman on my right, is sorter inconsistent. I don't mind treatin' the crowd, gentlemen, but this yer platform and resolutions don't seem to keep step."

This appeal to the *Demos* of every American crowd, of course, precluded any reply from the Gentleman of La Porte, but left it to the palpable chairman—the barkeeper, Mr. William Parker.

"Young man," he replied severely, "*when* ye can wear yaller kids like *that* man and make 'em hover in the air like summer lightnin', and strike in four places to onct!—*then* ye kin talk! *Then* ye kin wear your shirt half-masted if ye like!" A sentiment to which the crowd assenting, the meek man paid for the drinks, and would have, in addition, taken off his mourning-band, but was courteously stopped by the Gentleman of La Porte.

And yet, I protest, there was little suggestive of this baleful prowess in his face and figure. He was loose-jointed and long-limbed, yet with a certain mechanical, slow rigidity of movement that seemed incompatible with alacrity and dexterity. His arms were unusually long, and his hands hung with their palms forward. In walking his feet "toed in," suggesting an aboriginal ancestry. His face, as I remember it, was equally inoffensive. Thin and melancholy, the rare smile that lit it up was only a courteous reception of some attribute of humor in another which he was unable himself to appreciate. His straight black hair and high cheek-bones would have heightened his Indian resemblance; but these were offset by two most extraordinary eyes that were utterly at variance with this, or, indeed, any other, suggestion of his features. They were yellowish-blue, globular, and placidly staring. They expressed nothing that the Gentleman of La Porte thought—nothing that he did—nothing that he might reasonably be expected to do. They were at variance with his speech, his carriage, even his remarkable attire. More than one irreverent critic had suggested that he had probably lost his own eyes in some frontier difficulty, and had hurriedly replaced them with those of his antagonist.

Had this ingenious hypothesis reached the ears of the Gentleman, he would probably have contented himself with a simple denial of the fact, overlooking any humorous incongruity of statement. For, as has been already intimated, among his other privileges he enjoyed an absolute immunity from any embarrassing sense of the ludicrous. His deficient sense of humor and habitual gravity, in a community whose severest dramatic episodes were mitigated by some humorous detail, and whose customary relaxation was the playing of practical jokes, was marked with a certain frankness that was discomposing. "I think," he remarked to a well-known citizen of La Porte, "that, in alluding to the argumentative character of Mr. William Peghammer, you said you had found him lying awake at night contradicting the 'Katydids.' This he himself assures me is not true, and I may add that I passed the night with him in the woods without any such thing occurring. You seem to have *lied*." The severity of this reception checked further humorous exhibitions in his presence. Indeed, I am not certain but it invested him with a certain aristocratic isolation.

Thus identified with the earliest history of the Camp, Mr. Trott participated in its fortunes and shared its prosperity. As one of the original locators of the "Eagle Mine" he enjoyed a certain income which enabled him to live without labor and to freely indulge his few and inexpensive tastes. After his own personal adornment—which consisted chiefly in the daily wearing of spotless linen—he was fond of giving presents. These possessed, perhaps, a sentimental rather than intrinsic value. To an intimate friend he had once given a cane, the stick whereof was cut from a wild grapevine which grew above the spot where the famous "Eagle *lead*" was first discovered in La Porte; the head originally belonged to a cane presented to Mr. Trott's father, and the ferrule was made of the last silver half-dollar which he had brought to California. "And yet, do you know," said the indignant recipient of this touching gift, "I offered to put it down for a five-dollar ante last night over at Robinson's, and the boys wouldn't see it, and allowed I'd better leave the board. Thar's no appreciation of sacred things in this yer Camp."

It was in this lush growth and springtime of La Porte that the Gentleman was chosen Justice of the Peace by the unanimous voice of his fellow-citizens. That he should have exercised his functions with dignity was natural; that he should have shown a singular lenity in the levyings of fines and the infliction of penalties was, however, an unexpected and discomposing discovery to the settlement.

"The law requires me, sir," he would say to some unmistakable culprit, "to give you the option of ten days' imprisonment or the fine of ten dollars. If you have not the money with you, the clerk will doubtless advance it for you." It is needless to add that the clerk invariably advanced the money, or that when the Court adjourned the Judge instantly reimbursed him. In one instance only did the sturdy culprit—either from "pure cussedness" or a weaker desire to spare the Judge the expense of his conviction—*refuse* to borrow the amount of the fine from the clerk. He was accordingly remanded to the County Jail. It is related—on tolerably good authority—that when the Court had adjourned the Court was seen, in spotless linen and yellow gloves, making in the direction of the County Jail—a small *adobe* building, which also served as a Hall of Records; that, after ostentatiously consulting certain records, the Court entered the Jail as if in casual official inspection; that, later in the evening, the Deputy Sheriff having charge of the prisoner was dispatched for a bottle of whiskey and a pack of cards. But as the story here alleges that the Deputy, that evening, lost the amount of his month's stipend and the Court its entire yearly salary to the prisoner, in a friendly game of "cut-throat euchre," to relieve the tedium of the prisoner's confinement, the whole story has been denied, as incompatible with Judge Trott's dignity, though not inconsistent with his kindliness of nature.

It is certain, however, that his lenity would have brought him into disfavor but for a redeeming exhibition of his unofficial strength. A young and talented lawyer from Sacramento had been detained in some civil case before Judge Trott, but, confident of his success on appeal from this primitive tribunal, he had scarcely concealed his contempt for it in his closing argument. Judge Trott, when he had finished, sat unmoved save for a slight coloring of his high cheek-bones. But here I must again borrow the graphic language of a spectator: "When the Judge had hung out them air red danger signals he sez, quite peaceful-like, to that yer Sacramento Shrimp, sez he, 'Young gentleman,' sez he, 'do you know that I could fine ye fifty dollars for contempt o' Court?' 'And if ye could,' sez the shrimp, peart and sassy as a hossfly, 'I reckon I could pay it,' 'But I ought to add,' sez the Gentleman, sad-like, 'that I don't purpose to do it. I believe in freedom of speech and—action!' He then rises up, on limbers hisself, so to speak, stretches out that yer Hand o' Providence o' his, lites into that yer shrimp, lifts him up and scoots him through the window twenty feet into the ditch. 'Call the next case,' sez he, sittin' down again, with them big white eyes o' his looking peaceful-like ez if nothin' partikler had happened."

Happy would it have been for the Gentleman had these gentle eccentricities produced no greater result. But a fatal and hitherto unexpected weakness manifested itself in the very court in which he had triumphed, and for a time imperiled his popularity. A lady of dangerous antecedents and great freedom of manner, who was the presiding goddess of the "Wheel of Fortune" in the principal gambling-saloon of La Porte, brought an action against several of its able-bodied citizens for entering the saloon with "force and arms" and destroying the peculiar machinery of her game. She was ably supported by counsel, and warmly sympathized with by a gentleman who was not her husband. Yet in spite of this valuable coöperation she was not successful. The offense was clearly proved; but the jury gave a verdict in favor of the *defendants,* without leaving their seats.

Judge Trott turned his mild, inoffensive eyes upon them.

"Do I understand you to say that this is your final verdict?"

"You kin bet your boots, Your Honor," responded the foreman with cheerful but well-meaning irreverence, "that that's about the way the thing points."

"Mr. Clerk," said Judge Trott, "record the verdict, and then enter my resignation as Judge of this court."

He rose and left the bench. In vain did various influential citizens follow him with expostulations; in vain did they point out the worthlessness of the plaintiff and the worthlessness of her cause—in which he had sacrificed himself. In vain did the jury intimate that his resignation was an insult to *them*. Judge Trott turned abruptly upon the foreman, with the old ominous glow in his high cheek-bones.

"I didn't understand you," said he.

"I was saying," said the foreman hastily, "that it was useless to argue the case any longer." And withdrew slightly in advance of the rest of the jury, as became his official position. But Judge Trott never again ascended the bench.

It was quite a month after his resignation, and the Gentleman was sitting in the twilight "under the shadow of his own vine and fig tree,"—a figure of speech locally interpreted as a "giant redwood" and a mossy creeper,—before the door of that cabin in which he was first introduced to the reader, when he was faintly conscious of the outlines of a female form and the tones of a female voice.

The Gentleman hesitated, and placed over his right eye a large gold eyeglass, which had been lately accepted by the Camp as his most recent fashionable folly. The form was unfamiliar, but the voice the Gentleman instantly recognized as belonging to the plaintiff in his late momentous judicial experience. It is proper to say here that it was the voice of Mademoiselle Clotilde Montmorency; it is only just to add that, speaking no French, and being of unmistakable Anglo-Saxon origin, her name was evidently derived from the game over which she had presided, which was, in the baleful estimation of the Camp, of foreign extraction.

"I wanted to know," said Miss Clotilde, sitting down on a bench beside the Gentleman—"that is, me and Jake Woods thought we'd like to know—*how much* you consider yourself out of pocket by this yer resignation of yours?"

Scarcely hearing the speech, and more concerned with the apparition itself, Judge Trott stammered vaguely, "I have the pleasure of addressing Miss—"

"If you mean by that that you think you don't know me, never saw me before, and don't want to see me ag'in, why, I reckon that's the polite way o' putting it," said Miss Montmorency, with enforced calmness, scraping some dead leaves together with the tip of her parasol as if she were covering up her emotions. "But I'm Miss Montmorency. I was saying that Jake and me thought that—seein' as you stood by us when them hounds on the jury give in their hellish lying verdict—Jake and me thought it wasn't the square thing for you to lose your situation just for me. 'Find out from the Judge,' sez he, 'jist what he reckons he's lost by this yer resignation—

putting it at his own figgers.' That's what Jake said. Jake's a square man —I kin say *that* of him, anyhow."

"I don't think I understand you," said Judge Trott simply.

"That's it! That's just it!" continued Miss Clotilde, with only half-suppressed bitterness. "That's what I told Jake. I sez, 'The Judge won't understand you nor me. He's that proud he won't have anything to say to us. Didn't he meet me square on the street last Tuesday and never let on that he saw me—never even nodded when I nodded to him?' "

"My dear madam," said Judge Trott hurriedly, "I assure you you are mistaken. I did *not* see you. Pray believe me. The fact is—I am afraid to confess it even to myself—but I find that, day by day, my eyesight is growing weaker and weaker." He stopped and sighed.

Miss Montmorency, glancing upward at his face, saw it was pale and agitated. With a woman's swift intuition, she believed this weakness explained the otherwise gratuitous effrontery of his incongruous eyes, and it was to her a sufficient apology. It is only the inexplicable in a man's ugliness that a woman never pardons.

"Then ye really don't recognize me?" said Miss Clotilde, a little softened, and yet a little uneasy.

"I—am—afraid—not," said Trott, with an apologetic smile.

Miss Clotilde paused. "Do you mean to say you couldn't see me when I was in court during the trial?"

Judge Trott blushed. "I am afraid I saw only—an—outline."

"I had on," continued Miss Clotilde rapidly, "a straw hat, with magenta silk lining, turned up so—magenta ribbons tied here"—indicating her round throat—"a reg'lar 'Frisco hat—don't you remember?"

"I—that is—I am afraid—"

"And one of them figgered silk 'Dollar Vardens,' " continued Miss Clotilde anxiously.

Judge Trott smiled politely, but vaguely. Miss Clotilde saw that he evidently had not recognized this rare and becoming costume. She scattered the leaves again and dug her parasol into the ground.

"Then you never saw me at all?"

"Never distinctly."

"Ef it's a fair question betwixt you and me," she said suddenly, "what made you resign?"

"I could not remain Judge of a court that was obliged to record a verdict so unjust as that given by the jury in your case," replied Judge Trott warmly.

"Say that ag'in, old man," said Miss Clotilde, with an admiration which half apologized for the irreverence of epithet.

Judge Trott urbanely repeated the substance of his remark in another form.

Miss Montmorency was silent a moment. "Then it wasn't *me*?" she said finally.

"I don't think I catch your meaning," replied the Judge, a little awkwardly.

"Why—ME. It wasn't on account of *me* you did it?"

"No," said the Judge pleasantly.

There was another pause. Miss Montmorency balanced her parasol on the tip of her toe. "Well," she said finally, "this isn't getting much information for Jake."

"For whom?"

"Jake."

"Oh—your husband?"

Miss Montmorency clicked the snap of her bracelet smartly on her wrist and said sharply, "Who said he was 'my husband?' "

"Oh, I beg your pardon."

"I said Jake Woods. He's a square man—I can say *that* for him. He sez to me, 'You kin tell the Judge that whatever he chooses to take from us—it ain't no bribery nor corruption, nor nothin' o' that kind. It's all on the square. The trial's over; he isn't Judge any longer; he can't do anything for us—he ain't expected to do anything for us but one thing. And that is to give us the satisfaction of knowing that he hasn't lost anything by us—that he hasn't lost anything by being a square man and acting on the square.' There! that's what he said. I've said it! Of course I know what *you'll* say. I know you'll get wrathy. I know you're mad now! I know you're too proud to touch a dollar from the like of us—if you were starving. I know you'll tell Jake to go to hell, and me with him! And who the hell cares?"

She had worked herself up to this passion so suddenly, so outrageously and inconsistently, that it was not strange that it ended in an hysterical burst of equally illogical tears. She sank down again on the bench she had gradually risen from, and applied the backs of her yellow-gloved hands to her eyes, still holding the parasol at a rigid angle with her face. To her infinite astonishment Judge Trott laid one hand gently upon her shoulder and with the other possessed himself of the awkward parasol, which he tactfully laid on the bench beside her.

"You are mistaken, my dear young lady," he said, with a respectful gravity,—"deeply mistaken, if you think I feel anything but kindness and gratitude for your offer—an offer so kind and unusual that even you yourself feel that I could not accept it. No! Let me believe that in doing what

I thought was only my duty as a *Judge,* I gained your good-will, and let me feel that in doing my duty now as a *man,* I shall still keep it."

Miss Clotilde had lifted her face towards his, as if deeply and wonderingly following his earnest words. But she only said, "Can you see me in this light?—at this distance? Put up your glass and try."

Her face was not far from his. I have forgotten whether I have said that she was a pretty woman. She had been once prettier. But she retained enough of her good looks to invest the "Wheel of Fortune," over which she had presided, with a certain seductive and bewildering uncertainty, which increased the risk of the players. It was, in fact, this unhallowed combination of Beauty and Chance that excited the ire of La Porte—who deemed it unprofessional and not "on the square."

She had fine eyes. Possibly Judge Trott had never before been so near eyes that were so fine and so—expressive. He lifted his head with some embarrassment and a blush on his high cheek-bones. Then, partly from instinctive courtesy, partly from a desire to bring in a third party to relieve his embarrassment, he said—

"I hope you will make your friend, Mr.——, understand that I appreciate his kindness, even if I can't accept it."

"Oh, you mean Jake," said the lady. "Oh, *he's* gone home to the States. I'll make it all right with *him!*"

There was another embarrassing pause—possibly over the absence of Jake. At last it was broken by Miss Montmorency. "You must take care of your eyes, for I want you to know me the next time you see me."

So they parted. The Judge *did* recognize her on several other occasions. And then La Porte was stirred to its depths in hillside and tunnel with a strange rumor. Judge Trott had married Miss Jane Thomson, *alias* Miss Clotilde Montmorency—in San Francisco! For a few hours a storm of indignation and rage swept over the town; it was believed to have been a deep-laid plan and conspiracy. It was prefectly well understood that Judge Trott's resignation was the price of her hand—and of the small fortune she was known to be possessed of. Of his character nothing remained that was assailable. A factitious interest and pathos were imported into the character and condition of her last lover—Jake Woods—the victim of the double treachery of Judge Trott and Miss Clotilde. A committee was formed to write a letter of sympathy to this man, who, a few months before, had barely escaped lynching at their hands. The angry discussion was at last broken by the voice of the first speaker in this veracious narrative, Captain Henry Symes—

"Thar's one feature in this yer case that ye don't seem to know, and that oughter be considered. The day she married him in San Francisco she had just come from the doctor's, who had told her that Trott was *help-*

lessly blind! Gentlemen, when a gal like that throws over her whole life, her whole perfession, and a square man like Jake Woods, to marry a blind man without a dollar—just because he once stood up for her—*on principle,* damn me ef I see any man good enough to go back on her for it! Ef the Judge is willing to kinder overlook little bygone eccentricities o' hers for the sake o' being cared for and looked arter by her, that's his lookout! And you'll excoose me if, arter my experience, I reckon it ain't exactly a healthy business to interfere with the domestic concerns of the Gentleman of La Porte."

A Horseman in the Sky

AMBROSE BIERCE
(1842–1914?)

One sunny afternoon in the autumn of the year 1861, a soldier lay in a clump of laurel by the side of a road in Western Virginia. He lay at full length, upon his stomach, his feet resting upon the toes, his head upon the left forearm. His extended right hand loosely grasped his rifle. But for the somewhat methodical disposition of his limbs and a slight rhythmic movement of the cartridge-box at the back of his belt, he might have been thought to be dead. He was asleep at his post of duty. But if detected he would be dead shortly afterward, that being the just and legal penalty of his crime.

The clump of laurel in which the criminal lay was in the angle of a road which, after ascending, southward, a steep acclivity to that point, turned sharply to the west, running along the summit for perhaps one hundred yards. There it turned southward again and went zigzagging downward through the forest. At the salient of that second angle was a large flat rock, jutting out from the ridge to the northward, overlooking the deep valley from which the road ascended. The rock capped a high cliff; a stone dropped from its outer edge would have fallen sheer downward one thousand feet to the tops of the pines The angle where the soldier lay was on another spur of the same cliff. Had he been awake he would have commanded a view, not only of the short arm of the road and the jutting rock but of the entire profile of the cliff below it. It might well have made him giddy to look.

The country was wooded everywhere except at the bottom of the valley to the northward, where there was a small natural meadow, through which flowed a stream scarcely visible from the valley's rim. This open ground looked hardly larger than an ordinary door-yard, but was really several acres in extent. Its green was more vivid than that of the enclosing forest. Away beyond it rose a line of giant cliffs similar to those upon which we are supposed to stand in our survey of the savage scene, and through which the road had somehow made its climb to the summit. The configuration of the valley, indeed, was such that from our point of observation it seemed entirely shut in, and one could not but have wondered how the road which found a way out of it had found a way into it, and whence came and whither went the waters of the stream that parted the meadow two thousand feet below.

No country is so wild and difficult but men will make it a theatre of war; concealed in the forest at the bottom of that military rat-trap, in which half a hundred men in possession of the exits might have starved an army to submission, lay five regiments of Federal infantry. They had marched all the previous day and night and were resting. At nightfall they would take to the road again, climb to the place where their unfaithful sentinel now slept, and, descending the other slope of the ridge, fall upon a camp of the enemy at about midnight. Their hope was to surprise it, for the road led to the rear of it. In case of failure their position would be perilous in the extreme; and fail they surely would should accident or vigilance apprise the enemy of the movement.

The sleeping sentinel in the clump of laurel was a young Virginian named Carter Druse. He was the son of wealthy parents, an only child, and had known such ease and cultivation and high living as wealth and taste were able to command in the mountain country of Western Virginia. His home was but a few miles from where he now lay. One morning he had risen from the breakfast table and said, quietly and gravely: "Father, a Union regiment has arrived at Grafton. I am going to join it."

The father lifted his leonine head, looked at the son a moment in silence, and replied: "Go, Carter, and, whatever may occur, do what you conceive to be your duty. Virginia, to which you are a traitor, must get on without you. Should we both live to the end of the war, we will speak further of the matter. Your mother, as the physician has informed you, is in a most critical condition; at the best she cannot be with us longer than a few weeks, but that time is precious. It would be better not to disturb her."

So Carter Druse, bowing reverently to his father, who returned the salute with a stately courtesy which masked a breaking heart, left the home of his childhood to go soldiering. By conscience and courage, by deeds of devotion and daring, he soon commended himself to his fellows and his officers; and it was to these qualities and to some knowledge of the country that he owed his selection for his present perilous duty at the extreme outpost. Nevertheless, fatigue had been stronger than resolution, and he had fallen asleep. What good or bad angel came in a dream to rouse him from his state of crime who shall say? Without a movement, without a sound, in the profound silence and the languor of the late afternoon, some invisible messenger of fate touched with unsealing finger the eyes of his consciousness—whispered into the ear of his spirit the mysterious awakening word which no human lips have ever spoken, no human memory ever has recalled. He quietly raised his forehead from his arm and looked between the masking stems of the laurels, instinctively closing his right hand about the stock of his rifle.

His first feeling was a keen artistic delight. On a colossal pedestal, the cliff, motionless at the extreme edge of the capping rock and sharply outlined against the sky, was an equestrian statue of impressive dignity. The figure of the man sat the figure of the horse, straight and soldierly, but with the repose of a Grecian god carved in the marble which limits the suggestion of activity. The grey costume harmonised with its aerial background; the metal of accoutrement and caparison was softened and subdued by the shadow; the animal's skin had no points of high light. A carbine, strikingly foreshortened, lay across the pommel of the saddle, kept in place by the right hand grasping it at the "grip"; the left hand, holding the bridle rein, was invisible. In silhouette against the sky, the profile of the horse was cut with the sharpness of a cameo; it looked across the heights of air to the confronting cliffs beyond. The face of the rider, turned slightly to the left, showed only an outline of temple and beard; he was looking downward to the bottom of the valley. Magnified by its lift against the sky and by the soldier's testifying sense of the formidableness of a near enemy, the group appeared of heroic, almost colossal, size.

For an instant Druse had a strange, half-defined feeling that he had slept to the end of the war and was looking upon a noble work of art reared upon that commanding eminence to commemorate the deeds of an heroic past of which he had been an inglorious part. The feeling was dispelled by a slight movement of the group; the horse, without moving its feet, had drawn its body slightly backward from the verge; the man remained immobile as before. Broad awake and keenly alive to the significance of the situation, Druse now brought the butt of his rifle against his cheek by cautiously pushing the barrel forward through the bushes, cocked the piece, and, glancing through the sights, covered a vital spot of the horseman's breast. A touch upon the trigger and all would have been well with Carter Druse. At that instant the horseman turned his head and looked in the direction of his concealed foeman—seemed to look into his very face, into his eyes, into his brave compassionate heart.

Is it, then, so terrible to kill an enemy in war—an enemy who has surprised a secret vital to the safety of oneself and comrades—an enemy more formidable for his knowledge than all his army for its numbers? Carter Druse grew deathly pale; he shook in every limb, turned faint, and saw the statuesque group before him as black figures, rising, falling, moving unsteadily in arcs of circles in a fiery sky. His hand fell away from his weapon, his head slowly dropped until his face rested on the leaves in which he lay. This courageous gentleman and hardy soldier was near swooning from intensity of emotion.

It was not for long; in another moment his face was raised from earth, his hands resumed their places on the rifle, his forefinger sought the trigger; mind, heart, and eyes were clear, conscience and reason sound. He could not hope to capture that enemy; to alarm him would but send him dashing to his camp with his fatal news. The duty of the soldier was plain: the man must be shot dead from ambush—without warning, without a moment's spiritual preparation, with never so much as an unspoken prayer, he must be sent to his account. But no—there is a hope; he may have discovered nothing—perhaps he is but admiring the sublimity of the landscape. If permitted, he may turn and ride carelessly away in the direction whence he came. Surely it will be possible to judge at the instant of his withdrawing whether he knows. It may well be that his fixity of attention—Druse turned his head and looked below, through the deeps of air downward, as from the surface to the bottom of a translucent sea. He saw creeping across the green meadow a sinuous line of figures of men and horses—some foolish commander was permitting the soldiers of his escort to water their beasts in the open, in plain view from a hundred summits!

Druse withdrew his eyes from the valley and fixed them again upon the group of man and horse in the sky, and again it was through the sights of his rifle. But this time his aim was at the horse. In his memory, as if they were a divine mandate, rang the words of his father at their parting: "Whatever may occur, do what you conceive to be your duty." He was calm now. His teeth were firmly but not rigidly closed; his nerves were as tranquil as a sleeping babe's—not a tremor affected any muscle of his body; his breathing, until suspended in the act of taking aim, was regular and slow. Duty had conquered; the spirit had said to the body: "Peace, be still." He fired.

At that moment an officer of the Federal force, who, in a spirit of adventure or in quest of knowledge, had left the hidden bivouac in the valley, and, with aimless feet, had made his way to the lower edge of a small open space near the foot of the cliff, was considering what he had to gain by pushing his exploration farther. At a distance of a quarter-mile before him, but apparently at a stone's-throw, rose from its fringe of pines the gigantic face of rock, towering to so great a height above him that it made him giddy to look up to where its edge cut a sharp, rugged line against the sky. At some distance away to his right it presented a clean, vertical profile against a background of blue sky to a point half of the way down, and of distant hills hardly less blue thence to the tops of the trees at its base. Lifting his eyes to the dizzy altitude of its summit, the officer saw an astonishing sight—a man on horseback riding down into the valley through the air!

Straight upright sat the rider, in military fashion, with a firm seat in the saddle, a strong clutch upon the rein to hold his charger from too impetuous a plunge. From his bare head his long hair streamed upward, waving like a plume. His right hand was concealed in the cloud of the horse's lifted mane. The animal's body was as level as if every hoof-stroke encountered the resistant earth. Its motions were those of a wild gallop, but even as the officer looked they ceased, with all the legs thrown sharply forward as in the act of alighting from a leap. But this was a flight!

Filled with amazement and terror by this apparition of a horseman in the sky—half believing himself the chosen scribe of some new Apocalypse, the officer was overcome by the intensity of his emotions; his legs failed him and he fell. Almost at the same instant he heard a crashing sound in the trees—a sound that died without an echo, and all was still.

The officer rose to his feet, trembling. The familiar sensation of an abraded shin recalled his dazed faculties. Pulling himself together, he ran rapidly obliquely away from the cliff to a point a half-mile from its foot; thereabout he expected to find his man; and thereabout he naturally failed. In the fleeting instant of his vision his imagination had been so wrought upon by the apparent grace and ease and intention of the marvellous performance that it did not occur to him that the line of march of aerial cavalry is directed downward, and that he could find the objects of his search at the very foot of the cliff. A half-hour later he returned to camp.

This officer was a wise man; he knew better than to tell an incredible truth. He said nothing of what he had seen. But when the commander asked him if in his scout he had learned anything of advantage to the expedition, he answered:

"Yes, sir; there is no road leading down into this valley from the southward."

The commander, knowing better, smiled.

After firing his shot Private Carter Druse reloaded his rifle and resumed his watch. Ten minutes had hardly passed when a Federal sergeant crept cautiously to him on hands and knees. Druse neither turned his head nor looked at him, but lay without motion or sign of recognition.

"Did you fire?" the sergeant whispered.

"Yes."

"At what?"

"A horse. It was standing on yonder rock—pretty far out. You see it is no longer there. It went over the cliff."

The man's face was white, but he showed no other sign of emotion. Having answered, he turned away his face and said no more. The sergeant did not understand.

"See here, Druse," he said, after a moment's silence, "it's no use making a mystery. I order you to report. Was there anybody on the horse?"

"Yes."

"Who?"

"My father."

The sergeant rose to his feet and walked away. "Good God!" he said.

The Real Thing

HENRY JAMES

(1843–1916)

When the porter's wife who used to answer the house-bell, announced "A gentleman and a lady, sir," I had, as I often had in those days—the wish being father to the thought—an immediate vision of sitters. Sitters my visitors in this case proved to be; but not in the sense I should have preferred. There was nothing at first however to indicate that they mightn't have come for a portrait. The gentleman, a man of fifty, very high and very straight, with a moustache slightly grizzled and a dark grey walking-coat admirably fitted, both of which I noted professionally—I don't mean as a barber or yet as a tailor—would have struck me as a celebrity if celebrities often were striking. It was a truth of which I had for some time been conscious that a figure with a good deal of frontage was, as one might say, almost never a public institution. A glance at the lady helped to remind me of this paradoxical law: she also looked too distinguished to be a "personality." Moreover one would scarcely come across two variations together.

Neither of the pair immediately spoke—they only prolonged the preliminary gaze suggesting that each wished to give the other a chance. They were visibly shy; they stood there letting me take them in—which, as I afterwards perceived, was the most practical thing they could have done. In this way their embarrassment served their cause. I had seen people painfully reluctant to mention that they desired anything so gross as to be represented on canvas; but the scruples of my new friends appeared almost insurmountable. Yet the gentleman might have said "I should like a portrait of my wife," and the lady might have said "I should like a portrait of my husband." Perhaps they weren't husband and wife—this naturally would make the matter more delicate. Perhaps they wished to be done together—in which case they ought to have brought a third person to break the news.

"We come from Mr. Rivet," the lady finally said with a dim smile that had the effect of a moist sponge passed over a "sunk" piece of painting, as well as of a vague allusion to vanished beauty. She was as tall and straight, in her degree, as her companion, and with ten years less to carry. She looked as sad as a woman could look whose face was not charged with expression; that is her tinted oval mask showed waste as an exposed surface shows friction. The hand of time had played over her freely, but to an effect of elimination. She was slim and stiff, and so well-dressed, in dark blue cloth, with lappets and pockets and buttons, that it was clear she employed the same tailor as her husband. The couple had an indefinable air of prosperous thrift—they evidently got a good deal of luxury for their money. If I was to be one of their luxuries, it would behoove me to consider my terms.

"Ah, Claude Rivet recommended me?" I echoed; and I added that it was very kind of him, though I could reflect that, as he only painted landscape, this wasn't a sacrifice.

The lady looked very hard at the gentleman, and the gentleman looked round the room. Then, staring at the door a moment and stroking his moustache, he rested his pleasant eyes on me with the remark: "He said you were the right one."

"I try to be, when people want to sit."

"Yes, we should like to," said the lady anxiously.

"Do you mean together?"

My visitors exchanged a glance. "If you could do anything with *me* I suppose it would be double," the gentleman stammered.

"Oh, yes, there's naturally a higher charge for two figures than for one."

"We should like to make it pay," the husband confessed.

"That's very good of you," I returned, appreciating so unwonted a sympathy—for I supposed he meant pay the artist.

A sense of strangeness seemed to dawn on the lady. "We mean for the illustrations—Mr. Rivet said you might put one in."

"Put in—an illustration?" I was equally confused.

"Sketch her off, you know," said the gentleman, colouring.

It was only then that I understood the service Claude Rivet had rendered me; he had told them how I worked in black and white, for magazines, for storybooks, for sketches of contemporary life, and consequently had copious employment for models. These things were true, but it was not less true—I may confess it now; whether because the aspiration was to lead to everything or to nothing I leave the reader to guess—that I couldn't get the honours, to say nothing of the emoluments, of a great painter of portraits out of my head. My "illustrations" were my pot-boilers; I looked to a different branch of art—far and away the most interesting it had always seemed to me—to perpetuate my fame. There was no shame in looking to it also to make my fortune; but that fortune was by so much further from being made from the moment my visitors wished to be "done" for something. I was disappointed; for in the pictorial sense I had immediately seen them. I had seized their type—I had already settled what I would do with it. Something that wouldn't absolutely have pleased them, I afterwards reflected.

"Ah, you're—you're—a—?" I began as soon as I had mastered my surprise. I couldn't bring out the dingy word "models": it seemed so little to fit the case.

"We haven't had much practice," said the lady.

"We've got to *do* something, and we've thought that an artist in your line might perhaps make something of us," her husband threw off. He further mentioned that they didn't know many artists and that they had gone first, on the off chance—he painted views of course, but sometimes put in figures; perhaps I remembered—to Mr. Rivet, whom they had met a few years before at a place in Norfolk where he was sketching.

"We used to sketch a little ourselves," the lady hinted.

"It's very awkward, but we absolutely *must* do something," her husband went on.

"Of course we're not so *very* young," she admitted with a wan smile.

With the remark that I might as well know something more about them the husband had handed me a card extracted from a neat new pocketbook—their appurtenances were all of the freshest—and inscribed with the words "Major Monarch." Impressive as these words were they didn't carry my knowledge much further; but my visitor presently added: "I've left the army and we've had the misfortune to lose our money. In fact our means are dreadfully small."

"It's awfully trying—a regular strain," said Mrs. Monarch.

They evidently wished to be discreet—to take care not to swagger because they were gentlefolk. I felt them willing to recognise this as something of a drawback, at the same time that I guessed at an underlying sense—their consolation in adversity—that they *had* their points. They certainly had; but these advantages struck me as preponderantly social; such, for instance, as would help to make a drawing-room look well. However, a drawing-room was always, or ought to be, a picture.

In consequence of his wife's allusion to their age Major Monarch observed: "Naturally it's more for the figure that we thought of going in. We can still hold ourselves up." On the instant I saw the figure was indeed their strong point. His "naturally" didn't sound vain, but it lighted up the question. "*She* has the best one," he continued, nodding at his wife with a pleasant after-dinner absence of circumlocution. I could only reply, as if we were in fact sitting over our wine, that this didn't prevent his own from being very good; which led him in turn to make answer: "We thought that if you ever have to do people like us we might be something like it. *She* particularly—for a lady in a book, you know."

I was so amused by them that, to get more of it, I did my best to take their point of view; and though it was an embarrassment to find myself appraising physically, as if they were animals on hire or useful blacks, a pair whom I should have expected to meet only in one of the relations in which criticism is tacit, I looked at Mrs. Monarch judicially enough to be able to exclaim after a moment with conviction: "Oh, yes, a lady in a book!" She was singularly like a bad illustration.

"We'll stand up, if you like," said the Major; and he raised himself before me with a really grand air.

I could take his measure at a glance—he was six feet two and a perfect gentleman. It would have paid any club in process of formation and in want of a stamp to engage him at a salary to stand in the principal window. What struck me at once was that in coming to me they had rather missed their vocation; they could surely have been turned to better account for advertising purposes. I couldn't of course see the thing in detail, but I could see them make somebody's fortune—I don't mean their own. There was something in them for a waistcoat-maker, an hotel-keeper or a soap-vendor. I could imagine "We always use it" pinned on their bosoms with the greatest effect; I had a vision of the brilliancy with which they would launch a table d'hôte.

Mrs. Monarch sat still, not from pride but from shyness, and presently her husband said to her: "Get up, my dear, and show how smart you are." She obeyed, but she had no need to get up to show it. She walked to the end of the studio and then came back blushing, her fluttered eyes on the partner of her appeal. I was reminded of an incident I had accidentally had a glimpse of in Paris—being with a friend there, a dramatist about to produce a play, when an actress came to him to ask to be entrusted with a part. She went through her paces before him, walked up and down as Mrs. Monarch was doing. Mrs. Monarch did it quite as well, but I abstained from applauding. It was very odd to see such people apply for such poor pay. She looked as if she had ten thousand a year. Her husband had used the word that described her: she was in the London current jargon essentially and typically "smart." Her figure was, in the same order of ideas, conspicuously and irreproachably "good." For a woman of her age her waist was surprisingly small; her elbow moreover had the orthodox crook. She held her head at the conventional angle, but why did she come to *me?* She ought to have tried on jackets at a big shop. I feared my visitors were not only destitute but "artistic"—which would be a great complication. When she sat down again I thanked her, observing that what a draughtsman most valued in his model was the faculty of keeping quiet.

"Oh, *she* can keep quiet," said Major Monarch. Then he added jocosely: "I've always kept her quiet."

"I'm not a nasty fidget, am I?" It was going to wring tears from me, I felt, the way she hid her head, ostrich-like, in the other broad bosom.

The owner of this expanse addressed his answer to me. "Perhaps it isn't out of place to mention—because we ought to be quite businesslike, oughtn't we?—that when I married her she was known as the Beautiful Statue."

"Oh dear!" said Mrs. Monarch ruefully.

"Of course I should want a certain amount of expression," I rejoined.

"Of *course!*"—and I had never heard such unanimity.

"And then I suppose you know that you'll get awfully tired."

"Oh, we *never* get tired!" they eagerly cried.

"Have you had any kind of practice?"

They hesitated—they looked at each other. "We've been photographed—*immensely,*" said Mrs. Monarch.

"She means the fellows have asked us themselves," added the Major.

"I see—because you're so good-looking."

"I don't know what they thought, but they were always after us."

"We always got our photographs for nothing," smiled Mrs. Monarch.

"We might have brought some, my dear," her husband remarked.

"I'm not sure we have any left. We've given quantities away," she explained to me.

"With our autographs and that sort of thing," said the Major.

"Are they to be got in the shops?" I inquired as a harmless pleasantry.

"Oh, yes, *hers*—they used to be."

"Not now," said Mrs. Monarch with her eyes on the floor.

II

I could fancy the "sort of thing" they put on the presentation copies of their photographs, and I was sure they wrote a beautiful hand. It was odd how quickly I was sure of everything that concerned them. If they were now so poor as to have to earn shillings and pence they could never have had much of a margin. Their good looks had been their capital, and they had good-naturedly made the most of the career that this resource marked out for them. It was in their faces, the blankness, the deep intellectual repose of the twenty years of country-house visiting that had given them pleasant intonations. I could see the sunny drawing-rooms, sprinkled with periodicals she didn't read, in which Mrs. Monarch had continuously sat; I could see the wet shrubberies in which she had walked, equipped to admiration for either exercise. I could see the rich covers the Major had helped to shoot and the wonderful garments in which, late at night, he repaired to the smoking-room to talk about them. I could imagine their leggings and waterproofs, their knowing tweeds and rugs, their rolls of sticks and cases of tackle and neat umbrellas; and I could evoke the exact appearance of their servants and the compact variety of their luggage on platforms of country stations.

They gave small tips, but they were liked; they didn't do anything themselves, but they were welcome. They looked so well everywhere; they gratified the general relish for stature, complexion and "form." They knew it without fatuity or vulgarity, and they respected themselves in consequence. They weren't superficial; they were thorough and kept themselves up—it had been their line. People with such a taste for activity had to have some line. I could feel how even in a dull house they could have been counted on for the joy of life. At present something had happened—it didn't matter what, their little income had grown less, it had grown least—and they had to do something for pocket-money. Their friends could like them, I made out, without liking to support them. There was something about them that represented credit—their clothes, their manners, their type; but if credit is a large empty pocket in which an occasional chink reverberates, the chink at least must be audible. What they wanted of me was help to make it so. Fortunately they had no children—I soon divined that. They would also perhaps wish our relations to be kept secret: this was why it was "for the figure"—the reproduction of the face would betray them.

I liked them—I felt, quite as their friends must have done—they were so simple; and I had no objection to them if they would suit. But somehow with all their perfections I didn't easily believe in them. After all they were amateurs, and the ruling passion of my life was the detestation of the amateur. Combined with this was another perversity—an innate preference for the represented subject over the real one: the defect of the real one was so apt to be a lack of representation. I liked things that appeared; then one was sure. Whether they *were* or not was a subordinate and almost always a profitless question. There were other considerations, the first of which was that I already had two or three recruits in use, notably a young person with big feet, in alpaca, from Kilburn, who for a couple of years had come to me regularly for my illustrations and with whom I was still—perhaps ignobly—satisfied. I frankly explained to my visitors how the case stood, but they had taken more precautions than I supposed. They had reasoned out their opportunity, for Claude Rivet had told them of the projected *édition de luxe* of one of the writers of our day—the rarest of the novelists—who, long neglected by the multitudinous vulgar and dearly prized by the attentive (need I mention Philip Vincent?), had had the happy fortune of seeing, late in life, the dawn and then the full light of a higher criticism; an estimate in which on the part of the public there was something really of expiation. The edition preparing, planned by a publisher of taste, was practically an act of high reparation; the woodcuts with which it was to be enriched were the homage of English art to one of the most independent representatives of English letters. Major and Mrs. Monarch confessed to me they had hoped I might be able to work *them* into my branch of the enterprise. They knew I was to do the first of the books, "Rutland Ramsay," but I had to make clear to them that my participation in the rest of the affair—this first book was to be a test—must depend on the satisfaction I should give. If this should be limited my employers would drop me with scarce common forms. It was therefore a crisis for me, and naturally I was making special preparations, looking about for new people, should they be necessary, and securing the best types. I admitted however that I should like to settle down to two or three good models who would do for everything.

"Should we have often—a—put on special clothes?" Mrs. Monarch timidly demanded.

"Dear, yes—that's half the business."

"And should we be expected to supply our own costumes?"

"Oh, no; I've got a lot of things. A painter's models put on—or put off—anything he likes."

"And you mean—a—the same?"

"The same?"

Mrs. Monarch looked at her husband again.

"Oh, she was just wondering," he explained, "if the costumes are in *general* use." I had to confess that they were, and I mentioned further that some of them—I had a lot of genuine greasy last-century things—had served their time, a hundred years ago, on living world-stained men and women; on figures not perhaps so far removed, in that vanished world, from *their* type, the Monarchs', *quoi!* of a breeched and bewigged age. "We'll put on anything that *fits*," said the Major.

"Oh, I arrange that—they fit in the pictures."

"I'm afraid I should do better for the modern books. I'd come as you like," said Mrs. Monarch.

"She has got a lot of clothes at home: they might do for contemporary life," her husband continued.

"Oh, I can fancy scenes in which you'd be quite natural." And indeed I could see the slipshod rearrangements of stale properties—the stories I tried to produce pictures for without the exasperation of reading them—whose sandy tacts the good lady might help to people. But I had to return to the fact that for this sort of work—the daily mechanical grind—I was already equipped: the people I was working with were fully adequate.

"We only thought we might be more like *some* characters," said Mrs. Monarch mildly, getting up.

Her husband also rose; he stood looking at me with a dim wistfulness that was touching in so fine a man. "Wouldn't it be rather a pull sometimes to have—a—to have—?" He hung fire; he wanted me to help him by phrasing what he meant. But I couldn't—I didn't know. So he brought it out awkwardly: "The *real* thing; a gentleman, you know, or a lady." I was quite ready to give a general assent—I admitted that there was a great deal in that. This encouraged Major Monarch to say, following up his appeal with an unacted gulp: "It's awfully hard—we've tried everything." The gulp was communicative; it proved too much for his wife. Before I knew it Mrs. Monarch had dropped again upon a divan and burst into tears. Her husband sat down beside her, holding one of her hands; whereupon she quickly dried her eyes with the other, while I felt embarrassed as she looked up at me. "There isn't a confounded job I haven't applied for—waited for—prayed for. You can fancy we'd be pretty bad first. Secretaryships and that sort of thing? You might as well ask for a peerage. I'd be *anything*—I'm strong; a messenger or a coal-heaver. I'd put on a gold-laced cap and open carriage-doors in front of the haberdasher's; I'd hang about a station to carry portmanteaus; I'd be a postman. But they won't *look* at you; there are thousands as good as yourself already on the ground. *Gentlemen,* poor beggars, who've drunk their wine, who've kept their hunters!"

I was as reassuring as I know how to be, and my visitors were presently on their feet again while, for the experiment, we agreed on an hour. We were discussing it when the door opened and Miss Churm came in with a wet umbrella. Miss Churm had to take the omnibus to Maida Vale and then walk half a mile. She looked a trifle blowsy and slightly splashed. I scarcely ever saw her come in without thinking afresh how odd it was that, being so little in herself, she should yet be so much in others. She was a meagre little Miss Churm, but was such an ample heroine of romance. She was only a freckled cockney, but she could represent everything, from a fine lady to a shepherdess; she had the faculty as she might have had a fine voice or long hair. She couldn't spell and she loved beer, but she had two or three "points," and practice, and a knack, and mother-wit, and a whimsical sensibility, and a love of the theatre, and seven sisters, and not an ounce of respect, especially for the *h*. The first thing my visitors saw was that her umbrella was wet, and in their spotless perfection they visibly winced at it. The rain had come on since their arrival.

"I'm all in a soak; there *was* a mess of people in the bus. I wish you lived near a stytion," said Miss Churm. I requested her to get ready as quickly as possible, and she passed into the room in which she always changed her dress. But before going out she asked me what she was to get into this time.

"It's the Russian princess, don't you know?" I answered; "the one with the 'golden eyes,' in black velvet, for the long thing in the *Cheapside*."

"Golden eyes? I *say!*" cried Miss Churm, while my companions watched her with intensity as she withdrew. She always arranged herself, when she was late, before I could turn round; and I kept my visitors a little on purpose, so that they might get an idea, from seeing her, what would be expected of themselves. I mentioned that she was quite my notion of an excellent model—she was really very clever.

"Do you think she looks like a Russian princess?" Major Monarch asked with lurking alarm.

"When I make her, yes."

"Oh, if you have to *make* her—!" he reasoned, not without point.

"That's the most you can ask. There are so many who are not makable."

"Well, now, *here's* a lady"—and with a persuasive smile he passed his arm into his wife's—"who's already made!"

"Oh, I'm not a Russian princess," Mrs. Monarch protested a little coldly. I could see she had known some and didn't like them. There at once was a complication of a kind I never had to fear with Miss Churm.

This young lady came back in black velvet—the gown was rather rusty and very low on her lean shoulders—and with a Japanese fan in her red hands. I reminded her that in the scene I was doing she had to look over someone's head. "I forget whose it is; but it doesn't matter. Just look over a head."

"I'd rather look over a stove," said Miss Churm; and she took her station near the fire. She fell into position, settled herself into a tall attitude, gave a certain backward inclination to her head and a certain forward droop to her fan, and looked, at least to my prejudiced sense, distinguished and charming, foreign and dangerous. We left her looking so while I went downstairs with Major and Mrs. Monarch.

"I believe I could come about as near it as that," said Mrs. Monarch.

"Oh, you think she's shabby, but you must allow for the alchemy of art."

However, they went off with an evident increase of comfort founded on their demonstrable advantage in being the real thing. I could fancy them shuddering over Miss Churm. She was very droll about them when I went back, for I told her what they wanted.

"Well, if *she* can sit I'll tyke to bookkeeping," said my model.

"She's very ladylike," I replied as an innocent form of aggravation.

"So much the worse for *you*. That means she can't turn round."

"She'll do for the fashionable novels."

"Oh, yes, she'll *do* for them!" my model humorously declared. "Ain't they bad enough without her?" I had often sociably denounced them to Miss Churm.

III

It was for the elucidation of a mystery in one of these works that I first tried Mrs. Monarch. Her husband came with her, to be useful if necessary—it was sufficiently clear that as a general thing he would prefer to come with her. At first I wondered if this were for "propriety's" sake—if he were going to be jealous and meddling. The idea was too tiresome, and if it had been confirmed it would speedily have brought our acquaintance to a close. But I soon saw there was nothing in it and that if he accompanied Mrs. Monarch it was—in addition to the chance of being wanted—simply because he had nothing else to do. When they were separate his occupation was gone, and they never *had* been separate. I judged rightly that in their awkward situation their close union was their main comfort and that this union had no weak spot. It was a real marriage, an encouragement to the hesitating, a nut for pessimists to crack. Their address was humble—I remember afterwards thinking it had been the only thing about them that was really professional—and I could fancy the lamentable lodgings in which the Major would have been left alone. He could sit there more or less grimly with his wife—he couldn't sit there anyhow without her.

He had too much tact to try and make himself agreeable when he couldn't be useful; so when I was too absorbed in my work to talk he simply sat and waited. But I liked to hear him talk—it made my work, when not interrupting it, less mechanical, less special. To listen to him was to combine the excitement of going out with the economy of staying at home. There was only one hindrance—that I seemed not to know any of the people this brilliant couple had known. I think he wondered extremely, during the term of our intercourse, whom the deuce I *did* know. He hadn't a stray sixpence of an idea to fumble for, so we didn't spin it very fine; we confined ourselves to questions of leather and even of liquor—saddlers and breeches-makers and how to get excellent claret cheap—and matters like "good trains" and the habits of small game. His lore on these last subjects was astonishing—he managed to interweave the stationmaster with the ornithologist. When he couldn't talk about greater things he could talk cheerfully about small, and since I couldn't accompany him into reminscences of the fashionable world he could lower the conversation without a visible effort to my level.

So earnest a desire to please was touching in a man who could so easily have knocked one down. He looked after the fire and had an opinion on the draught of the stove without my asking him, and I could see that he thought many of my arrangements not half knowing. I remember telling him that if I were only rich I'd offer him a salary to come and teach me how to live. Sometimes he gave a random sigh of which the essence might have been: "Give me even such a bare old barrack as *this,* and I'd do something with it!" When I wanted to use him he came alone; which was an illustration of the superior courage of women. His wife could bear her solitary second floor, and she was in general more discreet; showing by various small reserves that she was alive to the propriety of keeping our relations markedly professional—not letting them slide into sociability. She wished it to remain clear that she and the Major were employed, not cultivated, and if she approved of me as a superior, who could be kept in his place, she never thought me quite good enough for an equal.

She sat with great intensity, giving the whole of her mind to it, and was capable of remaining for an hour almost as motionless as before a photographer's lens. I could see she had been photographed often, but somehow the very habit that made her good for that purpose unfitted her for mine. At first I was extremely pleased with her ladylike air, and it was a satisfaction, on coming to follow her lines, to see how good they were and how far they could lead the pencil. But after a little skirmishing I began to find her too insurmountably stiff; do what I would with it my drawing looked like a photograph or a copy of a photograph. Her figure had no variety of expression—she herself had no sense of variety. You may say that this was my business and was only a question of placing her. Yet I placed her in every conceivable position and she managed to obliterate their differences. She was always a lady certainly, and into the bargain was always the same lady. She was the real thing, but always the same thing. There were moments when I rather writhed under the serenity of her confidence that she *was* the real thing. All her dealings with me and all her husband's were an implication that this was lucky for *me*. Meanwhile I found myself trying to invent types that approached her own, instead of making her own transform itself—in the clever way that was not impossible for instance to poor Miss Churm. Arrange as I would and take the precautions I would, she always came out, in my pictures, too tall—landing me in the dilemma of having represented a fascinating woman as seven feet high, which (out of respect perhaps to my own very much scantier inches) was far from my idea of such a personage.

The case was worse with the Major—nothing I could do would keep *him* down, so that he became useful only for representation of brawny giants. I adored variety and range, I cherished human accidents, the illustrative note; I wanted to characterise closely, and the thing in the world I most hated was the danger of being ridden by a type. I had quarrelled with some of my friends about it; I had parted company with them for maintaining that one *had* to be, and that if the type was beautiful—witness Raphael and Leonardo—the servitude was only a gain. I was neither Leonardo nor Raphael—I might only be a presumptuous young modern searcher; but I held that everything was to be sacrificed sooner than character. When they claimed that the obsessional form could easily *be* character I retorted, perhaps superficially, "Whose?" It couldn't be everybody's—it might end in being nobody's.

After I had drawn Mrs. Monarch a dozen times I felt surer even than before that the value of such a model as Miss Churm resided precisely in the fact that she had no positive stamp, combined of course with the other fact that what she did have was a curious and inexplicable talent for imitation. Her usual appearance was like a curtain which she could draw up at request for a capital performance. This performance was simply suggestive; but it was a word to the wise—it was vivid and pretty. Sometimes even I thought it, though she was plain herself, too insipidly pretty; I made it a reproach to her that the figures drawn from her were monotonously (*bêtement,* as we used to say) graceful. Nothing made her more angry: it was so much her pride to feel she could sit for characters that had nothing in common with each other. She would accuse me at such moments of taking away her "reputytion."

It suffered a certain shrinkage, this queer quantity, from the repeated visits of my new friends. Miss Churm was greatly in demand, never in want of employment, so I had no scruple in putting her off occasionally, to try them more at my ease. It was certainly amusing at first to do the real thing—it was amusing to do Major Monarch's trousers. They *were* the real thing, even if he did come out colossal. It was amusing to do his wife's back hair—it was so mathematically neat—and the particular "smart" tension of her tight stays. She lent herself especially to positions in which the face was somewhat averted or blurred; she abounded in ladylike back views and *profils perdus.* When she stood erect she took naturally one of the attitudes in which court painters represent queens and princesses; so that I found myself wondering whether, to draw out this accomplishment, I couldn't get the editor of the *Cheapside* to publish a really royal romance, "A Tale of Buckingham Palace." Sometimes, however, the real thing and the make-believe came into contact; by which I mean that Miss Churm, keeping an appointment or coming to make one on days when I had much work in hand, encountered her invidious rivals. The encounter was not on their part, for they noticed her no more than if she had been the housemaid; not from intentional loftiness, but simply because as yet, professionally, they didn't know how to fraternise, as I could imagine they would have liked—or at least that the Major would. They couldn't talk about the omnibus—they always walked; and they didn't know what else to try—she wasn't interested in good trains or cheap claret. Besides, they must have felt—in the air—that she was amused at them, secretly derisive of their ever knowing how. She wasn't a person to conceal the limits of her faith if she had had a chance to show them. On the other hand Mrs. Monarch didn't think her tidy; for why else did she take pains to say to me—it was going out of the way, for Mrs. Monarch—that she didn't like dirty women?

One day when my young lady happened to be present with my other sitters—she even dropped in, when it was convenient, for a chat—I asked her to be so good as to lend a hand in getting tea, a service with which she was familiar and which was one of a class that, living as I did in my small way, with slender domestic resources, I often appealed to my models to render. They liked to lay hands on my property, to break the sitting, and sometimes the china—it made them feel Bohemian. The next time I saw Miss Churm after this incident she surprised me greatly by making a scene about it—she accused me of having wished to humiliate her. She hadn't resented the outrage at the time, but had seemed obliging and amused, enjoying the comedy of asking Mrs. Monarch, who sat vague and silent, whether she would have cream and sugar, and putting an exaggerated simper into the question. She had tried intonations—as if she too wished to pass for the real thing—till I was afraid my other visitors would take offence.

Oh, they were determined not to do this, and their touching patience was the measure of their great need. They would sit by the hour, uncomplaining, till I was ready to use them; they would come back on the chance of being wanted and would walk away cheerfully if it failed. I used to go to the door with them to see in what magnificent order they retreated. I tried to find other employment for them—I introduced them to several artists. But they didn't "take," for reasons I could appreciate, and I became rather anxiously aware that after such disappointments they fell back upon me with a heavier weight. They did me the honour to think me most *their* form. They weren't romantic enough for the painters, and in those days there were few serious workers in black-and-white. Besides, they had an eye to the great job I had mentioned to them—they had secretly set their hearts on supplying the right essence for my pictorial vindication of our fine novelist. They knew that for this undertaking I should want no costume effects, none of the frippery of past ages—that it was a case in which everything would be contemporary and satirical and presumably genteel. If I could work them into it their future would be assured, for the labour would of course be long and the occupation steady.

One day Mrs. Monarch came without her husband—she explained his absence by his having had to go to the City. While she sat there in her usual relaxed majesty there came at the door a knock which I immediately recognized as the subdued appeal of a model out of work. It was followed by the entrance of a young man whom I at once saw to be a foreigner and who proved in fact an Italian acquainted with no English word but my name, which he uttered in a way that made it seem to include all others. I hadn't then visited his country, nor was I proficient in his tongue; but as he was not so meanly constituted—what Italian is?—as to depend only on that member for expression he conveyed to me, in familiar but graceful mimicry, that he was in search of exactly the employment in which the lady before me was engaged. I was not struck with him at first, and while I continued to draw I dropped few signs of interest or encouragement. He stood his ground, however—not importunately, but with a dumb dog-like fidelity in his eyes that amounted to innocent impudence, the manner of a devoted servant—he might have been in the house for years—unjustly suspected. Suddenly it struck me that this very attitude and expression made a picture; whereupon I told him to sit down and wait till I should be free. There was another picture in the way he obeyed me, and I observed as I worked that there were others still in the way he looked wonderingly, with his head thrown back, about a high studio. He might have been crossing himself in Saint Peter's. Before I finished I said to myself, "The fellow's a bankrupt orange-monger, but a treasure."

When Mrs. Monarch withdrew he passed across the room like a flash to open the door for her, standing there with the rapt, pure gaze of the young Dante spellbound by the young Beatrice. As I never insisted, in such situations, on the blankness of the British domestic, I reflected that he had the making of a servant—and I needed one, but couldn't pay him to be only that—as well as of a model; in short I resolved to adopt my bright adventurer if he would agree to officiate in the double capacity. He jumped at my offer, and in the event my rashness—for I had really known nothing about him—wasn't brought home to me. He proved a sympathetic though a desultory ministrant, and had in a wonderful degree the *sentiment de la pose*. It was uncultivated, instinctive, a part of the happy instinct that had guided him to my door and helped him to spell out my name on the card nailed to it. He had had no other introduction to me than a guess, from the shape of my high north window, seen outside, that my place was a studio and that as a studio it would contain an artist. He had wandered to England in search of fortune, like other itinerants, and had embarked, with a partner and a small green handcart, on the sale of penny ices. The ices had melted away and the partner had dissolved in their train. My young man wore tight yellow trousers with reddish stripes and his name was Oronte. He was sallow but fair, and when I put him into some old clothes of my own he looked like an Englishman. He was as good as Miss Churm, who could look, when requested, like an Italian.

IV

I thought Mrs. Monarch's face slightly convulsed when, on her coming back with her husband, she found Oronte installed. It was strange to have to recognize in a scrap of a lazzarone a competitor to her magnificent Major. It was she who scented danger first, for the Major was anecdotically unconscious. But Oronte gave us tea, with a hundred eager confusions—he had never been concerned in so queer a process—and I think she thought better of me for having at last an "establishment." They saw a couple of drawings that I had made of the establishment, and Mrs. Monarch hinted that it never would have struck her he had sat for them." Now the drawings you make from *us,* they look exactly like us," she reminded me, smiling in triumph; and I recognized that this was indeed just their defect. When I drew the Monarchs I couldn't anyhow get away from them—get into the character I wanted to represent; and I hadn't the least desire my model should be discoverable in my picture. Miss Churm never was, and Mrs. Monarch thought I hid her, very properly, because she was vulgar; whereas if she was lost it was only as the dead who go to heaven are lost—in the gain of an angel the more.

By this time I had got a certain start with "Rutland Ramsay," the first novel in the great projected series; that is, I had produced a dozen drawings, several with the help of the Major and his wife, and I had sent them in for approval. My understanding with the publishers, as I have already hinted, had been that I was to be left to do my work, in this particular case, as I liked, with the whole book committed to me; but my connexion with the rest of the series was only contingent. There were moments when, frankly, it was a comfort to have the real thing under one's hand; for there were characters in "Rutland Ramsay" that were very much like it. There were people presumably as erect as the Major and women of as good a fashion as Mrs. Monarch. There was a great deal of country-house life—treated, it is true, in a fine fanciful ironical generalized way—and there was a considerable implication of knickerbockers and kilts. There were certain things I had to settle at the outset; such things for instance as the exact appearance of the hero and the particular bloom and figure of the heroine. The author of course gave me a lead, but there was a margin for interpretation. I took the Monarchs into my confidence, I told them frankly what I was about, I mentioned my embarrassments and alternatives. "Oh, take *him!*" Mrs. Monarch murmured sweetly, looking at her husband; and "What could you want better than my wife?" the Major inquired with the comfortable candour that now prevailed between us.

I wasn't obliged to answer these remarks—I was only obliged to place my sitters. I wasn't easy in mind, and I postponed a little timidly perhaps the solving of my question. The book was a large canvas, the other figures were numerous, and I worked off at first some of the episodes in which the hero and the heroine were not concerned. When once I had set *them* up I should have to stick to them—I couldn't make my young man seven feet high in one place and five feet nine in another. I inclined on the whole to the latter measurement, though the Major more than once reminded me that *he* looked about as young as any one. It was indeed quite possible to arrange him, for the figure, so that it would have been difficult to detect his age. After the spontaneous Oronte had been with me a month, and after I had given him to understand several times over that his native exuberance would presently constitute an insurmountable barrier to our further intercourse, I waked to a sense of his heroic capacity. He was only five feet seven, but the remaining inches were latent. I tried him almost secretly at first, for I was really rather afraid of the judgment my other models would pass on such a choice. If they regarded Miss Churm as little better than a snare what would they think of the representation of a person so little the real thing as an Italian street-vendor of a protagonist formed by a public school?

If I went a little in fear of them it wasn't because they bullied me, because they had got an oppressive foothold, but because in their really pathetic decorum and mysteriously permanent newness they counted on me so intensely. I was therefore very glad when Jack Hawley came home: he was always of such good counsel. He painted badly himself, but there was no one like him for putting his finger on the place. He had been absent from England for a year; he had been somewhere—I don't remember where—to get a fresh eye. I was in a good deal of dread of any such organ, but we were old friends; he had been away for months and a sense of emptiness was creeping into my life. I hadn't dodged a missile for a year.

He came back with a fresh eye, but with the same old black velvet blouse, and the first evening he spent in my studio we smoked cigarettes till the small hours. He had done no work himself, he had only got the eye; so the field was clear for the production of my little things. He wanted to see what I had produced for the *Cheapside*, but he was disappointed in the exhibition. That at least seemed the meaning of two or three comprehensive groans which, as he lounged on my big divan, his leg folded under him, looking at my latest drawings, issued from his lips with the smoke of the cigarette.

"What's the matter with you?" I asked.

"What's the matter with *you?*"

"Nothing save that I'm mystified."

"You are indeed. You're quite off the hinge. What's the meaning of this new fad?" And he tossed me, with visible irreverence, a drawing in which I happened to have depicted both my elegant models. I asked if he didn't think it good, and he replied that it struck him as execrable, given the sort of thing I had always represented myself to him as wishing to arrive at; but I let that pass—I was so anxious to see exactly what he meant. The two figures in the picture looked colossal, but I supposed this was *not* what he meant, inasmuch as, for aught he knew to the contrary, I might have been trying for some such effect. I maintained that I was working exactly in the same way as when he last had done me the honour to tell me I might do something some day. "Well, there's a screw loose somewhere," he answered; "wait a bit and I'll discover it." I depended upon him to do so; where else was the fresh eye? But he produced at last nothing more luminous than "I don't know—I don't like your types." This was lame for a critic who had never consented to discuss with me anything but the question of execution, the direction of strokes and the mystery of values.

"In the drawings you've been looking at I think my types are very handsome."

"Oh, they won't do!"

"I've been working with new models."

"I see you have. *They* won't do."

"Are you very sure of that?"

"Absolutely—they're stupid."

"You mean *I* am—for I ought to get round that."

"You *can't*—with such people. Who are they?"

I told him, so far as was necessary, and he concluded heartlessly: *"Ce sont des gens qu'il faut mettre à la porte."*

"You've never seen them; they're awfully good"—I flew to their defense.

"Not seen them? Why, all this recent work of yours drops to pieces with them. It's all I want to see of them."

"No one else has said anything against it—the *Cheapside* people are pleased."

"Every one else is an ass, and the *Cheapside* people the biggest asses of all. Come, don't pretend at this time of day to have pretty illusions about the public, especially about publishers and editors. It's not for *such* animals you work—it's for those who know, *coloro che sanno;* so keep straight for *me* if you can't keep straight for yourself. There was a certain sort of thing you used to try for—and a very good thing it was. But this twaddle isn't *in* it." When I talked with Hawley later about "Rutland Ramsay" and its possible successors he declared that I must get back into my boat again or I should go to the bottom. His voice was the voice of warning.

I noted the warning, but I didn't turn my friends out of doors. They bored me a good deal; but the very fact that they bored me admonished me not to sacrifice them—if there was anything to be done with them—simply to irritation. As I look back at this phase they seem to me to have pervaded my life not a little. I have a vision of them as most of the time in my studio, seated against the wall on an old velvet bench to be out of the way, and resembling the while a pair of patient courtiers in a royal ante-chamber. I'm convinced that during the coldest weeks of the winter they held their ground because it saved them fire. Their newness was losing its gloss, and it was impossible not to feel them objects of charity. Whenever Miss Churm arrived they went away, and after I was fairly launched in "Rutland Ramsey" Miss Churm arrived pretty often. They managed to express to me tacitly that they supposed I wanted her for the low life of the book, and I let them suppose it, since they had attempted to study the work—it was lying about the studio—without discovering that it dealt only with the highest circles. They had dipped into the most brilliant of our novelists without deciphering many passages. I still took an hour from them, now and again, in spite of Jack Hawley's warning: it would be time enough to dismiss them, if dismissal should be necessary, when the rigour of the season was over. Hawley had made their acquaintance—he had met them at my fireside—and thought them a ridiculous pair. Learning that he was a painter they tried to approach him, to show him too that they were the real thing; but he looked at them, across the big room, as if they were miles away; they were a compendium of everything he most objected to in the social system of his country. Such people as that, all convention and patent-leather, with ejaculations that stopped conversation, had no business in a studio. A studio was a place to learn to see, and how could you see through a pair of feather-beds?

The main inconvenience I suffered at their hands was that at first I was shy of letting it break upon them that my artful little servant had begun to sit for me for "Rutland Ramsay." They knew I had been odd enough—they were prepared by this time to allow oddity to artists—to pick a foreign vagabond out of the streets when I might have had a person with whiskers and credentials; but it was some time before they learned how high I rated his accomplishments. They found him in an attitude more than once, but they never doubted I was doing him as an organ-grinder. There were several things they never guessed, and one of them was that for a striking scene in the novel, in which a footman briefly figured, it occurred to me to make use of Major Monarch as the menial. I kept putting this off, I didn't like to ask him to don the livery—besides the difficulty of finding a livery to fit him. At last, one day late in the winter, when I was at work on the despised Oronte, who caught one's idea on the wing, and was in the glow of feeling myself go very straight, they came in, the Major and his wife, with their society laugh about nothing (there was less and less to laugh at); came in like country-callers—they always reminded me of that—who have walked across the park after church and are presently persuaded to stay to luncheon. Luncheon was over, but they could stay to tea—I knew they wanted it. The fit was on me, however, and I couldn't let my ardour cool and my work wait, with the fading daylight, while my model prepared it. So I asked Mrs. Monarch if she would mind laying it out—a request which for an instant brought all the blood to her face. Her eyes were on her husband's for a second, and some mute telegraphy passed between them. Their folly was over the next instant; his cheerful shrewdness put an end to it. So far from pitying their wounded pride, I must add, I was moved to give it as complete a lesson as I could. They bustled about together and got out the cups and saucers and made the kettle boil. I know they felt as if they were waiting on my servant, and when the tea was prepared, I said: "He'll have a cup, please—he's tired." Mrs. Monarch brought him one where he stood, and he took it from her as if he had been a gentleman at a party squeezing a crush-hat with an elbow.

Then it came over me that she had made a great effort for me—made it with a kind of nobleness—and that I owed her a compensation. Each time I saw her after this I wondered what the compensation could be. I couldn't go on doing the wrong thing to oblige them. Oh, it was the wrong thing, the stamp of the work for which they sat—Hawley was not the only person to say it now. I sent in a large number of the drawings I had made for "Rutland Ramsay," and I received a warning that was more to the point than Hawley's. The artistic adviser of the house for which I was working was of opinion that many of my illustrations were not what had been looked for. Most of these illustrations were the subjects in which the Monarchs had figured. Without going into the question of what *had* been looked for, I had to face the fact that at this rate I shouldn't get the other books to do. I hurled myself in despair on Miss Churm—I put her through all her paces. I not only adopted Oronte publicly as my hero, but one morning when the Major looked in to see if I didn't require him to finish a *Cheapside* figure for which he had begun to sit the week before, I told him I had changed my mind—I'd do the draw-from my man. At this my visitor turned pale and stood looking at me. "Is *he* your idea of an English gentleman?" he asked.

I was disappointed, I was nervous, I wanted to get on with my work; so I replied with irritation: "Oh my dear Major—I can't be ruined for *you!*"

It was a horrid speech, but he stood another moment—after which, without a word, he quitted the studio. I drew a long breath, for I said to myself that I shouldn't see him again. I hadn't told him definitely that I was in danger of having my work rejected, but I was vexed at his not having felt the catastrophe in the air, read with me the moral of our fruitless collaboration, the lesson that in the deceptive atmosphere of art even the highest respectability may fail of being plastic.

I didn't owe my friends money, but I did see them again. They reappeared together three days later, and, given all the other facts, there was something tragic in that one. It was a clear proof they could find nothing else in life to do. They had threshed the matter out in a dismal conference—they had digested the bad news that they were not in for the series. If they weren't useful to me even for the *Cheapside*, their function seemed difficult to determine, and I could only judge at first that they had come, forgivingly, decorously, to take a last leave. This made me rejoice in secret that I had little leisure for a scene; I had placed both my other models in position together and I was pegging away at a drawing from which I hoped to derive glory. It had been suggested by the passage in which Rutland Ramsay, drawing up a chair to Artemisia's piano-stool, says extraordinary things to her while she ostensibly fingers out a difficult piece of music. I had done Miss Churm at the piano before—it was an attitude in which she knew how to take on an absolutely poetic grace. I wished the two figures to "compose" together with intensity, and my little Italian had entered perfectly into my conception. The pair were vividly before me, the piano had been pulled out; it was a charming show of blended youth and murmured love, which I had only to catch and keep. My visitors stood and looked at it, and I was friendly to them over my shoulder.

They made no response, but I was used to silent company and went on with my work, only a little disconcerted—even though exhilarated by the sense that *this* was at least the ideal thing—at not having got rid of them after all. Presently I heard Mrs. Monarch's sweet voice beside or rather above me: "I wish her hair were a little better done." I looked up and she was staring with a strange fixedness at Miss Churm, whose back was turned to her. "Do you mind my just touching it?" she went on—a question which made me spring up for an instant as with the instinctive fear that she might do the young lady a harm. But she quieted me with a glance I shall never forget—I confess I should like to have been able to paint *that*—and went for a moment to my model. She spoke to her softly, laying a hand on her shoulder and bending over her; and as the girl, understanding, gratefully assented, she disposed her rough curls, with a few quick passes, in such a way as to make Miss Churm's head twice as charming. It was one of the most heroic personal services I've ever seen rendered. Then Mrs. Monarch turned away with a low sigh and, looking about her as if for something to do, stooped to the floor with a noble humility and picked up a dirty rag that had dropped out of my paint-box.

The Major meanwhile had also been looking for something to do, and, wandering to the other end of the studio, saw before him my breakfast-things neglected, unremoved. "I say, can't I be useful *here?*" he called out to me with an irrepressible quaver. I assented with a laugh that I fear was awkward, and for the next ten minutes, while I worked, I heard the light clatter of china and the tinkle of spoons and glass. Mrs. Monarch assisted her husband—they washed up my crockery, they put it away. They wandered off into my little scullery, and I afterwards found that they had cleaned my knives and that my slender stock of plates had an unprecedented surface. When it came over me, the latent eloquence of what they were doing, I confess that my drawing was blurred for a moment—the picture swam. They had accepted their failure, but they couldn't accept their fate. They had bowed their heads in bewilderment to the perverse and cruel law in virtue of which the real thing could be so much less precious than the unreal; but they didn't want to starve. If my servants were my models, then my models might be my servants. They would reverse the parts—the others would sit for the ladies and gentlemen and *they* would do the work. They would still be in the studio—it was an intense dumb appeal to me not to turn them out. "Take us on," they wanted to say—"we'll do *anything*."

My pencil dropped from my hand; my sitting was spoiled and I got rid of my sitters, who were also evidently rather mystified and awestruck. Then, alone with the Major and his wife I had a most uncomfortable moment. He put their prayer into a single sentence: "I say, you know—just let *us* do for you, can't you?" I couldn't—it was dreadful to see them emptying my slops; but I pretended I could, to oblige them, for about a week. Then I gave them a sum of money to go away, and I never saw them again. I obtained the remaining books, but my friend Hawley repeats that Major and Mrs. Monarch did me a permanent harm, got me into false ways. If it be true I'm content to have paid the price—for the memory.

The Hiltons' Holiday

SARAH ORNE JEWETT

(1849–1909)

I

There was a bright, full moon in the clear sky, and the sunset was still shining faintly in the west. Dark woods stood all about the old Hilton farmhouse, save down the hill, westward, where lay the shadowy fields which John Hilton, and his father before him, had cleared and tilled with much toil—the small fields to which they had given the industry and even affection of their honest lives.

John Hilton was sitting on the doorstep of his house. As he moved his head in and out of the shadows, turning now and then to speak to his wife, who sat just within the doorway, one could see his good face, rough and somewhat unkempt, as if he were indeed a creature of the shady woods and brown earth, instead of the noisy town. It was late in the long spring evening, and he had just come from the lower field as cheerful as a boy, proud of having finished the planting of his potatoes.

"I had to do my last row mostly by feelin'," he said to his wife. "I'm proper glad I pushed through, an' went back an' ended off after supper. 'Twould have taken me a good part o' to-morrow mornin', an' broke my day."

"'Tain't no use for ye to work yourself all to pieces, John," answered the woman, quickly. "I declare it does seem harder than ever that we couldn't have kep' our boy; he'd been comin' fourteen years old this fall, most a grown man, and he'd work right 'longside of ye now the whole time."

"'Twas hard to lose him; I do seem to miss little John," said the father, sadly. "I expect there was reasons why 'twas best. I feel able an' smart to work; my father was a girt strong man, an' a monstrous worker afore me. 'Tain't that; but I was thinkin' myself to-day what a sight o' company the boy would ha' been. You know, small's he was, how I could trust him to leave anywheres with the team, and how he'd beseech to go with me wherever I was goin'; always right in my tracks I used to tell 'em. Poor little John, for all he was so young he had a great deal o' judgment; he'd ha' made a likely man."

The mother sighed heavily as she sat within the shadow.

"But then there's the little girls, a sight o' help an' company," urged the father, eagerly, as if it were wrong to dwell upon sorrow and loss. "Katy, she's most as good as a boy, except that she ain't very rugged. She's a real little farmer, she's helped me a sight this spring; an' you've got Susan Ellen, that makes a complete little housekeeper for ye as far as she's learnt. I don't see but we're better off than most folks, each on us having a workmate."

"That's so, John," acknowledged Mrs. Hilton, wistfully, beginning to rock steadily in her straight splint-bottom chair. It was always a good sign when she rocked.

"Where be the little girls so late?" asked their father. "'Tis gettin' long past eight o'clock. I don't know when we've all set up so late, but it's so kind o' summer-like an' pleasant. Why, where be they gone?"

"I've told ye; only over to Becker's folks," answered the mother. "I don't see myself what keeps 'em so late; they beseeched me after supper till I let 'em go. They're all in a dazzle with the new teacher; she asked 'em to come over. They say she's unusual smart with 'rethmetic, but she has a kind of gorpen look to me. She's goin' to give Katy some pieces for her doll, but I told Katy she ought to be ashamed wantin' dolls' pieces, big as she's gittin' to be. I don't know's she ought, though; she ain't but nine this summer."

"Let her take her comfort," said the kind-hearted man. "Them things draws her to the teacher, an' makes them acquainted. Katy's shy with new folks, more so'n Susan Ellen, who's of the business kind. Katy's shy-feelin' and wishful."

"I don't know but she is," agreed the mother slowly. "Ain't it sing'lar how well acquainted you be with that one, an' I with Susan Ellen? 'Twas always so from the first. I'm doubtful sometimes our Katy ain't one that'll be like to get married—anyways not about here. She lives right with herself, but Susan Ellen ain't nothin' when she's alone, she's always after company; all the boys is waitin' on her a'ready. I ain't afraid but she'll take her pick when the time comes. I expect to see Susan Ellen well settled—she feels grown up now—but Katy don't care one mite 'bout none o' them things. She wants to be rovin' out o' doors. I do believe she'd stand an' hark to a bird the whole forenoon."

"Perhaps she'll grow up to be a teacher," suggested John Hilton. "She takes to her books more'n the other one. I should like one on 'em to be a teacher same's my mother was. They're good girls as anybody's got."

"So they be," said the mother, with unusual gentleness, and the creak of her rocking-chair was heard, regular as the ticking of a clock. The night breeze stirred in the great woods, and the sound of a brook that went falling down the hillside grew louder and louder. Now and then one could hear the plaintive chirp of a bird. The moon glittered with whiteness like a winter moon, and shone upon the low-roofed house until its small window-panes gleamed like silver, and one could almost see the colours of a blooming bush of lilac that grew in a sheltered angle by the kitchen door. There was an incessant sound of frogs in the lowlands.

"Be you sound asleep, John?" asked the wife presently.

"I don't know but what I was a'most," said the tired man, starting a little. "I should laugh if I was to fall sound asleep right here on the step; 'tis the bright night, I expect, makes my eyes feel heavy, an' 'tis so peaceful. I was up an' dressed a little past four an' out to work. Well, well!" and he laughed sleepily and rubbed his eyes. "Where's the little girls? I'd better step along an' meet 'em."

"I wouldn't just yet; they'll get home all right, but 'tis late for 'em certain. I don't want 'em keepin' Mis' Becker's folks up neither. There, le's wait a few minutes," urged Mrs. Hilton.

"I've be'n a-thinkin' all day I'd like to give the child'n some kind of a treat," said the father, wide awake now. "I hurried up my work 'cause I had it so in mind. They don't have the opportunities some do, an' I want 'em to know the world, an' not stay right here on the farm like a couple o' bushes."

"They're a sight better off not to be so full o' notions as some is," protested the mother, suspiciously.

"Certain," answered the farmer; "but they're good, bright child'n, an' commencin' to take a sight o' notice. I want 'em to have all we can give 'em. I want 'em to see how other folks does things."

"Why, so do I"—here the rocking-chair stopped ominously—"but so long's they're contented——"

"Contented ain't all in this world; hopper-toads may have that quality an' spend all their time a-blinkin'. I don't know's bein' contented is all there is to look for in a child. Ambition's somethin' to me."

"Now you've got your mind on to some plot or other." (The rocking-chair began to move again.) "Why can't you talk right out?"

"'Tain't nothin' special," answered the good man, a little ruffled; he was never prepared for his wife's mysterious powers of divination. "Well there, you do find things out the master! I only thought perhaps I'd take 'em to-morrow, an' go off somewhere if 'twas a good day. I've been promisin' for a good while I'd take 'em to Topham Corners; they've never been there since they was very small."

"I believe you want a good time yourself. You ain't never got over bein' a boy." Mrs. Hilton seemed much amused. "There, go if you want to an' take 'em; they've got their summer hats an' new dresses. I don't know o' nothin' that stands in the way. I should sense it better if there was a circus or anythin' to go to. Why don't you wait an' let the girls pick 'em some strawberries or nice ros'berries, and then they could take an' sell 'em to the stores?"

John Hilton reflected deeply. "I should like to get me some good yellow-turnip seed to plant late. I ain't more'n satisfied with what I've been gettin' o' late years o' Ira Speed. An' I'm goin' to provide me with a good hoe; mine's gettin' wore out an' all shackly. I can't seem to fix it good."

"Them's excuses," observed Mrs. Hilton, with friendly tolerance. "You just cover up the hoe with somethin', if you get it—I would. Ira Speed's so jealous he'll remember it of you this twenty year, your goin' an' buyin' a new hoe o' anybody but him."

"I've always thought 'twas a free country," said John Hilton, soberly. "I don't want to vex Ira neither; he favours us all he can in trade. 'Tis difficult for him to spare a cent, but he's as honest as daylight."

At this moment there was a sudden sound of young voices, and a pair of young figures came out from the shadow of the woods into the moonlighted open space. An old cock crowed loudly from his perch in the shed, as if he were a herald of royalty. The little girls were hand in hand, and a brisk young dog capered about them as they came.

"Wa'n't it dark gittin' home through the woods this time o' night?" asked the mother, hastily, and not without reproach.

"I don't love to have you gone so late; mother an' me was timid about ye, and you've kep' Mis' Becker's folks up, I expect," said their father, regretfully. "I don't want to have it said that my little girls ain't got good manners."

"The teacher had a party," chirped Susan Ellen, the elder of the two children. "Goin' home from school she asked the Grover boys, an' Mary an' Sarah Speed. An' Mis' Becker was real pleasant to us: she passed round some cake, an' handed us sap sugar on one of her best plates, an' we played games an' sung some pieces too. Mis' Becker thought we did real well. I can pick out most of a tune on the cabinet organ; teacher says she'll give me lessons."

"I want to know, dear!" exclaimed John Hilton.

"Yes, an' we played Copenhagen, an' took sides spellin', an' Katy beat everybody spellin' there was there."

Katy had not spoken, she was not so strong as her sister, and while Susan Ellen stood a step or two away addressing her eager little audience, Katy had seated herself close to her father on the doorstep. He put his arm around her shoulder, and drew her close to his side, where she stayed.

"Ain't you got nothin' to tell, daughter?" he asked, looking down fondly, and Katy gave a pleased little sigh for answer.

"Tell 'em what's goin' to be the last day o' school, and about our trimmin' the schoolhouse," she said, and Susan Ellen gave the programme in most spirited fashion.

" 'Twill be a great time," said the mother, when she had finished. "I don't see why folks want to go trapesin' off to strange places when such things is happenin' right about 'em." But the children did not observe her mysterious air. "Come, you must step yourselves right to bed."

They all went into the dark, warm house, the bright moon shone upon it steadily all night, and the lilac flowers were shaken by no breath of wind until the early dawn.

II

The Hiltons always waked early. So did their neighbours, the crows and song-sparrows and robins, the light-footed foxes and squirrels in the woods. When John Hilton waked, before five o'clock, an hour later than usual because he had sat up so late, he opened the house door and came out into the yard, crossing the short green turf hurriedly as if the day were too far spent for any loitering. The magnitude of the plan for taking a whole day of pleasure confronted him seriously, but the weather was fair, and his wife, whose disapproval could not have been set aside, had accepted and even smiled upon the great project. It was inevitable now that he and the children should go to Topham Corners. Mrs. Hilton had the pleasure of waking them, and telling the news.

In a few minutes they came frisking out to talk over the great plans. The cattle were already fed, and their father was milking. The only sign of high festivity was the wagon pulled out into the yard, with both seats put in as if it were Sunday; but Mr. Hilton still wore his everyday clothes, and Susan Ellen suffered instantly from disappointment.

"Ain't we goin', father?" she asked, complainingly, but he nodded and smiled at her, even though the cow, impatient to get to pasture, kept whisking her rough tail across his face. He held his head down and spoke cheerfully, in spite of this vexation.

"Yes, sister, we're goin' certain, an' goin' to have a great time, too." Susan Ellen thought that he seemed like a boy at that delightful moment, and felt new sympathy and pleasure at once. "You go an' help mother about breakfast an' them things; we want to get off quick's we can. You coax mother now, both on ye, an' see if she won't go with us."

"She said she wouldn't be hired to," responded Susan Ellen. "She says it's goin' to be hot, an' she's laid out to go over an' see how her aunt Tamsen Brooks is this afternoon."

The father gave a little sigh; then he took heart again. The truth was that his wife made light of the contemplated pleasure, and, much as he usually valued her companionship and approval, it was sure that they should have a better time without her. It was impossible, however, not to feel guilty of disloyalty at the thought. Even though she might be completely unconscious of his best ideals, he only loved her and the ideals the more, and bent his energies to satisfying her indefinite expectations. His wife still kept much of that youthful beauty which Susan Ellen seemed likely to reproduce.

An hour later the best wagon was ready, and the great expedition set forth. The little dog sat apart, and barked as if it fell entirely upon him to voice the general excitement. Both seats were in the wagon, but the empty place testified to Mrs. Hilton's unyielding disposition. She had wondered why one broad seat would not do, but John Hilton meekly suggested that the wagon looked better. The little girls sat on the back seat dressed alike in their Sunday hats of straw with blue ribbons, and their little plaid shawls pinned neatly about their small shoulders. They wore grey thread gloves, and sat very straight. Susan Ellen was half a head the taller, but otherwise, from behind, they looked much alike. As for their father, he was in his Sunday best—a plain black coat, and a winter hat of felt, which was heavy and rusty-looking for that warm early-summer day. He had it in mind to buy a new straw hat at Topham, so that this with the turnip-seed and the hoe made three important reasons for going.

"Remember an' lay off your shawls when you get there, an' carry them over your arms," said the mother, clucking like an excited hen to her chickens. "They'll do to keep the dust off your new dresses goin' and comin'. An' when you eat your dinners don't get spots on you, an' don't point at folks as you ride by, an' stare, or they'll know you came from the country. An' John, you call into Cousin Ad'line Marlow's an' see how they all be, an' tell her I expect her over certain to stop a while before hayin'. It always eases her phthisic to git up here on the highland, an' I've got a new notion about doin' over her best-room carpet sence I see her that'll save rippin' one breadth. An' don't come home all wore out; an', John, don't you go an' buy me no kickshaws to fetch home. I ain't a child, an' you ain't got no money to waste. I expect you'll go, like's not, an' buy you some kind of a foolish boy's hat; do look an' see if it's reasonable good straw, an' won't splinter all off round the edge. An' you mind, John—"

"Yes, yes, hold on!" cried John, impatiently; then he cast a last affectionate, reassuring look at her face, flushed with the hurry and responsibility of starting them off in proper shape. "I wish you was goin' too," he said, smiling. "I do so!" Then the old horse started, and they went out at the bars, and began the careful long descent of the hill. The young dog, tethered to the lilac bush, was frantic with piteous appeals; the little girls piped their eager good-byes again and again, and their father turned many times to look back and wave his hand. As for their mother, she stood alone and watched them out of sight.

There was one place far out on the high road where she could catch a last glimpse of the wagon, and she waited what seemed a very long time until it appeared and then was lost to sight again behind a low hill.

"They're nothing' but a pack o' child'n together," she said aloud, and then felt lonelier than she expected. She even stooped and patted the unresigned little dog as she passed him, going into the house.

The occasion was so much more important than anyone had foreseen that both the little girls were speechless. It seemed at first like going to church in new clothes, or to a funeral; they hardly knew how to behave at the beginning of a whole day of pleasure. They made grave bows at such persons of their acquaintance as happened to be straying in the road. Once or twice they stopped before a farmhouse, while their father talked an inconsiderately long time with someone about the crops and the weather and even dwelt upon town business and the doings of the selectmen, which might be talked of at any time. The explanations that he gave of their excursion seemed quite unnecessary. It was made entirely clear that he had a little business to do at Topham Corners, and thought he had better give the little girls a ride; they had been very steady at school, and he had finished planting, and could take the day as well as not. Soon, however, they all felt as if such an excursion were an everyday affair, and Susan Ellen began to ask eager questions, while Katy silently sat apart enjoying herself as she never had done before. She liked to see the strange houses, and the children who belonged to them; it was delightful to find flowers that she knew growing all along the road, no matter how far she went from home. Each small homestead looked its best and pleasantest, and shared the exquisite beauty that early summer made, shared the luxury of greenness and floweriness that decked the rural world. There was an early peony or a late lilac in almost every dooryard.

It was seventeen miles to Topham. After a while they seemed very far from home, having left the hills far behind, and descended to a great level country with fewer tracts of woodland, and wider fields where the crops were much more forward. The houses were all painted, and the roads were smoother and wider. It had been so pleasant driving along that Katy dreaded going into the strange town when she first caught sight of it, though Susan Ellen kept asking with bold fretfulness if they were not almost there. They counted the steeples of four churches, and their father presently showed them the Topham Academy, where their grandmother once went to school, and told them that perhaps some day they would go there too. Katy's heart gave a strange leap; it was such a tremendous thing to think of, but instantly the suggestion was transformed for her into one of the certainties of life. She looked with solemn awe at the tall belfry, and the long rows of windows in the front of the academy, there where it stood high and white among the clustering trees. She hoped that they were going to drive by, but something forbade her taking the responsibility of saying so.

Soon the children found themselves among the crowded village houses. Their father turned to look at them with affectionate solicitude.

"Now sit up straight and appear pretty," he whispered to them. "We're among the best people now, an' I want folks to think well of you."

"I guess we're just as good as they be," remarked Susan Ellen, looking at some innocent passers-by with dark suspicion, but Katy tried indeed to sit straight, and folded her hands prettily in her lap, and wished with all her heart to be pleasing for her father's sake. Just then an elderly woman saw the wagon and the sedate party it carried, and smiled so kindly that it seemed to Katy as if Topham Corners had welcomed and received them. She smiled back again as if this hospitable person were an old friend, and entirely forgot that the eyes of all Topham had been upon her.

"There, now we're coming to an elegant house that I want you to see; you'll never forget it," said John Hilton. "It's where Judge Masterson lives, the great lawyer; the handsomest house in the county, everybody says."

"Do you know him, father?" asked Susan Ellen.

"I do," answered John Hilton, proudly. "Him and my mother went to school together in their young days, and were always called the two best scholars of their time. The judge called to see her once; he stopped to our house to see her when I was a boy. An' then, some years ago—you've heard me tell how I was on the jury, an' when he heard my name spoken he looked at me sharp, and asked if I wa'n't the son of Catharine Winn, an' spoke most beautiful of your grandmother, an' how well he remembered their young days together."

"I like to hear about that," said Katy.

"She had it pretty hard, I'm afraid, up on the old farm. She was keepin' school in our district when father married her—that's the main reason I backed 'em down when they wanted to tear the old schoolhouse all to pieces," confided John Hilton, turning eagerly. "They all say she lived longer up here on the hill than she could anywhere, but she never had her health. I wa'n't but a boy when she died. Father an' me lived alone afterward till the time your mother come; 'twas a good while, too; I wa'n't married so young as some. 'Twas lonesome, I tell you; father was plumb discouraged losin' of his wife, an' her long sickness an' all set him back, an' we'd work all day on the land an' never say a word. I s'pose 'tis bein' so lonesome early in life that makes me so pleased to have some nice girls growin' up around me now."

There was a tone in her father's voice that drew Katy's heart toward him with new affection. She dimly understood, but Susan Ellen was less interested. They had often heard this story before, but to one child it was always new and to the other old. Susan Ellen was apt to think it tiresome to hear about her grandmother, who, being dead, was hardly worth talking about.

"There's Judge Masterson's place," said their father in an everyday manner, as they turned a corner, and came into full view of the beautiful old white house standing behind its green trees and terraces and lawns. The children had never imagined anything so stately and fine, and even Susan Ellen exclaimed with pleasure. At that moment they saw an old gentleman, who carried himself with great dignity, coming slowly down the wide, box-bordered path toward the gate.

"There he is now, there's the judge!" whispered John Hilton, excitedly, reining his horse quickly to the green roadside. "He's goin' downtown to his office; we can wait right here an' see him. I can't expect him to remember me; it's been a good many years. Now you are goin' to see the great Judge Masterson!"

There was a quiver of expectation in their hearts. The judge stopped at his gate, hesitating a moment before he lifted the latch, and glanced up the street at the country wagon with its two prim little girls on the back seat, and the eager man who drove. They seemed to be waiting for something; the old horse was nibbling at the fresh roadside grass. The judge was used to being looked at with interest, and responded now with a smile as he came out to the sidewalk, and unexpectedly turned their way. Then he suddenly lifted his hat with grave politeness, and came directly toward them.

"Good morning, Mr. Hilton," he said. "I am very glad to see you, sir," and Mr. Hilton, the little girls' own father, took off his hat with equal courtesy, and bent forward to shake hands.

Susan Ellen cowered and wished herself away, but little Katy sat straighter than ever, with joy in her father's pride and pleasure shining in her pale, flower-like little face.

"These are your daughters, I am sure," said the old gentleman, kindly, taking Susan Ellen's limp and reluctant hand; but when he looked at Katy, his face brightened. "How she recalls your mother!" he said with great feeling. "I am glad to see this dear child. You must come to see me with your father, my dear," he added, still looking at her. "Bring both little girls, and let them run about the old garden; the cherries will soon be getting ripe," said Judge Masterson, hospitably. "Perhaps you will have time to stop this afternoon as you go home?"

"I should call it a great pleasure if you would come and see us again some time. You may be driving our way, sir," said John Hilton.

"Not very often in these days," answered the old judge. "I thank you for the kind invitation. I should like to see the fine view again from your hill westward. Can I serve you in any way while you are in town? Good-bye, my little friends!"

Then they parted, but not before Katy, the shy Katy, whose hand the judge still held unconsciously while he spoke, had reached forward as he said good-bye, and lifted her face to kiss him. She could not have told why, except that she felt drawn to something in the serious, worn face. For the first time in her life the child had felt the charm of manners; perhaps she owned a kinship between that which made him what he was, and the spark of nobleness and purity in her own simple soul. She turned again and again to look back at him as they drove away.

"Now you have seen one of the first gentlemen in the country," said their father. "It was worth comin' twice as far——" But he did not say any more, nor turn as usual to look in the children's faces.

In the chief business street of Topham a great many country wagons like the Hiltons' were fastened to the posts, and there seemed to our holiday-makers to be a great deal of noise and excitement.

"Now I've got to do my errands, and we can let the horse rest and feed," said John Hilton. "I'll slip his headstall right off, an' put on his halter. I'm goin' to buy him a real good treat o' oats. First we'll go an' buy me my straw hat; I feel as if this one looked a little past to wear in Topham. We'll buy the things we want, an' then we'll walk all along the street, so you can look in the windows an' see the han'some things, same's your mother likes to. What was it mother told you about your shawls?"

"To take 'em off an' carry 'em over our arms," piped Susan Ellen, without comment, but in the interest of alighting and finding themselves afoot upon the pavement the shawls were forgotten. The children stood at the doorway of a shop while their father went inside, and they tried to see what the Topham shapes of bonnets were like, as their mother had advised them; but everything was exciting and confusing, and they could arrive at no decision. When Mr. Hilton came out with a hat in his hand to be seen in a better light, Katy whispered that she wished he would buy a shiny one like Judge Masterson's; but her father only smiled and shook his head, and said that they were plain folks, he and Katy. There were dry-goods for sale in the same shop, and a young clerk who was measuring linen kindly pulled off some pretty labels with gilded edges and gay pictures, and gave them to the little girls, to their exceeding joy. He may have had small sisters at home, this friendly lad, for he took pains to find two pretty blue boxes besides, and was rewarded by their beaming gratitude.

It was a famous day; they even became used to seeing so many people pass. The village was full of its morning activity, and Susan Ellen gained a new respect for her father, and an increased sense of her own consequence, because even in Topham several persons knew him and called him familiarly by name. The meeting with an old man who had once been a neighbour seemed to give Mr. Hilton the greatest pleasure. The old man called to them from a house doorway as they were passing, and they all went in. The children seated themselves wearily on the wooden step, but their father shook his old friend eagerly by the hand, and declared that he was delighted to see him so well and enjoying the fine weather.

"Oh, yes," said the old man, in a feeble, quavering voice, "I'm astonishin' well for my age. I don't complain, John, I don't complain."

They talked long together of people whom they had known in the past, and Katy, being a little tired, was glad to rest, and sat still with her hands folded, looking about the front yard. There were some kinds of flowers that she never had seen before.

"This is the one that looks like my mother," her father said, and touched Katy's shoulder to remind her to stand up and let herself be seen. "Judge Masterson saw the resemblance; we met him at his gate this morning."

"Yes, she certain does look like your mother, John," said the old man, looking pleasantly at Katy, who found that she liked him better than at first. "She does, certain; the best of young folks is, they remind us of the old ones. 'Tis nateral to cling to life, folks say, but for me, I git impatient at times. Most everybody's gone now, an' I want to be goin'. 'Tis somethin' before me, an' I want to have it over with. I want to be there 'long o' the rest o' the folks. I expect to last quite a while though; I may see ye couple o' times more, John."

John Hilton responded cheerfully, and the children were urged to pick some flowers. The old man awed them with his impatience to be gone. There was such a townful of people about him and he seemed as lonely as if he were the last survivor of a former world. Until that moment they had felt as if everything was just beginning.

"Now I want to buy somethin' pretty for your mother," said Mr. Hilton as they went soberly away down the street, the children keeping fast hold of his hands. "By now the old horse will have eat his dinner and had a good rest, so pretty soon we can jog along home. I'm goin' to take you round by the academy, and the old North meeting-house where Dr. Barstow used to preach. Can't you think o' somethin' that your mother 'd want?" he asked suddenly, confronted by a man's difficulty of choice.

"She was talkin' about wantin' a new pepper-box, one day; the top o' the old one won't stay on," suggested Susan Ellen, with delightful readiness. "Can't we have some candy, father?"

"Yes, ma'am," said John Hilton, smiling and swinging her hand to and fro as they walked. "I feel as if some would be good myself. What's all this?" They were passing a photographer's doorway with its enticing array of portraits. "I do declare!" he exclaimed, excitedly, "I'm goin' to have our pictures taken; 'twill please your mother more'n a little."

This was, perhaps, the greatest triumph of the day, except the delightful meeting with the judge; they sat in a row, with the father in the middle, and there was no doubt as to the excellence of the likeness. The best hats had to be taken off because they cast a shadow, but they were not missed, as their owners had feared. Both Susan Ellen and Katy looked their brightest and best; their eager young faces would forever shine there; the joy of the holiday was mirrored in the little picture. They did not know why their father was so pleased with it; they would not know until age had dowered them with the riches of association and remembrance.

Just at nightfall the Hiltons reached home again, tired out and happy. Katy had climbed over into the front seat beside her father, because that was always her place when they went to church on Sundays. It was a cool evening, there was a fresh sea wind that brought a light mist with it, and the sky was fast growing cloudy. Somehow the children looked different; it seemed to their mother as if they had grown older and taller since they went away in the morning, and as if they belonged to the town now as much as to the country. The greatness of their day's experience had left her far behind, the day had been silent and lonely without them, and she had had their supper ready, and been watching anxiously, ever since five o'clock. As for the children themselves they had little to say at first—they had eaten their luncheon early on the way to Topham. Susan Ellen was childishly cross, but Katy was pathetic and wan. They could hardly wait to show the picture, and their mother was as much pleased as everybody had expected.

"There, what did make you wear your shawls?" she exclaimed a moment afterward, reproachfully. "You ain't been an' wore 'em all day long? I wanted folks to see how pretty your new dresses was, if I did make 'em. Well, well! I wish more'n ever now I'd gone an' seen to ye!"

"An' here's the pepper-box!" said Katy, in a pleased, unconscious tone.

"That really is what I call beautiful," said Mrs. Hilton, after a long and doubtful look. "Our other one was only tin. I never did look so high as a chiny one with flowers, but I can get us another any time for every day. That's a proper hat, as good as you could have got, John. Where's your new hoe?" she asked, as he came toward her from the barn, smiling with satisfaction.

"I declare to Moses if I didn't forget all about it," meekly acknowledged the leader of the great excursion. "That an' my yellow-turnip seed, too; they went clean out o' my head, there was so many other things to think of. But 'tain't no sort o' matter; I can get a hoe just as well to Ira Speed's."

His wife could not help laughing. "You an' the little girls have had a great time. They was full o' wonder to me about everythin', and I expect they'll talk about it for a week. I guess we was right about havin' 'em see somethin' more o' the world."

"Yes," answered John Hilton, with humility, "yes, we did have a beautiful day. I didn't expect so much. They looked as nice as anybody, and appeared so modest an' pretty. The little girls will remember it perhaps by an' by. I guess they won't never forget this day they had 'long o' father."

It was evening again, the frogs were piping in the lower meadows, and in the woods, higher up the great hill, a little owl began to hoot. The sea air, salt and heavy, was blowing in over the country at the end of the hot, bright day. A lamp was lighted in the house, the happy children were chatting together, and supper was waiting. The father and mother lingered for a moment outside and looked down over the shadowy fields; then they went in, without speaking. The great day was over, and they shut the door.

A Shameful Affair

KATE CHOPIN

(1851–1904)

Mildred Orme, seated in the snuggest corner of the big front porch of the Kraummer farmhouse, was as content as a girl need hope to be.

This was no such farm as one reads about in humorous fiction. Here were swelling acres where the undulating wheat gleamed in the sun like a golden sea. For silver there was the Meramec—or, better, it was pure crystal, for here and there one might look clean through it down to where the pebbles lay like green and yellow gems. Along the river's edge trees were growing to the very water, and in it, sweeping it when they were willows.

The house itself was big and broad, as country houses should be. The master was big and broad, too. The mistress was small and thin, and it was always she who went out at noon to pull the great clanging bell that called the farmhands in to dinner.

From her agreeable corner where she lounged with her Browning or her Ibsen, Mildred watched the woman do this every day. Yet when the clumsy farmhands all came tramping up the steps and crossed the porch in going to their meal that was served within, she never looked at them. Why should she? Farmhands are not so very nice to look at, and she was nothing of an anthropologist. But once when the half dozen men came along, a paper which she had laid carelessly upon the railing was blown across their path. One of them picked it up, and when he had mounted the steps restored it to her. He was young, and brown, of course, as the sun had made him. He had nice blue eyes. His fair hair was dishevelled. His shoulders were broad and square and his limbs strong and clean. A not unpicturesque figure in the rough attire that bared his throat to view and gave perfect freedom to his every motion.

Mildred did not make these several observations in the half second that she looked at him in courteous acknowledgment. It took her as many days to note them all. For she signaled him out each time that he passed her, meaning to give him a condescending little smile, as she knew how. But he never looked at her. To be sure, clever young women of twenty, who are handsome, besides, who have refused their half dozen offers and are settling down to the conviction that life is a tedious affair, are not going to care a straw whether farmhands look at them or not. And Mildred did not care, and the thing would not have occupied her a moment if Satan had not intervened, in offering the employment which natural conditions had failed to supply. It was summer time; she was idle; she was piqued, and that was the beginning of the shameful affair.

"Who are these men, Mrs. Kraummer, that work for you? Where do you pick them up?"

"Oh, ve picks 'em up everyvere. Some is neighbors, some is tramps, and so."

"And that broad-shouldered young fellow—is he a neighbor? The one who handed me my paper the other day—you remember?"

"Gott, no! You might yust as well say he vas a tramp. Aber he vorks like a steam ingine."

"Well, he's an extremely disagreeable-looking man. I should think you'd be afraid to have him about, not knowing him."

"Vat you vant to be 'fraid for?" laughed the little woman. "He don't talk no more un ven he vas deef und dumb. I didn't t'ought you vas sooch a baby."

"But, Mrs. Kraummer, I don't want you to think I'm a baby, as you say —a coward, as you mean. Ask the man if he will drive me to church tomorrow. You see, I'm not so very much afraid of him," she added with a smile.

The answer which this unmannerly farmhand returned to Mildred's request was simply a refusal. He could not drive her to church because he was going fishing.

"Aber," offered good Mrs. Kraummer, "Hans Platzfeldt will drive you to church, oder verever you vants. He vas a goot boy vat you can trust, dat Hans."

"Oh, thank him very much. But I find I have so many letters to write tomorrow, and it promises to be hot, too. I shan't care to go to church after all.

She could have cried for vexation. Snubbed by a farmhand! a tramp, perhaps. She, Mildred Orme, who ought really to have been with the rest of the family at Narragansett—who had come to seek in this retired spot the repose that would enable her to follow exalted lines of thought. She marveled at the problematic nature of farmhands.

After sending her the uncivil message already recorded, and as he passed beneath the porch where she sat, he did look at her finally, in a way to make her positively gasp at the sudden effrontery of the man.

But the inexplicable look stayed with her. She could not banish it.

II

It was not so very hot after all, the next day, when Mildred walked down the long narrow footpath that led through the bending wheat to the river. High above her waist reached the yellow grain. Mildred's brown eyes filled with a reflected golden light as they caught the glint of it, as she heard the trill that it answered to the gentle breeze. Anyone who has walked through the wheat in midsummer-time knows that sound.

In the woods it was sweet and solemn and cool. And there beside the river was the wretch who had annoyed her, first, with his indifference, then with the sudden boldness of his glance.

"Are you fishing?" she asked politely and with kindly dignity, which she supposed would define her position toward him. The inquiry lacked not pertinence, seeing that he sat motionless, with a pole in his hand and his eyes fixed on a cork that bobbed aimlessly on the water.

"Yes, madam," was his brief reply.

"It won't disturb you if I stand here a moment, to see what success you will have?"

"No, madam."

She stood very still, holding tight to the book she had brought with her.

Her straw hat had slipped disreputably to one side, over the wavy bronze-brown bang that half covered her forehead. Her cheeks were ripe with color that the sun had coaxed there; so were her lips.

All the other farmhands had gone forth in Sunday attire. Perhaps this one had none better than these working clothes that he wore. A feminine commiseration swept her at the thought. He spoke never a word. She wondered how many hours he could sit there, so patiently waiting for fish to come to his hook. For her part, the situation began to pall, and she wanted to change it at last.

"Let me try a moment, please? I have an idea."

"Yes, madam."

"The man is surely an idiot, with his monosyllables," she commented inwardly. But she remembered that monosyllables belong to a boor's equipment.

She laid her book carefully down and took the pole gingerly that he came to place in her hands. Then it was his turn to stand back and look respectfully and silently on at the absorbing performance.

"Oh!" cried the girl, suddenly, seized with excitement upon seeing the line dragged deep in the water.

"Wait, wait! Not yet."

He sprang to her side. With his eyes eagerly fastened on the tense line, he grasped the pole to prevent her drawing it, as her intention seemed to be. That is, he meant to grasp the pole, but instead, his brown hand came down upon Mildred's white one.

He started violently at finding himself so close to a bronze-brown tangle that almost swept his chin—to a hot cheek only a few inches away from his shoulder, to a pair of young, dark eyes that gleamed for an instant unconscious things into his own.

Then, why ever it happened, or how ever it happened, his arms were holding Mildred and he kissed her lips. She did not know if it was ten times or only once.

She looked around—her face milk-white—to see him disappear with rapid strides through the path that had brought her there. Then she was alone.

Only the birds had seen, and she could count on their discretion. She was not wildly indignant, as many would have been. Shame stunned her. But through it she gropingly wondered if she should tell the Kraummers that her chaste lips had been rifled of their innocence. Publish her own confusion? No! Once in her room she would give calm thought to the situation, and determine then how to act. The secret must remain her own: a hateful burden to bear alone until she could forget it.

III

And because she feared not to forget it, Mildred wept that night. All day long a hideous truth had been thrusting itself upon her that made her ask herself if she could be mad. She feared it. Else why was that kiss the most delicious thing she had known in her twenty years of life? The sting of it had never left her lips since it was pressed into them. The sweet trouble of it banished sleep from her pillow.

But Mildred would not bend the outward conditions of her life to serve any shameful whim that chanced to visit her soul, like an ugly dream. She would avoid nothing. She would go and come as always.

In the morning she found in her chair upon the porch the book she had left by the river. A fresh indignity! But she came and went as she intended to, and sat as usual upon the porch amid her familiar surroundings. When the Offender passed her by she knew it, though her eyes were never lifted. Are there only sight and sound to tell such things? She discerned it by a wave that swept her with confusion and she knew not what besides.

She watched him furtively, one day, when he talked with Farmer Kraummer out in the open. When he walked away she remained like one who has drunk much wine. Then unhesitatingly she turned and began her preparations to leave the Kraummer farmhouse.

When the afternoon was far spent they brought letters to her. One of them read like this:

"My Mildred, deary! I am only now at Narragansett, and so broke up not to find you. So you are down at that Kraummer farm, on the Iron Mountain. Well! What do you think of that delicious crank, Fred Evelyn? For a man must be a crank who does such things. Only fancy! Last year he chose to drive an engine back and forth across the plains. This year he tills the soil with laborers. Next year it will be something else as insane—because he likes to live more lives than one kind, and other Quixotic reasons. We are great chums. He writes me he's grown as strong as an ox. But he hasn't mentioned that you are there. I know you don't get on with him, for he isn't a bit intellectual—detests Ibsen and abuses Tolstoi. He doesn't read 'in books'—says they are spectacles for the shortsighted to look at life through. Don't snub him, dear, or be too hard on him; he has a heart of gold, if he is the first crank in America."

Mildred tried to think—to feel that the intelligence which this letter brought to her would take somewhat of the sting from the shame that tortured her. But it did not. She knew that it could not.

In the gathering twilight she walked again through the wheat that was heavy and fragrant with dew. The path was very long and very narrow. When she was midway she saw the Offender coming toward her. What could she do? Turn and run, as a little child might? Spring into the wheat, as some frightened four-footed creature would? There was nothing but to pass him with the dignity which the occasion clearly demanded.

But he did not let her pass. He stood squarely in the pathway before her, hat in hand, a perturbed look upon his face.

"Miss Orme," he said, "I have wanted to say to you, every hour of the past week, that I am the most consummate hound that walks the earth."

She made no protest. Her whole bearing seemed to indicate that her opinion coincided with his own.

"If you have a father, or brother, or any one, in short, to whom you may say such things—"

"I think you aggravate the offense, sir, by speaking of it. I shall ask you never to mention it again. I want to forget that it ever happened. Will you kindly let me by."

"Oh," he ventured eagerly, "you want to forget it! Then, maybe, since you are willing to forget, you will be generous enough to forgive the offender some day?"

"Some day," she repeated, almost inaudibly, looking seemingly through him, but not at him—"some day—perhaps; when I shall have forgiven myself."

He stood motionless, watching her slim, straight figure lessening by degrees as she walked slowly away from him. He was wondering what she meant. Then a sudden, quick wave came beating into his brown throat and staining it crimson, when he guessed what it might be.

The World and the Door

O. HENRY

(1862–1910)

A favourite dodge to get your story read by the public is to assert that it is true, and then add that Truth is stranger than Fiction. I do not know if the yarn I am anxious for you to read is true; but the Spanish purser of the fruit steamer *El Carrero* swore to me by the shrine of Santa Guadalupe that he had the facts from the U.S. vice-consul at La Paz—a person who could not possibly have been cognizant of half of them.

As for the adage quoted above, I take pleasure in puncturing it by affirming that I read in a purely fictional story the other day the line: "'Be it so,' said the policeman." Nothing so strange has yet cropped out in Truth.

When H. Ferguson Hedges, millionaire promoter, investor and man-about-New-York, turned his thoughts upon matters convivial, and word of it went "down the line," bouncers took a precautionary turn at the Indian clubs, waiters put ironstone china on his favourite tables, cab drivers crowded close to the curbstone in front of all-night cafés, and careful cashiers in his regular haunts charged up a few bottles to his account by way of preface and introduction.

As a money power a one-millionaire is of small account in a city where the man who cuts your slice of beef behind the free-lunch counter rides to work in his own automobile. But Hedges spent his money as lavishly, loudly and showily as though he were only a clerk squandering a week's wages. And, after all, the bartender takes no interest in your reserve fund. He would rather look you up on his cash register than in Bradstreet.

On the evening that the material allegation of facts begins, Hedges was bidding dull care begone on the company of five or six good fellows—acquaintances and friends who had gathered in his wake.

Among them were two younger men—Ralph Merriam, a broker, and Wade, his friend.

Two deep-sea cabmen were chartered. At Columbus Circle they hove to long enough to revile the statue of the great navigator, unpatriotically rebuking him for having voyaged in search of land instead of liquids. Midnight overtook the party marooned in the rear of a cheap café far uptown.

Hedges was arrogant, overriding and quarrelsome. He was burly and tough, iron-gray but vigorous, "good" for the rest of the night. There was a dispute—about nothing that matters—and the five-fingered words were passed—the words that represent the glove cast into the lists. Merriam played the rôle of the verbal Hotspur.

Hedges rose quickly, seized his chair, swung it once and smashed wildly down at Merriam's head. Merriam dodged, drew a small revolver and shot Hedges in the chest. The leading roysterer stumbled, fell in a wry heap, and lay still.

Wade, a commuter, had formed that habit of promptness. He juggled Merriam out a side door, walked him to the corner, ran him a block and caught a hansom. They rode five minutes and then got out on a dark corner and dismissed the cab. Across the street the lights of a small saloon betrayed its hectic hospitality.

"Go in the back room of that saloon," said Wade, "and wait. I'll go find out what's doing and let you know. You may take two drinks while I am gone—no more."

At ten minutes to one o'clock Wade returned.

"Brace up, old chap," he said. "The ambulance got there just as I did. The doctor says he's dead. You may have one more drink. You let me run this thing for you. You've got to skip. I don't believe a chair is legally a deadly weapon. You've got to make tracks, that's all there is to it."

Merriam complained of the cold querulously, and asked for another drink. "Did you notice what big veins he had on the back of his hands?" he said. "I never could stand—I never could——"

"Take one more," said Wade, "and then come on. I'll see you through."

Wade kept his promise so well that at eleven o'clock the next morning Merriam, with a new suit case full of new clothes and hair-brushes, stepped quietly on board a little 500-ton fruit steamer at an East River pier. The vessel had brought the season's first cargo of limes from Port Limon, and was homeward bound. Merriam had his bank balance of $2,800 in his pocket in large bills, and brief instructions to pile up as much water as he could between himself and New York. There was no time for anything more.

From Port Limon Merriam worked down the coast by schooner and sloop to Colon, thence across the isthmus to Panama, where he caught a tramp bound for Callao and such intermediate ports as might tempt the discursive skipper from his course.

It was at La Paz that Merriam decided to land—La Paz the Beautiful, a little harbourless town smothered in a living green ribbon that banded the foot of a cloud-piercing mountain. Here the little steamer stopped to tread water while the captain's dory took him ashore that he might feel the pulse of the coconut market. Merriam went too, with his suit case, and remained.

Kalb, the vice-consul, a Græco-Armenian citizen of the United States, born in Hessen-Darmstadt, and educated in Cincinnati ward primaries, considered all Americans his brothers and bankers. He attached himself to Merriam's elbow, introduced him to every one in La Paz who wore shoes, borrowed ten dollars and went back to his hammock.

There was a little wooden hotel in the edge of a banana grove, facing the sea, that catered to the tastes of the few foreigners that had dropped out of the world into the *triste* Peruvian town. At Kalb's introductory: "Shake hands with——," he had obediently exchanged manual salutations with a German doctor, one French and two Italian merchants, and three or four Americans who were spoken of as gold men, rubber men, mahogany men—anything but men of living tissue.

After dinner Merriam sat in a corner of the broad front *galeria* with Bibb, a Vermonter interested in hydraulic mining, and smoked and drank Scotch "smoke." The moonlit sea, spreading infinitely before him, seemed to separate him beyond all apprehension from his old life. The horrid tragedy in which he had played such a disastrous part now began, for the first time since he stole on board the fruiter, a wretched fugitive, to lose its sharper outlines. Distance lent assuagement to his view. Bibb had opened the flood-gates of a stream of long-dammed discourse, overjoyed to have captured an audience that had not suffered under a hundred repetitions of his views and theories.

"One year more," said Bibb, "and I'll go back to God's country. Oh, I know it's pretty here, and you get *dolce far niente* handed to you in chunks, but this country wasn't made for a white man to live in. You've got to have to plug through snow now and then, and see a game of baseball and wear a stiff collar and have a policeman cuss you. Still, La Paz is a good sort of a pipe-dreamy old hole. And Mrs. Conant is here. When any of us feels particularly like jumping into the sea we rush around to her house and propose. It's nicer to be rejected by Mrs. Conant than it is to be drowned. And they say drowning is a delightful sensation."

"Many like her here?" asked Merriam.

"Not anywhere," said Bibb, with a comfortable sigh. "She's the only white woman in La Paz. The rest range from a dappled dun to the colour of a b-flat piano key. She's been her a year. Comes from—well, you know how a woman can talk—ask 'em to say 'string' and they'll say 'crow's foot' or 'cat's cradle.' Sometimes you'd think she was from Oshkosh, and again from Jacksonville, Florida, and the next day from Cape Cod."

"Mystery?" ventured Merriam.

"M—well, she looks it; but her talk's translucent enough. But that's a woman. I suppose if the Sphinx were to begin talking she'd merely say: 'Goodness me! more visitors coming for dinner, and nothing to eat but the sand which is here.' But you won't think about that when you meet her, Merriam. You'll propose to her too."

To make a hard story soft, Merriam did meet her and propose to her. He found her to be a woman in black with hair the colour of a bronze turkey's wings, and mysterious, *remembering* eyes that—well, that looked as if she might have been a trained nurse looking on when Eve was created. Her words and manner, though, were translucent, as Bibb had said. She spoke, vaguely, of friends in California and some of the lower parishes in Louisiana. The tropical climate and indolent life suited her; she had thought of buying an orange grove later on; La Paz, all in all, charmed her.

Merriam's courtship of the Sphinx lasted three months, although he did not know that he was courting her. He was using her as antidote for remorse, until he found, too late, that he had acquired the habit. During that time he had received no news from home. Wade did not know where he was; and he was not sure of Wade's exact address, and was afraid to write. He thought he had better let matters rest as they were for a while.

One afternoon he and Mrs. Conant hired two ponies and rode out along the mountain trail as far as the little cold river that came tumbling down the foothills. There they stopped for a drink, and Merriam spoke his piece—he proposed, as Bibb had prophesied.

Mrs. Conant gave him one glance of brilliant tenderness, and then her face took on such a strange, haggard look that Merriam was shaken out of his intoxication and back to his senses.

"I beg your pardon, Florence," he said, releasing her hand; "but I'll have to hedge on part of what I said. I can't ask you to marry me, of course. I killed a man in New York—a man who was my friend—shot him down—in quite a cowardly manner, I understand. Of course, the drinking didn't excuse it. Well, I couldn't resist having my say; and I'll always mean it. I'm here as a fugitive from justice, and—I suppose that ends our acquaintance."

Mrs. Conant plucked little leaves assiduously from the low-hanging branch of a lime tree.

"I suppose so," she said, in low and oddly uneven tones; "but that depends upon you. I'll be as honest as you were. I poisoned my husband. I am a self-made widow. A man cannot love a murderess. So I suppose that ends our acquaintance."

She looked up at him slowly. His face turned a little pale, and he stared at her blankly, like a deaf-and-dumb man who was wondering what it was all about.

She took a swift step toward him, with stiffened arms and eyes blazing. "Don't look at me like that!" she cried, as though she were in acute pain. "Curse me, or turn your back on me, but don't look that way. Am I a woman to be beaten? If I could show you—here on my arms, and on my back are scars—and it has been more than a year—scars that he made in his brutal rages. A holy nun would have risen and struck the fiend down. Yes, I killed him. The foul and horrible words that he hurled at me that last day are repeated in my ears every night when I sleep. And then came his blows, and the end of my endurance. I got the poison that afternoon. It was his custom to drink every night in the library before going to bed a hot punch made of rum and wine. Only from my fair hands would he receive it—because he knew the fumes of spirits always sickened me. That night when the maid brought it to me I sent her downstairs on an errand. Before taking him his drink I went to my little private cabinet and poured into it more than a teaspoonful of tincture of aconite—enough to kill three men, so I had learned. I had drawn $6,000 that I had in bank, and with that and a few things in a satchel I left the house without any one seeing me. As I passed the library I heard him stagger up and fall heavily on a couch. I took a night train for New Orleans, and from there I sailed to the Bermudas. I finally cast anchor in La Paz. And now what have you to say? Can you open your mouth?"

Merriam came back to life.

"Florence," he said earnestly, "I want you. I don't care what you've done. If the world——"

"Ralph," she interrupted, almost with a scream, "be my world!"

Her eyes melted; she relaxed magnificently and swayed toward Merriam so suddenly that he had to jump to catch her.

Dear me! in such scenes how the talk runs into artificial prose. But it can't be helped. It's the subconscious smell of the footlights' smoke that's in all of us. Stir the depths of your cook's soul sufficiently and she will discourse in Bulwer-Lyttonese.

Merriam and Mrs. Conant were very happy. He announced their engagement at the Hotel Orilla del Mar. Eight foreigners and four native Astors pounded his back and shouted insincere congratulations at him. Pedrito, the Castilian-mannered barkeep was goaded to extra duty until his agility would have turned a Boston cherry-phosphate clerk a pale lilac with envy.

They were both very happy. According to the strange mathematics of the god of mutual affinity, the shadows that clouded their pasts when united became only half as dense instead of darker. They shut the world out and bolted the doors. Each was the other's world. Mrs. Conant lived again. The remembering look left her eyes. Merriam was with her every moment that was possible. On a little plateau under a grove of palms and calabash trees they were going to build a fairy bungalow. They were to be married in two months. Many hours of the day they had their heads together over the house plans. Their joint capital would set up a business in fruit or woods that would yield a comfortable support. "Good night, my world," would say Mrs. Conant every evening when Merriam left her for his hotel. They were very happy. Their love had, circumstantially, that element of melancholy in it that it seems to require to attain its supremest elevation. And it seemed that their mutual great misfortune or sin was a bond that nothing could sever.

One day a steamer hove in the offing. Bare-legged and bare-shouldered La Paz scampered down to the beach, for the arrival of a steamer was their loop-the-loop, circus, Emancipation Day and four-o'clock tea.

When the steamer was near enough, wise ones proclaimed that she was the *Pajaro,* bound up-coast from Callao to Panama.

The *Pajaro* put on brakes a mile off shore. Soon a boat came bobbing shoreward. Merriam strolled down on the beach to look on. In the shallow water the Carib sailors sprang out and dragged the boat with a mighty rush to the firm shingle. Out climbed the purser, the captain and two passengers ploughing their way through the deep sand toward the hotel. Merriam glanced toward them with the mild interest due to strangers. There was something familiar to him in the walk of one of the passengers. He looked again, and his blood seemed to turn to strawberry ice cream in his veins. Burly, arrogant, debonair as ever, H. Ferguson Hedges, the man he had killed, was coming toward him ten feet away.

When Hedges saw Merriam his face flushed a dark red. Then he shouted in his old, bluff way: "Hello, Merriam. Glad to see you. Didn't expect to find you out here. Quinby, this is my old friend Merriam, of New York–Merriam, Mr. Quinby."

Merriam gave Hedges and then Quinby an ice-cold hand.

"Br-r-r-r!" said Hedges. "But you've got a frappéd flipper! Man, you're not well. You're as yellow as a Chinaman. Malarial here? Steer us to a bar if there is such a thing, and let's take a prophylactic."

Merriam, still half comatose, led them toward the Hotel Orilla del Mar.

"Quinby and I," explained Hedges, puffing through the slippery sand, "are looking out along the coast for some investments. We've just come up from Concepción and Valparaiso and Lima. The captain of this subsidized ferry boat told us there was some good picking around here in silver mines. So we got off. Now, where is that café, Merriam? Oh, in this portable soda-water pavilion?"

Leaving Quinby at the bar, Hedges drew Merriam aside.

"Now, what does this mean?" he said, with gruff kindness. "Are you sulking about that fool row we had?"

"I thought," stammered Merriam–"I heard–they told me you were–that I had––"

"Well, you didn't, and I'm not," said Hedges. "That fool young ambulance surgeon told Wade I was a candidate for a coffin just because I'd got tired and quit breathing. I laid up in a private hospital for a month; but here I am, kicking as hard as ever. Wade and I tried to find you, but couldn't. Now, Merriam, shake hands and forget it all. I was as much to blame as you were; and the shot really did me good–I came out of the hospital as healthy and fit as a cab horse. Come on; that drink's waiting."

"Old man," said Merriam, brokenly, "I don't know how to thank you—I—well, you know——"

"Oh, forget it," boomed Hedges. "Quinby'll die of thirst if we don't join him."

Bibb was sitting on the shady side of the gallery waiting for the eleven-o'clock breakfast. Presently Merriam came out and joined him. His eye was strangely bright.

"Bibb, my boy," said he, slowly waving his hand, "do you see those mountains and that sea and sky and sunshine?—they're mine, Bibbsy—all mine."

"You go in," said Bibb, "and take eight grains of quinine, right away. It won't do in this climate for a man to get to thinking he's Rockefeller, or James O'Neill either."

Inside, the purser was untying a great roll of newspapers, many of them weeks old, gathered in the lower ports by the *Pajaro* to be distributed at casual stopping-places. Thus do the beneficent voyagers scatter news and entertainment among the prisoners of sea and mountains.

Tio Pancho, the hotel proprietor, set his great silver-rimmed *anteojos* upon his nose and divided the papers into a number of smaller rolls. A barfooted *muchacho* dashed in, desiring the post of messenger.

"Bien venido," said Tio Pancho. "This is to Señora Conant; that to el Doctor S-S-Schlegel—*Dios!* what a name to say!—that to Señor Davis—one for Don Alberto. These two for the *Casa de Huespedes, Numero* 6, *en la calle de las Buenas Gracias*. And say to them all, *muchacho,* that the *Pajaro* sails for Panama at three this afternoon. If any have letters to send by the post, let them come quickly, that they may first pass through the *correo."*

Mrs. Conant received her roll of newspapers at four o'clock. The boy was late in delivering them, because he had been deflected from his duty by an iguana that crossed his path and to which he immediately gave chase. But it made no hardship, for she had no letters to send.

She was idling in a hammock in the *patio* of the house that she occupied, half awake, half happily dreaming of the paradise that she and Merriam had created out of the wrecks of their pasts. She was content now for the horizon of that shimmering sea to be the horizon of her life. They had shut out the world and closed the door.

Merriam was coming to her house at seven, after his dinner at the hotel. She would put on a white dress and an apricot-coloured lace mantilla, and they would walk an hour under the cocoanut palms by the lagoon. She smiled contentedly, and chose a paper at random from the roll the boy had brought.

At first the words of a certain headline of a Sunday newspaper meant nothing to her; they conveyed only a visualized sense of familiarity. The largest type ran thus: "Lloyd B. Conant secures divorce." And then the subheadings: "Well-known Saint Louis paint manufacturer wins suit, pleading one year's absence of wife." "Her mysterious disappearance recalled." "Nothing has been heard of her since."

Twisting herself quickly out of the hammock, Mrs. Conant's eye soon traversed the half-column of the "Recall." It ended thus: "It will be remembered that Mrs. Conant disappeared one evening in March of last year. It was freely rumoured that her marriage with Lloyd B. Conant resulted in much unhappiness. Stories were not wanting to the effect that his cruelty toward his wife had more than once taken the form of physical abuse. After her departure a full bottle of tincture of aconite, a deadly poison, was found in a small medicine cabinet in her bedroom. This might have been an indication that she meditated suicide. It is supposed that she abandoned such an intention if she possessed it, and left her home instead."

Mrs. Conant slowly dropped the paper, and sat on a chair, clasping her hands tightly.

"Let me think—O God!—let me think," she whispered. "I took the bottle with me . . . I threw it out of the window of the train . . . I— . . . there was another bottle in the cabinet . . . there were two, side by side—the aconite—and the valerian that I took when I could not sleep . . . If they found the aconite bottle full, why—but, he is alive, of course —I gave him only a harmless dose of valerian . . . I am not a murderess in fact . . . Ralph, I—O God, don't let this be a dream!"

She went into the part of the house that she rented from the old Peruvian man and his wife, shut the door, and walked up and down her room swiftly and feverishly for half an hour. Merriam's photograph stood in a frame on a table. She picked it up, looked at it with a smile of exquisite tenderness, and—dropped four tears on it. And Merriam only twenty rods away! Then she stood still for ten minutes, looking into space. She looked into space through a slowly opening door. On her side of the door was the building material for a castle of Romance—love, an Arcady of waving palms, a lullaby of waves on the shore of a haven of rest, respite, peace, a lotus land of dreamy ease and security—a life of poetry and heart's ease and refuge. Romanticist, will you tell me what Mrs. Conant saw on the other side of the door? You cannot?—that is, you will not? Very well; then listen.

She saw herself go into a department store and buy five spools of silk thread and three yards of gingham to make an apron for the cook. "Shall I charge it, ma'am?" asked the clerk. As she walked out a lady whom she met greeted her cordially. "Oh, where did you get the pattern for those sleeves, dear Mrs. Conant?" she said. At the corner a policeman helped her across the street and touched his helmet. "Any callers?" she asked the maid when she reached home. "Mrs. Waldron," answered the maid, "and the two Misses Jenkinson." "Very well," she said. "You may bring me a cup of tea, Maggie."

Mrs. Conant went to the door and called Angela, the old Peruvian woman. "If Mateo is there send him to me." Mateo, a half-breed, shuffling and old but efficient, came.

"Is there a steamer or a vessel of any kind leaving this coast to-night or to-morrow that I can get passage on?" she asked.

Mateo considered.

"At Punta Reina, thirty miles down the coast, señora," he answered, "there is a small steamer loading with cinchona and dyewoods. She sails for San Francisco to-morrow at sunrise. So says my brother, who arrived in his sloop to-day, passing by Punta Reina."

"You must take me in that sloop to that steamer to-night. Will you do that?"

"Perhaps——" Mateo shrugged a suggestive shoulder. Mrs. Conant took a handful of money from a drawer and gave it to him.

"Get the sloop ready behind the little point of land below the town," she ordered. "Get sailors, and be ready to sail at six o'clock. In half an hour bring a cart partly filled with straw into the *patio* here, and take my trunk to the sloop. There is more money yet. Now, hurry."

For one time Mateo walked away without shuffling his feet.

"Angela," cried Mrs. Conant, almost fiercely, "come and help me pack. I am going away. Out with this trunk. My clothes first. Stir yourself. Those dark dresses first. Hurry."

From the first she did not waver from her decision. Her view was clear and final. Her door had opened and let the world in. Her love for Merriam was not lessened; but it now appeared a hopeless and unrealizable thing. The visions of their future that had seemed so blissful and complete had vanished. She tried to assure herself that her renunciation was rather for his sake than for her own. Now that she was cleared of her burden—at least, technically—would not his own weigh too heavily upon him? If she should cling to him, would not the difference forever silently mar and corrode their happiness? Thus she reasoned; but there were a thousand little voices calling to her that she could feel rather than hear, like the hum of distant, powerful machinery—the little voices of the world, that, when raised in unison, can send their insistent call through the thickest door.

Once while packing, a brief shadow of the lotus dream came back to her. She held Merriam's picture to her heart with one hand, while she threw a pair of shoes into the trunk with her other.

At six o'clock Mateo returned and reported the sloop ready. He and his brother lifted the trunk into the cart, covered it with straw and conveyed it to the point of embarkation. From there they transferred it on board in the sloop's dory. Then Mateo returned for additional orders.

Mrs. Conant was ready. She had settled all business matters with Angela, and was impatiently waiting. She wore a long, loose black-silk duster that she often walked about in when the evenings were chilly. On her head was a small round hat, and over it the apricot-coloured lace mantilla.

Dusk had quickly followed the short twilight. Mateo led her by dark and grass-grown streets toward the point behind which the sloop was anchored. On turning a corner they beheld the Hotel Orilla del Mar three streets away, nebulously aglow with its array of kerosene lamps.

Mrs. Conant paused, with streaming eyes. "I must, *I must* see him once before I go," she murmured in anguish. But even then she did not falter in her decision. Quickly she invented a plan by which she might speak to him, and yet make her departure without his knowing. She would walk past the hotel, ask some one to call him out and talk a few moments on some trivial excuse, leaving him expecting to see her at her home at seven.

She unpinned her hat and gave it to Mateo. "Keep this, and wait here till I come," she ordered. Then she draped the mantilla over her head as she usually did when walking after sunset, and went straight to the Orilla del Mar.

She was glad to see the bulky, white-clad figure of Tio Pancho standing alone on the gallery.

"Tio Pancho," she said, with a charming smile, "may I trouble you to ask Mr. Merriam to come out for just a few moments that I may speak with him?"

Tio Pancho bowed as an elephant bows.

"*Buenas tardes,* Señora Conant," he said, as a cavalier talks. And then he went on, less at his ease:

"But does not the señora know that Señor Merriam sailed on the *Pajaro* for Panama at three o'clock of this afternoon?"

After Holbein

EDITH WHARTON

(1862–1937)

I

Anson Warley had had his moments of being a rather remarkable man; but they were only intermittent; they recurred at ever-lengthening intervals; and between times he was a small poor creature, chattering with cold inside, in spite of his agreeable and even distinguished exterior.

He had always been perfectly aware of these two sides of himself (which, even in the privacy of his own mind, he contemptuously refused to dub a dual personality); and as the rather remarkable man could take fairly good care of himself, most of Warley's attention was devoted to ministering to the poor wretch who took longer and longer turns at bearing his name, and was more and more insistent in accepting the invitations which New York, for over thirty years, had tirelessly poured out on him. It was in the interest of this lonely fidgety unemployed self that Warley, in his younger days, had frequented the gaudiest restaurants and the most glittering Palace Hotels of two hemispheres, subscribed to the most advanced literary and artistic reviews, bought the pictures of the young painters who were being the most vehemently discussed, missed few of the showiest first nights in New York, London or Paris, sought the company of the men and women—especially the women—most conspicuous in fashion, scandal, or any other form of social notoriety, and thus tried to warm the shivering soul within him at all the passing bonfires of success.

The original Anson Warley had begun by staying at home in his little flat, with his books and his thoughts, when the other poor creature went forth; but gradually—he hardly knew when or how—he had slipped into the way of going too, till finally he made the bitter discovery that he and the creature had become one, except on the increasingly rare occasions when, detaching himself from all casual contingencies, he mounted to the lofty water-shed which fed the sources of his scorn. The view from there was vast and glorious, the air was icy but exhilarating; but soon he began to find the place too lonely, and too difficult to get to, especially as the lesser Anson not only refused to go up with him but began to sneer, at first ever so faintly, then with increasing insolence, at this affectation of a taste for the heights.

"What's the use of scrambling up there, anyhow? I could understand it if you brought down anything worth while—a poem or a picture of your own. But just climbing and staring: what does it lead to? Fellows with the creative gift have got to have their occasional Sinaïs; I can see that. But for a mere looker-on like you, isn't that sort of thing rather a pose? You talk awfully well—brilliantly, even (oh, my dear fellow, no false modesty between you and *me*, please!). But who the devil is there to listen to you, up there among the glaciers? And sometimes, when you come down, I notice that you're rather—well, heavy and tongue-tied. Look out, or they'll stop asking us to dine! And sitting at home every evening—brr! Look here, by the way; if you've got nothing better for tonight, come along with me to Chrissy Torrance's—or the Bob Briggses'—or Princess Kate's; anywhere where there's lots of racket and sparkle, places that people go to in Rollses, and that are smart and hot and overcrowded, and you have to pay a lot—in one way or another—to get in."

Once and again, it is true, Warley still dodged his double and slipped off on a tour to remote uncomfortable places, where there were churches or pictures to be seen, or shut himself up at home for a good bout of reading, or just, in sheer disgust at his companion's platitude, spent an evening with people who were doing or thinking real things. This happened seldomer than of old, however, and more clandestinely; so that at last he used to sneak away to spend two or three days with an archæologically-minded friend, or an evening with a quiet scholar, as furtively as if he were stealing to a lover's tryst; which, as lovers' trysts were now always kept in the limelight, was after all a fair exchange. But he always felt rather apologetic to the other Warley about these escapades—and, if the truth were known, rather bored and restless before they were over. And in the back of his mind there lurked an increasing dread of missing something hot and noisy and overcrowded when he went off to one of his mountain-tops. "After all, that high-brow business has been awfully overdone—now hasn't it?" the little Warley would insinuate, rummaging for his pearl studs, and consulting his flat evening watch as nervously as if it were a railway time-table. "If only we haven't missed something really jolly by all this backing and filling . . ."

"Oh, you poor creature, you! Always afraid of being left out, aren't you? Well—just for once, to humour you, and because I happen to be feeling rather stale myself. But only to think of a sane man's wanting to go to places just because they're hot and smart and overcrowded!" And off they would dash together . . .

II

All that was long ago. It was years now since there had been two distinct Anson Warleys. The lesser one had made away with the other, done him softly to death without shedding of blood; and only a few people suspected (and they no longer cared) that the pale white-haired man, with the small slim figure, the ironic smile and the perfect evening clothes, whom New York still indefatigably invited, was nothing less than a murderer.

Anson Warley—Anson Warley! No party was complete without Anson Warley. He no longer went abroad now; too stiff in the joints; and there had been two or three slight attacks of dizziness . . . Nothing to speak of, nothing to think of, even; but somehow one dug one's self into one's comfortable quarters, and felt less and less like moving out of them, except to motor down to Long Island for weekends, or to Newport for a few visits in summer. A trip to the Hot Springs, to get rid of the stiffness, had not helped much, and the ageing Anson Warley (who really, otherwise, felt as young as ever) had developed a growing dislike for the promiscuities of hotel life and the monotony of hotel food.

Yes; he was growing more fastidious as he grew older. A good sign, he thought. Fastidious not only about food and comfort but about people also. It was still a privilege, a distinction, to have him to dine. His old friends were faithful, and the new people fought for him, and often failed to get him; to do so they had to offer very special inducements in the way of *cuisine*, conversation or beauty. Young beauty; yes, that would do it. He did like to sit and watch a lovely face, and call laughter into lovely eyes. But no dull dinners for *him*, not even if they fed you off gold. As to that he was as firm as the other Warley, the distant aloof one with whom he had—er, well, parted company, oh, quite amicably, a good many years ago . . .

On the whole, since that parting, life had been much easier and pleasanter; and by the time the little Warley was sixty-three he found himself looking forward with equanimity to an eternity of New York dinners.

Oh, but only at the right houses—always at the right houses; that was understood! The right people—the right setting—the right wines . . . He smiled a little over his perennial enjoyment of them; said "Nonsense, Filmore," to his devoted tiresome man-servant, who was beginning to hint that really, every night, sir, and sometimes a dance afterward, was too much, especially when you kept at it for months on end; and Dr.—

"Oh, damn your doctors!" Warley snapped. He was seldom ill-tempered; he knew it was foolish and upsetting to lose one's self-control. But Filmore began to be a nuisance, nagging him, preaching at him. As if he himself wasn't the best judge . . .

Besides, he chose his company. He'd stay at home any time rather than risk a boring evening. Damned rot, what Filmore had said about his going out every night. Not like poor old Mrs. Jaspar, for instance . . . He smiled self-approvingly as he evoked her tottering image. "That's the kind of fool Filmore takes me for," he chuckled, his good-humour restored by an analogy that was so much to his advantage.

Poor old Evelina Jaspar! In his youth, and even in his prime, she had been New York's chief entertainer—"leading hostess," the newspapers called her. Her big house in Fifth Avenue had been an entertaining machine. She had lived, breathed, invested and reinvested her millions, to no other end. At first her pretext had been that she had to marry her daughters and amuse her sons; but when sons and daughters had married and left her she had seemed hardly aware of it; she had just gone on entertaining. Hundreds, no, thousands of dinners (on gold plate, of course, and with orchids, and all the delicacies that were out of season), had been served in that vast pompous dining-room, which one had only to close one's eyes to transform into a railway buffet for millionaires, at a big junction, before the invention of restaurant trains . . .

Warley closed his eyes, and did so picture it. He lost himself in amused computation of the annual number of guests, of saddles of mutton, of legs of lamb, of terrapin, canvas-backs, magnums of champagne and pyramids of hot-house fruit that must have passed through that room in the last forty years.

And even now, he thought—hadn't one of old Evelina's nieces told him the other day, half bantering, half shivering at the avowal, that the poor old lady, who was gently dying of softening of the brain, still imagined herself to be New York's leading hostess, still sent out invitations (which of course were never delivered), still ordered terrapin, champagne and orchids, and still came down every evening to her great shrouded drawingrooms, with her tiara askew on her purple wig, to receive a stream of imaginary guests?

Rubbish, of course—a macabre pleasantry of the extravagant Nelly Pierce, who had always had her joke at Aunt Evelina's expense . . . But Warley could not help smiling at the thought that those dull monotonous dinners were still going on in their hostess's clouded imagination. Poor old

Evelina, he thought! In a way she was right. There was really no reason why that kind of standardized entertaining should ever cease; a performance so undiscriminating, so undifferentiated, that one could almost imagine, in the hostess's tired brain, all the dinners she had ever given merging into one Gargantuan pyramid of food and drink, with the same faces, perpetually the same faces, gathered stolidly about the same gold plate.

Thank heaven, Anson Warley had never conceived of social values in terms of mass and volume. It was years since he had dined at Mrs. Jaspar's. He even felt that he was not above reproach in that respect. Two or three times, in the past, he had accepted her invitations (always sent out weeks ahead), and then chucked her at the eleventh hour for something more amusing. Finally, to avoid such risks, he had made it a rule always to refuse her dinners. He had even—he remembered—been rather funny about it once, when someone had told him that Mrs. Jaspar couldn't understand . . . was a little hurt . . . said it couldn't be true that he always had another engagement the nights she asked him . . . "*True?* Is the truth what she wants? All right! Then the next time I get a 'Mrs. Jaspar requests the pleasure' I'll answer it with a 'Mr. Warley declines the boredom.' Think she'll understand that, eh?" And the phrase became a catchword in his little set that winter. " 'Mr. Warley declines the boredom'—good, good, *good!*" "Dear Anson, I do hope you won't decline the boredom of coming to lunch next Sunday to meet the new Hindu Yoghi"—or the new saxophone soloist, or that genius of a mulatto boy who plays Negro spirituals on a toothbrush; and so on and so on. He only hoped poor old Evelina never heard of it . . .

"Certainly I shall *not* stay at home tonight—why, what's wrong with me?" he snapped, swinging round on Filmore.

The valet's long face grew longer. His way of answering such questions was always to pull out his face; it was his only means of putting any expression into it. He turned away into the bedroom, and Warley sat alone by his library fire . . . Now what did the man see that was wrong with him, he wondered? He had felt a little confusion that morning, when he was doing his daily sprint around the Park (his exercise was reduced to that!); but it had been only a passing flurry, of which Filmore could of course know nothing. And as soon as it was over his mind had seemed more lucid, his eye keener, than ever; as sometimes (he reflected) the electric light in his library lamps would blaze up too brightly after a break in the current, and he would say to himself, wincing a little at the sudden glare on the page he was reading: "That means that it'll go out again in a minute."

Yes; his mind, at that moment, had been quite piercingly clear and perceptive; his eye had passed with a renovating glitter over every detail of the daily scene. He stood still for a minute under the leafless trees of the Mall, and looking about him with the sudden insight of age, understood that he had reached the time of life when Alps and cathedrals become as transient as flowers.

Everything was fleeting, fleeting . . . yes, that was what had given him the vertigo. The doctors, poor fools, called it the stomach, or high blood-pressure; but it was only the dizzy plunge of the sands in the hour-glass, the everlasting plunge that emptied one of heart and bowels, like the drop of an elevator from the top floor of a sky-scraper.

Certainly, after that moment of revelation, he had felt a little more tired than usual for the rest of the day; the light had flagged in his mind as it sometimes did in his lamps. At Chrissy Torrance's, where he had lunched, they had accused him of being silent, his hostess had said that he looked pale; but he had retorted with a joke, and thrown himself into the talk with a feverish loquacity. It was the only thing to do; for he could not tell all these people at the lunch table that very morning he had arrived at the turn in the path from which mountains look as transient as flowers—and that one after another they would all arrive there too.

He leaned his head back and closed his eyes, but not in sleep. He did not feel sleepy, but keyed up and alert. In the next room he heard Filmore reluctantly, protestingly, laying out his evening clothes . . . He had no fear about the dinner tonight; a quiet intimate little affair at an old friend's house. Just two or three congenial men, and Elfmann, the pianist (who would probably play), and that lovely Elfrida Flight. The fact that people asked him to dine to meet Elfrida Flight seemed to prove pretty conclusively that he was still in the running! He chuckled softly at Filmore's pessimism, and thought: "Well, after all, I suppose no man seems young to his valet . . . Time to dress very soon," he thought; and luxuriously postponed getting up out of his chair . . .

III

"She's worse than usual tonight," said the day nurse, laying down the evening paper as her colleague joined her. "Absolutely determined to have her jewels out."

The night nurse, fresh from a long sleep and an afternoon at the movies with a gentleman friend, threw down her fancy bag, tossed off her hat and rumpled up her hair before old Mrs. Jaspar's tall toilet mirror. "Oh, I'll settle that—don't you worry," she said brightly.

"Don't you fret her, though, Miss Cress," said the other, getting wearily out of her chair. "We're very well off here, take it as a whole, and I don't want her pressure rushed up for nothing."

Miss Cress, still looking at herself in the glass, smiled reassuringly at Miss Dunn's pale reflection behind her. She and Miss Dunn got on very well together, and knew on which side their bread was buttered. But at the end of the day Miss Dunn was always fagged out and fearing the worst. The patient wasn't as hard to handle as all that. Just let her ring for her old maid, old Lavinia, and say: "My sapphire velvet tonight, with the diamond stars"—and Lavinia would know exactly how to manage her.

Miss Dunn had put on her hat and coat, and crammed her knitting, and the newspaper, into her bag, which, unlike Miss Cress's, was capacious and shabby; but she still loitered undecided on the threshold. "I could stay with you till ten as easy as not . . ." She looked almost reluctantly about the big high-studded dressing-room (everything in the house was high-studded), with its rich dusky carpet and cutains, and its monumental dressing-table draped with lace and laden with gold-backed brushes and combs, gold-stoppered toilet-bottles, and all the charming paraphernalia of beauty at her glass. Old Lavinia even renewed every morning the roses and carnations in the slim crystal vases between the powder boxes and the nail polishers. Since the family had shut down the hothouses at the uninhabited country place on the Hudson, Miss Cress suspected that old Lavinia bought these flowers out of her own pocket.

"Cold out tonight?" queried Miss Dunn from the door.

"Fierce . . . Reg'lar blizzard at the corners. Say, shall I lend you my fur scarf?" Miss Cress, pleased with the memory of her afternoon (they'd be engaged soon, she thought), and with the drowsy prospect of an evening in a deep arm-chair near the warm gleam of the dressing-room fire, was disposed to kindliness toward that poor thin Dunn girl, who supported her mother, and her brother's idiot twins. And she wanted Miss Dunn to notice her new fur.

"My! Isn't it too lovely? No, not for worlds, thank you . . ." Her hand on the door-knob, Miss Dunn repeated: "Don't you cross her now," and was gone.

Lavinia's bell rang furiously, twice; then the door between the dressing-room and Mrs. Jaspar's bedroom opened, and Mrs. Jaspar herself emerged.

"Lavinia!" she called, in a high irritated voice; then, seeing the nurse, who had slipped into her print dress and starched cap, she added in a lower tone: "Oh, Miss Lemoine, good evening." Her first nurse, it appeared, had been called Miss Lemoine; and she gave the same name to all the others, quite unaware that there had been any changes in the staff.

"I heard talking, and carriages driving up. Have people begun to arrive?" she asked nervously. "Where is Lavinia? I still have my jewels to put on."

She stood before the nurse, the same petrifying apparition which always, at this hour, struck Miss Cress to silence. Mrs. Jaspar was tall; she had been broad; and her bones remained impressive though the flesh had withered on them. Lavinia had encased her, as usual, in her low-necked purple velvet dress, nipped in at the waist in the old-fashioned way, expanding in voluminous folds about the hips and flowing in a long train over the darker velvet of the carpet. Mrs. Jaspar's swollen feet could no longer be pushed into the high-heeled satin slippers which went with the dress; but her skirts were so long and spreading that, by taking short steps, she managed (so Lavinia daily assured her) entirely to conceal the broad round tips of her black orthopædic shoes.

"Your jewels, Mrs. Jaspar? Why, you've got them on," said Miss Cress brightly.

Mrs. Jaspar turned her porphyry-tinted face to Miss Cress, and looked at her with a glassy incredulous gaze. Her eyes, Miss Cress thought, were the worst . . . She lifted one old hand, veined and knobbed as a raised map, to her elaborate purple-black wig, groped among the puffs and curls and undulations (queer, Miss Cress thought, that it never occurred to her to look into the glass), and after an interval affirmed: "You must be mistaken, my dear. Don't you think you ought to have your eyes examined?"

The door opened again, and a very old woman, so old as to make Mrs. Jaspar appear almost young, hobbled in with sidelong steps. "Excuse me, madam. I was downstairs when the bell rang."

Lavinia had probably always been small and slight: now, beside her towering mistress, she looked a mere feather, a straw. Everything about her had dried, contracted, been volatilized into nothingness, except her watchful gray eyes, in which intelligence and comprehension burned like two fixed stars. "Do excuse me, madam," she repeated.

Mrs. Jaspar looked at her despairingly. "I hear carriages driving up. And Miss Lemoine says I have my jewels on; and I know I haven't."

"With that lovely necklace!" Miss Cress ejaculated.

Mrs. Jaspar's twisted hand rose again, this time to her denuded shoulders, which were as stark and barren as the rock from which the hand might have been broken. She felt and felt, and tears rose in her eyes . . .

"Why do you lie to me?" she burst out passionately.

Lavinia softly intervened. "Miss Lemoine meant how lovely you'll be when you get the necklace on, madam."

"Diamonds, diamonds," said Mrs. Jaspar with an awful smile.

"Of course, madam."

Mrs. Jaspar sat down at the dressing-table, and Lavinia, with eager random hands, began to adjust the *point de Venise* about her mistress's shoulders, and to repair the havoc wrought in the purple-black wig by its wearer's gropings for her tiara.

"Now you do look lovely, madam," she sighed.

Mrs. Jaspar was on her feet again, stiff but incredibly active. ("Like a cat she is," Miss Cress used to relate.) "I do hear carriages—or is it an automobile? The Magraws, I know, have one of those new-fangled automobiles. And now I hear the front door opening. Quick, Lavinia! My fan, my gloves, my handkerchief . . . how often have I got to tell you? I used to have a *perfect* maid—"

Lavinia's eyes brimmed. "That was me, madam," she said, bending to straighten out the folds of the long purple velvet train. ("To watch the two of 'em," Miss Cress used to tell a circle of appreciative friends, "is a lot better than any circus.")

Mrs. Jaspar paid no attention. She twitched the train out of Lavinia's vacillating hold, swept to the door, and then paused there as if stopped by a jerk of her constricted muscles. "Oh, but my diamonds—you cruel woman, you! You're letting me go down without my diamonds!" Her ruined face puckered up in a grimace like a new-born baby's, and she began to sob despairingly. "Everybody . . . Every . . . body's . . . against me . . ." she wept in her powerless misery.

Lavinia helped herself to her feet and tottered across the floor. It was almost more than she could bear to see her mistress in distress. "Madam, madam—if you'll just wait till they're got out of the safe," she entreated.

The woman she saw before her, the woman she was entreating and consoling, was not the old petrified Mrs. Jaspar with porphyry face and wig awry whom Miss Cress stood watching with a smile, but a young proud creature, commanding and splendid in her Paris gown of amber *moiré*, who, years ago, had burst into just such furious sobs because, as she was sweeping down to receive her guests, the doctor had told her that little Grace, with whom she had been playing all the afternoon, had a diphtheritic throat, and no one must be allowed to enter. "Everybody's against me, everybody . . ." she had sobbed in her fury; and the young Lavinia, stricken by such Olympian anger, had stood speechless, longing to comfort her, and secretly indignant with little Grace and the doctor . . .

"If you'll just wait, madam, while I go down and ask Munson to open the safe. There's no one come yet, I do assure you . . ."

Munson was the old butler, the only person who knew the combination of the safe in Mrs. Jaspar's bedroom. Lavinia had once known it too, but now she was no longer able to remember it. The worst of it was that she feared lest Munson, who had been spending the day in the Bronx, might not have returned. Munson was growing old too, and he did sometimes forget about these dinner-parties of Mrs. Jaspar's, and then the stupid footman, George, had to announce the names; and you couldn't be sure that Mrs. Jaspar wouldn't notice Munson's absence, and be excited and angry. These dinner-party nights were killing old Lavinia, and she did so want to keep alive; she wanted to live long enough to wait on Mrs. Jaspar to the last.

She disappeared, and Miss Cress poked up the fire, and persuaded Mrs. Jaspar to sit down in an armchair and "tell her who was coming." It always amused Mrs. Jaspar to say over the long list of her guests' names, and generally she remembered them fairly well, for they were always the same—the last people, Lavinia and Munson said, who had dined at the house, on the very night before her stroke. With recovered complacency she began, counting over one after another on her ring-laden fingers: "The Italian Ambassador, the Bishop, Mr. and Mrs. Torrington Bligh, Mr. and Mrs. Fred Amesworth, Mr. and Mrs. Mitchell Magraw, Mr. and Mrs. Torrington Bligh . . ." ("You've said them before," Miss Cress interpolated, getting out her fancy knitting—a necktie for her friend—and beginning to count the stitches.) And Mrs. Jaspar, distressed and bewildered by the interruption, had to repeat over and over: "Torrington Bligh, Torrington Bligh," till the connection was re-established, and she went on again swimmingly with "Mr. and Mrs. Fred Amesworth, Mr. and Mrs. Mitchell Magraw, Miss Laura Ladew, Mr. Harold Ladew, Mr. and Mrs. Benjamin Bronx, Mr. and Mrs. Torrington Bl—no, I mean, Mr. Anson Warley. Yes, Mr. Anson Warley; that's it," she ended complacently.

Miss Cress smiled and interrupted her counting. "No, that's *not* it."

"What do you mean, my dear—not it?"

"Mr. Anson Warley. He's not coming."

Mrs. Jaspar's jaw fell, and she stared at the nurse's coldly smiling face. "Not coming?"

"No. He's not coming. He's not on the list." (That old list! As if Miss Cress didn't know it by heart! Everybody in the house did, except the booby, George, who heard it reeled off every other night by Munson, and who was always stumbling over the names, and having to refer to the written paper.)

"Not on the list?" Mrs. Jaspar gasped.

Miss Cress shook her pretty head.

Signs of uneasiness gathered on Mrs. Jaspar's face and her lip began to tremble. It always amused Miss Cress to give her these little jolts, though she knew Miss Dunn and the doctors didn't approve of her doing so. She knew also that it was against her own interests, and she did try to bear in mind Miss Dunn's oft-repeated admonition about not sending up the patient's blood pressure; but when she was in high spirits, as she was tonight (they would certainly be engaged), it was irresistible to get a rise out of the old lady. And she thought it funny, this new figure unexpectedly appearing among those time-worn guests. ("I wonder what the rest of 'em 'll say to him," she giggled inwardly.)

"No; he's not on the list." Mrs. Jaspar, after pondering deeply, announced the fact with an air of recovered composure.

"That's what I told you," snapped Miss Cress.

"He's not on the list; but he promised me to come. I saw him yesterday," continued Mrs. Jaspar, mysteriously.

"You *saw* him—where?"

She considered. "Last night, at the Fred Amesworths' dance."

"Ah," said Miss Cress, with a little shiver; for she knew that Mrs. Amesworth was dead, and she was the intimate friend of the trained nurse who was keeping alive, by dint of *piqûres* and high frequency, the inarticulate and inanimate Mr. Amesworth. "It's funny," she remarked to Mrs. Jaspar, "that you'd never invited Mr. Warley before."

"No, I hadn't; not for a long time. I believe he felt I'd neglected him; for he came up to me last night, and said he was so sorry he hadn't been able to call. It seems he's been ill, poor fellow. Not as young as he was! So of course I invited him. He was very much gratified."

Mrs. Jaspar smiled at the remembrance of her little triumph; but Miss Cress's attention had wandered, as it always did when the patient became docile and reasonable. She thought: "Where's old Lavinia? I bet she can't find Munson." And she got up and crossed the floor to look into Mrs. Jaspar's bedroom, where the safe was.

There an astonishing sight met her, Munson, as she had expected, was nowhere visible; but Lavinia, on her knees before the safe, was in the act of opening it herself, her twitching hand slowly moving about the mysterious dial.

"Why, I thought you'd forgotten the combination!" Miss Cress exclaimed.

Lavinia turned a startled face over her shoulder. "So I had, Miss. But I've managed to remember it, thank God. I *had* to, you see, because Munson's forgot to come home."

"Oh," said the nurse incredulously. ("Old fox," she thought, "I wonder why she's always pretended she'd forgotten it.") For Miss Cress did not know that the age of miracles is not yet past.

Joyous, trembling, her cheeks wet with grateful tears, the little old woman was on her feet again, clutching to her breast the diamond stars, the necklace of *solitaires,* the tiara, the earrings. One by one she spread them out on the velvet-lined tray in which they always used to be carried from the safe to the dressing-room; then, with rambling fingers, she managed to lock the safe again, and put the keys in the drawer where they belonged, while Miss Cress continued to stare at her in amazement. "I don't believe the old witch is as shaky as she makes out," was her reflection as Lavinia passed her, bearing the jewels to the dressing-room where Mrs. Jaspar, lost in pleasant memories, was still computing: "The Italian Ambassador, the Bishop, the Torrington Blighs, the Mitchell Magraws, the Fred Amesworths . . ."

Mrs. Jaspar was allowed to go down to the drawing-room alone on dinner-party evenings because it would have mortified her too much to receive her guests with a maid or a nurse at her elbow; but Miss Cress and Lavinia always leaned over the stair-rail to watch her descent, and make sure it was accomplished in safety.

"She do look lovely yet, when all her diamonds is on," Lavinia sighed, her purblind eyes bedewed with memories, as the bedizened wig and purple velvet disappeared at the last bend of the stairs. Miss Cress, with a shrug, turned back to the fire and picked up her knitting, while Lavinia set about the slow ritual of tidying up her mistress's room. From below they heard the sound of George's stentorian monologue: "Mr. and Mrs. Torrington Bligh, Mr. and Mrs. Mitchell Magraw . . . Mr. Ladew, Miss Laura Ladew . . ."

IV

Anson Warley, who had always prided himself on his equable temper, was conscious of being on edge that evening. But it was an irritability which did not frighten him (in spite of what those doctors always said about the importance of keeping calm) because he knew it was due merely to the unusual lucidity of his mind. He was in fact feeling uncommonly well, his brain clear and all his perceptions so alert that he could positively hear the thoughts passing through his man-servant's mind on the other side of the door, as Filmore grudgingly laid out the evening clothes.

Smiling at the man's obstinacy, he thought: "I shall have to tell them tonight that Filmore thinks I'm no longer fit to go into society." It was always pleasant to hear the incredulous laugh with which his younger friends received any allusion to his supposed senility. "What, *you?* Well, that's a good one!" And he thought it was, himself.

And then, the moment he was in his bedroom, dressing, the sight of Filmore made him lose his temper again. "No; *not* those studs, confound it. The black onyx ones—haven't I told you a hundred times? Lost them,

I suppose? Sent them to the wash again in a soiled shirt? That it?" He laughed nervously, and sitting down before his dressing-table began to brush back his hair with short angry strokes.

"Above all," he shouted out suddenly, "don't stand there staring at me as if you were watching to see exactly at what minute to telephone for the undertaker!"

"The under—? Oh, sir!" gasped Filmore.

"The—the—damn it, are you *deaf* too? Who said undertaker? I said *taxi*; can't you hear what I say?"

"You want me to call a taxi, sir?"

"No; I don't. I've already told you so. I'm going to walk." Warley straightened his tie, rose and held out his arms toward his dress-coat.

"It's bitter cold, sir; better let me call a taxi all the same."

Warley gave a short laugh. "Out with it, now! What you'd really like to suggest is that I should telephone to say I can't dine out. You'd scramble me some eggs instead, eh?"

"I wish you would stay in, sir. There's eggs in the house."

"My overcoat," snapped Warley.

"Or else let me call a taxi; now do, sir."

Warley slipped his arms into his overcoat, tapped his chest to see if his watch (the thin evening watch) and his note-case were in their proper pockets, turned back to put a dash of lavender on his handkerchief, and walked with stiff quick steps toward the front door of his flat.

Filmore, abashed, preceded him to ring for the lift; and then, as it quivered upward through the long shaft, said again: "It's a bitter cold night, sir; and you've had a good deal of exercise today."

Warley levelled a contemptuous glance at him. "Daresay that's why I'm feeling so fit," he retorted as he entered the lift.

It *was* bitter cold; the icy air hit him in the chest when he stepped out of the overheated building, and he halted on the doorstep and took a long breath. "Filmore's missed his vocation; ought to be nurse to a paralytic," he thought. "He'd love to have to wheel me about in a chair."

After the first shock of the biting air he began to find it exhilarating, and walked along at a good pace, dragging one leg ever so little after the other. (The *masseur* had promised him that he'd soon be rid of that stiffness.) Yes—decidedly a fellow like himself ought to have a younger valet; a more cheerful one, anyhow. He felt like a young'un himself this evening; as he turned into Fifth Avenue he rather wished he could meet some one he knew, some man who'd say afterward at his club: "Warley? Why, I saw him sprinting up Fifth Avenue the other night like a two-year-old; that night it was four or five below . . ." He needed a good counter-irritant for Filmore's gloom. "Always have young people about you," he thought as he walked along; and at the words his mind turned to Elfrida Flight, next to whom he would soon be sitting in a warm pleasantly lit dining-room—*where?*

It came as abruptly as that: the gap in his memory. He pulled up at it as if his advance had been checked by a chasm in the pavement at his feet. Where the dickens was he going to dine? And with whom was he going to dine? God! But things didn't happen in that way; a sound strong man didn't suddenly have to stop in the middle of the street and ask himself where he was going to dine . . .

"Perfect in mind, body and understanding." The old legal phrase bobbed up inconsequently into his thoughts. Less than two minutes ago he had answered in every particular to that description; what was he now? He put his hand to his forehead, which was bursting; then he lifted his hat and let the cold air blow for a while on his overheated temples. It was queer, how hot he'd got, walking. Fact was, he'd been sprinting along at a damned good pace. In future he must try to remember not to hurry . . . Hang it—one more thing to remember! . . . Well, but what was all the fuss about? Of course, as people got older their memories were subject to these momentary lapses; he'd noticed it often enough among his contemporaries. And, brisk and alert though he still was, it wouldn't do to imagine himself totally exempt from human ills . . .

Where was it he was dining? Why, somewhere farther up Fifth Avenue; he was perfectly sure of that. With that lovely . . . that lovely . . . No; better not make any effort for the moment. Just keep calm, and stroll slowly along. When he came to the right street corner of course he'd spot it; and then everything would be perfectly clear again. He walked on, more deliberately, trying to empty his mind of all thoughts. "Above all," he said to himself, "don't worry."

He tried to beguile his nervousness by thinking of amusing things. "Decline the boredom—" He thought he might get off that joke tonight. "Mrs. Jaspar requests the pleasure—Mr. Warley declines the boredom." Not so bad, really; and he had an idea he'd never told it to the people . . . what in hell *was* their name? . . . the people he was on his way to dine with . . . *Mrs. Jaspar requests the pleasure.* Poor old Mrs. Jaspar; again it occurred to him that he hadn't always been very civil to her in old times. When everybody's running after a fellow it's pardonable now and then to chuck a boring dinner at the last minute; but all the same as one grew older one understood better how an unintentional slight of that sort might cause offense, cause even pain. And he hated to cause people pain . . . He thought perhaps he'd better call on Mrs. Jaspar some afternoon. She'd be surprised! Or ring her up, poor old girl, and propose himself, just informally, for dinner. One dull evening wouldn't kill him—

and how pleased she'd be! Yes—he thought decidedly . . . When he got to be her age, he could imagine how much he'd like it if somebody still in the running should ring him up unexpectedly and say—

He stopped, and looked up, slowly, wonderingly, at the wide illuminated façade of the house he was approaching. Queer coincidence—it was the Jaspar house. And all lit up; for a dinner evidently. And that was queerer yet; almost uncanny; for here he was, in front of the door, as the clock struck a quarter past eight; and of course—he remembered it quite clearly now—it was just here, it was with Mrs. Jasper, that he was dining . . . Those little lapses of memory never lasted more than a second or two. How right he'd been not to let himself worry. He pressed his hand on the door-bell.

"God," he thought, as the double doors swung open, "but it's good to get in out of the cold."

V

In that hushed sonorous house the sound of the door-bell was as loud to the two women upstairs as if it had been rung in the next room.

Miss Cress raised her head in surprise, and Lavinia dropped Mrs. Jaspar's other false set (the more comfortable one) with a clatter on the marble wash-stand. She stumbled across the dressing-room, and hastened out to the landing. With Munson absent, there was no knowing how George might muddle things . . .

Miss Cress joined her. "Who is it?" she whispered excitedly. Below, they heard the sound of a hat and a walking stick being laid down on the big marble-topped table in the hall, and then George's stentorian drone: "Mr. Anson Warley."

"It is—it *is!* I can see him—a gentleman in evening clothes," Miss Cress whispered, hanging over the stair-rail.

"Good gracious—mercy me! And Munson not here! Oh, whatever, whatever shall we do?" Lavinia was trembling so violently that she had to clutch the stair-rail to prevent herself from falling. Miss Cress thought, with her cold lucidity: "She's a good deal sicker than the old woman."

"What shall we do, Miss Cress? That fool of a George—he's showing him in! Who could have thought it?" Miss Cress knew the images that were whirling through Lavinia's brain: the vision of Mrs. Jaspar's having another stroke at the sight of this mysterious intruder, of Mr. Anson Warley's seeing her there, in her impotence and her abasement, of the family's being summoned, and rushing in to exclaim, to question, to be horrified and furious—and all because poor old Munson's memory was going, like his mistress's, like Lavinia's, and because he had forgotten that it was one of the *dinner nights*. Oh, misery! . . . The tears were running down Lavinia's cheeks, and Miss Cress knew she was thinking: "If the daughters send him off—and they will—where's he going to, old and deaf as he is, and all his people dead? Oh, if only he can hold on till she dies, and get his pension . . ."

Lavinia recovered herself with one of her supreme efforts. "Miss Cress, we must go down at once, at once! Something dreadful's going to happen . . ." She began to totter toward the little velvet-lined lift in the corner of the landing.

Miss Cress took pity on her. "Come along," she said. "But nothing dreadful's going to happen. You'll see."

"Oh, thank you, Miss Cress. But the shock—the awful shock to her—of seeing that strange gentleman walk in."

"Not a bit of it." Miss Cress laughed as she stepped into the lift. "He's not a stranger. She's expecting him."

"Expecting him? Expecting Mr. Warley?"

"Sure she is. She told me so just now. She says she invited him yesterday."

"But, Miss Cress, what are you thinking of? Invite him—how? When you know she can't write nor telephone?"

"Well, she says she saw him; she saw him last night at a dance."

"Oh, God," murmured Lavinia, covering her eyes with her hands.

"At a dance at the Fred Amesworths'—that's what she said," Miss Cress pursued, feeling the same little shiver run down her back as when Mrs. Jaspar had made the statement to her.

"The Amesworths—oh, not the Amesworths?" Lavinia echoed, shivering too. She dropped her hands from her face, and followed Miss Cress out of the lift. Her expression had become less anguished, and the nurse wondered why. In reality, she was thinking, in a sort of dreary beatitude: "But if she's suddenly got as much worse as this, she'll go before me, after all, my poor lady, and I'll be able to see to it that she's properly laid out and dressed, and nobody but Lavinia's hands'll touch her."

"You'll see—if she was expecting him, as she says, it won't give her a shock, anyhow. Only, how did *he* know?" Miss Cress whispered, with an acuter renewal of her shiver. She followed Lavinia with muffled steps down the passage to the pantry, and from there the two women stole into the dining-room, and placed themselves noiselessly at its farther end, behind the tall Coromandel screen through the cracks of which they could peep into the empty room.

The long table was set, as Mrs. Jaspar always insisted that it should be on these occasions; but old Munson not having returned, the gold plate (which his mistress also insisted on) had not been got out, and all down the table, as Lavinia saw with horror, George had laid the coarse blue and white plates from the servants' hall. The electric wall-lights were on, and the candles lit in the branching Sèvres candelabra—so much at least had been done. But the flowers in the great central dish of Rose Dubarry porcelain, and in the smaller dishes which accompanied it—the flowers, oh, shame, had been forgotten! They were no longer real flowers; the family had long since suppressed that expense; and no wonder, for Mrs. Jaspar always insisted on orchids. But Grace, the youngest daughter who was the kindest, had hit on the clever device of arranging three beautiful clusters of artificial orchids and maiden hair, which had only to be lifted from their shelf in the pantry and set in the dishes—only, of course, that imbecile footman had forgotten, or had not known where to find them. And, oh, horror, realizing his oversight too late, no doubt, to appeal to Lavinia, he had taken some old newspapers and bunched them up into something that he probably thought resembled a bouquet, and crammed one into each of the priceless Rose Dubarry dishes.

Lavinia clutched at Miss Cress's arm. "Oh, look—look what he's done; I shall die of the shame of it . . . Oh, Miss, hadn't we better slip around to the drawing-room and try to coax my poor lady upstairs again, afore she ever notices?"

Miss Cress, peering through the crack of the screen, could hardly suppress a giggle. For at that moment the double doors of the dining-room were thrown open, and George, shuffling about in a baggy livery inherited from a long-departed predecessor of more commanding build, bawled out in his loud singsong: "Dinner is served, madam."

"Oh, it's too late," moaned Lavinia. Miss Cress signed to her to keep silent, and the two watchers glued their eyes to their respective cracks of the screen.

What they saw, far off down the vista of empty drawing-rooms, and after an interval during which (as Lavinia knew) the imaginary guests were supposed to file in and take their seats, was the entrance, at the end of the ghostly cortège, of a very old woman, still tall and towering, on the arm of a man somewhat smaller than herself, with a fixed smile on a darkly pink face, and a slim erect figure clad in perfect evening clothes, who advanced with short measured steps, profiting (Miss Cress noticed) by the support of the arm he was supposed to sustain. "Well—I never!" was the nurse's inward comment.

The couple continued to advance, with rigid smiles and eyes staring straight ahead. Neither turned to the other, neither spoke. All their attention was concentrated on the immense, the almost unachievable effort of reaching that point, half way down the long dinner table, opposite the big

Dubarry dish, where George was drawing back a gilt armchair for Mrs. Jaspar. At last they reached it, and Mrs. Jaspar seated herself, and waved a stony hand to Mr. Warley. "On my right." He gave a little bow, like the bend of a jointed doll, and with infinite precaution let himself down into his chair. Beads of perspiration were standing on his forehead, and Miss Cress saw him draw out his handkerchief and wipe them stealthily away. He then turned his head somewhat stiffly toward his hostess.

"Beautiful flowers," he said, with great precision and perfect gravity, waving his hand toward the bunched-up newspaper in the bowl of Sèvres.

Mrs. Jaspar received the tribute with complacency. "So glad . . . orchids . . . From High Lawn . . . every morning," she simpered.

"Mar-vellous," Mr. Warley completed.

"I always say to the Bishop . . ." Mrs. Jaspar continued.

"Ha—of course," Mr. Warley warmly assented.

"Not that I don't think . . ."

"Ha—rather!"

George had reappeared from the pantry with a blue crockery dish of mashed potatoes. This he handed in turn to one after another of the imaginary guests, and finally presented to Mrs. Jaspar and her right-hand neighbour.

They both helped themselves cautiously, and Mrs. Jaspar addressed an arch smile to Mr. Warley. " 'Nother month—no more oysters."

"Ha—no more!"

George, with a bottle of Apollinaris wrapped in a napkin, was saying to each guest in turn: "Perrier-Jouet, 'ninety-five." (He had picked that up, thought Miss Cress, from hearing old Munson repeat it so often.)

"Hang it—well, then just a sip," murmured Mr. Warley.

"Old times," bantered Mrs. Jaspar; and the two turned to each other and bowed their heads and touched glasses.

"I often tell Mrs. Amesworth . . ." Mrs. Jaspar continued, bending to an imaginary presence across the table.

"Ha—*ha!*" Mr. Warley approved.

George reappeared and slowly encircled the table with a dish of spinach. After the spinach the Apollinaris also went the rounds again, announced successively as Château Lafite, 'seventy-four, and "the old Newbold Madeira." Each time that George approached his glass, Mr. Warley made a feint of lifting a defensive hand, and then smiled and yielded. "Might as well—hanged for a sheep . . ." he remarked gaily; and Mrs. Jaspar giggled.

Finally a dish of Malaga grapes and apples was handed. Mrs. Jaspar, now growing perceptibly languid, and nodding with more and more effort at Mr. Warley's pleasantries, transferred a bunch of grapes to her plate, but nibbled only two or three. "Tired," she said suddenly, in a whimper like a child's; and she rose, lifting herself up by the arms of her chair, and leaning over to catch the eye of an invisible lady, presumably Mrs. Amesworth, seated opposite to her. Mr. Warley was on his feet too, supporting himself by resting one hand on the table in a jaunty attitude. Mrs. Jaspar waved to him to be reseated. "Join us—after cigars," she smilingly ordained; and with a great and concentrated effort he bowed to her as she passed toward the double doors which George was throwing open. Slowly, majestically, the purple velvet train disappeared down the long enfilade of illuminated rooms, and the last door closed behind her.

"Well, I do believe she's enjoyed it!" chuckled Miss Cress, taking Lavinia by the arm to help her back to the hall. Lavinia, for weeping, could not answer.

VI

Anson Warley found himself in the hall again, getting into his fur-lined overcoat. He remembered suddenly thinking that the rooms had been intensely over-heated, and that all the other guests had talked very loud and laughed inordinately. "Very good talk though, I must say," he had to acknowledge.

In the hall, as he got his arms into his coat (rather a job, too, after that Perrier-Jouet) he remembered saying to somebody (perhaps it was to the old butler): "Slipping off early—going on; 'nother engagement," and thinking to himself the while that when he got out into the fresh air again he would certainly remember where the other engagement was. He smiled a little while the servant, who seemed a clumsy fellow, fumbled with the fastening of the door. "And Filmore, who thought I wasn't well enough to dine out! Damned ass! What would he say if he knew I was going on?"

The door opened, and with an immense sense of exhilaration Mr. Warley issued forth from the house and drew in a first deep breath of night air. He heard the door closed and bolted behind him, and continued to stand motionless on the step, expanding his chest, and drinking in the icy draught.

"'Spose it's about the last house where they give you 'ninety-five Perrier-Jouet," he thought; and then: "Never heard better talk either . . ."

He smiled again with satisfaction at the memory of the wine and the wit. Then he took a step forward, to where a moment before the pavement had been—and where now there was nothing.

The Bride Comes to Yellow Sky

STEPHEN CRANE

(1871–1900)

I

The great Pullman was whirling onward with such dignity of motion that a glance from the window seemed simply to prove that the plains of Texas were pouring eastward. Vast flats of green grass, dull-hued spaces of mesquite and cactus, little groups of frame houses, woods of light and tender trees, all were sweeping into the east, sweeping over the horizon, a precipice.

A newly married pair had boarded this coach at San Antonio. The man's face was reddened from many days in the wind and sun, and a direct result of his new black clothes was that his brick-colored hands were constantly performing in a most conscious fashion. From time to time he looked down respectfully at his attire. He sat with a hand on each knee, like a man waiting in a barber's shop. The glances he devoted to other passengers were furtive and shy.

The bride was not pretty, nor was she very young. She wore a dress of blue cashmere, with small reservations of velvet here and there, and with steel buttons abounding. She continually twisted her head to regard her puff sleeves, very stiff, straight, and high. They embarrassed her. It was quite apparent that she had cooked, and that she expected to cook, dutifully. The blushes caused by the careless scrutiny of some passengers as she had entered the car were strange to see upon this plain, underclass countenance, which was drawn in placid, almost emotionless lines.

They were evidently very happy. "Ever been in a parlor car before?" he asked, smiling with delight.

"No," she answered. "I never was. It's fine, ain't it?"

"Great! And then after a while we'll go forward to the diner, and get a big layout. Finest meal in the world. Charge a dollar."

"Oh, do they?" cried the bride. "Charge a dollar? Why, that's too much—for us—ain't it, Jack?"

"Not this trip, anyhow," he answered bravely. "We're going to go the whole thing."

Later, he explained to her about the trains. "You see, it's a thousand miles from one end of Texas to the other; and this train runs right across it, and never stops but four times." He had the pride of an owner. He pointed out to her the dazzling fittings of the coach; and in truth her eyes opened wider as she contemplated the sea-green figured velvet, the shining brass, silver, and glass, the wood that gleamed as darkly brilliant as the surface of a pool of oil. At one end a bronze figure sturdily held a support for a separated chamber, and at convenient places on the ceiling were frescoes in olive and silver.

To the minds of the pair, their surroundings reflected the glory of their marriage that morning in San Antonio. This was the environment of their new estate, and the man's face in particular beamed with an elation that made him appear ridiculous to the negro porter. This individual at times surveyed them from afar with an amused and superior grin. On other occasions he bullied them with skill in ways that did not make it exactly plain to them that they were being bullied. He subtly used all the manners of the most unconquerable kind of snobbery. He oppressed them; but of this oppression they had small knowledge, and they speedily forgot that infrequently a number of travelers covered them with stares of derisive enjoyment. Historically there was supposed to be something infinitely humorous in their situation.

"We are due in Yellow Sky at 3:42," he said, looking tenderly into her eyes.

"Oh, are we?" she said, as if she had not been aware of it. To evince surprise at her husband's statement was part of her wifely amiability. She took from a pocket a little silver watch; and as she held it before her, and stared at it with a frown of attention, the new husband's face shone.

"I bought it in San Anton' from a friend of mine," he told her gleefully.

"It's seventeen minutes past twelve," she said, looking up at him with a kind of shy and clumsy coquetry. A passenger, noting this play, grew excessively sardonic, and winked at himself in one of the numerous mirrors.

At last they went to the dining car. Two rows of negro waiters, in glowing white suits, surveyed their entrance with the interest, and also the equanimity, of men who had been forewarned. The pair fell to the lot of a waiter who happened to feel pleasure in steering them through their meal. He viewed them with the manner of a fatherly pilot, his countenance radiant with benevolence. The patronage, entwined with the ordinary deference, was not plain to them. And yet, as they returned to their coach, they showed in their faces a sense of escape.

To the left, miles down a long purple slope, was a little ribbon of mist where moved the keening Rio Grande. The train was approaching it at an angle, and the apex was Yellow Sky. Presently it was apparent that, as the distance from Yellow Sky grew shorter, the husband became commensurately restless. His brick-red hands were more insistent in their prominence. Occasionally he was even rather absent-minded and faraway when the bride leaned forward and addressed him.

As a matter of truth, Jack Potter was beginning to find the shadow of a deed weigh upon him like a leaden slab. He, the town marshal of Yellow Sky, a man known, liked, and feared in his corner, a prominent person, had gone to San Antonio to meet a girl he believed he loved, and there, after the usual prayers, had actually induced her to marry him, without consulting Yellow Sky for any part of the transaction. He was now bringing his bride before an innocent and unsuspecting community.

Of course people in Yellow Sky married as it pleased them, in accordance with a general custom; but such was Potter's thought of his duty to his friends, or of their idea of his duty, or of an unspoken form which does not control men in these matters, that he felt he was heinous. He had committed an extraordinary crime. Face to face with this girl in San Antonio, and spurred by his sharp impulse, he had gone headlong over all the social hedges. At San Antonio he was like a man hidden in the dark. A knife to sever any friendly duty, any form, was easy to his hand in that remote city. But the hour of Yellow Sky—the hour of daylight—was approaching.

He knew full well that his marriage was an important thing to his town. It could only be exceeded by the burning of the new hotel. His friends could not forgive him. Frequently he had reflected on the advisability of telling them by telegraph, but a new cowardice had been upon him. He feared to do it. And now the train was hurrying him toward a scene of amazement, glee, and reproach. He glanced out of the window at the line of haze swinging slowly in toward the train.

Yellow Sky had a kind of brass band, which played painfully, to the delight of the populace. He laughed without heart as he thought of it. If the citizens could dream of his prospective arrival with his bride, they would parade the band at the station and escort them, amid cheers and laughing congratulations, to his adobe home.

He resolved that he would use all the devices of speed and plains-craft in making the journey from the station to his house. Once within that safe citadel, he could issue some sort of a vocal bulletin, and then not go among the citizens until they had time to wear off a little of their enthusiasm.

The bride looked anxiously at him. "What's worrying you, Jack?"

He laughed again. "I'm not worrying, girl. I'm only thinking of Yellow Sky."

She flushed in comprehension.

A sense of mutual guilt invaded their minds and developed a finer tenderness. They looked at each other with eyes softly aglow. But Potter often laughed the same nervous laugh. The flush upon the bride's face seemed quite permanent.

The traitor to the feelings of Yellow Sky narrowly watched the speeding landscape. "We're nearly there," he said.

Presently the porter came and announced the proximity of Potter's home. He held a brush in his hand, and, with all his airy superiority gone, he brushed Potter's new clothes as the latter slowly turned this way and that way. Potter fumbled out a coin and gave it to the porter, as he had seen others do. It was a heavy and muscle-bound business, as that of a man shoeing his first horse.

The porter took their bag, and as the train began to slow they moved forward to the hooded platform of the car. Presently the two engines and their long string of coaches rushed into the station of Yellow Sky.

"They have to take water here," said Potter, from a constricted throat and in mournful cadence, as one announcing death. Before the train stopped, his eye had swept the length of the platform, and he was glad and astonished to see there was none upon it but the station-agent, who, with a slightly hurried and anxious air, was walking toward the water tanks. When the train had halted, the porter alighted first, and placed in position a little temporary step.

"Come on, girl," said Potter, hoarsely. As he helped her down they each laughed on a false note. He took the bag from the negro, and bade his wife cling to his arm. As they slunk rapidly away, his hangdog glance perceived that they were unloading the two trunks, and also that the station-agent, far ahead near the baggage car, had turned and was running toward him, making gestures. He laughed, and groaned as he laughed, when he noted the first effect of his marital bliss upon Yellow Sky. He gripped his wife's arm firmly to his side, and they fled. Behind them the porter stood, chuckling fatuously.

II

The California express on the Southern Railway was due at Yellow Sky in twenty-one minutes. There were six men at the bar of the Weary

Gentleman saloon. One was a drummer who talked a great deal and rapidly; three were Texans who did not care to talk at that time; and two were Mexican sheepherders, who did not talk as a general practice in the Weary Gentleman saloon. The barkeeper's dog lay on the boardwalk that crossed in front of the door. His head was on his paws, and he glanced drowsily here and there with the constant vigilance of a dog that is kicked on occasion. Across the sandy street were some vivid green grass-plots, so wonderful in appearance, amid the sands that burned near them in a blazing sun, that they caused a doubt in the mind. They exactly resembled the grass mats used to represent lawns on the stage. At the cooler end of the railway station, a man without a coat sat in a tilted chair and smoked his pipe. The fresh-cut bank of the Rio Grande circled near the town, and there could be seen beyond it a great plum-colored plain of mesquite.

Save for the busy drummer and his companions in the saloon, Yellow Sky was dozing. The newcomer leaned gracefully upon the bar, and recited many tales with the confidence of a bard who has come upon a new field.

"—and at the moment that the old man fell downstairs with the bureau in his arms, the old woman was coming up with two scuttles of coal, and of course—"

The drummer's tale was interrupted by a young man who suddenly appeared in the open door. He cried: "Scratchy Wilson's drunk, and has turned loose with both hands." The two Mexicans at once set down their glasses and faded out of the rear entrance of the saloon.

The drummer, innocent and jocular, answered: "All right, old man. S'pose he has? Come in and have a drink, anyhow."

But the information had made such an obvious cleft in every skull in the room that the drummer was obliged to see its importance. All had become instantly solemn. "Say," said he, mystified, "what is this?" His three companions made the introductory gesture of eloquent speech, but the young man at the door forestalled them.

"It means, my friend," he answered, as he came into the saloon, "that for the next two hours this town won't be a health resort."

The barkeeper went to the door and locked and barred it. Reaching out of the window, he pulled in heavy wooden shutters and barred them. Immediately a solemn chapel-like gloom was upon the place. The drummer was looking from one to another.

"But say," he cried, "what is this, anyhow? You don't mean there is going to be a gunfight?"

"Don't know whether there'll be a fight or not," answered one man, grimly. "But there'll be some shootin'—some good shootin'."

The young man who had warned them waved his hand. "Oh, there'll be a fight fast enough, if any one wants it. Anybody can get a fight out there in the street. There's a fight just waiting."

The drummer seemed to be swayed between the interest of a foreigner and a perception of personal danger.

"What did you say his name was?" he asked.

"Scratchy Wilson," they answered in chorus.

"And will he kill anybody? What are you going to do? Does this happen often? Does he rampage around like this once a week or so? Can he break in that door?"

"No; he can't break down that door," replied the barkeeper. "He's tried it three times. But when he comes you'd better lay down on the floor, stranger. He's dead sure to shoot at it, and a bullet may come through."

Thereafter the drummer kept a strict eye upon the door. The time had not yet been called for him to hug the floor, but, as a minor precaution, he sidled near to the wall. "Will he kill anybody?" he said again.

The men laughed low and scornfully at the question.

"He's out to shoot, and he's out for trouble. Don't see any good in experimentin' with him."

"But what do you do in a case like this? What do you do?"

A man responded: "Why, he and Jack Potter—"

"But," in chorus the other men interrupted, "Jack Potter's in San Anton'."

"Well, who is he? What's he got to do with it?"

"Oh, he's the town marshal. He goes out and fights Scratchy when he gets on one of these tears."

"Wow!" said the drummer, mopping his brow. "Nice job he's got."

The voices had toned away to mere whisperings. The drummer wished to ask further questions, which were born of an increasing anxiety and bewilderment; but when he attempted them, the men merely looked at him in irritation and motioned him to remain silent. A tense waiting hush was upon them. In the deep shadows of the room their eyes shone as they listened for sounds from the street. One man made three gestures at the barkeeper; and the latter, moving like a ghost, handed him a glass and a bottle. The man poured a full glass of whiskey, and set down the bottle noiselessly. He gulped the whiskey in a swallow, and turned again toward the door in immovable silence. The drummer saw that the barkeeper, without a sound, had taken a Winchester from beneath the bar. Later he saw this individual beckoning to him, so he tiptoed across the room.

"You better come with me back of the bar."

"No, thanks," said the drummer, perspiring. "I'd rather be where I can make a break for the back door."

Whereupon the man of bottles made a kindly but peremptory gesture.

The drummer obeyed it, and, finding himself seated on a box with his head below the level of the bar, balm was laid upon his soul at sight of various zinc and copper fittings that bore a resemblance to armor plate. The barkeeper took a seat comfortably upon an adjacent box.

"You see," he whispered, "this here Scratchy Wilson is a wonder with a gun—a perfect wonder—and when he goes on the war trail, we hunt our holes—naturally. He's about the last one of the old gang that used to hang out along the river here. He's a terror when he's drunk. When he's sober he's all right—kind of simple—wouldn't hurt a fly—nicest fellow in town. But when he's drunk—whoo!"

There were periods of stillness. "I wish Jack Potter was back from San Anton'," said the barkeeper. "He shot Wilson up once—in the leg—and he would sail in and pull out the kinks in this thing."

Presently they heard from a distance the sound of a shot, followed by three wild yowls. It instantly removed a bond from the men in the darkened saloon. There was a shuffling of feet. They looked at each other. "Here he comes," they said.

III

A man in a maroon-colored flannel shirt, which had been purchased for purposes of decoration, and made principally by some Jewish women on the East Side of New York, rounded a corner and walked into the middle of the main street of Yellow Sky. In either hand the man held a long, heavy, blue-black revolver. Often he yelled, and these cries rang through a semblance of a deserted village, shrilly flying over the roofs in a volume that seemed to have no relation to the ordinary vocal strength of a man. It was as if the surrounding stillness formed the arch of a tomb over him. These cries of ferocious challenge rang against walls of silence. And his boots had red tops with gilded imprints, of the kind beloved in winter by little sledding boys on the hillsides of New England.

The man's face flamed in a rage begot of whiskey. His eyes, rolling, and yet keen for ambush, hunted the still doorways and windows. He walked with the creeping movement of the midnight cat. As it occurred to him, he roared menacing information. The long revolvers in his hands were as easy as straws; they were moved with an electric swiftness. The little fingers of each hand played sometimes in a musician's way. Plain from the low collar of the shirt, the cords of his neck straightened and sank, straightened and sank, as passion moved him. The only sounds were his terrible invitations. The calm adobes preserved their demeanor at the passing of this small thing in the middle of the street.

There was no offer of fight—no offer of fight. The man called to the sky. There were no attractions. He bellowed and fumed and swayed his revolvers here and everywhere.

The dog of the barkeeper of the Weary Gentleman saloon had not appreciated the advance of events. He yet lay dozing in front of his master's door. At sight of the dog, the man paused and raised his revolver humorously. At sight of the man, the dog sprang up and walked diagonally away, with a sullen head, and growling. The man yelled, and the dog broke into a gallop. As it was about to enter an alley, there was a loud noise, a whistling, and something spat the ground directly before it. The dog screamed, and, wheeling in terror, galloped headlong in a new direction. Again there was a noise, a whistling, and sand was kicked viciously before it. Fear-stricken, the dog turned and flurried like an animal in a pen. The man stood laughing, his weapons at his hips.

Ultimately the man was attracted by the closed door of the Weary Gentleman saloon. He went to it and, hammering with a revolver, demanded drink.

The door remaining imperturbable, he picked a bit of paper from the walk, and nailed it to the framework with a knife. He then turned his back contemptuously upon this popular resort and, walking to the opposite side of the street and spinning there on his heel quickly and lithely, fired at the bit of paper. He missed it by a half-inch. He swore at himself, and went away. Later, he comfortably fusilladed the windows of his most intimate friend. The man was playing with this town. It was a toy for him.

But still there was no offer of fight. The name of Jack Potter, his ancient antagonist, entered his mind, and he concluded that it would be a glad thing if he should go to Potter's house, and by bombardment induce him to come out and fight. He moved in the direction of his desire, chanting Apache scalp-music.

When he arrived at it, Potter's house presented the same still front as had the other adobes. Taking up a strategic position, the man howled a challenge. But this house regarded him as might a great stone god. It gave no sign. After a decent wait, the man howled further challenges, mingling with them wonderful epithets.

Presently there came the spectacle of a man churning himself into deepest rage over the immobility of a house. He fumed at it as the winter wind attacks a prairie cabin in the North. To the distance there should have gone the sound of a tumult like the fighting of two hundred Mexicans. As necessity bade him, he paused for breath or to reload his revolvers.

IV

Potter and his bride walked sheepishly and with speed. Sometimes they laughed together shamefacedly and low.

"Next corner, dear," he said finally.

They put forth the efforts of a pair walking bowed against a strong wind. Potter was about to raise a finger to point the first appearance of the new home when, as they circled the corner, they came face to face with a man in a maroon-colored shirt, who was feverishly pushing cartridges into a large revolver. Upon the instant the man dropped his revolver to the ground, and, like lightning, whipped another from its holster. The second weapon was aimed at the bridegroom's chest.

There was a silence. Potter's mouth seemed to be merely a grave for his tongue. He exhibited an instinct to at once loosen his arm from the woman's grip, and he dropped the bag to the sand. As for the bride, her face had gone as yellow as old cloth. She was a slave to hideous rites, gazing at the apparitional snake.

The two men faced each other at a distance of three paces. He of the revolver smiled with a new and quiet ferocity.

"Tried to sneak up on me," he said. "Tried to sneak up on me!" His eyes grew more baleful. As Potter made a slight movement, the man thrust his revolver venomously forward. "No; don't you do it, Jack Potter. Don't you move a finger toward a gun just yet. Don't you move an eyelash. The time has come for me to settle with you, and I'm goin' to do it my own way, and loaf along with no interferin'. So if you don't want a gun bent on you, just mind what I tell you."

Potter looked at his enemy. "I ain't got a gun on me, Scratchy," he said. "Honest, I ain't." He was stiffening and steadying, but yet somewhere at the back of his mind a vision of the Pullman floated: the sea-green figured velvet, the shining brass, silver, and glass, the wood that gleamed as darkly brilliant as the surface of a pool of oil—all the glory of the marriage, the environment of the new estate. "You know I fight when it comes to fighting, Scratchy Wilson; but I ain't got a gun on me. You'll have to do all the shootin' yourself."

His enemy's face went livid. He stepped forward, and lashed his weapon to and fro before Potter's chest. "Don't you tell me you ain't got no gun on you, you whelp. Don't tell me no lie like that. There ain't a man in Texas ever seen you without no gun. Don't take me for no kid." His eyes blazed with light, and his throat worked like a pump.

"I ain't takin' you for no kid," answered Potter. His heels had not moved an inch backward. "I'm takin' you for a damn fool. I tell you I ain't got a gun, and I ain't. If you're goin' to shoot me up, you better begin now. You'll never get a chance like this again."

So much enforced reasoning had told on Wilson's rage. He was calmer. "If you ain't got a gun, why ain't you got a gun?" he sneered. "Been to Sunday school?"

"I ain't got a gun because I've just come from San Anton' with my wife. I'm married," said Potter. "And if I'd thought there was going to be any galoots like you prowling around when I brought my wife home, I'd had a gun, and don't you forget it."

"Married!" said Scratchy, not at all comprehending.

"Yes, married. I'm married," said Potter, distinctly.

"Married?" said Scratchy. Seemingly for the first time, he saw the drooping, drowning woman at the other man's side. "No!" he said. He was like a creature allowed a glimpse of another world. He moved a pace backward, and his arm, with the revolver, dropped to his side. "Is this the lady?" he asked.

"Yes; this is the lady," answered Potter.

There was another period of silence.

"Well," said Wilson at last, slowly, "I s'pose it's all off now."

"It's all off if you say so, Scratchy. You know I didn't make the trouble." Potter lifted his valise.

"Well, I 'low it's off, Jack," said Wilson. He was looking at the ground. "Married!" He was not a student of chivalry; it was merely that in the presence of this foreign condition he was a simple child of the earlier plains. He picked up his starboard revolver, and, placing both weapons in their holsters, he went away. His feet made funnel-shaped tracks in the heavy sand.

The Lost Phoebe

THEODORE DREISER

(1871–1945)

They lived together in a part of the country which was not so prosperous as it had once been, about three miles from one of those small towns that, instead of increasing in population, is steadily decreasing. The territory was not very thickly settled; perhaps a house every other mile or so, with large areas of corn- and wheat-land and fallow fields that at odd seasons had been sown to timothy and clover. Their particular house was part log and part frame, the log portion being the old original home of Henry's grandfather. The new portion, of now rain-beaten, time-worn slabs, through which the wind squeaked in the chinks at times, and which several overshadowing elms and a butternut-tree made picturesque and reminiscently pathetic, but a little damp, was erected by Henry when he was twenty-one and just married.

That was forty-eight years before. The furniture inside, like the house outside, was old and mildewy and reminiscent of an earlier day. You have seen the what-not of cherry wood, perhaps, with spiral legs and fluted top. It was there. The old-fashioned four poster bed, with its ball-like protuberances and deep curving incisions, was there also, a sadly alienated descendant of an early Jacobean ancestor. The bureau of cherry was also high and wide and solidly built, but faded-looking, and with a musty odor. The rag carpet that underlay all these sturdy examples of enduring furniture was a weak, faded, lead-and-pink-colored affair woven by Phœbe Ann's own hands, when she was fifteen years younger than she was when she died. The creaky wooden loom on which it had been done now stood like a dusty, bony skeleton, along with a broken rocking-chair, a worm-eaten clothes-press—Heaven knows how old—a lime-stained bench that had once been used to keep flowers on outside the door, and other decrepit factors of household utility, in an east room that was a lean-to against this so-called main portion. All sorts of other broken-down furniture were about this place; an antiquated clothes-horse, cracked in two of its ribs; a broken mirror in an old cherry frame, which had fallen from a nail and cracked itself three days before their youngest son, Jerry, died; an extension hat-rack, which once had had porcelain knobs on the ends of its pegs; and a sewing-machine, long since outdone in its clumsy mechanism by rivals of a newer generation.

The orchard to the east of the house was full of gnarled old apple-trees, worm-eaten as to trunks and branches, and fully ornamented with green and white lichens, so that it had a sad, greenish-white, silvery effect in moonlight. The low outhouses, which had once housed chickens, a horse or two, a cow, and several pigs, were covered with patches of moss as to their roof, and the sides had been free of paint for so long that they were blackish gray as to color, and a little spongy. The picket-fence in front, with its gate squeaky and askew, and the side fences of the stake-and-rider type were in an equally run-down condition. As a matter of fact, they had aged synchronously with the persons who lived here, old Henry Reifsneider and his wife Phœbe Ann.

They had lived here, these two, ever since their marriage, forty-eight years before, and Henry had lived here before that from his childhood up. His father and mother, well along in years when he was a boy, had invited him to bring his wife here when he had first fallen in love and decided to marry; and he had done so. His father and mother were the companions of himself and his wife for ten years after they were married, when both died; and then Henry and Phœbe were left with their five children growing lustily apace. But all sorts of things had happened since then. Of the seven children, all told, that had been born to them, three had died; one girl had gone to Kansas; one boy had gone to Sioux Falls, never even to be heard of after; another boy had gone to Washington; and the last girl lived five counties away in the same State, but was so burdened with cares of her own that she rarely gave them a thought. Time and a commonplace home life that had never been attractive had weaned them thoroughly, so that, wherever they were, they gave little thought as to how it might be with their father and mother.

Old Henry Reifsneider and his wife Phœbe were a loving couple. You perhaps know how it is with simple natures that fasten themselves like lichens on the stones of circumstance and weather their days to a crumbling conclusion. The great world sounds widely, but it has no call for them. They have no soaring intellect. The orchard, the meadow, the corn-field, the pig-pen, and the chicken-lot measure the range of their human activities. When the wheat is headed it is reaped and threshed; when the corn is browned and frosted it is cut and shocked; when the timothy is in full head it is cut, and the hay-cock erected. After that comes winter, with the hauling of grain to market, the sawing and splitting of wood, the simple chores of fire-building, meal-getting, occasional repairing, and visiting. Beyond these and the changes of weather—the snows, the rains, and the fair days—there are no immediate, significant things. All the rest of life is a far-off, clamorous phantasmagoria, flickering like Northern lights in the night, and sounding as faintly as cow-bells tinkling in the distance.

Old Henry and his wife Phœbe were as fond of each other as it is possible for two old people to be who have nothing else in this life to be fond of. He was a thin old man, seventy when she died, a queer, crotchety person with coarse gray-black hair and beard, quite straggly and unkempt. He looked at you out of dull, fishy, watery eyes that had deep-brown crow's-feet at the sides. His clothes, like the clothes of many farmers, were aged and angular and baggy, standing out at the pockets, not fitting about the neck, protuberant and worn at elbow and knee. Phœbe Ann was thin and shapeless, a very umbrella of a woman, clad in shabby black, and with a black bonnet for her best wear. As time had passed, and they had only themselves to look after, their movements had become slower and slower, their activities fewer and fewer. The annual keep of pigs had been reduced from five to one grunting porker, and the single horse which Henry now retained was a sleepy animal, not overnourished and not very clean. The chickens, of which formerly there was a large flock, had almost disappeared, owing to ferrets, foxes, and the lack of proper care, which produces disease. The former healthy garden was now a straggling memory of itself, and the vines and flower-beds that formerly ornamented the windows and dooryard had now become choking thickets. A will had been made which divided the small tax-eaten property equally among the remaining four, so that it was really of no interest to any of them. Yet these two lived together in peace and sympathy, only that now and then old Henry would become unduly cranky, complaining almost invariably that something had been neglected or mislaid which was of no importance at all.

"Phœbe, where's my corn-knife? You ain't never minded to let my things alone no more."

"Now you hush, Henry," his wife would caution him in a cracked and squeaky voice. "If you don't, I'll leave yuh. I'll git up and walk out of here some day, and then where would y' be? Y' ain't got anybody but me to look after yuh, so yuh just behave yourself. Your corn-knife's on the mantel where it's allus been unless you've gone an' put it summers else."

Old Henry, who knew his wife would never leave him in any circumstances, used to speculate at times as to what he would do if she were to die. That was the one leaving that he really feared. As he climbed on the chair at night to wind the old, long-pendulumed, double-weighted clock, or went finally to the front and the back door to see that they were safely shut in, it was a comfort to know that Phœbe was there, properly ensconced on her side of the bed, and that if he stirred restlessly in the night, she would be there to ask what he wanted.

"Now, Henry, do lie still! You're as restless as a chicken."

"Well, I can't sleep, Phœbe."

"Well, yuh needn't roll so, anyhow. Yuh kin let me sleep."

This usually reduced him to a state of somnolent ease. If she wanted a pail of water, it was a grumbling pleasure for him to get it; and if she did rise first to build the fires, he saw that the wood was cut and placed within easy reach. They divided this simple world nicely between them.

As the years had gone on, however, fewer and fewer people had called. They were well-known for a distance of as much as ten square miles as old Mr. and Mrs. Reifsneider, honest, moderately Christian, but too old to be really interesting any longer. The writing of letters had become an almost impossible burden too difficult to continue or even negotiate via others, although an occasional letter still did arrive from the daughter in Pemberton County. Now and then some old friend stopped with a pie or cake or a roasted chicken or duck, or merely to see that they were well; but even these kindly minded visits were no longer frequent.

One day in the early spring of her sixty-fourth year Mrs. Reifsneider took sick, and from a low fever passed into some indefinable ailment which, because of her age, was no longer curable. Old Henry drove to Swinnerton, the neighboring town, and procured a doctor. Some friends called, and the immediate care of her was taken off his hands. Then one chill spring night she died, and old Henry, in a fog of sorrow and uncertainty, followed her body to the nearest graveyard, an unattractive space with a few pines growing in it. Although he might have gone to the daughter in Pemberton or sent for her, it was really too much trouble and he was too weary and fixed. It was suggested to him at once by one friend and another that he come to stay with them awhile, but he did not see fit. He was so old and so fixed in his notions and so accustomed to the exact surroundings he had known all his days, that he could not think of leaving. He wanted to remain near where they had put his Phœbe; and the fact that he would have to live alone did not trouble him in the least. The living children were notified and the care of him offered if he would leave, but he would not.

"I kin make a shift for myself," he continually announced to old Dr. Morrow, who had attended his wife in this case. "I kin cook a little, and, besides, it don't take much more'n coffee an' bread in the mornin's to satisfy me. I'll get along now well enough. Yuh just let me be." And after many pleadings and proffers of advice, with supplies of coffee and bacon and baked bread duly offered and accepted, he was left to himself. For a while he sat idly outside his door brooding in the spring sun. He tried to revive his interest in farming, and to keep himself busy and free from thought by looking after the fields, which of late had been much neglected. It was a gloomy thing to come in of an evening, however, or in the afternoon and find no shadow of Phœbe where everything suggested her. By degrees he put a few of her things away. At night he sat beside his lamp and read in the papers that were left him occasionally or in a Bible that he had neglected for years, but he could get little solace from these things. Mostly he held his hand over his mouth and looked at the floor as he sat and thought of what had become of her, and how soon he himself would die. He made a great business of making his coffee in the morning and frying himself a little bacon at night; but his appetite was gone. The shell in which he had been housed so long seemed vacant, and its shadows were suggestive of immedicable griefs. So he lived quite dolefully for five long months, and then a change began.

It was one night, after he had looked after the front and the back door, wound the clock, blown out the light, and gone through all the selfsame motions that he had indulged in for years, that he went to bed not so much to sleep as to think. It was a moonlight night. The green-lichen-covered orchard just outside and to be seen from his bed where he now lay was a silvery affair, sweetly spectral. The moon shone through the east windows, throwing the pattern of the panes on the wooden floor, and making the old furniture, to which he was accustomed, stand out dimly in the room. As usual he had been thinking of Phœbe and the years when they had been young together, and of the children who had gone, and the poor shift he was making of his present days. The house was coming to be in a very bad state indeed. The bed-clothes were in disorder and not clean, for he made a wretched shift of washing. It was a terror to him. The roof leaked, causing things, some of them, to remain damp for weeks at a time, but he was getting into that brooding state where he would accept anything rather than exert himself. He preferred to pace slowly to and fro or to sit and think.

By twelve o'clock of this particular night he was asleep, however, and by two had waked again. The moon by this time had shifted to a position on the western side of the house, and it now shone in through the windows of the living-room and those of the kitchen beyond. A certain combination of furniture—a chair near a table, with his coat on it, the half-open kitchen door casting a shadow, and the position of a lamp near a paper—gave him an exact representation of Phœbe leaning over the table as he had often seen her do in life. It gave him a great start. Could it be she—or her ghost? He had scarcely ever believed in spirits; and still—— He looked at her fixedly in the feeble half-light, his old hair tingling oddly at the roots, and then sat up. The figure did not move. He put his thin legs out of the bed and sat looking at her, wondering if this could really be Phœbe. They had talked of ghosts often in their lifetime, of apparitions and omens; but they had never agreed that such things could be. It had never been a part of his wife's creed that she could have a spirit that could return to walk the earth. Her after-world was quite a different affair, a vague heaven, no less, from which the righteous did not trouble to return. Yet here she was now, bending over the table in her black skirt and gray shawl, her pale profile outlined against the moonlight.

"Phœbe," he called, thrilling from head to toe and putting out one bony hand, "have yuh come back?"

The figure did not stir, and he arose and walked uncertainly to the door, looking at it fixedly the while. As he drew near, however, the apparition resolved itself into its primal content—his old coat over the high-backed chair, the lamp by the paper, the half-open door.

"Well," he said to himself, his mouth open, "I thought shore I saw her." And he ran his hand strangely and vaguely through his hair, the while his nervous tension relaxed. Vanished as it had, it gave him the idea that she might return.

Another night, because of this first illusion, and because his mind was now constantly on her and he was old, he looked out of the window that was nearest his bed and commanded a hen-coop and pig-pen and a part of the wagon-shed, and there, a faint mist exuding from the damp of the ground, he thought he saw her again. It was one of those little wisps of mist, one of those faint exhalations of the earth that rise in a cool night after a warm day, and flicker like small white cypresses of fog before they disappear. In life it had been a custom of hers to cross this lot from her kitchen door to the pig-pen to throw in any scrap that was left from her cooking, and here she was again. He sat up and watched it strangely, doubtfully, because of his previous experience, but inclined, because of the nervous titillation that passed over his body, to believe that spirits really were, and that Phœbe, who would be concerned because of his lonely state, must be thinking about him, and hence returning. What other way would she have? How otherwise could she express herself? It would be within the province of her charity so to do, and like her loving interest in him. He quivered and watched it eagerly; but, a faint breath of air stirring, it wound away toward the fence and disappeared.

A third night, as he was actually dreaming, some ten days later, she came to his bedside and put her hand on his head.

"Poor Henry!" she said. "It's too bad."

He roused out of his sleep, actually to see her, he thought, moving from his bed-room into the one living-room, her figure a shadowy mass of black. The weak straining of his eyes caused little points of light to flicker about the outlines of her form. He arose, greatly astonished, walked the floor in the cool room, convinced that Phœbe was coming back to him. If he only thought sufficiently, if he made it perfectly clear by his feeling that he needed her greatly, she would come back, this kindly wife, and tell him what to do. She would perhaps be with him much of the time, in the night, anyhow; and that would make him less lonely, this state more endurable.

In age and with the feeble it is not such a far cry from the subtleties of illusion to actual hallucination, and in due time this transition was made for Henry. Night after night he waited, expecting her return. Once in his weird mood he thought he saw a pale light moving about the room, and another time he thought he saw her walking in the orchard after dark. It was one morning when the details of his lonely state were virtually unendurable that he woke with the thought that she was not dead. How he had arrived at this conclusion it is hard to say. His mind had gone. In its place was a fixed illusion. He and Phœbe had had a senseless quarrel. He had reproached her for not leaving his pipe where he was accustomed to find it, and she had left. It was an aberrated fulfillment of her old jesting threat that if he did not behave himself she would leave him.

"I guess I could find yuh ag'in," he had always said. But her cackling threat had always been.

"Yuh'll not find me if I ever leave yuh. I guess I kin git some place where yuh can't find me."

This morning when he arose he did not think to build the fire in the customary way or to grind his coffee and cut his bread, as was his wont, but solely to meditate as to where he should search for her and how he should induce her to come back. Recently the one horse had been dispensed with because he found it cumbersome and beyond his needs. He took down his soft crush hat after he had dressed himself, a new glint of interest and determination in his eye, and taking his black crook cane from behind the door, where he had always placed it, started out briskly to look for her among the nearest neighbors. His old shoes clumped soundly in the dust as he walked, and his gray-black locks, now grown rather long, straggled out in a dramatic fringe or halo from under his hat. His short coat stirred busily as he walked, and his hands and face were peaked and pale.

"Why, hello, Henry! Where're yuh goin' this mornin'?" inquired Farmer Dodge, who, hauling a load of wheat to market, encountered him on the public road. He had not seen the aged farmer in months, not since his wife's death, and he wondered now, seeing him looking so spry.

"Yuh ain't seen Phœbe, have yuh?" inquired the old man, looking up quizzically.

"Phœbe who?" inquired Farmer Dodge, not for the moment connecting the name with Henry's dead wife.

"Why, my wife Phœbe, o' course. Who do yuh s'pose I mean?" He stared up with a pathetic sharpness of glance from under his shaggy, gray eyebrows.

"Wall, I'll swan, Henry, yuh ain't jokin', are yuh?" said the solid Dodge, a pursy man, with a smooth, hard, red face. "It can't be your wife yuh're talkin' about. She's dead."

"Dead! Shucks!" retorted the demented Reifsneider. "She left me early this mornin', while I was sleepin'. She allus got up to build the fire, but she's gone now. We had a little spat last night, an' I guess that's the reason. But I guess I kin find her. She's gone over to Matilda Race's; that's where she's gone."

He started briskly up the road, leaving the amazed Dodge to stare in wonder after him.

"Well, I'll be switched!" he said aloud to himself. "He's clean out'n his head. That poor old feller's been livin' down there till he's gone outen his mind. I'll have to notify the authorities." And he flicked his whip with great enthusiasm. "Geddap!" he said, and was off.

Reifsneider met no one else in this poorly populated region until he reached the whitewashed fence of Matilda Race and her husband three miles away. He had passed several other houses en route, but these not being within the range of his illusion were not considered. His wife, who had known Matilda well, must be here. He opened the picket-gate which guarded the walk, and stamped briskly up to the door.

"Why, Mr. Reifsneider," exclaimed old Matilda herself, a stout woman, looking out of the door in answer to his knock, "what brings yuh here this mornin'?"

"Is Phœbe here?" he demanded eagerly.

"Phœbe who? What Phœbe?" replied Mrs. Race, curious as to this sudden development of energy on his part.

"Why, my Phœbe, o' course. My wife Phœbe. Who do yuh s'pose? Ain't she here now?"

"Lawsy me!" exclaimed Mrs. Race, opening her mouth. "Yuh pore man! So you're clean out'n your mind now. Yuh come right in and sit down. I'll git yuh a cup o' coffee. O' course your wife ain't here; but yuh come in an' sit down. I'll find her fer yuh after a while. I know where she is."

The old farmer's eyes softened, and he entered. He was so thin and pale a specimen, pantalooned and patriarchal, that he aroused Mrs. Race's extremest sympathy as he took off his hat and laid it on his knees quite softly and mildly.

"We had a quarrel last night, an' she left me," he volunteered.

"Laws! laws!" sighed Mrs. Race, there being no one present with whom to share her astonishment as she went to her kitchen. "The pore man! Now somebody's just got to look after him. He can't be allowed to run around the country this way lookin' for his dead wife. It's turrible."

She boiled him a pot of coffee and brought in some of her new-baked bread and fresh butter. She set out some of her best jam and put a couple of eggs to boil, lying whole-heartedly the while.

"Now yuh stay right there, Uncle Henry, till Jake comes in, an' I'll send him to look for Phœbe. I think it's more'n likely she's over to Swinnerton with some o' her friends. Anyhow, we'll find out. Now yuh just drink this coffee an' eat this bread. Yuh must be tired. Yuh've had a long walk this mornin'." Her idea was to take counsel with Jake, "her man," and perhaps have him notify the authorities.

She bustled about, meditating on the uncertainties of life, while old Reifsneider thrummed on the rim of his hat with his pale fingers and later ate abstractedly of what she offered. His mind was on his wife, however, and since she was not here, or did not appear, it wandered vaguely away to a family by the name of Murray, miles away in another direction. He decided after a time that he would not wait for Jake Race to hunt his wife but would seek her for himself. He must be on, and urge her to come back.

"Well, I'll be goin'," he said, getting up and looking strangely about him. "I guess she didn't come here after all. She went over to the Murrays', I guess. I'll not wait any longer, Mis' Race. There's a lot to do over to the house to-day." And out he marched in the face of her protests taking to the dusty road again in the warm spring sun, his cane striking the earth as he went.

It was two hours later that this pale figure of a man appeared in the Murrays' doorway, dusty, perspiring, eager. He had tramped all of five miles, and it was noon. An amazed husband and wife of sixty heard his strange query, and realized also that he was mad. They begged him to stay to dinner, intending to notify the authorities later and see what could be done; but though he stayed to partake of a little something, he did not stay long, and was off again to another distant farmhouse, his idea of many things to do and his need of Phœbe impelling him. So it went for that day and the next and the next, the circle of his inquiry every widening.

The process by which a character assumes the significance of being peculiar, his antics weird, yet harmless, in such a community is often involute and pathetic. This day, as has been said, saw Reifsneider at other doors, eagerly asking his unnatural question, and leaving a trail of amazement, sympathy, and pity in his wake. Although the authorities were informed—the county sheriff, no less—it was not deemed advisable to take him into custody; for when those who knew old Henry, and had for so long, reflected on the condition of the county insane asylum, a place which, because of the poverty of the district, was of staggering aberration and sickening environment, it was decided to let him remain at large; for, strange to relate, it was found on investigation that at night he returned peaceably enough to his lonesome domicile there to discover whether his wife had returned, and to brood in loneliness until the morning. Who would lock up a thin, eager, seeking old man with iron-gray hair and an attitude of kindly, innocent inquiry, particularly when he was well known for a past of only kindly servitude and reliability? Those who had known him best rather agreed that he should be allowed to roam at large. He could do no harm. There were many who were willing to help him as to food, old clothes, the odds and ends of his daily life—at least at first. His figure after a time became not so much a common-place as an accepted curiosity, and the replies, "Why, no, Henry; I ain't see her," or "No, Henry; she ain't been here to-day," more customary.

For several years thereafter then he was an odd figure in the sun and rain, on dusty roads and muddy ones, encountered occasionally in strange and unexpected places, pursuing his endless search. Undernourishment, after a time, although the neighbors and those who knew his history gladly contributed from their store, affected his body; for he walked much and ate little. The longer he roamed the public highway in this manner, the deeper became his strange hallucination; and finding it harder and harder to return from his more and more distant pilgrimages, he finally began taking a few utensils with him from his home, making a small package of them, in order that he might not be compelled to return. In an old tin coffee-pot of large size he placed a small tin cup, a knife, fork, and spoon, some salt and pepper, and to the outside of it, by a string forced through a pierced hole, he fastened a plate, which could be released, and which was his woodland table. It was no trouble for him to secure the little food that he needed, and with a strange, almost religious dignity, he had no hesitation in asking for that much. By degrees his hair became longer and longer, his once black hat became an earthen brown, and his clothes threadbare and dusty.

For all of three years he walked, and none knew how wide were his perambulations, nor how he survived the storms and cold. They could not see him, with homely rural understanding and forethought, sheltering himself in hay-cocks, or by the sides of cattle, whose warm bodies protected him from the cold, and whose dull understandings were not opposed to his harmless presence. Overhanging rocks and trees kept him at times from the rain, and a friendly hay-loft or corn-crib was not above his humble consideration.

The involute progression of hallucination is strange. From asking at doors and being constantly rebuffed or denied, he finally came to the conclusion that although his Phœbe might not be in any of the houses at the doors of which he inquired, she might nevertheless be within the sound of his voice. And so, from patient inquiry, he began to call sad, occasional cries, that ever and anon waked the quiet landscapes and ragged hill regions, and set to echoing his thin "O-o-o Phœbe! O-o-o Phœbe!" It had a pathetic, albeit insane, ring, and many a farmer or plowboy came to know it even from afar and say, "There goes old Reifsneider."

Another thing that puzzled him greatly after a time and after many hundreds of inquiries was, when he no longer had any particular dooryard in view and no special inquiry to make, which way to go. These cross-roads, which occasionally led in four or even six directions, came after a time to puzzle him. But to solve this knotty problem, which became more and more of a puzzle, there came to his aid another hallucination. Phœbe's spirit or some power of the air or wind or nature would tell him. If he stood at the center of the parting of the ways, closed his eyes, turned thrice about, and called "O-o-o Phœbe!" twice, and then threw his cane straight before him, that would surely indicate which way to go for Phœbe, or one of these mystic powers would surely govern its direction and fall! In whichever direction it went, even though, as was not infrequently the case, it took him back along the path he had already come, or across fields, he was not so far gone in his mind but that he gave himself ample time to search before he called again. Also the hallucination seemed to persist that at some time he would surely find her. There were hours when his feet were sore, and his limbs weary, when he would stop in the heat to wipe his seamed brow, or in the cold to beat his arms. Sometimes, after throwing away his cane, and finding it indicating the direction from which he had just come, he would shake his head wearily and philosophically, as if contemplating the unbelievable or an untoward fate, and then start briskly off. His strange figure came finally to be known in the farthest reaches of three or four counties. Old Reifsneider was a pathetic character. His fame was wide.

Near a little town called Watersville, in Green County, perhaps four miles from that minor center of human activity, there was a place or precipice locally known as the Red Cliff, a sheer wall of red sandstone, perhaps a hundred feet high, which raised its sharp face for half a mile or more above the fruitful cornfields and orchards that lay beneath, and which was surmounted by a thick grove of trees. The slope that slowly led up to it from the opposite side was covered by a rank growth of beech, hickory, and ash, through which threaded a number of wagon-tracks crossing at various angles. In fair weather it had become old Reifsneider's habit, so inured was he by now to the open, to make his bed in some such patch of trees as this to fry his bacon or boil his eggs at the foot of some tree before laying himself down for the night. Occasionally, so light and inconsequential was his sleep, he would walk at night. More often, the moonlight or some sudden wind stirring in the trees or a reconnoitering animal arousing him, he would sit up and think, or pursue his quest in the moonlight or the dark, a strange, unnatural, half wild, half savage-looking but utterly harmless creature, calling at lonely road crossings, staring at dark and shuttered houses, and wondering where, where Phœbe could really be.

That particular lull that comes in the systole-diastole of this earthly ball at two o'clock in the morning invariably aroused him, and though he might not go any farther he would sit up and contemplate the darkness or the stars, wondering. Sometimes in the strange processes of his mind he would fancy that he saw moving among the trees the figure of his lost wife, and then he would get up to follow, taking his utensils, always on a string, and his cane. If she seemed to evade him too easily he would run, or plead, or, suddenly losing track of the fancied figure, stand awed or disappointed, grieving for the moment over the almost insurmountable difficulties of his search.

It was in the seventh year of these hopeless peregrinations, in the dawn of a similar springtime to that in which his wife had died, that he came at last one night to the vicinity of this self-same patch that crowned the rise to the Red Cliff. His far-flung cane, used as a divining-rod at the last cross-roads, had brought him hither. He had walked many, many miles. It was after ten o'clock at night, and he was very weary. Long wandering and little eating had left him but a shadow of his former self. It was a question now not so much of physical strength but of spiritual endurance which kept him up. He had scarcely eaten this day, and now exhausted he set himself down in the dark to rest and possibly to sleep.

Curiously on this occasion a strange suggestion of the presence of his wife surrounded him. It would not be long now, he counseled with himself, although the long months had brought him nothing, until he should see her, talk to her. He fell asleep after a time, his head on his knees. At midnight the moon began to rise, and at two in the morning, his wakeful hour, was a large silver disk shining through the trees to the east. He opened his eyes when the radiance became strong, making a silver pattern at his feet and lighting the woods with strange lusters and silvery, shadowy forms. As usual, his old notion that his wife must be near occurred to him on this occasion, and he looked about him with a speculative, anticipatory eye. What was it that moved in the distant shadows along the path by which he had entered—a pale, flickering will-o'-the-wisp that bobbed gracefully among the trees and riveted his expectant gaze? Moonlight and shadows combined to give it a strange form and a stranger reality, this fluttering of bogfire or dancing of wandering fireflies. Was it truly his lost Phœbe? By a circuitous route it passed about him, and in his fevered state he fancied that he could see the very eyes of her, not as she was when he last saw her in the black dress and shawl but now a strangely younger Phœbe, gayer, sweeter, the one whom he had known years before as a girl. Old Reifsneider got up. He had been expecting and dreaming of this hour all these years, and now as he saw the feeble light dancing lightly before him he peered at it questioningly, one thin hand in his gray hair.

Of a sudden there came to him now for the first time in many years the full charm of her girlish figure as he had known it in boyhood, the pleasing, sympathetic smile, the brown hair, the blue sash she had once worn about her waist at a picnic, her gay, graceful movements. He walked around the base of the tree, straining with his eyes, forgetting for once his cane and utensils, and following eagerly after. On she moved before him, a will-o'-the-wisp of the spring, a little flame above her head, and it seemed as though among the small saplings of ash and beech and the thick trunks of hickory and elm that she signaled with a young, a lightsome hand.

"O Phœbe! Phœbe!" he called. "Have yuh really come? Have yuh really answered me?" And hurrying faster, he fell once, scrambling lamely to his feet, only to see the light in the distance dancing illusively on. On and on he hurried until he was fairly running, brushing his ragged arms against the trees, striking his hands and face against impeding twigs. His hat was gone, his lungs were breathless, his reason quite astray, when coming to the edge of the cliff he saw her below among a silvery bed of apple-trees now blooming in the spring.

"O Phœbe!" he called. "O Phœbe! Oh, no, don't leave me!" And feeling the lure of a world where love was young and Phœbe as this vision presented her, a delightful epitome of their quondam youth, he gave a gay cry of "Oh, wait, Phœbe!" and leaped.

Some farmer-boys, reconnoitering this region of bounty and prospect some few days afterward, found first the tin utensils tied together under the tree where he had left them, and then later at the foot of the cliff, pale, broken, but elate, a molded smile of peace and delight upon his lips, his body. His old hat was discovered lying under some low-growing saplings the twigs of which had held it back. No one of all the simple population knew how eagerly and joyously he had found his lost mate.

Neighbour Rosicky

WILLA CATHER

(1873–1947)

I

When Doctor Burleigh told neighbour Rosicky he had a bad heart, Rosicky protested.

"So? No, I guess my heart was always pretty good. I got a little asthma, maybe. Just a awful short breath when I was pitchin' hay last summer, dat's all."

"Well now, Rosicky, if you know more about it than I do, what did you come to me for? It's your heart that makes you short of breath, I tell you. You're sixty-five years old, and you've always worked hard, and your heart's tired. You've got to be careful from now on, and you can't do heavy work any more. You've got five boys at home to do it for you."

The old farmer looked up at the Doctor with a gleam of amusement in his queer triangular-shaped eyes. His eyes were large and lively, but the lids were caught up in the middle in a curious way, so that they formed a triangle. He did not look like a sick man. His brown face was creased but not wrinkled, he had a ruddy colour in his smooth-shaven cheeks and in his lips, under his long brown moustache. His hair was thin and ragged around his ears, but very little grey. His forehead, naturally high and crossed by deep parallel lines, now ran all the way up to his pointed crown. Rosicky's face had the habit of looking interested,—suggested a contented disposition and a reflective quality that was gay rather than grave. This gave him a certain detachment, the easy manner of an onlooker and observer.

"Well, I guess you ain't got no pills fur a bad heart, Doctor Ed. I guess the only thing is fur me to git me a new one."

Doctor Burleigh swung round in his desk-chair and frowned at the old farmer. "I think if I were you I'd take a little care of the old one, Rosicky."

Rosicky shrugged. "Maybe I don't know how. I expect you mean fur me not to drink my coffee no more."

"I wouldn't, in your place. But you'll do as you choose about that. I've never yet been able to separate a Bohemian from his coffee or his pipe. I've quit trying. But the sure thing is you've got to cut out farm work. You can feed the stock and do chores about the barn, but you can't do anything in the fields that makes you short of breath."

"How about shelling corn?"

"Of course not!"

Rosicky considered with puckered brows.

"I can't make my heart go no longer'n it wants to, can I, Doctor Ed?"

"I think it's good for five or six years yet, maybe more, if you'll take the strain off it. Sit around the house and help Mary. If I had a good wife like yours, I'd want to stay around the house."

His patient chuckled. "It ain't no place fur a man. I don't like no old man hanging round the kitchen too much. An' my wife, she's a awful hard worker her own self."

"That's it; you can help her a little. My Lord, Rosicky, you are one of the few men I know who has a family he can get some comfort out of; happy dispositions, never quarrel among themselves, and they treat you right. I want to see you live a few years and enjoy them."

"Oh, they're good kids, all right," Rosicky assented.

The Doctor wrote him a prescription and asked him how his oldest son, Rudolph, who had married in the spring, was getting on. Rudolph had struck out for himself, on rented land. "And how's Polly? I was afraid Mary mightn't like an American daughter-in-law, but it seems to be working out all right."

"Yes, she's a fine girl. Dat widder woman bring her daughters up very nice. Polly got lots of spunk, an' she got some style, too. Da's nice, for young folks to have some style." Rosicky inclined his head gallantly. His voice and his twinkly smile were an affectionate compliment to his daughter-in-law.

"It looks like a storm, and you'd better be getting home before it comes. In town in the car?" Doctor Burleigh rose.

"No, I'm in de wagon. When you got five boys, you ain't got much chance to ride round in de Ford. I ain't much for cars, noway."

"Well, it's a good road out to your place; but I don't want you bumping around in a wagon much. And never again on a hay-rake, remember!"

Rosicky placed the Doctor's fee delicately behind the desk-telephone, looking the other way, as if this were an absent-minded gesture. He put on his plush cap and his corduroy jacket with a sheepskin collar, and went out.

The Doctor picked up his stethoscope and frowned at it as if he were seriously annoyed with the instrument. He wished it had been telling tales about some other man's heart, some old man who didn't look the Doctor in the eye so knowingly, or hold out such a warm brown hand when he said good-bye. Doctor Burleigh had been a poor boy in the country before he went away to medical school; he had known Rosicky almost ever since he could remember, and he had a deep affection for Mrs. Rosicky.

Only last winter he had had such a good breakfast at Rosicky's, and that when he needed it. He had been out all night on a long, hard confinement case at Tom Marshall's,—a big rich farm where there was plenty of stock and plenty of feed and a great deal of expensive farm machinery of the newest model, and no comfort whatever. The woman had too many children and too much work, and she was no manager. When the baby was born at last, and handed over to the assisting neighbour woman, and the mother was properly attended to, Burleigh refused any breakfast in that slovenly house, and drove his buggy—the snow was too deep for a car—eight miles to Anton Rosicky's place. He didn't know another farm-house where a man could get such a warm welcome, and such good strong coffee with rich cream. No wonder the old chap didn't want to give up his coffee!

He had driven in just when the boys had come back from the barn and were washing up for breakfast. The long table, covered with a bright oilcloth, was set out with dishes waiting for them, and the warm kitchen was full of the smell of coffee and hot biscuit and sausage. Five big handsome boys, running from twenty to twelve, all with what Burleigh called natural good manners,—they hadn't a bit of the painful self-consciousness he himself had to struggle with when he was a lad. One ran to put his horse away, another helped him off with his fur coat and hung it up, and Josephine, the youngest child and the only daughter, quickly set another place under her mother's direction.

With Mary, to feed creatures was the natural expression of affection,—her chickens, the calves, her big hungry boys. It was a rare pleasure to feed a young man whom she seldom saw and of whom she was as proud as if he belonged to her. Some country housekeepers would have stopped to spread a white cloth over the oilcloth, to change the thick cups and plates for their best china, and the wooden-handled knives for plated ones. But not Mary.

"You must take us as you find us, Doctor Ed. I'd be glad to put out my good things for you if you was expected, but I'm glad to get you any way at all."

He knew she was glad,—she threw back her head and spoke out as if she were announcing him to the whole prairie. Rosicky hadn't said anything at all; he merely smiled his twinkling smile, put some more coal on the fire, and went into his own room to pour the Doctor a little drink in a medicine glass. When they were all seated, he watched his wife's face from his end of the table and spoke to her in Czech. Then, with the instinct of politeness which seldom failed him, he turned to the Doctor and said slyly: "I was just tellin' her not to ask you no question about Mrs. Marshall till you eat some breakfast. My wife, she's terrible fur to ask questions."

The boys laughed, and so did Mary. She watched the Doctor devour her biscuit and sausage, too much excited to eat anything herself. She drank her coffee and sat taking in everything about her visitor. She had known him when he was a poor country boy, and was boastfully proud of his success, always saying: "What do people go to Omaha for, to see a doctor, when we got the best one in the State right here?" If Mary liked people at all, she felt physical pleasure in the sight of them, personal exultation in any good fortune that came to them. Burleigh didn't know many women like that, but he knew she was like that.

When his hunger was satisfied, he did, of course, have to tell them about Mrs. Marshall, and he noticed what a friendly interest the boys took in the matter.

Rudolph, the oldest one (he was still living at home then), said: "The last time I was over there, she was lifting them big heavy milk-cans, and I knew she oughtn't to be doing it."

"Yes, Rudolph told me about that when he came home, and I said it wasn't right," Mary put in warmly. "It was all right for me to do them things up to the last, for I was terrible strong, but that woman's weakly. And do you think she'll be able to nurse it, Ed?" She sometimes forgot to give him the title she was so proud of. "And to think of your being up all night and then not able to get a decent breakfast! I don't know what's the matter with such people."

"Why, Mother," said one of the boys, "if Doctor Ed had got breakfast there, we wouldn't have him here. So you ought to be glad."

"He knows I'm glad to have him, John, any time. But I'm sorry for that poor woman, how bad she'll feel the Doctor had to go away in the cold without his breakfast."

"I wish I'd been in practice when these were getting born." The doctor looked down the row of close-clipped heads. "I missed some good breakfasts by not being."

The boys began to laugh at their mother because she flushed so red, but she stood her ground and threw up her head. "I don't care, you wouldn't have got away from this house without breakfast. No doctor ever did. I'd have had something ready fixed that Anton could warm up for you."

The boys laughed harder than ever, and exclaimed at her: "I'll bet you would!" "She would, that!"

"Father, did you get breakfast for the doctor when we were born?"

"Yes, and he used to bring me my breakfast, too, mighty nice. I was always awful hungry!" Mary admitted with a guilty laugh.

While the boys were getting the Doctor's horse, he went to the window to examine the house plants. "What do you do to your geraniums to keep them blooming all winter, Mary? I never pass this house that from the road I don't see your windows full of flowers."

She snapped off a dark red one, and a ruffled new green leaf, and put them in his buttonhole. "There, that looks better. You look too solemn for a young man, Ed. Why don't you git married? I'm worried about you. Settin' at breakfast, I looked at you real hard, and I seen you've got some grey hairs already."

"Oh, yes! They're coming. Maybe they'd come faster if I married."

"Don't talk so. You'll ruin your health eating at the hotel. I could send your wife a nice loaf of nut bread, if you only had one. I don't like to see a young man getting grey. I'll tell you something, Ed; you make some strong black tea and keep it handy in a bowl, and every morning just brush it into your hair, an' it'll keep the grey from showin' much. That's the way I do!

Sometimes the Doctor heard the gossipers in the drug-store wondering why Rosicky didn't get on faster. He was industrious, and so were his boys, but they were rather free and easy, weren't pushers, and they didn't always show good judgment. They were comfortable, they were out of debt, but they didn't get much ahead. Maybe, Doctor Burleigh reflected, people as generous and warm-hearted and affectionate as the Rosickys never got ahead much; maybe you couldn't enjoy your life and put it into the bank, too.

II

When Rosicky left Doctor Burleigh's office he went into the farm-implement store to light his pipe and put on his glasses and read over the list Mary had given him. Then he went into the general merchandise place next door and stood about until the pretty girl with the plucked eyebrows, who always waited on him, was free. Those eyebrows, two thin India-ink strokes, amused him, because he remembered how they used to be. Rosicky always prolonged his shopping by a little joking; the girl knew the old fellow admired her, and she liked to chaff with him.

"Seems to me about every other week you buy ticking, Mr. Rosicky, and always the best quality," she remarked as she measured off the heavy bolt with red stripes.

"You see, my wife is always makin' goose-fedder pillows, an' de thin stuff don't hold in dem little down-fedders."

"You must have lots of pillows at your house."

"Sure. She makes quilts of dem, too. We sleeps easy. Now she's makin' a fedder quilt for my son's wife. You know Polly, that married my Rudolph. How much my bill, Miss Pearl?"

"Eight eighty-five."

"Chust make it nine, and put in some candy fur de women."

"As usual. I never did see a man buy so much candy for his wife. First thing you know, she'll be getting too fat."

"I'd like dat. I ain't much fur all dem slim women like what de style is now."

"That's one for me, I suppose, Mr. Bohunk!" Pearl sniffed and elevated her India-ink strokes.

When Rosicky went out to his wagon, it was beginning to snow,—the first snow of the season, and he was glad to see it. He rattled out of town and along the highway through a wonderfully rich stretch of country, the finest farms in the county. He admired this High Prairie, as it was called, and always liked to drive through it. His own place lay in a rougher territory, where there was some clay in the soil and it was not so productive. When he bought his land, he hadn't the money to buy on High Prairie; so he told his boys, when they grumbled, that if their land hadn't some clay in it, they wouldn't own it at all. All the same, he enjoyed looking at these fine farms, as he enjoyed looking at a prize bull.

After he had gone eight miles, he came to the graveyard, which lay just at the edge of his own hay-land. There he stopped his horses and sat still on his wagon seat, looking about at the snowfall. Over yonder on the hill he could see his own house, crouching low, with the clump of orchard behind and the windmill before, and all down the gentle hill-slope the rows of pale gold cornstalks stood out against the white field. The snow was falling over the cornfield and the pasture and the hay-land, steadily, with very little wind,—a nice dry snow. The graveyard had only a light wire fence about it and was all overgrown with long red grass. The fine snow, settling into this red grass and upon the few little evergreens and the headstones, looked very pretty.

It was a nice graveyard, Rosicky reflected, sort of snug and homelike, not cramped or mournful,—a big sweep all round it. A man could lie down in the long grass and see the complete arch of the sky over him, hear the wagons go by; in summer the mowing-machine rattled right up to the wire fence. And it was so near home. Over there across the cornstalks his own roof and windmill looked so good to him that he promised himself to mind the Doctor and take care of himself. He was awful fond of his place, he admitted. He wasn't anxious to leave it. And it was a comfort to think that he would never have to go farther than the edge of his own hayfield. The snow, falling over his barnyard and the graveyard, seemed to draw things together like. And they were all old neighbours in the graveyard, most of them friends; there was nothing to feel awkward or embarrassed about. Embarrassment was the most disagreeable feeling Rosicky knew. He didn't often have it,—only with certain people whom he didn't understand at all.

Well, it was a nice snowstorm; a fine sight to see the snow falling so quietly and graciously over so much open country. On his cap and shoulders, on the horses' backs and manes, light, delicate, mysterious it fell; and with it a dry cool fragrance was released into the air. It meant rest for vegetation and men and beasts, for the ground itself; a season of long nights for sleep, leisurely breakfasts, peace by the fire. This and much more went through Rosicky's mind, but he merely told himself that winter was coming, clucked to his horses, and drove on.

When he reached home, John, the youngest boy, ran out to put away his team for him, and he met Mary coming up from the outside cellar with her apron full of carrots. They went into the house together. On the table, covered with oilcloth figured with clusters of blue grapes, a place was set, and he smelled hot coffee-cake of some kind. Anton never lunched in town; he thought that extravagant, and anyhow he didn't like the food. So Mary always had something ready for him when he got home.

After he was settled in his chair, stirring his coffee in a big cup, Mary took out of the oven a pan of *kolache* stuffed with apricots, examined them anxiously to see whether they had got too dry, put them beside his plate, and then sat down opposite him.

Rosicky asked her in Czech if she wasn't going to have any coffee.

She replied in English, as being somehow the right language for transacting business: "Now what did Doctor Ed say, Anton? You tell me just what."

"He said I was to tell you some compliments, but I forgot 'em." Rosicky's eyes twinkled.

"About you, I mean. What did he say about your asthma?"

"He says I ain't got no asthma." Rosicky took one of the little rolls in his broad brown fingers. The thickened nail of his right thumb told the story of his past.

"Well, what is the matter? And don't try to put me off."

"He don't say nothing much, only I'm a little older, and my heart ain't so good like it used to be."

Mary started and brushed her hair back from her temples with both hands as if she were a little out of her mind. From the way she glared, she might have been in a rage with him.

"He says there's something the matter with your heart? Doctor Ed says so?"

"Now don't yell at me like I was a hog in de garden, Mary. You know I always did like to hear a woman talk soft. He didn't say anything de matter wid my heart, only it ain't so young like it used to be, an' he tell me not to pitch hay or run de corn-sheller."

Mary wanted to jump up, but she sat still. She admired the way he never under any circumstances raised his voice or spoke roughly. He was city-bred, and she was country-bred; she often said she wanted her boys to have their papa's nice ways.

"You never have no pain there, do you? It's your breathing and your stomach that's been wrong. I wouldn't believe nobody but Doctor Ed about it. I guess I'll go see him myself. Didn't he give you no advice?"

"Chust to take it easy like, an' stay round de house dis winter. I guess you got some carpenter work for me to do. I kin make some new shelves for you, and I want dis long time to build a closet in de boys' room and make dem two little fellers keep dere clo'es hung up."

Rosicky drank his coffee from time to time, while he considered. His moustache was of the soft long variety and came down over his mouth like the teeth of a buggy-rake over a bundle of hay. Each time he put down his cup, he ran his blue handkerchief over his lips. When he took a drink of water, he managed very neatly with the back of his hand.

Mary sat watching him intently, trying to find any change in his face. It is hard to see anyone who has become like your own body to you. Yes, his hair had got thin, and his high forehead had deep lines running from left to right. But his neck, always clean shaved except in the busiest seasons, was not loose or baggy. It was burned a dark reddish brown, and there were deep creases in it, but it looked firm and full of blood. His cheeks had a good colour. On either side of his mouth there was a half-moon down the length of his cheek, not wrinkles, but two lines that had come there from his habitual expression. He was shorter and broader than when she married him; his back had grown broad and curved, a good deal like the shell of an old turtle, and his arms and legs were short.

He was fifteen years older than Mary, but she had hardly ever thought about it before. He was her man, and the kind of man she liked. She was rough, and he was gentle,—city-bred, as she always said. They had been shipmates on a rough voyage and had stood by each other in trying times.

Life had gone well with them because, at bottom, they had the same ideas about life. They agreed, without discussion, as to what was most important and what was secondary. They didn't often exchange opinions, even in Czech,—it was as if they had thought the same thought together. A good deal had to be sacrificed and thrown overboard in a hard life like theirs, and they had never disagreed as to the things that could go. It had been a hard life, and a soft life, too. There wasn't anything brutal in the short, broad-backed man with the three-cornered eyes and the forehead that went on to the top of his skull. He was a city man, a gentle man, and though he had married a rough farm girl, he had never touched her without gentleness.

They had been at one accord not to hurry through life, not to be always skimping and saving. They saw their neighbours buy more land and feed more stock than they did, without discontent. Once when the creamery agent came to the Rosickys to persuade them to sell him their cream, he told them how much money the Fasslers, their nearest neighbours, had made on their cream last year.

"Yes," said Mary, "and look at them Fassler children! Pale, pinched little things, they look like skimmed milk. I'd rather put some colour into my children's faces than put money into the bank."

The agent shrugged and turned to Anton.

"I guess we'll do like she says," said Rosicky.

III

Mary very soon got into town to see Doctor Ed, and then she had a talk with her boys and set a guard over Rosicky. Even John, the youngest, had his father on his mind. If Rosicky went to throw hay down from the loft, one of the boys ran up the ladder and took the fork from him. He sometimes complained that though he was getting to be an old man, he wasn't an old woman yet.

That winter he stayed in the house in the afternoons and carpentered, or sat in the chair between the window full of plants and the wooden bench where the two pails of drinking water stood. This spot was called "Father's corner," though it was not a corner at all. He had a shelf there, where he kept his Bohemian papers and his pipes and tobacco, and his shears and needles and thread and tailor's thimble. Having been a tailor in his youth, he couldn't bear to see a woman patching at his clothes, or at the boys'. He liked tailoring, and always patched all the overalls and jackets and work shirts. Occasionally he made over a pair of pants one of the older boys had outgrown, for the little fellow.

While he sewed, he let his mind run back over his life. He had a good deal to remember, really; life in three countries. The only part of his youth he didn't like to remember was the two years he had spent in London, in Cheapside, working for a German tailor who was wretchedly poor. Those days, when he was nearly always hungry, when his clothes were dropping off him for dirt, and the sound of a strange language kept him in continual bewilderment, had left a sore spot in his mind that wouldn't bear touching.

He was twenty when he landed at Castle Garden in New York, and he had a protector who got him work in a tailor shop in Vesey Street, down near the Washington Market. He looked upon that part of his life as very happy. He became a good workman, he was industrious, and his wages were increased from time to time. He minded his own business and envied nobody's good fortune. He went to night school and learned to read English. He often did overtime work and was well paid for it, but somehow he never saved anything. He couldn't refuse a loan to a friend, and he was self-indulgent. He liked a good dinner, and a little went for beer, a little for tobacco; a good deal went to the girls. He often stood through an opera on Saturday nights; he could get standing-room for a dollar. Those were the great days of opera in New York, and it gave a fellow something to think about for the rest of the week. Rosicky had a quick ear, and a childish love of all the stage splendour; the scenery, the costumes, the ballet. He usually went with a chum, and after the performance they had beer and maybe some oysters somewhere. It was a fine life; for the first five years or so it satisfied him completely. He was never hungry or cold or dirty, and everything amused him: a fire, a dog fight, a parade, a storm, a ferry ride. He thought New York the finest, richest, friendliest city in the world.

Moreover, he had what he called a happy home life. Very near the tailor shop was a small furniture-factory, where an old Austrian, Loeffler, employed a few skilled men and made unusual furniture, most of it to order, for the rich German housewives up-town. The top floor of Loeffler's five-storey factory was a loft, where he kept his choice lumber and stored the odd pieces of furniture left on his hands. One of the young workmen he employed was a Czech, and he and Rosicky became fast friends. They persuaded Loeffler to let them have a sleeping-room in one corner of the loft. They bought good beds and bedding and had their pick of the furniture kept up there. The loft was low-pitched, but light and airy, full of windows, and good-smelling by reason of the fine lumber put up there to season. Old Loeffler used to go down to the docks and buy wood from South America and the East from the sea captains. The young men were as foolish about their house as a bridal pair. Zichec, the young cabinet-maker, devised every sort of convenience, and Rosicky kept their clothes in order. At night and on Sundays, when the quiver of machinery underneath was still, it was the quietest place in the world, and on summer nights all the sea winds blew in. Zichec often practised on his flute in the evening. They were both fond of music and went to the opera together. Rosicky thought he wanted to live like that for ever.

But as the years passed, all alike, he began to get a little restless. When spring came round, he would begin to feel fretted, and he got to drinking. He was likely to drink too much of a Saturday night. On Sunday he was languid and heavy, getting over his spree. On Monday he plunged into work again. So he never had time to figure out what ailed him, though he knew something did. When the grass turned green in Park Place, and the lilac hedge at the back of Trinity churchyard put out its blossoms, he was tormented by a longing to run away. That was why he drank too much; to get a temporary illusion of freedom and wide horizons.

Rosicky, the old Rosicky, could remember as if it were yesterday the day when the young Rosicky found out what was the matter with him. It was on a Fourth of July afternoon, and he was sitting in Park Place in the sun. The lower part of New York was empty. Wall Street, Liberty Street, Broadway, all empty. So much stone and asphalt with nothing going on, so many empty windows. The emptiness was intense, like the stillness in a great factory when the machinery stops and the belts and bands cease running. It was too great a change, it took all the strength out of one. Those blank buildings, without the stream of life pouring through them, were like empty jails. It struck young Rosicky that this was the trouble with big cities; they built you in from the earth itself, cemented you away from any contact with the ground. You lived in an unnatural world, like the fish in an aquarium, who were probably much more comfortable than they ever were in the sea.

On that very day he began to think seriously about the articles he had read in the Bohemian papers, describing prosperous Czech farming communities in the West. He believed he would like to go out there as a farm hand; it was hardly possible that he could ever have land of his own. His people had always been workmen; his father and grandfather had worked in shops. His mother's parents had lived in the country, but they rented their farm and had a hard time to get along. Nobody in his family had ever owned any land,—that belonged to a different station of life altogether. Anton's mother died when he was little, and he was sent into the country to her parents. He stayed with them until he was twelve, and formed those ties with the earth and the farm animals and growing things which are never made at all unless they are made early. After his grandfather died, he went back to live with his father and stepmother, but she was very hard on him, and his father helped him to get passage to London.

After that Fourth of July day in Park Place, the desire to return to the country never left him. To work on another man's farm would be all he asked; to see the sun rise and set and to plant things and watch them grow. He was a very simple man. He was like a tree that has not many roots, but one tap-root that goes down deep. He subscribed for a Bohemian paper printed in Chicago, then for one printed in Omaha. His mind got farther and farther west. He began to save a little money to buy his liberty. When he was thirty-five, there was a great meeting in New York of Bohemian athletic societies, and Rosicky left the tailor shop and went home with the Omaha delegates to try his fortune in another part of the world.

IV

Perhaps the fact that his own youth was well over before he began to have a family was one reason why Rosicky was so fond of his boys. He had almost a grandfather's indulgence for them. He had never had to worry about any of them—except, just now, a little about Rudolph.

On Saturday night the boys always piled into the Ford, took little Josephine, and went to town to the moving-picture show. One Saturday morning they were talking at the breakfast table about starting early that evening, so that they would have an hour or so to see the Christmas things in the stores before the show began. Rosicky looked down the table.

"I hope you boys ain't disappointed, but I want you to let me have de car tonight. Maybe some of you can go in with de neighbours."

Their faces fell. They worked hard all week, and they were still like children. A new jackknife or a box of candy pleased the older ones as much as the little fellow.

"If you and Mother are going to town," Frank said, "maybe you could take a couple of us along with you, anyway."

"No, I want to take de car down to Rudolph's, and let him an' Polly go in to de show. She don't git into town enough, an' I'm afraid she's gettin' lonesome, an' he can't afford no car yet."

That settled it. The boys were a good deal dashed. Their father took another piece of apple-cake and went on: "Maybe next Saturday night de two little fellers can go along wid dem."

"Oh, is Rudolph going to have the car every Saturday night?"

Rosicky did not reply at once; then he began to speak seriously: "Listen, boys; Polly ain't lookin' so good. I don't like to see nobody lookin' sad. It comes hard fur a town girl to be a farmer's wife. I don't want no trouble to start in Rudolph's family. When it starts, it ain't so easy to stop. An American girl don't git used to our ways all at once. I like to tell Polly she and Rudolph can have the car every Saturday night till after New Year's, if it's all right with you boys."

"Sure it's all right, Papa," Mary cut in. "And it's good you thought about that. Town girls is used to more than country girls. I lay awake nights, scared she'll make Rudolph discontented with the farm."

The boys put as good a face on it as they could. They surely looked forward to their Saturday nights in town. That evening Rosicky drove the car the half-mile down to Rudolph's new, bare little house.

Polly was in a short-sleeved gingham dress, clearing away the supper dishes. She was a trim, slim little thing, with blue eyes and shingled yellow hair, and her eyebrows were reduced to a mere brush-stroke, like Miss Pearl's.

"Good evening, Mr. Rosicky. Rudolph's at the barn, I guess." She never called him father, or Mary mother. She was sensitive about having married a foreigner. She never in the world would have done it if Rudolph hadn't been such a handsome, persuasive fellow and such a gallant lover. He had graduated in her class in the high school in town, and their friendship began in the ninth grade.

Rosicky went in, though he wasn't exactly asked. "My boys ain't goin' to town tonight, an' I brought de car over fur you two to go in to de picture show."

Polly, carrying dishes to the sink, looked over her shoulder at him. "Thank you. But I'm late with my work tonight, and pretty tired. Maybe Rudolph would like to go in with you."

"Oh, I don't go to de shows! I'm too old-fashioned. You won't feel so tired after you ride in de air a ways. It's a nice clear night, an' it ain't cold. You go an' fix yourself up, Polly, an' I'll wash de dishes an' leave everything nice fur you."

Polly brushed and tossed her bob. "I couldn't let you do that, Mr. Rosicky. I wouldn't think of it."

Rosicky said nothing. He found a bib apron on a nail behind the kitchen door. He slipped it over his head and then took Polly by her two elbows and pushed her gently toward the door of her own room. "I washed up de kitchen many times for my wife, when de babies was sick or somethin'. You go an' make yourself look nice. I like you to look prettier'n any of dem town girls when you go in. De young folks must have some fun, an' I'm goin' to look out fur you, Polly."

That kind, reassuring grip on her elbows, the old man's funny bright eyes made Polly want to drop her head on his shoulder for a second. She restrained herself, but she lingered in his grasp at the door of her room, murmuring tearfully: "You always lived in the city when you were young, didn't you? Don't you ever get lonesome out here?"

As she turned round to him, her hand fell naturally into his, and he stood holding it and smiling into her face with his peculiar, knowing, indulgent smile without a shadow of reproach in it. "Dem big cities is all right fur de rich, but dey is terrible hard fur de poor."

"I don't know. Sometimes I think I'd like to take a chance. You lived in New York, didn't you?"

"An' London. Da's bigger still. I learned my trade dere. Here's Rudolph comin', you better hurry."

"Will you tell me about London some time?"

"Maybe. Only I ain't no talker, Polly. Run an' dress yourself up."

The bedroom door closed behind her, and Rudolph came in from the outside, looking anxious. He had seen the car and was sorry any of his family should come just then. Supper hadn't been a very pleasant occasion. Halting in the doorway, he saw his father in a kitchen apron, carrying dishes to the sink. He flushed crimson and something flashed in his eye. Rosicky held up a warning finger.

"I brought de car over fur you an' Polly to go to de picture show, an' I made her let me finish here so you won't be late. You go put on a clean shirt, quick!"

"But don't the boys want the car, Father?"

"Not tonight dey don't." Rosicky fumbled under his apron and found his pants pocket. He took out a silver dollar and said in a hurried whisper: "You go an' buy dat girl some ice cream an' candy tonight, like you was courtin'. She's awful good friends wid me."

Rudolph was very short of cash, but he took the money as if it hurt him. There had been a crop failure all over the county. He had more than once been sorry he'd married this year.

In a few minutes the young people came out, looking clean and a little stiff. Rosicky hurried them off, and then he took his own time with the dishes. He scoured the pots and pans and put away the milk and swept the kitchen. He put some coal in the stove and shut off the draughts, so the place would be warm for them when they got home late at night. Then he sat down and had a pipe and listened to the clock tick.

Generally speaking, marrying an American girl was certainly a risk. A Czech should marry a Czech. It was lucky that Polly was the daughter of a poor widow woman; Rudolph was proud, and if she had a prosperous family to throw up at him, they could never make it go. Polly was one of four sisters, and they all worked; one was book-keeper in the bank, one taught music, and Polly and her younger sister had been clerks, like Miss Pearl. All four of them were musical, had pretty voices, and sang in the Methodist choir, which the eldest sister directed.

Polly missed the sociability of a store position. She missed the choir, and the company of her sisters. She didn't dislike housework, but she disliked so much of it. Rosicky was a little anxious about this pair. He was afraid Polly would grow so discontented that Rudy would quit the farm and take a factory job in Omaha. He had worked for a winter up there, two years ago, to get money to marry on. He had done very well, and they would always take him back at the stockyards. But to Rosicky that meant the end of everything for his son. To be a landless man was to be a wage-earner, a slave, all your life; to have nothing, to be nothing.

Rosicky thought he would come over and do a little carpentering for Polly after the New Year. He guessed she needed jollying. Rudolph was a serious sort of chap, serious in love and serious about his work.

Rosicky shook out his pipe and walked home across the fields. Ahead of him the lamplight shone from his kitchen windows. Suppose he were still in a tailor shop on Vesey Street, with a bunch of pale, narrow-chested sons working on machines, all coming home tired and sullen to eat supper in a kitchen that was a parlour also; with another crowded, angry family quarrelling just across the dumb-waiter shaft, and squeaking pulleys at the windows where dirty washings hung on dirty lines above a court full of old brooms and mops and ash-cans. . . .

He stopped by the windmill to look up at the frosty winter stars and draw a long breath before he went inside. That kitchen with the shining windows was dear to him; but the sleeping fields and bright stars and the noble darkness were dearer still.

V

On the day before Christmas the weather set in very cold; no snow, but a bitter, biting wind that whistled and sang over the flat land and lashed one's face like fine wires. There was baking going on in the Rosicky kitchen all day, and Rosicky sat inside, making over a coat that Albert had outgrown into an overcoat for John. Mary had a big red geranium in bloom for Christmas, and a row of Jerusalem cherry trees, full of berries. It was the first year she had ever grown these; Doctor Ed brought her the seeds from Omaha when he went to some medical convention. They reminded Rosicky of plants he had seen in England; and all afternoon, as he stitched, he sat thinking about those two years in London, which his mind usually shrank from even after all this while.

He was a lad of eighteen when he dropped down into London, with no money and no connexions except the address of a cousin who was supposed to be working at a confectioner's. When he went to the pastry shop, however, he found that the cousin had gone to America. Anton tramped the streets for several days, sleeping in doorways and on the Embankment, until he was in utter despair. He knew no English, and the sound of the strange language all about him confused him. By chance he met a poor German tailor who had learned his trade in Vienna, and could speak a little Czech. This tailor, Lifschnitz, kept a repair shop in a Cheapside basement, underneath a cobbler. He didn't much need an apprentice, but he was sorry for the boy and took him in for no wages but his keep and what he could pick up. The pickings were supposed to be coppers given you when you took work home to a customer. But most of the customers called for their clothes themselves, and the coppers that came Anton's way were very few. He had, however, a place to sleep. The tailor's family lived upstairs in three rooms; a kitchen, a bedroom, where Lifschnitz and his wife and five children slept, and a living-room. Two corners of this living-room were curtained off for lodgers; in one Rosicky slept on an old horsehair sofa, with a feather quilt to wrap himself in. The other corner was rented to a wretched, dirty boy, who was studying the violin. He actually practised there. Rosicky was dirty, too. There was no way to be anything else. Mrs. Lifschnitz got the water she cooked and washed with from a pump in a brick court, four flights down. There were bugs in the place, and multitudes of fleas, though the poor woman did the best she could. Rosicky knew she often went empty to give another potato or a spoonful of dripping to the two hungry, sad-eyed boys who lodged with her. He used to think he would never get out of there, never get a clean shirt to his back again. What would he do, he wondered, when his clothes actually dropped to pieces and the worn cloth wouldn't hold patches any longer?

It was still early when the old farmer put aside his sewing and his recollections. The sky had been a dark grey all day, with not a gleam of sun, and the light failed at four o'clock. He went to shave and change his shirt while the turkey was roasting. Rudolph and Polly were coming over for supper.

After supper they sat round in the kitchen, and the younger boys were saying how sorry they were it hadn't snowed. Everybody was sorry. They wanted a deep snow that would lie long and keep the wheat warm, and leave the ground soaked when it melted.

"Yes, sir!" Rudolph broke out fiercely; "if we have another dry year like last year, there's going to be hard times in this country."

Rosicky filled his pipe. "You boys don't know what hard times is. You don't owe nobody, you got plenty to eat an' keep warm, an' plenty water to keep clean. When you got them, you can't have it very hard."

Rudolph frowned, opened and shut his big right hand, and dropped it clenched upon his knee. "I've got to have a good deal more than that, Father, or I'll quit this farming gamble. I can always make good wages railroading, or at the packing house, and be sure of my money."

"Maybe so," his father answered dryly.

Mary, who had just come in from the pantry and was wiping her hands on the roller towel, thought Rudy and his father were getting too serious. She brought her darning-basket and sat down in the middle of the group.

"I ain't much afraid of hard times, Rudy," she said heartily. "We've had a plenty, but we've always come through. Your father wouldn't never take nothing very hard, not even hard times. I got a mind to tell you a story on him. Maybe you boys can't hardly remember the year we had that terrible hot wind, that burned everything up on the Fourth of July? All the corn an' the gardens. An' that was in the days when we didn't have alfalfa yet,—I guess it wasn't invented.

"Well, that very day your father was out cultivatin' corn, and I was here in the kitchen makin' plum preserves. We had bushels of plums that year. I noticed it was terrible hot, but it's always hot in the kitchen when you're preservin', an' I was too busy with my plums to mind. Anton come in from the field about three o'clock, an' I asked him what was the matter.

"'Nothin',' he says, 'but it's pretty hot, an' I think I won't work no more today.' He stood round for a few minutes, an' then he says: 'Ain't you near through? I want you should git up a nice supper for us tonight. It's Fourth of July.'

"I told him to git along, that I was right in the middle of preservin', but the plums would taste good on hot biscuit. 'I'm goin' to have fried chicken, too,' he says, and he went off an' killed a couple. You three oldest boys was little fellers, playin' round outside, real hot an' sweaty, an' your father took you to the horse tank down by the windmill an' took off your clothes an' put you in. Them two box-elder trees was little then, but they made shade over the tank. Then he took off all his own clothes, an' got in with you. While he was playin' in the water with you, the Methodist preacher drove into our place to say how all the neighbours was goin' to meet at the schoolhouse that night, to pray for rain. He drove right to the windmill, of course, and there was your father and you three with no clothes on. I was in the kitchen door, an' I had to laugh, for the preacher acted like he ain't never seen a naked man before. He surely was embarrassed, an' your father couldn't get to his clothes; they was all hangin' up on the windmill to let the sweat dry out of 'em. So he laid in the tank where he was, an' put one of you boys on top of him to cover him up a little, an' talked to the preacher.

"When you got through playin' in the water, he put clean clothes on you and a clean shirt on himself, an' by that time I'd begun to get supper. He says: 'It's too hot in here to eat comfortable. Let's have a picnic in the orchard. We'll eat our supper behind the mulberry hedge, under them linden trees.'

"So he carried our supper down, an' a bottle of my wild-grape wine, an' everything tasted good, I can tell you. The wind got cooler as the sun was goin' down, and it turned out pleasant, only I noticed how the leaves was curled up on the linden trees. That made me think, an' I asked your father if that hot wind all day hadn't been terrible hard on the gardens an' the corn.

" 'Corn,' he says, 'there ain't no corn.'

" 'What you talkin' about?' I said. 'Ain't we got forty acres?'

" 'We ain't got an ear,' he says, 'nor nobody else ain't got none. All the corn in this country was cooked by three o'clock today, like you'd roasted it in an oven.'

" 'You mean you won't get no crop at all?' I asked him. I couldn't believe it, after he'd worked so hard.

" 'No crop this year,' he says. 'That's why we're havin' a picnic. We might as well enjoy what we got.'

"An' that's how your father behaved, when all the neighbours was so discouraged they couldn't look you in the face. An' we enjoyed ourselves that year, poor as we was, an' our neighbours wasn't a bit better off for bein' miserable. Some of 'em grieved till they got poor digestions and couldn't relish what they did have."

The younger boys said they thought their father had the best of it. But Rudolph was thinking that, all the same, the neighbours had managed to get ahead more, in the fifteen years since that time. There must be something wrong about his father's way of doing things. He wished he knew what was going on in the back of Polly's mind. He knew she liked his father, but he knew, too, that she was afraid of something. When his mother sent over coffee-cake or prune tarts or a loaf of fresh bread, Polly seemed to regard them with a certain suspicion. When she observed to him that his brothers had nice manners, her tone implied that it was remarkable they should have. With his mother she was stiff and on her guard. Mary's hearty frankness and gusts of good humour irritated her. Polly was afraid of being unusual or conspicuous in any way, of being "ordinary," as she said!

When Mary had finished her story, Rosicky laid aside his pipe.

"You boys like me to tell you about some of dem hard times I been through in London?" Warmly encouraged, he sat rubbing his forehead along the deep creases. It was bothersome to tell a long story in English (he nearly always talked to the boys in Czech), but he wanted Polly to hear this one.

"Well, you know about dat tailor shop I worked in in London? I had one Christmas dere I ain't never forgot. Times was awful bad before Christmas; de boss ain't got much work, an' have it awful hard to pay his rent. It ain't so much fun, bein' poor in a big city like London, I'll say! All de windows is full of good t'ings to eat, an' all de pushcarts in de streets is full, an' you smell 'em all de time, an' you ain't got no money,—not a damn bit. I didn't mind de cold so much, though I didn't have no overcoat, chust a short jacket I'd outgrowed so it wouldn't meet on me, an' my hands was chapped raw. But I always had a good appetite, like you all know, an' de sight of dem pork pies in de windows was awful fur me!

"Day before Christmas was terrible foggy dat year, an' dat fog gits into your bones and makes you all damp like. Mrs. Lifschnitz didn't give us nothin' but a little bread an' drippin' for supper, because she was savin' to try for to give us a good dinner on Christmas Day. After supper de boss say I can go an' enjoy myself, so I went into de streets to listen to de Christmas singers. Dey sing old songs an' make very nice music, an' I run round after dem a good ways, till I got awful hungry. I t'ink maybe if I go home, I can sleep till morning an' forgit my belly.

"I went into my corner real quiet, and roll up in my fedder quilt. But I ain't got my head down, till I smell somet'ing good. Seem like it git stronger an' stronger, an' I can't git to sleep noway. I can't understand dat smell. Dere was a gas light in a hall across de court, dat always shine in at my window a little. I got up an' look round. I got a little wooden box in my corner fur a stool, 'cause I ain't got no chair. I picks up dat box, and under it dere is a roast goose on a platter! I can't believe my eyes. I carry it to de window where de light comes in, an' touch it and smell it to find out, an' den I taste it to be sure. I say, I will eat chust one little bite of dat goose, so I can go to sleep, and tomorrow I won't eat none at all. But I tell you, boys, when I stop, one half of dat goose was gone!"

The narrator bowed his head, and the boys shouted. But little Josephine slipped behind his chair and kissed him on the neck beneath his ear.

"Poor little Papa, I don't want him to be hungry!"

"Da's long ago, child. I ain't never been hungry since I had your mudder to cook fur me."

"Go on and tell us the rest, please," said Polly.

"Well, when I come to realize what I done, of course, I felt terrible. I felt better in de stomach, but very bad in de heart. I set on my bed wid dat platter on my knees, an' it all come to me; how hard dat poor woman save to buy dat goose, and how she get some neighbour to cook it dat got more fire, an' how she put it in my corner to keep it away from dem hungry children. Dey was a old carpet hung up to shut my corner off, an' de children wasn't allowed to go in dere. An' I know she put it in my corner because she trust me more'n she did de violin boy. I can't stand it to face her after I spoil de Christmas. So I put on my shoes and go out into de city. I tell myself I better throw myself in de river; but I guess I ain't dat kind of a boy.

"It was after twelve o'clock, an' terrible cold, an' I start out to walk about London all night. I walk along de river awhile, but dey was lots of drunks all along; men, and women too. I chust move along to keep away from de police. I git onto de Strand, an' den over to New Oxford Street, where dere was a big German restaurant on de ground floor, wid big windows all fixed up fine, an' I could see de people havin' parties inside. While I was lookin' in, two men and two ladies come out, laughin' and talkin' and feelin' happy about all dey been eatin' an' drinkin', and dey was speakin' Czech,—not like de Austrians, but like de home folks talk it.

"I guess I went crazy, an' I done what I ain't never done before nor since. I went right up to dem gay people an' begun to beg dem: 'Fellow-countrymen, for God's sake give me money enough to buy a goose!'

"Dey laugh, of course, but de ladies speak awful kind to me, an' dey take me back into de restaurant and give me hot coffee and cakes, an' make me tell all about how I happened to come to London, an' what I was doin' dere. Dey take my name and where I work down on paper, an' both of dem ladies give me ten shillings.

"De big market at Covent Garden ain't very far away, an' by dat time it was open. I go dere an' buy a big goose an' some pork pies, an' potatoes and onions, an' cakes an' oranges fur de children,—all I could carry! When I git home, everybody is still asleep. I pile all I bought on de kitchen table, an' go in an' lay down on my bed, an' I ain't waken up till I hear dat woman scream when she come out into her kitchen. My goodness, but she was surprise! She laugh an' cry at de same time, an' hug me and waken all de children. She ain't stop fur no breakfast; she git de Christmas dinner ready dat morning, and we all sit down an' eat all we can hold. I ain't never seen dat violin boy have all he can hold before.

"Two three days after dat, de two men come to hunt me up, an' dey ask my boss, and he give me a good report an' tell dem I was a steady boy all right. One of dem Bohemians was very smart an' run a Bohemian newspaper in New York, an' de odder was a rich man, in de importing business, an' dey been travelling togedder. Dey told me how t'ings was easier in New York, an' offered to pay my passage when dey was goin' home soon on a boat. My boss say to me: 'You go. You ain't got no chance here, an' I like to see you git ahead, fur you always been a good boy to my woman, and fur dat fine Christmas dinner you give us all.' An' da's how I got to New York."

That night when Rudolph and Polly, arm in arm, were running home across the fields with the bitter wind at their backs, his heart leaped for joy when she said she thought they might have his family come over for supper on New Year's Eve. "Let's get up a nice supper, and not let your mother help at all; make her be company for once."

"That would be lovely of you, Polly," he said humbly. He was a very simple, modest boy, and he, too, felt vaguely that Polly and her sisters were more experienced and worldly than his people.

VI

The winter turned out badly for farmers. It was bitterly cold, and after the first light snows before Christmas there was no snow at all,—and no rain. March was as bitter as February. On those days when the wind fairly punished the country, Rosicky sat by his window. In the fall he and the boys had put in a big wheat planting, and now the seed had frozen in the ground. All that land would have to be ploughed up and planted over again, planted in corn. It had happened before, but he was younger then, and he never worried about what had to be. He was sure of himself and of Mary; he knew they could bear what they had to bear, that they would always pull through somehow. But he was not so sure about the young ones, and he felt troubled because Rudolph and Polly were having such a hard start.

Sitting beside his flowering window while the panes rattled and the wind blew in under the door, Rosicky gave himself to reflection as he had not done since those Sundays in the loft of the furniture-factory in New York, long ago. Then he was trying to find what he wanted in life for himself; now he was trying to find what he wanted for his boys, and why it was he so hungered to feel sure they would be here, working this very land, after he was gone.

They would have to work hard on the farm, and probably they would never do much more than make a living. But if he could think of them as staying here on the land, he wouldn't have to fear any great unkindness for them. Hardships, certainly; it was a hardship to have the wheat freeze in the ground when seed was so high; and to have to sell your stock because you had no feed. But there would be other years when everything came along right, and you caught up. And what you had was your own. You didn't have to choose between bosses and strikers, and go wrong either way. You didn't have to do with dishonest and cruel people. They were the only things in his experience he had found terrifying and horrible; the look in the eyes of a dishonest and crafty man, of a scheming and rapacious woman.

In the country, if you had a mean neighbour, you could keep off his land and make him keep off yours. But in the city, all the foulness and misery and brutality of your neighbours was part of your life. The worst things he had come upon in his journey through the world were human, —depraved and poisonous specimens of man. To this day he could recall certain terrible faces in London streets. There were mean people everywhere, to be sure, even in their own country town here. But they weren't tempered, hardened, sharpened, like the treacherous people in cities who live by grinding or cheating or poisoning their fellow-men. He had helped to bury two of his fellow-workmen in the tailoring trade, and he was distrustful of the organized industries that see one out of the world in big cities. Here, if you were sick, you had Doctor Ed to look after you; and if you died, fat Mr. Haycock, the kindest man in the world, buried you.

It seemed to Rosicky that for good, honest boys like his, the worst they could do on the farm was better than the best they would be likely to do in the city. If he'd had a mean boy, now, one who was crooked and sharp and tried to put anything over on his brothers, then town would be the place for him. But he had no such boy. As for Rudolph, the discontented one, he would give the shirt off his back to anyone who touched his heart. What Rosicky really hoped for his boys was that they could get through the world without ever knowing much about the cruelty of human beings. "Their mother and me ain't prepared them for that," he sometimes said to himself.

These thoughts brought him back to a grateful consideration of his own case. What an escape he had had, to be sure! He, too, in his time, had had to take money for repair work from the hand of a hungry child who let it go so wistfully; because it was money due his boss. And now, in all these years, he had never had to take a cent from any one in bitter need, —never had to look at the face of a woman become like a wolf's from struggle and famine. When he thought of these things, Rosicky would put on his cap and jacket and slip down to the barn and give his workhorses a little extra oats, letting them eat it out of his hand in their slobbery fashion. It was his way of expressing what he felt, and made him chuckle with pleasure.

The spring came warm, with blue skies,—but dry, dry as a bone. The boys began ploughing up the wheat-fields to plant them over in corn. Rosicky would stand at the fence corner and watch them, and the earth was so dry it blew up in clouds of brown dust that hid the horses and the sulky plough and the driver. It was a bad outlook.

The big alfalfa-field that lay between the home place and Rudolph's came up green, but Rosicky was worried because during that open windy winter a great many Russian thistle plants had blown in there and lodged. He kept asking the boys to rake them out; he was afraid their seed would root and "take the alfalfa." Rudolph said that was nonsense. The boys were working so hard planting corn, their father felt he couldn't insist about the thistles, but he set great store by that big alfalfa field. It was a feed you could depend on,—and there was some deeper reason, vague, but strong. The peculiar green of that clover woke early memories in old Rosicky, went back to something in his childhood in the old world. When he was a little boy, he had played in fields of that strong blue-green colour.

One morning, when Rudolph had gone to town in the car, leaving a work-team idle in his barn, Rosicky went over to his son's place, put the horses to the buggy-rake, and set about quietly raking up those thistles. He behaved with guilty caution, and rather enjoyed stealing a march on Doctor Ed, who was just then taking his first vacation in seven years of practice and was attending a clinic in Chicago. Rosicky got the thistles raked up, but did not stop to burn them. That would take some time, and his breath was pretty short, so he thought he had better get the horses back to the barn.

He got them into the barn and to their stalls, but the pain had come on so sharp in his chest that he didn't try to take the harness off. He started for the house, bending lower with every step. The cramp in his chest was shutting him up like a jack-knife. When he reached the windmill, he swayed and caught at the ladder. He saw Polly coming down the hill, running with the swiftness of a slim greyhound. In a flash she had her shoulder under his armpit.

"Lean on me, Father, hard! Don't be afraid. We can get to the house all right."

Somehow they did, though Rosicky became blind with pain; he could keep on his legs, but he couldn't steer his course. The next thing he was conscious of was lying on Polly's bed, and Polly bending over him wringing out bath towels in hot water and putting them on his chest. She stopped only to throw coal into the stove, and she kept the tea-kettle and the black pot going. She put these hot applications on him for nearly an hour, she told him afterwards, and all that time he was drawn up stiff and blue, with the sweat pouring off him.

As the pain gradually loosed its grip, the stiffness went out of his jaws, the black circles round his eyes disappeared, and a little of his natural colour came back. When his daughter-in-law buttoned his shirt over his chest at last, he sighed.

"Da's fine, de way I feel now, Polly. It was a awful bad spell, an' I was so sorry it all come on you like it did."

Polly was flushed and excited. "Is the pain really gone? Can I leave you long enough to telephone over to your place?"

Rosicky's eyelids fluttered. "Don't telephone, Polly. It ain't no use to scare my wife. It's nice and quiet here, an' if I ain't too much trouble to you, just let me lay still till I feel like myself. I ain't got no pain now. It's nice here."

Polly bent over him and wiped the moisture from his face. "Oh, I'm so glad it's over!" she broke out impulsively. "It just broke my heart to see you suffer so, Father."

Rosicky motioned her to sit down on the chair where the tea-kettle had been, and looked up at her with that lively affectionate gleam in his eyes. "You was awful good to me, I won't never forgit dat. I hate it to be sick on you like dis. Down at de barn I say to myself, dat young girl ain't had much experience in sickness, I don't want to scare her, an' maybe she's got a baby comin' or somet'ing."

Polly took his hand. He was looking at her so intently and affectionately and confidingly; his eyes seemed to caress her face, to regard it with pleasure. She frowned with her funny streaks of eyebrows, and then smiled back at him.

"I guess maybe there is something of that kind going to happen. But I haven't told anyone yet, not my mother or Rudolph. You'll be the first to know."

His hand pressed hers. She noticed that it was warm again. The twinkle in his yellow-brown eyes seemed to come nearer.

"I like mighty well to see dat little child, Polly," was all he said. Then he closed his eyes and lay half-smiling. But Polly sat still, thinking hard. She had a sudden feeling that nobody in the world, not her mother, not Rudolph, or anyone, really loved her as much as old Rosicky did. It perplexed her. She sat frowning and trying to puzzle it out. It was as if Rosicky had a special gift for loving people, something that was like an ear for music or an eye for colour. It was quiet, unobtrusive; it was merely there. You saw it in his eyes,—perhaps that was why they were merry. You felt it in his hands, too. After he dropped off to sleep, she sat holding his warm, broad, flexible brown hand. She had never seen another in the least like it. She wondered if it wasn't a kind of gypsy hand, it was so alive and quick and light in its communications,—very strange in a farmer. Nearly all the farmers she knew had huge lumps of fists, like mauls, or they were knotty and bony and uncomfortable-looking, with stiff fingers. But Rosicky's was like quicksilver, flexible, muscular, about the colour of a pale cigar, with deep, deep creases across the palm. It wasn't nervous, it wasn't a stupid lump; it was a warm brown human hand, with some cleverness in it, a great deal of generosity, and something else which Polly could only call "gypsy-like,"—something nimble and lively and sure, in the way that animals are.

Polly remembered that hour long afterwards; it had been like an awakening to her. It seemed to her that she had never learned so much about life from anything as from old Rosicky's hand. It brought her to herself; it communicated some direct and untranslatable message.

When she heard Rudolph coming in the car, she ran out to meet him.

"Oh, Rudy, your father's been awful sick! He raked up those thistles he's been worrying about, and afterwards he could hardly get to the house. He suffered so I was afraid he was going to die."

Rudolph jumped to the ground. "Where is he now?"

"On the bed. He's asleep. I was terribly scared, because, you know, I'm so fond of your father." She slipped her arm through his and they went into the house. That afternoon they took Rosicky home and put him to bed, though he protested that he was quite well again.

The next morning he got up and dressed and sat down to breakfast with his family. He told Mary that his coffee tasted better than usual to him, and he warned the boys not to bear any tales to Doctor Ed when he got home. After breakfast he sat down by his window to do some patching and asked Mary to thread several needles for him before she went to feed her chickens,—her eyes were better than his, and her hands steadier. He lit his pipe and took up John's overalls. Mary had been watching him anxiously all morning, and as she went out of the door with her bucket of scraps, she saw that he was smiling. He was thinking, indeed, about Polly, and how he might never have known what a tender heart she had if he hadn't got sick over there. Girls nowadays didn't wear their heart on their sleeve. But now he knew Polly would make a fine woman after the foolishness wore off. Either a woman had that sweetness at her heart or she hadn't. You couldn't always tell by the look of them; but if they had that, everything came out right in the end.

After he had taken a few stitches, the cramp began in his chest, like yesterday. He put his pipe cautiously down on the window-sill and bent over to ease the pull. No use,—he had better try to get to his bed if he could. He rose and groped his way across the familiar floor, which was rising and falling like the deck of a ship. At the door he fell. When Mary came in, she found him lying there, and the moment she touched him she knew that he was gone.

Doctor Ed was away when Rosicky died, and for the first few weeks after he got home he was hard driven. Every day he said to himself that he must get out to see that family that had lost their father. One soft, warm moonlight night in early summer he started for the farm. His mind was on other things, and not until his road ran by the graveyard did he realize that Rosicky wasn't over there on the hill where the red lamplight shone, but here, in the moonlight. He stopped his car, shut off the engine, and sat there for a while.

A sudden hush had fallen on his soul. Everything here seemed strangely moving and significant, though signifying what, he did not know. Close by the wire fence stood Rosicky's mowing-machine, where one of the boys had been cutting hay that afternoon; his own work-horses had been going up and down there. The new-cut hay perfumed all the night air. The moonlight silvered the long, billowy grass that grew over the graves and hid the fence; the few little evergreens stood out black in it, like shadows in a pool. The sky was very blue and soft, the stars rather faint because the moon was full.

For the first time it struck Doctor Ed that this was really a beautiful graveyard. He thought of city cemeteries; acres of shrubbery and heavy stone, so arranged and lonely and unlike anything in the living world. Cities of the dead, indeed; cities of the forgotten, of the "put away." But this was open and free, this little square of long grass which the wind for ever stirred. Nothing but the sky overhead, and the many-coloured fields running on until they met that sky. The horses worked here in summer; the neighbours passed on their way to town; and over yonder, in the cornfield, Rosicky's own cattle would be eating fodder as winter came on. Nothing could be more undeathlike than this place; nothing could be more right for a man who had helped to do the work of great cities and had always longed for the open country and had got to it at last. Rosicky's life seemed to him complete and beautiful.

The Egg

SHERWOOD ANDERSON

(1876–1941)

My father was, I am sure, intended by nature to be a cheerful, kindly man. Until he was thirty-four years old he worked as a farm-hand for a man named Thomas Butterworth whose place lay near the town of Bidwell, Ohio. He had then a horse of his own and on Saturday evenings drove into town to spend a few hours in social intercourse with other farm-hands. In town he drank several glasses of beer and stood about in Ben Head's saloon—crowded on Saturday evenings with visiting farm-hands. Songs were sung and glasses thumped on the bar. At ten o'clock father drove home along a lonely country road, made his horse comfortable for the night and himself went to bed, quite happy in his position in life. He had at that time no notion of trying to rise in the world.

It was in the spring of his thirty-fifth year that father married my mother, then a country school-teacher, and in the following spring I came wriggling and crying into the world. Something happened to the two people. They became ambitious. The American passion for getting up in the world took possession of them.

It may have been that mother was responsible. Being a school-teacher she had no doubt read books and magazines. She had, I presume, read of how Garfield, Lincoln, and other Americans rose from poverty to fame and greatness and as I lay beside her—in the days of her lying-in—she may have dreamed that I would some day rule men and cities. At any rate she induced father to give up his place as a farm-hand, sell his horse and embark on an independent enterprise of his own. She was a tall silent woman with a long nose and troubled grey eyes. For herself she wanted nothing. For father and myself she was incurably ambitious.

The first venture into which the two people went turned out badly. They rented ten acres of poor stony land on Grigg's Road, eight miles from Bidwell, and launched into chicken raising. I grew into boyhood on the place and got my first impressions of life there. From the beginning they were impressions of disaster and if, in my turn, I am a gloomy man inclined to see the darker side of life, I attribute it to the fact that what should have been for me the happy joyous days of childhood were spent on a chicken farm.

One unversed in such matters can have no notion of the many and tragic things that can happen to a chicken. It is born out of an egg, lives for a few weeks as a tiny fluffy thing such as you will see pictured on Easter cards, then becomes hideously naked, eats quantities of corn and meal bought by the sweat of your father's brow, gets diseases called pip, cholera, and other names, stands looking with stupid eyes at the sun, becomes sick and dies. A few hens and now and then a rooster, intended to serve God's mysterious ends, struggle through to maturity. The hens lay eggs out of which come other chickens and the dreadful cycle is thus made complete. It is all unbelievably complex. Most philosophers must have been raised on chicken farms. One hopes for so much from a chicken and is so dreadfully disillusioned. Small chickens, just setting out on the journey of life, look so bright and alert and they are in fact so dreadfully stupid. They are so much like people they mix one up in one's judgments of life. If disease does not kill them they wait until your expectations are thoroughly aroused and then walk under the wheels of a wagon—to go squashed and dead back to their maker. Vermin infest their youth, and fortunes must be spent for curative powders. In later life I have seen how a literature has been built up on the subject of fortunes to be made out of the raising of chickens. It is intended to be read by the gods who have just eaten of the tree of the knowledge of good and evil. It is a hopeful literature and declares that much may be done by simple ambitious people who own a few hens. Do not be led astray by it. It was not written for you. Go hunt for gold on the frozen hills of Alaska, put your faith in the honesty of a politician, believe if you will that the world is daily growing better and that good will triumph over evil, but do not read and believe the literature that is written concerning the hen. It was not written for you.

I, however, digress. My tale does not primarily concern itself with the hen. If correctly told it will centre on the egg. For ten years my father and mother struggled to make our chicken farm pay and then they gave up that struggle and began another. They moved into the town of Bidwell, Ohio, and embarked in the restaurant business. After ten years of worry with incubators that did not hatch, and with tiny—and in their own way lovely—balls of fluff that passed on into semi-naked pullethood and from that into dead henhood, we threw all aside and packing our belongings on a wagon drove down Grigg's Road toward Bidwell, a tiny caravan of hope looking for a new place from which to start on our upward journey through life.

We must have been a sad looking lot, not, I fancy, unlike refugees fleeing from a battlefield. Mother and I walked in the road. The wagon that contained our goods had been borrowed for the day from Mr. Albert Griggs, a neighbor. Out of its sides stuck the legs of cheap chairs and at the back of the pile of beds, tables, and boxes filled with kitchen utensils was a crate of live chickens, and on top of that the baby carriage in which I had been wheeled about in my infancy. Why we stuck to the baby carriage I don't know. It was unlikely other children would be born and the wheels were broken. People who have few possessions cling tightly to those they have. That is one of the facts that make life so discouraging.

Father rode on top of the wagon. He was then a bald-headed man of forty-five, a little fat and from long association with mother and the chickens he had become habitually silent and discouraged. All during our ten years on the chicken farm he had worked as a laborer on neighboring farms and most of the money he had earned had been spent for remedies to cure chicken diseases, on Wilmer's White Wonder Cholera Cure or Professor Bidlow's Egg Producer or some other preparations that mother found advertised in the poultry papers. There were two little patches of hair on father's head just above his ears. I remember that as a child I used to sit looking at him when he had gone to sleep in a chair before the stove on Sunday afternoons in the winter. I had at that time already begun to read books and have notions of my own and the bald path that led over the top of his head was, I fancied, something like a broad road, such a road as Caesar might have made on which to lead his legions out of Rome and into the wonders of an unknown world. The tufts of hair that grew above father's ears were, I thought, like forests. I fell into a half-sleeping, half-waking state and dreamed I was a tiny thing going along the road into a far beautiful place where there were no chicken farms and where life was a happy eggless affair.

One might write a book concerning our flight from the chicken farm into town. Mother and I walked the entire eight miles—she to be sure that nothing fell from the wagon and I to see the wonder of the world. On the seat of the wagon beside father was his greatest treasure. I will tell you of that.

On a chicken farm where hundreds and even thousands of chickens come out of eggs surprising things sometimes happen. Grotesques are born out of eggs as out of people. The accident does not often occur—perhaps once in a thousand births. A chicken is, you see, born that has four legs, two pairs of wings, two heads or what not. The things do not live. They go quickly back to the hand of their maker that has for a moment trembled. The fact that the poor little things could not live was one of the tragedies of life to father. He had some sort of notion that if he could but bring into henhood or roosterhood a five-legged hen or a two-headed rooster his fortune would be made. He dreamed of taking the wonder about to county fairs and of growing rich by exhibiting it to other farm-hands.

At any rate he saved all the little monstrous things that had been born on our chicken farm. They were preserved in alcohol and put each in its own glass bottle. These he had carefully put into a box and on our journey into town it was carried on the wagon seat beside him. He drove the horses with one hand and with the other clung to the box. When we got to our destination the box was taken down at once and the bottles removed. All during our days as keepers of a restaurant in the town of Bidwell, Ohio, the grotesques in their little glass bottles sat on a shelf back of the counter. Mother sometimes protested but father was a rock on the subject of his treasure. The grotesques were, he declared, valuable. People, he said, liked to look at strange and wonderful things.

Did I say that we embarked in the restaurant business in the town of Bidwell, Ohio? I exaggerated a little. The town itself lay at the foot of a low hill and on the shore of a small river. The railroad did not run through the town and the station was a mile away to the north at a place called Pickleville. There had been a cider mill and pickle factory at the station, but before the time of our coming they had both gone out of business. In the morning and in the evening busses came down to the station along a road called Turner's Pike from the hotel on the main street of Bidwell. Our going to the out of the way place to embark in the restaurant business was mother's idea. She talked of it for a year and then one day went off and rented an empty store building opposite the railroad station. It was her idea that the restaurant would be profitable. Travelling men, she said, would be always waiting around to take trains out of town and town people would come to the station to await incoming trains. They would come to the restaurant to buy pieces of pie and drink coffee. Now that I am older I know that she had another motive in going. She was ambitious for me. She wanted me to rise in the world, to get into a town school and become a man of the towns.

At Pickleville father and mother worked hard as they always had done. At first there was the necessity of putting our place into shape to be a restaurant. That took a month. Father built a shelf on which he put tins of vegetables. He painted a sign on which he put his name in large red letters. Below his name was the sharp command—"EAT HERE"—that was so seldom obeyed. A show case was bought and filled with cigars and tobacco. Mother scrubbed the floor and the walls of the room. I went to school in the town and was glad to be away from the farm and from the presence of the discouraged, sad-looking chickens. Still I was not very joyous. In the evening I walked home from school along Turner's Pike and remembered the children I had seen playing in the town school yard. A troop of little girls had gone hopping about and singing. I tried that. Down along the frozen road I went hopping solemnly on one leg. "Hippity Hop To The Barber Shop," I sang shrilly. Then I stopped and looked doubtfully about. I was afraid of being seen in my gay mood. It must have seemed to me that I was doing a thing that should not be done by one who, like myself, had been raised on a chicken farm where death was a daily visitor.

Mother decided that our restaurant should remain open at night. At ten in the evening a passenger train went north past our door followed by a local freight. The freight crew had switching to do in Pickleville and when the work was done they came to our restaurant for hot coffee and food. Sometimes one of them ordered a fried egg. In the morning at four they returned north-bound and again visited us. A little trade began to grow up. Mother slept at night and during the day tended the restaurant and fed our boarders while father slept. He slept in the same bed mother had occupied during the night and I went off to the town of Bidwell and to school. During the long nights, while mother and I slept, father cooked meats that were to go into sandwiches for the lunch baskets of our boarders. Then an idea in regard to getting up in the world came into his head. The American spirit took hold of him. He also became ambitious.

In the long nights when there was little to do father had time to think. That was his undoing. He decided that he had in the past been an unsuccessful man because he had not been cheerful enough and that in the future he would adopt a cheerful outlook on life. In the early morning he came upstairs and got into bed with mother. She woke and the two talked. From my bed in the corner I listened.

It was father's idea that both he and mother should try to entertain the people who came to eat at our restaurant. I cannot now remember his words, but he gave the impression of one about to become in some obscure way a kind of public entertainer. When people, particularly young people from the town of Bidwell, came into our place, as on very rare occasions they did, bright entertaining conversation was to be made. From father's words I gathered that something of the jolly innkeeper effect was to be sought. Mother must have been doubtful from the first, but she said nothing discouraging. It was father's notion that a passion for the company of himself and mother would spring up in the breasts of the younger people of the town of Bidwell. In the evening bright happy groups would come singing down Turner's Pike. They would troop shouting with joy and laughter into our place. There would be song and festivity. I do not mean to give the impression that father spoke so elaborately of the matter. He was as I have said an uncommunicative man. "They want some place to go. I tell you they want some place to go," he said over and over. That was as far as he got. My own imagination has filled in the blanks.

For two or three weeks this notion of father's invaded our house. We did not talk much, but in our daily lives tried earnestly to make smiles take the place of glum looks. Mother smiled at the boarders and I, catching the infection, smiled at our cat. Father became a little feverish in his anxiety to please. There was no doubt, lurking somewhere in him, a touch of the spirit of the showman. He did not waste much of his ammunition on the railroad men he served at night but seemed to be waiting for a young man or woman from Bidwell to come in to show what he could do. On the counter in the restaurant there was a wire basket kept always filled with eggs, and it must have been before his eyes when the idea of being entertaining was born in his brain. There was something pre-natal about the way eggs kept themselves connected with the development of his idea. At any rate an egg ruined his new impulse in life. Late one night I was awakened by a roar of anger coming from father's throat. Both mother and I sat upright in our beds. With trembling hands she lighted a lamp that stood on a table by her head. Downstairs the front door of our restaurant went shut with a bang and in a few minutes father tramped up the stairs. He held an egg in his hand and his hand trembled as though he were having a chill. There was a half insane light in his eyes. As he stood glaring at us I was sure he intended throwing the egg at either mother or me. Then he laid it gently on the table beside the lamp and dropped on his knees beside mother's bed. He began to cry like a boy and I, carried away by his grief, cried with him. The two of us filled the little upstairs room with our wailing voices. It is ridiculous, but of the picture we made I can remember only the fact that mother's hand continually stroked the bald patch that ran across the top of his head. I have forgotten what mother said to him and how she induced him to tell her of what had happened downstairs. His explanation also had gone out of my mind. I remember only my own grief and fright and the shiny path over father's head glowing in the lamp light as he knelt by the bed.

As to what happened downstairs. For some unexplainable reason I know the story as well as though I had been a witness to my father's discomfiture. One in time gets to know many unexplainable things. On that evening young Joe Kane, son of a merchant of Bidwell, came to Pickleville to meet his father, who was expected on the ten o'clock evening train from the South. The train was three hours late and Joe came into our place to loaf about and to wait for its arrival. The local freight train came in and the freight crew were fed. Joe was left alone in the restaurant with father.

From the moment he came into our place the Bidwell young man must have been puzzled by my father's actions. It was his notion that father was angry at him for hanging around. He noticed that the restaurant keeper was apparently disturbed by his presence and he thought of going out. However, it began to rain and he did not fancy the long walk to town and back. He bought a five-cent cigar and ordered a cup of coffee. He had a newspaper in his pocket and took it out and began to read. "I'm waiting for the evening train. It's late," he said apologetically.

For a long time father, whom Joe Kane had never seen before, remained silently gazing at his visitor. He was no doubt suffering an attack of stage fright. As so often happens in life he had thought so much and so often of the situation that now confronted him that he was somewhat nervous in its presence.

For one thing, he did not know what to do with his hands. He thrust one of them nervously over the counter and shook hands with Joe Kane. "How-de-do," he said. Joe Kane put his newspaper down and stared at him. Father's eyes lighted on the basket of eggs that sat on the counter and he began to talk. "Well," he began hesitatingly, "well, you have heard of Christopher Columbus, eh?" He seemed to be angry. "That Christopher Columbus was a cheat," he declared emphatically. "He talked of making an egg stand on its end. He talked, he did and then he went and broke the end of the egg."

My father seemed to his visitor to be beside himself at the duplicity of Christopher Columbus. He muttered and swore. He declared it was wrong to teach children that Christopher Columbus was a great man when, after all, he cheated at the critical moment. He had declared he would make an egg stand on end and then when his bluff had been called he had done a trick. Still grumbling at Columbus, father took an egg from the basket on the counter and began to walk up and down. He rolled the egg between the palms of his hands. He smiled genially. He began to mumble words regarding the effect to be produced on an egg by the electricity that comes out of the human body. He declared that without breaking its shell and by virtue of rolling it back and forth in his hands he could stand the egg on its end. He explained that the warmth of his hands and the gentle rolling movement he gave the egg created a new centre of gravity, and Joe Kane was mildly interested. "I have handled thousands of eggs," father said. "No one knows more about eggs than I do."

He stood the egg on the counter and it fell on its side. He tried the trick again and again, each time rolling the egg between the palms of his hands and saying the words regarding the wonders of electricity and the laws of gravity. When after a half hour's effort he did succeed in making the egg stand for a moment he looked up to find that his visitor was no longer watching. By the time he had succeeded in calling Joe Kane's attention to the success of his effort the egg had again rolled over and lay on its side.

Afire with the showman's passion and at the same time a good deal disconcerted by the failure of his first effort, father now took the bottles containing the poultry monstrosities down from their place on the shelf and began to show them to his visitor. "How would you like to have seven legs and two heads like this fellow?" he asked, exhibiting the most remarkable of his treasures. A cheerful smile played over his face. He reached over the counter and tried to slap Joe Kane on the shoulder as he had seen men do in Ben Head's saloon when he was a young farm-hand and drove to town on Saturday evenings. His visitor was made a little ill by the sight of the body of the terribly deformed bird floating in the alcohol in the bottle and got up to go. Coming from behind the counter father took hold of the young man's arm and led him back to his seat. He grew a little angry and for a moment had to turn his face away and force himself to smile. Then he put the bottles back on the shelf. In an outburst of generosity he fairly compelled Joe Kane to have a fresh cup of coffee and another cigar at his expense. Then he took a pan and filling it with vinegar, taken from a jug that sat beneath the counter, he declared himself about to do a new trick. "I will heat this egg in this pan of vinegar," he said. "Then I will put it through the neck of a bottle without breaking the shell. When the egg is inside the bottle it will resume its normal shape and the shell will become hard again. Then I will give the bottle with the egg in it to you. You can take it about with you wherever you go. People will want to know how you got the egg in the bottle. Don't tell them. Keep them guessing. This is the way to have fun with this trick."

Father grinned and winked at his visitor. Joe Kane decided that the man who confronted him was mildly insane but harmless. He drank the cup of coffee that had been given him and began to read his paper again. When the egg had been heated in vinegar father carried it on a spoon to the counter and going into a back room got an empty bottle. He was angry because his visitor did not watch him as he began to do his trick, but nevertheless went cheerfully to work. For a long time he struggled, trying to get the egg to go through the neck of bottle. He put the pan of vinegar back on the stove, intending to reheat the egg, then picked it up and burned his fingers. After a second bath in the hot vinegar the shell of the egg had been softened a little but not enough for his purpose. He worked and worked and a spirit of desperate determination took possession of him. When he thought that at last the trick was about to be consummated the delayed train came in at the station and Joe Kane started to go nonchalantly out at the door. Father made a last desperate effort to conquer the egg and make it do the things that would establish his reputation as one who knew how to entertain guests who came into his restaurant. He worried the egg. He attempted to be somewhat rough with it. He swore and the sweat stood out on his forehead. The egg broke under his hand. When the contents spurted over his clothes, Joe Kane, who had stopped at the door, turned and laughed.

A roar of anger rose from my father's throat. He danced and shouted a string of inarticulate words. Grabbing another egg from the basket on the counter, he threw it, just missing the head of the young man as he dodged through the door and escaped.

Father came upstairs to mother and me with an egg in his hand. I do not know what he intended to do. I imagine he had some idea of destroying it, of destroying all eggs, and that he intended to let mother and me see him begin. When, however, he got into the presence of mother something happened to him. He laid the egg gently on the table and dropped on his knees by the bed as I have already explained. He later decided to close the restaurant for the night and to come upstairs and get into bed. When he did so he blew out the light and after much muttered conversation both he and mother went to sleep. I suppose I went to sleep also, but my sleep was troubled. I awoke at dawn and for a long time looked at the egg that lay on the table. I wondered why eggs had to be and why from the egg came the hen who again laid the egg. The question got into my blood. It has stayed there, I imagine, because I am the son of my father. At any rate, the problem remains unsolved in my mind. And that, I conclude, is but another evidence of the complete and final triumph of the egg—at least as far as my family is concerned.

The God of His Fathers

JACK LONDON
(1876–1916)

I

On every hand stretched the forest primeval—the home of noisy comedy and silent tragedy. Here the struggle for survival continued to wage with all its ancient brutality. Briton and Russian were still to overlap in the land of the Rainbow's End—and this was the very heart of it—nor had Yankee gold yet purchased its vast domain. The wolf pack still clung to the flank of the cariboo herd, singling out the weak and the big with calf, and pulling them down as remorselessly as it were a thousand, thousand generations into the past. The sparse aborigines still acknowledged the rule of their chiefs and medicine men, drove out bad spirits, burned their witches, fought their neighbours, and ate their enemies with a relish which spoke well of their bellies. But it was at the moment when the stone age was drawing to a close. Already, over unknown trails and chartless wildernesses, were the harbingers of the steel arriving—fair-faced, blue-eyed, indomitable men, incarnations of the unrest of their race. By accident or design, single-handed and in twos and threes, they came from no one knew whither, and fought, or died, or passed on, no one knew whence. The priests raged against them, the chiefs called forth their fighting men, and stone clashed with steel; but to little purpose. Like water seeping from some mighty reservoir they trickled through the dark forests and mountain passes, treading the highways in bark canoes, or with their moccasined feet breaking trail for the wolf-dogs. They came of a great breed, and their mothers were many; but the fur-clad denizens of the Northland had this yet to learn. So many an unsung wanderer fought his last and died under the cold fire of the aurora, as did his brothers in burning sands and reeking jungles, and as they shall continue to do till in the fullness of time the destiny of their race be achieved.

It was near twelve. Along the northern horizon a rosy glow, fading to the west and deepening to the east, marked the unseen dip of the midnight sun. The gloaming and the dawn were so commingled that there was no night—simply a wedding of day with day, a scarcely perceptible blending of two circles of the sun. A kildee timidly chirped good-night; the full, right throat of a robin proclaimed good-morrow. From an island on the breast of the Yukon a colony of wild fowl voiced its interminable wrongs, while a loon laughed mockingly back across a still stretch of river.

In the foreground, against the bank of a lazy eddy, birch-bark canoes were lined two and three deep. Ivory-bladed spears, bone-barbed arrows, buckskin-thronged bows, and simple basket-woven traps bespoke the fact that in the muddy current of the river the salmon-run was on. In the background, from the tangle of skin tents and drying frames, rose the voices of the fisher-folk. Bucks skylarked with bucks or flirted with the maidens, while the older squaws, shut out from this by virtue of having fulfilled the end of their existence in reproduction, gossiped as they braided rope from the green roots of trailing vines. At their feet their naked progeny played and squabbled, or rolled in the muck with the tawny wolf-dogs.

To one side of the encampment, and conspicuously apart from it, stood a second camp of two tents. But it was a white man's camp. If nothing else, the choice of position at least bore convincing evidence of this. In case of offence, it commanded the Indian quarters a hundred yards away; of defence, a rise to the ground and the cleared intervening space; and last, of defeat, the swift slope of a score of yards to the canoes below.

From one of the tents came the petulant cry of a sick child and the crooning song of a mother. In the open, over the smouldering embers of a fire, two men held talk.

"Eh! I love the church like a good son. *Bien!* So great a love that my days have been spent in fleeing away from her, and my nights in dreaming dreams of reckoning. Look you!" The half-breed's voice rose to an angry snarl. "I am Red River born. My father was white—as white as you. But you are Yankee, and he was British bred, and a gentleman's son. And my mother was the daughter of a chief, and I was a man. Ay, and one had to look the second time to see what manner of blood ran in my veins; for I lived with the whites, and was one of them, and my father's heart beat in me. It happened there was a maiden—white—who looked on me with kind eyes. Her father had much land and many horses; also he was a big man among his people, and his blood was the blood of the French. He said the girl knew not her own mind, and talked over-much with her, and became wroth that such things should be.

"But she knew her mind, for we came quick before the priest. And quicker had come her father, with lying words, false promises, I know not what; so that the priest stiffened his neck and would not make us that we might live one with the other. As at the beginning it was the church which would not bless my birth, so now it was the church which refused me marriage and put the blood of men upon my hands. *Bien!* Thus have I cause to love the church. So I struck the priest on his woman's mouth, and we took swift horses, the girl and I, to Fort Pierre, where was a minister of good heart. But hot on our trail was her father, and brothers, and other men he had gathered to him. And we fought, our horses on the run, till I emptied three saddles and the rest drew off, and went on to Fort Pierre. Then we took east, the girl and I, to the hills and forests, and we lived one with the other, and we were not married—the work of the good church which I love like a son.

"But mark you, for this is the strangeness of woman, the way of which no man may understand. One of the saddles I emptied was that of her father, and the hoofs of those who came behind had pounded him into the earth. This we saw, the girl and I, and this I had forgot had she not remembered. And in the quiet of the evening, after the day's hunt were done, it came between us, and in the silence of the night when we lay beneath the stars and should have been one. It was there always. She never spoke, but it sat by our fire and held us ever apart. She tried to put it aside; but at such times it would rise up till I could read it in the look of her eyes, in the very intake of her breath.

"So in the end she bore me a child, a woman-child, and died. Then I went among my mother's people, that it might nurse at a warm breast and live. But my hands were wet with the blood of men, look you, because of the church, wet with the blood of men. And the riders of the North came for me, but my mother's brother, who was then chief in his own right, hid me and gave me horses and food. And we went away, my woman-child and I, even to the Hudson Bay Country, where white men were few and the questions they asked not many. And I worked for the company as a hunter, as a guide, as a driver of dogs, till my woman-child was become a woman, tall and slender, and fair to the eye.

"You know the winter, long and lonely, breeding evil thoughts and bad deeds. The chief factor was a hard man, and bold. And he was not such that a woman would delight in looking upon. But he cast eyes upon my woman-child who was become a woman. Mother of God! he sent me away on a long trip with the dogs, that he might—you understand, he was a hard man and without heart. She was most white, and her soul was white, and a good woman, and—well, she died.

"It was bitter cold the night of my return and I had been away months, and the dogs were limping sore when I came to the fort. The Indians and breeds looked on me in silence, and I felt the fear of I knew not what, but I said nothing till the dogs were fed and I had eaten as a man with work before him should. Then I spoke up, demanding the word, and they shrank from me, afraid of my anger and what I should do; but the story came out, the pitiful story, word for word and act for act, and they marvelled that I should be so quiet.

"When they had done I went to the factor's house, calmer than now in the telling of it. He had been afraid, and called upon the breeds to help him; but they were not pleased with the deed, and had left him to lie on the bed he had made. So he had fled to the house of the priest. Thither I followed. But when I was come to that place, the priest stood in my way, and spoke soft words, and said a man in anger should go neither to the right nor left, but straight to God. I asked by the right of a father's wrath that he give me past, but he said only over his body, and besought with me to pray. Look you, it was the church, always the church; for I passed over his body and sent the factor to meet my woman-child before his god, which is a bad god, and the god of the white men.

"Then was there hue and cry, for word was sent to the station below, and I came away. Through the Land of the Great Slave, down the Valley of the Mackenzie to the never-opening ice, over the White Rockies, past the Great Curve of the Yukon, even to this place did I come. And from that day to this, yours is the first face of my father's people I have looked upon. May it be the last! These people, which are my people, are a simple folk, and I have been raised to honour among them. My word is their law, and their priests but do my bidding, else would I not suffer them. When I speak for them I speak for myself. We ask to be let alone. We do not want your kind. If we permit you to sit by our fires, after you will come your church, your priests, and your gods. And know this, for each white man who comes to my village, him will I make deny his god. You are the first, and I give you grace. So it were well you go, and go quickly."

"I am not responsible for my brothers," the second man spoke up, filling his pipe in a meditative manner. Hay Stockard was at times as thoughtful of speech as he was wanton of action; but only at times.

"But I know your breed," responded the other. "Your brothers are many, and it is you and yours who break the trail for them to follow. In time they shall come to possess the land, but not in my time. Already, have I heard, are they on the head-reaches of the Great River, and far away below are the Russians."

Hay Stockard lifted his head with a quick start. This was startling geographical information. The Hudson Bay post at Fort Yukon had other notions concerning the course of the river, believing it to flow into the Arctic.

"Then the Yukon empties into Bering Sea?" he asked.

"I do not know, but below there are Russians, many Russians. Which is neither here nor there. You may go on and see for yourself; you may go back to your brothers; but up the Koyukuk you shall not go while the priests and fighting men do my bidding. Thus do I command, I, Baptiste the Red, whose word is law and who am head man over this people."

"And should I not go down to the Russians, or back to my brothers?"

"Then shall you go swift-footed before your god, which is a bad god, and the god of the white men."

The red sun shot up above the northern skyline, dripping and bloody. Baptiste the Red came to his feet, nodded curtly, and went back to his camp amid the crimson shadows and the singing of the robins.

Hay Stockard finished his pipe by the fire, picturing in smoke and coal the unknown upper reaches of the Koyukuk, the strange stream which ended here its arctic travels and merged its waters with the muddy Yukon flood. Somewhere up there, if the dying words of a shipwrecked sailorman, who had made the fearful overland journey, were to be believed, and if the vial of golden grains in his pouch attested anything—somewhere up there, in that home of winter, stood the Treasure House of the North. And as keeper of the gate, Baptiste the Red, English half-breed and renegade, barred the way.

"Bah!" He kicked the embers apart and rose to his full height, arms lazily outstretched, facing the flushing north with careless soul.

II

Hay Stockard swore, harshly, in the rugged monosyllables of his mother tongue. His wife lifted her gaze from the pots and pins, and followed his in a keen scrutiny of the river. She was a woman of the Teslin Country, wise in the ways of her husband's vernacular when it grew intensive. From the slipping of a snow-shoe thong to the forefront of sudden death, she could gauge occasion by the pitch and volume of his blasphemy. So she knew the present occasion merited attention. A long canoe, with paddles flashing back the rays of the westering sun, was crossing the current from above and urging in for the eddy. Hay Stockard watched it intently. Three men rose and dipped, rose and dipped, in rhythmical precision; but a red bandanna, wrapped about the head of one, caught and held his eye.

"Bill!" he called. "Oh, Bill!"

A shambling, loose-jointed giant rolled out of one of the tents, yawning and rubbing the sleep from his eyes. Then he sighted the strange canoe and was wide awake on the instant.

"By the jumping Methuselah! That damned sky-pilot!"

Hay Stockard nodded his head bitterly, half-reached for his rifle, then shrugged his shoulders.

"Pot-shot him," Bill suggested, "and settle the thing out of hand. He'll spoil us sure if we don't."

But the other declined this drastic measure and turned away, at the same time bidding the woman return to her work, and calling Bill back from the bank. The two Indians in the canoe moored it on the edge of the eddy, while its white occupant, conspicuous by his gorgeous headgear, came up the bank.

"Like Paul of Tarsus, I give you greeting. Peace be unto you and grace before the Lord."

His advances were met sullenly, and without speech.

"To you, Hay Stockard, blasphemer and Philistine, greeting. In your heart is the lust of Mammon, in your mind cunning devils, in your tent this woman whom you live with in adultery; yet of these divers sins, even here in the wilderness, I, Sturges Owen, apostle to the Lord, bid you to repent and cast from you your iniquities."

"Save your cant! Save your cant!" Hay Stockard broke in testily. "You'll need all you've got, and more, for the Red Baptiste over yonder."

He waved his hand toward the Indian camp, where the half-breed was looking steadily across, striving to make out the new-comers. Sturges Owen, disseminator of light and apostle to the Lord, stepped to the edge of the steep and commanded his men to bring up the camp outfit. Stockard followed him.

"Look here," he demanded, plucking the missionary by the shoulder and twirling him about. "Do you value your hide?"

"My life is in the Lord's keeping, and I do but work in His vineyard," he replied solemnly.

"Oh, stow that! Are you looking for a job of martyrship?"

"If He so wills."

"Well, you'll find it right here, but I'm going to give you some advice first. Take it or leave it. If you stop here, you'll be cut off in the midst of your labours. And not you alone, but your men, Bill, my wife—"

"Who is a daughter of Belial and hearkeneth not to the true Gospel."

"And myself. Not only do you bring trouble upon yourself, but upon us. I was frozen in with you last winter, as you will well recollect, and I know you for a good man and a fool. If you think it your duty to strive with the heathen, well and good; but do exercise some wit in the way you go about it. This man, Red Baptiste, is no Indian. He comes of our common stock, is as bull-necked as I ever dared be, and as wild a fanatic the one way as you are the other. When you two come together, hell'll be to pay, and I don't care to be mixed up in it. Understand? So take my advice and go away. If you go down-stream, you'll fall in with the Russians. There's bound to be Greek priests among them, and they'll see you safe through to Bering Sea—that's where the Yukon empties—and from there it won't be hard to get back to civilisation. Take my word for it, and get out of here as fast as God'll let you."

"He who carries the Lord in his heart and the Gospel in his hand hath no fear of the machinations of man or devil," the missionary answered stoutly. "I will see this man and wrestle with him. One backslider returned to the fold is a greater victory than a thousand heathen. He who is strong for evil can be as mighty for good, witness Saul when he journeyed up to Damascus to bring Christian captives to Jerusalem. And the voice of the Saviour came to him, crying, 'Saul, Saul, why persecutest thou Me?' And therewith Paul arrayed himself on the side of the Lord, and thereafter was most mighty in the saving of souls. And even as thou, Paul of Tarsus, even so do I work in the vineyard of the Lord, bearing trials and tribulations, scoffs and sneers, stripes and punishments, for His dear sake."

"Bring up the little bag with the tea and a kettle of water," he called the next instant to his boatmen; "not forgetting the haunch of cariboo and the mixing-pan."

When his men, converts by his own hand, had gained the bank, the trio fell to their knees, hands and backs burdened with camp equipage, and offered up thanks for their passage through the wilderness and their safe arrival. Hay Stockard looked upon the function with sneering disapproval, the romance and solemnity of it lost to his matter-of-fact soul. Baptiste the Red, still gazing across, recognised the familiar postures, and remembered the girl who had shared his star-roofed couch in the hills and forests, and the woman-child who lay somewhere by bleak Hudson's Bay.

III

"Confound it, Baptiste, couldn't think of it. Not for a moment. Grant that this man is a fool and of small use in the nature of things; but still, you know, I can't give him up."

Hay Stockard paused, striving to put into speech the rude ethics of his heart.

"He's worried me, Baptiste, in the past and now, and caused me all manner of troubles; but can't you see, he's my own breed—white—and—and—why, I couldn't buy my life with his, not if he was a nigger."

"So be it," Baptiste the Red made answer. "I have given you grace and choice. I shall come presently, with my priests and fighting men, and either shall I kill you, or you deny your god. Give up the priest to my pleasure, and you shall depart in peace. Otherwise your trail ends here. My people are against you to the babies. Even now have the children stolen away your canoes."

He pointed down to the river. Naked boys had slipped down the water from the point above, cast loose the canoes, and by then had worked them into the current. When they had drifted out of rifle-shot they clambered over the sides and paddled ashore.

"Give me the priest, and you may have them back again. Come! Speak your mind, but without haste."

Stockard shook his head. His glance dropped to the woman of the Teslin Country with his boy at her breast, and he would have wavered had he not lifted his eyes to the men before him.

"I am not afraid," Sturges Owen spoke up. "The Lord bears me in His right hand, and alone am I ready to go into the camp of the unbeliever. It is not too late. Faith may move mountains. Even in the eleventh hour may I win his soul to the true righteousness."

"No," Stockard answered. "I gave him my word that he could speak with us unmolested. Rules of warfare, Bill; rules of warfare. He's been on the square, given us warning, and all that, and—why, damn it, man, I can't break my word."

"He'll keep his, never fear."

"Don't doubt it, but I won't let a half-breed outdo me in fair dealing. Why not do what he wants,—give him the missionary and be done with it?"

"N-no," Bill hesitated doubtfully.

"Shoe pinches, eh?"

Bill flushed a little and dropped the discussion. Baptiste the Red was still waiting the final decision. Stockard went up to him.

"It's this way, Baptiste. I came to your village minded to go up the Koyukuk. I intended no wrong. My heart was clean of evil. It is still clean. Along comes this priest, as you call him. I didn't bring him here. He'd have come whether I was here or not. But now that he is here, being of my people, I've got to stand by him. And I'm going to. Further, it will be no child's play. When you have done, your village will be silent and empty, your people wasted as after a famine. True, we will be gone; likewise the pick of your fighting men——"

"But those who remain shall be in peace, nor shall the word of strange gods and the tongue of strange priests be buzzing in their ears."

Both men shrugged their shoulders and turned away, the half-breed going back to his own camp. The missionary called his two men to him, and they fell into prayer. Stockard and Bill attacked the few standing pines with their axes, felling them into convenient breastworks. The child had fallen asleep, so the woman placed it on a heap of furs and lent a hand in fortifying the camp. Three sides were thus defended, the steep declivity at the rear precluding attack from that direction. When these arrangements had been completed, the two men stalked into the open, clearing away, here and there, the scattered under-brush. From the opposing camp came the booming of war-drums and the voices of the priests stirring the people to anger.

"Worst of it is they'll come in rushes," Bill complained, as they walked back with shouldered axes.

"And wait till midnight, when the light gets dim for shooting."

"Can't start the ball a-rolling too early, then." Bill exchanged the axe for a rifle, and took a careful rest. One of the medicine-men, towering above his tribesmen, stood out distinctly. Bill drew a bead on him.

"All ready?" he asked.

Stockard opened the ammunition box, placed the woman where she could reload in safety, and gave the word. The medicine-man dropped. For a moment there was silence, then a wild howl went up and a flight of bone arrows fell short.

"I'd like to take a look at the beggar," Bill remarked throwing a fresh shell into place. "I'll swear I drilled him clean between the eyes."

"Didn't work." Stockard shook his head gloomily. Baptiste had evidently quelled the more warlike of his followers, and instead of precipitating an attack in the bright light of day, the shot had caused a hasty exodus, the Indians drawing out of the village beyond the zone of fire.

In the full tide of his proselytising fervour, borne along by the hand of God, Sturges Owen would have ventured alone into the camp of the unbeliever, equally prepared for miracle or martyrdom; but in the waiting which ensued, the fever of conviction died away gradually, as the natural man asserted itself. Physical fear replaced spiritual hope; the love of life, the love of God. It was no new experience. He could feel his weakness coming on, and knew it of old time. He had struggled against it and been overcome by it before. He remembered when the other men had driven their paddles like mad in the van of a roaring ice-flood, how, at the critical moment, in a panic of worldly terror, he had dropped his paddle and besought wildly with his God for pity. And there were other times. The recollection was not pleasant. It brought shame to him that his spirit should be so weak and his flesh so strong. But the love of life! the love of life! He could not strip it from him. Because of it had his dim ancestors perpetuated their line; because of it was he destined to perpetuate his. His courage, if courage it might be called, was bred of fanaticism. The courage of Stockard and Bill was the adherence to deep-rooted ideals. Not that the love of life was less, but the love of race tradition more! not that they were unafraid to die, but that they were brave enough not to live at the price of shame.

The missionary rose, for the moment swayed by the mood of sacrifice. He half crawled over the barricade to proceed to the other camp, but sank back, a trembling mass, wailing. "As the spirit moves! As the spirit moves! Who am I that I should set aside the judgments of God? Before the foundations of the world were all things written in the book of life. Worm that I am, shall I erase the page or any portion thereof? As God wills, so shall the spirit move!"

Bill reached over, plucked him to his feet, and shook him, fiercely, silently. Then he dropped the bundle of quivering nerves and turned his attention to the two converts. But they showed little fright and a cheerful alacrity in preparing for the coming passage at arms.

Stockard, who had been talking in undertones with the Teslin woman, now turned to the missionary.

"Fetch him over here," he commanded of Bill.

"Now," he ordered, when Sturges Owen had been duly deposited before him, "make us man and wife, and be lively about it." Then he added apologetically to Bill: "No telling how it's to end, so I just thought I'd get my affairs straightened up."

The woman obeyed the behest of her white lord. To her the ceremony was meaningless. By her lights she was his wife, and had been from the day they first foregathered. The converts served as witnesses. Bill stood over the missionary, prompting him when he stumbled. Stockard put the responses in the woman's mouth, and when the time came, for want of better, ringed her finger with thumb and forefinger of his own.

"Kiss the bride!" thundered Bill, and Sturges Owen was too weak to disobey.

"Now baptise the child!"

"Neat and tidy," Bill commented.

"Gathering the proper outfit for a new trail," the father explained, taking the boy from the mother's arms. "I was grub-staked, once, into the Cascades, and had everything in the kit except salt. Never shall forget it. And if the woman and the kid cross the divide to-night they might as well be prepared for potluck. A long shot, Bill, between ourselves, but nothing lost if it misses."

A cup of water served the purpose, and the child was laid away in a secure corner of the barricade. The men built the fire, and the evening meal was cooked.

The sun hurried round to the north, sinking closer to the horizon. The heavens in that quarter grew red and bloody. The shadows lengthened, the light dimmed, and in the sombre recesses of the forest, life slowly died away. Even the wild fowl in the river softened their raucous chatter and feigned the nightly farce of going to bed. Only the tribesmen increased their clamour, war-drums booming and voices raised in savage folk-songs. But as the sun dipped they ceased their tumult. The rounded hush of midnight was complete. Stockard rose to his knees and peered over the logs. Once the child wailed in pain and disconcerted him. The mother bent over it, but it slept again. The silence was interminable, profound. Then, of a sudden, the robins burst into full-throated song. The night had passed.

A flood of dark figures boiled across the open. Arrows whistled and bow-thongs sang. The shrill-tongued rifles answered back. A spear, and a mighty cast, transfixed the Teslin woman as she hovered above the child. A spent arrow, diving between the logs, lodged in the missionary's arm.

There was no stopping the rush. The middle distance was cumbered with bodies, but the rest surged on, breaking against and over the barricade like an ocean wave. Sturges Owen fled to the tent, while the men were swept from their feet, buried beneath the human tide. Hay Stockard alone regained the surface, flinging the tribesmen aside like yelping curs. He had managed to seize an axe. A dark hand grasped the child by a naked foot, and drew it from beneath its mother. At arm's length its puny body circled through the air, dashing to death against the logs. Stockard clove the man to the chin and fell to clearing space. The ring of savage faces closed in, raining upon him spear-thrusts and bone-barbed arrows. The sun shot up, and they swayed back and forth in the crimson shadows. Twice, with his axe blocked by too deep a blow, they rushed him; but each time he flung them clear. They fell under foot and he trampled dead and dying, the way slippery with blood. And still the day brightened and the robins sang. Then they drew back from him in awe, and he leaned breathless upon his axe.

"Blood of my soul!" cried Baptiste the Red. "But thou art a man. Deny thy god, and thou shalt yet live."

Stockard swore his refusal, feebly but with grace.

"Behold! A woman!" Sturges Owen had been brought before the half-breed.

Beyond a scratch on the arm, he was uninjured, but his eyes roved about him in an ecstasy of fear. The heroic figure of the blasphemer, bristling with wounds and arrows, leaning defiantly upon his axe, indifferent, indomitable, superb, caught his wavering vision. And he felt a great envy of the man who could go down serenely to the dark gates of death. Surely Christ, and not he, Sturges Owen, had been moulded in such manner. And why not he? He felt dimly the curse of ancestry, the feebleness of spirit which had come down to him out of the past, and he felt an anger at the creative force, symbolise it as he would, which had formed him, its servant, so weakly. For even a stronger man, this anger and the stress of circumstance were sufficient to breed apostasy, and for Sturges Owen it was inevitable. In the fear of man's anger he would dare the wrath of God. He had been raised up to serve the Lord only that he might be cast down. He had been given faith without the strength of faith; he had been given spirit without the power of spirit. It was unjust.

"Where now is thy god?" the half-breed demanded.

"I do not know." He stood straight and rigid, like a child, repeating a catechism.

"Hast thou then a god at all?"

"I had."

"And now?"

"No."

Hay Stockard swept the blood from his eyes and laughed. The missionary looked at him curiously, as in a dream. A feeling of infinite distance came over him, as though of a great remove. In that which had transpired, and which was to transpire, he had no part. He was a spectator—at a distance, yes, at a distance. The words of Baptiste came to him faintly:

"Very good. See that this man go free, and that no harm befall him. Let him depart in peace. Give him a canoe and food. Set his face toward the Russians, that he may tell their priests of Baptiste the Red, in whose country there is no god."

They led him to the edge of the steep, where they paused to witness the final tragedy. The half-breed turned to Hay Stockard.

"There is no god," he prompted.

The man laughed in reply. One of the young men poised a war-spear for the cast.

"Hast thou a god?"

"Ay, the God of my fathers."

He shifted the axe for a better grip. Baptiste the Red gave the sign, and the spear hurtled full against his breast. Sturges Owen saw the ivory head stand out beyond his back, saw the man sway, laughing, and snap the shaft short as he fell upon it. Then he went down to the river, that he might carry to the Russians the message of Baptiste the Red, in whose country there was no god.

Life Isn't a Short Story

CONRAD AIKEN
(1889–1973)

The short story writer had run out of ideas; he had used them all; he was feeling as empty as a bathtub and as blue as an oyster. He stirred his coffee without gusto and looked at his newspaper without reading it, only noting (but with a lackluster eye) that Prohibition was finally dead. He was having his breakfast at one of those white-tiled restaurants which are so symbolic of America—with an air of carbolic purity at the entrance, but steamy purlieus at the rear which imagination trembles to investigate. His breakfast was alway the same: two two-minute eggs, a little glass of chilled tomato juice, dry toast, and coffee. The only change, this morning, lay in the fact that he was having these simple things in a new place—it was a somewhat humbler restaurant than the one he usually entered at eight-thirty. He had looked in through the window appraisingly, and had a little hesitantly entered. But the ritual turned out to be exactly the same as at the others—a ticket at the entrance, where the cashier sat behind a glass case which was filled with cigarettes, chewing gum, and silver-papered cakes of chocolate; a tray at the counter; the precise intonation of *"Two twos, with."* The only difference, in fact, was that the china was of a pale smoke-blue, a soft and dim blue which, had it been green, would have been pistachio. This gave his coffee a new appearance.

He sat at the marble-topped table near the window, and looked out at the crowded square. A light soft drizzle was falling on the morning rush of cars, wagons, pedestrians, newsboys; before the window bobbed a continuous procession of men and women; and he watched them over the half-seen headlines of his newspaper. A middle-aged woman, walking quickly, her umbrella pulled low over her head, so that the whiteness of her profile was sharp and immediate against the purple shadow. She vanished past the range of his vision before he had had time to see her properly—and for a moment after she had gone he went on thinking about her. She might do for the physical model of his story; but she wasn't fat enough, nor was she blonde, and for some obscure reason he had decided that the heroine must be fat and blonde. Just the same, she was real, she had come from somewhere and was going somewhere, and she was doing it with obvious concentration and energy. The rhythm of her gait was unusually pronounced, each shoulder swayed slightly but emphatically sideways, as if in a series of quick and aggressive but cheerful greetings—the effect, if not quite graceful, was individual and charming. He stopped thinking about her, and recovered his powers of observation, just in time to see a gray Irish face, middle-aged, hook-nosed, under a dirty felt hat, a hand quickly removing the pipe from the mouth, and the lips pouting to eject a long bright arc of spit, which fell heavily out of sight, the pipe then replaced. Such a quantity of spit he could not have imagined—his mouth felt dry at the mere thought of it. Where had it been stored and for how long? and with increasing pleasure, or increasing annoyance? The act itself had been unmistakably a pleasure, and had probably had its origins in pride; one could imagine him having competed, as a boy, in spitting through a knot-hole in a fence. He had trained himself, all his life, in the power of retention; his mouth had become a kind of reservoir.

II

But the "story" came back to him. It had waked him up as a feeling of obscure weight at the back of his head or on the back of his tongue; it had seemed also to be in one corner of the shadowy ceiling above the bookcase, like a cobweb to be removed with a long brush. He had lain in bed looking at it, now and then turning his head to right or left on the pillow as if precisely to turn it away from the idea. It might be Elmira, it might be Akron, it might be Fitchburg—it was a small provincial city, at any rate, the sort of small town that looks its most characteristic in a brick-red postcard of hard straight streets and ugly red houses. But she wouldn't be living in one of these—she would be living in an apartment house of shabby stucco, and the entrance would be through a door of grained varnish and plate glass. It would have an air of jaded superiority. And as for her apartment itself, on the second floor, with a little curly brass number on the door——

The idea had first occurred to him in the lobby of the Orpheum. He had paused to light a cigarette in the passage that led past the lounge, where parrots squawked in cages, and canaries trilled, and goldfish swam in an ornate aquarium, at the bottom of which, dimly seen through the heavy green water, was a kind of crumbling Gothic castle. He was standing there, looking at this, when the two groups of people had suddenly encountered each other with such hearty and heavy surprise. He had caught merely the phrases *"as I live and breathe!"* and *"in the flesh!"* The two men and the two women he had scarcely looked at—the phrases themselves had so immediately assumed an extraordinary importance. They would both, he at once saw, make good titles—it was only later that he had seen that they both had the same meaning. They both simply meant—*alive.*

Alive. And that was the difference between life, as one conceived it in a story, and life as it was, for example, in the restaurant in which he was sitting, or in the noisy square at which he was looking. As I live and breathe—I am standing here living and breathing, you are standing there living and breathing, and it's a surprise and a delight to both of us. In the flesh, too—death hasn't yet stripped our bones, or the crematory tried out our fats. We haven't seen each other for a long while, we didn't know whether we were dead or not, but here we are.

At the same time, there was the awful commonplaceness of the two phrases, the cheapness of them, the vulgarity—they were as old as the hills, and as worn; æons of weather and æons of handshake lay upon them; one witnessed, in the mere hearing of them, innumerable surprised greetings, innumerable mutual congratulations on the mere fact of being still alive. The human race seemed to extend itself backwards through them, in time, as along a road—if one pursued the thought one came eventually to a vision of two small apes peering at each other round the cheeks of a cocoanut and making a startled noise that sounded like *"yoicks!"* Or else, one simply saw, in the void, one star passing another, with no vocal interchange at all, nothing but a mutual exacerbation of heat. . . . It was very puzzling.

He stirred his coffee, wondered if he had sweetened it, reassured himself by tasting it. Yes. But in this very commonplaceness lay perhaps the idea, he had begun to see, as he lay in bed in the morning, watching the rain: and as he wondered about the large blonde lady in Fitchburg, he had begun to see that Gladys (for that was her name) was just the sort of hopelessly vulgar and commonplace person who would pride herself on her superiority in such matters. She would dislike such phrases, they would disgust her. After the first two or three years of her marriage to Sidney, when the romance had worn off and the glamor had fallen like a mask from his lean Yankee trader's face, when the sense of time had begun to be obtrusive, and the deadly round of the merely quotidian had replaced the era of faint orchids and bright bracelets and expensive theater tickets, it was then that she became conscious of certain tedious phrases he was in the habit of using. There was no concealing the fact any longer that they really came of separate and different worlds; Sidney had had little more than a high-school education, he had no "culture," he had never read a book in his life. He had walked straight from school into his father's hardware shop. What there was to know about cutlery, tools, grass seed, lawn mowers, washing machines, wire nails, white lead paint, and sandpaper, he knew. He was a loyal Elk, a shrewd and honest business man, a man of no vices (unless one counted as a vice a kind of Hoosier aridity) and few pleasures. Occasionally he went to the bowling alleys, a pastime which she had always considered a little vulgar; he enjoyed a good hockey match; he liked a good thriller in the talkies (one of the few tastes they actually shared); and now and then he wanted to sit in the front row at a musical comedy. On these occasions, there was a definite sparkle or gleam about him, a lighting up of his sharp gray eyes, which reminded her of the Sidney to whom she had become engaged. This both puzzled and annoyed her; she felt, as she looked at him, a vague wave of jealousy and hatred. It must have been this gleam which, when focused intently on herself, had misled her into thinking him something that he wasn't and never would be.

III

As I live and breathe.

The story might even be called that.

A horse and wagon drew up at the curbstone outside the window. On the side of the wagon was inscribed, "Acme Towel Supply Company." Of course; it was one of those companies which supply towels and napkins and dishcloths to hotels and restaurants. The driver had jumped down, dropping his reins, and was opening the little pair of shabby wooden doors at the back of the wagon. The brown horse, his head down, his eyes invisible behind blinkers, stood perfectly still, as if deep in thought. His back and sides were shiny with rain, the worn harness dripped, now and then he twitched his shoulder muscles, as if in a slight shiver. Why did towel-supply companies always deliver towels in horse-drawn wagons? It was one of the minor mysteries; a queer sort of survival, for which one saw no possible reason. Beyond the wagon and the horse, the traffic was beginning to move forward again in response to a shrill birdcall from the policeman's whistle. A man in a black slicker had come close to the window and was reading the "specials" which were placarded in cinnamon-colored paper on the glass. When this had been done, he peered into the restaurant between two squares of paper; the quick sharp eyes looked straight at him and then past him and were as quickly gone. This meeting of his eyes had very likely prevented him from coming in; it was precisely such unexpected encounters with one's own image, as seen in the returned glance of another, that changed the course of one's life. And the restaurant had perhaps lost the sale of a couple of doughnuts and a "cup of coffee, half cream."

The way to get at Gladys's character, perhaps, was through her environment, the kind of place she lived in, her street, her apartment, her rooms. First of all, the stucco apartment house, the glass door, on which the name "Saguenay" was written obliquely in large gilt script, with a flourish of broad gilt underneath. Inside the door, a flight of shallow stairs, made of imitation marble, superficially clean, but deeply ingrained with dirt. Her apartment, now that she lived alone, was small, of course—it consisted of a bedroom, a sitting room, a bathroom, and a kitchenette. One's immediate feeling, on entering the sitting room from the varnished hallway, was that the occupant must be a silly woman. It was plushy, it was perfumed, there was a bead curtain trembling between the sitting room and the kitchenette, at either side of the lace-curtained window hung a golden-wired birdcage, in which rustled a canary, and on the window-sill was a large bowl of goldfish. The ornaments were very ornamental and very numerous; the mantel groaned with souvenirs and photographs; the pictures were uniformly sentimental—several were religious. It was clear that she doted, simply doted, on birds and flowers—talked baby-talk to the canaries and the goldfish, even to the azalea, and always of course in that offensive, little, high-pitched fat-woman's coo. She would come in to them in the morning, wearing a pink flannel wrapper, brushing her hair, and would talk to them or wag a coy finger at them. And how's my sweet little dicky bird this morning? and have they slept well and been good in the night? and have they kept their little eyes shut tight to keep out the naughty bogey-man? And then at once she would forget them entirely, begin singing softly, walk with her head tilted on one side to the bathroom to turn on the bath, return to the kitchen to filch a cookie from the bread-box, and then go languidly to the front door for the milk and the newspaper.

The newspaper was the *Christian Science Monitor*; she took it, not because she was a Scientist, though she had an open mind, but because it was so "cultured." She liked to read about books and music and foreign affairs, and it frequently gave her ideas for little talks to the Women's Club. She had talked about the dole in England, and its distressing effect on the morals of the young men, and she had made a sensation by saying that she thought one should not too hastily condemn the nudist cult in Germany. Everyone knew that the human body craved sunlight, that the ultra-violet rays, or was it the infra-red, were most beneficial, so the idea was at least a healthy one, wasn't it? And the beautiful purity of Greek life was surely an answer to those who thought the human body in itself impure. It raised the whole question of what was purity, anyway! Everyone knew that purity was in the heart, in the attitude, and not really in the body. She thought the idea of playing croquet in the nude, queer as it might seem to us in Fitchburg, most interesting. One ought to think less about the body and more about the mind.

IV

The towel-supply man seemed to have disappeared; perhaps he was getting a cup of coffee at the Waldorf next door. Or making a round of several of the adjacent restaurants all at once. The horse waited patiently, was absolutely still, didn't even stamp a foot. He looked as if he were thinking about the rain. Or perhaps, dismayed by the senseless noise of all the traffic about him, he was simply thinking about his stall, wherever it was. Or more likely, not thinking anything at all. He just stood.

To her friends, of course, and to her sister Emma (who was her chief reason for living in Fitchburg) she posed as a woman with a broken heart, a woman tragically disillusioned, a beautiful romantic who had found that love was dust and ashes and that men were—well, creatures of a lower order. It was all very sad, very pitiful. One ought to have foreseen it, perhaps, or one ought not to have been born so sensitive, but there it was. If you had a soul, if you had perceptions, and loved beautiful things, and if you fell in love while you were still inexperienced and trusting, while you still looked at a world of violets through violet eyes, this was what happened. You gave your heart to someone who didn't deserve it. But what man ever *did* deserve it? Only the poets, perhaps, or the composers, Chopin for instance, those rare creatures, half angel and half man (or was it half bird?), who had great and deep and tender souls. And how many such men could one find in Massachusetts? It was all so impossible, it was all so dreadful. Everyone knew that in America the women were infinitely more refined and sensitive than the men, you had only to look about you. What man ever wanted to talk about poetry with you, or listen to an evening of the Preludes, or to a lecture about the love affair of George Sand and Alfred de Musset? They wouldn't know what you meant; they wanted to go to the bowling alley or talk about the stock market; or else to sit in the front row of the Follies and look at the legs. They were vulgar, they had no imaginations. And she remembered that time at Emma's when Sidney had got so angry and gone on so in that common and vulgar way and made such a scene—whenever she thought of it she got hot all over. Absolutely, it was the most vulgar scene! And done deliberately, too, just because he was so jealous about their having a refined conversation. And when she tried to stop him talking about it, he just went on, getting stubborner and stubborner, and all simply to make her feel ashamed. As if any of them had wanted to hear about those cheap drinking parties of his in Ohio. And that dreadful word, burgoo, that was it, which they had all laughed at, and tried to shame him out of, why what do you mean, burgoo, why Sidney what are you talking about, who ever heard such a word as *burgoo, burgoo!* And even that hadn't been enough, he got red and angry and went on saying it, burgoo, what's wrong with burgoo, of course there is such a word, and damned fine parties they were, too, and if they only had burgoos in Massachusetts life here would be a damned sight better. The idea! It served him right that she got mad and jumped up and said what she did. If you can't talk politely like a gentleman, or let others talk, then I think you had better leave those who will. Why don't you go back to your hardware shop, or back to Ohio, it doesn't seem this is the right environment for you. Or *anywhere* where you can have your precious burgoo.

But of course that was only one incident among so many, it was happening all the time; anybody could see that Sidney was not the man to ever appreciate her. What she always said was that nobody outside a marriage could ever possibly have any *real* idea of the things that went on there, could they. It was just impossible for them even to conceive of it. All those little things that you wouldn't think of—like Sidney's always leaving the dirty lather and little black hairs in the wash-basin after he shaved. Or the way he never noticed when she had on a new hat or ever said anything nice about the meals she got for him, just simply not noticing anything at all. That was a part of it, but much more was his simply not ever being able to talk to her, or to take any interest in intellectual things. And his vulgarity, the commonness of his speech, his manners! Every time she introduced him to somebody he would put his head down and take that ridiculous little confidential step toward them and say, "What was the name? I didn't get the name?" The idea! And if you told him about it he got mad. And as for the number of times every day that he said "as I live and breathe"—!

V

It had begun to rain harder. The sound of it rushed through the opening door as a small man, very dark, a Syrian perhaps, came in shaking his sodden hat so that the drops fell in a curve on the floor. A bright spray was dancing on the roof of the towel wagon, and a heavy stream fell splattering from one corner of an awning. People had begun to run, to scurry, in one's and two's and three's, exactly like one of those movies of the Russian Revolution, when invisible machine guns were turned on the crowds. One would not be surprised to see them fall down, or crawl away on their bellies.

Or to see the whole square emptied of human beings in the twinkling of an eye. Nor would one be surprised to see a lightning flash, either, for it had suddenly become astonishingly dark—the whole dismal scene had that ominous look which seems to wait, in a melodrama, for a peal of thunder. The light was sulphur-colored; it was terrifying; and he watched with fascination all the little windshield wipers wagging agitatedly on the fronts of cars—it gave one the feeling that the poor things were actually frightened, and were breathing faster. As for the horse, he stood unmoving, unmoved. His head was down, and he seemed to be studying with an extraordinary concentration the torrent of muddy water which rushed past his feet. Perhaps he was enjoying it; perhaps he even liked to feel all that tropic weight of rain on his back, experiencing in it a renewal of contact with the real, the elemental. Or perhaps he merely enjoyed standing still. Or perhaps he simply *was*.

But the question arose, ought one now to switch the point of view in the story, and do something more about Sidney? What about Sidney? Where on earth was Sidney all this while? and doing what? Presumably, running his hardware shop—and presumably again in Boston—but this was a little meager, one wanted to know something more than that. One ought to give him a special sort of appearance—a pencil behind his ear, a tuft of white hair over his sallow forehead, sharply pointed brown shoes. Perhaps he was something of a dandy, with a vivid corner of striped handkerchief pointing from his breast pocket; and perhaps he was by no means such a dull fellow as Gladys thought. But this *would* involve a shift in point of view, which was a mistake; it was no doubt better to stick to Gladys, in Fitchburg, and to see Sidney wholly as *she* saw him, to think of him only as *she* thought of him. She would almost certainly, from time to time (self-absorbed as she was, and vain, and vulgar, and with her silly small-town pretensions to culture), she would almost certainly, nevertheless, give him credit for a few virtues. He was generous: he had offered her a divorce, as soon as he knew how she felt about it; and he had behaved like a lamb, really, if she did say so, like a lamb, about the separation. He had done everything he could think of to make it easier for her.

In fact, one thing you *could* say for Sidney was, that he was generous —generous to a fault. She often thought of that. She always thought of it especially on the first of the month, when the check for the separation allowance turned up, as punctually as the calendar—sometimes he even sent her something extra. On these days, when she bustled to the bank with the check tucked into her glove to deposit it and pay the rent, she always felt so secure and happy that she had a very special state of mind about Sidney, something that was almost affection. Of course, it couldn't *be* affection, but it was *like* it—and it was just that feeling, with perhaps the loneliness which had upset her to begin with, which had misled her at last into writing him. It was easy enough now, as she had so often said to Emma, to see what had made her do it; she was sorry for him; but it only went to show how right she had been in the whole idea.

Just the same, it had been natural enough to write to him in that affectionate and grateful way; and when he had answered by so pathetically asking her to let him come to see her she had certainly thought it might be worth trying; even Emma had thought so; perhaps they would find after all that the differences between them were superficial; they could patch things up, maybe she would go back to Boston to live with him. The idea actually excited her—she remembered how she had found herself looking forward to having him come. Emma had offered to put him up for the night, so as to prevent embarrassment. And the thought of having him see her new apartment for the first time, with the canaries and the goldfish and the oriental rugs, and the Encyclopædia Britannica, had given her a very funny feeling, almost like being unfaithful. The day before he came she could hardly sit still. She kept walking to and fro round the apartment, moving the rugs and the chairs, and patting the cushions—and all the time wondering if two years would have changed him much, and what they would say. Naturally, she hadn't held out any real hope to him in her letter, she had only told him she would be willing to talk with him, that was all. He had no right to expect anything else, she had made that clear. However, there was no sense in not being friendly about these things, was there? Even if you were separated you could behave like a civilized human being; Emma agreed with her about that. It was the only decent thing to do. But when the day came, and when finally that afternoon she heard him breeze into Emma's front hall, stamping his feet, and went out to meet him, and saw him wearing the wing collar and the stringy little white tie, and the rubbers, and his little gray eyes shining behind the glasses with the cord, and when the very first thing he said was, just as if nothing at all had ever happened, "Well, as I live and breathe, if it isn't Gladys!"—and then stood there, not knowing whether to kiss her or shake hands—it was just a misdeal, that was all, just another misdeal.

The whole thing went down, smack, like a house of cards. She could hardly bring herself to shake hands with him, or look at him—she suddenly wanted to cry. She rushed into Emma's room and stayed there on the bed for an hour, crying—Emma kept running in and saying for God's sake pull yourself together, at least go out and talk to him for a while, he's hurt, you can't treat him like this; the poor man doesn't know whether he's going or coming; come on now, Gladys, and be a good sport. He's sitting on the sofa in there with his head down like a horse, not knowing what to say; you simply can't treat him like that. The least you can do is go out and tell him you're sorry and that it was a mistake, and that he'd better not stay, or take him round to your apartment and talk it over with him quietly and then send him back to Boston. Come on now.

But of course she couldn't do it—she couldn't even go with him to the station. Emma went with him, and told him on the platform while they were waiting for the train that it was no use, it had all been a terrible mistake, and she was sorry, they were both sorry, Gladys sent word that she was very sorry. And afterwards, she had said it was so pathetic seeing him with his brand-new suitcase there beside him on the platform, his suitcase which he hadn't even opened, just taking it back to Boston where he came from. . . . When the train finally came, he almost forgot his suitcase; she thought he would have liked to leave it behind.

The towel-supply man came running back with a basket, flung it into the wagon, banged the dripping doors shut, and then jumped nimbly up to his seat, unhooking the reins. Automatically, but as if still deep in thought, the horse leaned slowly forward, lowered his head a little, and began to move. A long day was still ahead of him, a day of crowded and noisy streets, streets full of surprises and terrors and rain, muddy uneven cobbles and greasy smooth asphalt. The wagon and the man would be always there behind him; an incalculable sequence of accidents and adventures was before him. What did he think about, as he plodded from one dirty restaurant to another, one hotel to another, carrying towels? Probably nothing at all; certainly no such sentimental thing as a green meadow, nor anything so ridiculous as a story about living and breathing. It was enought, even if one was a slave, to live and breathe. For life, after all, isn't a short story.

The Grave
KATHERINE ANNE PORTER
(1890–1980)

The grandfather, dead for more than thirty years, had been twice disturbed in his long repose by the constancy and possessiveness of his widow. She removed his bones first to Louisiana and then to Texas as if she had set out to find her own burial place, knowing well she would never return to the places she had left. In Texas she set up a small cemetery in a corner of her first farm, and as the family connection grew, and oddments of relations came over from Kentucky to settle, it contained at last about twenty graves. After the grandmother's death, part of her land was to be sold for the benefit of certain of her children, and the cemetery happened to lie in the part set aside for sale. It was necessary to take up the bodies and bury them again in the family plot in the big new public cemetery, where the grandmother had been buried. At last her husband was to lie beside her for eternity, as she had planned.

The family cemetery had been a pleasant small neglected garden of tangled rose bushes and ragged cedar trees and cypress, the simple flat stones rising out of uncropped sweet-smelling wild grass. The graves were lying open and empty one burning day when Miranda and her brother Paul, who often went together to hunt rabbits and doves, propped their twenty-two Winchester rifles carefully against the rail fence, climbed over and explored among the graves. She was nine years old and he was twelve.

They peered into the pits all shaped alike with such purposeful accuracy, and looking at each other with pleased adventurous eyes, they said in solemn tones: "These were graves!" trying by words to shape a special, suitable emotion in their minds, but they felt nothing except an agreeable thrill of wonder: they were seeing a new sight, doing something they had not done before. In them both there was also a small disappointment at the entire commonplaceness of the actual spectacle. Even if it had once contained a coffin for years upon years, when the coffin was gone a grave was just a hole in the ground. Miranda leaped into the pit that had held her grandfather's bones. Scratching around aimlessly and pleasurably as any young animal, she scooped up a lump of earth and weighted it in her palm. It had a pleasantly sweet, corrupt smell, being mixed with cedar needles and small leaves, and as the crumbs fell apart, she saw a silver dove no larger than a hazel nut, with spread wings and a neat fan-shaped tail. The breast had a deep round hollow in it. Turning it up to the fierce sunlight, she saw that the inside of the hollow was cut in little whorls. She scrambled out, over the pile of loose earth that had fallen back into one end of the grave, calling to Paul that she had found something, he must guess what . . . His head appeared smiling over the rim of another grave. He waved a closed hand at her. "I've got something too!" They ran to compare treasures, making a game of it, so many guesses each, all wrong, and a final showdown with opened palms. Paul had found a thin wide gold ring carved with intricate flowers and leaves. Miranda was smitten at sight of the ring and wished to have it. Paul seemed more impressed by the dove. They made a trade, with some little bickering. After he had got the dove in his hand, Paul said, "Don't you know what this is? This is a screw head for a *coffin!* . . . I'll bet nobody else in the world has one like this!"

Miranda glanced at it without covetousness. She had the gold ring on her thumb; it fitted perfectly. "Maybe we ought to go now," she said, "maybe one of the niggers'll see us and tell somebody." They knew the land had been sold, the cemetery was no longer theirs, and they felt like trespassers. They climbed back over the fence, slung their rifles loosely under their arms—they had been shooting at targets with various kinds of firearms since they were seven years old—and set out to look for the rabbits and doves or whatever small game might happen along. On these expeditions Miranda always followed at Paul's heels along the path, obeying instructions about handling her gun when going through fences; learning how to stand it up properly so it would not slip and fire unexpectedly; how to wait her time for a shot and not just bang away in the air without looking, spoiling shots for Paul, who really could hit things if given a chance. Now and then, in her excitement at seeing birds whizz up suddenly before her face, or a rabbit leap across her very toes, she lost her head, and almost without sighting she flung her rifle up and pulled the trigger. She hardly ever hit any sort of mark. She had no proper sense of hunting at all. Her brother would be often completely disgusted with her. "You don't care whether you get your bird or not," he said. "That's no way to hunt." Miranda could not understand his indignation. She had seen him smash his hat and yell with fury when he had missed his aim. "What I like about shooting," said Miranda, with exasperating inconsequence, "is pulling the trigger and hearing the noise."

"Then, by golly," said Paul, "whyn't you go back to the range and shoot at bullseyes?"

"I'd just as soon," said Miranda, "only like this, we walk around more."

"Well, you just stay behind and stop spoiling my shots," said Paul, who, when he made a kill, wanted to be certain he had made it. Miranda, who alone brought down a bird once in twenty rounds, always claimed as her own any game they got when they fired at the same moment. It was tiresome and unfair and her brother was sick of it.

"Now, the first dove we see, or the first rabbit, is mine," he told her. "And the next will be yours. Remember that and don't get smarty."

"What about snakes?" asked Miranda idly. "Can I have the first snake?"

Waving her thumb gently and watching her gold ring glitter, Miranda lost interest in shooting. She was wearing her summer roughing outfit: dark blue overalls, a light blue shirt, a hired-man's straw hat, and thick brown sandals. Her brother had the same outfit except his was a sober hickory-nut color. Ordinarily Miranda preferred her overalls to any other dress, though it was making rather a scandal in the countryside, for the year was 1903, and in the back country the law of female decorum had teeth in it. Her father had been criticized for letting his girls dress like boys and go careering around astride barebacked horses. Big sister Maria, the really independent and fearless one, in spite of her rather affected ways, rode at a dead run with only a rope knotted around her horse's nose. It was said the motherless family was running down, with the Grandmother no longer there to hold it together. It was known that she had discriminated against her son Harry in her will, and that he was in straits about money. Some of his old neighbors reflected with vicious satisfaction that now he would probably not be so stiff-necked, nor have any more high-stepping horses either. Miranda knew this, though she could not say how. She had met along the road old women of the kind who smoked corn-cob pipes, who had treated her grandmother with most sincere respect. They slanted their gummy old eyes side-ways at the granddaughter and said, "Ain't you ashamed of yoself, Missy? It's aginst the Scriptures to dress like that. Whut yo Pappy thinkin about?" Miranda, with her powerful social sense, which was like a fine set of antennae radiating from every pore of her skin, would feel ashamed because she knew well it was rude and ill-bred to shock anybody, even bad-tempered old crones, though she had faith in her father's judgment and was perfectly comfortable in the clothes. Her father had said, "They're just what you need, and they'll save your dresses for school . . ." This sounded quite simple and natural to her. She had been brought up in rigorous economy. Wastefulness was vulgar. It was also a sin. These were truths; she had heard them repeated many times and never once disputed.

Now the ring, shining with the serene purity of fine gold on her rather grubby thumb, turned her feelings against her overalls and sockless feet, toes sticking through the thick brown leather straps. She wanted to go back to the farmhouse, take a good cold bath, dust herself with plenty of Maria's violet talcum powder—provided Maria was not present to object, of course—put on the thinnest, most becoming dress she owned, with a big sash, and sit in a wicker chair under the trees . . . These things were not all she wanted, of course; she had vague stirrings of desire for luxury and a grand way of living which could not take precise form in her imagination but were founded on family legend of past wealth and leisure. These immediate comforts were what she could have, and she wanted them at once. She lagged rather far behind Paul, and once she thought of just turning back without a word and going home. She stopped, thinking that Paul would never do that to her, and so she would have to tell him. When a rabbit leaped, she let Paul have it without dispute. He killed it with one shot.

When she came up with him, he was already kneeling, examining the wound, the rabbit trailing from his hands. "Right through the head," he said complacently, as if he had aimed for it. He took out his sharp, competent bowie knife and started to skin the body. He did it very cleanly and quickly. Uncle Jimbilly knew how to prepare the skins so that Miranda always had fur coats for her dolls, for though she never cared much for her dolls she liked seeing them in fur coats. The children knelt facing each other over the dead animal. Miranda watched admiringly while her brother stripped the skin away as if he were taking off a glove. The flayed flesh emerged dark scarlet, sleek, firm; Miranda with thumb and finger felt the long fine muscles with the silvery flat strips binding them to the joints. Brother lifted the oddly bloated belly. "Look," he said, in a low amazed voice. "It was going to have young ones."

Very carefully he slit the thin flesh from the center ribs to the flanks, and a scarlet bag appeared. He slit again and pulled the bag open, and there lay a bundle of tiny rabbits, each wrapped in a thin scarlet veil. The brother pulled these off and there they were, dark gray, their sleek wet down lying in minute even ripples, like a baby's head just washed, their unbelievably small delicate ears folded close, their little blind faces almost featureless.

Miranda said, "Oh, I want to *see*," under her breath. She looked and looked—excited but not frightened, for she was accustomed to the sight of animals killed in hunting—filled with pity and astonishment and a kind of shocked delight in the wonderful little creatures for their own sakes, they were so pretty. She touched one of them ever so carefully, "Ah, there's blood running over them," she said and began to tremble without knowing why. Yet she wanted most deeply to see and to know. Having seen, she felt at once as if she had known all along. The very memory of her former ignorance faded, she had always known just this. No one had ever told her anything outright, she had been rather unobservant of the animal life around her because she was so accustomed to animals. They seemed simply disorderly and unaccountably rude in their habits, but altogether natural and not very interesting. Her brother had spoken as if he had known about everything all along. He may have seen all this before. He had never said a word to her, but she knew now a part at least of what he knew. She understood a little of the secret, formless intuitions in her own mind and body, which had been clearing up, taking form, so gradually and so steadily she had not realized that she was learning what she had to know. Paul said cautiously, as if he were talking about something forbidden: "They were just about ready to be born." His voice dropped on the last word. "I know," said Miranda, "like kittens. I know, like babies." She was quietly and terribly agitated, standing again with her rifle under her arm, looking down at the bloody heap. "I don't want the skin," she said, "I won't have it." Paul buried the young rabbits again in their mother's body, wrapped the skin around her, carried her to a clump of sage bushes, and hid her away. He came out again at once and said to Miranda, with an eager friendliness, a confidential tone quite unusual in him, as if he were taking her into an important secret on equal terms: "Listen now. Now you listen to me, and don't ever forget. Don't you ever tell a living soul that you saw this. Don't tell a soul. Don't tell Dad because I'll get into trouble. He'll say I'm leading you into things you ought not to do. He's always saying that. So now don't you go and forget and blab out sometime the way you're always doing . . . Now, that's a secret. Don't you tell."

Miranda never told, she did not even wish to tell anybody. She thought about the whole worrisome affair with confused unhappiness for a few days. Then it sank quietly into her mind and was heaped over by accumulated thousands of impressions, for nearly twenty years. One day she was picking her path among the puddles and crushed refuse of a market street in a strange city of a strange country, when without warning, plain and clear in its true colors as if she looked through a frame upon a scene that had not stirred nor changed since the moment it happened, the episode of that far-off day leaped from its burial place before her mind's eye. She was so reasonlessly horrified she halted suddenly staring, the scene before her eyes dimmed by the vision back of them. An Indian vendor had held up before her a tray of dyed sugar sweets, in the shapes of all kinds of small creatures: birds, baby chicks, baby rabbits, lambs, baby pigs. They were in gay colors and smelled of vanilla, maybe. . . . It was a very hot day and the smell in the market, with its piles of raw flesh and wilting flowers, was like the mingled sweetness and corruption she had smelled that other day in the empty cemetery at home: the day she had remembered always until now vaguely as the time she and her brother had found treasure in the opened graves. Instantly upon this thought the dreadful vision faded, and she saw clearly her brother, whose childhood face she had forgotten, standing again in the blazing sunshine, again twelve years old, a pleased sober smile in his eyes, turning the silver dove over and over in his hands.

You Were Perfectly Fine

DOROTHY PARKER

(1893–1967)

The pale young man eased himself carefully into the low chair, and rolled his head to the side, so that the cool chintz comforted his cheek and temple.

"Oh, dear," he said. "Oh, dear, oh, dear, oh, dear. Oh."

The clear-eyed girl, sitting light and erect on the couch, smiled brightly at him.

"Not feeling so well today?" she said.

"Oh, I'm great," he said. "Corking, I am. Know what time I got up? Four o'clock this afternoon, sharp. I kept trying to make it, and every time I took my head off the pillow, it would roll under the bed. This isn't my head I've got on now. I think this is something that used to belong to Walt Whitman. Oh, dear, oh, dear, oh, dear."

"Do you think maybe a drink would make you feel better?" she said.

"The hair of the mastiff that bit me?" he said. "Oh, no, thank you. Please never speak of anything like that again. I'm through. I'm all, all through. Look at that hand; steady as a humming-bird. Tell me, was I very terrible last night?"

"Oh, goodness," she said, "everybody was feeling pretty high. You were all right."

"Yeah," he said. "I must have been dandy. Is everybody sore at me?"

"Good heavens, no," she said. "Everyone thought you were terribly funny. Of course, Jim Pierson was a little stuffy, there, for a minute at dinner. But people sort of held him back in his chair, and got him calmed down. I don't think anybody at the other tables noticed it at all. Hardly anybody."

"He was going to sock me?" he said. "Oh, Lord. What did I do to him?"

"Why, you didn't do a thing," she said. "You were perfectly fine. But you know how silly Jim gets, when he thinks anybody is making too much fuss over Elinor."

"Was I making a pass at Elinor?" he said. "Did I do that?"

"Of course you didn't," she said. "You were only fooling, that's all. She thought you were awfully amusing. She was having a marvelous time. She only got a little tiny bit annoyed just once, when you poured the clam-juice down her back."

"My God," he said. "Clam-juice down that back. And every vertebra a little Cabot. Dear God. What'll I ever do?"

"Oh, she'll be all right," she said. "Just send her some flowers, or something. Don't worry about it. It isn't anything."

"No, I won't worry," he said. "I haven't got a care in the world. I'm sitting pretty. Oh, dear, oh, dear. Did I do any other fascinating tricks at dinner?"

"You were fine," she said. "Don't be so foolish about it. Everybody was crazy about you. The maître d'hôtel was a little worried because you wouldn't stop singing, but he really didn't mind. All he said was, he was afraid they'd close the place again, if there was so much noise. But he didn't care a bit, himself. I think he loved seeing you have such a good time. Oh, you were just singing away, there, for about an hour. It wasn't so terribly loud, at all."

"So I sang," he said. "That must have been a treat. I sang."

"Don't you remember?" she said. "You just sang one song after another. Everybody in the place was listening. They loved it. Only you kept insisting that you wanted to sing some song about some kind of fusiliers or other, and everybody kept shushing you, and you'd keep trying to start it again. You were wonderful. We were all trying to make you stop singing for a minute, and eat something, but you wouldn't hear of it. My, you were funny."

"Didn't I eat any dinner?" he said.

"Oh, not a thing," she said. "Every time the waiter would offer you something, you'd give it right back to him, because you said that he was your long-lost brother, changed in the cradle by a gypsy band, and that anything you had was his. You had him simply roaring at you."

"I bet I did," he said. "I bet I was comical. Society's Pet, I must have been. And what happened then, after my overwhelming success with the waiter?"

"Why, nothing much," she said. "You took a sort of dislike to some old man with white hair, sitting across the room, because you didn't like his necktie and you wanted to tell him about it. But we got you out, before he got really mad."

"Oh, we got out," he said. "Did I walk?"

"Walk! Of course you did," she said. "You were absolutely all right. There was that nasty stretch of ice on the sidewalk, and you did sit down awfully hard, you poor dear. But good heavens, that might have happened to anybody."

"Oh, sure," he said. "Louisa Alcott or anybody. So I fell down on the sidewalk. That would explain what's the matter with my—Yes. I see. And then what, if you don't mind?"

"Ah, now, Peter!" she said. "You can't sit there and say you don't remember what happened after that! I did think that maybe you were just a little tight at dinner—oh, you were perfectly all right, and all that, but I did know you were feeling pretty gay. But you were so serious, from the time you fell down—I never knew you to be that way. Don't you know, how you told me I had never seen your real self before? Oh, Peter, I just couldn't bear it, if you didn't remember that lovely long ride we took together in the taxi! Please, you do remember that, don't you? I think it would simply kill me, if you didn't."

"Oh, yes," he said. "Riding in the taxi. Oh, yes, sure. Pretty long ride, hmm?"

"Round and round and round the park," she said. "Oh, and the trees were shining so in the moonlight. And you said you never knew before that you really had a soul."

"Yes," he said. "I said that. That was me."

"You said such lovely, lovely things," she said. "And I'd never known, all this time, how you had been feeling about me, and I'd never dared to let you see how I felt about you. And then last night—oh, Peter dear, I think that taxi ride was the most important thing that ever happened to us in our lives."

"Yes," he said. "I guess it must have been."

"And we're going to be so happy," she said. "Oh, I just want to tell everybody! But I don't know—I think maybe it would be sweeter to keep it all to ourselves."

"I think it would be," he said.

"Isn't it lovely?" she said.

"Yes," he said. "Great."

"Lovely!" she said.

"Look here," he said, "do you mind if I have a drink? I mean, just medicinally, you know. I'm off the stuff for life, so help me. But I think I feel a collapse coming on."

"Oh, I think it would do you good," she said. "You poor boy, it's a shame you feel so awful. I'll go make you a whisky and soda."

"Honestly," he said, "I don't see how you could ever want to speak to me again, after I made such a fool of myself, last night. I think I'd better go join a monastery in Tibet."

"You crazy idiot!" she said. "As if I could ever let you go away now! Stop talking like that. You were perfectly fine."

She jumped up from the couch, kissed him quickly on the forehead, and ran out of the room.

The pale young man looked after her and shook his head long and slowly, then dropped it in his damp and trembling hands.

"Oh, dear," he said. "Oh, dear, oh, dear, oh, dear."

The Secret Life of Walter Mitty

JAMES THURBER

(1894–1961)

"We're going through!" The Commander's voice was like thin ice breaking. He wore his full-dress uniform, with the heavily braided white cap pulled down rakishly over one cold gray eye. "We can't make it, sir. It's spoiling for a hurricane, if you ask me." "I'm not asking you, Lieutenant Berg," said the Commander. "Throw on the power lights! Rev her up to 8,500! We're going through!" The pounding of the cylinders increased: ta-pocketa-pocketa-pocketa-*pocketa-pocketa.* The Commander stared at the ice forming on the pilot window. He walked over and twisted a row of complicated dials. "Switch on No. 8 auxiliary!" he shouted. "Switch on No. 8 auxiliary!" repeated Lieutenant Berg. "Full strength in No. 3 turret!" shouted the Commander. "Full strength in No. 3 turret!" The crew, bending to their various tasks in the huge, hurtling eight-engined Navy hydroplane, looked at each other and grinned. "The Old Man'll get us through," they said to one another. "The Old Man ain't afraid of Hell!" . . .

"Not so fast! You're driving too fast!" said Mrs. Mitty. "What are you driving so fast for?"

"Hmm?" said Walter Mitty. He looked at his wife, in the seat beside him, with shocked astonishment. She seemed grossly unfamiliar, like a strange woman who had yelled at him in a crowd. "You were up to fifty-five," she said. "You know I don't like to go more than forty. You were up to fifty-five." Walter Mitty drove on toward Waterbury in silence, the roaring of the SN202 through the worst storm in twenty years of Navy flying fading in the remote, intimate airways of his mind. "You're tensed up again," said Mrs. Mitty. "It's one of your days. I wish you'd let Dr. Renshaw look you over."

Walter Mitty stopped the car in front of the building where his wife went to have her hair done. "Remember to get those overshoes while I'm having my hair done," she said. "I don't need overshoes," said Mitty. She put her mirror back into her bag. "We've been all through that," she said, getting out of the car. "You're not a young man any longer." He raced the engine a little. "Why don't you wear your gloves? Have you lost your gloves?" Walter Mitty reached in a pocket and brought out the gloves. He put them on, but after she had turned and gone into the building and he had driven on to a red light, he took them off again. "Pick it up, brother!" snapped a cop as the light changed, and Mitty hastily pulled on his gloves and lurched ahead. He drove around the streets aimlessly for a time, and then he drove past the hospital on his way to the parking lot.

. . . "It's the millionaire banker, Wellington McMillan," said the pretty nurse. "Yes?" said Walter Mitty, removing his gloves slowly. "Who has the case?" "Dr. Renshaw and Dr. Benbow, but there are two specialists here, Dr. Remington from New York and Mr. Pritchard-Mitford from London. He flew over." A door opened down a long, cool corridor and Dr. Renshaw came out. He looked distraught and haggard. "Hello, Mitty," he said. "We're having the devil's own time with McMillan, the millionaire banker and close personal friend of Roosevelt. Obstreosis of the ductal tract. Tertiary. Wish you'd take a look at him." "Glad to," said Mitty.

In the operating room there were whispered introductions: "Dr. Remington, Dr. Mitty. Mr. Pritchard-Mitford, Dr. Mitty." "I've read your book on streptothricosis," said Pritchard-Mitford, shaking hands. "A brilliant performance, sir." "Thank you," said Walter Mitty. "Didn't know you were in the States, Mitty," grumbled Remington. "Coals to Newcastle, bringing Mitford and me here for a tertiary." "You are very kind," said Mitty. A huge, complicated machine, connected to the operating table, with many tubes and wires, began at this moment to go pocketa-

pocketa-pocketa. "The new anesthetizer is giving way!" shouted an interne. "There is no one in the East who knows how to fix it!" "Quiet, man!" said Mitty in a low, cool voice. He sprang to the machine, which was now going pocketa-pocketa-queep-pocketa-queep. He began fingering delicately a row of glistening dials. "Give me a fountain pen!" he snapped. Someone handed him a fountain pen. He pulled a faulty piston out of the machine and inserted the pen in its place. "That will hold for ten minutes," he said. "Get on with the operation." A nurse hurried over and whispered to Renshaw, and Mitty saw the man turn pale. "Coreopsis has set in," said Renshaw nervously. "If you would take over, Mitty?" Mitty looked at him and at the craven figure of Benbow, who drank, and at the grave, uncertain faces of the two great specialists. "If you wish," he said. They slipped a white gown on him; he adjusted a mask and drew on thin gloves; nurses handed him shining. . . .

"Back it up, Mac! Look out for that Buick!" Walter Mitty jammed on the brakes. "Wrong lane, Mac," said the parking-lot attendant, looking at Mitty closely. "Gee. Yeh," muttered Mitty. He began cautiously to back out of the lane marked "Exit Only." "Leave her sit there," said the attendant. "I'll put her away." Mitty got out of the car. "Hey, better leave the key." "Oh," said Mitty, handing the man the ignition key. The attendant vaulted into the car, backed it up with insolent skill, and put it where it belonged.

They're so damn cocky, thought Walter Mitty, walking along Main Street; they think they know everything. Once he had tried to take his chains off, outside New Milford, and he had got them wound around the axles. A man had had to come out in a wrecking car and unwind them, a young, grinning garageman. Since then Mrs. Mitty always made him drive to a garage to have the chains taken off. The next time, he thought, I'll wear my right arm in a sling; they won't grin at me then. I'll have my right arm in a sling and they'll see I couldn't possibly take the chains off myself. He kicked at the slush on the sidewalk. "Overshoes," he said to himself, and he began looking for a shoe store.

When he came out into the street again, with the overshoes in a box under his arm, Walter Mitty began to wonder what the other thing was his wife had told him to get. She had told him twice, before they set out from their house for Waterbury. In a way he hated these weekly trips to town—he was always getting something wrong. Kleenex, he thought, Squibb's, razor blades? No. Toothpaste, toothbrush, bicarbonate, carborundum, initiative and referendum? He gave it up. But she would remember it. "Where's the what's-its-name?" she would ask. "Don't tell me you forgot the what's-its-name?" A newsboy went by shouting something about the Waterbury trial.

. . . "Perhaps this will refresh your memory." The District Attorney suddenly thrust a heavy automatic at the quiet figure on the witness stand. "Have you ever seen this before?" Walter Mitty took the gun and examined it expertly. "This is my Webley-Vickers 50.80," he said calmly. An excited buzz ran around the courtroom. The judge rapped for order. "You are a crack shot with any sort of firearms, I believe?" said the District Attorney, insinuatingly. "Objection!" shouted Mitty's attorney. "We have shown that the defendant could not have fired the shot. We have shown that he wore his right arm in a sling on the night of the fourteenth of July." Walter raised his hand briefly and the bickering attorneys were stilled. "With any known make of gun," he said evenly, "I could have killed Gregory Fitzhurst at three hundred feet *with my left hand."* Pandemonium broke loose in the courtroom. A woman's scream rose above the bedlam and suddenly a lovely, dark-haired girl was in Walter Mitty's arms. The District Attorney struck at her savagely. Without rising from his chair, Mitty let the man have it on the point of the chin. "You miserable cur!" . . .

"Puppy biscuit," said Walter Mitty. He stopped walking and the buildings of Waterbury rose up out of the misty courtroom and surrounded him again. A woman who was passing laughed. "He said 'Puppy biscuit,'" she said to her companion. "That man said 'Puppy biscuit' to himself." Walter Mitty hurried on. He went into an A & P, not the first one he came to but a smaller one farther up the street. "I want some biscuit for small, young dogs," he said to the clerk. "Any special brand, sir?" The greatest pistol shot in the world through a moment. "It says 'Puppies Bark for It' on the box," said Walter Mitty.

His wife would be through at the hairdresser's in fifteen minutes, Mitty saw in looking at his watch, unless they had trouble drying it; sometimes they had trouble drying it. She didn't like to get to the hotel first; she would want him to be there waiting for her as usual. He found a big leather chair in the lobby, facing a window, and he put the overshoes and the puppy biscuit on the floor beside it. He picked up an old copy of *Liberty* and sank down into the chair. "Can Germany Conquer the World Through the Air?" Walter Mitty looked at the pictures of bombing planes and of ruined streets.

. . . "The cannonading has got the wind up in young Raleigh, sir," said the sergeant. Captain Mitty looked up at him through tousled hair. "Get him to bed," he said wearily. "With the others. I'll fly alone." "But you can't, sir," said the sergeant anxiously. "It takes two men to handle the bomber and the Archies are pounding hell out of the air. Von Richtman's circus is between here and Saulier." "Somebody's got to get that ammunition dump," said Mitty. "I'm going over. Spot of brandy?" He poured a drink for the sergeant and one for himself. War thundered and whined around the dugout and battered at the door. There was a rending of wood and splinters flew through the room. "A bit of a near thing," said Captain Mitty carelessly. "The box barrage is closing in," said the sergeant. "We only live once, Sergeant," said Mitty, with his faint, fleeting smile. "Or do we?" He poured another brandy and tossed it off. "I never see a man could hold his brandy like you, sir," said the sergeant. "Begging your pardon, sir." Captain Mitty stood up and strapped on his huge Webley-Vickers automatic. "It's forty kilometers through hell, sir," said the sergeant. Mitty finished one last brandy. "After all," he said softly, "what isn't?" The pounding of the cannon increased; there was the rat-tat-tatting of machine guns, and from somewhere came the menacing pocketa-pocketa-pocketa of the new flame-throwers. Walter Mitty walked to the door of the dugout humming "Auprès de Ma Blonde." He turned and waved to the sergeant. "Cheerio!" he said. . . .

Something struck his shoulder. "I've been looking all over this hotel for you," said Mrs. Mitty. "Why do you have to hide in this old chair? How did you expect me to find you?" "Things close in," said Walter Mitty vaguely. "What?" Mrs. Mitty said. "Did you get the what's-its-name? The puppy biscuit? What's in the box?" "Overshoes," said Mitty. "Couldn't you have put them on in the store?" "I was thinking," said Walter Mitty. "Does it ever occur to you that I am sometimes thinking?" She looked at him. "I'm going to take your temperature when I get you home," she said.

They went out through the revolving doors that made a faintly derisive whistling sound when you pushed them. It was two blocks to the parking lot. At the drugstore on the corner she said, "Wait here for me. I forgot something. I won't be a minute." She was more than a minute. Walter Mitty lighted a cigarette. It began to rain, rain with sleet in it. He stood up against the wall of the drugstore, smoking. . . . He put his shoulders back and his heels together. "To hell with the handkerchief," said Walter Mitty scornfully. He took one last drag on his cigarette and snapped it away. Then, with that faint, fleeting smile playing about his lips, he faced the firing squad; erect and motionless, proud and disdainful, Walter Mitty the Undefeated, inscrutable to the last.

The Baby Party

F. SCOTT FITZGERALD

(1896–1940)

When John Andros felt old he found solace in the thought of life continuing through his child. The dark trumpets of oblivion were less loud at the patter of his child's feet or at the sound of his child's voice babbling mad non sequiturs to him over the telephone. The latter incident occurred every afternoon at three when his wife called the office from the country, and he came to look forward to it as one of the vivid minutes of his day.

He was not physically old, but his life had been a series of struggles up a series of rugged hills, and here at thirty-eight having won his battles against ill-health and poverty he cherished less than the usual number of illusions. Even his feeling about his little girl was qualified. She had interrupted his rather intense love-affair with his wife, and she was the reason for their living in a suburban town, where they paid for country air with endless servant troubles and the weary merry-go-round of the commuting train.

It was little Ede as a definite piece of youth that chiefly interested him. He liked to take her on his lap and examine minutely her fragrant, downy scalp and her eyes with their irises of morning blue. Having paid this homage John was content that the nurse should take her away. After ten minutes the very vitality of the child irritated him; he was inclined to lose his temper when things were broken, and one Sunday afternoon when she had disrupted a bridge game by permanently hiding up the ace of spades, he had made a scene that had reduced his wife to tears.

This was absurd and John was ashamed of himself. It was inevitable that such things would happen, and it was impossible that little Ede should spend all her indoor hours in the nursery upstairs when she was becoming, as her mother said, more nearly a "real person" every day.

She was two and a half, and this afternoon, for instance, she was going to a baby party. Grown-up Edith, her mother, had telephoned the information to the office, and little Ede had confirmed the business by shouting "I yam going to a *pantry!*" into John's unsuspecting left ear.

"Drop in at the Markeys' when you get home, won't you, dear?" resumed her mother. "It'll be funny. Ede's going to be all dressed up in her new pink dress——"

The conversation terminated abruptly with a squawk which indicated that the telephone had been pulled violently to the floor. John laughed and decided to get an early train out; the prospect of a baby party in some one else's house amused him.

"What a peach of a mess!" he thought humorously. "A dozen mothers, and each one looking at nothing but her own child. All the babies breaking things and grabbing at the cake, and each mamma going home thinking about the subtle superiority of her own child to every other child there."

He was in a good humor today—all the things in his life were going better than they had ever gone before. When he got off the train at his station he shook his head at an importunate taxi man, and began to walk up the long hill toward his house through the crisp December twilight. It was only six o'clock but the moon was out, shining with proud brilliance on the thin sugary snow that lay over the lawns.

As he walked along drawing his lungs full of cold air his happiness increased, and the idea of a baby party appealed to him more and more. He began to wonder how Ede compared to other children of her own age, and if the pink dress she was to wear was something radical and mature. Increasing his gait he came in sight of his own house, where lights of a defunct Christmas tree still blossomed in the window, but he continued on past the walk. The party was at the Markeys' next door.

As he mounted the brick step and rang the bell he became aware of voices inside, and he was glad he was not too late. Then he raised his head and listened—the voices were not children's voices, but they were loud and pitched high with anger; there were at least three of them and one, which rose as he listened to a hysterical sob, he recognized immediately as his wife's.

"There's been some trouble," he thought quickly.

Trying the door, he found it unlocked and pushed it open.

The baby party began at half past four, but Edith Andros, calculating shrewdly that the new dress would stand out more sensationally against vestments already rumpled, planned the arrival of herself and little Ede for five. When they appeared it was already a flourishing affair. Four baby girls and nine baby boys, each one curled and washed and dressed with all the care of a proud and jealous heart, were dancing to the music of a phonograph. Never more than two or three were dancing at once, but as all were continually in motion running to and from their mothers for encouragement, the general effect was the same.

As Edith and her daughter entered, the music was temporarily drowned out by a sustained chorus, consisting largely of the word *cute* and directed toward little Ede, who stood looking timidly about and fingering the edges of her pink dress. She was not kissed—this is the sanitary age—but she was passed along a row of mammas each one of whom said "cu-u-ute" to her and held her pink little hand before passing her on to the next. After some encouragement and a few mild pushes she was absorbed into the dance, and became an active member of the party.

Edith stood near the door talking to Mrs. Markey, and keeping one eye on the tiny figure in the pink dress. She did not care for Mrs. Markey; she considered her both snippy and common, but John and Joe Markey were congenial and went in together on the commuting train every morning, so the two women kept up an elaborate pretense of warm amity. They were always reproaching each other for "not coming to see me," and they were always planning the kind of parties that began with "You'll have to come to dinner with us soon, and we'll go in to the theatre," but never matured further.

"Little Ede looks perfectly darling," siad Mrs. Markey, smiling and moistening her lips in a way that Edith found particularly repulsive. "So *grown-up*—I can't *believe* it!"

Edith wondered if "little Ede" referred to the fact that Billy Markey, though several months younger, weighed almost five pounds more. Accepting a cup of tea she took a seat with two other ladies on a divan and launched into the real business of the afternoon, which of course lay in relating the recent accomplishments and insouciances of her child.

An hour passed. Dancing palled and the babies took to sterner sport. They ran into the dining-room, rounded the big table, and essayed the kitchen door, from which they were rescued by an expeditionary force of mothers. Having been rounded up they immediately broke loose, and rushing back to the dining-room tried the familiar swinging door again. The word "overheated" began to be used, and small white brows were dried with small white handkerchiefs. A general attempt to make the babies sit down began, but the babies squirmed off laps with peremptory cries of "Down! Down!" and the rush into the fascinating dining-room began anew.

This phase of the party came to an end with the arrival of refreshments, a large cake with two candles, and saucers of vanilla ice cream. Billy Markey, a stout laughing baby with red hair and legs somewhat bowed, blew out the candles, and placed an experimental thumb on the white frosting. The refreshments were distributed, and the children ate, greedily but without confusion—they had behaved remarkably well all afternoon. They were modern babies who ate and slept at regular hours, so their dispositions were good, and their faces healthy and pink—such a peaceful party would not have been possible thirty years ago.

After the refreshments a gradual exodus began. Edith glanced anxiously at her watch—it was almost six, and John had not arrived. She wanted him to see Ede with the other children—to see how dignified and polite and intelligent she was, and how the only ice-cream spot on her dress was some that had dropped from her chin when she was joggled from behind.

"You're a darling," she whispered to her child, drawing her suddenly against her knee. "Do you know you're a darling? Do you *know* you're a darling?"

Ede laughed. "Bow-wow," she said suddenly.

"Bow-wow?" Edith looked around. "There isn't any bow-wow."

"Bow-wow," repeated Ede. "I want a bow-wow."

Edith followed the small pointing finger.

"That isn't a bow-wow, dearest, that's a teddy-bear."

"Bear?"

"Yes, that's a teddy-bear, and it belongs to Billy Markey. You don't want Billy Markey's teddy-bear, do you?"

Ede did want it.

She broke away from her mother and approached Billy Markey, who held the toy closely in his arms. Ede stood regarding him with inscrutable eyes, and Billy laughed.

Grown-up Edith looked at her watch again, this time impatiently.

The party had dwindled until, besides Ede and Billy, there were only two babies remaining—and one of the two remained only by virtue of having hidden himself under the dining-room table. It was selfish of John not to come. It showed so little pride in the child. Other fathers had come, half a dozen of them, to call for their wives, and they had stayed for a while and looked on.

There was a sudden wail. Ede had obtained Billy's teddy-bear by pulling it forcibly from his arms, and on Billy's attempt to recover it, she had pushed him casually to the floor.

"Why, Ede!" cried her mother, repressing an inclination to laugh.

Joe Markey, a handsome, broad-shouldered man of thirty-five, picked up his son and set him on his feet. "You're a fine fellow," he said jovially. "Let a girl knock you over! You're a fine fellow."

"Did he bump his head?" Mrs. Markey returned anxiously from bowing the next to last remaining mother out the door.

"No-o-o-o," exclaimed Markey. "He bumped something else, didn't you, Billy? He bumped something else."

Billy had so far forgotten the bump that he was already making an attempt to recover his property. He seized a leg of the bear which projected from Ede's enveloping arms and tugged at it but without success.

"No," said Ede emphatically.

Suddenly, encouraged by the success of her former half-accidental manœuvre, Ede dropped the teddy-bear, placed her hands on Billy's shoulders and pushed him backward off his feet.

This time he landed less harmlessly; his head hit the bare floor just off the rug with a dull hollow sound, whereupon he drew in his breath and delivered an agonized yell.

Immediately the room was in confusion. With an exclamation Markey hurried to his son, but his wife was first to reach the injured baby and catch him up into her arms.

"Oh, *Billy*," she cried, "what a terrible bump! She ought to be spanked."

Edith, who had rushed immediately to her daughter, heard this remark, and her lips came sharply together.

"Why, Ede," she whispered perfunctorily, "you bad girl!"

Ede put back her little head suddenly and laughed. It was a loud laugh, a triumphant laugh with victory in it and challenge and contempt. Unfortunately it was also an infectious laugh. Before her mother realized the delicacy of the situation, she too had laughed, an audible, distinct laugh not unlike the baby's, and partaking of the same overtones.

Then, as suddenly, she stopped.

Mrs. Markey's face had grown red with anger, and Markey, who had been feeling the back of the baby's head with one finger, looked at her, frowning.

"It's swollen already," he said with a note of reproof in his voice. "I'll get some witch-hazel."

But Mrs. Markey had lost her temper. "I don't see anything funny about a child being hurt!" she said in a trembling voice.

Little Ede meanwhile had been looking at her mother curiously. She noted that her own laugh had produced her mother's, and she wondered if the same cause would always produce the same effect. So she chose this moment to throw back her head and laugh again.

To her mother the additional mirth added the final touch of hysteria to the situation. Pressing her handkerchief to her mouth she giggled irrepressibly. It was more than nervousness—she felt that in a peculiar way she was laughing with her child—they were laughing together.

It was in a way a defiance—those two against the world.

While Markey rushed upstairs to the bathroom for ointment, his wife was walking up and down rocking the yelling boy in her arms.

"Please go home!" she broke out suddenly. "The child's badly hurt, and if you haven't the decency to be quiet, you'd better go home."

"Very well," said Edith, her own temper rising. "I've never seen any one make such a mountain out of—"

"Get out!" cried Mrs. Markey frantically. "There's the door, get out—I never want to see you in our house again. You or your brat either!"

Edith had taken her daughter's hand and was moving quickly toward the door, but at this remark she stopped and turned around, her face contracting with indignation.

"Don't you dare call her that!"

Mrs. Markey did not answer but continued walking up and down, muttering to herself and to Billy in an inaudible voice.

Edith began to cry.

"I will get out!" she sobbed, "I've never heard anybody so rude and c-common in my life. I'm glad your baby did get pushed down—he's nothing but a f-fat little fool anyhow."

Joe Markey reached the foot of the stairs just in time to hear this remark.

"Why, Mrs. Andros," he said sharply, "can't you see the child's hurt? You really ought to control yourself."

"Control m-myself!" exclaimed Edith brokenly. "You better ask her to c-control herself. I've never heard anybody so c-common in my life."

"She's insulting me!" Mrs. Markey was now livid with rage. "Did you hear what she said, Joe? I wish you'd put her out. If she won't go, just take her by the shoulders and put her out!"

"Don't you dare touch me!" cried Edith. "I'm going just as quick as I can find my c-coat!"

Blind with tears she took a step toward the hall. It was just at this moment that the door opened and John Andros walked anxiously in.

"John!" cried Edith, and fled to him wildly.

"What's the matter? Why, what's the matter?"

"They're—they're putting me out!" she wailed, collapsing against him. "He'd just started to take me by the shoulders and put me out. I want my coat!"

"That's not true," objected Markey hurriedly. "Nobody's going to put you out." He turned to John. "Nobody's going to put her out," he repeated. "She's—"

"What do you mean 'put her out'?" demanded John abruptly. "What's all this talk, anyhow?"

"Oh, let's go!" cried Edith. "I want to go. They're so *common*, John!"

"Look here!" Markey's face darkened. "You've said that about enough. You're acting sort of crazy."

"They called Ede a brat!"

For the second time that afternoon little Ede expressed emotion at an inopportune moment. Confused and frightened at the shouting voices, she began to cry, and her tears had the effect of conveying that she felt the insult in her heart.

"What's the idea of this?" broke out John. "Do you insult your guests in your own house?"

"It seems to me it's your wife that's done the insulting!" answered Markey crisply. "In fact, your baby there started all the trouble."

John gave a contemptuous snort. "Are you calling names at a little baby?" he inquired. "That's a fine manly business!"

"Don't talk to him, John," insisted Edith. "Find my coat!"

"You must be in a bad way," went on John angrily, "if you have to take out your temper on a helpless little baby."

"I never heard anything so damn twisted in my life," shouted Markey. "If that wife of yours would shut her mouth for a minute——"

"Wait a minute! You're not talking to a woman and child now——"

There was an incidental interruption. Edith had been fumbling on a chair for her coat, and Mrs. Markey had been watching her with hot, angry eyes. Suddenly she laid Billy down on the sofa, where he immediately stopped crying and pulled himself upright, and coming into the hall she quickly found Edith's coat and handed it to her without a word. Then she went back to the sofa, picked up Billy, and rocking him in her arms looked again at Edith with hot, angry eyes. The interruption had taken less than half a minute.

"Your wife comes in here and begins shouting around about how common we are!" burst out Markey violently. "Well, if we're so damn common, you'd better stay away! And, what's more, you'd better get out now!"

Again John gave a short, contemptuous laugh.

"You're not only common," he returned, "you're evidently an awful bully–when there's any helpless women and children around." He felt for the knob and swung the door open. "Come on, Edith."

Taking up her daughter in her arms, his wife stepped outside and John, still looking contemptuously at Markey, started to follow.

"Wait a minute!" Markey took a step forward; he was trembling slightly, and two large veins on his temple were suddenly full of blood. "You don't think you can get away with that, do you? With me?"

Without a word John walked out the door, leaving it open.

Edith, still weeping, had started for home. After following her with his eyes until she reached her own walk, John turned back toward the lighted doorway where Markey was slowly coming down the slippery steps. He took off his overcoat and hat, tossed them off the path onto the snow. Then, sliding a little on the iced walk, he took a step forward.

At the first blow, they both slipped and fell heavily to the sidewalk, half rising then, and again pulling each other to the ground. They found a better foothold in the thin snow to the side of the walk and rushed at each other, both swinging wildly and pressing out the snow into a pasty mud underfoot.

The street was deserted, and except for their short tired gasps and the padded sound as one or the other slipped down into the slushy mud, they fought in silence, clearly defined to each other by the full moonlight as well as by the amber glow that shone out of the open door. Several times they both slipped down together, and then for a while the conflict threshed about wildly on the lawn.

For ten, fifteen, twenty minutes they fought there senselessly in the moonlight. They had both taken off coats and vests at some silently agreed upon interval and now their shirts dripped from their backs in wet pulpy shreds. Both were torn and bleeding and so exhausted that they could stand only when by their position they mutually supported each other—the impact, the mere effort of a blow, would send them both to their hands and knees.

But it was not weariness that ended the business, and the very meaninglessness of the fight was a reason for not stopping. They stopped because once when they were straining at each other on the ground, they heard a man's footsteps coming along the sidewalk. They had rolled somehow into the shadow, and when they heard these footsteps they stopped fighting, stopped moving, stopped breathing, lay huddled together like two boys playing Indian until the footsteps had passed. Then, staggering to their feet, they looked at each other like two drunken men.

"I'll be damned if I'm going on with this thing any more," cried Markey thickly.

"I'm not going on any more either," said John Andros. "I've had enough of this thing."

Again they looked at each other, sulkily this time, as if each suspected the other of urging him to a renewal of the fight. Markey spat out a mouthful of blood from a cut lip; then he cursed softly, and picking up his coat and vest, shook off the snow from them in a surprised way, as if their comparative dampness was his only worry in the world.

"Want to come in and wash up?" he asked suddenly.

"No, thanks," said John. "I ought to be going home—my wife'll be worried."

He too picked up his coat and vest and then his overcoat and hat. Soaking wet and dripping with perspiration, it seemed absurd that less than half an hour ago he had been wearing all these clothes.

"Well—good night," he said hesitantly.

Suddenly they both walked toward each other and shook hands. It was no perfunctory hand-shake: John Andros's arm went around Markey's shoulder, and he patted him softly on the back for a little while.

"No harm done," he said brokenly.

"No—you?"

"No, no harm done."

"Well," said John Andros after a minute, "I guess I'll say good night."

"Good night."

Limping slightly and with his clothes over his arm, John Andros turned away. The moonlight was still bright as he left the dark patch of trampled ground and walked over the intervening lawn. Down at the station, half a mile away, he could hear the rumble of the seven o'clock train.

"But you must have been crazy," cried Edith brokenly, "I thought you were going to fix it all up there and shake hands. That's why I went away."

"Did you want us to fix it up?"

"Of course not, I never want to see them again. But I thought of course that was what you were going to do." She was touching the bruises on his neck and back with iodine as he sat placidly in a hot bath. "I'm going to get the doctor," she said insistently. "You may be hurt internally."

He shook his head. "Not a chance," he answered. "I don't want this to get all over town."

"I don't understand yet how it all happened."

"Neither do I." He smiled grimly. "I guess these baby parties are pretty rough affairs."

"Well, one thing—" suggested Edith hopefully, "I'm certainly glad we have beefsteak in the house for tomorrow's dinner."

"Why?"

"For your eye, of course. Do you know I came within an ace of ordering veal? Wasn't that the luckiest thing?"

Half an hour later, dressed except that his neck would accommodate no collar, John moved his limbs experimentally before the glass. "I believe I'll get myself in better shape," he said thoughtfully. "I must be getting old."

"You mean so that next time you can beat him?"

"I did beat him," he announced. "At least, I beat him as much as he beat me. And there isn't going to be any next time. Don't you go calling people common any more. If you get in any trouble, you just take your coat and go home. Understand?"

"Yes, dear," she said meekly. "I was very foolish and now I understand."

Out in the hall, he paused abruptly by the baby's door.

"Is she asleep?"

"Sound asleep. But you can go in and peek at her—just to say good night."

They tiptoed in and bent together over the bed. Little Ede, her cheeks flushed with health, her pink hands clasped tight together, was sleeping soundly in the cool, dark room. John reached over the railing of the bed and passed his hand lightly over the silken hair.

"She's asleep," he murmured in a puzzled way.

"Naturally, after such an afternoon."

"Miz Andros," the colored maid's stage whisper floated in from the hall, "Mr. and Miz Markey downstairs an' want to see you. Mr. Markey he's all cut up in pieces, ma'am. His face look like a roast beef. An' Miz Markey she 'pear mighty mad."

"Why, what incomparable nerve!" exclaimed Edith. "Just tell them we're not home. I wouldn't go down for anything in the world."

"You most certainly will." John's voice was hard and set.

"What?"

"You'll go down right now, and, what's more, whatever that other woman does, you'll apologize for what you said this afternoon. After that you don't ever have to see her again."

"Why—John, I can't."

"You've got to. And just remember that she probably hated to come over here just twice as much as you hate to go downstairs."

"Aren't you coming? Do I have to go alone?"

"I'll be down—in just a minute."

John Andros waited until she had closed the door behind her; then he reached over into the bed, and picking up his daughter, blankets and all, sat down in the rocking-chair holding her tightly in his arms. She moved a little, and he held his breath, but she was sleeping soundly, and in a moment she was resting quietly in the hollow of his elbow. Slowly he bent his head until his cheek was against her bright hair. "Dear little girl," he whispered. "Dear little girl, dear little girl."

John Andros knew at length what it was he had fought for so savagely that evening. He had it now, he possessed it forever, and for some time he sat there rocking very slowly to and fro in the darkness.

That Evening Sun

WILLIAM FAULKNER

(1897–1962)

I

Monday is no different from any other weekday in Jefferson now. The streets are paved now, and the telephone and electric companies are cutting down more and more of the shade trees—the water oaks, the maples and locusts and elms—to make room for iron poles bearing clusters of bloated and ghostly and bloodless grapes, and we have a city laundry which makes the rounds on Monday morning, gathering the bundles of clothes into bright-colored, specially-made motor cars: the soiled wearing of a whole week now flees apparitionlike behind alert and irritable electric horns, with a long diminishing noise of rubber and asphalt like tearing silk, and even the Negro women who still take in white people's washing after the old custom, fetch and deliver it in automobiles.

But fifteen years ago, on Monday morning the quiet, dusty, shady streets would be full of Negro women with, balanced on their steady, turbaned heads, bundles of clothes tied up in sheets, almost as large as cotton bales, carried so without touch of hand between the kitchen door of the white house and the blackened washpot beside a cabin door in Negro Hollow.

Nancy would set her bundle on the top of her head, then upon the bundle in turn she would set the black straw sailor hat which she wore winter and summer. She was tall, with a high, sad face sunken a little where her teeth were missing. Sometimes we would go a part of the way down the lane and across the pasture with her, to watch the balanced bundle and the hat that never bobbed nor wavered, even when she walked down into the ditch and up the other side and stooped through the fence. She would go down on her hands and knees and crawl through the gap, her head rigid, uptilted, the bundle steady as a rock or a balloon, and rise to her feet again and go on.

Sometimes the husbands of the washing women would fetch and deliver the clothes, but Jesus never did that for Nancy, even before father told him to stay away from our house, even when Dilsey was sick and Nancy would come to cook for us.

And then about half the time we'd have to go down the lane to Nancy's cabin and tell her to come on and cook breakfast. We would stop at the ditch, because father told us to not have anything to do with Jesus —he was a short black man, with a razor scar down his face—and we would throw rocks at Nancy's house until she came to the door, leaning her head around it without any clothes on.

"What yawl mean, chunking my house?" Nancy said. "What you little devils mean?"

"Father says for you to come on and get breakfast," Caddy said. "Father says it's over a half an hour now, and you've got to come this minute."

"I aint studying no breakfast," Nancy said. "I going to get my sleep out."

"I bet you're drunk," Jason said. "Father says you're drunk. Are you drunk, Nancy?"

"Who says I is?" Nancy said. "I got to get my sleep out. I aint studying no breakfast."

So after a while we quit chunking the cabin and went back home. When she finally came, it was too late for me to go to school. So we thought it was whisky until that day they arrested her again and they were taking her to jail and they passed Mr Stovall. He was the cashier in the bank and a deacon in the Baptist church, and Nancy began to say:

"When you going to pay me, white man? When you going to pay me, white man? It's been three times now since you paid me a cent—" Mr Stovall knocked her down, but she kept on saying, "When you going to pay me, white man? It's been three times now since—" until Mr Stovall kicked her in the mouth with his heel and the marshal caught Mr Stovall back, and Nancy lying in the street, laughing. She turned her head and spat out some blood and teeth and said, "It's been three times now since he paid me a cent."

That was how she lost her teeth, and all that day they told about Nancy and Mr Stovall, and all that night the ones that passed the jail could hear Nancy singing and yelling. They could see her hands holding to the window bars, and a lot of them stopped along the fence, listening to her and to the jailer trying to make her stop. She didn't shut up until almost daylight, when the jailer began to hear a bumping and scraping upstairs and he went up there and found Nancy hanging from the window bar. He said that it was cocaine and not whisky, because no nigger would try to commit suicide unless he was full of cocaine, because a nigger full of cocaine wasn't a nigger any longer.

The jailer cut her down and revived her; then he beat her, whipped her. She had hung herself with her dress. She had fixed it all right, but when they arrested her she didn't have on anything except a dress and so she didn't have anything to tie her hands with and she couldn't make her hands let go of the window ledge. So the jailer heard the noise and ran up there and found Nancy hanging from the window, stark naked, her belly already swelling out a little, like a little balloon.

When Dilsey was sick in her cabin and Nancy was cooking for us, we could see her apron swelling out; that was before father told Jesus to stay away from the house. Jesus was in the kitchen, sitting behind the stove, with his razor scar on his black face like a piece of dirty string. He said it was a watermelon that Nancy had under her dress.

"It never come off of your vine, though," Nancy said.

"Off of what vine?" Caddy said.

"I can cut down the vine it did come off of," Jesus said.

"What makes you want to talk like that before these chillen?" Nancy said. "Whyn't you go on to work? You done et. You want Mr Jason to catch you hanging around his kitchen, talking that way before these chillen?"

"Talking what way?" Caddy said. "What vine?"

"I cant hang around white man's kitchen," Jesus said. "But white man can hang around mine. White man can come in my house, but I cant stop him. When white man want to come in my house, I aint got no house. I cant stop him, but he cant kick me outen it. He cant do that."

Dilsey was still sick in her cabin. Father told Jesus to stay off our place. Dilsey was still sick. It was a long time. We were in the library after supper.

"Isn't Nancy through in the kitchen yet?" mother said. "It seems to me that she has had plenty of time to have finished the dishes."

"Let Quentin go and see," father said. "Go and see if Nancy is through, Quentin. Tell her she can go on home."

I went to the kitchen. Nancy was through. The dishes were put away and the fire was out. Nancy was sitting in a chair, close to the cold stove. She looked at me.

"Mother wants to know if you are through," I said.

"Yes," Nancy said. She looked at me. "I done finished." She looked at me.

"What is it?" I said. "What is it?"

"I aint nothing but a nigger," Nancy said. "It aint none of my fault."

She looked at me, sitting in the chair before the cold stove, the sailor hat on her head. I went back to the library. It was the cold stove and all, when you think of a kitchen being warm and busy and cheerful. And with a cold stove and the dishes all put away, and nobody wanting to eat at that hour.

"Is she through?" mother said.

"Yessum," I said.

"What is she doing?" mother said.

"She's not doing anything. She's through."

"I'll go and see," father said.

"Maybe she's waiting for Jesus to come and take her home," Caddy said.

"Jesus is gone," I said. Nancy told us how one morning she woke up and Jesus was gone.

"He quit me," Nancy said. "Done gone to Memphis, I reckon. Dodging them city *po*-lice for a while, I reckon."

"And a good riddance," father said. "I hope he stays there."

"Nancy's scaired of the dark," Jason said.

"So are you," Caddy said.

"I'm not," Jason said.

"Scairy cat," Caddy said.

"I'm not," Jason said.

"You, Candace!" mother said. Father came back.

"I am going to walk down the lane with Nancy," he said. "She says that Jesus is back."

"Has she seen him?" mother said.

"No. Some Negro sent her word that he was back in town. I wont be long."

"You'll leave me alone, to take Nancy home?" mother said. "Is her safety more precious to you than mine?"

"I wont be long," father said.

"You'll leave these children unprotected, with that Negro about?"

"I'm going too," Caddy said. "Let me go, Father."

"What would he do with them, if he were unfortunate enough to have them?" father said.

"I want to go, too," Jason said.

"Jason!" mother said. She was speaking to father. You could tell that by the way she said the name. Like she believed that all day father had been trying to think of doing the thing she wouldn't like the most, and that she knew all the time that after a while he would think of it. I stayed quiet, because father and I both knew that mother would want him to make me stay with her if she just thought of it in time. So father didn't look at me. I was the oldest. I was nine and Caddy was seven and Jason was five.

"Nonsense," father said. "We wont be long."

Nancy had her hat on. We came to the lane. "Jesus always been good to me," Nancy said. "Whenever he had two dollars, one of them was mine." We walked in the lane. "If I can just get through the lane," Nancy said, "I be all right then."

The lane was always dark. "This is where Jason got scared on Hallowe'en," Caddy said.

"I didn't," Jason said.

"Cant Aunt Rachel do anything with him?" father said. Aunt Rachel was old. She lived in a cabin beyond Nancy's, by herself. She had white hair and she smoked a pipe in the door, all day long; she didn't work any more. They said she was Jesus' mother. Sometimes she said she was and sometimes she said she wasn't any kin to Jesus.

"Yes, you did," Caddy said. "You were scairder than Frony. You were scairder than T.P. even. Scairder than niggers."

"Cant nobody do nothing with him," Nancy said. "He say I done woke up the devil in him and aint but one thing going to lay it down again."

"Well, he's gone now," father said. "There's nothing for you to be afraid of now. And if you'd just let white men alone."

"Let what white men alone?" Caddy said. "How let them alone?"

"He aint gone nowhere," Nancy said. "I can feel him. I can feel him now, in this lane. He hearing us talk, every word, hid somewhere, waiting. I aint seen him, and I aint going to see him again but once more, with that razor in his mouth. That razor on that string down his back, inside his shirt. And then I aint going to be even surprised."

"I wasn't scaired," Jason said.

"If you'd behave yourself, you'd have kept out of this," father said. "But it's all right now. He's probably in St. Louis now. Probably got another wife by now and forgot all about you."

"If he has, I better not find out about it," Nancy said. "I'd stand there right over them, and every time he wropped her, I'd cut that arm off. I'd cut his head off and I'd slit her belly and I'd shove—"

"Hush," father said.

"Slit whose belly, Nancy?" Caddy said.

"I wasn't scaired," Jason said. "I'd walk right down this lane by myself."

"Yah," Caddy said. "You wouldn't dare to put your foot down in it if we were not here too."

II

Dilsey was still sick, so we took Nancy home every night until mother said, "How much longer is this going on? I to be left alone in this big house while you take home a frightened Negro?"

We fixed a pallet in the kitchen for Nancy. One night we waked up, hearing the sound. It was not singing and it was not crying, coming up the dark stairs. There was a light in mother's room and we heard father going down the hall, down the back stairs, and Caddy and I went into the hall. The floor was cold. Our toes curled away from it while we listened to the sound. It was like singing and it wasn't like singing, like the sounds that Negroes make.

Then it stopped and we heard father going down the back stairs, and we went to the head of the stairs. Then the sound began again, in the stairway, not loud, and we could see Nancy's eyes halfway up the stairs, against the wall. They looked like cat's eyes do, like a big cat against the wall, watching us. When we came down the steps to where she was, she quit making the sound again, and we stood there until father came back up from the kitchen, with his pistol in his hand. He went back down with Nancy and they came back with Nancy's pallet.

We spread the pallet in our room. After the light in mother's room went off, we could see Nancy's eyes again. "Nancy," Caddy whispered, "are you asleep, Nancy?"

Nancy whispered something. It was oh or no, I dont know which. Like nobody had made it, like it came from nowhere and went nowhere, until it was like Nancy was not there at all; that I had looked so hard at her eyes on the stairs that they had got printed on my eyeballs, like the sun does when you have closed your eyes and there is no sun. "Jesus," Nancy whispered. "Jesus."

"Was it Jesus?" Caddy said. "Did he try to come into the kitchen?"

"Jesus," Nancy said. Like this: Jeeeeeeeeeeeeeeeesus, until the sound went out, like a match or a candle does.

"It's the other Jesus she means," I said.

"Can you see us, Nancy?" Caddy whispered. "Can you see our eyes too?"

"I aint nothing but a nigger," Nancy said. "God knows. God knows."

"What did you see down there in the kitchen?" Caddy whispered. "What tried to get in?"

"God knows," Nancy said. We could see her eyes. "God knows."

Dilsey got well. She cooked dinner. "You'd better stay in bed a day or two longer," father said.

"What for?" Dilsey said. "If I had been a day later, this place would be to rack and ruin. Get on out of here now, and let me get my kitchen straight again."

Dilsey cooked supper too. And that night, just before dark, Nancy came into the kitchen.

"How do you know he's back?" Dilsey said. "You aint seen him."

"Jesus is a nigger," Jason said.

"I can feel him," Nancy said. "I can feel him laying yonder in the ditch."

"Tonight?" Dilsey said. "Is he there tonight?"

"Dilsey's a nigger too," Jason said.

"You try to eat something," Dilsey said.

"I don't want nothing," Nancy said.

"I ain't a nigger," Jason said.

"Drink some coffee," Dilsey said. She poured a cup of coffee for Nancy. "Do you know he's out there tonight? How come you know it's tonight?"

"I know," Nancy said. "He's there, waiting. I know. I done lived with him too long. I know what he is fixing to do fore he know it himself."

"Drink some coffee," Dilsey said. Nancy held the cup to her mouth and blew into the cup. Her mouth pursed out like a spreading adder's, like a rubber mouth, like she had blown all the color out of her lips with blowing the coffee.

"I aint a nigger," Jason said. "Are you a nigger, Nancy?"

"I hellborn, child," Nancy said. "I wont be nothing soon. I going back where I come from soon."

III

She began to drink the coffee. While she was drinking, holding the cup in both hands, she began to make the sound again. She made the sound into the cup and the coffee sploshed out onto her hands and her dress. Her eyes looked at us and she sat there, her elbows on her knees, holding the cup in both hands, looking at us across the wet cup, making the sound. "Look at Nancy," Jason said. "Nancy cant cook for us now. Dilsey's got well now."

"You hush up," Dilsey said. Nancy held the cup in both hands, looking at us, making the sound, like there were two of them: one looking at us and the other making the sound. "Whyn't you let Mr. Jason telefoam the marshal?" Dilsey said. Nancy stopped then, holding the cup in her long brown hands. She tried to drink some coffee again, but it sploshed out of the cup, onto her hands and her dress, and she put the cup down. Jason watched her.

"I cant swallow it," Nancy said. "I swallows but it wont go down me."

"You go down to the cabin," Dilsey said. "Frony will fix you a pallet and I'll be there soon."

"Wont no nigger stop him," Nancy said.

"I aint a nigger," Jason said. "Am I, Dilsey?"

"I reckon not," Dilsey said. She looked at Nancy. "I dont reckon so. What you going to do, then?"

Nancy looked at us. Her eyes went fast, like she was afraid there wasn't time to look, without hardly moving at all. She looked at us, at all three of us at one time. "You member that night I stayed in yawls' room?" she said. She told about how we waked up early the next morning, and played. We had to play quiet, on her pallet, until father woke up and it was time to get breakfast. "Go and ask your maw to let me stay here tonight," Nancy said. "I won't need no pallet. We can play some more."

Caddy asked mother. Jason went too. "I cant have Negroes sleeping in the bedrooms," mother said. Jason cried. He cried until mother said he couldn't have any dessert for three days if he didn't stop. Then Jason said he would stop if Dilsey would make a chocolate cake. Father was there.

"Why dont you do something about it?" mother said. "What do we have officers for?"

"Why is Nancy afraid of Jesus?" Caddy said. "Are you afraid of father, mother?"

"What could the officers do?" father said. "If Nancy hasn't seen him, how could the officers find him?"

"Then why is she afraid?" mother said.

"She says he is there. She says she knows he is there tonight."

"Yet we pay taxes," mother said. "I must wait here alone in this big house while you take a Negro woman home."

"You know that I am not lying outside with a razor," father said.

"I'll stop if Dilsey will make a chocolate cake," Jason said. Mother told us to go out and father said he didn't know if Jason would get a chocolate cake or not, but he knew what Jason was going to get in about a minute. We went back to the kitchen and told Nancy.

"Father said for you to go home and lock the door, and you'll be all right," Caddy said. "All right from what, Nancy? Is Jesus mad at you?" Nancy was holding the coffee cup in her hands again, her elbows on her knees and her hands holding the cup between her knees. She was looking into the cup. "What have you done that made Jesus mad?" Caddy said. Nancy let the cup go. It didn't break on the floor, but the coffee spilled out, and Nancy sat there with her hands still making the shape of the cup. She began to make the sound again, not loud. Not singing and not unsinging. We watched her.

"Here," Dilsey said. "You quit that, now. You get aholt of yourself. You wait here. I going to get Versh to walk home with you." Dilsey went out.

We looked at Nancy. Her shoulders kept shaking, but she quit making the sound. We watched her. "What's Jesus going to do to you?" Caddy said. "He went away."

Nancy looked at us. "We had fun that night I stayed in yawls' room, didn't we?"

"I didn't," Jason said. "I didn't have any fun."

"You were asleep in mother's room," Caddy said. "You were not there."

"Let's go down to my house and have some more fun," Nancy said.

"Mother wont let us," I said. "It's too late now."

"Dont bother her," Nancy said. "We can tell her in the morning. She wont mind."

"She wouldn't let us," I said.

"Dont ask her now," Nancy said. "Dont bother her now."

"She didn't say we couldn't go," Caddy said.

"We didn't ask," I said.

"If you go, I'll tell," Jason said.

"We'll have fun," Nancy said. "They won't mind, just to my house. I been working for yawl a long time. They won't mind."

"I'm not afraid to go," Caddy said. "Jason is the one that's afraid. He'll tell."

"I'm not," Jason said.

"Yes, you are," Caddy said. "You'll tell."

"I won't tell," Jason said. "I'm not afraid."

"Jason ain't afraid to go with me," Nancy said. "Is you, Jason?"

"Jason is going to tell," Caddy said. The lane was dark. We passed the pasture gate. "I bet if something was to jump out from behind that gate, Jason would holler."

"I wouldn't," Jason said. We walked down the lane. Nancy was talking loud.

"What are you talking so loud for, Nancy?" Caddy said.

"Who; me?" Nancy said. "Listen at Quentin and Caddy and Jason saying I'm talking loud."

"You talk like there was five of us here," Caddy said. "You talk like father was here too."

"Who; me talking loud, Mr Jason?" Nancy said.

"Nancy called Jason 'Mister,'" Caddy said.

"Listen how Caddy and Quentin and Jason talk," Nancy said.

"We're not talking loud," Caddy said. "You're the one that's talking like father—"

"Hush," Nancy said; "hush, Mr Jason."

"Nancy called Jason 'Mister' aguh—"

"Hush," Nancy said. She was talking loud when we crossed the ditch and stooped through the fence where she used to stoop through with the clothes on her head. Then we came to her house. We were going fast then. She opened the door. The smell of the house was like the lamp and the smell of Nancy was like the wick, like they were waiting for one another to begin to smell. She lit the lamp and closed the door and put the bar up. Then she quit talking loud, looking at us.

"What're we going to do?" Caddy said.

"What do yawl want to do?" Nancy said.

"You said we would have some fun," Caddy said.

There was something about Nancy's house; something you could smell besides Nancy and the house. Jason smelled it, even. "I don't want to stay here," he said. "I want to go home."

"Go home, then," Caddy said.

"I don't want to go by myself," Jason said.

"We're going to have some fun," Nancy said.

"How?" Caddy said.

Nancy stood by the door. She was looking at us, only it was like she had emptied her eyes, like she had quit using them. "What do you want to do?" she said.

"Tell us a story," Caddy said. "Can you tell a story?"

"Yes," Nancy said.

"Tell it," Caddy said. We looked at Nancy. "You don't know any stories."

"Yes," Nancy said. "Yes, I do."

She came and sat in a chair before the hearth. There was a little fire there. Nancy built it up, when it was already hot inside. She built a good blaze. She told a story. She talked like her eyes looked, like her eyes watching us and her voice talking to us did not belong to her. Like she was living somewhere else, waiting somewhere else. She was outside the cabin. Her voice was inside and the shape of her, the Nancy that could stoop under a barbed wire fence with a bundle of clothes balanced on her head as though without weight, like a balloon, was there. But that was all. "And so this here queen come walking up to the ditch, where that bad man was hiding. She was walking up to the ditch, and she say, 'If I can just get past this here ditch,' was what she say . . ."

"What ditch?" Caddy said. "A ditch like that one out there? Why did a queen want to go into a ditch?"

"To get to her house," Nancy said. She looked at us. "She had to cross the ditch to get into her house quick and bar the door."

"Why did she want to go home and bar the door?" Caddy said.

IV

Nancy looked at us. She quit talking. She looked at us. Jason's legs stuck straight out of his pants where he sat on Nancy's lap. "I don't think that's a good story," he said. "I want to go home."

"Maybe we had better," Caddy said. She got up from the floor. "I bet they are looking for us right now." She went toward the door.

"No," Nancy said. "Don't open it." She got up quick and passed Caddy. She didn't touch the door, the wooden bar.

"Why not?" Caddy said.

"Come back to the lamp," Nancy said. "We'll have fun. You don't have to go."

"We ought to go," Caddy said. "Unless we have a lot of fun." She and Nancy came back to the fire, the lamp.

"I want to go home," Jason said. "I'm going to tell."

"I know another story," Nancy said. She stood close to the lamp. She looked at Caddy, like when your eyes look up at a stick balanced on your nose. She had to look down to see Caddy, but her eyes looked like that, like when you are balancing a stick.

"I won't listen to it," Jason said. "I'll bang on the floor."

"It's a good one," Nancy said. "It's better than the other one."

"What's it about?" Caddy said. Nancy was standing by the lamp. Her hand was on the lamp, against the light, long and brown.

"Your hand is on that hot globe," Caddy said. "Don't it feel hot to your hand?"

Nancy looked at her hand on the lamp chimney. She took her hand away, slow. She stood there, looking at Caddy, wringing her long hand as though it were tied to her wrist with a string.

"Let's do something else," Caddy said.

"I want to go home," Jason said.

"I got some popcorn," Nancy said. She looked at Caddy and then at Jason and then at me and then at Caddy again. "I got some popcorn."

"I don't like popcorn," Jason said. "I'd rather have candy."

Nancy looked at Jason. "You can hold the popper." She was still wringing her hand; it was long and limp and brown.

"All right," Jason said. "I'll stay a while if I can do that. Caddy can't hold it. I'll want to go home again if Caddy holds the popper."

Nancy built up the fire. "Look at Nancy putting her hands in the fire," Caddy said. "What's the matter with you, Nancy?"

"I got popcorn," Nancy said. "I got some." She took the popper from under the bed. It was broken. Jason began to cry.

"Now we can't have any popcorn," he said.

"We ought to go home, anyway," Caddy said. "Come on, Quentin."

"Wait," Nancy said; "wait. I can fix it. Don't you want to help me fix it?"

"I don't think I want any," Caddy said. "It's too late now."

"You help me, Jason," Nancy said. "Don't you want to help me?"

"No," Jason said. "I want to go home."

"Hush," Nancy said; "hush. Watch. Watch me. I can fix it so Jason can hold it and pop the corn." She got a piece of wire and fixed the popper.

"It won't hold good," Caddy said.

"Yes, it will," Nancy said. "Yawl watch. Yawl help me shell some corn."

The popcorn was under the bed too. We shelled it into the popper and Nancy helped Jason hold the popper over the fire.

"It's not popping," Jason said. "I want to go home."

"You wait," Nancy said. "It'll begin to pop. We'll have fun then." She was sitting close to the fire. The lamp was turned up so high it was beginning to smoke.

"Why don't you turn it down some?" I said.

"It's all right," Nancy said. "I'll clean it. Yawl wait. The popcorn will start in a minute."

"I don't believe it's going to start," Caddy said. "We ought to start home, anyway. They'll be worried."

"No," Nancy said. "It's going to pop. Dilsey will tell um yawl with me. I been working for yawl long time. They won't mind if yawl at my house. You wait, now. It'll start popping any minute now."

Then Jason got some smoke in his eyes and he began to cry. He dropped the popper into the fire. Nancy got a wet rag and wiped Jason's face, but he didn't stop crying.

"Hush," she said. "Hush." But he didn't hush. Caddy took the popper out of the fire.

"It's burned up," she said. "You'll have to get some more popcorn, Nancy."

"Did you put all of it in?" Nancy said.

"Yes," Caddy said. Nancy looked at Caddy. Then she took the popper and opened it and poured the cinders into her apron and began to sort the grains, her hands long and brown, and we watching her.

"Haven't you got any more?" Caddy said.

"Yes," Nancy said; "yes. Look. This here ain't burnt. All we need to do is—"

"I want to go home," Jason said. "I'm going to tell."

"Hush," Caddy said. We all listened. Nancy's head was already turned toward the barred door, her eyes filled with red lamplight. "Somebody is coming," Caddy said.

Then Nancy began to make that sound again, not loud, sitting there above the fire, her long hands dangling between her knees; all of a sudden water began to come out on her face in big drops, running down her face, carrying in each one a little turning ball of firelight like a spark until it dropped off her chin. "She's not crying," I said.

"I ain't crying," Nancy said. Her eyes were closed. "I ain't crying. Who is it?"

"I don't know," Caddy said. She went to the door and looked out. "We've got to go now," she said. "Here comes father."

"I'm going to tell," Jason said. "Yawl made me come."

The water still ran down Nancy's face. She turned in her chair. "Listen. Tell him. Tell him we going to have fun. Tell him I take good care of yawl until in the morning. Tell him to let me come home with yawl and sleep on the floor. Tell him I won't need no pallet. We'll have fun. You member last time how we had so much fun?"

"I didn't have fun," Jason said. "You hurt me. You put smoke in my eyes. I'm going to tell."

V

Father came in. He looked at us. Nancy did not get up.

"Tell him," she said.

"Caddy made us come down here," Jason said. "I didn't want to."

Father came to the fire. Nancy looked up at him. "Can't you go to Aunt Rachel's and stay?" he said. Nancy looked up at father, her hands between her knees. "He's not here," father said. "I would have seen him. There's not a soul in sight."

"He in the ditch," Nancy said. "He waiting in the ditch yonder."

"Nonsense," father said. He looked at Nancy. "Do you know he's there?"

"I got the sign," Nancy said.

"What sign?"

"I got it. It was on the table when I come in. It was a hog-bone, with blood meat still on it, laying by the lamp. He's out there. When yawl walk out that door, I gone."

"Gone where, Nancy?" Caddy said.

"I'm not a tattletale," Jason said.

"Nonsense," father said.

"He out there," Nancy said. "He looking through that window this minute, waiting for yawl to go. Then I gone."

"Nonsense," father said. "Lock up your house and we'll take you on to Aunt Rachel's."

"'Twont do no good," Nancy said. She didn't look at father now, but he looked down at her, at her long, limp, moving hands. "Putting it off wont do no good."

"Then what do you want to do?" father said.

"I don't know," Nancy said. "I can't do nothing. Just put it off. And that don't do no good. I reckon it belong to me. I reckon what I going to get ain't no more than mine."

"Get what?" Caddy said. "What's yours?"

"Nothing," father said. "You all must get to bed."

"Caddy made me come," Jason said.

"Go on to Aunt Rachel's," father said.

"It won't do no good," Nancy said. She sat before the fire, her elbows on her knees, her long hands between her knees. "When even your own kitchen wouldn't do no good. When even if I was sleeping on the floor in the room with your chillen, and the next morning there I am, and blood—"

"Hush," father said. "Lock the door and put out the lamp and go to bed."

"I scared of the dark," Nancy said. "I scared for it to happen in the dark."

"You mean you're going to sit right here with the lamp lighted?" father said. Then Nancy began to make the sound again, sitting before the fire, her long hands between her knees. "Ah, damnation," father said. "Come along, chillen. It's past bedtime."

"When yawl go home, I gone," Nancy said. She talked quieter now, and her face looked quiet, like her hands. "Anyway, I got my coffin money saved up with Mr. Lovelady." Mr. Lovelady was a short, dirty man who collected the Negro insurance, coming around to the cabins or the kitchens every Saturday morning, to collect fifteen cents. He and his wife lived at the hotel. One morning his wife committed suicide. They had a child, a little girl. He and the child went away. After a week or two he came back alone. We would see him going along the lanes and the back streets on Saturday mornings.

"Nonsense," father said. "You'll be the first thing I'll see in the kitchen tomorrow morning."

"You'll see what you'll see, I reckon," Nancy said. "But it will take the Lord to say what that will be."

VI

We left her sitting before the fire.

"Come and put the bar up," father said. But she didn't move. She didn't look at us again, sitting quietly there between the lamp and the fire. From some distance down the lane we could look back and see her through the open door.

"What, Father?" Caddy said. "What's going to happen?"

"Nothing," father said. Jason was on father's back, so Jason was the tallest of all of us. We went down into the ditch. I looked at it, quiet. I couldn't see much where the moonlight and the shadows tangled.

"If Jesus is hid here, he can see us, cant he?" Caddy said.

"He's not there," father said. "He went away a long time ago."

"You made me come," Jason said, high; against the sky it looked like father had two heads, a little one and a big one. "I didn't want to."

We went up out of the ditch. We could still see Nancy's house and the open door, but we couldn't see Nancy now, sitting before the fire with the door open, because she was tired. "I just done got tired," she said. "I just a nigger. It ain't no fault of mine."

But we could hear her, because she began just after we came up out of the ditch, the sound that was not singing and not unsinging. "Who will do our washing now, Father?" I said.

"I'm not a nigger," Jason said, high and close above father's head.

"You're worse," Caddy said, "you are a tattletale. If something was to jump out, you'd be scairder than a nigger."

"I wouldn't," Jason said.

"You'd cry," Caddy said.

"Caddy," father said.

"I wouldn't!" Jason said.

"Scairy cat," Caddy said.

"Candace!" father said.

The Light of the World

ERNEST HEMINGWAY

(1899–1961)

When he saw us come in the door the bartender looked up and then reached over and put the glass covers on the two free-lunch bowls.

"Give me a beer," I said. He drew it, cut the top off with the spatula and then held the glass in his hand. I put the nickel on the wood and he slid the beer toward me.

"What's yours?" he said to Tom.

"Beer."

He drew that beer and cut it off and when he saw the money he pushed the beer across to Tom.

"What's the matter?" Tom asked.

The bartender didn't answer him. He just looked over our heads and said, "What's yours?" to a man who'd come in.

"Rye," the man said. The bartender put out the bottle and glass and a glass of water.

Tom reached over and took the glass off the free-lunch bowl. It was a bowl of pickled pig's feet and there was a wooden thing that worked like a scissors, with two wooden forks at the end to pick them up with.

"No," said the bartender and put the glass cover back on the bowl. Tom held the wooden scissors fork in his hand. "Put it back," said the bartender.

"You know where," said Tom.

The bartender reached a hand forward under the bar, watching us both. I put fifty cents on the wood and he straightened up.

"What was yours?" he said.

"Beer," I said, and before he drew the beer he uncovered both the bowls.

"Your goddam pig's feet stink," Tom said, and spit what he had in his mouth on the floor. The bartender didn't say anything. The man who had drunk the rye paid and went out without looking back.

"You stink yourself," the bartender said. "All you punks stink."

"He says we're punks," Tommy said to me.

"Listen," I said. "Let's get out."

"You punks clear the hell out of here," the bartender said.

"I said we were going out," I said. "It wasn't your idea."

"We'll be back," Tommy said.

"No you won't," the bartender told him.

"Tell him how wrong he is," Tom turned to me.

"Come on," I said.

Outside it was good and dark.

"What the hell kind of place is this?" Tommy said.

"I don't know," I said. "Let's go down to the station."

We'd come in that town at one end and we were going out the other. It smelled of hides and tan bark and the big piles of sawdust. It was getting dark as we came in, and now that it was dark it was cold and the puddles of water in the road were freezing at the edges.

Down at the station there were five whores waiting for the train to come in, and six white men and four Indians. It was crowded and hot from the stove and full of stale smoke. As we came in nobody was talking and the ticket window was down.

"Shut the door, can't you?" somebody said.

I looked to see who said it. It was one of the white men. He wore stagged trousers and lumbermen's rubbers and a mackinaw shirt like the others, but he had no cap and his face was white and his hands were white and thin.

"Aren't you going to shut it?"

"Sure," I said, and shut it.

"Thank you," he said. One of the other men snickered.

"Ever interfere with a cook?" he said to me.

"No."

"You can interfere with this one," he looked at the cook. "He likes it."

The cook looked away from him holding his lips tight together.

"He puts lemon juice on his hands," the man said. "He wouldn't get them in dishwater for anything. Look how white they are."

One of the whores laughed out loud. She was the biggest whore I ever saw in my life and the biggest woman. And she had on one of those silk dresses that change colors. There were two other whores that were nearly as big but the big one must have weighed three hundred and fifty pounds. You couldn't believe she was real when you looked at her. All three had those changeable silk dresses. They sat side by side on the bench. They were huge. The other two were just ordinary looking whores, peroxide blondes.

"Look at his hands," the man said and nodded his head at the cook. The whore laughed again and shook all over.

The cook turned and said to her quickly, "You big disgusting mountain of flesh."

She just keep on laughing and shaking.

"Oh, my Christ," she said. She had a nice voice. "Oh, my sweet Christ."

The two other whores, the big ones, acted very quiet and placid as though they didn't have much sense, but they were big, nearly as big as the biggest one. They'd have both gone well over two hundred and fifty pounds. The other two were dignified.

Of the men, besides the cook and the one who talked, there were two other lumberjacks, one that listened, interested but bashful, and the other that seemed getting ready to say something, and two Swedes. Two Indians were sitting down at the end of the bench and one standing up against the wall.

The man who was getting ready to say something spoke to me very low, "Must be like getting on top of a hay mow." I laughed and said it to Tommy.

"I swear to Christ I've never been anywhere like this," he said. "Look at the three of them." Then the cook spoke up.

"How old are you boys?"

"I'm ninety-six and he's sixty-nine," Tommy said.

"Ho! Ho! Ho!" the big whore shook with laughing. She had a really pretty voice. The other whores didn't smile.

"Oh, can't you be decent?" the cook said. "I asked just to be friendly."

"We're seventeen and nineteen," I said.

"What's the matter with you?" Tommy turned to me.

"That's all right."

"You can call me Alice," the big whore said and then she began to shake again.

"Is that your name?" Tommy asked.

"Sure," she said. "Alice. Isn't it?" she turned to the man who sat by the cook.

"Alice. That's right."

"That's the sort of name you'd have," the cook said.

"It's my real name," Alice said.

"What's the other girls' names?" Tom asked.

"Hazel and Ethel," Alice said. Hazel and Ethel smiled. They weren't very bright.

"What's your name?" I said to one of the blondes.

"Frances," she said.

"Frances what?"

"Frances Wilson. What's it to you?"

"What's yours?" I asked the other one.

"Oh, don't be fresh," she said.

"He just wants us all to be friends," the man who talked said. "Don't you want to be friends?"

"No," the peroxide one said. "Not with you."

"She's just a spitfire," the man said. "A regular little spitfire."

The one blonde looked at the other and shook her head.

"Goddamned mossbacks," she said.

Alice commenced to laugh again and to shake all over.

"There's nothing funny," the cook said. "You all laugh but there's nothing funny. You two young lads; where are you bound for?"

"Where are you going yourself?" Tom asked him.

"I want to go to Cadillac," the cook said. "Have you ever been there? My sister lives there."

"He's a sister himself," the man in the stagged trousers said.

"Can't you stop that sort of thing?" the cook asked. "Can't we speak decently?"

"Cadillac is where Steve Ketchel came from and where Ad Wolgast is from," the shy man said.

"Steve Ketchel," one of the blondes said in a high voice as though the name had pulled a trigger in her. "His own father shot and killed him. Yes, by Christ, his own father. There aren't any more men like Steve Ketchel."

"Wasn't his name Stanley Ketchel?" asked the cook.

"Oh, shut up," said the blonde. "What do you know about Steve? Stanley. He was no Stanley. Steve Ketchel was the finest and most beautiful man that ever lived. I never saw a man as clean and as white and as beautiful as Steve Ketchel. There never was a man like that. He moved just like a tiger and he was the finest, free-est, spender that ever lived."

"Did you know him?" one of the men asked.

"Did I know him? Did I know him? Did I love him? You ask me that? I knew him like you know nobody in the world and I loved him like you love God. He was the greatest, finest, whitest, most beautiful man that ever lived, Steve Ketchel, and his own father shot him down like a dog."

"Were you out on the coast with him?"

"No. I knew him before that. He was the only man I ever loved."

Every one was very respectful to the peroxide blonde, who said all this in a high stagey way, but Alice was beginning to shake again. I felt it sitting by her.

"You should have married him," the cook said.

"I wouldn't hurt his career," the peroxide blonde said. "I wouldn't be a drawback to him. A wife wasn't what he needed. Oh, my God, what a man he was."

"That was a fine way to look at it," the cook said. "Didn't Jack Johnson knock him out though?"

"It was a trick," Peroxide said. "That big dinge took him by surprise. He'd just knocked Jack Johnson down, the big black bastard. That nigger beat him by a fluke."

The ticket window went up and the three Indians went over to it.

"Steve knocked him down," Peroxide said. "He turned to smile at me."

"I thought you said you weren't on the coast," some one said.

"I went out just for that fight. Steve turned to smile at me and that black son of a bitch from hell jumped up and hit him by surprise. Steve could lick a hundred like that black bastard."

"He was a great fighter," the lumberjack said.

"I hope to God he was," Peroxide said. "I hope to God they don't have fighters like that now. He was like a god, he was. So white and clean and beautiful and smooth and fast and like a tiger or like lightning."

"I saw him in the moving pictures of the fight," Tom said. We were all very moved. Alice was shaking all over and I looked and saw she was crying. The Indians had gone outside on the platform.

"He was more than any husband could ever be," Peroxide said. "We were married in the eyes of God and I belong to him right now and always will and all of me is his. I don't care about my body. They can take my body. My soul belongs to Steve Ketchel. By God, he was a man."

Everybody felt terribly. It was sad and embarrassing. Then Alice, who was still shaking, spoke. "You're a dirty liar," she said in that low voice. "You never layed Steve Ketchel in your life and you know it."

"How can you say that?" Peroxide said proudly.

"I say it because it's true," Alice said. "I'm the only one here that ever knew Steve Ketchel and I come from Mancelona and I knew him there and it's true and you know it's true and God can strike me dead if it isn't true."

"He can strike me too," Peroxide said.

"This is true, true, true, and you know it. Not just made up and I know exactly what he said to me."

"What did he say?" Peroxide asked, complacently.

Alice was crying so she could hardly speak from shaking so. "He said 'You're a lovely piece, Alice.' That's exactly what he said."

"It's a lie," Peroxide said.

"It's true," Alice said. "That's truly what he said."

"It's a lie," Peroxide said proudly.

"No, it's true, true, true, to Jesus and Mary true."

"Steve couldn't have said that. It wasn't the way he talked," Peroxide said happily.

"It's true," said Alice in her nice voice. "And it doesn't make any difference to me whether you believe it or not." She wasn't crying any more and she was calm.

"It would be impossible for Steve to have said that," Peroxide declared.

"He said it," Alice said and smiled. "And I remember when he said it and I *was* a lovely piece then exactly as he said, and right now I'm a better piece than you, you dried up old hot-water bottle."

"You can't insult me," said Peroxide. "You big mountain of pus. I have my memories."

"No," Alice said in that sweet lovely voice, "you haven't got any real memories except having your tubes out and when you started C. and M. Everything else you just read in the papers. I'm clean and you know it and men like me, even though I'm big, and you know it, and I never lie and you know it."

"Leave me with my memories," Peroxide said. "With my true, wonderful memories."

Alice looked at her and then at us and her face lost that hurt look and she smiled and she had about the prettiest face I ever saw. She had a pretty face and a nice smooth skin and a lovely voice and she was nice all right and really friendly. But my God she was big. She was as big as three women. Tom saw me looking at her and he said, "Come on. Let's go."

"Good-bye," said Alice. She certainly had a nice voice.

"Good-bye," I said.

"Which way are you boys going?" asked the cook.

"The other way from you," Tom told him.

Nothing Ever Breaks Except the Heart

KAY BOYLE

(1903–)

Perhaps you have been there, and you know the Avenida and the way the trees grow the length of it—palm trees and the foreign varieties of hawthorn and maple. Perhaps you've drunk iced coffee under a colored umbrella there, with your back turned to the traffic's noise and the sight of the horses and your face turned to the strips of green, fresh-watered grass. The trees make the long avenues of shade that flow like a dark stream through the city, and on the edges of them stagger the horses, knee-deep in burning, if imaginary, sands. Perhaps you've walked up the avenue through the leafy jungle-dark toward where the American flag hangs, heavy with summer, on its white pole in this foreign city's air. Either children or tropical mirages of them must have run barefoot and scrofulous after you, asking for something as cool as money, and if you were there this summer, you must have seen Miss Del Monte eating ice cream at one of the tiny tables under the trees.

Miss Del Monte used to buy all the American picture magazines there were, and she would sit there looking at them, so as not to think of the horses, with the carts they drew breaking their backs and crippling their limbs beneath them, nor of the lather frothing under the harness that bound them irrevocably to man. Something was always doing it to her, taking the heart out of her breast and tearing it apart, and now she had come to the end. The first day she arrived, she told this to Mr. McCloskey. She said, "You can have the horses and the children with pellagra. I'll take the mint juleps," and Mr. McCloskey stopped looking at the German and the Polish and the Czech and the Russian refugees for a moment and decided, without much interest in it, that she was probably the prettiest woman he had ever seen.

Perhaps you even know Mr. McCloskey—the set of his shoulders in his American businessman's suit, and the rather jaded look in his eyes, and the thick hair just beginning to go gray. He had a roll-top desk to himself, but he never sat down at it, because for eight hours a day he stood behind the elegant, glass-topped counter in the airways office and told the roomful of foreigners, and Americans even, that they wouldn't be able to board a plane and go where they wanted to go for at least another month or two. Miss Del Monte went into the office in June, the first day she got to the city, and spun the propeller of the miniature plane with one finger as she waited there. She had left her stockings at the hotel because of the heat, and her arms and legs and her head were bare and cool enough looking; her nails were long and immaculately done, and her mouth was far too brilliant. Once you'd seen her, you watched for her everywhere you went: at the Tivoli Bar before dinner, or at the Aquarium, dining on the balcony, and after that playing at the Casino, or dancing at the Palace or the Atlantico. But she was never anywhere like that. She was always in the airways office, talking to Mr. McCloskey or waiting to talk to Mr. McCloskey, smoking one cigarette after another and putting fresh lip rouge on from time to time.

"I'd like to get over by Saturday," Miss Del Monte had said to him the first day, and when she said it all the refugees sitting on the benches along the wall stopped breathing for a moment and looked at something that wasn't bitterness and hopelessness at last.

"Look," said Mr. McCloskey, making a gesture. "Everyone in this country's trying to get over." His eyes were haggard and his face was a little gaunt from the heat and the amount of talking he had to do. There were three telephone calls waiting for him on three different desks and fifteen people at the counter where Miss Del Monte stood. "It's either the language that's driving them out, or else it's because they don't kill their bulls in the *corsos* here," he said.

"They broke my heart every Sunday afternoon in Spain," said Miss Del Monte. "They dragged it out with the horses, and now I'm not having any more." She took another cigarette and she said, "On account my show's opening up, I'd like to get over by Saturday."

"Saturday!" a little man in a pongee suit behind her cried out, and for a moment Miss Del Monte thought he had been stabbed. "I've been three monce waiting here—three monce!" he said, and he held up that number of fingers. He didn't speak English very well, but he had diamonds on his hand.

That was the first day, and the second day, in the morning, they were standing three deep around the counter, so Miss Del Monte gave it up after an hour and came back in the afternoon. When she got opposite Mr. McCloskey at last, she lit a cigarette and looked at him carefully and evenly. He must have been just over thirty, in spite of the gray in his hair, and his shoulders would probably have looked too broad for any chair he sat in.

"I'm not prepared for summer," she said. "Monday's the latest I can wait. I haven't a single sharkskin to put on."

"Do you know Mr. Sumner Welles?" said Mr. McCloskey, and for the first time Miss Del Monte saw the madness in his eye. "Have you influential friends in Washington?" he asked, and Miss Del Monte shook her head. "Then perhaps I can help you out," he said, and he walked rather handsomely to his desk, passing Mr. Concachina at the counter on his way.

Mr. Concachina was native, and his head was bald, and his mind was going. "I'm just now speaking four different languages at the same time to five different parties, Mr. McCloskey," he said, and there was sweat on his forehead. "I tell you, I can't do it much longer. I'm at the breaking point."

"You've been saying that for a year and a half," said Mr. McCloskey. He was looking among the other papers for the typewritten list of names. "But nothing ever breaks, nothing," he said, and he repeated it vaguely. "Nothing ever breaks," and he held the list in one hand while he said "Hello there" into one of the three telephones. When he came back to the counter, he looked at Miss Del Monte. "We have a very nice opening for the seventeenth of November," he said.

This went on for a week or more, and then, one Monday morning, Miss Del Monte felt she was getting somewhere at last. She was on her fourth cigarette, and she had combed back her hair and put fresh lipstick on her mouth, and she looked more beautiful than ever.

"Just a minute," said Mr. McCloskey, studying the list. "How old are you? How much do you weigh?"

"A hundred and fifteen," said Miss Del Monte quickly. "I'm twenty-four, but I feel a lot older."

Mr. McCloskey pondered for a moment, and then he said, "Did you ever think of trying a boat, Miss Del Monte?"

"A boat? Do you mean a boat?" she said.

"Yes," said Mr. McCloskey. He looked at her and moved his hand in a swaying motion. "You'd be surprised. You might like a boat."

Mr. Concachina, a little way down the counter, had a telephone receiver in one hand and a fountain pen in the other, and he was writing something down. But still he had time enough to look up at Miss Del Monte. "You know about Pola Negri?" he said, and then he spoke the other language into the mouthpiece. "Well, Pola Negri got fed up," he said, after a moment. "She went out of here in a huff this morning. She's going to take a boat."

"I'd just as soon go out of here in a huff as in what I have on," said Miss Del Monte, evenly. "I'm sure it would be cooler."

"It ought to be awfully cool on shipboard," Mr. McCloskey said.

It was never Mr. McCloskey's intention to start going out in the evening with Miss Del Monte, but by the second week he had got so accustomed to seeing her around that it seemed the natural thing to find her on the Avenida one evening after dinner and walk back and forth with her beneath the trees. She carried a guidebook in one hand, with a cablegram marking a page in it, and she said she'd just had a double whiskey and soda.

"It breaks my heart to talk shop," she said, "but my show's opening on the first of September."

"It can't if you're not there," said Mr. McCloskey. Behind them, in the fountains, illuminated water lilies with iron stems and china petals floated monstrously through the night, and the bookstalls, each one shaped like a book, and the leather tooled across the back, were open.

"If I stay much longer, I'll be right in time for the summer season," said Miss Del Monte. "It says so in the guidebook on page twenty-three. It says there are always balls and processions, varinos exhibitions, gymkhanas, and firelarks. However they want to spell it, I'd give up the varinos exhibitions any day if I could see a gymkhana or a firelark."

"You probably will without a bit of trouble if you have another double whiskey," said Mr. McCloskey, but Miss Del Monte said she'd rather hear a *fado* sung.

Mr. McCloskey had never been to a *fado* café before, but Miss Del Monte seemed quite familiar with the back street where one was. The lights were still on when they walked in and took a table, and all the men in their pongee suits and their white silk shoes turned to watch Miss Del Monte go past. The only other women there were the female *fado* singers, with their Spanish-looking shawls on their shoulders, sitting there rather grimly at separate tables, some with their fathers keeping an eye on them and some with their entrepreneurs, either sitting silent or writing out *fados* while they waited for their turn to come. In a minute the lights went out, and two guitar players mounted a little platform and sat down on the chairs that were placed on opposite sides of it and tuned their instruments up. No one looked very pleased about it, not even when the *fado* singer himself ran quickly up the steps in his patent-leather shoes and stood in the spotlight between the two guitarists on the platform's boards. He was a short, evil-looking man in a black suit, and his hair was wavy and very well greased, and he kept his hands in his trousers' pockets all the time.

"If he takes his hands out of his pockets, he isn't a *fado* singer," said Miss Del Monte, and although the man hadn't yet started to sing, someone behind her hissed.

Presently the singer announced the title of the *fado* and added that this was the first time it had been sung in public, for it was about a stabbing that had occurred near the fish market that day. But when he opened his mouth he might just as well have been telling them all what he thought of them, one minute facing half of the room with his neck going red, and then one minute berating the other half with the veins in his forehead beginning to swell. He said the same words over and over to them, so that there could be no mistake, breaking the rhythm savagely and throwing it in their faces while the throbbing of the guitars wove steadily and systematically upward and, finding no foothold, wove steadily and carefully down again.

When he was done, the lights sprang up all over, and the applause scattered about him, and Miss Del Monte lit another cigarette.

"Did you find this in the guidebook?" Mr. McCloskey asked. He removed the crockery jug from its pail of ice and poured the green wine out.

"Don't be absurd," said Miss Del Monte. "This is neither a bewildering panorama nor a rendezvous of the elite, nor is it an imposing terrace overlooking the sea."

"It might be a gymkhana," said Mr. McCloskey, and he took another drink of wine.

The second night they went out together, again to one of the back-street cafés, Miss Del Monte explained to him further about the *fados*. She said the better ones were either patriotic or heroic, and these had been handed down from generation to generation. The ones they sat writing out quickly at the tables were only the personal ones, she told him.

"You simply have to sense which kind it is," she said.

This time it was a girl who sang first, standing up on the platform between the two seated guitarists, with the fringe of the black Spanish shawl hanging just below her knees. Her throat was bare and broad, and her face was primitive under the *maquillage,* and it was only the feet that had nothing to do with the rest. She wore pink stockings, and her feet were as small as mice and twisted like mice in the traps of the open-toed, cork-soled shoes she had on. She began her statement of fact with her teeth showing white in her mouth, and her voice was husky. She said it beautifully, repeating it first to one side of the room and then to the other, with her hands clasped on her stomach, holding the shawl.

"This is a personal one," said Miss Del Monte in a whisper to Mr. McCloskey.

"I'd be interested to know," said Mr. McCloskey rather wearily, "if she makes any mention of Mr. Sumner Welles."

"It's something she read in the paper," said Miss Del Monte. "It's about a girl whose financé kills her sister because she takes the bracelets he'd given the other one and wears them to go out dancing with another man. He couldn't stand it."

Mr. McCloskey filled their glasses up again. "Miss Del Monte," he said, "I don't know how your public's getting on without you."

It may have been later in the summer, perhaps it was in July, that Mr. McCloskey took her across on the ferry to have dinner on the other shore. They were probably sitting on the open part of the ferry's deck when Mr. McCloskey said, "She's over there." He didn't look toward the city's delicately starred hills but off into the darkness. "The only thing in life I care about is over there," he said, and as he spoke the strung lights of the battleship and the cutter went running past.

He said it again, after they had left the ferry and left the taxi and were walking down through the grass to the river's edge. The moon had risen now, and everything was as brilliantly lit as if by daylight, and although no explanation had been asked for or given as to why they had come here, and why they went down through the night-drenched grass to where the bright stream of water lay, still it seemed, and singularly without question, the one thing left for them to do.

"She's out there, tethered on the water," Mr. McCloskey said. "The plane," he said, a little impatiently, because Miss Del Monte didn't seem to be able to understand English any more. "She's out there. You can see her just to the left of the jetty." They stood on a footpath at the water's edge, where a half-dozen dories, white-flanked and rocking empty on the tide, were chained up to the shore. "We can row out to her," he said, and Miss Del Monte stepped into the boat that he held steady with his foot and sat down on the cross seat, doing it slowly and without wonder, like one hypnotized.

Mr. McCloskey followed her in and fitted the oars in their rowlocks and then pushed off from shore. The water was smooth, and the light and the dark moved clearly in broken pieces on it, first light and then dark around them as the oars dipped softly in the night. Every now and then he turned partway in his seat and feathered the oars while he looked ahead at the suave, enormous body of the plane.

"I love her," he said. "I love her," and Miss Del Monte couldn't think of the right thing to say. As they drew nearer he pulled hard and in silence on one oar so as to bring them up against the wing.

"Have you ever piloted one?" Miss Del Monte asked, and Mr.

McCloskey didn't say anything for a little while. They were riding close to the plane and he had pulled the oars in, and, until the water began drying on them, the splays of them looked as bright as glass.

"That's what's the matter with me," he said after a moment. "I used to be one. I used to fly them across." He did not move from his seat, but he raised one hand and ran it along the hard, sweet, sloping, metallic breast. "I didn't have what it takes," he said, and his voice was bitter to hear. "Or, rather, I gave away what it takes. I had it. I had it." The dory gyrated slowly and without direction near the marvelously still body of the plane. "One or two whiskeys too much every now and then, and jitters," he said. "Single whiskeys when I was tired and double ones to get me out of whatever trouble I happened to be in. Jitters," he said. "So now I'm just good enough to stand up all day behind a counter and tell them what day the company's going to let them fly."

When Miss Del Monte got to the airways office the next morning, there was one Frenchwoman talking faster and better than the others, leaning across to Mr. McCloskey, with her hand in the black fish-net glove closed sharply on his arm. She was telling him, in French, that she knew Mr. Sumner Welles and that she'd been to school with Eve Curie, and Mr. McCloskey was saying nothing in French or in any other language. He simply stood there looking at her with a rather faded, hopeless look around his eyes.

One for the Road

JOHN O'HARA

(1905–1970)

One for the road, kiddie. One for the road and I just happen to think of one happen to me only about a month ago. This might interest you. I doubt it, but it might. You've a rye, I'll have a rye. In my case, soda. In your case, whatever in the name of William Wadsworth Longfellow Shubert. You go right ahead and have whatever you prefer, and by the way, old chum, if I want to call you old chum or kiddie I shall continue to do so, because in my estimation I can always do and continue to do whatsoever I may please. You may be bigger than I, but I was telling you a story. Innaruptions not necessary. I stood here and listen to your dull goddam anecdote, so you will kindly remain here while I airy persiflage. Put in your own verb, son.

Mm. Hoom. Don't look at me if you don't want to, *mon vieux*. Also in any case don't patronize me. You're bigger, but by God I was always a better press agent than you are. I made more money and et settra.

Something you said a minute ago. I forget . . . Well, cheers, and here's how it was.

Wud I tell you? Happen a couple months ago? The hell it did. It happened quite a few years ago, but I thought I'd bring it up to date. No matter. Preten' it happened in the very recent past.

I had a couple shows then, doing a gray deal better than I am now, because in spite of the fact that I'm making more money now, I didn't have to work hard *then* and *now* I don't have to work at *all*. No week went by when I didn't extract a fast four or five c's, even in July. Before that I ud been poor, 'tis true. I shall attempt to give you some background, *mon vieux*.

When I was a kid in this shoe town in Mass. where I come from I was in love with a doll from the right side of the tracks. All I can say about her was she was the loveliest thing I ever saw in my whole life, which covers a great many years. Not beautiful. I didn't say that, but what is worse than beautiful? I'll tell you. It's lovely. This doll was sheer poetry, and I was a sheer nothing. My background was I was poor, I din have any money, I was a mick. My own grandfather couldn't read or write, my own grandmother could read or write but just barely. And she was sheer poetry, this doll. And to make the story worse, I was what you'd expect. A very handsome young man from the wrong side of the tracks.

I met her, and it was whack! I can't snap my fingers, so you snap your fingers. I'd a cousin worked for them in their garage and I went up to see 'im one day and I met her. Whack! It use to be a stable and they still had two horses, and a Mayo man by birth or by ancestry, I knew a fetlock from a crupper, but if I didn't know a fetlock from an I dono what—distributor—id still be the same. We'd a moment's chat and then I said I'll see you tomorrow back of the boat-club clubhouse, and by God she did.

Love, *mon vieux*, it stard then and it stard then and continued. I was a very bad little boy, acting up all the time, but valedictorian of our class at St. Rose of Lima, the high school. I was the unusual combination of bright boy and the girls' garters. I think we had either fourteen or fifteen girls in my class. I don't know what's the matter with you Pronnasuns. You certainly do miss a hell of a lot.

They sent her to a school down in Connecticut, but she'd no sooner be off the train than back of the boathouse or right on her own front porch, so what could they do? I mean her family. They finally said we could get married. They said, all right, marry Pat, but first Pat has to earn five thousand dollars. Oh, sure. Go on, Pat, earn five thousand dollars. Not only earn it, but have it saved up. Sure. My old man was dead and my old lady was coughing blood, and I had a job clerking in the goddam shoe factory, and her family partly owned the shoe factory. Go right ahead, Pat. Embezzle yourself five g's. Wah-wah. I dono, you Pronnasuns have a wry sense of humor. They put it up to me. *I*, my old lady coughing blood and I pulling down the munficent sum of twenty-two a week, I'm suppose to amass the munficent sum of five thousand dollars. I couldn't amass fifty dollars, let alone any five thousand. On the two-two a week I was getting I could have made a showing, might have bought a car or go to Boston or New York, which I later did, but not while the old lady is alive. The doll and I figured it out one night and it was going to take me at the very least forty years, so the smart Yankees beat the smart mick.

The hell they did. Naturally she married some guy, not from our town, but he was helping his old man when they were putting in some new machinery in the shoe factory, and he was studying engineering, too. This doll's people, you know, they weren't any Governor Bradfords. Just Yankees. And no objection raised when this Ralph came along. A Canuck! Rafe, she called him.

I even sent them a wedding present, or her.

Then I ran for selectman, and I got it, and I thought aw the hell with this. I didn't think I'd get elected dogketcher, but I breezed in, so I went to the lousy Yankee that ran the paper and told him I'd prefer to be in the newspaper business. I got the lousy job, and if you can't learn the newspaper business in a year you might as well give up. This son of a bitch even offered me stock to stay, but no. Not me. I stashed a few bucks and came to New York and got to be a press agent.

Now we have two ryes to denote lapse of none of your goddam business how many years. I go around corrupting the press more and more, making myself more valuable by and large, to the point where I can command a *pourboire* running around thirty thousand dollars per annum. *That* was around the kind of money her old man was extricating from his paltry shoe factory. She by this time is in residence in the Province of Ontario. *I* have this two-room suite, the same lousy two-room suite in the same lousy hotel where I stayed the first night I got to New York. I got married one little time and it ran me around fifteen thousand dollars, but we parted amicably when we decided—well, what we decided. The whole thing ran about five months, and we parted amicably. It was all right with me, it was all right with her. I din lose anything, barring the fifteen g's, and she didn't lose anything, unless you call losing me losing.

So, as they say, I played the field. More to my style anyway.

Then the night came I'm talking about.

I was around, talking to this one and that one. Stage doormen, treasurers. Got a half promise from a kid in a show I had, a musical, but I knew that wasn't going to amount to anything. And I dono, aside from passing the time of day with a cop or two, I didn't feel like talking much, or picking up tabs for the newspaper crowd, and so what did I do? I went over on the East Side. Spot where I knew the press corrupter and the barkeep. It was too early to go home, and anyway I din have anything to read at home. Barkeep and I exchange the time of day and I'm about to end up reading the labels on the booze when this worthy taps me on the shoulder. Calls me by name. Yeah, I said, that's me. Clean-looking fellow, not looking for trouble. Standing there and heard the barkeep call me by name.

"You know who I am?" he said.

"Your identity eludes me," I said.

"It won't," he said. "All I have to tell you is I married"—mentioning the doll by name.

"You're Rafe," I said.

He laughed and he said yeah. He said he heard a lot about me. So I tried to make polite conversation and bought the fellow a drink. We had three or four mutually and in the course of the conversation I found out he was just in town on his way to another town. The other town is where his wife, my girl, or *old* girl, she was moving their things from Canada to —well, a little city not too far from right here. I asked him how she was, and the kid, and everything was fine. Then he got an earnest face on him and asked me, he said, "I understand you have something to do with such-and-such a show."

"That's right," I said. "Why?"

"Well, I saw the show last night," he said. "You know as one man to another," he said, "I'd settle for any one of those chorines."

"Oh," I said. I knew the show had about twenty minutes to run, and I guess he surmised that, too. "See what I can do about that," I said.

So I went to the phone, out in the booth. And if you think I called the theatre . . . I called the little city I was talking about, and I got his wife, my old girl. I gave her my addresses and phone numbers and told her for God's sake. "No, Pat," she said, "I could never do that."

I stard to tell her, I mean I was going to start to tell her what I was supposed to be doing in the phone booth, and then I thought—I don't know what the hell I thought. I went back and told Rafe it was no cigar. All the kids dated up.

Jerk probly thinks I'm a great friend of his. Mm. Hoom . . . Two ryes.

A Walk With Raschid

JOSEPHINE JACOBSEN

(1908–)

When the muezzin began to call, James got out of bed and went to the window. Tracy shifted as he did so, murmuring and giving a light shiver, and he pulled the sheet over her body, which looked bright in the moonlight; the iron grillwork barred it.

The call, a rough, unhuman, melancholy, hornlike sound, fell and rose, with a breathstopping pause between phrases. It appeared to take up, in a strange tongue, an unsettled theme. That it referred to a god could never be doubted. It insisted, accused, identified, summoned. No matter that he couldn't get so much as his toe into Moulay Idriss, shoeless or shod.

They had turned off the fountain just below, and the tiled courtyard, where he and Tracy and Mr. and Mrs. Neeson had sipped mint tea at noon in a daze of color, was absolutely still. The bone-blue of the medina slept; anyway, was silent. Not a bawl, not a bark. That extraordinary voice, not like a reed or a ram's horn, but more like both than a voice, proceeded powerfully up and down its ways. Were the tanners asleep, bright yellow and red, peacefully stinking? Did the single-toothed coppersmith rise and kneel to the east? Did it wake Raschid? At the thought of Raschid asleep or awake in that visible bone-blue city, James thought immediately of Oliver, asleep or awake in a home once as familiar to James as his fingers, now distant in a variety of ways. This had happened three or four times. Beyond the fact that Raschid and Oliver both belonged to the human species and were ten-year-old males, it was hard to see a connection.

Shivering a little in the three o'clock air, he heard the phrase end, on a wild deep braying gasp; a pause, and then a high climb. He stared through the grill at the blaze of moonlight; all the dark seemed to have contracted into the cypresses. A small dizzy sense of ridiculousness wafted over him: James Gantry, naked, immaculately shaved, hearing the news of Allah and his Prophet, while his wife, bright as a minted penny, slept behind him, and his honeymoon rose in the blanched Moroccan night. Here every known thing seemed to have its alien echo: his feet, the brilliant geometry of the tiles; Tracy, the carved and gilded and painted bed; his son's pale square-set image, Raschid.

Raschid wore a striped djellabah; it was too small, but looked dignified. He never (when James had seen him) raised the hood. He had small bones, extended eyelashes, and a left thumb flattened in some mishap. His eyes (differing in this from his face, which was somber) were lighthearted in their darkness; unlike those of Oliver, which were of a pale and steadfast blue.

Hastily choosing the lighter confusion, James pressed down on the thought of Raschid. He didn't understand Raschid. Political prejudice aside, he did consider Arabs decorative; and then, Oliver's lack of childish charm had only lucklessly sharpened James's love of it. So he was prepared for that aspect of Raschid. But although he was gloomily convinced that the man who wasn't a scoundrel was apt to be a boob, he didn't want to be a boob, and he was alert for Raschid's angle. It could hardly be other than money, and when James found it apparently wasn't, he was thrown into unease. The whole of Fez contributed to this.

Fez was all there, close, breathing, smelling and moving, and yet he felt unsure what was real, where, exactly, the fraud began. The dyers and tanners were real; standing high above the stench, on narrow pitted steps with Tracy gamely clutching his elbow, the guide waiting, and Raschid gesticulating one step below, he saw them, inside their own lives; but, too, in some circle of Dante's. And in the cavern of trays the coppersmith, with his one tooth and serene eyes, looked at once like a tourist's artisan and a disguised and saintly magician.

Raschid had cut himself out from the horde of children by an incident common between the sexes, and not unknown between adults and children strange to each other—a sudden wordless intimacy, based on a mutual attraction solid as an electric shock.

Raschid's reaction, James perfectly well knew, was inevitably rooted in a lack in the past, and a hunger for the future. His own, he faced with a familiar stale qualm, was at least the former. The future, now, was Tracy. He had never been truly equipped to love Oliver, if love entailed satisfaction. But, unrejected, he would have offered as fine substitutes as his nature would provide and guilt could prompt. But he *had* been rejected;

first somewhere in secret, and then verbally. It was odd how clearly he knew that it was he who had been rejected, rather than Louise who had been chosen. If Louise had never found their son a very interest-compelling subject, she had maintained with him, during the periods when he attracted her attention, a mild-mannered friendliness. There were children who *did* interest her; but any comparison which she may have made in silence, or in dreams, never resulted in maternal animosity.

It had always been hard for Oliver to speak; and it was Tracy who had got him through the ordeal of his decision, by her ability to listen, an ability as native and as finely-honed as her tennis game. How a child of his and Louise's could be that inarticulate, passed James's understanding. Though he secretly thought of Louise's articulateness as facile (perhaps because it worked so well on her newly-privileged kindergarten listeners), there it was. Oliver gave, always, the impression of weighing. He was a sort of small, human, heavily constructed pair of scales, the results of whose balances were never disclosed. After the permissible baby age, he had been caught now and then telling stories, all involving possessions, material or animal; but until James had looked at them in the light of Tracy's sunny honesty, he had not called them lies. Like Tracy, he spontaneously believed lying to be the meanest of the vices. "Know the truth, and the truth shall make you free." It was Tracy's only biblical quotation.

One hot September afternoon she had said it to him, running her cool fingers over the pink shells of her toenails. James, waiting in his brown hateful bed-sitting room; Oliver, redelivered to the house which for twelve years had been James's home. Tracy had been standing at the window; he thought she appeared like Mercury, the gods' lissome and terrible messenger. She came over to the daybed, kicked off her pumps, curled up and seized her toes. Over them, half humorous, half tearful, she quoted her maxim.

"Well?" said James.

"He wants to stay with Louise."

The curious shaft, like dry ice, that burned through him, he could not have diagnosed for his life.

"I don't believe it."

"He told me so. In so many words."

There was a silence. Tracy kept it; she never blundered.

"Well," he said at last. "How hard was it—for him, I mean?"

"Very, I think," said Tracy softly. She looked, for her, tired, and James rushed toward her in his mind's eye. How much she gave, how little, without denigrating herself, she asked. She had not demanded commitment. Now that she had it, she would have shaped herself to another woman's heavy and taciturn child, if that was what James and Oliver wanted. Oliver had liked her at once. He was always looking for a new thing to belong to him, James glumly thought, and it was Tracy who had lifted from all three of them that most savage incident of a split marriage —self-declaration by offspring. Louise, conditioned to consult, in her warm-soup voice, finger-painters versus block-builders, had kindly said, "Oliver should choose, himself. He's ten. It's only a limited choice, it's not as though he'd never see the other."

"A child that age, even a *frank* child," Tracy had said as she and James turned it gently over and over, "can't get words around huge things, the things its life is made of. If you ask him about motorbike parts, or batting averages, it's a piece of cake. But fool, awful questions, like 'do you love your mother?' 'are you mad at your father?' . . . What we've *got* to have is the truth, that's the only thing that'll hold up. He can say to me 'my father' or 'my mother.' To you, or Louise, he'd have to say 'you.' That's where, perhaps, I helped. Getting 'loyalty' out of it. Poor Oliver. Christ, the things people do in the name of loyalty. Pulling live tissue apart. I said it was a temporary pattern; just that. No great, permanent decision. That you and Louise wanted to stand enough aside to give him room to breathe and think. This way, he needn't say to either, 'I don't want to live with you.' "

"It's just," said James lamely, "that he seems so remote from Louise."

Tracy laid her weary head back against the brown cushions of the daybed.

"Louise really only likes them at the pre-judgment age," she said astutely. "It makes her nervous to be sized up. Children are death on that."

"Did he say anything about me?" he after a while asked.

"Bang!" went knuckles on the door. James rose; it was their ice. Conveniently later she said gently, "He was embarrassed. He's only ten. And he sometimes finds it hard to be honest. This was one of the hard times."

James raised his amber glass and drank. Tracy, too, raised her glass. "To Oliver," she said slowly. They drank. Suddenly a wild relief—the die cast, that inn of decision in which the mind sleeps well—flooded James. "To Morocco," he said. But the second toast was too soon for Tracy. She set her glass softly by the icebucket, and closed her green eyes.

The chanting had stopped. The muezzin had gone back to wherever he had come from. The moonlight had withdrawn; Tracy was only a dark corner. James, who had sat down on a sighing hassock, got up. A light burst out in a kitty-cornered window in the lower garden, and Mrs. Neeson, in flamingo chiffon panels, went across it. How very gorgeous, James thought meanly. Mrs. Neeson was too much for him. The effect was flawless, but though effortless in appearance, seemed to spring from a vast hidden machinery. Surely Nubian slaves must have toiled for centuries, computers made hairline decisions, sleep, reading and eating have been forsworn for plans. Was Mr. Neeson the machinery?

Mrs. Neeson's references were too oblique and intimate to be name-dropping; nothing so cut-rate fell from her lips. The Palais Jamai, reprieved by quaintness and the lovely tokens of old Moorish lusts, amused her in an endearing way. "How we do envy you dear old number seven," she had said at once. "We cabled just too late." Tracy, with her candid gaze, had subsequently reexamined their small lustrous room. "Well, now we have the Good Housekeeping Seal," James said nastily. It had amused him that Mrs. Neeson should cause Tracy to reassess anything.

Did that flamingo vision arise, from the first sweet sleep of night, to perform esoteric rites of beautification? Or was she merely en route to the bathroom? The light still burned. The medina still slept. In an orgy of pre-dawn slackness, James wondered, abashed, if Raschid dreamed of the American who spoke French, who, infinitely powerful, infinitely just, was an enormous sudden friend. James was as beautiful as Raschid, though at thirty-three it would never have occurred to him that this was true.

In the morning, the courtyard tiles shone from the hose. The fountain, released, sprang up and fell, and distant noises came from the medina.

Raschid came to the outer entrance about ten o'clock. James, who had gone out to treat with a taxi-driver, saw his striped djellabah swerve out of the medina-alley. The taxi-driver said at once, "The guides will get police if he keeps does so. He can't guide. Beggars, beggars."

"He is not a beggar," said James shortly. He decided to ignore the taxi-driver's opinions. "At eleven-thirty, then," he said haughtily, and turned toward Raschid.

Day before yesterday, when he had first joined them (doubling their steps quietly along the stony way, regarded sideways by a James enchanted, apprehensive, waiting for the story and the brown small palm) he had worried about James's French. "Vous comprenez?" he asked, drawing up his short nose as though smelling language deficiencies. "Vous comprenez ce que j'ai dit?" Then he began to worry about Tracy, but not much. "Expliquez à votre femme," he said once or twice rather perfunctorily, as if she might be dangerous if too much excluded.

He made the stale standard joke, pushing a donkey aside, "Ce sont les petits taxis de la medina!" and his eyes laughing at James, at himself, at the donkeys, at the prostrate jest, took James into a dazzling intimacy.

At the end of their stroll through the bleak biblical landscape of stones, bare earth and bleached sun, James extracted a handful of change. Instantly a cloud passed over Raschid's brown eyes, muddying their color.

He put both hands behind his back and looked sullenly down at his feet under the djellabah's dirty edge.

"J'ai voulu faire votre connaissance," he said. "C'était tout simplement ça."

Amazed, pleased, uneasy, James had returned his dirhams to his pocket.

"What did he say?" asked Tracy, smiling at Raschid.

"He said he wished to make my acquaintance, that was his only purpose."

They shook hands with him, first James, then Tracy, and he asked James when he would care to go through the medina. They were going the next morning, said James, but with a guide, it was already arranged. Raschid murmured something in Arabic. Then he lifted his head and said clearly in French, looking James straight in the eye, that he would like, once, to take them himself into the medina. They would go to certain places the guide would not have time for; then, when that was finished, they would go to un restaurant typique, très typique, très petit, très bon, and there they would prendre le déjeuner ensemble. "Demain, peutêtre?"

That they could not do, Tracy, easily snared, having commited them to lunch with the Neesons. "Alors, le jour après . . ." said Raschid.

"Hélas, nous allons à Meknès."

"Alors, le jour après ça . . ."

"But that's our last day," said Tracy, guessing.

James said to her in rapid English, "We could go in the afternoon, late, and have supper instead of lunch. I'd really like to. That would leave practically the whole day free."

"Good," she said instantly. She grinned affirmatively at Raschid; but his face, direly balanced between their glances, stayed dark until James committed them: "Eh bien, d'accord. À quatre heures et demi. Après, nous pouvons diner ensemble. Le jour après le lendemain."

The next day he came with them and their outraged guide. He pointed now and then, but did not speak except to say, with taciturn authority, "Moulay Idriss, c'est le plus beau de tous."

As they peered over the shoulders of a picture-snapping compatriot, into that vast, ordered, brilliant coolness, Tracy said a little crossly, "I don't see why they let people take *pictures* and not go in—if they take their shoes off, I mean. My husband went into one in Alexandria," she told the guide.

He gave them a bland frown. "Fez is a more holy city," he said. "Very holy." Raschid stared at James to see how he received this statement.

Disoriented, they trudged behind their towering and animated guide: coppersmiths, tinsmiths; souks, weavers, tanners, dyers. They debouched, helpless, into lavish rooms at the end of sinister entrances; undesired rugs, glowing like radiant signals, unfurled by rapid boys; mint tea; unstuffed hassocks, cast upon the floor to sink in gorgeous slow motion; mint tea. They flattened themselves against stone to let donkeys pass. The donkeys' aristocratic legs supported immense piles of planks, towering baskets, piles of colored cloth. "Ce sont les petits taxis de la medina," said the guide.

Tracy, golden, in white linen, stayed cool and happy. James was battling a sense of disequilibrium. It seemed to have darted like a shadowy fish in deep water ever since the hour when he had heard the muezzin's raucous wandering call, when he had been alone at the window. He was summoned, yet he was not. He could touch people at any minute—indeed, it was impossible not to; but he should have been closer, or more distant. This way, it needed to be a travelogue, a chapter: the medina, Fez. The place hummed, milled, teemed; all the travelogue words. But the eyes that met his, over yashmak and under turban, slid over human material borne past them by a guide.

His elbow was jerked; on his arm the soiled brown hand with the smashed thumbnail rested, pressing. "Voilà! C'est notre restaurant futur. Quand nous faisons ensemble notre promenade."

He could see nothing but a blind darkness beyond an open doorway; and they were past it, anyway. But it was an engagement; and it was as though at last he were identified.

They had not gone to Meknès, after all. Something had upset Tracy, and she lay all day, qualmish and languid, not even much reading. She urged James to go anyway, but he suddenly realized how much he did not want to. He wanted to stay still. The Neesons *had* gone to Meknès, causing Tracy to remark, childishly, that if she *were* going to be sick, it seemed like a good day.

James sat in the shadow by the fountain and read *The Tale of Genji*. Ravished by a paragraph, he stared from his shade into a daze of sun. He jumped up, and went in to read to Tracy about the little maids going into the dim early garden, carrying their cricket-cages; but she had fallen asleep, her pale hair lightly snarled on the punched-up pillow. He stared at his future, awed. The simple, unambiguous, exquisite, and here-present future. He went back, through the cool splendors of the hall, into the courtyard, sat down and read the passage again. But this time it had thinned out. He shut the book, and then as two couples paused, staring lovingly around them, raised it.

He had not heard his muezzin again, except the night before, when, a semi-circular foursome, they were having coffee in the small bar. Then, though faint, the hard distant wail had caused them slightly to raise their voices.

It annoyed James that he did not enjoy the Neesons. He credited them with being out of the run; *more* of something, if not of something different. Mr. Neeson, who looked as though he had had his blood painlessly extracted and then been sealed again, had a small, pungent speech. It admitted of no qualifications, but it was lively. Mrs. Neeson, whose anecdotes, never blasting, were pleasantly penultimate, glowed and breathed. Perhaps Mrs. Neeson had all that blood?

A friend of hers, a more-than-promising young French film director (formerly a Godard protégé, but now intransigently individualistic), was, or might be, at Marrakesh; the Neesons were waiting for a call. Against the embroidered cushions, Mrs. Neeson appeared to have been incarnated from an absolutely first-class original. Lustrously, she leaned toward James, with a luminous-lipped air of barely pre-coital chic.

"He's very ready," she said. "Very open-ended. But there's a terrific thrust. He used color-change for mood long before Antonioni."

"Film is exciting," said Tracy. James saw with love that she felt uncertain, but not totally docile, in her habitual self-underestimation.

"It's the camera. It's knowing how not to interfere with what the camera sees." A turbaned head appeared at her shoulder; it was the Mamounia, calling from Marrakesh.

The Gantrys were halfway up the stairs when she returned. "Jean-Paul!" she cried softly after them. "It was! His art man is going to do some sketches of a palace in Meknès, and we're going back to Meknès, and meet him at a friend's place outside, where we can go for cocktails, and then drive on late to Rabat, all of us."

Back at the foot of the stairs again, the Gantrys glanced at each other, reapproaching the bar. Could she mean "all"?

"I've told him about you both." So she did. "And you were going to Rabat anyway, the next day."

James said at once, "How nice of him, and of you. But tomorrow, we can't." He saw Tracy's eyes cloud. "We're tied up." he nevertheless said. It sounded lame. Somehow he could not get a grip on Raschid which could produce him for the Neesons in the guise of an engagement.

But Mrs. Neeson was incurious and easy. "Oh dear, if we'd only known a bit sooner."

Behind the big carved door of number 7, James said guiltily, "Why on earth don't you go? You can take a car back here."

Tracy had crossed to the window-grille. The fountain was still playing. "Darling, don't be ridiculous. 'Jean-Paul' doesn't want to see me. It might have been fun—but not just me, with them."

He joined her at the window. The cypresses pointed straight at a great many stars.

"I mean," said James, "he's been counting on it for three days. A kid that age . . ."

"Heavens, yes," she instantly agreed. "We couldn't change him to lunch, you don't suppose?"

He was somehow relieved that evidently it wasn't that she hankered for the Neesons in exchange for Raschid, as that she had a generous appetite for both. "We can't get *hold* of him. I've no idea where he lives, in the medina. Do you know," he said, surprised, "I can't even remember his last name. He told me twice, but Arabic names . . ." But it still seemed to him strange.

"Oh well," said Tracy mildly, and taking her kimono she disappeared into the bathroom, through whose open overhead arch he could hear her running the shower and cheerfully whistling.

He dreamed of Mercury. The god's heels, conventionally wing-tipped, barely rested on the kindergarten floor. The small black faces stared, not truly frightened. "And *this,*" said Louise's breathy voice, "is *Mercury*. He is a messenger. He is the gods' *messenger*. He is a god, too. He is the god of lovers, and of thieves. We will draw that thing on his head. With our crayons. It is a helmet. A *golden helmet*. Oliver, will you turn him sideways for us, please." As Oliver moved to do so, James woke, coldly clear. Mercury had been beautiful. The small black faces had been beautiful; open, dark, turned like royal pansies toward Louise's sun. Louise's son. James's son. Not that pale, really, not in real life; not that squat, not that shut.

He had had one tantrum, Louise wrote. Only one. He bought a snake, sent from an unscrupulous snake farm in Florida. It had to be fed live mice. Regularly. The whole thing was psychologically wrong at the moment. Cruel, stupid and inefficient. She had returned the snake, collect. Oliver had exploded. He had called her a white mouse. A white rat. For the snake to eat. He wanted to live with his father. His father was, actually, coming to take him away.

Louise, rancorless, and encouraged by this purging, had reminded him of his choice. It was a lie. He began to weep. He had never never said that, never, never. She had not said, "Then why hasn't your father come to get you?" And a little later, when she came back to the room he hugged her violently and explained that he had said it because his snake had been returned. He had chosen her because he loved her. Since then he was friendly, and was saving for a Siamese kitten.

For an awful day James had wondered if, in his rage and frustration, Oliver had lived through minutes of believing his own invention; that he had summoned a father who, silently, never arrived; received a disprized home, nursed a secret he could never admit. Tracy had gone quite white over this story. But she did not think that, even in his rage, Oliver believed it. "That's his weak spot. It's because he's inarticulate. I'm sure. He lies sometimes, like about the raccoon—because he can't fully express things."

Faces such as Raschid's did not, basically, need words; but he had them, correct, lucid, formal. It was a curious rendezvous; beyond the afternoon, the walk, the dinner, the farewell, what did Raschid want? A different memory? A promise? A bond outside his arc? Yes, he had brothers, he had answered. Six. Two sisters. No father. (Gone? Dead?) An aunt. A mother.

What sort of present could Raschid be given? He was extraordinarily intelligent. He spoke well. He had fire, grace. He was dirty; but small boys got dirty. But this was settled dirt. And the djellabah was mildly ragged. Would he like James to meet his mother? To what purpose? Was this really a friendship? Wild as that seemed. What would they eat? What on earth would the restaurant through that dark doorway be like? But then the inner shops. . . . He felt a tremendous hot gaiety, a sense of some light-hearted reprieve, that spilled into his sleep. He was amused to find he was thinking in terms of "not letting Raschid down."

Their last day came over the gardens like a single jewel. After lunch they went down to the lower level to say goodbye to the Neesons, later departing for Meknès and Jean-Paul. The Gantrys had an hour before Raschid's arrival. The lower garden was cool and dusty; the Gantrys, faced with a long, sunny trek, slumped peacefully in wicker chairs. Tracy thought of the postcards she had meant to get. "I could do it now," she said. "Oh sit still," said Mrs. Neeson affably, but Tracy went on mournfully remembering that she would *not* want to write them tonight, and God knew, not before leaving early in the morning. Finally, she went to get them. When she came back, some time later, she was dissatisfied. Having searched, she had ended up with pictures taken from curious angles, denigrating the courtyard and its views. Nevertheless, she scribbled laxly, stopping to sigh, in the fragrant heat.

At quarter past four, James rose. "Well," he said, "have a fine trip. I hope . . ." But the Neesons were coming up, too. At five, the car for Meknès would be there; they would wait by the fountain. "Those streets must be death, in this sun," said Mrs. Neeson. It was hotter in the upper courtyard, an intimation of outside.

"You go and see," said Tracy to James. "He mightn't be there yet."

James secretly had a feeling that he would have been there for some time. He went out through the flower-beds, past the lily-pool, along the tiled way, to the outside glare. Raschid had not yet arrived. There were two taxis (neither the one driven by Raschid's foe), a motorcycle, loiterers in the narrow shade thrown by the wall. He went back to the courtyard. Tracy had finished her cards. She stuffed them in her purse, slung it on her shoulder, and looked ready.

Suddenly James was anxious. It was like one of those dreadful, contrived stories in which at the last moment someone is run over, his mother falls dead, he is arrested, or locked in a windowless room.

"He *must* be there now," said Tracy. She had evidently explained things to the Neesons, since they looked only interested. "If your small Arab doesn't show, you'll get to Rabat with us yet," said Mrs. Neeson amiably.

"It's twenty-five to five," said Tracy. "You know he'd be there by now. Go see."

One of the taxis was gone. The shade along the wall had widened. He could not see Raschid. Perhaps the boy had come during James's return to the courtyard and dashed away for a minute. His breath felt odd. I am *not* meeting a general to negotiate for peace, he reproved himself, a little amused and puzzled. The taxi-driver stared at him. James looked fiercely at the ground; the man knew perfectly well that his cab was not wanted. Then he raised his eyes quickly to his watch. It was a quarter to five, and a weight like a concrete block fell on him. Something *had* happened. And he would never know. That was the only part that was really bad. The truth, he thought, joking, can't make me free if I don't know it. Couldn't Raschid have sent him word? But he knew that an alley tart would have had more chance of penetrating the late sultan's harem, than Raschid or a friend, of penetrating the courtyard.

A taxi drew up, and two black and enormous women got out, one magnificent in royal blue, the other towering in a bone-crushing pink. They were mammoth, handsome, ferociously powerful. They began pulling bundles from the taxi, roped huge mounds, baskets, bags with knotted necks. Their driver had disappeared into the medina. James looked gratefully at this diversion. Raschid had no watch. Time, to an Arab child . . . But he did not believe it.

The taxi-driver reappeared from the medina entrance, followed by a man in a soiled white djellabah, leading two donkeys. The man and the driver began to load the bundles onto the donkeys, higher and higher; last came a roped trunk. Finally, when only the huge heads and delicate legs were visible, the man struck each donkey a blow with a large stick and they lurched, and then swayed, sagging, forward down the sloping alley and out of sight. The taxi backed, ground gears, rushed off. The driver of the parked taxi addressed James.

"Berbers," he said. "Berbers. No damn good." He spat from the taxi window. "Bad people around," he said.

James looked at him. The man stared into his eyes. "Bad boys, too," he said. "That boy, he kicked your wife."

"What?" said James.

"He kicked her," repeated the driver. "Police fix him soon, I say it. She speak to him nice, and he yelling, Non, non, non. And then she try to give him something. Give him American money. Goddam fool, he kick and yell."

"I don't know what you are talking about," said James.

"Not one hour gone by," said the taxi-driver with care. "Not one hour. He yelling at her, *menteuse, menteuse!* That's 'liar' he says. In French, crying and yelling. Then he pull up his hood, and kick her leg and run away. She smile at me, this way," he lifted his shoulders to his ears. "Very nice lady, not to get police."

James went over to the alley and looked down it. The Berbers and their donkeys had disappeared; other figures, other donkeys, strode and swayed. Hooded heads turned corners. Under a djellabah-hood, dark eyes, now turned a light, steadfast blue, raced away, raced away. The wall had cut off the sun, and a faint fresh coolness rose from the stones. As the taxi-driver watched him, he turned back and went toward the courtyard.

The Daring Young Man on the Flying Trapeze

WILLIAM SAROYAN

(1908–1981)

I. SLEEP

Horizontally wakeful amid universal widths, practising laughter and mirth, satire, the end of all, of Rome and yes of Babylon, clenched teeth, remembrance, much warmth volcanic, the streets of Paris, the plains of Jericho, much gliding as of reptile in abstraction, a gallery of watercolors, the sea and the fish with eyes, symphony, a table in the corner of the

Eiffel Tower, jazz at the opera house, alarm clock and the tap-dancing of doom, conversation with a tree, the river Nile, Cadillac coupe to Kansas, the roar of Dostoyevsky, and the dark sun.

This earth, the face of one who lived, the form without the weight, weeping upon snow, white music, the magnified flower twice the size of the universe, black clouds, the caged panther staring, deathless space, Mr. Eliot with rolled sleeves baking bread, Flaubert and Guy de Maupassant, a wordless rhyme of early meaning, Finlandia, mathematics highly polished and slick as a green onion to the teeth, Jerusalem, the path to paradox.

The deep song of man, the sly whisper of someone unseen but vaguely known, hurricane in the cornfield, a game of chess, hush the queen, the king, Karl Franz, black Titanic, Mr. Chaplin weeping, Stalin, Hitler, a multitude of Jews, tomorrow is Monday, no dancing in the streets.

O swift moment of life: it is ended, the earth is again now.

II. WAKEFULNESS

He (the living) dressed and shaved, grinning at himself in the mirror. Very unhandsome, he said; where is my tie? (He had but one.) Coffee and a gray sky, Pacific Ocean fog, the drone of a passing streetcar, people going to the city, time again, the day, prose and poetry. He moved swiftly down the stairs to the street and began to walk, thinking suddenly, *It is only in sleep that we may know that we live. There only, in that living death, do we meet ourselves and the far earth, God and the saints, the names of our fathers, the substance of remote moments; it is there that the centuries merge in the moment, that the vast becomes the tiny, tangible atom of eternity.*

He walked into the day as alertly as might be, making a definite noise with his heels, perceiving with his eyes the superficial truth of streets and structures, the trivial truth of reality. Helplessly his mind sang, *He flies through the air with the greatest of ease; the daring young man on the flying trapeze;* then laughed with all the might of his being. It was really a splendid morning: gray, cold, and cheerless, a morning for inward vigor; ah, Edgar Guest, he said, how I long for your music.

In the gutter he saw a coin which proved to be a penny dated 1923, and placing it in the palm of his hand he examined it closely, remembering that year and thinking of Lincoln whose profile was stamped upon the coin. There was almost nothing a man could do with a penny. I will purchase a motorcar, he thought. I will dress myself in the fashion of a fop, visit the hotel strumpets, drink and dine, and then return to the quiet. Or I will drop the coin into a slot and weigh myself.

It was good to be poor, and the Communists—but it was dreadful to be hungry. What appetites they had, how fond they were of food! Empty stomachs. He remembered how greatly he needed food. Every meal was bread and coffee and cigarettes, and now he had no more bread. Coffee without bread could never honestly serve as supper, and there were no weeds in the park that could be cooked as spinach is cooked.

If the truth were known, he was half starved, and yet there was still no end of books he ought to read before he died. He remembered the young Italian in a Brooklyn hospital, a small sick clerk named Mollica, who had said desperately, I would like to see California once before I die. And he thought earnestly, I ought at least to read *Hamlet* once again; or perhaps *Huckleberry Finn.*

It was then that he became thoroughly awake: at the thought of dying. Now wakefulness was a state in the nature of a sustained shock. A young man could perish rather unostentatiously, he thought; and already he was very nearly starved. Water and prose were fine, they filled much inorganic space, but they were inadequate. If there were only some work he might do for money, some trivial labor in the name of commerce. If they would only allow him to sit at a desk all day and add trade figures, subtract and multiply and divide, then perhaps he would not die. He would buy food, all sorts of it: untasted delicacies from Norway, Italy, and France; all manner of beef, lamb, fish, cheese; grapes, figs, pears, apples, melons, which he would worship when he had satisfied his hunger. He would place a bunch of red grapes on a dish beside two black figs, a large yellow pear, and a green apple. He would hold a cut melon to his nostrils for hours. He would buy great brown loaves of French bread, vegetables of all sorts, meat; he would buy life.

From a hill he saw the city standing majestically in the east, great towers, dense with his kind, and there he was suddenly outside of it all, almost definitely certain that he should never gain admittance, almost positive that somehow he had ventured upon the wrong earth, or perhaps into the wrong age, and now a young man of twenty-two was to be permanently ejected from it. This thought was not saddening. He said to himself, sometime soon I must write *An Application for Permission to Live*. He accepted the thought of dying without pity for himself or for man, believing that he would at least sleep another night. His rent for another day was paid; there was yet another tomorrow. And after that he might go where other homeless men went. He might even visit the Salvation Army—sing to God and Jesus (unlover of my soul), be saved, eat and sleep. But he knew that he would not. His life was a private life. He did not wish to destroy this fact. Any other alternative would be better.

Through the air on the flying trapeze, his mind hummed. Amusing it was, astoundingly funny. A trapeze to God, or to nothing, a flying trapeze to some sort of eternity; he prayed objectively for strength to make the flight with grace.

I have one cent, he said. It is an American coin. In the evening I shall polish it until it glows like a sun and I shall study the words.

He was now walking in the city itself, among living men. There were one or two places to go. He saw his reflection in the plate-glass windows of stores and was disappointed with his appearance. He seemed not at all as strong as he felt; he seemed, in fact, a trifle infirm in every part of his body, in his neck, his shoulders, arms, trunk, and knees. This will never do, he said, and with an effort he assembled all his disjointed parts and became tensely, artificially erect and solid.

He passed numerous restaurants with magnificent discipline, refusing even to glance into them, and at last reached a building which he entered. He rose in an elevator to the seventh floor, moved down a hall, and, opening a door, walked into the office of an employment agency. Already there were two dozen young men in the place; he found a corner where he stood waiting his turn to be interviewed. At length he was granted this great privilege and was questioned by a thin, scatterbrained miss of fifty.

Now tell me, she said; what can you do?

He was embarrassed. I can write, he said pathetically.

You mean your penmanship is good? Is that it? said the elderly maiden.

Well, yes, he replied. But I mean that I can write.

Write what? said the miss, almost with anger.

Prose, he said simply.

There was a pause. At last the lady said:

Can you use a typewriter?

Of course, said the young man.

All right, went on the miss, we have your address; we will get in touch with you. There is nothing this morning, nothing at all.

It was much the same at the other agency, except that he was questioned by a conceited young man who closely resembled a pig. From the agencies he went to the large department stores: there was a good deal of pomposity, some humiliation on his part, and finally the report that work was not available. He did not feel displeased, and strangely did not even feel that he was personally involved in all the foolishness. He was a living young man who was in need of money with which to go on being one, and there was no way of getting it except by working for it; and there was no work. It was purely an abstract problem which he wished for the last time to attempt to solve. Now he was pleased that the matter was closed.

He began to perceive the definiteness of the course of his life. Except for moments, it had been largely artless, but now at the last minute he was determined that there should be as little imprecision as possible.

He passed countless stores and restaurants on his way to the Y.M.C.A., where he helped himself to paper and ink and began to compose his *Application.* For an hour he worked on this document, then suddenly, owing to the bad air in the place and to hunger, he became faint. He seemed to be swimming away from himself with great strokes, and hurriedly left the building. In the Civic Center Park, across from the Public Library Building, he drank almost a quart of water and felt himself refreshed. An old man was standing in the center of the brick boulevard surrounded by sea gulls, pigeons, and robins. He was taking handfuls of bread crumbs from a large paper sack and tossing them to the birds with a gallant gesture.

Dimly he felt impelled to ask the old man for a portion of the crumbs, but he did not allow the thought even nearly to reach consciousness; he entered the Public Library and for an hour read Proust, then, feeling himself to be swimming away again, he rushed outdoors. He drank more water at the fountain in the park and began the long walk to his room.

I'll go and sleep some more, he said; there is nothing else to do. He knew now that he was much too tired and weak to deceive himself about being all right, and yet his mind seemed somehow still lithe and alert. It, as if it were a separate entity, persisted in articulating impertinent pleasantries about his very real physical suffering. He reached his room early in the afternoon and immediately prepared coffee on the small gas range. There was no milk in the can, and the half pound of sugar he had purchased a week before was all gone; he drank a cup of the hot black fluid, sitting on his bed and smiling.

From the Y.M.C.A. he had stolen a dozen sheets of letter paper upon which he hoped to complete his document, but now the very notion of writing was unpleasant to him. There was nothing to say. He began to polish the penny he had found in the morning, and this absurd act somehow afforded him great enjoyment. No American coin can be made to shine so brilliantly as a penny. How many pennies would he need to go on living? Wasn't there something more he might sell? He looked about the bare room. No. His watch was gone; also his books. All those fine books; nine of them for eighty-five cents. He felt ill and ashamed for having parted with his books. His best suit he had sold for two dollars, but that was all right. He didn't mind at all about clothes. But the books. That was different. It made him very angry to think that there was no respect for men who wrote.

He placed the shining penny on the table, looking upon it with the delight of a miser. How prettily it smiles, he said. Without reading them he looked at the words, *E Pluribus Unum One Cent United States of America,* and turning the penny over, he saw Lincoln and the words, *In God We Trust Liberty 1923*. How beautiful it is, he said.

He became drowsy and felt a ghastly illness coming over his blood, a feeling of nausea and disintegration. Bewildered, he stood beside his bed, thinking there *is nothing to do but sleep*. Already he felt himself making great strides through the fluid of the earth, swimming away to the beginning. He fell face down upon the bed, saying, I ought first at least to give the coin to some child. A child could buy any number of things with a penny.

Then swiftly, neatly, with the grace of the young man on the trapeze, he was gone from his body. For an eternal moment he was all things at once: the bird, the fish, the rodent, the reptile, and man. An ocean of print undulated endlessly and darkly before him. The city burned. The herded crowd rioted. The earth circled away, and knowing that he did so, he turned his lost face to the empty sky and became dreamless, unalive, perfect.

A Worn Path

EUDORA WELTY

(1909–   )

It was December—a bright frozen day in the early morning. Far out in the country there was an old Negro woman with her head tied in a red rag, coming along a path through the pinewoods. Her name was Phoenix Jackson. She was very old and small and she walked slowly in the dark pine shadows, moving a little from side to side in her steps, with the balanced heaviness and lightness of a pendulum in a grandfather clock. She carried a thin, small cane made from an umbrella, and with this she kept tapping the frozen earth in front of her. This made a grave and persistent noise in the still air, that seemed meditative like the chirping of a solitary little bird.

She wore a dark striped dress reaching down to her shoe tops, and an equally long apron of bleached sugar sacks, with a full pocket: all neat and tidy, but every time she took a step she might have fallen over her shoe-laces, which dragged from her unlaced shoes. She looked straight ahead. Her eyes were blue with age. Her skin had a pattern all its own of numberless branching wrinkles and as though a whole little tree stood in the middle of her forehead, but a golden color ran underneath, and the two knobs of her cheeks were illuminated by a yellow burning under the dark. Under the red rag her hair came down on her neck in the frailest of ringlets, still black, and with an odor like copper.

Now and then there was a quivering in the thicket. Old Phoenix said, "Out of my way, all you foxes, owls, beetles, jack rabbits, coons, and wild animals! . . . Keep out from under these feet, little bob-whites. . . . Keep the big wild hogs out of my path. Don't let none of those come running my direction. I got a long way." Under her small black-freckled hand her cane, limber as a buggy whip, would switch at the brush as if to rouse up any hiding things.

On she went. The woods were deep and still. The sun made the pine needles almost too bright to look at, up where the wind rocked. The cones dropped as light as feathers. Down in the hollow was the mourning dove --it was not too late for him.

The path ran up a hill. "Seem like there is chains about my feet, time I get this far," she said, in the voice of argument old people keep to use with themselves. "Something always take a hold of me on this hill—pleads I should stay."

After she got to the top she turned and gave a full, severe look behind her where she had come. "Up through pines," she said at length. "Now down through oaks."

Her eyes opened their widest, and she started down gently. But before she got to the bottom of the hill a bush caught her dress.

Her fingers were busy and intent, but her skirts were full and long, so that before she could pull them free in one place they were caught in another. It was not possible to allow the dress to tear. "I in the thorny bush," she said. "Thorns, you doing your appointed work. Never want to let folks pass—no sir. Old eyes thought you was a pretty little *green* bush."

Finally, trembling all over, she stood free, and after a moment dared to stoop for her cane.

"Sun so high!" she cried, leaning back and looking, while the thick tears went over her eyes. "The time getting all gone here."

At the foot of this hill was a place where a log was laid across the creek.

"Now comes the trial," said Phoenix.

Putting her right foot out, she mounted the log and shut her eyes. Lifting her skirt, levelling her cane fiercely before her, like a festival figure in some parade, she began to march across. Then she opened her eyes and she was safe on the other side.

"I wasn't as old as I thought," she said.

But she sat down to rest. She spread her skirts on the bank around her and folded her hands over her knees. Up above her was a tree in a pearly cloud of mistletoe. She did not dare to close her eyes, and when a little boy brought her a little plate with a slice of marble-cake on it she spoke to him. "That would be acceptable," she said. But when she went to take it there was just her own hand in the air.

So she left that tree, and had to go through a barbed-wire fence. There she had to creep and crawl, spreading her knees and stretching her fingers like a baby trying to climb the steps. But she talked loudly to herself: she could not let her dress be torn now, so late in the day, and she could not pay for having her arm ar her leg sawed off if she got caught fast where she was.

At last she was safe through the fence and risen up out in the clearing. Big dead trees, like black men with one arm, were standing in the purple stalks of the withered cotton field. There sat a buzzard.

"Who you watching?"

In the furrow she made her way along.

"Glad this not the season for bulls," she said, looking sideways, "and the good Lord made his snakes to curl up and sleep in the winter. A pleasure I don't see no two-headed snake coming around that tree, where it come once. It took a while to get by him, back in the summer."

She passed through the old cotton and went into a field of dead corn. It whispered and shook and was taller than her head. "Through the maze now," she said, for there was no path.

Then there was something tall, black, and skinny there, moving before her.

At first she took it for a man. It could have been a man dancing in the field. But she stood still and listened, and it did not make a sound. It was as silent as a ghost.

"Ghost," she said sharply, "who be you the ghost of? For I have heard of nary death close by."

But there was no answer—only the ragged dancing in the wind.

She shut her eyes, reached out her hand, and touched a sleeve. She found a coat and inside that an emptiness, cold as ice.

"You scarecrow," she said. Her face lighted. "I ought to be shut up for good," she said with laughter. "My senses is gone. I too old. I the oldest people I ever know. Dance, old scarecrow," she said, "while I dancing with you."

She kicked her foot over the furrow, and with mouth drawn down, shook her head once or twice in a little strutting way. Some husks blew down and whirled in streamers about her skirts.

Then she went on, parting her way from side to side with the cane, through the whispering field. At last she came to the end, to a wagon track where the silver grass blew between the red ruts. The quail were walking around like pullets, seeming all dainty and unseen.

"Walk pretty," she said. "This the easy place. This the easy going."

She followed the track, swaying through the quiet bare fields, through the little strings of trees silver in their dead leaves, past cabins silver from weather, with the doors and windows boarded shut, all like old women under a spell sitting there. "I walking in their sleep," she said, nodding her head vigorously.

In a ravine she went where a spring was silently flowing through a hollow log. Old Phoenix bent and drank. "Sweet-gum makes the water sweet," she said, and drank more. "Nobody know who made this well, for it was here when I was born."

The track crossed a swampy part where the moss hung as white as lace from every limb. "Sleep on, alligators, and blow your bubbles." Then the track went into the road.

Deep, deep the road went down between the high green-colored banks. Overhead the live-oaks met, and it was as dark as a cave.

A black dog with a lolling tongue came up out of the weeds by the ditch. She was meditating, and not ready, and when he came at her she only hit him a little with her cane. Over she went in the ditch, like a little puff of milk-weed.

Down there, her senses drifted away. A dream visited her, and she reached her hand up, but nothing reached down and gave her a pull. So she lay there and presently went to talking. "Old woman," she said to herself, "that black dog come up out of the weeds to stall you off, and now there he sitting on his fine tail, smiling at you."

A white man finally came along and found her—a hunter, a young man, with his dog on a chain.

"Well, Granny!" he laughed. "What are you doing there?"

"Lying on my back like a June-bug waiting to be turned over, mister," she said, reaching up her hand.

He lifted her up, gave her a swing in the air, and set her down, "Anything broken, Granny?"

"No sir, them old dead weeds is springy enough," said Phoenix, when she had got her breath. "I thank you for your trouble."

"Where do you live, Granny?" he asked, while the two dogs were growling at each other.

"Away back yonder, sir, behind the ridge. You can't even see it from here."

"On your way home?"

"No, sir, I going to town."

"Why, that's too far! That's as far as I walk when I come out myself, and I get something for my trouble." He patted the stuffed bag he carried, and there hung down a little closed claw. It was one of the bob-whites, with its beak hooked bitterly to show it was dead. "Now you go on home, Granny!"

"I bound to go to town, mister," said Phoenix. "The time come around."

He gave another laugh, filling the whole landscape. "I know you old colored people! Wouldn't miss going to town to see Santa Claus!"

But something held Old Phoenix very still. The deep lines in her face went into a fierce and different radiation. Without warning, she had seen with her own eyes a flashing nickel fall out of the man's pocket onto the ground.

"How old are you, Granny?" he was saying.

"There is no telling, mister," she said, "no telling."

Then she gave a little cry and clapped her hands and said, "Git on away from here, dog! Look! Look at that dog!" She laughed as if in admiration. "He ain't scared of nobody. He a big black dog." She whispered, "Sic him!"

"Watch me get rid of that cur," said the man. "Sic him, Pete! Sic him!"

Phoenix heard the dogs fighting, and heard the man running and throwing sticks. She even heard a gunshot. But she was slowly bending forward by that time, further and further forward, the lids stretched down over her eyes, as if she were doing this in her sleep. Her chin was lowered almost to her knees. The yellow palm of her hand came out from the fold of her apron. Her fingers slid down and along the ground under the piece of money with the grace and care they would have in lifting an egg from under a sitting hen. Then she slowly straightened up, she stood erect, and the nickel was in her apron pocket. A bird flew by. Her lips moved. "God watching me the whole time. I come to stealing."

The man came back, and his own dog panted about them. "Well, I scared him off that time," he said, and then he laughed and lifted his gun and pointed it at Phoenix.

She stood straight and faced him.

"Doesn't the gun scare you?" he said, still pointing it.

"No, sir, I seen plenty go off closer by, in my day, and for less than what I done," she said, holding utterly still.

He smiled, and shouldered the gun. "Well, Granny," he said, "you must be a hundred years old, and scared of nothing. I'd give you a dime if

I had any money with me. But you take my advice and stay home, and nothing will happen to you."

"I bound to go on my way, mister," said Phoenix. She inclined her head in the red rag. Then they went in different directions, but she could hear the gun shooting again and again over the hill.

She walked on. The shadows hung from the oak trees to the road like curtains. Then she smelled wood-smoke, and smelled the river, and she saw a steeple and the cabins on their steep steps. Dozens of little black children whirled around her. There ahead was Natchez shining. Bells were ringing. She walked on.

In the paved city it was Christmas time. There were red and green electric lights strung crisscrossed everywhere, and all turned on in the daytime. Old Phoenix would have been lost if she had not distrusted her eyesight and depended on her feet to know where to take her.

She paused quietly on the sidewalk where people were passing by. A lady came along in the crowd, carrying an armful of red-, green-, and silver-wrapped presents; she gave off perfume like the red roses in hot summer, and Phoenix stopped her.

"Please, missy, will you lace up my shoe?" She held up her foot.

"What do you want, Grandma?"

"See my shoe," said Phoenix. "Do all right for out in the country, but wouldn't look right to go in a big building."

"Stand still then, Grandma," said the lady. She put her packages down on the sidewalk beside her and laced and tied both shoes tightly.

"Can't lace 'em with a cane," said Phoenix. "Thank you, missy. I doesn't mind asking a nice lady to tie up my shoe, when I gets out on the street."

Moving slowly and from side to side, she went into the big building and into a tower of steps, where she walked up and around and around until her feet knew to stop.

She entered a door, and there she saw nailed up on the wall the document that had been stamped with the gold seal and framed in the gold frame, which matched the dream that was hung up in her head.

"Here I be," she said. There was a fixed and ceremonial stiffness over her body.

"A charity case, I suppose," said an attendant who sat at the desk before her.

But Phoenix only looked above her head. There was sweat on her face, the wrinkles in her skin shone like a bright net.

"Speak up, Grandma," the woman said. "What's your name? We must have your history, you know. Have you been here before? What seems to be the trouble with you?"

Old Phoenix only gave a twitch to her face as if a fly were bothering her.

"Are you deaf?" cried the attendant.

But then the nurse came in.

"Oh, that's just old Aunt Phoenix," she said. "She doesn't come for herself—she has a little grandson. She makes these trips just as regular as clockwork. She lives away back off the Old Natchez Trace." She bent down. "Well, Aunt Phoenix, why don't you just take a seat? We won't keep you standing after your long trip." She pointed.

The old woman sat down, bolt upright in the chair.

"Now, how is the boy?" asked the nurse.

Old Phoenix did not speak.

"I said, how is the boy?"

But Phoenix only waited and stared straight ahead, her face very solemn and withdrawn into rigidity.

"Is his throat any better?" asked the nurse. "Aunt Phoenix, don't you hear me? Is your grandson's throat any better since the last time you came for the medicine?"

With her hands on her knees, the old woman waited, silent, erect and motionless, just as if she were in armour.

"You mustn't take up our time this way, Aunt Phoenix," the nurse said. "Tell us quickly about your grandson, and get it over. He isn't dead, is he?"

At last there came a flicker and then a flame of comprehension across her face, and she spoke.

"My grandson. It was my memory had left me. There I sat and forgot why I made my long trip."

"Forgot?" The nurse frowned. "After you came so far?"

Then Phoenix was like an old woman begging a dignified forgiveness for waking up frightened in the night. "I never did go to school, I was too old at the Surrender," she said in a soft voice. "I'm an old woman without an education. It was my memory fail me. My little grandson, he is just the same, and I forgot it in the coming."

"Throat never heals, does it?" said the nurse, speaking in a loud, sure voice to Old Phoenix. By now she had a card with something written on it, a little list. "Yes. Swallowed lye. When was it—January—two-three years ago—"

Phoenix spoke unasked now. "No, missy, he not dead, he just the same. Every little while his throat begin to close up again, and he not able to swallow. He not get his breath. He not able to help himself. So the time come around, and I go on another trip for the soothing medicine."

"All right. The doctor said as long as you came to get it, you could have it," said the nurse. "But it's an obstinate case."

"My little grandson, he sit up there in the house all wrapped up, waiting by himself," Phoenix went on. "We is the only two left in the world. He suffer and it don't seem to put him back at all. He got a sweet look. He going to last. He wear a little patch quilt and peep out holding his mouth open like a little bird. I remembers so plain now. I not going to forget him again, no, the whole enduring time. I could tell him from all the others in creation."

"All right." The nurse was trying to hush her now. She brought her a bottle of medicine. "Charity," she said, making a check mark in a book.

Old Phoenix held the bottle close to her eyes and then carefully put it into her pocket.

"I thank you," she said.

"It's Christmas time, Grandma," said the attendant. "Could I give you a few pennies out of my purse?"

"Five pennies is a nickel," said Phoenix stiffly.

"Here's a nickel," said the attendant.

Phoenix rose carefully and held out her hand. She received the nickel and then fished the other nickel out of her pocket and laid it beside the new one. She stared at her palm closely, with her head on one side.

Then she gave a tap with her cane on the floor.

"This is what come to me to do," she said. "I going to the store and buy my child a little windmill they sells, made out of paper. He going to find it hard to believe there such a thing in the world. I'll march myself back where he waiting, holding it straight up in this hand."

She lifted her free hand, gave a little nod, turned round, and walked out of the doctor's office. Then her slow step began on the stairs, going down.

The Night Club in the Woods

HORTENSE CALISHER
(1911–)

We first saw her, Mrs. Hawthorn, sitting alone, the first one down in the tender that waited to take us off the Bermuda boat. She was wearing a quilted taffeta suit, expensively flared at shoulder and hip, and a matching hat—one of those deep, real hats we were all wearing in the fall of 1935—and her arms were full, crammed full of tea roses. Under a city marquee, she would have had an enviable chic, but on the white deck of the tender, in the buttery Bermuda sun, she looked outlandishly urban for that travel-folder scene. As the rest of us climbed down into the tender, she made room for us with an apologetic shifting of the roses, but one could see, as she nestled her long, rouge-assisted face into the buds, that she was pleased with them.

Later on, in the week that followed, we saw her at our hotel, and Luke and I, drifting in the ambience of our honeymooners' table, idly watched her dinner entrances. Each evening, appearing late but consciously unflurried, in a different gown—one always too dominantly colorful and sparkling for the off-season crowd—she crossed to the table reserved for her and her companion, a dark, pear-shaped man, shorter than she, who received her with an anxious, hesitant courtesy.

On the first evening, Luke, nudging me, had pointed to the single bird-of-paradise bud with which the hotel kept the tables adorned, each beaked bloom soaring from its coarse glass holder like an immoderately hued bird, and every evening thereafter, the analogy had kept us amused. One evening, however, as she passed us, her tall, haggard figure sheathed in green sequins that boomeranged the light, a child at a nearby table cried out: "Look, Mommy! Christmas tree!" As she stopped, and bent toward the child, the sequins not quite concealing the middle-aged line from breast to hip, we heard her say, in a mellow voice, as if she were indulgently amused at both the child and herself—"Yes, darling! Christmas tree!"—and we felt ashamed, and liked her.

We met the two of them again, as we were all herded docilely into one of the glass-bottomed sightseeing boats, and she told us her name. The little man, tentative and deferential in the background, was one of those hovering people whose names one never catches, and we never did, although she told us it too. Again we saw her, alone on the beach in front of the hotel, in a maillot that was still somewhat scandalous for that time. We were a little embarrassed for her, not at the suit, but at its cruel, sagging revelation, and I remember that both of us, looking away with the instinctive distaste of the young for the fading, glanced down with satisfaction at our own bodies. One of her arms was covered almost from wrist to elbow with diamond and sapphire bracelets, and she must have seen me staring at them, or trying not to. She laughed, on the same mellow note.

"I'd feel naked without them." She turned, and slid into the water. She swam well, better than either of us, her long, water-sallowed face, which once must have been very handsome, sinking deep into the fervid blue of the water, the one mailed arm flashing in the sun.

In those days, the thing to do was to go down on the *Monarch* and come back on the *Queen*. The little stenographers squandering their vacation on off-season rates, an "interchangeable" wardrobe, and one shattering evening dress, the honeymooners, intent on seeming otherwise, all said it airily: "We came down on the *Monarch* and will go back on the *Queen*." On the return voyage, we met Mrs. Hawthorn and her vague companion again. The ship had run into bad weather, the usual October storms of the Caribbean, and at dinnertime, the little stenographers had been unable to appear in their evening dresses after all.

Luke had been affected too, although I was not. After dinner alone, I wandered into one of the ornate lounges that hollowed the ship. Seated in one of the gold chairs, her lamé gown blending so well that at first I did not see her, was Mrs. Hawthorn. She beckoned to me.

"I see you're a good sailor, too," she said. "I never get sick. Dave—the friend who is traveling with me—is down in his cabin." There was the slightest emphasis on "his." "Women are the stronger sex, I always say. You two are newlyweds, aren't you?"

"Yes."

"Look," she said. "Why don't you and your husband come up to my stateroom and have champagne. It's the best thing in the world for seasickness—and after all we really should celebrate for you two. Yes, do! We really must!"

I went down to our cabin, and roused Luke. "You think you're inveigling me," he said. "But it's really Mrs. Hawthorn who intrigues me."

We climbed the ladders from D deck to A. Up there, with no feel of more ship above us, the ocean, silhouetted against the looming slant of the stacks, seemed to shift its dark obliques more pervasively near us.

"The water seems more intimate up here with the rich, doesn't it?" I said.

"Hmmm," said Luke, "but it's not an intimacy I care to develop at the moment." I giggled, and lurching together, hip to hip, half with love, half with the movement of the deck, we entered Mrs. Hawthorn's stateroom.

The room was banked with flowers. Mrs. Hawthorn and her companion were waiting for us, sitting stiffly in the center of the blooms like unintroduced visitors in the anteroom of a funeral chapel. Wedged behind a coffee table blocked with bottles, Mrs. Hawthorn did not rise, but we greeted each other with that air of confederate gaiety adopted by hostess and guest at parties of whose success neither is sure. Across from her, behind an imitation hearth, a gas log burned insolently, as if a fireplace burning in the middle of the sea might serve to keep the elements in their place.

"Life on the hypotenuse," said Luke. He retrieved a bunch of gladioli, and set them back on the erring horizontal of a table.

Mrs. Hawthorn shifted her bracelets. "Dave is the florist in our home town—Hawthornton, Connecticut. I needed a rest, so Dave came down with me. Senator Hawthorn couldn't get away. He's the senator from there, you know."

Luke and I nodded, eager to let her see that we took her explanation at its face value, unwilling to appear abashed at the malpractices of the rich and worn. I imagined her life—the idle, probably childless woman, burdened with an exuberance no longer matched by her exterior, drawing toward her, with the sequins of wealth and difference, the self-conscious little man who was doggedly trying to fill the gap between them with the only largesse at his command—his abracadabra of flowers. Luke and I exchanged looks across the flowers, secure in our cocoon of beginnings, seeing before us an itinerary that repudiated compromise, and made no concessions to the temporal.

As we drank, the fraudulent solidity of the room was displaced now and again by a deep, visceral sway that drained the chair arms from beneath our digging fingers, and the wine seemed only to accentuate the irrationality of the four of us so transiently, so unsuitably met. At one point, Mrs. Hawthorn told the blond, mild-featured Luke that he had a "sulphurous" look, which roused us all to unsteady laughter, and again I remember her asking, with the gaucherie so denied by her appearance, if he were a "college man."

Then, suddenly, with an incredulous look on his face, Dave, the little man, stood up. Edging backwards, he felt for the doorknob, caught it, and disappeared around it. Ignoring his defection, the three of us sat on; then Luke, with a wild look at me, lurched through the flapping door and was gone.

Mrs. Hawthorn and I sat on for a moment, united in that smug matriarchy which joins women whose men have acted similarly and disgracefully. The heat from the burning log brought out the reek of the flowers, until it seemed to me that I had drunk perfume instead of champagne. Slowly the log up-ended and pointed toward the ceiling, but this too had slid far to the right, so that the room hung in a momentary armistice with the storm, the implacable hearth still glowing in its center. I stood up, and moved toward the door. It sidled toward me, and I achieved the corridor, but not before I had caught a last glimpse of Mrs. Hawthorn. She was sitting there like one of those children one often sees at dusk in the playground or the corner lot, still concentrated in fierce, solitary energy on the spinning top or the chalked squares of the deserted game, unwilling to admit the default of the others who have wilted, conceded in the afternoon's end, and acquiescently gone home.

By the time Luke and I had made our separate ways to the cabin, the ship had ridden out the storm area and was running smoothly. We would dock next morning in New York Harbor. We greeted each other, and slid limply into bed. Luke put his arms around me with a protectiveness tinged, I could not help thinking, with a relief that I had not proved so indomitable after all. For a second, I held him at arm's length. "Tell me first," I said. "Are you a college man?" Then we nestled together, in the excluding, sure laughter of the young.

At the docking the next day, we got through the lines early, without seeing anyone we knew. We had exchanged addresses with Mrs. Hawthorn, never really expecting to see her again, and in the busy weeks after, during which we returned to our jobs and our life together, we forgot her completely.

About a month later, sometime in November, we got a note from her, written in a large, wasteful hand on highly colored, expensive notepaper, and followed, when we did not immediately answer, by a phone call, during which her voice came over the wire as gaily insistent as before. Would we come up for dinner and stay the night? We accepted without particular consideration, partly out of a reawakened interest in her and what she would be like at home with the Senator, and partly because it was a place to go with the Chevvie—and no sense of the stringency of time had led us as yet to a carping evaluation of the people with whom we spent it.

On the way up that Saturday, a run of about seventy miles, we drove steadily through a long, umber autumn afternoon. At our left the sun dropped slowly, a red disc without penumbra. Along the country roads, the escarpments of pines and firs were black-green, with the somber deadness of a tyro's painting of Italy. Lights popped up in the soiled gray backs of towns, and a presage of winter tingled in our minds, its remembered icicle sliding down our spines. I was twenty-two, free, still catching up with a childhood where hot dogs had been forbidden. I made Luke stop for them twice. After that we drove silently, my head on Luke's shoulder. Inside the chugging little car, the heater warmed us; we were each with the one necessary person; we had made love the night before.

At seven, when we were expected, we were still twenty miles away. Luke stopped to phone. He came back to the car. "She says dinner will wait for us, not to rush. We're to go on to a night club afterwards."

In a second my mind had raked over everything in my suitcase, had placed me at the dinner table—perhaps not quite at the Senator's right—had moved me on to the little round table on the dance floor.

"I just remembered," I said. "I didn't put in my evening shoes."

"*I* just remembered," said Luke. "I didn't bring a proper tie."

We burst into laughter, "We'll swing round by way of New London," said Luke. "We can get things there."

When we got to the main street of the town, it was crowded, but the clothing stores were closing. Luke rushed into a haberdashery shop and came out with a tie. At the dark end of the shopping district we found a shoe store whose proprietor, counting stock in his dim interior, opened his locked door. I bought a pair of silver, girl-graduate sandals, the first pair he showed me. "Gee, lady," he said, as we whisked out of his shop, "I wish every lady was as quick as you."

Smiling to ourselves. we reentered the car. There was a charm that hung about us then, and we were not insensible of it, even aware that it had more to do with our situation than ourselves. We were still guests in the adult world of "lady" and "gentleman"; lightly we rode anchor in their harbor, partook of its perquisites, and escaped again to our enviable truancy. The rest of the world—we saw it in their faces—would be like us if it could. On the way through Hawthornton, I looked for a florist shop, but we passed too quickly by.

Five miles through the woodland of the Hawthorns' private road brought us to the house. There had been no others along the way. But the house that loomed before us, in a cleared area rather bleak and shrubless after the woods behind us, had no baronial mystery about it. By the lights under its porte-cochere, it looked to be about forty years old—one of those rambling, tasteless houses, half timbered, with thick stone porches, which "comfortably off" people built around the turn of the century, more for summer use, but providently made habitable for all year round. As we came to a stop under the porte-cochere, and the coupe's engine died, I heard the rushing sound of water, and saw that we seemed to be on the tip of a promontory that ended several hundred feet beyond.

"We on a lake?"

"Only the Atlantic," said Luke. "Don't you ever know where you are? We've been driving toward it all afternoon."

"Hardly ever," I said. "But we seem to be fated to meet Mrs. H. on one ocean or another."

A capped maid opened the door. Mrs. Hawthorn stood at the foot of the stairs to greet us. It was the first time I had seen her in black, a very low-cut, smart black, enlivened only by the cuff of bracelets on her right arm. It made her seem less of a "character," placing her almost in my mother's generation, although she may not have been quite that, and a little unsettling me. In my world, the different generations did not much visit each other, at least did not seek each other's company as she had ours.

She made a breezy stir of our welcome, giving us each a hand, directing the houseman as to our bags, referring us to separate corners for a wash. "Drinks in the dining room. See you there."

When we entered, she was seated at the long dining table, alone. Three places were set, not at the head, but down toward the middle, ours opposite hers. There was no evidence that anyone else was to dine, or had.

I remember nothing of the room, except my surprise. As we clicked glasses, were served, I tried to recall her voice as it had come over the wire to New York; certainly her airy chitchat had given me the impression that we were to be members of a house party. Otherwise, considering the gap between us of situation, money, age—how odd it was of her to have singled us out! Her conversation seemed to be newly flecked with slang, a kind of slang she perhaps thought we used. "That way for the johns," she had said, directing us to the bathrooms, and now, speaking of Bermuda, she asked us if we had not thought it "simply terrif." She had found European travel "rather a frost."

"I get more of a boot out of cutting a dash at home," she said, grinning.

A second manservant and maid were serving us. "I keep the estate staffed the way it's always been," she said. "Even though a good bit of the time it's only just me. Of course we've had to draw in our horns in lots of ways, like everyone else. But I've washed enough dishes in Hawthornton, I always say." She smiled down at her bracelets.

"Have you always lived in Hawthornton?" said Luke.

She nodded. "The Senator's people have always had the mills here.

The Hawthorn Knitting Mills. And my father was the town parson—also the town drunk. But I married the mill-owner's son." She chuckled, and we had to laugh with her, at the picture she drew for us. It was the same with all her allusions to her possessions—allusions which were frequent and childlike. As they ballooned into boasting, she pricked them, careful to show that she claimed no kind of eminence because of them.

What she did claim was the puzzling thing, for I felt that "the estate" meant something to her beyond the ordinary, and that her choice of our company was somehow connected with that meaning. Certainly she was shrewd enough to see that our scale of living was not hers, although for a while I dallied with the idea that a real social ignorance—that of the daughter of the down-at-the-heel parson, suddenly transmuted into the mill-owner's wife—had kept her insensitive to all the economic gradations between, had made her assume that because we were "college people," had been on the Bermuda boat, and had an anonymous East Side address, our jobs and our battered Chevvie were only our way of drawing in our horns. But she did not seem to be really interested in who we were, or what our parents had been. Something about what we had, or were now, had drawn her to us; in her queer little overtures of slang she seemed to be wistfully ranging herself on our side. But I did not know what she imagined "our side" to be.

We took our coffee in what she referred to as "the big room"—at first it was hard to categorize as anything else. Large as a hotel lounge, it had something of the same imperviousness to personality. Sofas and club chairs, stodgy but solid, filled its middle spaces: there was a grand piano at either end, and all along the edges, beneath the irregularly nooked windows, there were many worn wicker-and-chintz settees. But, looking further, I saw the dark bookshelves filled with Elbert Hubbard editions, the burnt-leather cushions, of the kind that last a lifetime, scattering the wicker, the ponderous floor lamps, whose parchment umbrella shades were bound with fringe—and I began to recognize the room for what it was. This was a room from which the stags' heads, the Tiffany glass had been cleared, perhaps, but it was still that room which lurked in albums and memoirs, behind pictures labeled *The Family at ——. Summer of 1910. Bottom row my son Ned, later to fall in the Ardennes, daughters Julie and Christine, and their school friend, Mary X, now wife of my son George.*

"I never did much to this room except put in the pianos," said Mrs. Hawthorn. "It's practically the same as when we got married, the year Harry's mother died, and he came back from France. We had some helluva parties here, though. Wonderful!" And now, as I followed her glance, I fancied that I detected in the room a faint, raffish overglaze of the early twenties, when I was too young to go to parties—here and there a hassock, still loudly black-and-white, a few of those ballerina book ends everyone used to have, and yes, there, hung in a corner, a couple of old batiks. Dozens of people could have sprawled here, the young men with their bell-bottomed trousers, the girls with their Tutankhamen eardrops, pointed pumps, and orange-ice-colored silk knees. The weathered wicker would have absorbed the spilled drinks without comment, and cigarette burns would have been hilariously added to the burnt-leather cushions. Yes, it could have been a hell of a room for a party.

Mrs. Hawthorn led us to the windows and pointed out into the dark, staring through it with the sure, commanding eye of the householder. "You can't see, of course, but we're on three bodies of water here—the river, the Sound, and the ocean. There's the end of the dock—the Coast Guard still ties up there once in a while, although we don't keep it up any more. When I was a kid, it used to be fitted out like a summer hotel. I used to swim around the point and watch them." Then, I thought, she would not have been one of the three little girls in the bottom row of the picture—she would never have been in that picture at all.

She closed the curtain. "Let me show you your room, then we'll be off." She led us upstairs, into a comfortable, nondescript bedroom. "That's my door, across the hall. Knock when you're ready."

"Oh, it won't take a minute to change," I said.

"Change? Dear, you don't have to change."

"Oh, but we've brought our evening things," I said. "It'll only take us a minute." There was a slight wail to my voice.

"Really it won't," said Luke. "We're awfully sorry if we've delayed you, but we'll rush."

We continued our protests for a minute, standing there in the hall. She leaned down and patted my shoulder, looking at me with that musing smile older women wore when they leaned over baby carriages. I had encountered that look often that year, among my mother's friends. "No, run along, and never mind," she said. "Nobody else is going to be there."

In front of the mirror in our room, I ran a comb through my curls. "Nobody who *is* anybody, I suppose she meant. I can't imagine why else she picked on us. And when I think of those awful shoes!"

"You can wear them at home," said Luke. "I like women to be flashy around the house. Come on, you look wonderful."

"I'm going to change to them anyway. They'll dance better."

"You'll only have to dance half the dances."

"Luke—" I slid my feet into the shoes and twisted to check my stocking seams. "Do you suppose that little man, Dave, will be there? Do you suppose we're being used as a sort of *cover?*"

He laughed. "I don't know. Come on."

"Don't you think it's funny she doesn't say where the Senator is? At least make his excuses or something?"

"Away on business, probably."

"Well, why isn't she in Washington with him, then? I would be—if it were you."

"Thank *you,*" he said. "But how come you got through college? There's no Connecticut senator to Washington named Hawthorn."

"Luke! I knew there was something fishy! Maybe there isn't any Senator. Or maybe he's divorced her, and nobody around here will know her. Or maybe she's a little off, from his being dead, and wants to go on pretending he's alive. With people like us—who wouldn't know."

He put back his head in laughter. "Now I know how you did get through college." He kissed the back of my neck, and pushed me through the door. "State senator, dope," he whispered, as we knocked at Mrs. Hawthorn's.

"Ready?" She opened the door and held it back in such a way that we knew we were to look in. "This is the only room I changed," she said. "I had it done again last year, the same way. I thought the man from Sloane would drop in his tracks when I insisted on the same thing. All that pink. Ninety yards of it in the curtains alone." She laughed, as she had done at the child in Bermuda. "Of course I had no idea back then . . . I thought it was lovely, so help me. And now I'm used to it."

We looked around. All that pink, as she had said. The room, from its shape, must be directly above the big room below; its great windows jutted out like a huge pink prow, overlooking the three bodies of water. Chairs with the sickly sheen of hard candy pursed their Louis Quatorze legs on a rose madder rug, under lamps the tinge of old powder puffs. There were a few glossy prints on the walls—nymphs couched like bonbons in ambiguous verdure. Marble putti held back the curtains, and each morning, between ninety yards of rosy lingerie, there would rise the craggy, seamed face of the sea.

Mrs. Hawthorn put her hand on one of the cherubs, and looked out. "We sailed from there on our honeymoon," she said. "On the old Hawthorns' yacht, right from the end of the dock. I remember thinking it would give, there were so many people on the end of it." She took a fur from a chair, slung it around her shoulders, and walked to the door. At the door, she turned back and surveyed the room. "Ain't it orful!" she said, in her normal voice. "Harry can't bear it."

She had two voices, I thought, as we followed her downstairs and got in the car she referred to as her runabout, that she'd made Harry give her in place of the chauffeur-driven Rolls. One voice for that tranced tale of first possession—when the house, the dock, the boudoir, Harry were new. And one for now—slangy, agnostic, amused.

She drove well, the way she swam, with a crisp, physical intensity. There had been bridle paths through these woods, she told us, but she hadn't really minded giving up the horses; swimming was the only thing she liked to do alone. She swam every day; it kept her weight down to the same as when she married. "You'll be having to pick yourself some exercise now too, honey," she said, sighing. "And stick to it the rest of your days."

We would turn on to the main road soon, I thought, probably to one of those roadhouses full of Saturday night daters such as Luke and I had been the year before, spinning out the evening on the cover charge and a couple of setups, and looking down our noses at the fat middle-agers who didn't have to watch the tab, but were such a nuisance on the floor.

The car veered suddenly to the left, and reduced speed. Now we seemed to be riding on one of the overgrown paths. Twigs whipped through the open window and slurred out again as we passed. Beside me, Luke rolled up the window. We were all in the front seat together. No one spoke.

We stopped. We must be in the heart of the woods, I thought. There was nothing except the blind probe of the headlamps against leaves, the scraping of the November wind.

"Guess the switch from the house doesn't work any more," she said, half to herself. She took a flashlight from the compartment. "Wait here," she said, and got out of the car. After she had gone, I opened the window and leaned across Luke, holding on to his hand. Above me, the stars were enlarged by the pure air. Off somewhere to the right, the flashlight made a weak, disappearing nimbus.

Then, suddenly, the woods were *en fête*. Festoons of lights spattered from tree to tree. Ahead of us, necromanced from the dark wood, the pattern of a house sprang on the air. After a moment our slow eyes saw that strings of lights garlanded its low log-cabin eaves, and twined up the two thick thrusts of chimney at either end. The flashlight wigwagged to us. We got out of the car, and walked toward it. Mrs. Hawthorn was leaning against one of the illuminated trees, looking up at the house. The furs slung back from her shoulders in a conqueror's arc. As we approached, she shook her head, in a swimmer's shake. "Well, ladies and gents," she said, in the cool, the vinaigrette voice, "here it is."

"Is it—is this the night club?" I said.

"This is it, baby," she said, and the way she said it made me feel as if she'd reached down and ruffled my curls. Instead, she reached up, and pressed a fuse box attached to the tree. For a minute, the red dazzle of the sign on the roof of the house made us blink. GINGER AND HARRY'S it said. There were one or two gaps in GINGER, and the second R of HARRY'S was gone, but the AND was perfect.

"Woods are death on electric lines," she said. Leading the way up the flagged path to the door, she bent down, muttering, and twitched at the weeds that had pushed up between the flags.

She unlocked the door. "We no longer heat it, of course. The pipes are drained. But I had them build fires this afternoon."

It was cold in the vestibule, just as it often was in the boxlike entrances of the roadhouses we knew, and, with its bare wood and plaster, it was just like them too—as if the flash and the jump were reserved for the sure customers inside. To our right was the hatcheck stall, with its brass tags hung on hooks, and a white dish for quarters and dimes.

"I never had any servants around here," said Mrs. Hawthorn. "The girls used to take turns in the cloakroom, and the men used to tumble over themselves for a chance to tend bar, or be bouncer. Lord, it was fun. We had a kid from Hollywood here one night, one of the Wampas stars, and we sneaked her in as ladies' matron, before anyone knew who she was. What a stampede there was, when the boys found out!"

I bent down to decipher a tiled plaque in the plaster, with three initials and a date—1918. Mrs. Hawthorn saw me looking at it.

"As my mother used to say," she said. "Never have your picture taken in a hat."

Inside, she showed us the lounges for the men and the women—the men's in red leather, hunting prints, and green baize. In the powder room, done in magenta and blue, with girandoles and ball fringe, with poufs and mirrored dressing tables, someone had hit even more precisely the exact note of the smart public retiring room—every woman a Pompadour, for ten minutes between dances.

"I did this all myself," she said. "From top to bottom. Harry had a bad leg when he came back—he was in an army hospital before we got married. He gave me my wedding present ahead of time—enough to remodel the old place, or build a new one. I surprised him. I built this place instead."

"Is his leg all right now?" I said.

"What?" she said.

"His leg. Is it all right now?"

"Yes, of course. That was donkey's years ago." She was vague, as if about a different person. Behind her, Luke shook his head at me.

"And now . . ." she said. "Now . . . come in where it's warm." And this time my ear picked up that tone of hers as it might a motif—that deep, rubato tone of possession fired by memory. She opened the door for us, but for a scant moment before, with her hand on the knob, she approached it as a curator might pause before his Cellini, or a hostess before the lion of her afternoon.

And here it was. The two fires burned at either end; the sultry hooded sidelights reflected here and there on the pale, unscarred dance floor. The little round tables were neatly stacked at its edge, all but one table that was set for service, as if now that it was 3 A.M. or four, the fat proprietor and his headwaiter might just be sitting down for their morning bowl of soup. On the wall, behind the tables, flickered the eternal mural, elongated bal-masqué figures and vaudeville backdrops, painted dim even when new, and never meant to be really seen. It could be the one of the harlequin-faced young men with top hats and canes, doing a soft-shoe routine against an after-dark sky. Or it might be the one of the tapering Venuses with the not-quite bodies, behind prussian-blue intimations of Versailles. It didn't matter. Here was the "Inn," the "Club," the "Spot," the Glen Island, where one danced to Ozzie Nelson, the Log Cabin at Armonk, the one near Rumson, with the hot guitarist, the innumerable ones where, for an evening or a week of evenings, Vincent Lopez's teeth glinted like piano keys under his mustache. The names would have varied somewhat from these names of the thirties, but here it was, with the orchestra shell waiting—the podium a little toward one end, so that the leader might ride sidesaddle, his suave cheek for the tables, his talented wrist for the band. Only the air was different, pure and still, without the hot, confectionery smell of the crowd. And the twin fires, though they were burning true and red, had fallen in a little, fallen back before the chill advance of the woods.

So, for the second time, we sat down to champagne with Mrs. Hawthorn. There was a big phonograph hidden in a corner; after a while she set it going, and we danced, Luke first with her, then with me. And now, as the champagne went to our heads, it was not the logs, or the chair arms that moved, but we who moved, looping and twirling to the succulent long-phrased music, laughing and excited with the extraordinary freedom of the floor. I thought of Dave, the little man, but Mrs. Hawthorn never mentioned his name. She was warm, gay—"like a young girl"—as I had heard it said now and then of an older woman. I had thought that this could not be so without grotesquerie, but now, with the wisdom of the wine, I imagined that it could—if it came from inside. She had the sudden, firm bloom of those people who really expand only in their own homes. For the first time, we were seeing her there.

Toward the evening's height, she brought out some old jazz records, made specially for her, with the drum and cymbal parts left out, and from the wings back of the podium she drew out the traps, the cymbals, and the snare. In the old days, she told us, everybody who came did a turn. The turn with the drums had been hers. We made her play some of the songs for us, songs I remembered, or thought I remembered, from childhood, things like *Dardanella* and *Jadda Jadda Jing Jing Jing*. She had some almost new ones too—*Melancholy Baby,* and *Those Little White Lies*. We gave her a big hand.

Then, just as we began to speak of tiring, of going to bed because we had to drive back early the next day, she let the drumsticks fall, and put her fingers to her mouth. "Why, I forgot it!" she said. "I almost forgot to show you the best thing of all!" She reached up with the other hand, and turned off the big spotlight over the orchestra shell.

Once more, only the sidelights glowed, behind their tinted shades. Then the center ceiling light began to move. I hadn't noticed it before; it was so much like what one expected of these places. That was the point—that it was. It was one of those fixtures made of several tiers of stained glass, with concealed slots of lights focused in some way, so that as it revolved, and the dancers revolved under it, bubbles of color would slide over their faces, run in chromatic patches over the tables, and dot the far corners of the room.

"Dance under it," she said. "I'll play for you." Obediently, we put our arms around one another, and danced. She played *Good Night, Ladies*. The drums hardly sounded at all. When it was over, she let the sticks rest in her lap. The chandelier turned, silently. Oval blobs of light passed over her face, greening it and flushing it like long, colored tears. Between the lights, I imagined that she was looking at us, as if she knew something about us that we ourselves did not know. "It was lovely," she said. "That first year." And this time I could not have said which of her two voices she had used.

We left early the next morning. By prearrangement, she was to sleep late and not bother about us, and in a sense we did not see her again. But, as we drove down the private road, we stopped for a moment at a gap in the trees, to see the sun shining, great, over the sea. There was a tall, gray matchstick figure on the end of the dock. As we watched, it dove. She could not have seen us; probably she would not have wanted to. She was doing the exercise to keep her weight down, perhaps, or swimming around the dock, as she had done as a child. Or perhaps she was doing the only thing she cared to do alone. It was certainly she. For as the figure came up, we saw its arm—the one mailed arm, flashing in the sun.

During the next few years I often used to tell the story of our visit to Hawthornton. So many casual topics brought it up so naturally—Bermuda, the people one meets when one travels, the magnified eccentricities of the rich. When it became fashionable to see the twenties as the great arterial spurt of the century's youth, I even told it that way, making her seem a symbol, a denizen of that time. I no longer speculated on why she had invited us; I never made that the point of the story. But for some time now I have known why, and now that I do, I know how to tell her story at last. For now that I know why, it is no longer Mrs. Hawthorn's story. It is ours.

It is almost eighteen years since we were at Mrs Hawthorn's, just as it was then almost eighteen years since Harry had come back from France. I was never to meet anyone who knew them, nor was I ever to see her again. But I know now that there was never any special mystery about her and Harry. Only the ordinary mystery of the distance that seeps between people, even while they live and lie together as close as knives.

Luke is in the garden now. His face passes the window, intent on raking the leaves. Yet he is as far from me now as ever Harry was from Hawthornton, wherever Harry was that day. He and I are not rich; we do not have the externalizations of the rich. Yet, silently, silently, we too have drawn in our horns.

So, sometimes, when I walk in the woods near our house, it is to a night club that I walk. I sit down on a patch of moss, and I am sitting at the little round table on the unscarred floor. I fold my hands. Above me, the glass dome turns. I watch them—the two people, about whom I know something they themselves do not know. This is what I see:

It is a long, umber autumn afternoon. To the left the sun drops slowly, a red disc without penumbra. Along the country roads, the pines and firs are black-green, with the somber deadness of a tyro's painting of Italy. Lights pop up in the soiled gray backs of towns. Inside the chugging little car the heater warms them; they are each with the one necessary person; they have made love the night before. The rest of the world, if it could, would be like them.

Torch Song

JOHN CHEEVER

(1912–)

After Jack Lorey had known Joan Harris in New York for a few years, he began to think of her as the Widow. She always wore black, and he was always given the feeling, by a curious disorder in her apartment, that the undertakers had just left. This impression did not stem from malice on his part, for he was fond of Joan. They came from the same city in Ohio and had reached New York at about the same time in the middle thirties. They were the same age, and during their first summer in the city they used to meet after work and drink Martinis in places like the Brevoort and Charles', and have dinner and play checkers at the Lafayette.

Joan went to a school for models when she settled in the city, but it turned out that she photographed badly, so after spending six weeks learning how to walk with a book on her head she got a job as a hostess in a Longchamps. For the rest of the summer she stood by the hatrack, bathed in an intense pink light and the string music of heartbreak, swinging her mane of dark hair and her black skirt as she moved forward to greet the customers. She was then a big, handsome girl with a wonderful voice, and her face, her whole presence, always seemed infused with a gentle and healthy pleasure at her surroundings, whatever they were. She was innocently and incorrigibly convivial, and would get out of bed and dress at three in the morning if someone called her and asked her to come out for a drink, as Jack often did. In the fall, she got some kind of freshman executive job in a department store. They saw less and less of each other and then for quite a while stopped seeing each other altogether. Jack was living with a girl he had met at a party, and it never occurred to him to wonder what had become of Joan.

Jack's girl had some friends in Pennsylvania, and in the spring and summer of his second year in town he often went there with her for weekends. All of this—the shared apartment in the Village, the illicit relationship, the Friday-night train to a country house—was what he had imagined life in New York to be, and he was intensely happy. He was returning to New York with his girl one Sunday night on the Lehigh line. It was one of those trains that move slowly across the face of New Jersey, bringing back to the city hundreds of people, like the victims of an immense and strenuous picnic, whose faces are blazing and whose muscles are lame. Jack and his girl, like most of the other passengers, were overburdened with vegetables and flowers. When the train stopped in Pennsylvania Station, they moved with the crowd along the platform, toward the escalator. As they were passing the wide, lighted windows of the diner, Jack turned his head and saw Joan. It was the first time he had seen her since Thanksgiving, or since Christmas. He couldn't remember.

Joan was with a man who had obviously passed out. His head was in his arms on the table, and an overturned highball glass was near one of his elbows. Joan was shaking his shoulders gently and speaking to him. She seemed to be vaguely troubled, vaguely amused. The waiters had cleared off all the other tables and were standing around Joan, waiting for her to resurrect her escort. It troubled Jack to see in these straits a girl who reminded him of the trees and the lawns of his home town, but there was nothing he could do to help. Joan continued to shake the man's shoulders, and the crowd pressed Jack past one after another of the diner's windows, past the malodorous kitchen, and up the escalator.

He saw Joan again, later that summer, when he was having dinner in a Village restaurant. He was with a new girl, a Southerner. There were many Southern girls in the city that year. Jack and his belle had wandered into the restaurant because it was convenient, but the food was terrible and the place was lighted with candles. Halfway through dinner, Jack noticed Joan on the other side of the room, and when he had finished eating, he crossed the room and spoke to her. She was with a tall man who was wearing a monocle. He stood, bowed stiffly from the waist, and said to Jack, "We are very pleased to meet you." Then he excused himself and headed for the toilet. "He's a count, he's a Swedish count," Joan said. "He's on the radio, Friday afternoons at four-fifteen. Isn't it exciting?" She seemed to be delighted with the count and the terrible restaurant.

Sometime the next winter, Jack moved from the Village to an apartment in the East Thirties. He was crossing Park Avenue one cold morning on his way to the office when he noticed, in the crowd, a woman he had a met a few times at Joan's apartment. He spoke to her and asked about his friend. "Haven't you heard?" she said. She pulled a long face. "Perhaps I'd better tell you. Perhaps you can help." She and Jack had breakfast in a drugstore on Madison Avenue and she unburdened herself of the story.

The count had a program called "The Song of the Fiords," or something like that, and he sang Swedish folk songs. Everyone suspected him of being a fake, but that didn't bother Joan. He had met her at a party and, sensing a soft touch, had moved in with her the following night. About a week later, he complained of pains in his back and said he must have some morphine. Then he needed morphine all the time. If he didn't get morphine, he was abusive and violent. Joan began to deal with those doctors and druggists who peddle dope, and when they wouldn't supply her, she went down to the bottom of the city. Her friends were afraid she would be found some morning stuffed in a drain. She got pregnant. She had an abortion. The count left her and moved to a flea bag near Times Square, but she was so impressed by then with his helplessness, so afraid that he would die without her, that she followed him there and shared his room and continued to buy his narcotics. He abandoned her again, and Joan waited a week for him to return before she went back to her place and her friends in the Village.

It shocked Jack to think of the innocent girl from Ohio having lived with a brutal dope addict and traded with criminals, and when he got to his office that morning, he telephoned her and made a date for dinner that night. He met her at Charles'. When she came into the bar, she seemed as wholesome and calm as ever. Her voice was sweet, and reminded him of elms, of lawns, of those glass arrangements that used to be hung from porch ceilings to tinkle in the summer wind. She told him about the count. She spoke of him charitably and with no trace of bitterness, as if her voice, her disposition, were incapable of registering anything beyond simple affection and pleasure. Her walk, when she moved ahead of him toward their table, was light and graceful. She ate a large dinner and talked enthusiastically about her job. They went to a movie and said goodbye in front of her apartment house.

That winter, Jack met a girl he decided to marry. Their engagement was announced in January and they planned to marry in July. In the spring, he received, in his office mail, an invitation to cocktails at Joan's. It was for a Saturday when his fiancée was going to Massachusetts to visit her parents, and when the time came and he had nothing better to do, he took a bus to the Village. Joan had the same apartment. It was a walk-up. You rang the bell above the mailbox in the vestibule and were answered with a death rattle in the lock. Joan lived on the third floor. Her calling card was in a slot in the mailbox, and above her name was written the name Hugh Bascomb.

Jack climbed the two flights of carpeted stairs, and when he reached Joan's apartment, she was standing by the open door in a black dress. After she greeted Jack, she took his arm and guided him across the room. "I want you to meet Hugh, Jack," she said.

Hugh was a big man with a red face and pale-blue eyes. His manner was courtly and his eyes were inflamed with drink. Jack talked with him for a little while and then went over to speak to someone he knew, who was standing by the mantelpiece. He noticed then, for the first time, the indescribable disorder of Joan's apartment. The books were in their shelves and the furniture was reasonably good, but the place was all wrong, somehow. It was as if things had been put in place without thought or real interest, and for the first time, too, he had the impression that there had been a death there recently.

As Jack moved around the room, he felt that he had met the ten or twelve guests at other parties. There was a woman executive with a fancy hat, a man who could imitate Roosevelt, a grim couple whose play was in rehearsal, and a newspaperman who kept turning on the radio for news of the Spanish Civil War. Jack drank Martinis and talked with the woman in the fancy hat. He looked out of the window at the back yards and the ailanthus trees and heard, in the distance, thunder exploding off the cliffs of the Hudson.

Hugh Bascomb got very drunk. He began to spill liquor, as if drinking, for him, were a kind of jolly slaughter and he enjoyed the bloodshed and the mess. He spilled whiskey from a bottle. He spilled a drink on his shirt and then tipped over someone else's drink. The party was not quiet, but Hugh's hoarse voice began to dominate the others. He attacked a photographer who was sitting in a corner explaining camera techniques to a homely woman. "What did you come to the party for if all you wanted to do was to sit there and stare at your shoes?" Hugh shouted. "What did you come for? Why don't you stay at home?"

The photographer didn't know what to say. He was not staring at his shoes. Joan moved lightly to Hugh's side. "Please don't get into a fight now, darling," she said. "Not this afternoon."

"Shut up," he said. "Let me alone. Mind your own business." He lost his balance, and in struggling to steady himself he tipped over a lamp.

"Oh, your lovely lamp, Joan," a woman sighed.

"Lamps!" Hugh roared. He threw his arms into the air and worked them around his head as if he were bludgeoning himself. "Lamps. Glasses. Cigarette boxes. Dishes. They're killing me. They're killing me, for Christ's sake. Let's all go up to the mountains and hunt and fish and live like men, for Christ's sake."

People were scattering as if a rain had begun to fall in the room. It had, as a matter of fact, begun to rain outside. Someone offered Jack a ride uptown, and he jumped at the chance. Joan stood at the door, saying goodbye to her routed friends. Her voice remained soft, and her manner, unlike that of those Christian women who in the face of disaster can summon new and formidable sources of composure, seemed genuinely simple. She appeared to be oblivious of the raging drunk at her back, who was pacing up and down, grinding glass into the rug, and haranguing one of the survivors of the party with a story of how he, Hugh, had once gone without food for three weeks.

In July, Jack was married in an orchard in Duxbury, and he and his wife went to West Chop for a few weeks. When they returned to town, their apartment was cluttered with presents, including a dozen after-dinner coffee cups from Joan. His wife sent her the required note, but they did nothing else.

Late in the summer, Joan telephoned Jack at his office and asked if he wouldn't bring his wife to see her; she named an evening the following week. He felt guilty about not having called her, and accepted the invitation. This made his wife angry. She was an ambitious girl who liked a social life that offered rewards, and she went unwillingly to Joan's Village apartment with him.

Written above Joan's name on the mailbox was the name Franz Denzel. Jack and his wife climbed the stairs and were met by Joan at the open door. They went into her apartment and found themselves among a group of people for whom Jack, at least, was unable to find any bearings.

Franz Denzel was a middle-aged German. His face was pinched with bitterness or illness. He greeted Jack and his wife with that elaborate and clever politeness that is intended to make guests feel that they have come too early or too late. He insisted sharply upon Jack's sitting in the chair in which he himself had been sitting, and then went and sat on a radiator. There were five other Germans sitting around the room, drinking coffee. In a corner was another American couple, who looked uncomfortable. Joan passed Jack and his wife small cups of coffee with whipped cream. "These cups belonged to Franz's mother," she said. "Aren't they lovely? They were the only things he took from Germany when he escaped from the Nazis."

Franz turned to Jack and said, "Perhaps you will give us your opinion on the American educational system. That is what we were discussing when you arrived."

Before Jack could speak, one of the German guests opened an attack on the American educational system. The other Germans joined in, and went on from there to describe every vulgarity that had impressed them in American life and to contrast German and American culture generally. Where, they asked one another passionately, could you find in America anything like the Mitropa dining cars, the Black Forest, the pictures in Munich, the music in Bayreuth? Franz and his friends began speaking in

German. Neither Jack nor his wife nor Joan could understand German, and the other American couple had not opened their mouths since they were introduced. Joan went happily around the room, filling everyone's cup with coffee, as if the music of a foreign language were enough to make an evening for her.

Jack drank five cups of coffee. He was desperately uncomfortable. Joan went into the kitchen while the Germans were laughing at their German jokes, and he hoped she would return with some drinks, but when she came back, it was with a tray of ice cream and mulberries.

"Isn't this pleasant?" Franz asked, speaking in English again.

Joan collected the coffee cups, and as she was about to take them back to the kitchen, Franz stopped her.

"Isn't one of those cups chipped?"

"No, darling," Joan said. "I never let the maid touch them. I wash them myself."

"What's that?" he asked, pointing at the rim of one of the cups.

"That's the cup that's always been chipped, darling. It was chipped when you unpacked it. You noticed it then."

"These things were perfect when they arrived in this country," he said.

Joan went into the kitchen and he followed her.

Jack tried to make conversation with the Germans. From the kitchen there was the sound of a blow and a cry. Franz returned and began to eat his mulberries greedily. Joan came back with her dish of ice cream. Her voice was gentle. Her tears, if she had been crying, had dried as quickly as the tears of a child. Jack and his wife finished their ice cream and made their escape. The wasted and unnerving evening enraged Jack's wife, and he supposed that he would never see Joan again.

Jack's wife got pregnant early in the fall, and she seized on all the prerogatives of an expectant mother. She took long naps, ate canned peaches in the middle of the night, and talked about the rudimentary kidney. She chose to see only other couples who were expecting children, and the parties that she and Jack gave were temperate. The baby, a boy, was born in May, and Jack was very proud and happy. The first party he and his wife went to after her convalescence was the wedding of a girl whose family Jack had known in Ohio.

The wedding was at St. James's, and afterward there was a big reception at the River Club. There was an orchestra dressed like Hungarians, and a lot of champagne and Scotch. Toward the end of the afternoon, Jack was walking down a dim corridor when he heard Joan's voice. "Please don't, darling," she was saying. "You'll break my arm. *Please* don't, darling." She was being pressed against the wall by a man who seemed to be twisting her arm. As soon as they saw Jack, the struggle stopped. All three of them were intensely embarrassed. Joan's face was wet and she made an effort to smile through her tears at Jack. He said hello and went on without stopping. When he returned, she and the man had disappeared.

When Jack's son was less than two years old, his wife flew with the baby to Nevada to get a divorce. Jack gave her the apartment and all its furnishings and took a room in a hotel near Grand Central. His wife got her decree in due course, and the story was in the newspapers. Jack had a telephone call from Joan a few days later.

"I'm awfully sorry to hear about your divorce, Jack," she said. "She seemed like *such* a nice girl. But that wasn't what I called you about. I want your help, and I wondered if you could come down to my place tonight around six. It's something I don't want to talk about over the phone."

He went obediently to the Village that night and climbed the stairs. Her apartment was a mess. The pictures and the curtains were down and the books were in boxes. "You moving, Joan?" he asked.

"That's what I wanted to see you about, Jack. First, I'll give you a drink." She made two Old-Fashioneds. "I'm being evicted, Jack," she said. "I'm being evicted because I'm an immoral woman. The couple who have the apartment downstairs—they're charming people, I've always thought—have told the real-estate agent that I'm a drunk and a prostitute and all kinds of things. Isn't that fantastic? This real-estate agent has always been so nice to me that I didn't think he'd believe them, but he's canceled my lease, and if I make any trouble, he's threatened to take the matter up with the store, and I don't want to lose my job. This nice real-estate agent won't even talk with me any more. When I go over to the office, the receptionist leers at me as if I were some kind of dreadful woman. Of course, there have been a lot of men here and we sometimes are noisy, but I can't be expected to go to bed at ten every night. Can I? Well, the agent who manages this building has apparently told all the other agents in the neighborhood that I'm an immoral and drunken woman, and none of them will give me an apartment. I went in to talk with one man—he seemed to be such a nice old gentleman—and he made me an indecent proposal. Isn't it fantastic? I have to be out of here on Thursday and I'm literally being turned out into the street."

Joan seemed as serene and innocent as ever while she described this scourge of agents and neighbors. Jack listened carefully for some sign of indignation or bitterness or even urgency in her recital, but there was none. He was reminded of a torch song, of one of those forlorn and touching ballads that had been sung neither for him nor for her but for their older brothers and sisters by Marion Harris. Joan seemed to be singing her wrongs.

"They've made my life miserable," she went on quietly. "If I keep the radio on after ten o'clock, they telephone the agent in the morning and tell him I had some kind of orgy here. One night when Philip—I don't think you've met Philip; he's in the Royal Air Force; he's gone back to England—one night when Philip and some other people were here, they called the police. The police came bursting in the door and talked to me as if I were I don't know what and then looked in the bedroom. If they think there's a man up here after midnight, they call me on the telephone and say all kinds of disgusting things. Of course, I can put my furniture into storage and go to a hotel, I guess. I guess a hotel will take a woman with my kind of reputation, but I thought perhaps you might know of an apartment. I thought—"

It angered Jack to think of this big, splendid girl's being persecuted by her neighbors, and he said he would do what he could. He asked her to have dinner with him, but she said she was busy.

Having nothing better to do, Jack decided to walk uptown to his hotel. It was a hot night. The sky was overcast. On his way, he saw a parade in a dark side street off Broadway near Madison Square. All the buildings in the neighborhood were dark. It was so dark that he could not see the placards the marchers carried until he came to a street light. Their signs urged the entry of the United States into the war, and each platoon represented a nation that had been subjugated by the Axis powers. They marched up Broadway, as he watched, to no music, to no sound but their own steps on the rough cobbles. It was for the most part an army of elderly men and women—Poles, Norwegians, Danes, Jews, Chinese. A few idle people like himself lined the sidewalks, and the marchers passed between them with all the self-consciousness of enemy prisoners. There were children among them dressed in the costumes in which they had, for the newsreels, presented the Mayor with a package of tea, a petition, a protest, a constitution, a check, or a pair of tickets. They hobbled through the darkness of the loft neighborhood like a mortified and destroyed people, toward Greeley Square.

In the morning, Jack put the problem of finding an apartment for Joan up to his secretary. She started phoning real-estate agents, and by afternoon she had found a couple of available apartments in the West Twenties. Joan called Jack the next day to say that she had taken one of the apartments and to thank him.

Jack didn't see Joan again until the following summer. It was a Sunday evening; he had left a cocktail party in a Washington Square apartment and had decided to walk a few blocks up Fifth Avenue before he took a bus. As he was passing the Brevoort, Joan called to him. She was with a man at one of the tables on the sidewalk. She looked cool and fresh, and the man appeared to be respectable. His name, it turned out, was Pete Bristol. He invited Jack to sit down and join in a celebration. Germany had invaded Russia that weekend, and Joan and Pete were drinking champagne to celebrate Russia's changed position in the war. The three of them drank champagne until it got dark. They had dinner and drank champagne with their dinner. They drank more champagne afterward and then went over to the Lafayette and then to two or three other places. Joan had always been tireless in her gentle way. She hated to see the night end, and it was after three o'clock when Jack stumbled into his apartment. The following morning he woke up haggard and sick, and with no recollection of the last hour or so of the previous evening. His suit was soiled and he had lost his hat. He didn't get to his office until eleven. Joan had already called him twice, and she called him again soon after he got in. There was no hoarseness at all in her voice. She said that she had to see him, and he agreed to meet her for lunch in a seafood restaurant in the Fifties.

He was standing at the bar when she breezed in, looking as though she had taken no part in that calamitous night. The advice she wanted concerned selling her jewelry. Her grandmother had left her some jewelry, and she wanted to raise money on it but didn't know where to go. She took some rings and bracelets out of her purse and showed them to Jack. He said that he didn't know anything about jewelry but that he could lend her some money. "Oh, I couldn't borrow money from you, Jack," she said. "You see, I want to get the money for Pete. I want to help him. He wants to open an advertising agency, and he needs quite a lot to begin with." Jack didn't press her to accept his offer of a loan after that, and the project wasn't mentioned again during lunch.

He next heard about Joan from a young doctor who was a friend of theirs. "Have you seen Joan recently?" the doctor asked Jack one evening when they were having dinner together. He said no. "I gave her a checkup last week," the doctor said, "and while she's been through enough to kill the average mortal—and you'll never know what she's been through—she still has the constitution of a virtuous and healthy woman. Did you hear about the last one? She sold her jewelry to put him into some kind of business, and as soon as he got the money, he left her for another girl, who had a car—a convertible."

Jack was drafted into the Army in the spring of 1942. He was kept at Fort Dix for nearly a month, and during this time he came to New York in the evening whenever he could get permission. Those nights had for him the intense keenness of a reprieve, a sensation that was heightened by the fact that on the train in from Trenton women would often press upon him dog-eared copies of *Life* and half-eaten boxes of candy, as though the brown clothes he wore were surely cerements. He telephoned Joan from Pennsylvania Station one night. "Come right over, Jack," she said. "Come right over. I want you to meet Ralph."

She was living in that place in the West Twenties that Jack had found for her. The neighborhood was a slum. Ash cans stood in front of her house, and an old woman was there picking out bits of refuse and garbage and stuffing them into a perambulator. The house in which Joan's apartment was located was shabby, but the apartment itself seemed familiar. The furniture was the same. Joan was the same big, easygoing girl. "I'm so glad you called me," she said. "It's so good to see you. I'll make you a drink. I was having one myself. Ralph ought to be here by now. He promised to take me to dinner." Jack offered to take her to Cavanagh's, but she said that Ralph might come while she was out. "If he doesn't come by nine, I'm going to make myself a sandwich. I'm not really hungry."

Jack talked about the Army. She talked about the store. She had been working in the same place for—how long was it? He didn't know. He had never seen her at her desk and he couldn't imagine what she did. "I'm terribly sorry Ralph isn't here," she said. "I'm sure you'd like him. He's not a young man. He's a heart specialist who loves to play the viola." She turned on some lights, for the summer sky had got dark. "He has this dreadful wife on Riverside Drive and four ungrateful children. He—"

The noise of an air-raid siren, lugubrious and seeming to spring from pain, as if all the misery and indecision in the city had been given a voice, cut her off. Other sirens, in distant neighborhoods, sounded, until the dark air was full of their noise. "Let me fix you another drink before I have to turn out the lights," Joan said, and took his glass. She brought the drink back to him and snapped off the lights. They went to the windows, and, as children watch a thunderstorm, they watched the city darken. All the lights nearby went out but one. Air-raid wardens had begun to sound their whistles in the street. From a distant yard came a hoarse shriek of anger. "Put out your lights, you Fascists!" a woman screamed. "Put out your lights, you Nazi Fascist Germans. Turn out your lights. Turn out your lights." The last light went off. They went away from the window and sat in the lightless room.

In the darkness, Joan began to talk about her departed lovers, and from what she said Jack gathered that they had all had a hard time. Nils, the suspect count, was dead. Hugh Bascomb, the drunk, had joined the Merchant Marine and was missing in the North Atlantic. Franz, the German, had taken poison the night the Nazis bombed Warsaw. "We listened to the news on the radio," Joan said, "and then he went back to his hotel and took poison. The maid found him dead in the bathroom the next morning." When Jack asked her about the one who was going to open an advertising agency, she seemed at first to have forgotten him. "Oh, Pete," she said after a pause. "Well, he was always very sick, you know. He was supposed to go to Saranac, but he kept putting it off and putting it off and–" She stopped talking when she heard steps on the stairs, hoping, he supposed, that it was Ralph, but whoever it was turned at the landing and continued to the top of the house. "I wish Ralph would come," she said, with a sigh. "I want you to meet him." Jack asked her again to go out, but she refused, and when the all-clear sounded, he said goodbye.

Jack was shipped from Dix to an infantry training camp in the Carolinas and from there to an infantry division stationed in Georgia. He had been in Georgia three months when he married a girl from the Augusta boarding-house aristocracy. A year or so later, he crossed the continent in a day coach and thought sententiously that the last he might see of the country he loved was the desert towns like Barstow, that the last he might hear of it was the ringing of the trolleys on the Bay Bridge. He was sent into the Pacific and returned to the United States twenty months later, uninjured and apparently unchanged. As soon as he received his furlough, he went to Augusta. He presented his wife with the souvenirs he had brought from the islands, quarreled violently with her and all her family, and, after making arrangements for her to get an Arkansas divorce, left for New York.

Jack was discharged from the Army at a camp in the East a few months later. He took a vacation and then went back to the job he had left in 1942. He seemed to have picked up his life at approximately the moment when it had been interrupted by the war. In time, everything came to look and feel the same. He saw most of his old friends. Only two of the men he knew had been killed in the war. He didn't call Joan, but he met her one winter afternoon on a crosstown bus.

Her fresh face, her black clothes, and her soft voice instantly destroyed the sense–if he had ever had such a sense–that anything had changed or intervened since their last meeting, three or four years ago. She asked him up for cocktails and he went to her apartment the next Saturday afternoon. Her room and her guests reminded him of the parties she had given when she had first come to New York. There was a woman with a fancy hat, an elderly doctor, and a man who stayed close to the radio, listening for news from the Balkans. Jack wondered which of the men belonged to Joan and decided on an Englishman who kept coughing into a handkerchief that he pulled out of his sleeve. Jack was right. "Isn't Stephen brilliant?" Joan asked him a little later, when they were alone in a corner. "He knows more about the Polynesians than anyone else in the world."

Jack had returned not only to his old job but to his old salary. Since living costs had doubled and since he was paying alimony to two wives, he had to draw on his savings. He took another job, which promised more money, but it didn't last long and he found himself out of work. This didn't bother him at all. He still had money in the bank, and anyhow it was easy to borrow from friends. His indifference was the consequence not of lassitude or despair but rather of an excess of hope. He had the feeling that he had only recently come to New York from Ohio. The sense that he was very young and that the best years of his life still lay before him was an illusion that he could not seem to escape. There was all the time in the world. He was living in hotels then, moving from one to another every five days.

In the spring, Jack moved to a furnished room in the badlands west of Central Park. He was running out of money. Then, when he began to feel that a job was a desperate necessity, he got sick. At first, he seemed to have only a bad cold, but he was unable to shake it and he began to run a fever and to cough blood. The fever kept him drowsy most of the time, but he roused himself occasionally and went out to a cafeteria for a meal. He felt sure that none of his friends knew where he was, and he was glad of this. He hadn't counted on Joan.

Late one morning, he heard her speaking in the hall with his landlady. A few moments later, she knocked on his door. He was lying on the bed in a pair of pants and a soiled pajama top, and he didn't answer. She knocked again and walked in. "I've been looking everywhere for you, Jack," she said. She spoke softly. "When I found out that you were in a place like this I thought you must be broke or sick. I stopped at the bank and got some money, in case you're broke. I've brought you some Scotch. I thought a little drink wouldn't do you any harm. Want a little drink?"

Joan's dress was black. Her voice was low and serene. She sat in a chair beside his bed as if she had been coming there every day to nurse him. Her features had coarsened, he thought, but there were still very few lines in her face. She was heavier. She was nearly fat. She was wearing black cotton gloves. She got two glasses and poured Scotch into them. He drank his whiskey greedily. "I didn't get to bed until three last night," she said. Her voice had once before reminded him of a gentle and despairing song, but now, perhaps because he was sick, her mildness, the mourning she wore, her stealthy grace, made him uneasy. "It was one of those nights," she said. "We went to the theatre. Afterward, someone asked us up to his place. I don't know who he was. It was one of those places. They're so strange. There were some meat-eating plants and a collection of Chinese snuff bottles. Why do people collect Chinese snuff bottles? We all autographed a lampshade, as I remember, but I can't remember much."

Jack tried to sit up in bed, as if there were some need to defend himself, and then fell back again, against the pillows. "How did you find me, Joan?" he asked.

"It was simple," she said. "I called that hotel. The one you were staying in. They gave me this address. My secretary got the telephone number. Have another little drink."

"You know, you've never come to a place of mine before—never," he said. "Why did you come now?"

"Why did I come, darling?" she asked. "What a question! I've known you for thirty years. You're the oldest friend I have in New York. Remember that night in the Village when it snowed and we stayed up until morning and drank whiskey sours for breakfast? That doesn't seem like twelve years ago. And that night—"

"I don't like to have you see me in a place like this," he said earnestly. He touched his face and felt his beard.

"And all the people who used to imitate Roosevelt," she said, as if she had not heard him, as if she were deaf. "And that place on Staten Island where we all used to go for dinner when Henry had a car. Poor Henry. He bought a place in Connecticut and went out there by himself one weekend. He fell asleep with a lighted cigarette and the house, the barn, everything burned. Ethel took the children out to California." She poured more Scotch into his glass and handed it to him. She lighted a cigarette and put it between his lips. The intimacy of this gesture, which made it seem not only as if he were deathly ill but as if he were her lover, troubled him.

"As soon as I'm better," he said, "I'll take a room at a good hotel. I'll call you then. It was nice of you to come."

"Oh, don't be ashamed of this room, Jack," she said. "Rooms never bother me. It doesn't seem to matter to me where I am. Stanley had a filthy room in Chelsea. At least, other people told me it was filthy. I never noticed it. Rats used to eat the food I brought him. He used to have to hang the food from the ceiling, from the light chain."

"I'll call you as soon as I'm better," Jack said. "I think I can sleep now if I'm left alone. I seem to need a lot of sleep."

"You really *are* sick, darling," she said. "You must have a fever." She sat on the edge of his bed and put a hand on his forehead.

"How is that Englishman, Joan?" he asked. "Do you still see him?"

"What Englishman?" she said.

"You know. I met him at your house. He kept a handkerchief up his sleeve. He coughed all the time. You know the one I mean."

"You must be thinking of someone else," she said. "I haven't had an Englishman at my place since the war. Of course, I can't remember everyone." She turned and, taking one of his hands, linked her fingers in his.

"He's dead, isn't he?" Jack said. "That Englishman's dead." He pushed her off the bed, and got up himself. "Get out," he said.

"You're sick, darling," she said. "I can't leave you alone here."

"Get out," he said again, and when she didn't move, he shouted, "What kind of an obscenity are you that you can smell sickness and death the way you do?"

"You poor darling."

"Does it make you feel young to watch the dying?" he shouted. "Is that the lewdness that keeps you young? Is that why you dress like a crow? Oh, I know there's nothing I can say that will hurt you. I know there's nothing filthy or corrupt or depraved or brutish or base that the others haven't tried, but this time you're wrong. I'm not ready. My life isn't ending. My life's beginning. There are wonderful years ahead of me. There are, there are wonderful, wonderful, wonderful years ahead of me, and when they're over, when it's time, then I'll call you. Then, as an old friend, I'll call you and give you whatever dirty pleasure you take in watching the dying, but until then, you and your ugly and misshappen forms will leave me alone."

She finished her drink and looked at her watch. "I guess I'd better show up at the office," she said. "I'll see you later. I'll come back tonight. You'll feel better then, you poor darling." She closed the door after her, and he heard her light step on the stairs.

Jack emptied the whiskey bottle into the sink. He began to dress. He stuffed his dirty clothes into a bag. He was trembling and crying with sickness and fear. He could see the blue sky from his window, and in his fear it seemed miraculous that the sky should be blue, that the white clouds should remind him of snow, that from the sidewalk he could hear the shrill voices of children shrieking, "I'm the king of the mountain, I'm the king of the mountain, I'm the king of the mountain." He emptied the ashtray containing his nail parings and cigarette butts into the toilet, and swept the floor with a shirt, so that there would be no trace of his life, of his body, when that lewd and searching shape of death came there to find him in the evening.

The Snowfall

JEAN GARRIGUE

(1912–1972)

She was very good-looking: anyone would have to admit that. But her good looks had come to her as a surprise for even through high school she had been thin and sharp-faced. The chagrin of her looks had so impressed her then that she had really never had time to adjust to the new face in her mirror. She still really saw a girl with big cat eyes and a cat-thin face, straw-colored hair lying in wispy uncertainties over the top of her head where sharp ears should have stayed. Her good looks had, in fact, come late: not really appeared until she was twenty-one or so. Suddenly then the hungry boniness of her had disappeared: her shoulders seemed less narrow and hunched, there were amazing tendernesses of contour at the waist, her hair had deepened in color and she had let it grow long.

She had gone through high school and college indifferent and cold, scornful of the tomfool, meaty boys so interested in games and machinery. At twenty she was still actually a child: her social vanities needed no reassurance for she was trying to be a good painter and succeeding—her teachers praised her. But then she had grown up into beauty. It made a great change in her life. She met Tom, who was determined to take her over and scout the nonsense out of her head. They spent an out-of-door summer together. She was good with a gun and had no squeamishness about breaking one syllable of a sparrow's note in two, bursting it midway in air. She was even better than Tom and he had gone to military school and worn royal blue capes! This prowess which—it is true—she bragged of, irritated him and he had set out to break her will in other ways: he realized that she was aloof, physically, not caring to be touched. So he was determined to get her that way, and he did. He was absolutely ruthless and remorseless, he did not care if he nearly broke her arms and when she would bite him because there was nothing else she could do, he was filled with such a pleasant rage that he nearly loved her more than ever.

She herself was painfully and bitterly confused, for she was able to mock him intellectually, to deplore his tastes and ambitions, and yet to welcome the savagery that exerted itself between them. Not that she ever admitted that she liked his callous way of saying: "Yes, you will," but the tension was harshly alive and exciting. Couldn't she admit that? It was exciting. She liked, suddenly, the contours of his mouth: heavy and wide, his hair falling flat over his eyes, the strange fur on his shoulders and back that made her feel as if she were touching a beast.

But the struggle exhausted her—this pure blank hatred she felt for him because he managed to be stronger than she and could pin her down like any sickly insect—and yet, on the other hand, this desire to struggle with him that her hatred might be inflamed so that later it could be subdued. Well, wasn't that it?

It worried her, as well, that there was no sweetness attached to her feelings: no kind of joy. He tormented her, taunted her, bullied her; he never spoke of her painting and she never permitted him to see anything she had done, as if that would be a last sacrilege. It was not until after she had known him for a year that it occurred to her that there was really a kind of immorality at hand, that she was bossed by him not because *she* loved him or even desired him, but because some black motion in her drove her toward him. Once she realized this, she considered it as an abasement and then at last was able to break it off. But the need for reassurance by the male had become a hunger she could not do without, and she had a series of affairs: getting great gifts, records and fountain pens and books.

This energy of interest served to extrovert her. She had not become proud of her looks but interested in them as if they were some distant favor conceded to her, like a newly discovered and romantic relation. Yet profoundly at heart she remained celibate and distrustful, distrustful not of those boys she knew who were incapable, in fact, of tricking or shocking her, for she had made certain, after Tom, to pick those more tractable; but distrustful of the good of the feelings they aroused in her.

She was wary, alert, high-strung, in short, a light sleeper, subject to sudden disorders, and picked at her food. On parting with Tom she had developed an illness that puzzled two doctors. They hesitated, actually, to call it only "nerves" and had put her to bed for a month. During that time she had wept regularly, had been unable to sleep or eat, had lain back against herself, a light shadow on the substantial bed, her lids protecting her eyes. "What is it, what is it, can't you tell me, if only you would tell me!" her father implored. He had taught her to beat him at tennis and shoot better than Tom. He took a presumptuous, passionate interest in her.

But she had not known herself: shaking her head slowly, as the tears seeped vulgarly out, the color of lilac or shadow, she had not been able to say.

She had met Nicholas in Chicago where she was teaching in a private school and at first she had believed that she might very possibly be able to love him. For he was an artist: she no longer had the problem of trying to make herself understood: he knew what subtleties might awake that gratitude so infrequent in her, and counted on the small: the flower or a print, the right silence, to accost her with the appreciation that was the nearest to love she had come. He was not always yearning at her feet. He was intelligent and immensely talented: a violinist, he played in the Symphony. This was the first man worthy of her, she might admit to herself! She had scorned and ridiculed those others until they had learned to ridicule themselves.

How near she was to love for Nicholas! But what was it—at some mysterious last point the reservation had to be made, the dread qualification. "I love you, however . . ." However, it was true that he was plain and underfed. However, it was true that she admitted once to a friend that she could not quite see taking him into a nightclub. But you never go to nightclubs, her friend answered, and that was true, she never did. She should be ashamed for making so feeble an excuse! Then what was it? What was it that stopped in her, on the threshold of declarations? She had no virginal reluctances, no qualms about committing herself to the long escapade of a love affair, bout after bout, sorty and sally and volley of wills. What was it that balked like the mule at that suggestion of the permanent? She could not say, except that it was the instant that had always moved her, never the funereal threat of continuity. It was the necessity of the endowed instant. As if music were suddenly remembered inside her when the right time for wooing occurred, when she, that is, willed it. She realized that the immense virtue of Nicholas lay in just his sensitivity to her: he actually waited for her first stalking move. His love was so strong and fearful that he dared not risk forcing what he valued upon her. She had to be willing and ready: he had to be sure of the fact. She had become, in her own nervous and resonant way, her own clanging, brisk and jaunty, cocksure fashion, the male and he the compliant, watchful, studious female. He reflected, then, her directions, and it was his task and cleverness to do so. This she immensely admired, and for the first time in her relations with any man felt strong and free. Luckily, too, he tempered his praise of her with occasional outbursts of chill and spare invective. She was not the bitch and louse of criticism's usual hurt spendthrifty. Those criticisms were but another way of expending admiration and demanded but laughter or the return of insult: bloody, murderous hacking: "You've got nothing in your head." "You're cold and dull." "You fool, you."

But his was reflective, bony comment. She feared his insights because they came from profundities in him that shamed her. She wished she could see him so clearly. It made her feel jealous and slightly inferior. At the same time, it was a consolation (despite her resentment of it) to know that he so had her "interests at heart." She really felt that he knew her better than she knew herself with whom she lived so irregularly. She asked him advice as she might have asked her father had he glossed her with as much clarity of love.

Yet she had taken the job at Yellow Springs, had precipitantly, in the month of September, left Nicholas to be alone in a small town to teach young girls the amenities of water colors.

In her heart she was fearful of going. Once she had made the decision she seriously wondered why she did not stay in Chicago and marry Nicholas. She did not really want to be alone. She felt that she should be but she did not want to be. She was forcing herself into a difficulty. And yet the decision was not a calculated one. A restlessness had made the decision. It awoke her at night and turned her from Nicholas. It criticized and belittled. It made Nicholas a foreign, slavish little dog. It detached her from him, making her cool to his enthusiasms. It made her think: no, this isn't my life yet. Besides, his parents hate me (which was true) and my parents think he is a lame duck (which was also true). It forced all kinds of ridiculous, out of the way and untrue judgments upon her. But in the end it remained that she had to get away.

She was even prepared to hate Yellow Springs. But that inland, sweetened country took her by surprise. It was morning-like and new. She felt that for a long while she could be content with her new, abstemious life: living in a girlish room in somebody's house, teaching classes and holding conferences, painting and saving her money so that soon she could take a year off and study seriously in New York. (Nicholas would come too.)

For as she had grown up belatedly and with a certain amount of aversion to the process, so she had timidly approached her talent, one hand held in back of her. Time? She had an infinite amount of it and as for those powers in herself—well, she firmly and uncritically believed that life would see to it that she deepened and darkened. So, at the age of twenty-three, she was not yet ready for the responsibilities of her desires and possibly Nicholas' eager willingness to assume responsibility for her, to wrap her around with his verities and hopes and to support her intellectually by all the thinking he had done on history, poetry and philosophy, had driven her from him. Possibly she had feared that she might not grow up with him. Possibly she feared that his love stood between her and the blows actuality had not yet given her. For she did fear the laziness in her that might prevent her from feeling all that she should feel. Oh, she had fine ways of protecting herself from the full consequences of situations! A healthy convenience for black-outs! How well the obdurate memory failed when the ego could profit therefrom!

Well, looking back upon it now, walking through the bitter-bright rindy leaves of first windfall, she could not really understand why she had left Nicholas. He had been the first not to force reproaches upon her, not to make her feel that she was lacking in primal femininities. Looking back over the laundry list, the library catalog of boys she had known since that unlucky initiation with Tom, she realized that she had permitted all of them to make love to her so that afterwards she would be unable to forgive them for it. But with Nicholas that action had not seemed a disguise for the attainment of blunt supremacy. But especially! she had not felt humiliated by being exposed to her own coldness. At last she did not feel that she was being the dupe of others' desires, the ready jewel-eyed player queen, a stake for others but heartless to herself. So she could then "afford" to be kind to him, could then relax for the first time, since she trusted him. The competitiveness and hostility, the sardonic allegations could be given back to their falsities. He loved what he saw and did not see. Indeed, how interesting to herself his love made her!

But yet—she had had to be free. His love still kept her away from the world. It was still the petition to her vanity, it was so pure and warm, so devoted and sorrowful—a kind of less complicated father-love.

Yes, she had bolted like a thief. Why did Nicholas allow her to go so easily? Possibly because he had reasoned: she is going to a small college town, to teach in a girls' school where they specialize in horseback riding and by the end of the year, after having met only young faculty darlings who sway as they walk, and young well-wived husbands and old salt and pepper deans, and having seen America's sons of the filling station and fire department, ruddy, agog young men born on another planet, she may know that, after all, it is I she has been searching for all her life and I who have accounted for all her unusual lonelinesses in the middle of her fashionable popularities.

And, parting with her, he casually turned over to her his battered but racy and strong Ford coupé. I would simply be paying garage rent here, you know, he said. Now that you won't be here to take rides I'll practice instead. What about other girls, Nicholas? she asked. They can walk, he said.

He wrote her daily, long journal-like letters. Sometimes he felt that he was the curator of a remarkable bird, the last of its species! Would not this account for his watchfulness? But the bird in order to live must go away, must understand more of the world before it could thrive in the great cage of air where he had willed that it must "settle." It must not be hungry for freedoms whose emptinesses it had never tested.

Yes, watchful Nicholas was also cunning, with the foresight and insight of great desire. It was as if his humility and generosity were not character traits but mere extracts and, at the same time, mere placations of the necessity she had become to him. Her ignorant wilfulness, her errancies—merely the excess of her charm! The headstrong moodiness with which she protected her sensitivities—it had frightened all away from that which she truly was. Let him be the Pygmalion to startle her soul!

And she, walking on streets of little houses where pear leaves, dark brown and red, like pyres of light were heaped, was happy and at peace. His letters like literature came, budding with comparison of her to the dark summer. It was wonderful to be away from him and to have only his letters, his thoughts and her memories. Could she not see him now in his true magnificence? She need never look up to find his eyes, full-lidded, mournful and black in the boniness of his face, fixed on her with an expression that was—really—spaniel-like. The way he dressed need not disparage him now—those shirts with flabby collars, the trousers that were always too long and the coat that made his shoulders narrow. Some people could not learn to dress. Nicholas was one. It was the same with his room. Cigarette ashes and dust. Unwashed milk bottles. Discarded razor blades. Month-old newspapers. Torn window blinds. And yet he lavished such care on a phrase, he would work hours to perfect a trill. There was no correlation, she knew, as he had told her. Nevertheless, it disturbed her, and always his slight smell of violinist's nervous sweat, the way he could get his fingers ashy putting out a cigarette! But now, in the absence of those irritations perhaps she could begin to see him with the joy of the soul's eye, she thought, having been educated by him to this.

And indeed she did. She even considered seriously for the first time fidelity. More than that, his ever-recurring appearance by letter fed and sustained her, an aerial diet delicately intoxicating! She went from letters to classes, zestful and proud, and, walking on the old Victorian campus, thought for the first time: I can really dispense with all but the world! Watching the bees stupefied by the rank sweetness of pears gone soft and brown, and grapes in arbors split open by the warmth of the sun, she was tenderly content as if the autumn promised improbable happiness she did not have to run to.

She went to her first party in Yellow Springs with a red-haired Professor of Radio, a spotty, conceited character lording it over with his voice as if every individual were a crowd. On meeting her he had decided immediately that she was to be his girl for the year. And she, observing distantly the standard ways he took to indicate his liveliness, thought: how is it that once I took pride in leading a fool by the nose?

At the party she was introduced to Luke Banford, who sat on a thin chair in a corner, idly fiddling with a pad of paper on which, as she noticed quickly, he had drawn a few caricatures. On seeing him in a gray checked suit which fitted so aptly his moderate tallness and flatness, on seeing his hair, black as a seal's wet fur, his high, polished dark forehead, his eyes, aloof and steely as a bird's with a glance that cut because of its brilliance, his full, wide mouth, so amply balanced and darkly molded, she felt a sudden anger of distaste. Male beauty, made by a watchmaker!

The party bored her and she soon acquired a headache. Do let us go, she said to the Professor who had been cracking jokes with Banford which she had not bothered to listen to. I suggest we all take a ride, the Professor said munificently. What about Starr Lake? It's the last night of Indian Summer they say. She looked up warily to intercept Banford's black glance like ice. Why not? he said, looking at her without smiling. She noticed then a deep, blunt scar on his forehead.

But she said: "Why not?" and turned away. The dark man flushed and the Professor frowned. A moment later he drew her away into the center of the room and said: "Hey, take it easy. He's really a nice guy. I knew him in New York."

"Then what's he doing in Yellow Springs?" she asked.

"He was in a crack-up last year. His wife was killed."

"A sad story," she said.

Riding in the Professor's roadster, a hostage between the two men, the Professor leaning warmly toward her, Banford drawn tautly into a corner, she suddenly felt enormously energetic and cruel. As her father had squeezed through the barbarities and inanimities of domestic depressions and business failures by kidding Existence, so she at such times took it out on the world with a brazen, vaudeville wit. Usually her excitement came from ambivalences of tensions, deploying between the erotic and sudden confusing memories that enraged her. She felt herself to be on a ferris wheel then, circling, lifting and dropping over areas of the unknowable. Frightened, she laughed it off, reforming and socializing the nightmare. At such times she wished to turn on herself and kill or mutilate and so chose the world as a worthier object. Nicholas had hated her in such moods but Tom had always laughed with her. Now she noticed that the Professor did too, though he was awkwardly interrupting to lean across her to say to Banford: "She's really got a heart like ducksoup. She's the kind to want to stop a car if she hears some animal crying in the woods."

But even to this Banford, for all his wealthy politeness, scarcely responded and the Professor laughed alone but perhaps more out of relief than enjoyment, for usually he was a part of the world her surgical humor gashed.

But as they stood out in the wind by the lake her jokebook mood dropped away. She was aware of the handsome man's silence and remembered what Nicholas had said of those parties of malice: "It is a way of defaming the world." The wind roughly blew at her and she wished to run straight to the cold mouth of the water.

Sometimes she would meet Luke Banford on the campus. He walked Indian straight, stepping as lightly, with narrow feet, usually his wristwatch hand in his pocket. He never wore a hat but the wind did not seem to touch him; his hair was always of a piece with his head, black and shining like mica, and his eyes so critical, so glittering beneath the evenness of his proud eyebrows. Occasionally he walked with her, but they never seemed to manage to say much— talking with him was like talking against a waterfall, difficult, as against frightful pressures he built up against her: of silence, of formality, the niceties of caution. She was ready to give it up, simply to pass him by briefly when they met. Besides, she thought, he must really be stupid. And she decided that he had no character.

Then she thought the more of Nicholas, hurrying to his image as if it were an icon in a corner. What an ample and noble life he lived! Always at the heart of sound! But she began to harry his image; she began to drive and hurry it. Less frequently would it appear between unexpected interstices of time, the rough dark head. And sometimes at night, thinking of him, she could find no flavor of joy at all. The image could then assume no life nor body of its own, could neither rustle with sound nor burn with light. My heart must be empty, she thought fiercely, putting her hand against it. And her mouth felt dry.

Suddenly the year began to hurry to its death. A cold wind one morning cut all the leaves down. Rain followed, to soil them. Midway from classes that afternoon she met Luke.

The melancholy of the day had quieted and humbled her. She shivered in the wind as she stood talking to him. He said: "Will you have a drink?" and took her by the arm. The warmth of his hard, delicate hand pierced through her coat and dress sleeves. The abrasive effect of his misfortune had, up till then, made him seem cold and self-insulated—as if by vanity, she had even thought! But now, walking in the sodden afternoon, he seemed less brittle, incalculably more free and direct with her. Perhaps the sadness of the rain!

And sitting with him in the dark light of a tavern she evasively looked from his scar to his mouth and then to his crisp collar. She noticed his fingers, pointed for a man, and the few small hairs on the back of his hand. Suddenly the sight of his scar pained her. The imperfection on perfection. And it seemed that from that short, blunt mark his pain must flow. For surely his silences covered over a dark space of what—some suffering no one could get to! And it seemed remarkable to her that so handsome a man should be so dark and unreachable—so alone, for instance, at the party!

The subtle and petty resentments she had held against him—those neat marriages of color in ties and socks, the hardness of his head and eye, the rebuke of his distant and impersonal indifference, were then revoked. Looking at his scar, she began to marvel as if he had been accused of some grotesquerie. Certainly it then distinguished him. Pity, pity! This is what she exclaimed later. I learned to pity him!

As he was lighting her cigarette, his hand touched hers, and the effect, as though he might have held the flame to her fingers, made her heart freeze with subtle fear and anticipation. They talked in many directions eagerly but carefully, until he said: "I had been planning to leave this town until I met you."

She trembled but sipped her martini as if she were concealing a tear. When finally she looked up at him his eyes were still on hers: black and tense as an animal's. She could not see beyond their surfaces of light. The black kept out the color of his thoughts.

From then on she saw him constantly, for dinner, for long walks, for drives in Nicholas' Ford to the show parts of the state. Those with whom she had been about to make friends she forgot had ever interested her. She went from classes to him. His looks made him seem remarkable, like some foreign trophy of war and honor. She felt that he wore armor, delicate, invisible, and his aloneness gave her a superstitious belief in his integrity. This exhilarated her because she felt that he had been wounded.

He did not mention what had—as she understood from the Professor—changed his life. He had only told her that he had moved around for the last year, had been up and down the West Coast, in Wyoming, St. Louis, all kinds of places he had never seen before. But it was those very allusions, intensities of gaps between the unfinished accounts of years, that touched her. What time she did not spend with him she spent in her mind with him, finishing out his history, supplying connectives between small anecdotes he related about Hartford, Connecticut, where he had grown up and the year he'd gambled in Wall Street and lost his shirt. But he treated his past gingerly as if it were unfriendly to him and so she too politely pretended to herself that she did not wish to know about it. Yet she conventionally wished him to move in her head sequentially when actually he seemed to have been born from the scar on his forehead. His Spanish eyes and English nose. His sad, cool blood and hawk-like heart.

In a month she was completely in love with him. It did not shock her when he asked her to marry him. She had been so taken by surprise that it seemed inevitable that at last she had pulled out of her sleeve the ace of hearts. In fact, for the first time in her life she did not think about herself. Luke's image completely objectified her. It concentrated her as well. All thought and emotion ran from her to him. She could have been fanatically happy. For at last she was directed, caught up in a single purity of attention and desire. But yet she would be threatened by tears as, sitting by Starr Lake on Saturday afternoons, geese flew over. Uncontrollable, unreasonable sadness! Was it because he was restless with his measly job and talked of Wall Street deals, thereby frightening her? She could only see money gained as money earned.

She wished to put her sadness to some practical cause. For her heart beat so fast, with such elation! And his delicate Indian tread, the steel in the center of his breast so compelled her to moody symbols. She dreamed of ways in which to paint him: with red silk scarves, a blasphemy of softness, tied round his throat.

In that month her looks changed. She grew rosy, and moved so tenderly that everyone remarked: She's a changed person—for one thing, always so gay! She put up her hair, which added a city dignity to her pointed, child-like face. But it was not that! A look in the eyes! The points of her pupils had been absorbed, as if she were always looking into the sun, and all the green of the iris suffused her glance.

Yes, for a month she had no time to think about herself and indeed continued to write to Nicholas as if nothing had happened to her or as if, rather, Luke had given her a new self which had nothing to do with the selves Nicholas had known. Then, in middle November, when he wrote her that he was coming down to see her, she awoke with a start and wired him that it was impossible for her to see him. After that she tried on several occasions to write him the letter that would cut him off from her but each letter was too blunt and exultant. She did not want to boast about her new-found happiness for then it seemed unreal. Actually, she did not want to talk about it at all. It was too private a revelation. When Nicholas finally called her long distance she was rude and stormy. He who had believed he could best keep her by leaving her alone when she made it clear that she wanted to be left alone, broke out into great anger and vowed that he was coming straight down to see what had happened to her. Freed by his rage, she was finally able to write him the letter that told him it was all over and that she was to be married soon. With that gesture she turned her back on all her past and made Luke the king of her eye.

Yet, had she not been able to pity him, who knows what would have happened? Pity was the solvent. The glamor of the automobile wreck! His wife killed by that! He, exempt, but not from remorse and pain, cast out like any wanderer by the guilt he felt. Yes! Pity for this aloof, metallic, glittering man who seemed, physically, as incorruptible as a statue, lent impulsiveness to caution. He was elusive. He was mysterious. He was not knowable because his very appearance so satisfied the eye that the eye wished to stop there, content with the secrecy and reserve that the beautiful must have for protection. As the thorn must safeguard and give dignity to its rose!

Commonplaces, homelinesses, like their cow-licks and ingenuously large ears, had been all the deeps of those she had known before she met Nicholas. Goodnesses and practicalities and shrewdnesses. That kind of single-hearted devotion, intent, possessive but also detached, she had known in Nicholas. But in Luke, there was the great feeling of the pit, that steep fall, that downward rush into perils and dangers, the gambled card, the risked life, the conquering contempt, the disdain, the destruction.

In a few weeks they were always together: she deserted her studio save for those occasions when he would come there to let her sketch him. He was in a dream, a masked dream, filled with loathing of what he had come to, teaching a class in radio in Yellow Springs after years of sailboating off Long Island and commanding stone houses on the seacoast. But the sickness still so hidden by his hard breast she would cure, she believed. That sense of responsibility for so obscure a charge exalted her. And he was good to her in a purely self-absorbed and penitent way; he permitted himself to be taken care of by her. When suddenly he had to go to New York on business he accepted the loan of Nicholas' car and even some money she jokingly gave him although he had flushed and had said crisply: "My poor foolish proper girl."

The week that he was gone she hated the canvas color of the sky and the bare, ruined trees and could think only of the fanciful, proportioned life he would, with casual elegance, ordain for her. And when he returned, having wrecked Nicholas' car on the way, she was only so glad that he had not been hurt that she could not fret over the embarrassment, to say the least, of the loss.

Of course he did drive ninety miles an hour!

But the car could be repaired. "Think nothing of it," she said. "I don't."

Yet her effort to steel herself against such concern robbed for a while her joy of some of its energy. This did vex for she was immoderately anxious to have everything perfect between them. She was as determined to have him as perfect as he could be and what he had done and had been did seem, in many ways, an intrusion upon the joy his presence brought her. Simply to be in the same room with him! Whereupon she remembered that her mother had said to her: "I just like to be where you are." Ah, well! Then she had turned disdainfully away.

And as when she talked about her own childhood she did not expect him to tell her about his, so she did not expect him to tell her why it had been so necessary for him to go to New York. He had the most subtle ways of keeping such areas of his life fenced off. A silence contacted around him which anguished her but for which she had total respect. He seemed, really, divested of background. She was certain that he had had an easy boyhood but this was simply because he dressed so well and had such fine, easy manners and, moreover, because he had such a talent for letting money go by him, out the window of hopes! This scornful unconsciousness about money worried her for she did feel that he might be the sort of person to get himself into trouble over what he, in his piratical dignity, deemed trifling, the care of bankclerks and prudential knaves.

So she had soon learned to live with a small, cold dread for him, unnamable, based upon nothing but fluctuations of intuition. Those fears accounted for sudden tendernesses toward him that were her own miracle. She had never before been so human, so "womanly." But those others had presented solid, impermeable surfaces; the face-hardened opinion, the dogged conviction. She in her uncertainties had had to proceed against such certitudes, her footing untenable on such resistant, tensile bluffs. But he was dark shade, the cool and fear of subtile caves. His silences were stony and hawk-like but softness also spread out from them. There were things he did not want to say. There were strengths he wished to preserve from glaring speech. He did not have to be anything with her but a breathing thing: a dark object of blood and black hair and bird-black, icy eyes.

Yet he saw that, at occasional parties, she did not drink too much, and he studied minor landscapes of hers or those sketches she was always making of him with long care and interest. "The sky is too cold here," he would say, or "if you could make this corner more interesting, I should like to hear the *sound* of the bells." "Now the value of El Greco's crooked beards—you make this face too symmetrical." It was his own, a fact both ignored.

Such criticisms seemed gilded. She saw him as the prince of good taste. She admired the disinterestedness with which he listened to scraps of her past: the rebellions at ten, the death of her grandmother, games in which she had won all the marbles from little boys. He was not anxious as Nicholas had been to verify an interpretation of her, painfully anxious to catch more light on the coils of her soul.

She invited him home for Christmas vacation. On Christmas Eve she was so excited, so happy, for snow had begun to fall at twilight and late that night they had gone out for a walk, running into bushes like children and throwing soft, tender bullets of snow at one another, that she said to herself: I fear: this joy brings me too close to sorrow. And at three o'clock that night had gone to his room, once her grandmother's.

"My dear!" he said, "this is incestuous," as he found her weeping beside him.

"Luke!" she begged, "do not leave me."

When Nicholas came down she was immediately outraged to see his dark face like her conscience against the general white.

"I hope you came to get your Ford," she said.

"You can keep the Ford. I wanted to see you."

"There's nothing worse than post-mortems. I said what I had to say in my letter."

"I know you did," he said, "but I didn't believe your truth. But it's true that you've changed. You're all dolled up. Let's see your finger nails."

He seized her hands. She tried to pull them away but he held on to them savagely. There was an intense, invisible motion about him. His rough, black hair looked uncombed. His shirt collar was, as usual, wilted and smudged. He looked into her face as if he held a bright light against it. She avoided his eyes and suddenly he let her hands go with a show of great disgust.

"Yes, I would say," he said methodically, "that there is a change. You have that well-loved look that pretty women around thirty so often get."

"You're insulting," she said.

"But where's the candidate?" he asked. "No pictures around?"

For a moment he paced up and down the room. How undersized and bony he looked! How shabby and hungry! She felt triumphant, thinking of Luke's long, flat and beautiful back, the wide wings of his shoulders. And his delicate, narrow ankles!

Suddenly Nicholas stood before her. "Why have you done this?"

"I am in love."

"But you have made a mistake," he said studiously. "There is only one for me and that is you and there is only one for you and that is me."

Her heart hardened. "I could never love you," she said.

"What does he want to give you? A house in Indian Hills?"

"Keep him out of it," she said fiercely.

"How could you have changed?" he asked thoughtfully. "I believed you wanted to be a painter. It seems you want to be a wife. Just a beautiful doll of a wife. Just a loving, fatuous spouse."

"Get out," she cried, pained and hurt.

"Now I have made you angry. But what have you done to me? You are going to make me suffer. I don't like that. Can you understand how I wish to protect myself and how I would do anything, anything, to make you realize that I am the one for you?"

"I have found the man I love," she said stonily.

"Was it such deception?" he asked, grimacing.

"Did I ever tell you I loved you?"

"But you might as well have. We might as well have been married. No one could have known you better than I! You allowed me to know you. All your miseries, ambitions and memories. If you can forget, do you think I can?"

"It was all a mistake."

He paled. "Then you are killing our two years. Two years is a great deal of space and time to kill. I don't think you will succeed."

"How dramatic you are."

He went on as if he did not hear her: "In the winter there is only One. Is it because the streets are so cold? The world shrivels up like an old orange. Passion becomes so inward, it is in all the pores and secret veins. It *is* the body. In the spring it is different when the world expands and goes outward. The wits of the heart get crafty then. Do you want me to forget you? Is that what you want?"

She looked at him hurriedly and then turned away. In her heart she could not find it possible to say yes! forget me! The way in which she knew her was a consolation! Even his ridiculous manner of treating her as a museum piece. Stay! Just that way! he had commanded her, just so against the light!

She looked out to the snow. Did she want him to forget her? He had discovered so much of herself for her.

He came up to her. She saw a heavy sorrow standing in his eyes. He took her by the shoulders. But the instant that his nervous touch was upon her she was glad. Oh, I cannot really love him, she knew. False sympathy! Sentimentality! He's nothing to me! He was never my soul. It's that he talked so well. His rhetoric bewitched me.

Please go! she said, and moved away from beneath his hands.

He said no more but looked at her. For a moment yet the reasonableness of his pain struggled with her. But suddenly realizing that what she wanted to do she did have the courage to do—but yet not want to do and cringed to do when he did not touch her but only looked at her—she said.

"Here are the keys to the Ford."

She threw them at his lank chest, and walked out of the room, leaving him there.

This then, more than anything, gave her completely and wholly over to Luke. She need not be obliged to remember Nicholas' nose when she admired Luke's; to think how both men were so dark, but Luke so golden dark and Nicholas so blackly dark, like a coal-miner; she need not remember that sometimes—such was the sad universality of language!—Luke said the phrase that Nicholas had once said.

But there was a difference! She felt obliged to consider the relation anew, from a distance. Nicholas' leavetaking had robbed her of some very imperceptible but dense and alive background. Now no one stood in the mirror but Luke and herself. That older, obscure penumbra of image, the subtle prod to her conscience, now gone, left her all the more dramatically alone when Luke was away. Now she was feverish, her body felt alone and abandoned. For two months the sun did not shine and Luke had resigned his job at Yellow Springs and had taken a job with the new radio station in her home town. It paid him better and he needed money, he jocularly confessed. He had debts in New York that might catch up with him.

But then he had turned around and bought a brisk and handsome second-hand roadster for them, as he put it. Every weekend he drove its wheels off to see her; two hundred miles each way. She knew how fast he drove and how destructive his impatience could be. But yet! the winter was so black and arid! What would she do without him? She had made no friends in Yellow Springs. She was absolutely dependent on him. The Professor, sternly disapproving of the choice she had made, avoided her. Two casual acquaintances—serious but charming young women—had said to her on separate occasions: "But he seems so superficial!" She had darkly thought that they had conspired together to present the same judgment to her, and had been bitterly offended as she had violently distrusted her father after he had said one night when Luke had gone out for cigarettes: "Are you sure he will make you happy?"

"Am I sure I will make him happy!" she had rejoined.

"No, my dear," he had begun with his best Polonius air, "a man does not depend on a woman for happiness. What a man wants is the difficult. He wants to fight. He wants to buck up against stone. He wants to feel his courage and muscle. Now Luke: are you sure he wants that? Are you sure he isn't looking for the perpetual golf course?"

Oh, she could have turned upon him! She could have said: You old cotton-mouthed fool! You kill-joy you! But she had not. Her father, for all his insulting sententiousness, loved her piously and wanted to see her well married to a home, wanted for her all the safeties he had sought so feverishly, and all the dullnesses. But that he had dared to speak of Luke! No one dared use his name but as she allowed them to. Oh! to answer him, to say: You don't even know whom you're speaking of, please dismiss the subject, I will not have the ignorant speaking of what I love—it was rude, too shocking. It would rankle in her conscience afterward. Thank God, at that minute Luke had come back, the brim of his hat holding snow like daisies. "Darling!" he had exclaimed. And that word, fallen so clemently, with the effect of propitiation, between them, a word he rarely confessed to before her parents, exposed the full humiliation of the injustice done him. She had gone up to him, kissing him straight on the mouth, and had stood there, against the tight glances of the two. Luke had stiffened beneath her kiss, which had increased her anger that he should have had to feel its apology.

So she was alone and every Friday night he raced like a speed-king to her. She was alone but yet she could have begged him not to come. For every late Friday night she felt gripped by some agony as if the car were driving through her brain. Occasionally she dared say: "I hope you want to live long, Luke."

"I'm careful," he would state. "I'm an expert."

And then she would be blankly silent.

Yet what would she do, she asked herself, if he did not come every week? For she was quite alone. Nicholas had been right. In the winter there was only One. The world contacted to One. And she waited each Friday for his arrival so that she might come alive.

At first Luke had said: "Let's marry at Christmas." But then she agreed with him later on that it would be better to wait until the summer.

"Why not a house in Indian Hills for a while?" he suggested.

"Oh, Luke," she had replied, abashed. "What do you want from life?"

"You," he had answered conventionally. "I'm spoiled. You're really all I want."

But looking up with the instant delight that statement had borne, she was oppressed by the look in his eye which had not become more brilliant from the influence of those gold words, and as he drew her to him was disappointed by the regular clop of his heart and his beautiful, bitter odor.

And what did he mean, that he was spoiled? she thought anxiously, remembering much later that quality of his voice which seemed to come through from another time, as if the words were too well known to him, through which, it could seem, another voice was speaking? Or was it merely the repetition of that ironic malice he had employed once before when he had said to her as she stood in a doorway in a green dress, putting up her hair: "How strong you are! It doesn't matter if I'm weak, does it?"

It was afterward that she thought: why did he choose February? Of all months dead in the calendar, when hope had been exhausted by the winter, when the long effort against the withering cold had all but mummied the flesh and the heart could do no more than keep up its life against the north, of all times, why had he told her then that it was not his wife who had been killed in the accident but a girl he had been in love with and that it was her death that had nearly knocked him in and that his wife was still in New York.

Oh, Luke! she had said. Oh! the lie! she had thought. The dishonor! she had thought. He had said she must understand: how the story had got started that it had been his wife; the Professor had got it wrong.

"I never wanted to talk about it," he said. "He didn't hear it from me. It was my business. I didn't want the blabbings of others about that. Their questionable condolences: O my God, I've just heard . . . That's why I got away. Everyone saying: tough luck. Her mother. Her sisters."

"You loved her," she said.

He looked up as if she had, in that withdrawn moment, touched him. "Yes."

"Then you met me," she persisted quietly.

He had not heard her. Sweat was on his upper lip.

"It was all useless," he said, "useless."

"Luke, tell me," she said. "I've got to know."

"Oh, the filthy details," he said, striking at the table softly. "Icy road. March.

"She lived in New London. I'd gone up to see her. Sunday night I was going back to New York."

She waited.

"I wasn't going fast. There was a curve. I skidded. Another car was coming. It skidded. We all met. Of course she was with me. I was the only one in the whole bunch to get out alive."

She looked at his scar with horror but then had no more reactions.

A great snow fell. It was thick and strong and broke many branches. It fell steadily on Thursday, stopped on Friday, and began again on Saturday, when Luke was with her in her studio. It made the whole world look like the inside of a great soft tomb, and what Luke had told her was jailed in it. She felt stunned, but by the snow.

Yet she listened to him as she watched the white grains fall over the sky panes. Were they not falling through? Could the glass stop them? The world was white like the inside of a tomb.

He was saying that he would save money like hell and get a divorce in six months. Idly she thought: he exaggerates. It will take a year. And he will never save the money. He cannot save. He's a prince with money. I can save. I'll buy his divorce.

But she lifted her hand and let it fall, imitating the descent of one particular flake.

"I am not jealous of your wife," she said. "She's a legal dear."

He smiled uneasily.

She looked at him but preferred the snow flakes. They were brilliant. His face had gone inward. In the gray light those individually bright and sharp flakes made, his face was blurred as if a heavy beard covered it over.

"I'm jealous only of what is like myself," she went on. "What was your girl like, Luke? I think she was like myself."

"She was," he said.

"But she's faceless. What was the color of her eyes? Was she tall?

"Luke," she said, starting, "did you like me because I was like her?"

"O God," he said.

She saw that he was bored.

As well he might be! The girl was gone!

She wanted to weep because the girl had died uselessly. Luke had loved her, had he not? He had gone up to see her on weekends. The girl had loved him. She too had feared his recklessness and had driven back with him on that icy night. Simply to save him from excesses of speed. But she had not! And she had not saved him! He had concealed the noble fact of her death for so long!

"If I am like her, Luke," she said, "I'm not real, am I? I'm the second-hand parody of her."

"You're out of your head," he said, smiling, and trying to touch her hair.

She averted her head quickly. "How can you love me if you loved her?" she cried. "I'm jealous but she's more jealous! The jealousy of the dead is lasting!"

He sought to take her hands. "Anybody loves more than once."

"But there is only One!" she answered. "In the winter there is only One. But in the spring too. In the summer too when swimming is the season and the natural sensuality of the pleasure-seeking will."

He smiled, attempting to draw her close and away from such abstractions.

"No," she said, "she makes you dead too. She loved you and you should suffer and you've not and that makes you dead too."

But he was still smiling, attempting to take her hands.

"Nicholas was right," she said. "Go away, Luke, I am very tired."

"You're sick," he said. "You've got to have a fever."

"I love you," she answered, "but your girl haunts me and I love her more."

Obediently he left. She locked the door of the studio which the school had so kindly given her. The gray, philosophic light of the snow came down.

That girl's the mercury for my looking glass, she thought. Now I know how cold, how practical, how shrewd his heart. I see now how he cares for me, she thought. He cannot care, she thought, as I could not care. Love is the image of ourself until ourself destroys us.

And she wept for the perfect love of the girl and for the perfect love of Nicholas.

In Dreams Begin Responsibilities

DELMORE SCHWARTZ
(1913–1966)

I

I think it is the year 1909. I feel as if I were in a moving-picture theater, the long arm of light crossing the darkness and spinning, my eyes fixed upon the screen. It is a silent picture, as if an old Biograph one, in which the actors are dressed in ridiculously old-fashioned clothes, and one flash succeeds another with sudden jumps, and the actors, too, seem to jump about, walking too fast. The shots are full of rays and dots, as if it had been raining when the picture was photographed. The light is bad.

It is Sunday afternoon, June 12th, 1909, and my father is walking down the quiet streets of Brooklyn on his way to visit my mother. His clothes are newly pressed and his tie is too tight in his high collar. He jingles the coins in his pocket, thinking of the witty things he will say. I feel as if I had by now relaxed entirely in the soft darkness of the theater; the organist peals out the obvious approximate emotions on which the audience rocks unknowingly. I am anonymous. I have forgotten myself: it is always so when one goes to a movie, it is, as they say, a drug.

My father walks from street to street of trees, lawns, and houses, once in a while coming to an avenue on which a street-car skates and gnaws, progressing slowly. The motorman, who has a handle-bar mustache, helps a young lady wearing a hat like a feathered bowl onto the car. He leisurely makes change and rings his bell as the passengers mount the car. It is obviously Sunday, for everyone is wearing Sunday clothes and the street-car's noises emphasize the quiet of the holiday (Brooklyn is said to be the city of churches). The shops are closed and their shades drawn but for an occasional stationery store or drugstore with great green balls in the window.

My father has chosen to take this long walk because he likes to walk and think. He thinks about himself in the future and so arrives at the place he is to visit in a mild state of exaltation. He pays no attention to the houses he is passing, in which the Sunday dinner is being eaten, nor to the many trees which line each street, now coming to their full green and the time when they will enclose the whole street in leafy shadow. An occasional carriage passes, the horses' hooves falling like stones in the quiet afternoon, and once in a while an automobile, looking like an enormous upholstered sofa, puffs and passes.

My father thinks of my mother, of how lady-like she is, and of the pride which will be his when he introduces her to his family. They are not yet engaged and he is not yet sure that he loves my mother, so that, once in a while, he becomes panicky about the bond already established. But then he reassures himself by thinking of the big men he admires who are married: William Randolph Hearst and William Howard Taft, who has just become the President of the United States.

My father arrives at my mother's house. He has come too early and so is suddenly embarrassed. My aunt, my mother's younger sister, answers the loud bell with her napkin in her hand, for the family is still at dinner. As my father enters, my grandfather rises from the table and shakes hands with him. My mother has run upstairs to tidy herself. My grandmother asks my father if he has had dinner and tells him that my mother will be down soon. My grandfather opens the conversation by remarking about the mild June weather. My father sits uncomfortably near the table, holding his hat in his hand. My grandmother tells my aunt to take my father's hat. My uncle, twelve years old, runs into the house, his hair tousled. He shouts a greeting to my father, who has often given him nickels, and then runs upstairs, as my grandmother shouts after him. It is evident that the respect in which my father is held in this house is tempered by a good deal of mirth. He is impressive, but also very awkward.

II

Finally my mother comes downstairs and my father, being at the moment engaged in conversation with my grandfather, is made uneasy by her entrance, for he does not know whether to greet my mother or to continue the conversation. He gets up from his chair clumsily and says "Hello" gruffly. My grandfather watches this, examining their congruence, such as it is, with a critical eye, and meanwhile rubbing his bearded cheek roughly, as he always does when he reasons. He is worried; he is afraid that my father will not make a good husband for his oldest daughter. At this point something happens to the film, just as my father says something funny to my mother: I am awakened to myself and my unhappiness just as my interest has become most intense. The audience begins to clap impatiently. Then the trouble is attended to, but the film has been returned to a portion just shown, and once more I see my grandfather rubbing his bearded cheek, pondering my father's character. It is difficult to get back into the picture once more and forget myself, but as my mother giggles at my father's words, the darkness drowns me.

My father and mother depart from the house, my father shaking hands with my grandfather once more, out of some unknown uneasiness. I stir uneasily also, slouched in the hard chair of the theater. Where is the older uncle, my mother's older brother? He is studying in his bedroom upstairs, studying for his final examinations at the College of the City of New York, having been dead of double pneumonia for the last twenty-one years. My mother and father walk down the same quiet streets once more. My mother is holding my father's arm and telling him of the novel she has been reading and my father utters judgments of the characters as the plot is made clear to him. This is a habit which he very much enjoys, for he feels the utmost superiority and confidence when he is approving or condemning the behavior of other people. At times he feels moved to utter a brief "Ugh," whenever the story becomes what he would call sugary. This tribute is the assertion of his manliness. My mother feels satisfied by the interest she has awakened; and she is showing my father how intelligent she is and how interesting.

They reach the avenue, and the street-car leisurely arrives. They are going to Coney Island this afternoon, although my mother really considers such pleasures inferior. She has made up her mind to indulge only in a walk on the boardwalk and a pleasant dinner, avoiding the riotous amusements as being beneath the dignity of so dignified a couple.

My father tells my mother how much money he has made in the week just past, exaggerating an amount which need not have been exaggerated. But my father has always felt that actualities somehow fall short, no matter how fine they are. Suddenly I begin to weep. The determined old lady who sits next to me in the theater is annoyed and looks at me with an angry face, and being intimidated, I stop. I drag out my handkerchief and dry my face, licking the drop which has fallen near my lips. Meanwhile I have missed something, for here are my father and mother alighting from the street-car at the last stop, Coney Island.

III

They walk toward the boardwalk and my mother commands my father to inhale the pungent air from the sea. They both breathe in deeply, both of them laughing as they do so. They have in common a great interest in health, although my father is strong and husky, and my mother is frail. They are both full of theories about what is good to eat and not good to eat, and sometimes have heated discussions about it, the whole matter ending in my father's announcement, made with a scornful bluster, that you have to die sooner or later anyway. On the boardwalk's flagpole, the American flag is pulsing in an intermittent wind from the sea.

My father and mother go to the rail of the boardwalk and look down on the beach where a good many bathers are casually walking about. A few are in the surf. A peanut whistle pierces the air with its pleasant and active whine, and my father goes to buy peanuts. My mother remains at the rail and stares at the ocean. The ocean seems merry to her; it pointedly sparkles and again and again the pony waves are released. She notices the children digging in the wet sand, and the bathing costumes of the girls who are her own age. My father returns with the peanuts. Overhead the sun's lightning strikes and strikes, but neither of them are at all aware of it. The boardwalk is full of people dressed in their Sunday clothes and casually strolling. The tide does not reach as far as the boardwalk, and the strollers would feel no danger if it did. My father and mother lean on the rail of the boardwalk and absently stare at the ocean. The ocean is becoming rough; the waves come in slowly, tugging strength from far back. The moment before they somersault, the moment when they arch their backs so beautifully, showing white veins in the green and black, that moment is intolerable. They finally crack, dashing fiercely upon the sand, actually driving, full force downward, against it, bouncing upward and forward, and at last petering out into a small stream of bubbles which slides up the beach and then is recalled. The sun overhead does not disturb my father and my mother. They gaze idly at the ocean, scarcely interested in its harshness. But I stare at the terrible sun which breaks up sight, and the fatal merciless passionate ocean. I forget my parents. I stare fascinated, and finally, shocked by their indifference, I burst out weeping once more. The old lady next to me pats my shoulder and says: "There, there, young man, all of this is only a movie, only a movie," but I look up once more at the terrifying sun and the terrifying ocean, and being unable to control my tears I get up and go to the men's room, stumbling over the feet of the other people seated in my row.

IV

When I return, feeling as if I had just awakened in the morning sick for lack of sleep, several hours have apparently passed and my parents are riding on the merry-go-round. My father is on a black horse, my mother on a white one, and they seem to be making an eternal circuit for the single purpose of snatching the nickel rings which are attached to an arm of one of the posts. A hand-organ is playing; it is inseparable from the ceaseless circling of the merry-go-round.

For a moment it seems that they will never get off the carousel, for it will never stop, and I feel as if I were looking down from the fiftieth story of a building. But at length they do get off; even the hand-organ has ceased for a moment. There is a sudden and sweet stillness, as if the achievement of so much motion. My mother has acquired only two rings, my father, however, ten of them, although it was my mother who really wanted them.

They walk on along the boardwalk as the afternoon descends by imperceptible degrees into the incredible violet of dusk. Everything fades into a relaxed glow, even the ceaseless murmuring from the beach. They look for a place to have dinner. My father suggests the best restaurant on the boardwalk and my mother demurs, according to her principles of economy and housewifeliness.

However they do go to the best place, asking for a table near the window so that they can look out upon the boardwalk and the mobile ocean. My father feels omnipotent as he places a quarter in the waiter's hand in asking for a table. The place is crowded and here too there is music, this time from a kind of string trio. My father orders with a fine confidence.

As their dinner goes on, my father tells of his plans for the future and my mother shows with expressive face how interested she is, and how impressed. My father becomes exultant, lifted up by the waltz that is being played and his own future begins to intoxicate him. My father tells my mother that he is going to expand his business, for there is a great deal of money to be made. He wants to settle down. After all, he is twenty-nine, he has lived by himself since his thirteenth year, he is making more and more money, and he is envious of his friends when he visits them in the security of their homes, surrounded, it seems, by the calm domestic pleasures, and by delightful children, and then as the waltz reaches the moment when the dancers all swing madly, then, then with awful daring, then he asks my mother to marry him, although awkwardly enough and puzzled as to how he had arrived at the question, and she, to make the whole business worse, begins to cry, and my father looks nervously about, not knowing at all what to do now, and my mother says: "It's all I've wanted from the first moment I saw you," sobbing, and he finds all of this very difficult, scarcely to his taste, scarcely as he thought it would be, on his long walks over Brooklyn Bridge in the revery of a fine cigar, and it was then, at that point, that I stood up in the theater and shouted: "Don't do it! It's not too late to change your minds, both of you. Nothing good will come of it, only remorse, hatred, scandal, and two children whose characters are monstrous." The whole audience turned to look at me, annoyed, the usher came hurrying down the aisle flashing his searchlight, and the old lady next to me tugged me down into my seat, saying: "Be quiet. You'll be put out, and you paid thirty-five cents to come in." And so I shut my eyes because I could not bear to see what was happening. I sat there quietly.

V

But after a while I begin to take brief glimpses and at length I watch again with thirsty interest, like a child who tries to maintain his sulk when he is offered the bribe of candy. My parents are now having their picture taken in a photographer's booth along the boardwalk. The place is shadowed in the mauve light which is apparently necessary. The camera is set to the side on its tripod and looks like a Martian man. The photographer is instructing my parents in how to pose. My father has his arm over my mother's shoulder, and both of them smile emphatically. The photographer brings my mother a bouquet of flowers to hold in her hand, but she holds it at the wrong angle. Then the photographer covers himself with the black cloth which drapes the camera and all that one sees of him is one protruding arm and his hand with which he holds tightly to the rubber ball which he squeezes when the picture is taken. But he is not satisfied with their appearance. He feels that somehow there is something wrong in their pose. Again and again he comes out from his hiding place with new directions. Each suggestion merely makes matters worse.

My father is becoming impatient. They try a seated pose. The photographer explains that he has his pride, he wants to make beautiful pictures, he is not merely interested in all of this for the money. My father says: "Hurry up, will you? We haven't got all night." But the photographer only scurries about apologetically, issuing new directions. The photographer charms me, and I approve of him with all my heart, for I know exactly how he feels, and as he criticizes each revised pose according to some obscure idea of rightness, I become quite hopeful. But then my father says angrily: "Come on, you've had enough time, we're not going to wait any longer." And the photographer, sighing unhappily, goes back into the black covering, and holds out his hand, saying: "One, two, three, Now!", and the picture is taken, with my father's smile turned to a grimace and my mother's bright and false. It takes a few minutes for the picture to be developed and as my parents sit in the curious light they become depressed.

VI

They have passed a fortune-teller's booth and my mother wishes to go in, but my father does not. They begin to argue about it. My mother becomes stubborn, my father once more impatient. What my father would like to do now is walk off and leave my mother there, but he knows that that would never do. My mother refuses to budge. She is near tears, but she feels an uncontrollable desire to hear what the palm-reader will say. My father consents angrily and they both go into the booth which is, in a way, like the photographer's, since it is draped in black cloth and its light is colored and shadowed. The place is too warm, and my father keeps saying that this is all nonsense, pointing to the crystal ball on the table. The fortune-teller, a short, fat woman garbed in robes supposedly exotic, comes into the room and greets them, speaking with an accent, but suddenly my father feels that the whole thing is intolerable; he tugs at my mother's arm but my mother refuses to budge. And then, in terrible anger, my father lets go of my mother's arm and strides out, leaving my mother stunned. She makes a movement as if to go after him, but the fortune-teller holds her and begs her not to do so, and I in my seat in the darkness am shocked and horrified. I feel as if I were walking a tight-rope one hundred feet over a circus audience and suddenly the rope is showing signs of breaking, and I get up from my seat and begin to shout once more the first words I can think of to communicate my terrible fear, and once more the usher comes hurrying down the aisle flashing his searchlight, and the old lady pleads with me, and the shocked audience has turned to stare at me, and I keep shouting: "What are they doing? Don't they know what they are doing? Why doesn't my mother go after my father and beg him not to be angry? If she does not do that, what will she do? Doesn't my father know what he is doing?" But the usher has seized my arm, and is dragging me away, and as he does so, he says: "What are *you* doing? Don't you know you can't do things like this, you can't do whatever you want to do, even if other people aren't about? You will be sorry if you do not do what you should do. You can't carry on like this, it is not right, you will find that out soon enough, everything you do matters too much," and as he said that, dragging me through the lobby of the theater, into the cold light, I woke up into the bleak winter morning of my twenty-first birthday, the windowsill shining with its lip of snow, and the morning already begun.

King of the Bingo Game

RALPH ELLISON

(1914–)

The woman in front of him was eating roasted peanuts that smelled so good that he could barely contain his hunger. He could not even sleep and wished they'd hurry and begin the bingo game. There, on his right, two fellows were drinking wine out of a bottle wrapped in a paper bag, and he could hear soft gurgling in the dark. His stomach gave a low, gnawing growl. "If this was down South," he thought, "all I'd have to do is lean over and say, 'Lady, gimme a few of those peanuts, please ma'm,' and she'd pass me the bag and never think nothing of it." Or he could ask the fellows for a drink in the same way. Folks down South stuck together that way; they didn't even have to know you. But up here it was different. Ask somebody for something, and they'd think you were crazy. Well, I ain't crazy. I'm just broke, 'cause I got no birth certificate to get a job, and Laura 'bout to die 'cause we got no money for a doctor. But I ain't crazy. And yet a pinpoint of doubt was focused in his mind as he glanced toward the screen and saw the hero stealthily entering a dark room and sending the beam of a flashlight along a wall of bookcases. This is where he finds the trapdoor, he remembered. The man would pass abruptly through the wall and find the girl tied to a bed, her legs and arms spread wide, and her clothing torn to rags. He laughed softly to himself. He had seen the picture three times, and this was one of the best scenes.

On his right the fellow whispered wide-eyed to his companion. "Man, look a-yonder!"

"Damn!"

"Wouldn't I like to have her tied up like that . . ."

"Hey! That fool's letting her loose!"

"Aw, man, he loves her."

"Love or no love!"

The man moved impatiently beside him, and he tried to involve himself in the scene. But Laura was on his mind. Tiring quickly of watching the picture he looked back to where the white beam filtered from the projection room above the balcony. It started small and grew large, specks of dust dancing in its whiteness as it reached the screen. It was strange how the beam always landed right on the screen and didn't mess up and fall somewhere else. But they had it all fixed. Everything was fixed. Now suppose when they showed that girl with her dress torn the girl started taking off the rest of her clothes, and when the guy came in he didn't untie her but kept her there and went to taking off his own clothes? *That* would be something to see. If a picture got out of hand like that those guys up there would go nuts. Yeah, and there'd be so many folks in here you couldn't find a seat for nine months! A strange sensation played over his skin. He shuddered. Yesterday he'd seen a bedbug on a woman's neck as they walked out into the bright street. But exploring his thigh through a hole in his pocket he found only goose pimples and old scars.

The bottle gurgled again. He closed his eyes. Now a dreamy music was accompanying the film and train whistles were sounding in the distance, and he was a boy again walking along a railroad trestle down South, and seeing the train coming, and running back as fast as he could go, and hearing the whistle blowing, and getting off the trestle to solid ground just in time, with the earth trembling beneath his feet, and feeling relieved as he ran down the cinder-strewn embankment onto the highway, and looking back and seeing with terror that the train had left the track and was following him right down the middle of the street, and all the white people laughing as he ran screaming . . .

"Wake up there, buddy! What the hell do you mean hollering like that! Can't you see we trying to enjoy this here picture?"

He stared at the man with gratitude.

"I'm sorry, old man," he said. "I musta been dreaming."

"Well, here, have a drink. And don't be making no noise like that, damn!"

His hands trembled as he tilted his head. It was not wine, but whiskey. Cold rye whiskey. He took a deep swoller, decided it was better not to take another, and handed the bottle back to its owner.

"Thanks, old man," he said.

Now he felt the cold whiskey breaking a warm path straight through the middle of him, growing hotter and sharper as it moved. He had not eaten all day, and it made him light-headed. The smell of the peanuts stabbed him like a knife, and he got up and found a seat in the middle aisle. But no sooner did he sit than he saw a row of intense-faced young girls, and got up again, thinking, "You chicks musta been Lindy-hopping somewhere." He found a seat several rows ahead as the lights came on, and he saw the screen disappear behind a heavy red and gold curtain; then the curtain rising, and the man with the microphone and a uniformed attendant coming on the stage.

He felt for his bingo cards, smiling. The guy at the door wouldn't like it if he knew about his having *five* cards. Well, not everyone played the bingo game; and even with five cards he didn't have much of a chance. For Laura, though, he had to have faith. He studied the cards, each with its different numerals, punching the free center hole in each and spreading them neatly across his lap; and when the lights faded he sat slouched in his seat so that he could look from his cards to the bingo wheel with but a quick shifting of his eyes.

Ahead, at the end of the darkness, the man with the microphone was pressing a button attached to a long cord and spinning the bingo wheel and calling out the number each time the wheel came to rest. And each time the voice rang out his finger raced over the cards for the number. With five cards he had to move fast. He became nervous; there were too many cards, and the man went too fast with his grating voice. Perhaps he should just select one and throw the others away. But he was afraid. He became warm. Wonder how much Laura's doctor would cost? Damn that, watch the cards! And with despair he heard the man call three in a row which he missed on all five cards. This way he'd never win . . .

When he saw the row of holes punched across the third card, he sat paralyzed and heard the man call three more numbers before he stumbled forward, screaming.

"Bingo! Bingo!"

"Let that fool up there," someone called.

"Get up there, man!"

He stumbled down the aisle and up the steps to the stage into a light so sharp and bright that for a moment it blinded him, and he felt that he had moved into the spell of some strange, mysterious power. Yet it was as familiar as the sun, and he knew it was the perfectly familiar bingo.

The man with the microphone was saying something to the audience as he held out his card. A cold light flashed from the man's finger as the card left his hands. His knees trembled. The man stepped closer, checking the card against the numbers chalked on the board. Suppose he had made a mistake? The pomade on the man's hair made him feel faint, and he backed away. But the man was checking the card over the microphone now, and he had to stay. He stood tense, listening.

"Under the O, forty-four," the man chanted. "Under the I, seven. Under the G, three. Under the B, ninety-six. Under the N, thirteen!"

His breath came easier as the man smiled at the audience.

"Yessir, ladies and gentlemen, he's one of the chosen people!"

The audience rippled with laughter and applause.

"Step right up to the front of the stage."

He moved slowly forward, wishing that the light was not so bright.

"To win tonight's jackpot of $36.90 the wheel must stop between the double zero, understand?"

He nodded, knowing the ritual from the many days and nights he had watched the winners march across the stage to press the button that controlled the spinning wheel and receive the prizes. And now he followed the instructions as though he'd crossed the slippery stage a million prize-winning times.

The man was making some kind of a joke, and he nodded vacantly. So tense had he become that he felt a sudden desire to cry and shook it away. He felt vaguely that his whole life was determined by the bingo wheel; not only that which would happen now that he was at last before it, but all that had gone before, since his birth, and his mother's birth and the birth of his father. It had always been there, even though he had not been aware of it, handing out the unlucky cards and numbers of his days. The feeling persisted, and he started quickly away. I better get down from here before I make a fool of myself, he thought.

"Here, boy," the man called. "You haven't started yet."

Someone laughed as he went hesitantly back.

"Are you all reet?"

He grinned at the man's jive talk, but no words would come, and he knew it was not a convincing grin. For suddenly he knew that he stood on the slippery brink of some terrible embarrassment.

"Where are you from, boy?" the man asked.

"Down South."

"He's from down South, ladies and gentlemen," the man said. "Where from? Speak right into the mike."

"Rocky Mont," he said. "Rock' Mont, North Car'lina."

"So you decided to come down off that mountain to the U.S.," the man laughed. He felt that the man was making a fool of him, but then something cold was placed in his hand, and the lights were no longer behind him.

Standing before the wheel he felt alone, but that was somehow right, and he remembered his plan. He would give the wheel a short quick twirl. Just a touch of the button. He had watched it many times, and always it came close to double zero when it was short and quick. He steeled himself; the fear had left, and he felt a profound sense of promise, as though he were about to be repaid for all the things he'd suffered all his life. Trembling, he pressed the button. There was a whirl of lights, and in a second he realized with finality that though he wanted to, he could not stop. It was as though he held a high-powered line in his naked hand. His nerves tightened. As the wheel increased its speed it seemed to draw him more and more into its power, as though it held his fate; and with it came a deep need to submit, to whirl, to lose himself in its swirl of color. He could not stop it now, he knew. So let it be.

The button rested snugly in his palm where the man had placed it. And now he became aware of the man beside him, advising him through the microphone, while behind the shadowy audience hummed with noisy voices. He shifted his feet. There was still that feeling of helplessness within him, making part of him desire to turn back, even now that the jackpot was right in his hand. He squeezed the button until his fist ached. Then, like the sudden shriek of a subway whistle, a doubt tore through his head. Suppose he did not spin the wheel long enough? What could he do, and how could he tell? And then he knew, even as he wondered, that as long as he pressed the button, he could control the jackpot. He and only he could determine whether or not it was to be his. Not even the man with the microphone could do anything about it now. He felt drunk. Then, as though he had come down from a high hill into a valley of people, he heard the audience yelling.

"Come down from there, you jerk!"

"Let somebody else have a chance . . ."

"Ole Jack thinks he done found the end of the rainbow . . ."

The last voice was not unfriendly, and he turned and smiled dreamily into the yelling mouths. Then he turned his back squarely on them.

"Don't take too long, boy," a voice said.

He nodded. They were yelling behind him. Those folks did not understand what had happened to him. They had been playing the bingo game day in and night out for years, trying to win rent money or hamburger change. But not one of those wise guys had discovered this wonderful thing. He watched the wheel whirling past the numbers and experienced a burst of exaltation: This is God! This is the really truly God! He said it aloud, "This is God!"

He said it with such absolute conviction that he feared he would fall fainting into the footlights. But the crowd yelled so loud that they could not hear. Those fools, he thought. I'm here trying to tell them the most wonderful secret in the world, and they're yelling like they gone crazy. A hand fell upon his shoulder.

"You'll have to make a choice now, boy. You've taken too long."

He brushed the hand violently away.

"Leave me alone, man. I know what I'm doing!"

The man looked surprised and held on to the microphone for support. And because he did not wish to hurt the man's feelings he smiled, realizing with a sudden pang that there was no way of explaining to the man just why he had to stand there pressing the button forever.

"Come here," he called tiredly.

The man approached, rolling the heavy microphone across the stage.

"Anybody can play this bingo game, right?" he said.

"Sure, but . . ."

He smiled, feeling inclined to be patient with this slick looking white man with his blue sport shirt and his sharp gabardine suit.

"That's what I thought," he said. "Anybody can win the jackpot as long as they get the lucky number, right?"

"That's the rule, but after all . . ."

"That's what I thought," he said. "And the big prize goes to the man who knows how to win it?"

The man nodded speechlessly.

"Well then, go on over there and watch me win like I want to. I ain't going to hurt nobody," he said, "and I'll show you how to win. I mean to show the whole world how it's got to be done."

And because he understood, he smiled again to let the man know that he held nothing against him for being white and impatient. Then he refused to see the man any longer and stood pressing the button, the voices of the crowd reaching him like sounds in distant streets. Let them yell. All the Negroes down there were just ashamed because he was black like them. He smiled inwardly, knowing how it was. Most of the time he was ashamed of what Negroes did himself. Well, let them be ashamed for something this time. Like him. He was like a long thin black wire that was being stretched and wound upon the bingo wheel; wound until he wanted to scream; wound, but this time himself controlling the winding and the sadness and the shame, and because he did, Laura would be all right. Suddenly the lights flickered. He staggered backwards. Had something gone wrong? All this noise. Didn't they know that although he controlled the wheel, it also controlled him, and unless he pressed the button forever and forever and ever it would stop, leaving him high and dry, dry and high on this hard high slippery hill and Laura dead? There was only once chance; he had to do whatever the wheel demanded. And gripping the button in despair, he discovered with surprise that it imparted a nervous energy. His spine tingled. He felt a certain power.

Now he faced the raging crowd with defiance, its screams penetrating his eardrums like trumpets shrieking from a jukebox. The vague faces glowing in the bingo lights gave him a sense of himself that he had never known before. He was running the show, by God! They had to react to him, for he was their luck. This is *me,* he thought. Let the bastards yell. Then someone was laughing inside him, and he realized that somehow he had forgotten his own name. It was a sad, lost feeling to lose your name, and a crazy thing to do. That name had been given him by the white man who had owned his grandfather a long lost time ago down South. But maybe those wise guys knew his name.

"Who am I?" he screamed.

"Hurry up and bingo, you jerk!"

They didn't know either, he thought sadly. They didn't even know their own names, they were all poor nameless bastards. Well, he didn't need that old name; he was reborn. For as long as he pressed the button he was The-man-who-pressed-the-button-who-held-the-prize-who-was-the-King-of-Bingo. That was the way it was, and he'd have to press the button even if nobody understood, even though Laura did not understand.

"Live!" he shouted.

The audience quieted like the dying of a huge fan.

"Live, Laura, baby. I got holt of it now, sugar. Live!"

He screamed it, tears streaming down his face. "I got nobody but YOU!"

The screams tore from his very guts. He felt as though the rush of blood to his head would burst out in baseball seams of small red droplets, like a head beaten by police clubs. Bending over he saw a trickle of blood splashing the toe of his shoe. With his free hand he searched his head. It was his nose. God, suppose something has gone wrong? He felt that the whole audience had somehow entered him and was stamping its feet in his stomach, and he was unable to throw them out. They wanted the prize, that was it. They wanted the secret for themselves. But they'd never get it; he would keep the bingo wheel whirling forever, and Laura would be safe in the wheel. But would she? It had to be, because if she were not safe the wheel would cease to turn; it could not go on. He had to get away, *vomit* all, and his mind formed an image of himself running with Laura in his arms down the tracks of the subway just ahead of an A train, running desperately *vomit* with people screaming for him to come out but knowing no way of leaving the tracks because to stop would bring the train crushing down upon him and to attempt to leave across the other tracks would mean to run into a hot third rail as high as his waist which threw blue sparks that blinded his eyes until he could hardly see.

He heard singing and the audience was clapping its hands.

Shoot the liquor to him, Jim, boy!
Clap-clap-clap
Well a-calla the cop
He's blowing his top!
Shoot the liquor to him, Jim, boy!

Bitter anger grew within him at the singing. They think I'm crazy. Well let 'em laugh. I'll do what I got to do.

He was standing in an attitude of intense listening when he saw that they were watching something on the stage behind him. He felt weak. But when he turned he saw no one. If only his thumb did not ache so. Now they were applauding. And for a moment he thought that the wheel had stopped. But that was impossible, his thumb still pressed the button. Then he saw them. Two men in uniform beckoned from the end of the stage. They were coming toward him, walking in step, slowly, like a tap dance team returning for a third encore. But their shoulders shot forward, and he backed away, looking wildly about. There was nothing to fight them with. He had only the long black cord which led to a plug somewhere back stage, and he couldn't use that because it operated the bingo wheel. He backed slowly, fixing the men with his eyes as his lips stretched over his teeth in a tight, fixed grin; moved toward the end of the stage and realizing that he couldn't go much further, for suddenly the cord became taut and he couldn't afford to break the cord. But he had to do something. The audience was howling. Suddenly he stopped dead, seeing the men halt, their legs lifted as in an interrupted step of a slow-motion dance. There was nothing to do but run in the other direction and he dashed forward, slipping and sliding. The men fell back, surprised. He struck out violently going past.

"Grab him!"

He ran, but all too quickly the cord tightened, resistingly, and he turned and ran back again. This time he slipped them, and discovered by running in a circle before the wheel he could keep the cord from tightening. But this way he had to flail his arms to keep the men away. Why couldn't they leave a man alone? He ran, circling.

"Ring down the curtain," someone yelled. But they couldn't do that. If they did the wheel flashing from the projection room would be cut off. But they had him before he could tell them so, trying to pry open his fist, and he was wrestling and trying to bring his knees into the fight and holding on to the button, for it was his life. And now he was down, seeing a foot coming down, crushing his wrist cruelly, down, as he saw the wheel whirling serenely above.

"I can't give it up," he screamed. Then quietly, in a confidential tone, "Boys, I really can't give it up."

It landed hard against his head. And in the blank moment they had it away from him, completely now. He fought them trying to pull him up from the stage as he watched the wheel spin slowly to a stop. Without surprise he saw it rest at double zero.

"You see," he pointed bitterly.

"Sure, boy, sure, it's O.K.," one of the men said smiling.

And seeing the man bow his head to someone he could not see, he felt very, very happy; he would receive what all the winners received.

But as he warmed in the justice of the man's tight smile he did not see the man's slow wink, nor see the bow-legged man behind him step clear of the swiftly descending curtain and set himself for a blow. He only felt the dull pain exploding in his skull, and he knew even as it slipped out of him that his luck had run out on the stage.

Black Is My Favorite Color

BERNARD MALAMUD

(1914–)

Charity Sweetness sits in the toilet eating her two hard-boiled eggs while I'm having my ham sandwich and coffee in the kitchen. That's how it goes only don't get the idea of ghettoes. If there's a ghetto I'm the one that's in it. She's my cleaning woman from Father Divine and comes in once a week to my small three-room apartment on my day off from the liquor store. "Peace," she says to me, "Father reached on down and took me right up in Heaven." She's a small person with a flat body, frizzy hair, and a quiet face that the light shines out of, and Mama had such eyes before she died. The first time Charity Sweetness came in to clean, a little more than a year and a half, I made the mistake to ask her to sit down at the kitchen table with me and eat her lunch. I was still feeling not so hot after Ornita left but I'm the kind of a man—Nat Lime, forty-four, a bachelor with a daily growing bald spot on the back of my head, and I could lose frankly fifteen pounds—who enjoys company so long as he has it. So she cooked up her two hard-boiled eggs and sat down and took a small bite out of one of them. But after a minute she stopped chewing and she got up and carried the eggs in a cup in the bathroom, and since then she eats there. I said to her more than once, "Okay, Charity Sweetness, so have it your way, eat the eggs in the kitchen by yourself and I'll eat when you're done," but she smiles absentminded and eats in the toilet. It's my fate with colored people.

Although black is still my favorite color you wouldn't know it from my luck except in short quantities even though I do all right in the liquor store business in Harlem, on Eighth Avenue between 110th and 111th. I speak with respect. A large part of my life I've had dealings with Negro people, most on a business basis but sometimes for friendly reasons with genuine feeling on both sides. I'm drawn to them. At this time of my life I should have one or two good colored friends but the fault isn't necessarily mine. If they knew what was in my heart towards them, but how can you tell that to anybody nowadays? I've tried more than once but the language of the heart either is a dead language or else nobody understands it the way you speak it. Very few. What I'm saying is, personally for me there's only one human color and that's the color of blood. I like a black person if not because he's black, then because I'm white. It comes to the same thing. If I wasn't white my first choice would be black. I'm satisfied to be white because I have no other choice. Anyway, I got an eye for color. I appreciate. Who wants everybody to be the same? Maybe it's like some kind of a talent. Nat Lime might be a liquor dealer in Harlem, but once in the jungle in New Guinea in the Second War, I got the idea when I shot at a running Jap and missed him, that I had some kind of a talent, though maybe it's the kind where you have a marvelous idea now and then but in the end what do they come to? After all, it's a strange world.

Where Charity Sweetness eats her eggs makes me think about Buster Wilson when we were both boys in the Williamsburg section of Brooklyn. There was this long block of run-down dirty frame houses in the middle of a not-so-hot white neighborhood full of pushcarts. The Negro houses looked to me like they had been born and died there, dead not long after the beginning of the world. I lived on the next street. My father was a cutter with arthritis in both hands, big red knuckles and swollen fingers so he didn't cut, and my mother was the one who went to work. She sold paper bags from a second-hand pushcart in Ellery Street. We didn't starve but nobody ate chicken unless we were sick or the chicken was. This was my first acquaintance with a lot of black people and I used to poke around on their poor block. I think I thought, brother, if there can be like this, what can't there be? I mean I caught an early idea what life was about. Anyway I met Buster Wilson there. He used to play marbles by himself. I sat on the curb across the street, watching him shoot one marble lefty and the other one righty. The hand that won picked up the marbles. It wasn't so much of a game but he didn't ask me to come over. My idea was to be friendly, only he never encouraged, he discouraged. Why did I pick him out for a friend? Maybe because I had no others then, we were new in the neighborhood, from Manhattan. Also I liked his type. Buster did everything alone. He was a skinny kid and his brothers' clothes hung on him like worn-out potato sacks. He was a beanpole boy, about twelve, and I was then ten. His arms and legs were burnt out matchsticks. He always wore a brown wool sweater, one arm half unraveled, the other went down to the wrist. His long and narrow head had a white part cut straight in the short woolly hair, maybe with a ruler there, by his father, a barber but too drunk to stay a barber. In those days though I had little myself I was old enough to know who was better off, and the whole block of colored houses made me feel bad in the daylight. But I went there as much as I could because the street was full of life. In the night it looked different, it's hard to tell a cripple in the dark. Sometimes I was afraid to walk by the houses when they were dark and quiet. I was afraid there were people looking at me that I couldn't see. I liked it better when they had parties at night and everybody had a good time. The musicians played their banjos and saxophones and the houses shook with the music and laughing. The young girls, with their pretty dresses and ribbons in their hair, caught me in my throat when I saw them through the windows.

But with the parties came drinking and fights. Sundays were bad days after the Saturday night parties. I remember once that Buster's father, also long and loose, always wearing a dirty gray Homburg hat, chased another black man in the street with a half-inch chisel. The other one, maybe five feet high, lost his shoe and when they wrestled on the ground he was already bleeding through his suit, a thick red blood smearing the sidewalk. I was frightened by the blood and wanted to pour it back in the man who was bleeding from the chisel. On another time Buster's father was playing in a crap game with two big bouncy red dice, in the back of an alley between two middle houses. Then about six men started fist-fighting there, and they ran out of the alley and hit each other in the street. The neighbors, including children, came out and watched, everybody afraid but nobody moving to do anything. I saw the same thing near my store in Harlem, years later, a big-crowd watching two men in the street, their breaths hanging in the air on a winter night, murdering each other with switch knives, but nobody moved to call a cop. I didn't either. Anyway, I was just a young kid but I still remember how the cops drove up in a police paddy wagon and broke up the fight by hitting everybody they could hit with big nightsticks. This was in the days before LaGuardia. Most of the fighters were knocked out cold, only one or two got away. Buster's father started to run back in his house but a cop ran after him and cracked him on his Homburg hat with a club, right on the front porch. Then the Negro men were lifted up by the cops, one at the arms and the other at the feet, and they heaved them in the paddy wagon. Buster's father hit the back of the wagon and fell, with his nose spouting very red blood, on top of three other men. I personally couldn't stand it, I was scared of the human race so I ran home, but I remember Buster watching without any expression in his eyes. I stole an extra fifteen cents from my mother's pocketbook and I ran back and asked Buster if he wanted to go to the movies. I would pay. He said yes. This was the first time he talked to me.

So we went more than once to the movies. But we never got to be friends. Maybe because it was a one-way proposition—from me to him. Which includes my invitations to go with me, my (poor mother's) movie money, Hershey chocolate bars, watermelon slices, even my best Nick Carter and Merriwell books that I spent hours picking up in the junk shops, and that he never gave me back. Once he let me go in his house to get a match so we could smoke some butts we found, but it smelled so heavy, so impossible, I died till I got out of there. What I saw in the way of furniture I won't mention—the best was falling apart in pieces. Maybe we went to the movies all together five or six matinees that spring and in the summertime, but when the shows were over he usually walked home by himself.

"Why don't you wait for me, Buster?" I said. "We're both going in the same direction."

But he was walking ahead and didn't hear me. Anyway he didn't answer.

One day when I wasn't expecting it he hit me in the teeth. I felt like crying but not because of the pain. I spit blood and said, "What did you hit me for? What did I do to you?"

"Because you a Jew bastard. Take your Jew movies and your Jew candy and shove them up your Jew ass."

And he ran away.

I thought to myself how was I to know he didn't like the movies. When I was a man I thought, you can't force it.

Years later, in the prime of my life, I met Mrs. Ornita Harris. She was standing by herself under an open umbrella at the bus stop, crosstown 110th, and I picked up her green glove that she had dropped on the wet sidewalk. It was the end of November. Before I could ask her was it hers, she grabbed the glove out of my hand, closed her umbrella, and stepped in the bus. I got on right after her.

I was annoyed so I said, "If you'll pardon me, Miss, there's no law that you have to say thanks, but at least don't make a criminal out of me."

"Well, I'm sorry," she said, "but I don't like white men trying to do me favors."

I tipped my hat and that was that. In ten minutes I got off the bus but she was already gone.

Who expected to see her again but I did. She came into my store about a week later for a bottle of scotch.

"I would offer you a discount," I told her, "but I know you don't like a certain kind of a favor and I'm not looking for a slap in the face."

Then she recognized me and got a little embarrassed.

"I'm sorry I misunderstood you that day."

"So mistakes happen."

The result was she took the discount. I gave her a dollar off.

She used to come in about every two weeks for a fifth of Haig and Haig. Sometimes I waited on her, sometimes my helpers, Jimmy or Mason, also colored, but I said to give the discount. They both looked at me but I had nothing to be ashamed. In the spring when she came in we used to talk once in a while. She was a slim woman, dark but not the most dark, about thirty years I would say, also well built, with a combination nice legs and good-size bosom that I like. Her face was pretty, with big eyes and high cheek bones, but lips a little thick and a nose a little broad. Sometimes she didn't feel like talking, she paid for the bottle, less discount, and walked out. Her eyes were tired and she didn't look to me like a happy woman.

I found out her husband was once a window cleaner on the big buildings, but one day his safety belt broke and he fell fifteen stories. After the funeral she got a job as a manicurist in a Times Square barber shop. I told her I was a bachelor and lived with my mother in a small three-room apartment on West Eighty-third near Broadway. My mother had cancer, and Ornita said she was very sorry.

One night in July we went out together. How that happened I'm still not so sure. I guess I asked her and she didn't say no. Where do you go out with a Negro woman? We went to the Village. We had a good dinner and walked in Washington Square Park. It was a hot night. Nobody was surprised when they saw us, nobody looked at us like we were against the law. If they looked maybe they saw my new lightweight suit that I bought yesterday and my shiny bald spot when we walked under a lamp, also how pretty she was for a man of my type. We went in a movie on West Eighth Street. I didn't want to go in but she said she had heard about the picture. We went in like strangers and we came out like strangers. I wondered what was in her mind and I thought to myself, whatever is in there it's not a certain white man that I know. All night long we went together like we were chained. After the movie she wouldn't let me take her back to Harlem. When I put her in a taxi she asked me, "Why did we bother?"

For the steak, I wanted to say. Instead I said, "You're worth the bother."

"Thanks anyway."

Kiddo, I thought to myself after the taxi left, you just found out what's what, now the best thing is forget her.

It's easy to say. In August we went out the second time. That was the night she wore a purple dress and I thought to myself, my God, what colors. Who paints that picture paints a masterpiece. Everybody looked at us but I had pleasure. That night when she took off her dress it was in a furnished room I had the sense to rent a few days before. With my sick mother, I couldn't ask her to come to my apartment, and she didn't want me to go home with her where she lived with her brother's family on West 115th near Lenox Avenue. Under her purple dress she wore a black slip, and when she took that off she had white underwear. When she took off the white underwear she was black again. But I know where the next white was, if you want to call it white. And that was the night I think I fell in love with her, the first time in my life though I have liked one or two nice girls I used to go with when I was a boy. It was a serious proposition. I'm the kind of a man when I think of love I'm thinking of marriage. I guess that's why I am a bachelor.

That same week I had a holdup in my place, two big men—both black—with revolvers. One got excited when I rang open the cash register so he could take the money and he hit me over the ear with his gun. I stayed in the hospital a couple of weeks. Otherwise I was insured. Ornita came to see me. She sat on a chair without talking much. Finally I saw she was uncomfortable so I suggested she ought to go home.

"I'm sorry it happened," she said.

"Don't talk like it's your fault."

When I got out of the hospital my mother was dead. She was a wonderful person. My father died when I was thirteen and all by herself she kept the family alive and together. I sat shive for a week and remembered how she sold paper bags on her pushcart. I remembered her life and what she tried to teach me. Nathan, she said, if you ever forget you are a Jew a goy will remind you. Mama, I said, rest in peace on this subject. But if I do something you don't like, remember, on earth it's harder than where you are. Then when my week of mourning was finished, one night I said, "Ornita, let's get married. We're both honest people and if you love me like I love you it won't be such a bad time. If you don't like New York I'll sell out here and we'll move someplace else. Maybe to San Francisco where nobody knows us. I was there for a week in the Second War and I saw white and colored living together."

"Nat," she answered me, "I like you but I'd be afraid. My husband woulda killed me."

"Your husband is dead."

"Not in my memory."

"In that case I'll wait."

"Do you know what it'd be like—I mean the life we could expect?"

"Ornita," I said, "I'm the kind of a man, if he picks his own way of life he's satisfied."

"What about children? Were you looking forward to half-Jewish polka dots?"

"I was looking forward to children."

"I can't," she said.

Can't is can't. I saw she was afraid and the best thing was not to push. Sometimes when we met she was so nervous that whatever we did she couldn't enjoy it. At the same time I still thought I had a chance. We were together more and more. I got rid of my furnished room and she came to my apartment—I gave away Mama's bed and bought a new one. She stayed with me all day on Sundays. When she wasn't so nervous she was affectionate, and if I know what love is, I had it. We went out a couple of times a week, the same way—usually I met her in Times Square and sent her home in a taxi, but I talked more about marriage and she talked less against it. One night she told me she was still trying to convince herself but she was almost convinced. I took an inventory of my liquor stock so I could put the store up for sale.

Ornita knew what I was doing. One day she quit her job, the next day she took it back. She also went away a week to visit her sister in Philadelphia for a little rest. She came back tired but said maybe. Maybe is maybe so I'll wait. The way she said it it was closer to yes. That was the winter two years ago. When she was in Philadelphia I called up a friend of mine from the Army, now CPA, and told him I would appreciate an invitation for an evening. He knew why. His wife said yes right away. When Ornita came back we went there. The wife made a fine dinner. It wasn't a bad time and they told us to come again. Ornita had a few drinks. She looked relaxed, wonderful. Later, because of a twenty-four hour taxi strike I had to take her home on the subway. When we got to the 116th Street station she told me to stay on the train, and she would walk the couple of blocks to her house. I didn't like a woman walking alone on the streets at that time of the night. She said she never had any trouble but I insisted nothing doing. I said I would walk to her stoop with her and when she went upstairs I would go back to the subway.

On the way there, on 115th in the middle of the block before Lenox, we were stopped by three men—maybe they were boys. One had a black hat with a half-inch brim, one a green cloth hat, and the third wore a black leather cap. The green hat was wearing a short coat and the other two had long ones. It was under a street light but the leather cap snapped a six-inch switchblade open in the light.

"What you doin' with this white son of a bitch?" he said to Ornita.

"I'm minding my own business," she answered him, "and I wish you would too."

"Boys," I said, "we're all brothers. I'm a reliable merchant in the neighborhood. This young lady is my dear friend. We don't want any trouble. Please let us pass."

"You talk like a Jew landlord," said the green hat. "Fifty a week for a single room."

"No charge fo' the rats," said the half-inch brim.

"Believe me, I'm no landlord. My store is 'Nathan's Liquors' between Hundred Tenth and Eleventh. I also have two colored clerks, Mason and Jimmy, and they will tell you I pay good wages as well as I give discounts to certain customers."

"Shut your mouth, Jewboy," said the leather cap, and he moved the knife back and forth in front of my coat button. "No more black pussy for you."

"Speak with respect about this lady, please."

I got slapped on my mouth.

"That ain't no lady," said the long face in the half-inch brim, "that's black pussy. She deserve to have evvy bit of her hair shave off. How you like to have evvy bit of your hair shave off, black pussy?"

"Please leave me and this gentleman alone or I'm gonna scream long and loud. That's my house three doors down."

They slapped her. I never heard such a scream. Like her husband was falling fifteen stories.

I hit the one that slapped her and the next I knew I was lying in the gutter with a pain in my head. I thought, goodbye, Nat, they'll stab me for sure, but all they did was take my wallet and run in three different directions.

Ornita walked back with me to the subway and she wouldn't let me go home with her again.

"Just get home safely."

She looked terrible. Her face was gray and I still remembered her scream. It was a terrible winter night, very cold February, and it took me an hour and ten minutes to get home. I felt bad for leaving her but what could I do?

We had a date downtown the next night but she didn't show up, the first time.

In the morning I called her in her place of business.

"For God's sake, Ornita, if we got married and moved away we wouldn't have that kind of trouble that we had. We wouldn't come in that neighborhood any more."

"Yes, we would. I have family there and don't want to move anyplace else. The truth of it is I can't marry you, Nat. I got troubles enough of my own."

"I coulda sworn you love me."

"Maybe I do but I can't marry you."

"For God's sake, why?"

"I got enough trouble of my own."

I went that night in a cab to her brother's house to see her. He was a quiet man with a thin mustache. "She gone," he said, "left for a long visit to some close relatives in the South. She said to tell you she appreciate your intentions but didn't think it will work out."

"Thank you kindly," I said.

Don't ask me how I got home.

Once on Eighth Avenue, a couple of blocks from my store, I saw a blind man with a white cane tapping on the sidewalk. I figured we were going in the same direction so I took his arm.

"I can tell you're white," he said.

A heavy colored woman with a full shopping bag rushed after us.

"Never mind," she said, "I know where he live."

She pushed me with her shoulder and I hurt my leg on the fire hydrant.

That's how it is. I give my heart and they kick me in my teeth.

"Charity Sweetness—you hear me?—come out of that goddamn toilet!"

A Silver Dish

SAUL BELLOW
(1915–)

What do you do about death—in this case, the death of an old father? If you're a modern person, sixty years of age, and a man who's been around, like Woody Selbst, what do you do? Take this matter of mourning, and take it against a contemporary background. How, against a contemporary background, do you mourn an octogenarian father, nearly blind, his heart enlarged, his lungs filling with fluid, who creeps, stumbles, gives off the odors, the moldiness or gassiness of old men. I *mean!* As Woody put it, be realistic. Think what times these are. The papers daily give it to you—the Lufthansa pilot in Aden is described by the hostages on his knees, begging the Palestinian terrorists not to execute him, but they shoot him through the head. Later they themselves are killed. And still others shoot others, or shoot themselves. That's what you read in the press, see on the tube, mention at dinner. We know now what goes daily through the whole of the human community, like a global death-peristalsis.

Woody, a businessman in South Chicago, was not an ignorant person. He knew more such phrases than you would expect a tile contractor (offices, lobbies, lavatories) to know. The kind of knowledge he had was not the kind for which you get academic degrees. Although Woody had studied for two years in a seminary, preparing to be a minister. Two years of college during the Depression was more than most high-school graduates could afford. After that, in his own vital, picturesque, original way (Morris, his old man, was also, in his days of nature, vital and picturesque) Woody had read up on many subjects, subscribed to *Science* and other magazines that gave real information, and had taken night courses at De Paul and Northwestern in ecology, criminology, existentialism. Also he had travelled extensively in Japan, Mexico, and Africa, and there was an African experience that was especially relevant to mourning. It was this: On a launch near the Murchison Falls in Uganda, he had seen a buffalo calf seized by a crocodile from the bank of the White Nile. There were giraffes along the tropical river, and hippopotamuses, and baboons, and flamingos and other brilliant birds crossing the bright air in the heat of the morning, when the calf, stepping into the river to drink, was grabbed by the hoof and dragged down. The parent buffaloes couldn't figure it out. Under the water the calf still threshed, fought, churned the mud. Woody, the robust traveller, took this in as he sailed by, and to him it looked as if the parent cattle were asking each other dumbly what had happened. He chose to assume that there was pain in this, he read brute grief into it. On the White Nile, Woody had the impression that he had gone back to the pre-Adamite past, and he brought reflections on this impression home to South Chicago. He brought also a bundle of hashish from Kampala. In this he took a chance with the customs inspectors, banking perhaps on his broad build, frank face, high color. He didn't look like a wrongdoer, a bad guy; he looked like a good guy. But he liked taking chances. Risk was a wonderful stimulus. He threw down his trenchcoat on the customs counter. If the inspectors searched the pockets, he was prepared to say that the coat wasn't his. But he got away with it, and the Thanksgiving turkey was stuffed with hashish. This was much enjoyed. That was practically the last feast at which Pop, who also relished risk or defiance, was present. The hashish Woody had tried to raise in his back yard from the Africa seeds didn't take. But behind his warehouse, where the Lincoln Continental was parked, he kept a patch of marijuana. There was no harm at all in Woody but he didn't like being entirely within the law. It was simply a question of self-respect.

After that Thanksgiving, Pop gradually sank as if he had a slow leak. This went on for some years. In and out of the hospital, he dwindled, his mind wandered, he couldn't even concentrate enough to complain, except in exceptional moments on the Sundays Woody regularly devoted to him. Morris, an amateur who once was taken seriously by Willie Hoppe, the great pro himself, couldn't execute the simplest billiard shots anymore. He could only conceive shots; he began to theorize about impossible three-cushion combinations. Halina, the Polish woman with whom Morris had lived for over forty years as man and wife, was too old herself now to run to the hospital. So Woody had to do it. There was Woody's mother, too—a Christian convert—needing care; she was over eighty and frequently hospitalized. Everybody had diabetes and pleurisy and arthritis and cataracts and cardiac pacemakers. And everybody had lived by the body, but the body was giving out.

There were Woody's two sisters as well, unmarried, in their fifties, very Christian, very straight, still living with Mama in an entirely Christian bungalow. Woody, who took full responsibility for them all, occasionally had to put one of the girls (they had become sick girls) in a mental institution. Nothing severe. The sisters were wonderful women, both of them gorgeous once, but neither of the poor things was playing with a full deck. And all the factions had to be kept separate—Mama, the Christian convert; the fundamentalist sisters; Pop, who read the Yiddish paper as long as he could still see print; Halina, a good Catholic. Woody, the seminary forty years behind him, described himself as an agnostic. Pop had no more religion than you could find in the Yiddish paper, but he made Woody promise to bury him among Jews, and that was where he lay now, in the Hawaiian shirt Woody had bought for him at the tilers' convention in Honolulu. Woody would allow no undertaker's assistant to dress him but came to the parlor and buttoned the stiff into the shirt himself, and the old man went down looking like Ben-Gurion in a simple wooden coffin, sure to rot fast. That was how Woody wanted it all. At the graveside, he had taken off and folded his jacket, rolled up his sleeves on thick freckled biceps, waved back the little tractor standing by, and shovelled the dirt himself. His big face, broad at the bottom, narrowed upward like a Dutch house. And, his small good lower teeth taking hold of the upper lip in his exertion, he performed the final duty of a son. He was very fit, so it must have been emotion, not the shovelling, that made him redden so. After the funeral, he went home with Halina and her son, a decent Polack like his mother, and talented, too—Mitosh played the organ at hockey and basketball games in the Stadium, which took a smart man because it was a rabble-rousing kind of occupation—and they had some drinks and comforted the old girl. Halina was true blue, always one hundred per cent for Morris.

Then for the rest of the week Woody was busy, had jobs to run, office responsibilities, family responsibilities. He lived alone; as did his wife; as did his mistress: everybody in a separate establishment. Since his wife, after fifteen years of separation, had not learned to take care of herself, Woody did her shopping on Fridays, filled her freezer. He had to take her this week to buy shoes. Also, Friday night he always spent with Helen—Helen was his wife de facto. Saturday he did his big weekly shopping. Saturday night he devoted to Mom and his sisters. So he was too busy to attend to his own feelings except, intermittently, to note to himself, "First

Thursday in the grave." "First Friday, and fine weather." "First Saturday; he's got to be getting used to it." Under his breath he occasionally said, "Oh, Pop."

But it was Sunday that hit him, when the bells rang all over South Chicago—the Ukrainian, Roman Catholic, Greek, Russian, African-Methodist churches, sounding off one after another. Woody had his offices in his warehouse, and there had built an apartment for himself, very spacious and convenient, in the top story. Because he left every Sunday morning at seven to spend the day with Pop, he had forgotten by how many churches Selbst Tile Company was surrounded. He was still in bed when he heard the bells, and all at once he knew how heartbroken he was. This sudden big heartache in a man of sixty, a practical, physical, healthy-minded, and experienced man, was deeply unpleasant. When he had an unpleasant condition, he believed in taking something for it. So he thought, What shall I take? There were plenty of remedies available. His cellar was stocked with cases of Scotch whiskey, Polish vodka, Armagnac, Moselle, Burgundy. There were also freezers with steaks and with game and with Alaskan king crab. He bought with a broad hand—by the crate and by the dozen. But in the end, when he got out of bed, he took nothing but a cup of coffee. While the kettle was heating, he put on his Japanese judo-style suit and sat down to reflect.

Woody was moved when things were *honest*. Bearing beams were honest, undisguised concrete pillars inside high-rise apartments were honest. It was bad to cover up anything. He hated faking. Stone was honest. Metal was honest. These Sunday bells were very straight. They broke loose, they wagged and rocked, and the vibrations and the banging did something for him—cleansed his insides, purified his blood. A bell was a one-way throat, had only one thing to tell you and simply told it. He listened.

He had had some connections with bells and churches. He was after all something of a Christian. Born a Jew, he was a Jew facially, with a hint of Iroquois or Cherokee, but his mother had been converted more than fifty years ago by her brother-in-law, the Reverend Dr. Kovner. Kovner, a rabbinical student who had left the Hebrew Union College in Cincinnati to become a minister and establish a mission, had given Woody a partly Christian upbringing. Now Pop was on the outs with these fundamentalists. He said that the Jews came to the mission to get coffee, bacon, canned pineapple, day-old bread, and dairy products. And if they had to listen to sermons, that was O.K.—this was the Depression and you couldn't be too particular—but he knew they sold the bacon.

The Gospels said it plainly: "Salvation is from the Jews."

Backing the Reverend Doctor were wealthy fundamentalists, mainly Swedes, eager to speed up the Second Coming by converting all Jews. The foremost of Kovner's backers was Mrs. Skoglund, who had inherited a large dairy business from her late husband. Woody was under her special protection.

Woody was fourteen years of age when Pop took off with Halina, who worked in his shop, leaving his difficult Christian wife and his converted son and his small daughters. He came to Woody in the back yard one spring day and said, "From now on you're the man of the house." Woody was practicing with a golf club, knocking off the heads of dandelions. Pop came into the yard in his good suit, which was too hot for the weather, and when he took off his fedora the skin of his head was marked with a deep ring and the sweat was sprinkled over his scalp—more drops than hairs. He said, "I'm going to move out." Pop was anxious, but he was set to go—determined. "It's no use. I can't live a life like this." Envisioning the life Pop simply *had* to live, his free life, Woody was able to picture him in the billiard parlor, under the "L" tracks in a crap game, or playing poker at Brown and Koppel's upstairs. "You're going to be the man of the house," said Pop. "It's O.K. I put you all on welfare. I just got back from Wabansia Avenue, from the Relief Station." Hence the suit and the hat. "They're sending out a caseworker." Then he said, "You got to lend me money to buy gasoline—the caddie money you saved."

Understanding that Pop couldn't get away without his help, Woody turned over to him all he had earned at the Sunset Ridge Country Club in Winnetka. Pop felt that the valuable life lesson he was transmitting was worth far more than these dollars, and whenever he was conning his boy a sort of high-priest expression came down over his bent nose, his ruddy face. The children, who got their finest ideas at the movies, called him Richard Dix. Later, when the comic strip came out, they said he was Dick Tracy.

As Woody now saw it, under the tumbling bells, he had bankrolled his own desertion. Ha ha! He found this delightful; and especially Pop's attitude of "That'll teach you to trust your father." For this was a demonstration on behalf of real life and free instincts, against religion and hypocrisy. But mainly it was aimed against being a fool, the disgrace of foolishness. Pop had it in for the Reverend Dr. Kovner, not because he was an apostate (Pop couldn't have cared less), not because the mission was a racket (he admitted that the Reverend Doctor was personally honest), but because Dr. Kovner behaved foolishly, spoke like a fool, and acted like a fiddler. He tossed his hair like a Paganini (this was Woody's addition; Pop had never even heard of Paganini). Proof that he was not a spiritual leader was that he converted Jewish women by stealing their hearts. "He works up all those broads," said Pop. "He doesn't even know it himself, I swear he doesn't know how he gets them."

From the other side, Kovner often warned Woody, "Your father is a dangerous person. Of course, you love him; you should love him and forgive him, Voodrow, but you are old enough to understand he is leading a life of wice."

It was all petty stuff: Pop's sinning was on a boy level and therefore made a big impression on a boy. And on Mother. Are wives children, or what? Mother often said, "I hope you put that brute in your prayers. Look what he has done to us. But only pray for him, don't see him." But he saw him all the time. Woodrow was leading a double life, sacred and profane. He accepted Jesus Christ as his personal redeemer. Aunt Rebecca took advantage of this. She made him work. He had to work under Aunt Rebecca. He filled in for the janitor at the mission and settlement house. In winter, he had to feed the coal furnace, and on some nights he slept near the furnace room, on the pool table. He also picked the lock of the storeroom. He took canned pineapple and cut bacon from the flitch with his pocketknife. He crammed himself with uncooked bacon. He had a big frame to fill out.

Only now, sipping Melitta coffee, he asked himself—had he been so hungry? No, he loved being reckless. He was fighting Aunt Rebecca Kovner when he took out his knife and got on a box to reach the bacon. She didn't know, she couldn't prove that Woody, such a frank, strong, positive boy who looked you in the eye, so direct, was a thief also. But he was also a thief. Whenever she looked at him, he knew that she was seeing his father. In the curve of his nose, the movements of his eyes, the thickness of his body, in his healthy face she saw that wicked savage, Morris.

Morris, you see, had been a street boy in Liverpool—Woody's mother and her sister were British by birth. Morris's Polish family, on their way to America, abandoned him in Liverpool because he had an eye infection and they would all have been sent back from Ellis Island. They stopped awhile in England, but his eyes kept running and they ditched him. They slipped away, and he had to make out alone in Liverpool at the age of twelve. Mother came of better people. Pop, who slept in the cellar of her house, fell in love with her. At sixteen, scabbing during a seamen's strike, he shovelled his way across the Atlantic and jumped ship in Brooklyn. He became an American, and America never knew it. He voted without papers, he drove without a license, he paid no taxes, he cut every corner. Horses, cards, billiards, and women were his lifelong interests, in ascending order. Did he love anyone (he was so busy)? Yes, he loved Halina.

He loved his son. To this day, Mother believed that he had loved her most and always wanted to come back. This gave her a chance to act the queen, with her plump wrists and faded Queen Victoria face. "The girls are instructed never to admit him," she said. The Empress of India, speaking.

Bell-battered Woodrow's soul was whirling this Sunday morning, indoors and out, to the past, back to his upper corner of the warehouse, laid out with such originality—the bells coming and going, metal on naked metal, until the bell circle expanded over the whole of steelmaking, oil-refining, power-producing mid-autumn South Chicago, and all its Croatians, Ukrainians, Greeks, Poles, and respectable blacks heading for their churches to hear Mass or to sing hymns.

Woody himself had been a good hymn singer. He still knew the hymns. He had testified, too. He was often sent by Aunt Rebecca to get up and tell a church full of Scandihoovians that he, a Jewish lad, accepted Jesus Christ. For this she paid him fifty cents. She made the disbursement. She was the bookkeeper, fiscal chief, general manager of the mission. The Reverend Doctor didn't know a thing about the operation. What the Doctor supplied was the fervor. He was genuine, a wonderful preacher. And what about Woody himself? He also had fervor. He was drawn to the Reverend Doctor. The Reverend Doctor taught him to lift up his eyes, gave him his higher life. Apart from this higher life, the rest was Chicago—the ways of Chicago, which came so natural that nobody thought to question them. So, for instance, in 1933 (what ancient, ancient times!) at the Century of Progress World's Fair, when Woody was a coolie and pulled a rickshaw, wearing a peaked straw hat and trotting with powerful, thick legs, while the brawny red farmers—his boozing passengers—were laughing their heads off and pestered him for whores, he, although a freshman at the seminary, saw nothing wrong, when girls asked him to steer a little business their way, in making dates and accepting tips from both sides. He necked in Grant Park with a powerful girl who had to go home quickly to nurse her baby. Smelling of milk, she rode beside him on the streetcar to the West Side, squeezing his rickshaw puller's thigh and wetting her blouse. This was the Roosevelt Road car. Then, in the apartment where she lived with her mother, he couldn't remember that there were any husbands around. What he did remember was the strong milk odor. Without inconsistency, next morning he did New Testament Greek: The light shineth in darkness—*to fos en te skotia fainei*—and the darkness comprehended it not.

And all the while he trotted between the shafts on the fairgrounds he had one idea—nothing to do with these horny giants having a big time in the city: that the goal, the project, the purpose was (and he couldn't explain why he thought so; all evidence was against it), God's idea was that this world should be a love-world, that it should eventually recover and be entirely a world of love. He wouldn't have said this to a soul, for he could see himself how stupid it was—personal and stupid. Nevertheless, there it was at the center of his feelings. And at the same time Aunt Rebecca was right when she said to him, strictly private, close to his ear even, "You're a little crook, like your father."

There was some evidence for this, or what stood for evidence to an impatient person like Rebecca. Woody matured quickly—he had to—but how could you expect a boy of seventeen, he wondered, to interpret the viewpoint, the feelings of a middle-aged woman, and one whose breast had been removed? Morris told him that this happened only to neglected women, and was a sign. Morris said that if titties were not fondled and kissed they got cancer in protest. It was a cry of the flesh. And this had seemed true to Woody. When his imagination tried the theory on the Reverend Doctor, it worked out—he couldn't see the Reverend Doctor behaving in that way to Aunt Rebecca's breasts! Morris's theory kept Woody looking from bosoms to husbands and from husbands to bosoms. He still did that. It's an exceptionally smart man who isn't marked forever by the sexual theories he hears from his father, and Woody wasn't all that smart. He knew this himself. Personally, he had gone far out of his way to do right by women in this regard. What nature demanded. He and Pop were common, thick men, but there's nobody too gross to have ideas of delicacy.

The Reverend Doctor preached, Rebecca preached, rich Mrs. Skoglund preached from Evanston, Mother preached. Pop also was on a soapbox. Everyone was doing it. Up and down Division Street, under every lamp, almost, speakers were giving out: anarchists, Socialists, Stalinists, single-taxers, Zionists, Tolstoyans, vegetarians, and fundamentalist Christian preachers—you name it. A beef, a hope, a way of life or salvation, a protest. How was it that the accumulated gripes of all the ages took off so when transplanted to America?

And that fine Swedish immigrant Aase (Osie, they pronounced it), who had been the Skoglunds' cook and married the eldest son to become his rich, religious widow—she supported the Reverend Doctor. In her time she must have been built like a chorus girl. And women seem to have lost the secret of putting up their hair in the high basketry fence of braid she wore. Aase took Woody under her special protection and paid his tuition at the seminary. And Pop said . . . But on this Sunday, at peace as soon as the bells stopped banging, this velvet autumn day when the grass was finest and thickest, silky green: before the first frost, and the blood in your lungs is redder than summer air can make it and smarts with oxygen, as if the iron in your system was hungry for it, and the chill was sticking it to you in every breath—Pop, six feet under, would never feel this blissful sting again. The last of the bells still had the bright air streaming with vibrations.

On weekends, the institutional vacancy of decades came back to the warehouse and crept under the door of Woody's apartment. It felt as empty on Sundays as churches were during the week. Before each business day, before the trucks and the crews got started, Woody jogged five miles in his Adidas suit. Not on this day still reserved for Pop, however. Although it was tempting to go out and run off the grief. Being alone hit Woody hard this morning. He thought, Me and the world; the world and me. Meaning that there always was some activity to interpose, an errand or a visit, a picture to paint (he was a creative amateur), a massage, a meal—a shield between himself and that troublesome solitude which used the world as its reservoir. But Pop! Last Tuesday, Woody had gotten into the hospital bed with Pop because he kept pulling out the intravenous needles. Nurses stuck them back, and then Woody astonished them all by climbing into bed to hold the struggling old guy in his arms. "Easy, Morris, Morris, go easy." But Pop still groped feebly for the pipes.

When the tolling stopped, Woody didn't notice that a great lake of quiet had come over his kingdom, the Selbst Tile Warehouse. What he heard and saw was an old red Chicago streetcar, one of those trams the color of a stockyard steer. Cars of this type went out before Pearl Harbor—clumsy, big-bellied, with tough rattan seats and brass grips for the standing passengers. Those cars used to make four stops to the mile, and ran with a wallowing motion. They stank of carbolic or ozone and throbbed when the air compressors were being charged. The conductor had his knotted signal cord to pull, and the motorman beat the foot gong with his mad heel.

Woody recognized himself on the Western Avenue line and riding through a blizzard with his father, both in sheepskins and with hands and faces raw, the snow blowing in from the rear platform when the doors opened and getting into the longitudinal cleats of the floor. There wasn't warmth enough inside to melt it. And Western Avenue was the longest car line in the world, the boosters said, as if it was a thing to brag about. Twenty-three miles long, made by a draftsman with a T-square, lined with factories, storage buildings, machine shops, used-car lots, trolley barns, gas stations, funeral parlors, six-flats, utility buildings, and junk yards, on and on from the prairies on the south to Evanston on the north. Woodrow and his father were going north to Evanston, to Howard Street, and then some, to see Mrs. Skoglund. At the end of the line they would still have about five blocks to hike. The purpose of the trip? To raise money for Pop. Pop had talked him into this. When they found out, Mother and Aunt Rebecca would be furious, and Woody was afraid, but he couldn't help it.

Morris had come and said, "Son, I'm in trouble. It's bad."

"What's bad, Pop?"

"Halina took money from her husband for me and has to put it back before old Bujak misses it. He could kill her."

"What did she do it for?"

"Son, you know how the bookies collect? They send a goon. They'll break my head open."

"Pop! You know I can't take you to Mrs. Skoglund."

"Why not? You're my kid, aren't you? The old broad wants to adopt you, doesn't she? Shouldn't I get something out of it for my trouble? What am I—outside? And what about Halina? She puts her life on the line, but my own kid says no."

"Oh, Bujak wouldn't hurt her."

"Woody, he'd beat her to death."

Bujak? Uniform in color with his dark-gray work clothes, short in the legs, his whole strength in his tool-and-die-maker's forearms and black fingers; and beat-looking—there was Bujak for you. But, according to Pop, there was big, big violence in Bujak, a regular boiling Bessemer inside his narrow chest. Woody could never see the violence in him. Bujak wanted no trouble. If anything, maybe he was afraid that Morris and Halina would gang up on him and kill him, screaming. But Pop was no desperado murderer. And Halina was a calm, serious woman. Bujak kept his savings in the cellar (banks were going out of business). The worst they did was to take some of his money, intending to put it back. As Woody saw him, Bujak was trying to be sensible. He accepted his sorrow. He set minimum requirements for Halina: cook the meals, clean the house, show respect. But at stealing Bujak might have drawn the line, for money was different, money was vital substance. If they stole his savings he might have had to take action, out of respect for the substance, for himself—self-respect. But you couldn't be sure that Pop hadn't invented the bookie, the goon, the theft—the whole thing. He was capable of it, and you'd be a fool not to suspect him. Morris knew that Mother and Aunt Rebecca had told Mrs. Skoglund how wicked he was. They had painted him for her in poster colors—purple for vice, black for his soul, red for Hell flames: a gambler, smoker, drinker, deserter, screwer of women, and atheist. So Pop was determined to reach her. It was risky for everybody. The Reverend Doctor's operating costs were met by Skoglund Dairies. The widow paid Woody's seminary tuition; she bought dresses for the little sisters.

Woody, now sixty, fleshy and big, like a figure for the victory of American materialism, sunk in his lounge chair, the leather of its armrests softer to his fingertips than a woman's skin, was puzzled and, in his depths, disturbed by certain blots within him, blots of light in his brain, a blot combining pain and amusement in his breast (how did *that* get there?). Intense thought puckered the skin between his eyes with a strain bordering on headache. Why had he let Pop have his way? Why did he agree to meet him that day, in the dim rear of the poolroom?

"But what will you tell Mrs. Skoglund?"

"The old broad? Don't worry, there's plenty to tell her, and it's all true. Ain't I trying to save my little laundry-and-cleaning shop? Isn't the bailiff coming for the fixtures next week?" And Pop rehearsed his pitch on the Western Avenue car. He counted on Woody's health and his freshness. Such a straightforward-looking boy was perfect for a con.

Did they still have such winter storms in Chicago as they used to have? Now they somehow seemed less fierce. Blizzards used to come straight down from Ontario, from the Arctic, and drop five feet of snow in an afternoon. Then the rusty green platform cars, with revolving brushes at both ends, came out of the barns to sweep the tracks. Ten or twelve streetcars followed in slow processions, or waited, block after block.

There was a long delay at the gates of Riverview Park, all the amusements covered for the winter, boarded up—the dragon's-back high-rides, the Bobs, the Chute, the Tilt-a-Whirl, all the fun machinery put together by mechanics and electricians, men like Bujak the tool-and-die-maker, good with engines. The blizzard was having it all its own way behind the gates, and you couldn't see far inside; only a few bulbs burned behind the palings. When Woody wiped the vapor from the glass, the wire mesh of the window guards was stuffed solid at eye level with snow. Looking higher, you saw mostly the streaked wind horizontally driving from the north. In the seat ahead, two black coal heavers both in leather Lindbergh flying helmets sat with shovels between their legs, returning from a job. They smelled of sweat, burlap sacking, and coal. Mostly dull with black dust, they also sparkled here and there.

There weren't many riders. People weren't leaving the house. This was a day to sit legs stuck out beside the stove, mummified by both the outdoor and the indoor forces. Only a fellow with an angle, like Pop, would go and buck such weather. A storm like this was out of the compass, and you kept the human scale by having a scheme to raise fifty bucks. Fifty soldiers! Real money in 1933.

"That woman is crazy for you," said Pop.

"She's just a good woman, sweet to all of us."

"Who knows what she's got in mind. You're a husky kid. Not such a kid either."

"She's a religious woman. She really has religion."

"Well, your mother isn't your only parent. She and Rebecca and Kovner aren't going to fill you up with their ideas. I know your mother wants to wipe me out of your life. Unless I take a hand, you won't even understand what life is. Because they don't know—those silly Christers."

"Yes Pop."

"The girls I can't help. They're too young. I'm sorry about them, but I can't do anything. With you it's different."

He wanted me like himself, an American.

They were stalled in the storm, while the cattle-colored car waited to have the trolley reset in the crazy wind, which boomed, tingled, blasted. At Howard Street they would have to walk straight into it, due north.

"You'll do the talking at first," said Pop.

Woody had the makings of a salesman, a pitchman. He was aware of this when he got to his feet in church to testify before fifty or sixty people. Even though Aunt Rebecca made it worth his while, he moved his own heart when he spoke up about his faith. But occasionally, without notice, his heart went away as he spoke religion and he couldn't find it anywhere. In its absence, sincere behavior got him through. He had to rely for delivery on his face, his voice—on behavior. Then his eyes came closer and closer together. And in this approach of eye to eye he felt the strain of hypocrisy. The twisting of his face threatened to betray him. It took everything he had to keep looking honest. So, since he couldn't bear the cynicism of it, he fell back on mischievousness. Mischief was where Pop came in. Pop passed straight through all those divided fields, gap after gap, and arrived at his side, bent-nosed and broad-faced. In regard to Pop, you thought of neither sincerity nor insincerity. Pop was like the man in the song: he wanted what he wanted when he wanted it. Pop was physical; Pop was digestive, circulatory, sexual. If Pop got serious, he talked to you about washing under the arms or in the crotch or of drying between your toes or of cooking supper, of baked beans and fried onions, of draw poker or of a certain horse in the fifth race at Arlington. Pop was elemental. That was why he gave such relief from religion and paradoxes, and things like that. Now Mother *thought* she was spiritual, but Woody knew that she was kidding herself. Oh, yes, in the British accent she never gave up she was always talking to God or about Him—please-God, God-willing, praise-God. But she was a big substantial bread-and-butter, down-to-earth woman, with down-to-earth duties like feeding the girls, protecting, refining, keeping pure the girls. And those two protected doves grew up so overweight, heavy in the hips and thighs, that their poor heads looked long and slim. And mad. Sweet but cuckoo—Paula cheerfully cuckoo, Joanna depressed and having episodes.

"I'll do my best by you, but you have to promise, Pop, not to get me in Dutch with Mrs. Skoglund."

"You worried because I speak bad English? Embarrassed? I have a mockie accent?"

"It's not that. Kovner has a heavy accent, and she doesn't mind."

"Who the hell are those freaks to look down on me? You're practically a man and your dad has a right to expect help from you. He's in a fix. And you bring him to her house because she's big-hearted, and you haven't got anybody else to go to."

"I got you, Pop."

The two coal trimmers stood up at Devon Avenue. One of them wore a woman's coat. Men wore women's clothing in those years, and women men's, when there was no choice. The fur collar was spiky with the wet, and sprinkled with soot. Heavy, they dragged their shovels and got off at the front. The slow car ground on, very slow. It was after four when they reached the end of the line, and somewhere between gray and black, with snow spouting and whirling under the street lamps. In Howard Street, autos were stalled at all angles and abandoned. The sidewalks were blocked. Woody led the way into Evanston, and Pop followed him up the middle of the street in the furrows made earlier by trucks. For four blocks they bucked the wind and then Woody broke through the drifts to the snowbound mansion, where they both had to push the wrought-iron gate because of the drift behind it. Twenty rooms or more in this dignified house and nobody in them but Mrs. Skoglund and her servant Hjordis, also religious.

As Woody and Pop waited, brushing the slush from their sheepskin collars and Pop wiping his big eyebrows with the ends of his scarf, sweating and freezing, the chains began to rattle and Hjordis uncovered the air holes of the glass storm door by turning a wooden bar. Woody called her "monk-faced." You no longer see women like that, who put no female touch on the face. She came plain, as God made her. She said, "Who is it and what do you want?"

"It's Woodrow Selbst. Hjordis? It's Woody."

"You're not expected."

"No, but we're here."

"What do you want?"

"We came to see Mrs. Skoglund."

"What for do you want to see her?"

"Just to tell her we're here."

"I have to tell her what you came for, without calling up first."

"Why don't you say it's Woody with his father, and we wouldn't come in a snowstorm like this if it wasn't important."

The understandable caution of women who live alone. Respectable old-time women, too. There was no such respectability now in those Evanston houses, with their big verandas and deep yards and with a servant like Hjordis, who carried at her belt keys to the pantry and to every closet and every dresser drawer and every padlocked bin in the cellar. And in High Episcopal Christian Science Women's Temperance Evanston no tradespeople rang at the front door. Only invited guests. And here, after a ten-mile grind through the blizzard, came two tramps from the West Side. To this mansion where a Swedish immigrant lady, herself once a cook and now a philanthropic widow, dreamed, snowbound, while frozen lilac twigs clapped at her storm windows, of a new Jerusalem and a Second Coming and a Resurrection and a Last Judgment. To hasten the Second Coming, and all the rest, you had to reach the hearts of these scheming bums arriving in a snowstorm.

Sure, they let us in.

Then in the heat that swam suddenly up to their mufflered chins Pop and Woody felt the blizzard for what it was; their cheeks were frozen slabs. They stood beat, itching, trickling in the front hall that *was* a hall, with a carved newel post staircase and a big stained-glass window at the top. Picturing Jesus with the Samaritan woman. There was a kind of Gentile closeness to the air. Perhaps when he was with Pop, Woody made more Jewish observations than he would otherwise. Although Pop's most Jewish characteristic was that Yiddish was the only language he could read a paper in. Pop was with Polish Halina, and Mother was with Jesus Christ, and Woody ate uncooked bacon from the flitch. Still now and then he had a Jewish impression.

Mrs. Skoglund was the cleanest of women—her fingernails, her white neck, her ears—and Pop's sexual hints to Woody all went wrong because she was so intensely clean, and made Woody think of a waterfall, large as she was, and grandly built. Her bust was big. Woody's imagination had investigated this. He thought she kept things tied down tight, very tight. But she lifted both arms once to raise a window and there it was, her bust, beside him, the whole unbindable thing. Her hair was like the raffia you had to soak before you could weave with it in a basket class—pale, pale. Pop, as he took his sheepskin off, was in sweaters, no jacket. His darting looks made him seem crooked. Hardest of all for these Selbsts with their bent noses and big, apparently straightforward faces was to look honest. All the signs of dishonesty played over them. Woody had often puzzled about it. Did it go back to the muscles, was it fundamentally a jaw problem—the projecting angles of the jaws? Or was it the angling that went on in the heart? The girls called Pop Dick Tracy, but Dick Tracy was a good guy. Whom could Pop convince? Here, Woody caught a possibility as it flitted by. Precisely because of the way Pop looked, a sensitive person might feel remorse for condemning unfairly or judging unkindly. Just because of a face? Some must have bent over backward. Then he had them. Not Hjordis. She would have put Pop into the street then and there, storm or no storm. Hjordis was religious, but she was wised up, too. She hadn't come over in steerage and worked forty years in Chicago for nothing.

Mrs. Skoglund, Aase (Osie), led the visitors into the front room. This, the biggest room in the house, needed supplementary heating. Because of fifteen-foot ceilings and high windows, Hjordis had kept the parlor stove burning. It was one of those elegant parlor stoves that wore a nickel crown, or mitre, and this mitre, when you moved it aside, automatically raised the hinge of an iron stove lid. That stove lid underneath the crown was all soot and rust, the same as any other stove lid. Into this hole you tipped the scuttle and the anthracite chestnut rattled down. It made a cake or dome of fire visible through the small isinglass frames. It was a pretty room, three-quarters panelled in wood. The stove was plugged into the flue of the marble fireplace, and there were parquet floors and Axminster carpets and cranberry-colored tufted Victorian upholstery, and a kind of Chinese étagère, inside a cabinet, lined with mirrors and containing silver pitchers, trophies won by Skoglund cows, fancy sugar tongs and cut-glass pitchers and goblets. There were Bibles and pictures of Jesus and the Holy Land and that faint Gentile odor, as if things had been rinsed in a weak vinegar solution.

"Mrs. Skoglund, I brought my dad to you. I don't think you ever met him," said Woody.

"Yes, Missus, that's me, Selbst."

Pop stood short but masterful in the sweaters, and his belly sticking out, not soft but hard. He was a man of the hard-bellied type. Nobody intimidated Pop. He never presented himself as a beggar. There wasn't a cringe in him anywhere. He let her see at once by the way he said "Missus" that he was independent and that he knew his way around. He communicated that he was able to handle himself with women. Handsome Mrs. Skoglund, carrying a basket woven out of her own hair, was in her fifties—eight, maybe ten years his senior.

"I asked my son to bring me because I know you do the kid a lot of good. It's natural you should know both of his parents."

"Mrs. Skoglund, my dad is in a tight corner and I don't know anybody else to ask for help."

This was all the preliminary Pop wanted. He took over and told the widow his story about the laundry-and-cleaning business and payments overdue, and explained about the fixtures and the attachment notice, and the bailiff's office and what they were going to do to him; and he said, "I'm a small man trying to make a living."

"You don't support your children," said Mrs. Skoglund.

"That's right," said Hjordis.

"I haven't got it. If I had it, wouldn't I give it? There's bread lines and soup lines all over town. Is it just me? What I have I divvy with. I give the kids. A bad father? You think my son would bring me if I was a bad father into your house? He loves his dad, he trusts his dad, he knows his dad is a good dad. Every time I start a little business going I get wiped out. This one is a good little business, if I could hold on to that little business. Three people work for me, I meet a payroll, and three people will be on the street, too, if I close down. Missus, I can sign a note and pay you in two months. I'm a common man, but I'm a hard worker and a fellow you can trust."

Woody was startled when Pop used the word "trust." It was as if from all four corners a Sousa band blew a blast to warn the entire world. "Crook! This is a crook!" But Mrs. Skoglund, on account of her religious preoccupations, was remote. She heard nothing. Although everybody in this part of the world, unless he was crazy, led a practical life, and you'd have nothing to say to anyone, your neighbors would have nothing to say to you if communications were not of a practical sort, Mrs. Skoglund, with all her money, was unworldly—two-thirds out of this world.

"Give me a chance to show what's in me," said Pop, "and you'll see what I do for my kids."

So Mrs. Skoglund hesitated, and then she said she'd have to go upstairs, she'd have to go to her room and pray on it and ask for guidance—would they sit down and wait. There were two rocking chairs by the stove. Hjordis gave Pop a grim look (a dangerous person) and Woody a blaming one (he brought a dangerous stranger and disrupter to injure two kind Christian ladies). Then she went out with Mrs. Skoglund.

As soon as they left, Pop jumped up from the rocker and said in anger, "What's this with the praying? She has to ask God to lend me fifty bucks?"

Woody said, "It's not you, Pop, it's the way these religious people do."

"No," said Pop. "She'll come back and say that God wouldn't let her."

Woody didn't like that; he thought Pop was being gross and he said, "No, she's sincere. Pop, try to understand; she's emotional, nervous, and sincere, and tries to do right by everybody."

And Pop said, "That servant will talk her out of it. She's a toughie. It's all over her face that we're a couple of chisellers."

"What's the use of us arguing," said Woody. He drew the rocker closer to the stove. His shoes were wet through and would never dry. The blue flames fluttered like a school of fishes in the coal fire. But Pop went over to the Chinese-style cabinet or étagère and tried the handle, and then opened the blade of his penknife and in a second had forced the lock of the curved glass door. He took out a silver dish.

"Pop, what is this?" said Woody.

Pop, cool and level, knew exactly what this was. He relocked the étagère, crossed the carpet, listened. He stuffed the dish under his belt and pushed it down into his trousers. He put the side of his short thick finger to his mouth.

So Woody kept his voice down, but he was all shook up. He went to Pop and took him by the edge of his hand. As he looked into Pop's face, he felt his eyes growing smaller and smaller, as if something were contracting all the skin on his head. They call it hyperventilation when everything feels tight and light and close and dizzy. Hardly breathing, he said, "Put it back, Pop."

Pop said, "It's solid silver; it's worth dough."

"Pop, you said you wouldn't get me in Dutch."

"It's only insurance in case she comes back from praying and tells me no. If she says yes, I'll put it back."

"How?"

"It'll get back. If I don't put it back, you will."

"You picked the lock. I couldn't. I don't know how."

"There's nothing to it."

"We're going to put it back now. Give it here."

"Woody, it's under my fly, inside my underpants, don't make such a noise about nothing."

"Pop, I can't believe this."

"For Cry-99, shut your mouth. If I didn't trust you I wouldn't have let you watch me do it. You don't understand a thing. What's with you?"

"Before they come down, Pop, will you dig that dish out of your long johns."

Pop turned stiff on him. He became absolutely military. He said, "Look, I order you!"

Before he knew it, Woody had jumped his father and begun to wrestle with him. It was outrageous to clutch your own father, to put a heel behind him, to force him to the wall. Pop was taken by surprise and said began to resist, angry, and they turned about several times when Woody, loudly, "You want Halina killed? Kill her! Go on, you be responsible." He with a trick he had learned in a Western movie and used once on the playground, tripped him and they fell to the ground. Woody, who already outweighed the old man by twenty pounds, was on the top. They landed on the floor beside the stove, which stood on a tray of decorated tin to protect the carpet. In this position, pressing Pop's hard belly, Woody recognized that to have wrestled him to the floor counted for nothing. It was impossible to thrust his hand under Pop's belt to recover the dish. And now Pop had turned furious, as a father has every right to be when his son is violent with him, and he freed his hand and hit Woody in the face. He hit him three or four times in mid-face. Then Woody dug his head into Pop's shoulder and held tight only to keep from being struck and began to say in his ear, "Jesus, Pop, for Christ sake remember where you are. Those women will be back!" But Pop brought up his short knee and fought and butted him with his chin and rattled Woody's teeth. Woody thought the old man was about to bite him. And, because he was a seminarian, he thought, "Like an unclean spirit." And held tight. Gradually Pop stopped threshing and struggling. His eyes stuck out and his mouth was open, sullen. Like a stout fish. Woody released him and gave him a hand up. He was then overcome with many many bad feelings of a sort he knew the old man never suffered. Never, never. Pop never had these grovelling emotions. There was his whole superiority. Pop had no such feelings. He was like a horseman from Central Asia, a bandit from China. It was Mother, from Liverpool, who had the refinement, the English manners. It was the preaching Reverend Doctor in his black suit. You have refinements, and all they do is oppress you? The hell with that.

The long door opened and Mrs. Skoglund stepped in, saying, "Did I imagine, or did something shake the house?"

"I was lifting the scuttle to put coal on the fire and it fell out of my hand. I'm sorry I was so clumsy," said Woody.

Pop was too huffy to speak. With his eyes big and sore and the thin hair down over his forehead, you could see by the tightness of his belly how angrily he was fetching his breath, though his mouth was shut.

"I prayed," said Mrs. Skoglund.

"I hope it came out well," said Woody.

"Well, I don't do anything without guidance, but the answer was yes, and I feel right about it now. So if you'll wait I'll go to my office and write a check. I asked Hjordis to bring you a cup of coffee. Coming in such a storm."

And Pop, consistently a terrible little man, as soon as she shut the door said, "A check? Hell with a check. Get me the greenbacks."

"They don't keep money in the house. You can cash it in her bank tomorrow. But if they miss that dish, Pop, they'll stop the check, and then where are you?"

As Pop was reaching below the belt Hjordis brought in the tray. She was very sharp with him. She said, "Is this a place to adjust clothing, Mister? A men's washroom?"

"Well, which way is the toilet, then?" said Pop.

She had served the coffee in the seamiest mugs in the pantry, and she bumped down the tray and led Pop down the corridor, standing guard at the bathroom door so that he shouldn't wander about the house.

Mrs. Skoglund called Woody to her office and after she had given him the folded check said that they should pray together for Morris. So once more he was on his knees, under rows and rows of musty marbled cardboard files, by the glass lamp by the edge of the desk, the shade with flounced edges, like the candy dish. Mrs. Skoglund, in her Scandinavian accent—an emotional contralto—raising her voice to Jesus-uh Christ-uh, as the wind lashed the trees, kicked the side of the house, and drove the snow seething on the windowpanes, to send light-uh, give guidance-uh, put a new heart-uh in Pop's bosom. Woody asked God only to make Pop put the dish back. He kept Mrs. Skoglund on her knees as long as possible. Then he thanked her, shining with candor (as much as he knew how) for her Christian generosity and he said, "I know that Hjordis has a cousin who works at the Evanston Y.M.C.A. Could she please phone him and try to get us a room tonight so that we don't have to fight the blizzard all the way back? We're almost as close to the Y as to the car line. Maybe the cars have even stopped running."

Suspicious Hjordis, coming when Mrs. Skoglund called to her, was burning now. First they barged in, made themselves at home, asked for money, had to have coffee, probably left gonorrhea on the toilet seat. Hjordis, Woody remembered, was a woman who wiped the doorknobs with rubbing alcohol after guests had left. Nevertheless, she telephoned the Y and got them a room with two cots for six bits.

Pop had plenty of time, therefore, to reopen the étagère, lined with reflecting glass or German silver (something exquisitely delicate and tricky), and as soon as the two Selbsts had said thank you and goodbye and were in mid-street again up to the knees in snow, Woody said, "Well, I covered for you. Is that thing back?"

"Of course it is," said Pop.

They fought their way to the small Y building, shut up in wire grille and resembling a police station—about the same dimensions. It was locked, but they made a racket on the grille, and a small black man let them in and shuffled them upstairs to a cement corridor with low doors. It was like the small mammal house in Lincoln Park. He said there was nothing to eat, so they took off their wet pants, wrapped themselves tightly in the khaki army blankets, and passed out on their cots.

First thing in the morning, they went to the Evanston National Bank and got the fifty dollars. Not without difficulties. The teller went to call

Mrs. Skoglund and was absent a long time from the wicket. "Where the hell has he gone," said Pop.

But when the fellow came back he said, "How do you want it?"

Pop said, "Singles." He told Woody, "Bujak stashes it in one-dollar bills."

But by now Woody no longer believed Halina had stolen the old man's money.

Then they went into the street, where the snow-removal crews were at work. The sun shone broad, broad, out of the morning blue, and all Chicago would be releasing itself from the temporary beauty of those vast drifts.

"You shouldn't have jumped me last night, Sonny."

"I know, Pop, but you promised you wouldn't get me in Dutch."

"Well, it's O.K., we can forget it, seeing you stood by me."

Only, Pop had taken the silver dish. Of course he had, and in a few days Mrs. Skoglund and Hjordis knew it, and later in the week they were all waiting for Woody in Kovner's office at the settlement house. The group included the Reverend Dr. Crabbie, head of the seminary, and Woody, who had been flying along, level and smooth, was shot down in flames. He told them he was innocent. Even as he was falling, he warned that they were wronging him. He denied that he or Pop had touched Mrs. Skoglund's property. The missing object—he didn't even know what it was—had probably been misplaced, and they would be very sorry on the day it turned up. After the others were done with him, Dr. Crabbie said until he was able to tell the truth he would be suspended from the seminary, where his work had been unsatisfactory anyway. Aunt Rebecca took him aside and said to him, "You are a little crook, like your father. The door is closed to you here."

To this Pop's comment was "So what, kid?"

"Pop, you shouldn't have done it."

"No? Well, I don't give a care, if you want to know. You can have the dish if you want to go back and square yourself with all those hypocrites."

"I didn't like doing Mrs. Skoglund in the eye, she was so kind to us."

"Kind?"

"Kind."

"Kind has a price tag."

Well, there was no winning such arguments with Pop. But they debated it in various moods and from various elevations and perspectives for forty years and more, as their intimacy changed, developed, matured.

"Why did you do it, Pop? For the money? What did you do with the fifty bucks?" Woody, decades later, asked him that.

"I settled with the bookie, and the rest I put in the business."

"You tried a few more horses."

"I maybe did. But it was a double, Woody. I didn't hurt myself, and at the same time did you a favor."

"It was for me?"

"It was too strange of a life. That life wasn't *you,* Woody. All those women—Kovner was no man, he was an in-between. Suppose they made you a minister? Some Christian minister! First of all, you wouldn't have been able to stand it, and, second, they would throw you out sooner or later."

"Maybe so."

"And you wouldn't have converted the Jews, which was the main thing they wanted."

"And what a time to bother the Jews," Woody said. "At least *I* didn't bug them."

Pop had carried him back to his side of the line, blood of his blood, the same thick body walls, the same coarse grain. Not cut out for a spiritual life. Simply not up to it.

Pop was no worse than Woody, and Woody was no better than Pop. Pop wanted no relation to theory, and yet he was always pointing Woody toward a position—a jolly, hearty, natural, likable, unprincipled position. If Woody had a weakness, it was to be unselfish. This worked to Pop's advantage, but he criticized Woody for it, nevertheless. "You take too much on yourself," Pop was always saying. And it's true that Woody gave Pop his heart because Pop was so selfish. It's usually the selfish people who are loved the most. They do what you deny yourself, and you love them for it. You give them your heart.

Remembering the pawn ticket for the silver dish, Woody startled himself with a laugh so sudden that it made him cough. Pop said to him after his expulsion from the seminary and banishment from the settlement house, "You want in again? Here's the ticket. I hocked that thing. It wasn't so valuable as I thought."

"What did they give?"

"Twelve-fifty was all I could get. But if you want it you'll have to raise the dough yourself, because I haven't got it anymore."

"You must have been sweating in the bank when the teller went to call Mrs. Skoglund about the check."

"I was a little nervous," said Pop. "But I didn't think they could miss the thing so soon."

That theft was part of Pop's war with Mother. With Mother, and Aunt Rebecca, and the Reverend Doctor. Pop took his stand on realism. Mother represented the forces of religion and hypochondria. In four decades, the fighting never stopped. In the course of time, Mother and the girls turned into welfare personalities and lost their individual outlines. Ah, the poor things, they became dependents and cranks. In the meantime, Woody, the sinful man, was their dutiful and loving son and brother. He maintained the bungalow—this took in roofing, pointing, wiring, insulation, air-conditioning—and he paid for heat and light and food, and dressed them all out of Sears, Roebuck and Wieboldt's, and bought them a TV, which they watched as devoutly as they prayed. Paula took courses to learn skills like macramé-making and needlepoint, and sometimes got a little job as recreational worker in a nursing home. But she wasn't steady enough to keep it. Wicked Pop spent most of his life removing stains from people's clothing. He and Halina in the last years ran a Cleanomat in West Rogers Park—a so-so business resembling a laundromat—which gave him leisure for billiards, the horses, rummy and pinochle. Every morning he went behind the partition to check out the filters of the cleaning equipment. He found amusing things that had been thrown into the vats with the clothing—sometimes, when he got lucky, a locket chain or a brooch. And when he had fortified the cleaning fluid, pouring all that blue and pink stuff in from plastic jugs, he read the *Forward* over a second cup of coffee, and went out, leaving Halina in charge. When they needed help with the rent, Woody gave it.

After the new Disney World was opened in Florida, Woody treated all his dependents to a holiday. He sent them down in separate batches, of course. Halina enjoyed this more than anybody else. She couldn't stop talking about the address given by an Abraham Lincoln automaton. "Wonderful, how he stood up and moved his hands, and his mouth. So real! And how beautiful he talked." Of them all, Halina was the soundest, the most human, the most honest. Now that Pop was gone, Woody and Halina's son, Mitosh, the organist at the Stadium, took care of her needs over and above Social Security, splitting expenses. In Pop's opinion, insurance was a racket. He left Halina nothing but some out-of-date equipment.

Woody treated himself, too. Once a year, and sometimes oftener, he left his business to run itself, arranged with the trust department at the bank to take care of his Gang, and went off. He did that in style, imaginatively, expensively. In Japan, he wasted little time on Tokyo. He spent three weeks in Kyoto and stayed at the Tawaraya Inn, dating from the seventeenth century or so. There he slept on the floor, the Japanese way, and bathed in scalding water. He saw the dirtiest strip show on earth, as well as the holy places and the temple gardens. He visited also Istanbul, Jerusalem, Delphi, and went to Burma and Uganda and Kenya on safari, on democratic terms with drivers, Bedouins, bazaar merchants. Open, lavish, familiar, fleshier and fleshier but (he jogged, he lifted weights) still muscular—in his naked person beginning to resemble a Renaissance courtier in full costume—becoming rudier every year, an outdoor type with freckles on his back and spots across the flaming forehead and the honest nose. In Addis Ababa he took an Ethiopian beauty to his room from the street and washed her, getting into the shower with her to soap her with his broad, kindly hands. In Kenya he taught certain American obscenities to a black woman so that she could shout them out during the act. On the Nile, below Murchison Falls, those fever trees rose huge from the mud, and hippos on the sandbars belched at the passing launch, hostile. One of them danced on his spit of sand, springing from the ground and coming down heavy, on all fours. There, Woody saw the buffalo calf disappear, snatched by the crocodile.

Mother, soon to follow Pop, was being light-headed these days. In company, she spoke of Woody as her boy—"What do you think of my Sonny?"—as though he was ten years old. She was silly with him, her behavior was frivolous, almost flirtatious. She just didn't seem to know the facts. And behind her all the others, like kids at the playground, were waiting their turn to go down the slide; one on each step, and moving toward the top.

Over Woody's residence and place of business there had gathered a pool of silence of the same perimeter as the church bells while they were ringing, and he mourned under it, this melancholy morning of sun and autumn. Doing a life survey, taking a deliberate look at the gross side of his case—of the other side as well, what there was of it. But if this heartache continued, he'd go out and run it off. A three-mile jog—five, if necessary. And you'd think that this jogging was an entirely physical activity, wouldn't you? But there was something else in it. Because, when he was a seminarian, between the shafts of his World's Fair rickshaw, he used to receive, pulling along (capable and stable), his religious experiences while he trotted. Maybe it was all a single experience repeated. He felt truth coming to him from the sun. He received a communication that was also light and warmth. It made him very remote from his horny Wisconsin passengers, those farmers whose whoops and whore-cries he could hardly hear when he was in one of his states. And again out of the flaming of the sun would come to him a secret certainty that the goal set for this earth was that it should be filled with good, saturated with it. After everything preposterous, after dog had eaten dog, after the crocodile death had pulled everyone into his mud. It wouldn't conclude as Mrs. Skoglund, bribing him to round up the Jews and hasten the Second Coming, imagined it but in another way. This was his clumsy intuition. It went no further. Subsequently, he proceeded through life as life seemed to want him to do it.

There remained one thing more this morning, which was explicitly physical, occurring first as a sensation in his arms and against his breast and, from the pressure, passing into him and going into his breast.

It was like this: When he came into the hospital room and saw Pop with the sides of his bed raised, like a crib, and Pop, so very feeble, and writhing, and toothless, like a baby, and the dirt already cast into his face, into the wrinkles—Pop wanted to pluck out the intravenous needles and he was piping his weak death noise. The gauze patches taped over the needles were soiled with dark blood. Then Woody took off his shoes, lowered the side of the bed, and climbed in and held him in his arms to soothe and still him. As if he were Pop's father, he said to him, "Now Pop. Pop." Then it was like the wrestle in Mrs. Skoglund's parlor, when Pop turned angry like an unclean spirit and Woody tried to appease him, and warn him, saying, "Those women will be back!" Beside the coal stove, when Pop hit Woody in the teeth with his head and then became sullen, like a stout fish. But this struggle in the hospital was weak—so weak! In his great pity, Woody held Pop, who was fluttering and shivering. From those people, Pop had told him, you'll never find out what life is, because they don't know what it is. Yes, Pop—well, what is it, Pop? Hard to comprehend that Pop, who was dug in for eighty-three years and had done all he could to stay, should now want nothing but to free himself. How could Woody allow the old man to pull the intravenous needles out? Willful Pop, he wanted what he wanted when he wanted it. But what he wanted at the very last Woody failed to follow, it was such a switch.

After a time, Pop's resistance ended. He subsided and subsided. He rested against his son, his small body curled there. Nurses came and looked. They disapproved, but Woody, who couldn't spare a hand to wave them out, motioned with his head toward the door. Pop, whom Woody thought he had stilled, only had found a better way to get around him. Loss of heat was the way he did it. His heat was leaving him. As can happen with small animals while you hold them in your hand, Woody presently felt him cooling. Then, as Woody did his best to restrain him, and thought he was succeeding, Pop divided himself. And when he was separated from his warmth he slipped into death. And there was his elderly, large, muscular son, still holding and pressing him when there was nothing anymore to press. You could never pin down that self-willed man. When he was ready to make his move, he made it—always on his own terms. And always, always, something up his sleeve. That was how he was.

The Jockey

CARSON McCULLERS

(1917–1967)

The jockey came to the doorway of the dining room, then after a moment stepped to one side and stood motionless, with his back to the wall. The room was crowded, as this was the third day of the season and all the hotels in the town were full. In the dining room bouquets of August roses scattered their petals on the white table linen and from the adjoining bar came a warm, drunken wash of voices. The jockey waited with his back to the wall and scrutinized the room with pinched, crêpy eyes. He examined the room until at last his eyes reached a table in a corner diagonally across from him, at which three men were sitting. As he watched, the jockey raised his chin and tilted his head back to one side, his dwarfed body grew rigid, and his hands stiffened so that the fingers curled inward like gray claws. Tense against the wall of the dining room, he watched and waited in this way.

He was wearing a suit of green Chinese silk that evening, tailored precisely and the size of a costume outfit for a child. The shirt was yellow, the tie striped with pastel colors. He had no hat with him and wore his hair brushed down in a stiff, wet bang on his forehead. His face was drawn, ageless, and gray. There were shadowed hollows at his temples and his mouth was set in a wiry smile. After a time he was aware that he had been seen by one of the three men he had been watching. But the jockey did not nod; he only raised his chin still higher and hooked the thumb of his tense hand in the pocket of his coat.

The three men at the corner table were a trainer, a bookie, and a rich man. The trainer was Sylvester—a large, loosely built fellow with a flushed nose and slow blue eyes. The bookie was Simmons. The rich man was the owner of a horse named Seltzer, which the jockey had ridden that afternoon. The three of them drank whisky with soda, and a white-coated waiter had just brought on the main course of the dinner.

It was Sylvester who first saw the jockey. He looked away quickly, put down his whisky glass, and nervously mashed the tip of his red nose with his thumb. "It's Bitsy Barlow," he said. "Standing over there across the room. Just watching us."

"Oh, the jockey," said the rich man. He was facing the wall and he half turned his head to look behind him. "Ask him over."

"God no," Sylvester said.

"He's crazy," Simmons said. The bookie's voice was flat and without inflection. He had the face of a born gambler, carefully adjusted, the expression a permanent deadlock between fear and greed.

"Well, I wouldn't call him that exactly," said Sylvester. "I've known him a long time. He was O.K. until about six months ago. But if he goes on like this, I can't see him lasting out another year. I just can't."

"It was what happened in Miami," said Simmons.

"What?" asked the rich man.

Sylvester glanced across the room at the jockey and wet the corner of his mouth with his red, fleshy tongue. "A accident. A kid got hurt on the track. Broke a leg and a hip. He was a particular pal of Bitsy's. A Irish kid. Not a bad rider, either."

"That's a pity," said the rich man.

"Yeah. They were particular friends," Sylvester said. "You would always find him up in Bitsy's hotel room. They would be playing rummy or else lying on the floor reading the sports page together."

"Well, those things happen," said the rich man.

Simmons cut into his beefsteak. He held his fork prongs downward on the plate and carefully piled on mushrooms with the blade of his knife. "He's crazy," he repeated. "He gives me the creeps."

All the tables in the dining room were occupied. There was a party at the banquet table in the center, and green-white August moths had found their way in from the night and fluttered about the clear candle flames. Two girls wearing flannel slacks and blazers walked arm in arm across the room into the bar. From the main street outside came the echoes of holiday hysteria.

"They claim that in August Saratoga is the wealthiest town per capita in the world." Sylvester turned to the rich man. "What do you think?"

"I wouldn't know," said the rich man. "It may very well be so."

Daintily, Simmons wiped his greasy mouth with the tip of his forefinger. "How about Hollywood? And Wall Street——"

"Wait," said Sylvester. "He's decided to come over here."

The jockey had left the wall and was approaching the table in the corner. He walked with a prim strut, swinging out his legs in a half-circle with each step, his heels biting smartly into the red velvet carpet on the floor. On the way over he brushed against the elbow of a fat woman in white satin at the banquet table; he stepped back and bowed with dandifield courtesy, his eyes quite closed. When he had crossed the room he drew up a chair and sat at a corner of the table, between Sylvester and the rich man, without a nod of greeting or a change in his set, gray face.

"Had dinner?" Sylvester asked.

"Some people might call it that." The jockey's voice was high, bitter, clear.

Sylvester put his knife and fork down carefully on his plate. The rich man shifted his position, turning sidewise in his chair and crossing his legs. He was dressed in twill riding pants, unpolished boots, and a shabby brown jacket—this was his outfit day and night in the racing season, although he was never seen on a horse. Simmons went on with his dinner.

"Like a spot of seltzer water?" asked Sylvester. "Or something like that?"

The jockey didn't answer. He drew a gold cigarette case from his pocket and snapped it open. Inside were a few cigarettes and a tiny gold penknife. He used the knife to cut a cigarette in half. When he had lighted his smoke he held up his hand to a waiter passing by the table. "Kentucky bourbon, please."

"Now, listen, kid," said Sylvester.

"Don't 'kid' me."

"Be reasonable. You know you got to behave reasonable."

The jockey drew up the left corner of his mouth in a stiff jeer. His eyes lowered to the food spread out on the table, but instantly he looked up again. Before the rich man was a fish casserole, baked in a cream sauce and garnished with parsley. Sylvester had ordered eggs Benedict. There were asparagus, fresh buttered corn, and a side dish of wet black olives. A plate of French-fried potatoes was in the corner of the table before the jockey. He didn't look at the food again but kept his pinched eyes on the centerpiece of full-blown lavender roses. "I don't suppose you remember a certain person by the name of McGuire," he said.

"Now, listen," said Sylvester.

The waiter brought the whisky, and the jockey sat fondling the glass with his small, strong, calloused hands. On his wrist was a gold link bracelet that clinked against the table edge. After turning the glass between his palms the jockey suddenly drank the whisky neat in two hard swallows. He set down the glass sharply. "No, I don't suppose your memory is that long and extensive," he said.

"Sure enough, Bitsy," said Sylvester. "What makes you act like this? You hear from the kid today?"

"I received a letter," the jockey said. "The certain person we were speaking about was taken out from the cast on Wednesday. One leg is two inches shorter than the other one. That's all."

Sylvester clucked his tongue and shook his head. "I realize how you feel."

"Do you?" The jockey was looking at the dishes on the table. His gaze passed from the fish casserole to the corn and finally fixed on the plate of fried potatoes. His face tightened and quickly he looked up again. A rose shattered and he picked up one of the petals, bruised it between his thumb and forefinger, and put it in his mouth.

"Well, those things happen," said the rich man.

The trainer and the bookie had finished eating, but there was food left on the serving dishes before their plates. The rich man dipped his buttery fingers in his water glass and wiped them with his napkin.

"Well," said the jockey, "doesn't somebody want me to pass them something? Or maybe perhaps you desire to reorder. Another hunk of beefsteak, gentlemen, or——"

"Please," said Sylvester. "Be reasonable. Why don't you go on upstairs?"

"Yes, why don't I?" the jockey said.

His prim voice had risen higher and there was about it the sharp whine of hysteria.

"Why don't I go up to my god-damn room and walk around and write some letters and go to bed like a good boy? Why don't I just——" He pushed his chair back and got up. "Oh, foo," he said. "Foo to you. I want a drink."

"All I can say is it's your funeral," said Sylvester. "You know what it does to you. You know well enough."

The jockey crossed the dining room and went into the bar. He ordered a Manhattan, and Sylvester watched him stand with his heels pressed tight together, his body hard as a lead soldier's, holding his little finger out from the cocktail glass and sipping the drink slowly.

"He's crazy," said Simmons. "Like I said."

Sylvester turned to the rich man. "If he eats a lamb chop, you can see the shape of it in his stomach a hour afterward. He can't sweat things out of him any more. He's a hundred and twelve and a half. He's gained three pounds since we left Miami."

"A jockey shouldn't drink," said the rich man.

"The food don't satisfy him like it used to, and he can't sweat it out. If he eats a lamb chop, you can watch it tooching out in his stomach and it don't go down."

The jockey finished his Manhattan. He swallowed, crushed the cherry in the bottom of the glass with his thumb, then pushed the glass away from him. The two girls in blazers were standing at his left, their faces turned toward each other, and at the other end of the bar two touts had started an argument about which was the highest mountain in the world.

Everyone was with somebody else; there was no other person drinking alone that night. The jockey paid with a brand-new fifty-dollar bill and didn't count the change.

He walked back to the dining room and to the table at which the three men were sitting, but he did not sit down. "No, I wouldn't presume to think your memory is that extensive," he said. He was so small that the edge of the table top reached almost to his belt, and when he gripped the corner with his wiry hands he didn't have to stoop. "No, you're too busy gobbling up dinners in dining rooms. You're too——"

"Honestly," begged Sylvester. "You've got to behave reasonable."

"Reasonable! Reasonable!" The jockey's gray face quivered, then set in a mean, frozen grin. He shook the table so that the plates rattled, and for a moment it seemed that he would push it over. But suddenly he stopped. His hand reached out toward the plate nearest to him and deliberately he put a few of the French-fried potatoes in his mouth. He chewed slowly, his upper lip raised, then he turned and spat out the pulpy mouthful on the smooth red carpet which covered the floor. "Libertines," he said, and his voice was thin and broken. He rolled the word in his mouth, as though it had a flavor and a substance that gratified him. "You libertines," he said again, and turned and walked with his rigid swagger out of the dining room.

Sylvester shrugged one of his loose, heavy shoulders. The rich man sopped up some water that had been spilled on the tablecloth, and they didn't speak until the waiter came to clear away.

The Valiant Woman

J. F. POWERS

(1917–)

They had come to the dessert in a dinner that was a shambles. "Well, John," Father Nulty said, turning away from Mrs. Stoner and to Father Firman, long gone silent as his own table. "You've got the bishop coming for confirmations next week."

"Yes," Mrs. Stoner cut in, "and for dinner. And if he don't eat any more than he did last year——"

Father Firman, in a rare moment, faced it. "Mrs. Stoner, the bishop is not well. You know that."

"And after I fixed that fine dinner and all." Mrs. Stoner pouted in Father Nulty's direction.

"I wouldn't feel bad about it, Mrs. Stoner," Father Nulty said. "He never eats much anywhere."

"It's funny. And that new Mrs. Allers said he ate just fine when he was there," Mrs. Stoner argued, and then spit out, "but she's a damned liar!"

Father Nulty, unsettled but trying not to show it, said, "Who's Mrs. Allers?"

"She's at Holy Cross," Mrs. Stoner said.

"She's the housekeeper," Father Firman added, thinking Mrs. Stoner made it sound as though Mrs. Allers were the pastor there.

"I swear I don't know what to do about the dinner this year," Mrs. Stoner said.

Father Firman moaned. "Just do as you've always done, Mrs. Stoner."

"Huh! And have it all to throw out! Is that any way to do?"

"Is there any dessert?" Father Firman asked coldly.

Mrs. Stoner leaped up from the table and bolted into the kitchen, mumbling. She came back with a birthday cake. She plunged it in the center of the table. She found a big wooden match in her apron pocket and thrust it at Father Firman.

"I don't like this bishop," she said. "I never did. And the way he went and cut poor Ellen Kennedy out of Father Doolin's will!"

She went back into the kitchen.

"Didn't they talk a lot of filth about Doolin and the housekeeper?" Father Nulty asked.

"I should think they did," Father Firman said. "All because he took her to the movies on Sunday night. After he died and the bishop cut her out of the will, though I hear he gives her a pension privately, they talked about the bishop."

"I don't like this bishop at all," Mrs. Stoner said, appearing with a cake knife. "Bishop Doran—there was the man!"

"We know," Father Firman said. "All man and all priest."

"He did know real estate," Father Nulty said.

Father Firman struck the match.

"Not on the chair!" Mrs. Stoner cried, too late.

Father Firman set the candle burning—it was suspiciously large and yellow, like a blessed one, but he could not be sure. They watched the fluttering flame.

"I'm forgetting the lights!" Mrs. Stoner said, and got up to turn them off. She went into the kitchen again.

The priests had a moment of silence in the candlelight.

"Happy birthday, John," Father Nulty said softly. "Is it fifty-nine you are?"

"As if you didn't know, Frank," Father Firman said, "and you the same but one."

Father Nulty smiled, the old gold of his incisors shining in the flickering light, his collar whiter in the dark, and raised his glass of water, which would have been wine or better in the bygone days, and toasted Father Firman.

"Many of 'em, John."

"Blow it out," Mrs. Stoner said, returning to the room. She waited by the light switch for Father Firman to blow out the candle.

Mrs. Stoner, who ate no desserts, began to clear the dishes into the kitchen, and the priests, finishing their cake and coffee in a hurry, went to sit in the study.

Father Nulty offered a cigar.

"John?"

"My ulcers, Frank."

"Ah, well, you're better off." Father Nulty lit the cigar and crossed his long black legs. "Fish Frawley has got him a Filipino, John. Did you hear?"

Father Firman leaned forward, interested. "He got rid of the woman he had?"

"He did. It seems she snooped."

"Snooped, eh?"

"She did. And gossiped. Fish introduced two town boys to her, said, 'Would you think these boys were my nephews?' That's all, and the next week the paper had it that his two nephews were visiting him from Erie. After that, he let her believe he was going East to see his parents, though both are dead. The paper carried the story. Fish returned and made a sermon out of it. Then he got the Filipino."

Father Firman squirmed with pleasure in his chair. "That's like Fish, Frank. He can do that." He stared at the tips of his fingers bleakly. "You could never get a Filipino to come to a place like this."

"Probably not," Father Nulty said. "Fish is pretty close to Minneapolis. Ah, say, do you remember the trick he played on us all in Marmion Hall!"

"That I'll not forget!" Father Firman's eyes remembered. "Getting up New Year's morning and finding the toilet seats all painted!"

"*Happy Circumcision!* Hah!" Father Nulty had a coughing fit.

When he had got himself together again, a mosquito came and sat on his wrist. He watched it a moment before bringing his heavy hand down.

He raised his hand slowly, viewed the dead mosquito, and sent it spinning with a plunk of his middle finger.

"Only the female bites," he said.

"I didn't know that," Father Firman said.

"Ah, yes . . ."

Mrs. Stoner entered the study and sat down with some sewing—Father Firman's black socks.

She smiled pleasantly at Father Nulty. "And what do you think of the atom bomb, Father?"

"Not much," Father Nulty said.

Mrs. Stoner had stopped smiling. Father Firman yawned.

Mrs. Stoner served up another: "Did you read about this communist convert, Father?"

"He's been in the Church before," Father Nulty said, "and so it's not a conversion, Mrs. Stoner."

"No? Well, I already got him down on my list of Monsignor's converts."

"It's better than a conversion, Mrs. Stoner, for there is more rejoicing in heaven over the return of . . . uh, he that was lost, Mrs. Stoner, is found."

"And that congresswoman, Father?"

"Yes. A convert—she."

"And Henry Ford's grandson, Father. I got him down."

"Yes, to be sure."

Father Firman yawned, this time audibly, and held his jaw.

"But he's one only by marriage, Father," Mrs. Stoner said. "I always say you got to watch those kind."

"Indeed you do, but a convert nonetheless, Mrs. Stoner. Remember, Cardinal Newman himself was one."

Mrs. Stoner was unimpressed. "I see where Henry Ford's making steering wheels out of soybeans, Father."

"I didn't see that."

"I read it in the *Reader's Digest* or some place."

"Yes, well . . ." Father Nulty rose and held his hand out to Father Firman. "John," he said. "It's been good."

"I heard Hirohito's next," Mrs. Stoner said, returning to converts.

"Let's wait and see, Mrs. Stoner," Father Nulty said.

The priests walked to the door.

"You know where I live, John."

"Yes. Come again, Frank. Good night."

Father Firman watched Father Nulty go down the walk to his car at the curb. He hooked the screen door and turned off the porch light. He hesitated at the foot of the stairs, suddenly moved to go to bed. But he went back into the study.

"Phew!" Mrs. Stoner said. "I thought he'd never go. Here it is after eight o'clock."

Father Firman sat down in his rocking chair. "I don't see him often," he said.

"I give up!" Mrs. Stoner exclaimed, flinging the holey socks upon the horsehair sofa. "I'd swear you had a nail in your shoe."

"I told you I looked."

"Well, you ought to look again. And cut your toenails, why don't you? Haven't I got enough to do?"

Father Firman scratched in his coat pocket for a pill, found one, swallowed it. He let his head sink back against the chair and closed his eyes. He could hear her moving about the room, making the preparations; and how he knew them—the fumbling in the drawer for a pencil with a point, the rip of the page from his daily calendar, and finally the leg of the card table sliding up against his leg.

He opened his eyes. She yanked the floor lamp alongside the table, setting the bead fringe tinkling on the shade, and pulled up her chair on the other side. She sat down and smiled at him for the first time that day. Now she was happy.

She swept up the cards and began to shuffle with the abandoned virtuosity of an old river-boat gambler, standing them on end, fanning them out, whirling them through her fingers, dancing them halfway up her arms, cracking the whip over them. At last they lay before him tamed into a neat deck.

"Cut?"

"Go ahead," he said. She liked to go first.

She gave him her faint, avenging smile and drew a card, cast it aside for another which he thought must be an ace from the way she clutched it face down.

She was getting all the cards, as usual, and would have been invincible if she had possessed his restraint and if her cunning had been of a higher order. He knew a few things about leading and lying back that she would never learn. Her strategy was attack, forever attack, with one baffling departure: she might sacrifice certain tricks as expendable if only she could have the last ones, the heartbreaking ones, if she could slap them down one after another, shatteringly.

She played for blood, no bones about it, but for her there was no other way; it was her nature, as it was the lion's, and for this reason he found her ferocity pardonable, more a defect of the flesh, venial, while his own trouble was all in the will, mortal. He did not sweat and pray over each card as she must, but he did keep an eye out for reneging and demanded a cut now and then just to aggravate her, and he was always secretly hoping for aces.

With one card left in her hand, the telltale trick coming next, she delayed playing it, showing him first the smile, the preview of defeat. She laid it on the table—so! She held one more trump than he had reasoned possible. Had she palmed it from somewhere? No, she would not go that far; that would not be fair, was worse than reneging, which so easily and often happened accidentally, and she believed in being fair. Besides he had been watching her.

God smote the vines with hail, the sycamore trees with frost, and offered up the flocks to the lightning—but Mrs. Stoner! What a cross Father Firman had from God in Mrs. Stoner! There were other housekeepers as bad, no doubt, walking the rectories of the world, yes, but . . . yes. He could name one and maybe two priests who were worse off. One, maybe two. Cronin. His scraggly blonde of sixty—take her, with her everlasting banging on the grand piano, the gift of the pastor; her proud talk about the goiter operation at the Mayo Brothers', also a gift; her honking the parish Buick at passing strange priests because they were all in the game together. She was worse. She was something to keep the home fires burning. Yes sir. And Cronin said she was not a bad person really, but what was he? He was quite a freak himself.

For that matter, could anyone say that Mrs. Stoner was a bad person? No. He could not say it himself, and he was no freak. She had her points, Mrs. Stoner. She was clean. And though she cooked poorly, could not play the organ, would not take up the collection in an emergency, and went to card parties, and told all—even so, she was clean. She washed everything. Sometimes her underwear hung down beneath her dress like a paratrooper's pants, but it and everything she touched was clean. She washed constantly. She was clean.

She had her other points, to be sure—her faults, you might say. She snooped—no mistake about it—but it was not snooping for snooping's sake; she had a reason. She did other things, always with a reason. She overcharged on rosaries and prayer books, but that was for the sake of the poor. She censored the pamphlet rack, but that was to prevent scandal. She pried into the baptismal and matrimonial records, but there was no other way if Father was out, and in this way she had once uncovered a bastard and flushed him out of the rectory, but that was the perverted decency of the times. She held her nose over bad marriages in the presence of the victims, but that was her sorrow and came from having her husband buried in a mine. And he had caught her telling a bewildered young couple that there was only one good reason for their wanting to enter into a mixed marriage—the child had to have a name, and that—that was what?

She hid his books, kept him from smoking, picked his friends (usually the pastors of her colleagues), bawled out people for calling after dark, had no humor, except at cards, and then it was grim, very grim, and she sat hatchet-faced every morning at Mass. But she went to Mass, which was all that kept the church from being empty some mornings. She did annoying things all day long. She said annoying things into the night. She said she had given him the best years of her life. Had she? Perhaps—for the miner had her only a year. It was too bad, sinfully bad, when he thought of it like that. But all talk of best years and life was nonsense. He had to consider the heart of the matter, the essence. The essence was that housekeepers were hard to get, harder to get than ushers, than willing workers, than organists, than secretaries—yes, harder to get than assistants or vocations.

And she was a *saver*—saved money, saved electricity, saved string, bags, sugar, saved—him. That's what she did. That's what she said she did, and she was right, in a way. In a way, she was usually right. In fact, she was always right—in a way. And you could never get a Filipino to come way out here and live. Not a young one anyway, and he had never seen an old one. Not a Filipino. They liked to dress up and live.

Should he let it drop about Fish having one, just to throw a scare into her, let her know he was doing some thinking? No. It would be a perfect cue for the one about a man needing a woman to look after him. He was not up to that again, not tonight.

Now she was doing what she liked most of all. She was making a grand slam, playing it out card for card, though it was in the bag, prolonging what would have been cut short out of mercy in gentle company. Father Firman knew the agony of losing.

She slashed down the last card, a miserable deuce trump, and did in the hapless king of hearts he had been saving.

"Skunked you!"

She was awful in victory. Here was the bitter end of their long day together, the final murderous hour in which all they wanted to say—all he wouldn't and all she couldn't—came out in the cards. Whoever won at honeymoon won the day, slept on the other's scalp, and God alone had to help the loser.

"We've been at it long enough, Mrs. Stoner," he said, seeing her assembling the cards for another round.

"Had enough, huh!"

Father Firman grumbled something.

"No?"

"Yes."

She pulled the table away and left it against the wall for the next time. She went out of the study carrying the socks, content and clucking. He closed his eyes after her and began to get under way in the rocking chair, the nightly trip to nowhere. He could hear her brewing a cup of tea in the kitchen and conversing with the cat. She made her way up the stairs, carrying the tea, followed by the cat, purring.

He waited, rocking out to sea, until she would be sure to be through in the bathroom. Then he got up and locked the front door (she looked after the back door) and loosened his collar going upstairs.

In the bathroom he mixed a glass of antiseptic, always afraid of pyorrhea, and gargled to ward off pharyngitis.

When he turned on the light in his room, the moths and beetles began to batter against the screens, the lighter insects humming. . . .

Yes, and she had the guest room. How did she come to get that? Why wasn't she in the back room, in her proper place? He knew, if he cared to remember. The screen in the back room—it let in mosquitoes, and if it didn't do that she'd love to sleep back there, Father, looking out at the steeple and the blessed cross on top, Father, if it just weren't for the screen, Father. Very well, Mrs. Stoner, I'll get it fixed or fix it myself. Oh, could you now, Father? I could, Mrs. Stoner, and I will. In the meantime you take the guest room. Yes, Father, and thank you, Father, the house ringing with amenities then. Years ago, all that. She was a pie-faced girl then, not really a girl perhaps, but not too old to marry again. But she never had. In fact, he could not remember that she had even tried for a husband since coming to the rectory, but, of course, he could be wrong, not knowing how they went about it. God! God save us! Had she got her wires crossed and mistaken him all these years for *that? That!* Him! Suffering God! No. That was going too far. That was getting morbid. No. He must not think of that again, ever. No.

But just the same she had got the guest room and she had it yet. Well, did it matter? Nobody ever came to see him any more, nobody to stay overnight anyway, nobody to stay very long . . . not any more. He knew how they laughed at him. He had heard Frank humming all right—before he saw how serious and sad the situation was and took pity—humming, "Wedding Bells Are Breaking Up That Old Gang of Mine." But then they'd always laughed at him for something—for not being an athlete, for wearing glasses, for having kidney trouble . . . and mail coming addressed to Rev. and Mrs. Stoner.

Removing his shirt, he bent over the table to read the volume left open from last night. He read, translating easily, "Eisdem licet cum illis . . . Clerics are allowed to reside only with women about whom there can be no suspicion, either because of a natural bond (as mother, sister, aunt) or of advanced age, combined in both cases with good repute."

Last night he had read it, and many nights before, each time as though this time to find what was missing, to find what obviously was not in the paragraph, his problem considered, a way out. She was not mother, not sister, not aunt, and *advanced age* was a relative term (why, she was younger than he was) and so, eureka, she did not meet the letter of the law—but, alas, how she fulfilled the spirit! And besides it would be a slimy way of handling it after all her years of service. He could not afford to pension her off, either.

He slammed the book shut. He slapped himself fiercely on the back, missing the wily mosquito, and whirled to find it. He took a magazine and folded it into a swatter. Then he saw it—oh, the preternatural cunning of it!—poised in the beard of St. Joseph on the bookcase. He could not hit it there. He teased it away, wanting it to light on the wall, but it knew his thoughts and flew high away. He swung wildly, hoping to stun it, missed, swung back, catching St. Joseph across the neck. The statue fell to the floor and broke.

Mrs. Stoner was panting in the hall outside his door.

"What is it!"

"Mosquitoes!"

"What is it, Father? Are you hurt?"

"Mosquitoes—damn it! And only the female bites!"

Mrs. Stoner, after a moment, said, "Shame on you, Father. She needs the blood for her eggs."

He dropped the magazine and lunged at the mosquito with his bare hand.

She went back to her room, saying, "Pshaw, I thought it was burglars murdering you in your bed."

He lunged again.

The Lottery

SHIRLEY JACKSON

(1919–1965)

The morning of June 27th was clear and sunny, with the fresh warmth of a full-summer day; the flowers were blossoming profusely and the grass was richly green. The people of the village began to gather in the square, between the post office and the bank, around ten o'clock; in some towns there were so many people that the lottery took two days and had to be started on June 26th, but in this village, where there were only about three hundred people, the whole lottery took less than two hours, so it could begin at ten o'clock in the morning and still be through in time to allow the villagers to get home for noon dinner.

The children assembled first, of course. School was recently over for the summer, and the feeling of liberty sat uneasily on most of them; they tended to gather together quietly for a while before they broke into boisterous play, and their talk was still of the classroom and the teacher, of books and reprimands. Bobby Martin had already stuffed his pockets full of stones, and the other boys soon followed his example, selecting the smoothest and roundest stones; Bobby and Harry Jones and Dickie Delacroix—the villagers pronounced his name "Dellacroy"—eventually made a great pile of stones in one corner of the square and guarded it against the raids of the other boys. The girls stood aside, talking among themselves, looking over their shoulders at the boys, and the very small children rolled in the dust or clung to the hands of their older brothers or sisters.

Soon the men began to gather, surveying their own children, speaking of planting and rain, tractors and taxes. They stood together, away from the pile of stones in the corner, and their jokes were quiet and they smiled rather than laughed. The women, wearing faded house dresses and sweaters, came shortly after their menfolk. They greeted one another and exchanged bits of gossip as they went to join their husbands. Soon the women, standing by their husbands, began to call to their children, and the children came reluctantly, having to be called four or five times.

Bobby Martin ducked under his mother's grasping hand and ran, laughing, back to the pile of stones. His father spoke up sharply, and Bobby came quickly and took his place between his father and his oldest brother.

The lottery was conducted—as were the square dances, the teen-age club, the Halloween program—by Mr. Summers, who had time and energy to devote to civic activities. He was a round-faced, jovial man and he ran the coal business, and people were sorry for him, because he had no children and his wife was a scold. When he arrived in the square, carrying the black wooden box, there was a murmur of conversation among the villagers, and he waved and called, "Little late today, folks." The postmaster, Mr. Graves, followed him, carrying a three-legged stool, and the stool was put in the center of the square and Mr. Summers set the black box down on it. The villagers kept their distance, leaving a space between themselves and the stool, and when Mr. Summers said, "Some of you fellows want to give me a hand?" there was a hesitation before two men, Mr. Martin and his oldest son, Baxter, came forward to hold the box steady on the stool while Mr. Summers stirred up the papers inside it.

The original paraphernalia for the lottery had been lost long ago, and the black box now resting on the stool had been put into use even before Old Man Warner, the oldest man in town, was born. Mr. Summers spoke frequently to the villagers about making a new box, but no one liked to upset even as much tradition as was represented by the black box. There was a story that the present box had been made with some pieces of the box that had preceded it, the one that had been constructed when the first people settled down to make a village here. Every year, after the lottery, Mr. Summers began talking again about a new box, but every year the subject was allowed to fade off without anything's being done. The black box grew shabbier each year; by now it was no longer completely black but splintered badly along one side to show the original wood color, and in some places faded or stained.

Mr. Martin and his oldest son, Baxter, held the black box securely on the stool until Mr. Summers had stirred the papers thoroughly with his hand. Because so much of the ritual had been forgotten or discarded, Mr. Summers had been successful in having slips of paper substituted for the chips of wood that had been used for generations. Chips of wood, Mr. Summers had argued, had been all very well when the village was tiny, but now that the population was more than three hundred and likely to keep on growing, it was necessary to use something that would fit more easily into the black box. The night before the lottery, Mr. Summers and Mr. Graves made up the slips of paper and put them in the box, and it was then taken to the safe of Mr. Summers' coal company and locked up until Mr. Summers was ready to take it to the square next morning. The rest of the year, the box was put away, sometimes one place, sometimes another; it had spent one year in Mr. Graves's barn and another year underfoot in the post office, and sometimes it was set on a shelf in the Martin grocery and left there.

There was a great deal of fussing to be done before Mr. Summers declared the lottery open. There were the lists to make up—of heads of families, heads of households in each family, members of each household in each family. There was the proper swearing-in of Mr. Summers by the postmaster, as the official of the lottery; at one time, some people remembered, there had been a recital of some sort, performed by the official of the lottery, a perfunctory, tuneless chant that had been rattled off duly each year; some people believed that the official of the lottery used to stand just so when he said or sang it, others believed that he was supposed to walk among the people, but years and years ago this part of the ritual had been allowed to lapse. There had been, also, a ritual salute, which the official of the lottery had had to use in addressing each person who came up to draw from the box, but this also had changed with time, until now it was felt necessary only for the official to speak to each person approaching. Mr. Summers was very good at all this; in his clean white shirt and blue jeans, with one hand resting carelessly on the black box, he seemed very proper and important as he talked interminably to Mr. Graves and the Martins.

Just as Mr. Summers finally left off talking and turned to the assembled villagers, Mrs. Hutchinson came hurriedly along the path to the square, her sweater thrown over her shoulders, and slid into place in the back of the crowd. "Clean forgot what day it was," she said to Mrs. Delacroix, who stood next to her, and they both laughed softly. "Thought my old man was out back stacking wood," Mrs. Hutchinson went on, "and then I looked out the window and the kids were gone, and then I remembered it was the twenty-seventh and came a-running." She dried her hands on her apron, and Mrs. Delacroix said, "You're in time, though. They're still talking away up there."

Mrs. Hutchinson craned her neck to see through the crowd and found her husband and children standing near the front. She tapped Mrs. Delacroix on the arm as a farewell and began to make her way through the crowd. The people separated good-humoredly to let her through; two or three people said, in voices just loud enough to be heard across the crowd, "Here comes your Missus, Hutchinson," and "Bill, she made it after all." Mrs. Hutchinson reached her husband, and Mr. Summers, who had been waiting, said cheerfully, "Thought we were going to have to get on without you, Tessie." Mrs. Hutchinson said, grinning, "Wouldn't have me leave m'dishes in the sink, now, would you, Joe?," and soft laughter ran through the crowd as the people stirred back into position after Mrs. Hutchinson's arrival.

"Well, now," Mr. Summers said soberly, "guess we better get started, get this over with, so's we can go back to work. Anybody ain't here?"

"Dunbar," several people said. "Dunbar, Dunbar."

Mr. Summers consulted his list. "Clyde Dunbar," he said. "That's right. He's broke his leg, hasn't he? Who's drawing for him?"

"Me, I guess," a woman said, and Mr. Summers turned to look at her. "Wife draws for her husband," Mr. Summers said. "Don't you have a grown boy to do it for you, Janey?" Although Mr. Summers and everyone else in the village knew the answer perfectly well, it was the business of the official of the lottery to ask such questions formally. Mr. Summers waited with an expression of polite interest while Mrs. Dunbar answered.

"Horace's not but sixteen yet," Mrs. Dunbar said regretfully. "Guess I gotta fill in for the old man this year."

"Right," Mr. Summers said. He made a note on the list he was holding. Then he asked, "Watson boy drawing this year?"

A tall boy in the crowd raised his hand. "Here," he said. "I'm drawing for m'mother and me." He blinked his eyes nervously and ducked his head as several voices in the crowd said things like "Good fellow, Jack," and "Glad to see your mother's got a man to do it."

"Well," Mr. Summers said, "guess that's everyone. Old Man Warner make it?"

"Here," a voice said, and Mr. Summers nodded.

A sudden hush fell on the crowd as Mr. Summers cleared his throat and looked at the list. "All ready?" he called. "Now, I'll read the names—heads of families first—and the men come up and take a paper out of the box. Keep the paper folded in your hand without looking at it until everyone has had a turn. Everything clear?"

The people had done it so many times that they only half listened to the directions; most of them were quiet, wetting their lips, not looking around. Then Mr. Summers raised one hand high and said, "Adams." A man disengaged himself from the crowd and came forward. "Hi, Steve," Mr. Summers said, and Mr. Adams said, "Hi, Joe." They grinned at one another humorlessly and nervously. Then Mr. Adams reached into the black box and took out a folded paper. He held it firmly by one corner as he turned and went hastily back to his place in the crowd, where he stood a little apart from his family, not looking down at his hand.

"Allen." Mr. Summers said. "Anderson. . . . Bentham."

"Seems like there's no time at all between lotteries any more," Mrs.

Delacroix said to Mrs. Graves in the back row. "Seems like we got through with the last one only last week."

"Time sure goes fast," Mrs. Graves said.

"Clark. . . . Delacroix."

"There goes my old man," Mrs. Delacroix said. She held her breath while her husband went forward.

"Dunbar," Mr. Summers said, and Mrs. Dunbar went steadily to the box while one of the women said, "Go on, Janey," and another said, "There she goes."

"We're next," Mrs. Graves said. She watched while Mr. Graves came around from the side of the box, greeted Mr. Summers gravely, and selected a slip of paper from the box. By now, all through the crowd there were men holding the small folded papers in their large hands, turning them over and over nervously. Mrs. Dunbar and her two sons stood together, Mrs. Dunbar holding the slip of paper.

"Harburt. . . . Hutchinson."

"Get up there, Bill," Mrs. Hutchinson said, and the people near her laughed.

"Jones."

"They do say," Mr. Adams said to Old Man Warner, who stood next to him, "that over in the north village they're talking of giving up the lottery."

Old Man Warner snorted. "Pack of crazy fools," he said. "Listening to the young folks, nothing's good enough for *them*. Next thing you know, they'll be wanting to go back to living in caves, nobody work any more, live *that* way for a while. Used to be a saying about 'Lottery in June, corn be heavy soon.' First thing you know, we'd all be eating stewed chickweed and acorns. There's *always* been a lottery," he added petulantly. "Bad enough to see young Joe Summers up there joking with everybody."

"Some places have already quit lotteries," Mrs. Adams said.

"Nothing but trouble in *that,*" Old Man Warner said stoutly. "Pack of young fools."

"Martin." And Bobby Martin watched his father go forward. "Overdyke. . . . Percy."

"I wish they'd hurry," Mrs. Dunbar said to her older son. "I wish they'd hurry."

"They're almost through," her son said.

"You get ready to run tell Dad," Mrs. Dunbar said.

Mr. Summers called his own name and then stepped forward precisely and selected a slip from the box. Then he called, "Warner."

"Seventy-seventh year I been in the lottery," Old Man Warner said as he went through the crowd. "Seventy-seventh time."

"Watson." The tall boy came awkwardly through the crowd. Someone said, "Don't be nervous, Jack." Mr. Summers said, "Take your time, son."

"Zanini."

After that, there was a long pause, a breathless pause, until Mr. Summers, holding his slip of paper in the air, said, "All right, fellows." For a minute, no one moved, and then all the slips of paper were opened. Suddenly, all the women began to speak at once, saying, "Who is it?," "Who's got it?," "Is it the Dunbars?," "Is it the Watsons?" Then the voices began to say, "It's Hutchinson. It's Bill," "Bill Hutchinson's got it."

"Go tell your father," Mrs. Dunbar said to her older son.

People began to look around to see the Hutchinsons. Bill Hutchinson was standing quiet, staring down at the paper in his hand. Suddenly, Tessie Hutchinson shouted to Mr. Summers, "You didn't give him time enough to take any paper he wanted. I saw you. It wasn't fair!"

"Be a good sport, Tessie," Mrs. Delacroix called, and Mrs. Graves said, "All of us took the same chance."

"Shut up, Tessie," Bill Hutchinson said.

"Well, everyone," Mr. Summers said, "that was done pretty fast, and now we've got to be hurrying a little more to get it done in time." He consulted his next list. "Bill," he said, "you draw for the Hutchinson family. You got any other households in the Hutchinsons?"

"There's Don and Eva," Mrs. Hutchinson yelled. "Make *them* take their chance!"

"Daughters draw with their husbands' families, Tessie," Mr. Summers said gently. "You know that as well as anyone else."

"I guess not, Joe," Bill Hutchinson said regretfully. "My daughter draws with her husband's family, that's only fair. And I've got no other family except the kids."

"Then, as far as drawing for families is concerned, it's you," Mr. Summers said in explanation, "and as far as drawing for households is concerned, that's you, too. Right?"

"Right," Bill Hutchinson said.

"How many kids, Bill?" Mr. Summers asked formally.

"Three," Bill Hutchinson said. "There's Bill, Jr., and Nancy, and little Dave. And Tessie and me."

"All right, then," Mr. Summers said. "Harry, you got their tickets back?"

Mr. Graves nodded and held up the slips of paper. "Put them in the box, then," Mr. Summers directed. "Take Bill's and put it in."

"I think we ought to start over," Mrs. Hutchinson said, as quietly as she could. "I tell you it wasn't *fair*. You didn't give him time enough to choose. *Every*body saw that."

Mr. Graves had selected the five slips and put them in the box, and he dropped all the papers but those onto the ground, where the breeze caught them and lifted them off.

"Listen, everybody," Mrs. Hutchinson was saying to the people around her.

"Ready, Bill?" Mr. Summers asked, and Bill Hutchinson, with one quick glance around at his wife and children, nodded.

"Remember," Mr. Summers said, "take the slips and keep them folded until each person has taken one. Harry, you help little Dave." Mr. Graves took the hand of the little boy, who came willingly with him up to the box. "Take a paper out of the box, Davy," Mr. Summers said. Davy put his hand into the box and laughed. "Take just *one* paper," Mr. Summers said. "Harry, you hold it for him." Mr. Graves took the child's hand and removed the folded paper from the tight fist and held it while little Dave stood next to him and looked up at him wonderingly.

"Nancy next," Mr. Summers said. Nancy was twelve, and her school friends breathed heavily as she went forward, switching her skirt, and took a slip daintily from the box. "Bill, Jr.," Mr. Summers said, and Billy, his face red and his feet over-large, nearly knocked the box over as he got a paper out. "Tessie," Mr. Summers said. She hesitated for a minute, looking around defiantly, and then set her lips and went up to the box. She snatched a paper out and held it behind her.

"Bill," Mr. Summers said, and Bill Hutchinson reached into the box and felt around, bringing his hand out at last with the slip of paper in it.

The crowd was quiet. A girl whispered, "I hope it's not Nancy," and the sound of the whisper reached the edges of the crowd.

"It's not the way it used to be," Old Man Warner said clearly. "People ain't the way they used to be."

"All right," Mr. Summers said. "Open the papers. Harry, you open little Dave's."

Mr. Graves opened the slip of paper and there was a general sigh through the crowd as he held it up and everyone could see that it was blank. Nancy and Bill, Jr., opened theirs at the same time, and both beamed and laughed, turning around to the crowd and holding their slips of paper above their heads.

"Tessie," Mr. Summers said. There was a pause, and then Mr. Summers looked at Bill Hutchinson, and Bill unfolded his paper and showed it. It was blank.

"It's Tessie," Mr. Summers said, and his voice was hushed. "Show us her paper, Bill."

Bill Hutchinson went over to his wife and forced the slip of paper out of her hand. It had a black spot on it, the black spot Mr. Summers had made the night before with the heavy pencil in the coal-company office. Bill Hutchinson held it up, and there was a stir in the crowd.

"All right, folks," Mr. Summers said. "Let's finish quickly."

Although the villagers had forgotten the ritual and lost the original black box, they still remembered to use stones. The pile of stones the boys had made earlier was ready; there were stones on the ground with the blowing scraps of paper that had come out of the box. Mrs. Delacroix selected a stone so large she had to pick it up with both hands and turned to Mrs. Dunbar. "Come on," she said. "Hurry up."

Mrs. Dunbar had small stones in both hands, and she said, gasping for breath, "I can't run at all. You'll have to go ahead and I'll catch up with you."

The children had stones already, and someone gave little Davy Hutchinson a few pebbles.

Tessie Hutchinson was in the center of a cleared space by now, and she held her hands out desperately as the villagers moved in on her. "It isn't fair," she said. A stone hit her on the side of the head.

Old Man Warner was saying, "Come on, come on, everyone." Steve Adams was in the front of the crowd of villagers, with Mrs. Graves beside him.

"It isn't fair, it isn't right," Mrs. Hutchinson screamed, and then they were upon her.

Three Heroines

PETER TAYLOR

(1919–)

Dedicated to the memory of Lily Heth Dabney,
another of my heroines

Dressed to the nines, and she is eighty-six!
A gold lamé gown,
Savage pearls in her pierced earlobes!
Diamonds blazing

That her Grandmother Haynes wore
A century ago!
In Washington City!
Before the War!

The exclamations are all mine, not hers—
And silent. My questions all silent, too:
Who does the woman think she is?
Where does she think she's going in that outfit,
At her age, in her health?
It's not as though *I* don't know, her son,
And *she* doesn't herself know
And the black maid who dresses her, Willie Mae,
And everybody else who cares at all to,
Does not know
In precisely what plot of cemetery ground
This woman will be lying six weeks hence
. . . at most.

"Let me do it," says Willie Mae
About everything. Snapping the golden snaps
As she stands behind her mistress, towering above her,
Towering even in heel-less carpet slippers
("Where does Willie Mae find such slippers any more?"),
Pulling the snaps together with her powerful brown hands,
Pulling the gold cloth over the white powdered back
Of my beautiful mother.

I stand in the doorway, watching, watching,
Waiting in my black tie and dinner jacket
Which I have not worn in ten years till tonight
But which I brought with me on the plane
For her sake, at her request.

And Willie Mae arranging the almost too silvery-white mane
(Silvery. Almost like, but not quite like, the blue heads
Of her "less well-bred contemporaries"
With whom she is "reduced to associating"—
So few of her very own sort are left.)
The long silvery-white hair thinned by time and perhaps by hats
(Party hats, shopping hats, church hats—
Wide-brimmed hats, cloche hats, turbans,

Whatever the fashion is)
But hair thickened tonight, filled in, ratted by Willie till it can deceive
Even me, who remember the old real thickness
The old burnt-umber color, everything, how every hair
And every strand once grew and fell, fell tenderly and attentively
Over a child that had mumps or measles
And needed attention
And no doubt once upon a time
Over a lover, a husband.

And now Willie Mae's handsome hands
Pushing her down onto the dressing-table stool
Like a child. But she is not yielding like a child.
Her knees and her hips yield,
But her posture is unaffected by standing or sitting.
With her long body and short legs she sits
Almost as high as she stands.
When I remark on this, she says,
"A long torso means a long life—
Plenty of room for all the vital organs."
It is one of her jokes.
It is something, in fact, that her Grandmother Haynes used to say
About herself, in *her* late eighties, too,
Not before the War, in Washington City
But back in Tennessee, the War over
And everything gone but her diamonds (raked from the ashes)
And her flat silver (buried and then a year later exhumed
"Thirty yards N.E. walking in a straight line from the sycamore")
And her faded finery, including the black lace mantilla
(From which she was never parted by war or economic pestilence),
Proud and witty till the end, that old lady,
Herself finally buried in the shade of that same sycamore,
Proud till the end of what she had endured,
Proud of all she had survived.

In her gold lamé, my mother recalls it all
And regales us with it one more time, me and Willie Mae.
Seated there on the silk-skirted dressing-table stool
With Willie Mae kneeling before her, sitting
Straight as if corseted, which of course she isn't,
With the false hair Willie has piled on her head
And the false figure just as deceiving

Which Willie also has arranged,
The dress cut low in front, though not so low as to reveal
The old scar from her mastectomy (forty years back
When I was twelve, the operation that she survived
When others were not surviving it).

Willie Mae is massaging her miniature feet,
Working them into the miniature gold slippers, tiny feet
But swollen, almost beyond recognition as feet
Until they shall be forcibly shod by the firm hand of Willie Mae.
One feels the pain in the room. In one's own feet.
But my mother doesn't bat an eye. Not a wince from her.
Willie hesitates considerately,
Balancing the right slipper lightly in her gentle palm,
Looking up, questioningly.
But Mother, not returning the look, says,
"Go ahead please, Willie Mae."
And herself goes ahead with whatever the funny thing is
She is saying to me.
"There!" Willie Mae says at last. "There you are.
We've got you in them. Now you can go to the ball, Cinderella."
And to me: "Ain't she a pretty thing?"
(Archly, knowing how little I like her to play the black-nigger.)
My mother gazes down at her swollen feet.
"Ah," she sighs. And then suddenly she is laughing:
"This is one Cinderella who won't lose a slipper at the ball.
We'll have to take them off with the can opener, Willie Mae."
And Willie laughs so hard she has to hide her face
In her hands, still squatting there. She rocks back and forth.
I *think* she is laughing. I *hope* she is laughing.
Then her frizzy old wig goes askew on her head
And she throws up her hands to hold it on.
She's like a madwoman, there on her haunches
Her whole body throbbing and shaking,
Her big hands holding her head on
. . . And Mother sits very erect, watching her.
Wearing her most serious expression, she watches Willie Mae.

Now we are standing in the narrow side hall, Mother and I.
We are almost on our way. The car and driver
Are patient outside in the porte-cochere.
Suddenly I remember where it is we're going.

I'd never thought we'd really go. Not
When she telephoned long-distance and asked I come out
And play her escort: the Golden Wedding Reception
Of a couple she hardly knew the names of.
Still, it was to be at the Club, wasn't it?
Everyone would be there, wouldn't they?
"And I might possibly never go to such a grand affair
Again." Incredible words, I say to myself.
Imagine! But we keep it up, she and I.
And now I see the whole evening before me,
See just how it will be. "Are you sure you want to go, Mother?
Are you sure you ought to go, after all?" I ask
With a forced smile, dropping down before her on a straight hall chair.

"Why, sure, she ought to go!" cries Willie Mae,
Appearing from nowhere, the Fairy Godmother.
Holding wide the silk-lined mink cape,
She swoops down upon Mother,
Enfolds her in the cape.
For a moment the leathery-brown arms are wrapped
About the lighter brown fur like a belt.
She holds Mother as if she were a baby
In a blanket. She all but kisses her
But doesn't want to spoil the rouged cheek.
She says: "Sure, she ought to go.
My darlin's going to have the time of her life."
Now I am on my feet again.
Mother stares up at me with eyes bright as a child's.
The coloring of her rouge and lipstick seems real—
More than real.
As real as a doll's coloring.
She is more real than life.
She is something Willie Mae has put together
To amuse a sick child with.

It is such a party as one goes to in one's dreams.
That is, in nightmares of a milder sort.
At most there are six faces
In all the vast clutter of faces
Which I think that I can match with names
And in half that number
It is the wrong name I actually come up with.

Yet, sticking like pitch to Mother,
I am smiled upon by everyone.
A faithful son at such an affair as this
Is everybody's hero. And my beautiful mother
Is everybody's heroine. They flock to her
And stand about listening to her famous bon-mots,
Her jokes, her stories. When it is crudely suggested by someone
That she might be the oldest person present, she says:
"I don't mind being old;
There's just no future in it."
—A moment's hush, then a burst of laughter.
"Dear lady, with your high-piled silver tresses
And your golden draperies, you are
Like a Greek goddess mingling tonight
Amongst the mere mortals of the Country Club."
—He is "some old professor emeritus
From the University." Or so someone whispers in my ear.
I feel myself blushing. She blinks at him
Twice or three times.
And then, after only a moment's reflection:
"As to my golden draperies—
Greek accusative, Herr Professor—
They are of course in honor of the occasion,
Bought new for our dear friend's wedding anniversary. . . .
Something old—that's me.
Something new—that's the dress.
Something borrowed—that's my son's strength.
Something blue—that's the hair piled so high on my old head."

She is the belle of the ball, without rival.
Everyone comes paying homage to her.
Almost everyone. Only her "medicine man,"
As she calls him, her beloved doctor
Keeps his distance,
He whom we met on the steps outside the Club
And had our exchanges with, brief and awkward,
Out there in the vestibule. I see him eyeing her
From far across the room, and again from a nearer point,
Eyeing her with dark, deep-set eyes
Out of his long, sad face.
Twice at least I see him moving toward her.
He is a man my age. I watch him closely.

Each time he approaches us he lets himself be intercepted,
Averted, drawn aside. How easily
He permits it. How eagerly he greets
Those who intercept him and keep him from us—from her.
They, too, no doubt are his aging patients.
But to my mother he will not come. Never.
And of course I have known all along he would not.
From the moment I saw his face
In the dim light on the outside steps I knew.
He looked at her as though he had seen a ghost.
He could not believe his eyes.
She? At such an affair? Dressed to the nines?
With what she had *inside* her?
He gave no sign of recognition.
This woman who resembled his dying patient
Whom he regarded as already dead, really
He would be a fool to mistake the one for the other.

Then, face to face with her
In the bright light of the vestibule
His curt greeting to her is all but insulting.
He cannot help it, though.
He wishes only to turn, with his knowledge,
Back into the uncertain dimness on the steps outside
And on back into the blissful darkness of his primitive profession.
What does he know of death? Certainly nothing at all, he says to himself.
He knows only about the cessation of life.
She must not ask him to go beyond that with her.
The terror seen in the eyes of most patients
Is no less repulsive to him than its opposite
Whatever the opposite might be called.
There can be no *proper* greeting for death.
There can be no *attitude* at all toward death.
If there is any real way of dealing with death,
Says her beloved doctor to himself,
Then all his success at preventing and relieving pain,
Even at saving life,
Is such a small thing. Hardly worth considering, by comparison.
. . . But the beloved doctor could not turn back into the dimness
And he could not brush past my mother in the vestibule.
For one awful moment his eyes met mine.
All that could pass between us was our disbelief—

I don't know of what precisely–and
I don't know which of us
Pitied the other more.
And then the arriving guests
Pushed us on inside and into the party
And parted us. . . . And the evening became an eternity
In which the stricken doctor could not even manage,
Could not *bring* himself
To say goodnight to Mother.

Home at last, though.
She *had* done it!
In the car, sitting together in the back seat,
She held my hand tight, never slackening, all the way.
A kind of thing she hadn't done in years,
And then only when I was in trouble,
When I was waiting to face Father
Over my newest act of rebellion
Or my latest incompetence.
The clasp of the hand
Brings it all back:
My foolish first marriage that wasn't really a marriage,
Flunking out of college,
Hitchhiking to the Gulf Coast,
Shipping out work-a-way on a Waterman Line freighter
Never writing them a word about where I was
Then rolling in home
In dirty clothes and too drunk to speak
And finally, worst of all, deserting to the literati.
And then at last forgiveness:
Father forgiving me, because he was dying
(Tears streaming down his cheeks–his only words since he could
No longer speak), me forgiving Father because he was dying
(Myself speechless too),
Mother forgiving both
And saying there was nothing to forgive.
. . . But all the way home she holds my hand
And talks again of her Grandmother Haynes, only
Of her Grandmother Haynes.

Of *her* bravery during the War,
Her husband on the Union side,
Off lecturing at Boston and Philadelphia,

Raising money to relieve the suffering
Of loyalist up-country Southerners,
And her own twin brother, the Confederate Senator,
His musical voice and old-fashioned rhetoric
Resounding through the halls of the Capitol at Richmond.
She adored them both, husband and brother,
Wrote each of them a letter every day that passed,
And suffered for them both,
Staying at home with the eleven children and the freed slaves,
Persecuted by her neighbors on both sides,
Accused by each side of supporting the other,
Even of spying,
Of sending information from Boston to Richmond
And from Richmond to Boston, and so on to Washington.
Two of her children died, and one freed slave went berserk,
Thought he was Jeff Davis and tried to surrender to *everybody*.
But she, Grandmother Haynes, never surrendered
To either side, and never betrayed either side.
She looked after her children, ran the farm,
And gave a dance in the parlor at least once a month.
People said she was vain and frivolous.
She was most assuredly both—and capable and hardworking
And brave, too. Toward the end of the War,
Sometime during the last weeks of it,
Her neighbors burned the house and barn,
And even set fire to the summer kitchen and the smokehouse.
Then her husband, Grandfather Haynes, came down
And took her and the children through the lines
To Princeton. "It's a pretty place," she wrote her brother.
"To see it, you wouldn't suppose there had been a War."
But now the War was over
She and Grandfather Haynes and the children
Had to go back to Tennessee and be poor as church mice.

They were as poor as if Grandfather Haynes had been on the losing side.
All she had was her flat silver and her diamonds and her faded finery.
They say she wore her black lace mantilla
To do the milking in.
And her brocades and silks to hoe corn
And chop cotton.
Her husband turned Methodist
And took up preaching seriously,

Preaching religion to the covites
And to the mountain folks and the Black Republicans
"Who were in sore need of it," his wife pronounced.
But she approved. "It's doing good where good is needed,"
She said. "Besides, there's more money in preaching
Than in farming—nowadays." One day her brother, the twin,
His whereabouts unknown to her for more than a year,
Appeared in the cowshed doorway
In his cutaway and starched shirtfront,
His silk hat in his hand. He had been to Brazil.
He was on his way out West now, to make a new beginning,
Traveling under an assumed name: Ben Smith.
"What a pity," she said to him,
"To have to be known as Ben Smith the rest of your life
When you are really Landon Carter of Tennessee."
They embraced, shedding tears for their happy reunion,
As she reported it,
And then parted without tears
But with long looks as he retreated on foot
Out of the barn lot and down the Valley Road,
Both of them knowing they would never meet again
In this life.

Home at last, yes,
And I have almost forgotten whether
It is my mother I am with
Or my Great-grandmother Haynes.
Though I have heard it all recited before
Time and again, and in the same words,
It never seemed so real.
The two women never seemed so nearly one.
Franklin, her driver, is at her other elbow.
Together, we very nearly carry her inside.
"She was vain and frivolous—and brave,"
Mother says, as much to Franklin as to me.
(Franklin knows the stories, too. He and the good doctor together
Have been more son to her than I, in these last years.)
"It's a combination people find it hard to understand.
But they shouldn't. It's not uncommon, do you think?"

Willie is waiting in the lighted doorway.
We traverse that last ten feet
Under the porte-cochere and across the porch.

As we make our way with her
It comes over me how near the end she is.
More than that, it sweeps over me how little even there has been
In her life. Wars have raged
Always on the other side of the world for her.
She has not even had to choose
Between neighbors, or not choose.
She did not even have a twin brother
To be torn away from.
Or an idealistic, impractical husband
To stand behind. (Hers was faithful,
Adoring, and a good provider.) Her only child
Never even gave her a scare—not of dying, anyway.
Even his rebellions and desertions and incompetences
Were healthy in their way!
But what is evident somehow
Is that she is every bit the heroine
She would have been had she been called upon to show
Her colors. She has been always ready
And would have been up to whatever
Might have come. And all this she knows! She *knows.*
Yet she is not jaded or disappointed
At not having had her chance to show.
And that, what is that?
Why, that is better than having shown.
It is something more than life.
Death doesn't exist for it, Beloved Doctor.

Just inside the door to the side hall, Willie
Is waiting. She does not take one step forward.
She waits in her self-appointed place
For us to deliver our charge.
She does not even open her arms
Until we are in the doorway and standing before her.
Then she throws wide her arms and clasps her mistress to her bosom
As though she were herself the angel waiting on the other side.
"My honey, my darlin'," she says, hugging her, petting her.
And I hear Mother's muffled voice: "Willie Mae, I'm so tired."

"Of course. Sure you are," says Willie Mae.
I stand there beside Franklin, feeling empty-handed.
There is nothing else for me to do.
"I'll put up the car," says Franklin. He is lucky.

And he leaves me alone with just Mother and Willie Mae.
"Maybe she ought not to have gone, after all," I say,
Not knowing anything else to say.
"She *had* to go," Willie says.
"I think she had a wonderful time," I say,
Not thinking of anything else to say.
"Of *course* she had a wonderful time,"
Says Willie, still holding Mother, and looks at me over Mother's head.
As if to say, What *else* did you expect of *her*?
"Anyway, I'm glad you waited up for her," I say.
And Willie, with a look of even deeper wonder,
Asks with her eyes: What else did you expect of *me*?

An Old-Fashioned Story

JANE MAYHALL
(1922–)

When Clorinda's letter came, Jackie was fourteen. The idea of having a memory had just begun to be exotic. You could remember and it was a feeling of conceit, an aberration, a limitless unfixed disguise that made things seem what they were not. Would you know yourself as once you might have been? Jackie tapped the letter on her tooth and let the voluptuous sensation of Clorinda envelop vast roomy mirrors outside the commonplace.

That was dippy thinking, and dead-end. In plain terms, they had not met since they were seven. Both were now fourteen. There was something embarrassing, mawkish, too realistic about the years that divided. But as Jackie still felt that every friend was the big experience, hotshot soul mate (precociously admitted, the arrows always pointing to your own self-interests), she could afford to give in a little to childish sentiment. There was much to be gained, and the thought that Clorinda still wanted to see her. After all these years, Jackie plowing through her life in the same old place, not quite middle-South, and Clorinda off on unknown rounds in Terre Haute, Indiana.

Clorinda did not send a photograph, and she invited Jackie to come visit next week. Jackie's stomach slightly turned. To think that Clorinda would have grown taller, slimmer, blonder, curly-headedy-er. Jackie reconstructed Clorinda's elfin features. Secretly, she was the elf of the second grade. As Jackie was the black cat tiger. Clorinda, tiny and sprigs of golden curls, and Jackie was the suave black tiger. They were both little white girls in a white girl neighborhood, but that was the part that Jackie played. She didn't figure why. Clorinda was light and pixie with a husky pixie voice and Jackie was the black cat river. Tigers and rivers and skulking underground. Clorinda danced and Jackie swam. But they complemented each other, knowing it very well.

"Do you want to go?" said Jackie's mother. "I wonder what Mr. Harper is doing."

"What did he do?" said Jackie. "I remember, he ran trains."

"He was an engineer on the L & N, I think."

"Mrs. Harper, I remember her, was plenty tall."

"Yes," said Jackie's mother. "She was raw-boned, gaunt. But attractive in her way."

Jackie said, "Clorinda was pretty."

"And the boy, wasn't he younger?"

"Yes."

"Kevin. He was one of those children whose face looks as if it never fits together. Probably changed by now."

"Yes."

"Do you," said Jackie's mother, "want to go?"

"Yes." Jackie's stomach gave the same unpleasant heave. It was like seeing something perfect in your mind, that was going to happen outside. She didn't know if she could face it. Another way to think was, nothing ever changed. Clorinda in the playfield, in a starched lavender-flowered dress. The tiny, dainty, thin-dainty legs, as she ran up to catch a volleyball toss. Clorinda had always reminded of morning glories strung on the wire school-fence. Memory again, and Jackie could feel contemptuous of herself. The silly, childish past. What did Clorinda know about boys? She did not know about boys, and how they smelled and tasted. Chewing-gum lips, and the flat buckles on their skinny leather belts. Clorinda didn't know about chasing in the alley, and the sly electric welcome of fingers slightly touching. Grabbing around, and everybody running off again. Jackie held back, not only to entice the flood that was finally coming. At this age, of course, she depended on her own hypocrisy. She recognized to what uses she put it, deciding for a little while longer to play it safe. She had her technique, and time enough for later.

Clorinda did not know any of this yet. She knew nothing about Jackie, their letters never said. Jackie anticipated for a moment unfolding her own deepest, most wry cleverness, to show off her experience and prowess. For Clorinda's piquant wonder, the shining elfin eyes which Jackie, overwhelmingly, recalled were gray.

The contempt for her own true-heartedness came back. You get along in this world only by denying what you felt. That was one of the tricky rules, meanwhile snatching when you could one fast drink of feeling, when nobody watched or knew. She stood at the table, quizzically, and gave her mother a disinterested smile.

"Sure," she said. "I'd like to go. Even if I don't like Clorinda, or she thinks I'm a bore." Mechanical phrases sealed the issue. "I'll just go along for the trip."

The next week, Jackie was on the bus. Out of her suitcase, she sneaked a homemade sausage sandwich wrapped in wax paper and a German sour pickle. (This was a period in America when some people could not afford bus station snacks, but it wasn't considered respectable to bring your own.) Goodbye, farewell. Jackie had given strict orders against her mother that she not be accompanied by any family person. Goodbye, farewell. The bus jiggled along, tears formed in the hot corners of her eyes. Jackie was not much used to travel and led a sheltered life. But more due to money lack than cowardly inhibition. Jackie felt sorry for her parents who never had a break, but now let their undeserving daughter take a four-day fling. Phooey, rat, hell, bitch. A string of off-color words flattered her into composure. Rat, phooey, hell. She gobbled the sour pickle.

Her thoughts reverted to Clorinda, then were lost in the yellow-green spring countryside. There were a few men on the bus, too middle-aged to be interesting. Although, this idea was just a pose. And if Jackie looked at some man with crossed knees long enough, she could imagine actively putting the palms of her hands on his legs. She tried to curb herself, but could not stop thinking what she liked to. Getting her hands around the lovely-meated knees, and also squeezing his wrists and elbows; and kissing the harsh, smooth-shaven cheeks of men. Often these attacks of desire could nearly swallow up reason. As, when she was a little child, she liked to hug a tree.

When the bus stopped at Terre Haute, Clorinda and her younger brother were waiting. Jackie was not surprised. It was a funny thing, and she let the fact sink in. She recognized Clorinda, by not recognizing her. She knew she would be changed, and Jackie let the galloping uneasy feeling simply run over her for a moment. She felt remorse too, the way you feel guilty for being mean. Clorinda was no longer pretty. She was absolutely glumpy, and stood on the platform, peering with large be-spectacled eyes. What had been elfin had turned into raw bones. Maybe not so bad, but it matched somebody else. Her blond hair had darkened, and the light freckled skin was just mottled, drab. She and Kevin waved. Jackie dragged over her suitcase. Kevin was about her height, still a little boy. But Clorinda was a big, bungling woman.

"Did you know me?" asked Jackie.

"Sort of." Clorinda examined her with slow incurious eyes, which at first looked too big, popped. Jackie searched for her beauty. Defiance made her do it, like being determined to put a picture back in its frame. If she said that, would Clorinda know what she meant? She felt a hovering indecision, whether or not to trust (as it used to be) how the other thought no matter what. She could not find a way to speak the subject.

"I knew you," said Jackie.

"Mother is at home. She said to take a taxi."

The town was like a movie that seemed strange. All the time the three of them walked, aiming for a taxi, Kevin lugging the bag, Jackie had this double vision. It was like everything you knew was building up and disappearing—a kind of idea she had just come on recently. Unexpected developments, and Jackie loved thinking in these terms. But could leave it alone if she wanted. Clorinda wore a print dress, with a white collar around the gawky neck. She was at an awkward age, Jackie's mother would say. Jackie had never grown any taller past the age of eleven, but was not quite a runt and normal-short. They had plenty to talk about, Clorinda asking about the trip. At the same time, she seemed cagey and remote. That was what caused the strangeness, or maybe it was her different appearance. Still, somewhere in that big ungainly girl was the shiny little drop of elfin gold.

Mrs. Harper welcomed Jackie. She asked about Jackie's mother and father. Only Mrs. Harper, Jackie could estimate, was definitely real. It was not that she looked exactly the same as she did seven years ago. Jackie had no memory for other people's mothers. But it was how red and slightly flushed Mrs. Harper's face was. That made her seem real, and the nub of some experience Jackie didn't have to embroider on. Mrs. Harper sat down earnestly and asked what she and her mother and father had been doing all these years.

Jackie said that her father still had his lumberyard job over at Kretchmer's. Her mother stuck around the house, doing housework. Jackie rattled on, everything feeling important that she mentioned.

"What have you been doing?"

Jackie said, "I play the violin. But not very good." Privately she thought she did better. But it was not a thing to say.

Mrs. Harper nodded, the perfect audience. All the news was taken right. Kevin stood shyly in the corner. It was true, his face had not yet come together. The gray eyes too wide, and the tufted brown hair made the skull seem lopsided. He was gallantly aware of not being usual looking. But Kevin kept himself a gentleman, and was not going to get mad at what other people thought.

These ideas flitted through Jackie's mind. Clorinda sat on the divan, and Jackie noticed how thoroughly a woman she was. Clorinda looked about eighteen. Neither of the girls wanted to make an effort to live up to the past. Any references to, or images of what Jackie might have considered before, shriveled in her head like burnt paper.

As soon as they were alone in the guest room (Kevin's, and lent for the visit) Clorinda said:

"Jackie, do you have any dates?"

"Yes. My mother lets me. Yours?"

Behind the glasses, Clorinda rolled sophisticated eyes.

"Sure. What else is there?"

Jackie had a slight sense of distaste. Why? In the double-track way, her mind crossed over again. She felt she had to protect the seven-year-old elf that Clorinda was from the big gangling woman she'd become. Thinking like that wasn't just dumb, it was crazy.

"I got a couple of dates lined up for you," Clorinda said.

What else should she have said? Nothing wrong with that. But Jackie felt faintly pressured, hemmed-in.

"Well," she said. "I'll see."

"What do you mean? They're nice kids."

"I know," said Jackie. Her words vaporized. "I mean, all right."

That night Mrs. Harper cooked a chicken with creamed gravy, and had green beans and then cherry tarts for dessert. The Harpers were not rich either, and seemed even worse off than Jackie's people. Mr. Harper was sick and had been let go from his railroad job, only doing part-time work. But he still wore his railroad cap that Jackie remembered. She always thought he was not dressed up because he wore the gray-striped gingham cap inside the house. He had a sick-looking color, and looked older than anybody Jackie had ever known. The change had made him very old.

He sat down and belched. It was indigestion and not bad manners. Mrs. Harper handed him some medicine. Clorinda did not pay any attention to anybody, she sat at the table putting on fingernail polish, even a few seconds before supper was served. It seemed terrible and sordid, and Jackie had a chilly feeling. But also, she was thrilled. People so badly off, and everything running into like shabby poor-folks acting. It was not really too awful, or dangerous. Though, just seeing things so badly off, and the tablecloth with a hole neatly mended—that's the way it looked. This was not in Jackie's language yet, but she had a sense of the extravagant misery. It was a keen feeling of excitement, that families got poor. And she was torn between her fourteen-year-old contempt, and her inborn sense of importance about what people had to go through. Jackie didn't have the words for this either, but it was the spirit of the connoisseur.

She was a little afraid of Mr. Harper. Just because he was sick. She was afraid of people with whom she could not enter any give-and-take relation. Included, there was no possibility of feeling romantic about him. He was too sad, and out of work. There was nobody to be in love with, really. Clorinda had changed too much, although Jackie kept looking for glints. But even Clorinda's movements had slowed down. She wore heavy high heels, and had heavy woman's legs. The only thing that remained was her husky voice.

"Mom, Jackie and I are going to the movies," she said to Mrs. Harper.

"All right," said Mrs. Harper. "Jackie," she said, "I trust you to take care of Clorinda."

That was funny. Clorinda was twice as big. But maybe Mrs. Harper sensed the same thing. Jackie was the suave old tiger self, and Clorinda had been nothing but a fairy, a tinker-bell elf. She was clearly a dependent. Jackie tapped a front tooth with her fork. Maybe it was not loyal to Clorinda, having this idea. But Jackie would always take care of her, after all.

When they got alone again, Clorinda said:

"You don't think we're really going to the movies?"

"I don't care," said Jackie.

"Not the kids I know."

"All right."

Jackie was not as pleased as she might have been. But she was tired from the bus ride, and was therefore not getting the right bang out of an opportunity offered.

It was a big chance to be with boys. She never doubted that she was more than a little girl. She had never in her life felt like a child. It was Clorinda who'd been that. Not herself. Jackie was always being canny, and never innocent. And she played those games that were outlandish, of testing memory. And she could be perfectly calm and see the world falling apart. And nobody, especially not Clorinda, could see how sick and old her father, Mr. Harper, was. However, even seeing matters clearly, Jackie did not like the way Clorinda talked about boys. It was the slow motion, and how she moved her heavy legs. And everything was, for a moment, too unpleasantly in contrast to their grammar-school days.

She was walking on eggs of dreams. Clorinda set her hair, and Jackie went into the bathroom to wash her face. Mrs. Harper had hung up two towels, and a small, clean ragged washcloth. Jackie gritted her teeth, exalted. The sparseness and poverty of the bathroom felt enchanted. She frothed the soap in her hands, and rubbed it over her face. In the mirror, she saw her own black, humorless, terribly observing eyes. She feared that Clorinda was too lethargic in her own ways to make Jackie any better or different. Jackie glimpsed that she had actually made the trip in the hope of improving herself.

The boys came in a car, they must have been about nineteen years old. There were two of them, big dumb louts. As soon as Jackie saw them, she tried to imagine putting her hands on their knees. But they were so compulsively apish, with their swinging animal arms and leering smiles, their eyes dull-leaded—their souls, she felt, were composed of greasy soup. But they had a car, and their hair was slicked down. One boy was named Tom, and the other Red. Red was Clorinda's partner, they sat in the backseat and before the car was three blocks away they were locked in a writhing embrace. Jackie kept her eyes on the streets, passing unfamiliar corners.

"Where are we going?" she said.

"To get some beer. Then a place in the woods," her own delegated lout said.

Jackie felt a disapproval mixed with conscience. In spite of herself, what had she wanted? She knew. What she'd wanted was grown-up laughing and talking like in Scott Fitzgerald. This, where she was, was also different from the magic feeling of boys grabbing in the alley. They, at least, were friendly. The silence in the car was deadening. From the rear seat came the sound of kisses and rustling. Tom, her front-seat lout, reached over and yanked at Jackie's skirt.

"Cut it out," Jackie said.

"What's the matter? You yellow?"

Inwardly, she swore never to go out with anybody under thirty. Older people were more polite. Her mind ticked regulations. But in fact, Jackie might have guessed, and maybe it was Clorinda's lousy crowd. That was what Terre Haute boys were like.

"No, I'm not yellow."

"Then, what are you?"

"I'm somebody"—the words tumbled out, scathing. "I'm somebody that can't stand big apes."

"Why, you filthy ——" Jackie had always enjoyed the curse words that bubbled up in her head. But hearing them said aloud (and directed at her character) was something else. A stream was let loose. She didn't even know him and he was talking vicious as he could. The boy was driving faster and faster. She did not feel she ought to have kept quiet. She only hoped, though, she could get out before the car turned over. She didn't even know him. In the backseat, the other couple necked, oblivious.

"Pull over," said Jackie.

The boy drove on. Jackie's mind worked like a piston.

"Okay," she said. "Pardon me what I said. If you slow down, I'll act like you wanted."

"Huh—" he appeared disconcerted by the change. But he said, "You'd better." The boy eased his foot on the gas. At the same time, he was sullen. "You southern girls are too damned stuck up."

"Oh," said Jackie, "we're not that much. I just didn't know how to do."

"Up here," said Tom, "girls are good for just one thing. You know what that is."

"Sure," Jackie said. She felt an ecstasy of hate. "When you come down to it, I guess you're right."

They stopped at what looked like a main corner, waiting for a light. Jackie put her hand on the door handle and got out. In a flash, she was safe on the sidewalk.

"Now—" her companion sneered. "What's up?"

"Thanks," she said. "I gotta go back."

Clorinda was pulling out of her sleepy involvement. She put a disheveled head at the window. "Jackie," she said. "What's the matter?"

"Nothing," said Jackie. "I'm just tired. You all go along. I'll get back. See you, Clorinda, in the morning."

"What? Well, I think you're nuts."

"Yes, I am."

"Crap," said Tom. "She's a bitch. There's nothing I hate more than bitch and a tease. You're the kind of girl that can make a man sick."

"Okay," said Jackie. "See you, Clorinda." She stifled false apologies.

"Well," Clorinda put her head back down in the car. "I think you're nuts."

Jackie walked off. The car did not even pause. Ahead, it went in second gear. Jackie for a moment felt relieved. But the next instant, she opened her pocketbook. And into it, having swiftly removed wallet and lipstick, she was expertly sick.

Nobody apparently noticed. The sky was half-dark and everybody walking along was busy, heading for a movie or a store. Jackie took a streetcar to Clorinda's address. The motorman said where to transfer, and it was not very long. Her face, she felt, was either green or white.

Mrs. Harper was sitting on the porch. She did not act like anything was wrong.

"I see," she said, "you decided to come back."

"Yes," said Jackie. "I was sick."

Mrs. Harper did not comment.

But Jackie kept the pocketbook out of sight until she reached the bathroom. Then she found some Old Dutch Cleanser and set about her job. It was pretty hard cleaning all the guck out of the lining. Jackie felt perfectly well and calm. Why did she ever throw up? When the task was done, she returned to the guest room. Kevin was bunking on the sofa in the parlor and the Harpers had a bedroom down the hall. Clorinda's private quarters was a back-porch renovated and not big enough for two with any comfort. Jackie put on her pajamas and climbed into the small brown wooden bed. The clean sheets felt clean, with a nice blanket piled on. She had to clear her mind, and get some needed rest.

Jackie didn't know how much later, but Clorinda had opened the door. A slant of light went across the wall.

"Hey, you still awake?"

Jackie said, "I don't know. What's the trouble?"

Clorinda shut the door and came in. She said, "Don't turn on the light."

"I won't."

Clorinda said, "Oh well, turn it on."

"I don't know where it is."

Clorinda breathed around a little, and clicked a lamp.

Jackie said, "What's happened?"

"Nothing. You nearly ruined it. But Tom gave Red the car. We went on anyway."

"I'm glad."

Clorinda sat in silence. What she rested on was like a cedar chest, and her profile was rising out of bulky shadows. She had her glasses off and the big pop eyes looked naked. Jackie felt a twinge, she didn't know at what. Clorinda's bunched-up clothes and hair seemed unprotected. Though her manner was cold, officious.

"You want to hear something?"

Jackie said, "Sure."

"I've got caught."

"What's—?"

Clorinda turned, full on.

"You know what that means!"

Jackie sank, abashed. The waves of the other girl's wrath went over her.

"Yes. I guess I do."

"Don't you guess! You know."

Jackie felt astonished. But the way it was happening was also very cold. Clorinda's face was immobile in satisfaction.

"Now I've got them where they're going to be."

"Who?" Jackie propped herself on elbows. "Clorinda, who?"

"Don't call me Clorinda. Nobody calls your other name." Clorinda's voice mimicked the wayside problem. "It's Jackie, Jackie. But not me. Why do I be called this?"

Jackie listened carefully. It was like figuring out pig Latin. There was something flipping back, or in between. She ought to circumvent the trouble-making places.

She said, "Yes, okay. I don't like Jacqueline either. I'll call anything you want."

Clorinda shot a bitter glance, in charge of herself again. She said she hadn't told Red, but was going to.

"Even if it wasn't him."

She spat her feelings, jerky. Jackie accepted the way she talked. It was like taking things in through a sieve, not what you could put your mind on all at once. But Clorinda was testing her own courage, saying what she needed.

What Jackie spoke was not her real train of thought. She said, "You going to tell your mother?"

Clorinda looked at her blankly.

"Sure. She prob'ly knows."

"Will—?"

Clorinda gave a little laugh.

"Don't worry. I can wind her around my little finger."

The main thing was, though, she was going to tell her dad. He'd be plenty upset. *Upset* wasn't what Clorinda used, Jackie could almost hear the thinking better than words uttered. Clorinda's thoughts overflowed, and you couldn't hold them back. Mr. Harper would have it out with Red, and they'd have to get married.

Jackie said, "You want to get married. *Now?*"

"You bet your life I do." In the tone, there was no answer.

But everything that Jackie had ever pipe-dreamed about felt shrunk up. All of her expectations were a cause for self-distrust. Even if things like memories never quite came to the surface, tigers and elves and all that mushy stuff. Jackie's next question was a total giveaway. She felt in Clorinda the rebuff before she made it.

Jackie said, "You still going back to school?"

Clorinda said, "Heck no." She was done with that. School was a place for idiots. What good was going to school? She turned her bulging sad eyes straight on Jackie. Jackie felt the force. It was like a wheelbarrow emptying bricks. Jackie could not keep her gaze on the other girl's face. Nothing could be brought to terms, and it could not be summarized. By now, Jackie had had crushes on lots of teachers, and usually what they taught. Sports and mathematics, music, lab. But she sensed the violation toward her friends, it wasn't what you ought to feel. As—there was also a vague connection with the boys she liked in alleys. It was a transgression that she couldn't tell. Doing the way you felt was always forbidden. But just assuming that frame of mind was indulgent and wrong.

Considering the way that Clorinda felt.

What Jackie liked, Clorinda hated.

People could vanish from your life, and maybe not come back. And yet, Clorinda sat there like a big stuffed avenging angel. Was she in love with Red? It didn't matter to Clorinda (Jackie thought) if she was or not.

The lamp seemed muddier, draining. Through the dimity curtains were shreds of dawn.

Clorinda gave a yawn.

She said, "How long you going to stay?"

Jackie said, "I don't know. I've got to go and do some things. I thought I might get a bus tomorrow. They gave a round trip back."

Clorinda got up and lumbered toward the door.

She said, "If Red don't marry me, my dad'll beat him up."

Jackie almost did not say anything. The idea of Mr. Harper hitting anybody did not seem true.

She said, "I hope—" hesitating. "I hope he won't."

Clorinda shifted her eyes, pityingly.

"We got different ideas. You want the light put out?"

Jackie said yes.

She pulled the covers up. She looked around the room after Clorinda left. By the bureau she caught sight of something she'd noticed before. Kevin had cut out some newspaper pictures of dogs and tacked them on the wall. It didn't mean anything. Jackie felt submerged. Nothing would have helped. Even if she'd been smart, and called Clorinda another name. All that had been told seemed boring as the moon. And what Jackie had talked out too. It didn't mean anything.

She tried to wonder what it meant. It was like one of those old-fashioned stories that just went on and on. And nothing new to learn. Why was she going home? Jackie saw no point. There was no reason for going back. Or to stay at Clorinda's either. There ought to be someplace else, that wasn't here or home.

A Conversation With My Father

GRACE PALEY
(1922–)

My father is eighty-six years old and in bed. His heart, that bloody motor, is equally old and will not do certain jobs any more. It still floods his head with brainy light. But it won't let his legs carry the weight of his body around the house. Despite my metaphors, this muscle failure is not due to his old heart, he says, but to a potassium shortage. Sitting on one pillow, leaning on three, he offers last-minute advice and makes a request.

"I would like you to write a simple story just once more," he says, "the kind de Maupassant wrote, or Chekhov, the kind you used to write. Just recognizable people and then write down what happened to them next."

I say, "Yes, why not? That's possible." I want to please him, though I don't remember writing that way. I *would* like to try to tell such a story, if he means the kind that begins: "There was a woman . . ." followed by plot, the absolute line between two points which I've always despised. Not for literary reasons, but because it takes all hope away. Everyone, real or invented, deserves the open destiny of life.

Finally I thought of a story that had been happening for a couple of years right across the street. I wrote it down, then read it aloud. "Pa," I said, "how about this? Do you mean something like this?"

Once in my time there was a woman and she had a son. They lived nicely, in a small apartment in Manhattan. This boy at about fifteen became a junkie, which is not unusual in our neighborhood. In order to maintain her close friendship with him, she became a junkie too. She said it was part of the youth culture, with which she felt very much at home. After a while, for a number of reasons, the boy gave it all up and left the city and his mother in disgust. Hopeless and alone, she grieved. We all visit her.

"O.K., Pa, that's it," I said, "an unadorned and miserable tale."

"But that's not what I mean," my father said. "You misunderstood me on purpose. You know there's a lot more to it. You know that. You left everything out. Turgenev wouldn't do that. Chekhov wouldn't do that. There are in fact Russian writers you never heard of, you don't have an inkling of, as good as anyone, who can write a plain ordinary story, who would not leave out what you have left out. I object not to facts but to people sitting in trees talking senselessly, voices from who knows where . . ."

"Forget that one, Pa, what have I left out now? In this one?"

"Her looks, for instance."

"Oh. Quite handsome, I think. Yes."

"Her hair?"

"Dark, with heavy braids, as though she were a girl or a foreigner."

"What were her parents like, her stock? That she became such a person. It's interesting, you know."

"From out of town. Professional people. The first to be divorced in their county. How's that? Enough?" I asked.

"With you, it's all a joke," he said. "What about the boy's father? Why didn't you mention him? Who was he? Or was the boy born out of wedlock?"

"Yes," I said. "He was born out of wedlock."

"For Godsakes, doesn't anyone in your stories get married? Doesn't anyone have the time to run down to City Hall before they jump into bed?"

"No," I said. "In real life, yes. But in my stories, no."

"Why do you answer me like that?"

"Oh, Pa, this is a simple story about a smart woman who came to N.Y.C. full of interest love trust excitement very up to date, and about her son, what a hard time she had in this world. Married or not, it's of small consequence."

"It is of great consequence," he said.

"O.K.," I said.

"O.K. O.K. yourself," he said, "but listen. I believe you that she's good-looking, but I don't think she was so smart."

"That's true," I said. "Actually that's the trouble with stories. People start out fantastic. You think they're extraordinary, but it turns out as the work goes along, they're just average with a good education. Sometimes the other way around, the person's a kind of dumb innocent, but he outwits you and you can't even think of an ending good enough."

"What do you do then?" he asked. He had been a doctor for a couple of decades and then an artist for a couple of decades and he's still interested in details, craft, technique.

"Well, you just have to let the story lie around till some agreement can be reached between you and the stubborn hero."

"Aren't you talking silly, now?" he asked. "Start again," he said. "It so happens I'm not going out this evening. Tell the story again. See what you can do this time."

"O.K.," I said. "But it's not a five-minute job." Second attempt:

Once, across the street from us, there was a fine handsome woman, our neighbor. She had a son whom she loved because she'd known him since birth (in helpless chubby infancy, and in the wrestling, hugging ages, seven to ten, as well as earlier and later). This boy, when he fell into the fist of adolescence, became a junkie. He was not a hopeless one. He was in fact hopeful, an ideologue and successful converter. With his busy brilliance, he wrote persuasive articles for his high-school newspaper. Seeking a wider audience, using important connections, he drummed into Lower Manhattan newsstand distribution a periodical called *Oh! Golden Horse!*

In order to keep him from feeling guilty (because guilt is the stony heart of nine tenths of all clinically diagnosed cancers in America today, she said), and because she had always believed in giving bad habits room at home where one could keep an eye on them, she too became a junkie. Her kitchen was famous for a while—a center for intellectual addicts who knew what they were doing. A few felt artistic like Coleridge and others were scientific and revolutionary like Leary. Although she was often high herself, certain good mothering reflexes remained, and she saw to it that there was lots of orange juice around and honey and milk and vitamin pills. However, she never cooked anything but chili, and that no more than once a week. She explained, when we talked to her, seriously, with neighborly concern, that it was her part in the youth culture and she would rather be with the young, it was an honor, than with her own generation.

One week, while nodding through an Antonioni film, this boy was severely jabbed by the elbow of a stern and proselytizing girl, sitting beside him. She offered immediate apricots and nuts for his sugar level, spoke to him sharply, and took him home.

She had heard of him and his work and she herself published, edited, and wrote a competitive journal called *Man Does Live By Bread Alone.* In the organic heat of her continuous presence he could not help but become interested once more in his muscles, his arteries, and nerve connections. In fact he began to love them, treasure them, praise them with funny little songs in *Man Does Live* . . .

the fingers of my flesh transcend
my transcendental soul
the tightness in my shoulders end
my teeth have made me whole

To the mouth of his head (that glory of will and determination) he brought hard apples, nuts, wheat germ, and soy-bean oil. He said to his old friends, From now on, I guess I'll keep my wits about me. I'm going on the natch. He said he was about to begin a spiritual deep-breathing journey. How about you too, Mom? he asked kindly.

His conversion was so radiant, splendid, that neighborhood kids his age began to say that he had never been a real addict at all, only a journalist along for the smell of the story. The mother tried several times to give up what had become without her son and his friends a lonely habit. This effort only brought it to supportable levels. The boy and his girl took their electronic mimeograph and moved to the bushy edge of another borough. They were very strict. They said they would not see her again until she had been off drugs for sixty days.

At home alone in the evening, weeping, the mother read and reread the seven issues of *Oh! Golden Horse!* They seemed to her as truthful as ever. We often crossed the street to visit and console. But if we mentioned any of our children who were at college or in the hospital or dropouts at home, she would cry out, My baby! My baby! and burst into terrible, face-scarring, time-consuming tears. The End.

First my father was silent, then he said, "Number One: You have a nice sense of humor. Number Two: I see you can't tell a plain story. So don't waste time." Then he said sadly, "Number Three: I suppose that means she was alone, she was left like that, his mother. Alone. Probably sick?"

I said, "Yes."

"Poor woman. Poor girl, to be born in a time of fools, to live among fools. The end. The end. You were right to put that down. The end."

I didn't want to argue, but I had to say, "Well, it is not necessarily the end, Pa."

"Yes," he said, "what a tragedy. The end of a person."

"No, Pa," I begged him. "It doesn't have to be. She's only about forty. She could be a hundred different things in this world as time goes on. A teacher or a social worker. An ex-junkie! Sometimes it's better than having a master's in education."

"Jokes," he said. "As a writer that's your main trouble. You don't want to recognize it. Tragedy! Plain tragedy! Historical tragedy! No hope. The end."

"Oh, Pa," I said. "She could change."

"In your own life, too, you have to look it in the face. He took a couple of nitroglycerin. "Turn to five," he said, pointing to the dial on the oxygen tank. He inserted the tubes into his nostrils and breathed deep. He closed his eyes and said, "No."

I had promised the family to always let him have the last word when arguing, but in this case I had a different responsibility. That woman lives across the street. She's my knowledge and my invention. I'm sorry for her. I'm not going to leave her there in that house crying. (Actually neither would Life, which unlike me has no pity.)

Therefore: She did change. Of course her son never came home again. But right now, she's the receptionist in a storefront community clinic in the East Village. Most of the customers are young people, some old friends. The head doctor has said to her, "If we only had three people in this clinic with your experiences . . ."

"The doctor said that?" My father took the oxygen tubes out of his nostrils and said, "Jokes. Jokes again."

"No, Pa, it could really happen that way, it's a funny world nowadays."

"No," he said. "Truth first. She will slide back. A person must have character. She does not."

"No, Pa," I said. "That's it. She's got a job. Forget it. She's in that storefront working."

"How long will it be?" he asked. "Tragedy! You too. When will you look it in the face?"

Welcome to the Monkey House

KURT VONNEGUT, JR.

(1922–)

So Pete Crocker, the sheriff of Barnstable County, which was the whole of Cape Cod, came into the Federal Ethical Suicide Parlor in Hyannis one May afternoon—and he told the two six-foot Hostesses there that they weren't to be alarmed, but that a notorious nothinghead named Billy the Poet was believed headed for the Cape.

A nothinghead was a person who refused to take his ethical birth-control pills three times a day. The penalty for that was $10,000 and ten years in jail.

This was at a time when the population on Earth was 17 billion human beings. That was far too many mammals that big for a planet that small. The people were virtually packed together like drupelets.

Drupelets are the pulpy little knobs that compose the outside of a raspberry.

So the World Government was making a two-pronged attack on overpopulation. One pronging was the encouragement of ethical suicide, which consisted of going to the nearest Suicide Parlor and asking a Hostess to kill you painlessly while you lay on a Barcalounger. The other pronging was compulsory ethical birth control.

The sheriff told the Hostesses, who were pretty, tough-minded, highly intelligent girls, that roadblocks were being set up and house-to-house searches were being conducted to catch Billy the Poet. The main difficulty was that the police didn't know what he looked like. The few people who had seen him and known him for what he was were women—and they disagreed fantastically as to his height, his hair color, his voice, his weight, the color of his skin.

"I don't need to remind you girls," the sheriff went on, "that a nothinghead is very sensitive from the waist down. If Billy the Poet somehow slips in here and starts making trouble, one good kick in the right place will do wonders."

He was referring to the fact that ethical birth-control pills, the only legal form of birth control, made people numb from the waist down.

Most men said their bottom halves felt like cold iron or balsawood. Most women said their bottom halves felt like wet cotton or stale ginger ale. The pills were so effective that you could blindfold a man who had taken one, tell him to recite the Gettysburg Address, kick him in the balls while he was doing it, and he wouldn't miss a syllable.

The pills were ethical because they didn't interfere with a person's ability to reproduce, which would have been unnatural and immoral. All the pills did was take every bit of pleasure out of sex.

Thus did science and morals go hand in hand.

The two Hostesses there in Hyannis were Nancy McLuhan and Mary Kraft. Nancy was a strawberry blonde. Mary was a glossy brunette. Their uniforms were white lipstick, heavy eye makeup, purple body stockings with nothing underneath, and black-leather boots. They ran a small operation—with only six suicide booths. In a really good week, say the one before Christmas, they might put sixty people to sleep. It was done with a hypodermic syringe.

"My main message to you girls," said Sheriff Crocker, "is that everything's well under control. You can just go about your business here."

"Didn't you leave out part of your main message?" Nancy asked him.

"I don't get you."

"I didn't hear you say he was probably headed straight for us."

He shrugged in clumsy innocence. "We don't know that for sure."

"I thought that was all anybody *did* know about Billy the Poet: that he specializes in deflowering Hostesses in Ethical Suicide Parlors." Nancy was a virgin. All Hostesses were virgins. They also had to hold advanced degrees in psychology and nursing. They also had to be plump and rosy, and at least six feet tall.

America had changed in many ways, but it had yet to adopt the metric system.

Nancy McLuhan was burned up that the sheriff would try to protect her and Mary from the full truth about Bill the Poet—as though they might panic if they heard it. She told the sheriff so.

"How long do you think a girl would last in the E. S. S.," she said, meaning the Ethical Suicide Service, "if she scared that easy?"

The sheriff took a step backward, pulled in his chin. "Not very long, I guess."

"That's very true," said Nancy, closing the distance between them and offering him a sniff of the edge of her hand, which was poised for a karate chop. All Hostesses were experts at judo and karate. "If you'd like to find out how helpless we are, just come toward me, pretending you're Billy the Poet."

The sheriff shook his head, gave her a glassy smile. "I'd rather not."

"That's the smartest thing you've said today," said Nancy, turning her back on him while Mary laughed. "We're not scared—we're *angry*. Or we're not even *that*. He isn't *worth* that. We're *bored*. How boring that he should come a great distance, should cause all this fuss, in order to——" She let the sentence die there. "It's just too absurd."

"I'm not as mad at *him* as I am at the women who let him do it to them without a struggle"—said Mary—"who let him do it and then couldn't tell the police what he looked like. Suicide Hostesses at that!"

"Somebody hasn't been keeping up with her karate," said Nancy.

It wasn't just Billy the Poet who was attracted to Hostesses in Ethical Suicide Parlors. All nothingheads were. Bombed out of their skulls with the sex madness that came from taking nothing, they thought the white lips and big eyes and body stocking and boots of a Hostess spelled *sex, sex, sex.*

The truth was, of course, that sex was the last thing any Hostess ever had in mind.

"If Billy follows his usual M. O.," said the sheriff, "he'll study your habits and the neighborhood. And then he'll pick one or the other of you and he'll send her a dirty poem in the mail."

"Charming," said Nancy.

"He has also been known to use the telephone."

"How brave," said Nancy. Over the sheriff's shoulder, she could see the mailman coming.

A blue light went on over the door of a booth for which Nancy was responsible. The person in there wanted something. It was the only booth in use at the time.

The sheriff asked her if there was a possibility that the person in there was Billy the Poet, and Nancy said, "Well, if it is, I can break his neck with my thumb and forefinger."

"Foxy Grandpa," said Mary, who'd seen him, too. A Foxy Grandpa was any old man, cute and senile, who quibbled and joked and reminisced for hours before he let a Hostess put him to sleep.

Nancy groaned. "We've spent the past two hours trying to decide on a last meal."

And then the mailman came in with just one letter. It was addressed to Nancy in smeary pencil. She was splendid with anger and disgust as she opened it, knowing it would be a piece of filth from Billy.

She was right. Inside the envelope was a poem. It wasn't an original poem. It was a song from olden days that had taken on new meanings since the numbness of ethical birth control had become universal. It went like this, in smeary pencil again:

We were walking through the park,
A-goosing statues in the dark.
If Sherman's horse can take it,
So can you.

When Nancy came into the suicide booth to see what he wanted, the Foxy Grandpa was lying on the mint-green Barcalounger, where hundreds had died so peacefully over the years. He was studying the menu from the Howard Johnson's next door and beating time to the Muzak coming from the loudspeaker on the lemon-yellow wall. The room was painted cinder block. There was one barred window with a Venetian blind.

There was a Howard Johnson's next door to every Ethical Suicide Parlor, and vice versa. The Howard Johnson's had an orange roof and the

Suicide Parlor had a purple roof, but they were both the Government. Practically everything was the Government.

Practically everything was automated, too. Nancy and Mary and the sheriff were lucky to have jobs. Most people didn't. The average citizen moped around home and watched television, which was the Government. Every fifteen minutes his television would urge him to vote intelligently or consume intelligently, or worship in the church of his choice, or love his fellowmen, or obey the laws—or pay a call to the nearest Ethical Suicide Parlor and find out how friendly and understanding a Hostess could be.

The Foxy Grandpa was something of a rarity, since he was marked by old age, was bald, was shaky, had spots on his hands. Most people looked twenty-two, thanks to anti-aging shots they took twice a year. That the old man looked old was proof that the shots had been discovered after his sweet bird of youth had flown.

"Have we decided on a last supper yet?" Nancy asked him. She heard peevishness in her own voice, heard herself betray her exasperation with Billy the Poet, her boredom with the old man. She was ashamed, for this was unprofessional of her. "The breaded veal cutlet is very good."

The old man cocked his head. With the greedy cunning of second childhood, he had caught her being unprofessional, unkind, and he was going to punish her for it. "You don't sound very friendly. I thought you were all supposed to be friendly. I thought this was supposed to be a pleasant place to come."

"I beg your pardon," she said. "If I seem unfriendly, it has nothing to do with you."

"I thought maybe I bored you."

"No, no," she said gamely, "not at all. You certainly know some very interesting history." Among other things, the Foxy Grandpa claimed to have known J. Edgar Nation, the Grand Rapids druggist who was the father of ethical birth control.

"Then *look* like you're interested," he told her. He could get away with that sort of impudence. The thing was, he could leave any time he wanted to, right up to the moment he asked for the needle—and he had to *ask* for the needle. That was the law.

Nancy's art, and the art of every Hostess, was to see that volunteers didn't leave, to coax and wheedle and flatter them patiently, every step of the way.

So Nancy had to sit down there in the booth, to pretend to marvel at the freshness of the yarn the old man told, a story everybody knew, about how J. Edgar Nation happened to experiment with ethical birth control.

"He didn't have the slightest idea his pills would be taken by human beings someday," said the Foxy Grandpa. "His dream was to introduce morality into the monkey house at the Grand Rapids Zoo. Did you realize that?" he inquired severely.

"No. No, I didn't. That's very interesting."

"He and his eleven kids went to church one Easter. And the day was so nice and the Easter service had been so beautiful and pure that they decided to take a walk through the zoo, and they were just walking on clouds."

"Um." The scene described was lifted from a play that was performed on television every Easter.

The Foxy Grandpa shoehorned himself into the scene, had himself chat with the Nations just before they got to the monkey house. " 'Good morning, Mr. Nation,' I said to him. 'It certainly is a nice morning.' 'And a good morning to *you,* Mr. Howard,' he said to me. 'There is nothing like an Easter morning to make a man feel clean and reborn and at one with God's intentions.' "

"Um." Nancy could hear the telephone ringing faintly, naggingly, through the nearly soundproof door.

"So we went on to the monkey house together, and what do you think we saw?"

"I can't imagine." Somebody had answered the phone.

"We saw a monkey playing with his private parts!"

"No!"

"Yes! And J. Edgar Nation was so upset he went straight home and he started developing a pill that would make monkeys in the springtime fit things for a Christian family to see."

There was a knock on the door.

"Yes——?" said Nancy.

"Nancy," said Mary, "telephone for you."

When Nancy came out of the booth, she found the sheriff choking on little squeals of law-enforcement delight. The telephone was tapped by agents hidden in the Howard Johnson's. Billy the Poet was believed to be on the line. His call had been traced. Police were already on their way to grab him.

"Keep him on, keep him on," the sheriff whispered to Nancy, and he gave her the telephone as though it were solid gold.

"Yes–?" said Nancy.

"Nancy McLuhan?" said a man. His voice was disguised. He might have been speaking through a kazoo. "I'm calling for a mutual friend."

"Oh?"

"He asked me to deliver a message."

"I see."

"It's a poem."

"All right."

"Ready?"

"Ready." Nancy could hear sirens screaming in the background of the call.

The caller must have heard the sirens, too, but he recited the poem without any emotion. It went like this:

"Soak yourself in Jergen's Lotion.
Here comes the one-man population
explosion."

They got him. Nancy heard it all—the thumping and clumping, the argle-bargle and cries.

The depression she felt as she hung up was glandular. Her brave body had prepared for a fight that was not to be.

The sheriff bounded out of the Suicide Parlor, in such a hurry to see the famous criminal he'd helped catch that a sheaf of papers fell from the pocket of his trench coat.

Mary picked them up, called after the sheriff. He halted for a moment, said the papers didn't matter anymore, asked her if maybe she wouldn't like to come along. There was a flurry between the two girls, with Nancy persuading Mary to go, declaring that she had no curiosity about Billy. So Mary left, irrelevantly handing the sheaf to Nancy.

The sheaf proved to be photocopies of poems Billy had sent to Hostesses in other places. Nancy read the top one. It made much of a peculiar side effect of ethical birth-control pills: They not only made people numb—they also made people piss blue. The poem was called *What the Somethinghead Said to the Suicide Hostess,* and it went like this:

I did not sow, I did not spin,
And thanks to pills I did not sin.
I loved the crowds, the stink, the noise.
And when I peed, I peed turquoise.

I ate beneath a roof of orange;
Swung with progress like a door hinge.
'Neath purple roof I've come today
To piss my azure life away.

Virgin hostess, death's recruiter,
Life is cute, but you are cuter.
Mourn my pecker, purple daughter—
All it passed was sky-blue water.

"You never heard that story before—about how J. Edgar Nation came to invent ethical birth control?" the Foxy Grandpa wanted to know. His voice cracked.

"Never did," lied Nancy.

"I thought everybody knew that."

"It was news to me."

"When he got through with the monkey house, you couldn't tell it from the Michigan Supreme Court. Meanwhile, there was this crisis going on in the United Nations. The people who understood science said people had to quit reproducing so much, and the people who understood morals said society would collapse if people used sex for nothing but pleasure."

The Foxy Grandpa got off his Barcalounger, went over to the window, pried two slats of the blind apart. There wasn't much to see out there. The view was blocked by the backside of a mocked-up thermometer twenty feet high, which faced the street. It was calibrated in billions of people on Earth, from zero to twenty. The make-believe column of liquid was a strip of translucent red plastic. It showed how many people there were on Earth. Very close to the bottom was a black arrow that showed what the scientists thought the population ought to be.

The Foxy Grandpa was looking at the setting sun through that red plastic, and through the blind, too, so that his face was banded with shadows and red.

"Tell me—" he said, "when I die, how much will that thermometer go down? A foot?"

"No."

"An inch?"

"Not quite."

"You know what the answer is, don't you?" he said, and he faced her. The senility had vanished from his voice and eyes. "One inch on that thing equals 83,333 people. You knew that, didn't you?"

"That—that might be true," said Nancy, "but that isn't the right way to look at it, in my opinion."

He didn't ask her what the right way was, in her opinion. He completed a thought of his own, instead. "I'll tell you something else that's true: I'm Billy the Poet, and you're a very good-looking woman."

With one hand, he drew a snub-nosed revolver from his belt. With the other, he peeled off his bald dome and wrinkled forehead, which proved to be rubber. Now he looked twenty-two.

"The police will want to know exactly what I look like when this is all over," he told Nancy with a malicious grin. "In case you're not good at describing people, and it's surprising how many women aren't:

I'm five foot two,
With eyes of blue,
With Brown hair to my shoulders—
A manly elf
So full of self
The ladies say he smolders."

Billy was ten inches shorter than Nancy was. She had about forty pounds on him. She told him he didn't have a chance, but Nancy was much mistaken. He had unbolted the bars on the window the night before and he made her go out the window and then down a manhole that was hidden from the street by the big thermometer.

He took her down into the sewers of Hyannis. He knew where he was going. He had a flashlight and a map. Nancy had to go before him along the narrow catwalk, her own shadow dancing mockingly in the lead. She tried to guess where they were, relative to the real world above. She guessed correctly when they passed under the Howard Johnson's, guessed from noises she heard. The machinery that processed and served the food there was silent. But, so people wouldn't feel too lonesome when eating there, the designers had provided sound effects for the kitchen. It was these Nancy heard—a tape recording of the clashing of silverware and the laughter of Negroes and Puerto Ricans.

After that she was lost. Billy had very little to say to her other than "Right," or, "Left," or "Don't try anything funny, Juno, or I'll blow your great big fucking head off."

Only once did they have anything resembling a conversation. Billy began it, and ended it, too. "What in hell is a girl with hips like yours doing selling death?" he asked her from behind.

She dared to stop. "I can answer that," she told him. She was confident that she could give him an answer that would shrivel him like napalm.

But he gave her a shove, offered to blow her fucking head off again.

"You don't even want to hear my answer," she taunted him. "You're afraid to hear it."

"I never listen to a woman till the pills wear off," sneered Billy. That was his plan, then—to keep her a prisoner for at least eight hours. That was how long it took for the pills to wear off.

"That's a silly rule."

"A woman's not a woman till the pills wear off."

"You certainly manage to make a woman feel like an object rather than a person."

"Thank the pills for that," said Billy.

There were 80 miles of sewers under Greater Hyannis, which had a population of 400,000 drupelets, 400,000 souls. Nancy lost track of the time down there. When Billy announced that they had at last reached their destination, it was possible for Nancy to imagine that a year had passed.

She tested this spooky impression by pinching her own thigh, by feeling what the chemical clock of her body said. Her thigh was still numb.

Billy ordered her to climb iron rungs that were set in wet masonry. There was a circle of sickly light above. It proved to be moonlight filtered through the plastic polygons of an enormous geodesic dome. Nancy didn't have to ask the traditional victim's question, "Where am I?" There was only one dome like that on Cape Cod. It was in Hyannis Port and it sheltered the ancient Kennedy Compound.

It was a museum of how life had been lived in more expansive times. The museum was closed. It was open only in the summertime.

The manhole from which Nancy and then Billy emerged was set in an expanse of green cement, which showed where the Kennedy lawn had been. On the green cement, in front of the ancient frame houses, were statues representing the fourteen Kennedys who had been Presidents of the United States or the World. They were playing touch football.

The President of the World at the time of Nancy's abduction, incidentally, was an ex-Suicide Hostess named "Ma" Kennedy. Her statue would never join this particular touch-football game. Her name was Kennedy, all right, but she wasn't the real thing. People complained of her lack of style, found her vulgar. On the wall of her office was a sign that said, YOU DON'T HAVE TO BE CRAZY TO WORK HERE, BUT IT SURE HELPS, and another one that said THIMK!, and another one that said, SOME DAY WE'RE GOING TO HAVE TO GET ORGANIZED AROUND HERE.

Her office was in the Taj Mahal.

Until she arrived in the Kennedy Museum, Nancy McLuhan was confident that she would sooner or later get a chance to break every bone in Billy's little body, maybe even shoot him with his own gun. She wouldn't have minded doing those things. She thought he was more disgusting than a blood-filled tick.

It wasn't compassion that changed her mind. It was the discovery that

Billy had a gang. There were at least eight people around the manhole, men and women in equal numbers, with stockings pulled over their heads. It was the women who laid firm hands on Nancy, told her to keep calm. They were all at least as tall as Nancy and they held her in places where they could hurt her like hell if they had to.

Nancy closed her eyes, but this didn't protect her from the obvious conclusion: These perverted women were sisters from the Ethical Suicide Service. This upset her so much that she asked loudly and bitterly, "How can you violate your oaths like this?"

She was promptly hurt so badly that she doubled up and burst into tears.

When she straightened up again, there was plenty more she wanted to say, but she kept her mouth shut. She speculated silently as to what on Earth could make Suicide Hostesses turn against every concept of human decency. Nothingheadedness alone couldn't begin to explain it. They had to be drugged besides.

Nancy went over in her mind all the terrible drugs she'd learned about in school, persuaded herself that the women had taken the worst one of all. That drug was so powerful, Nancy's teachers had told her, that even a person numb from the waist down would copulate repeatedly and enthusiastically after just one glass. That had to be the answer: The women, and probably the men, too, had been drinking gin.

They hastened Nancy into the middle frame house, which was dark like all the rest, and Nancy heard the men giving Billy the news. It was in this news that Nancy perceived a glint of hope. Help might be on its way.

The gang member who had phoned Nancy obscenely had fooled the police into believing that they had captured Billy the Poet, which was bad for Nancy. The police didn't know yet that Nancy was missing, two men told Billy, and a telegram had been sent to Mary Kraft in Nancy's name, declaring that Nancy had been called to New York City on urgent family business.

That was where Nancy saw the glint of hope: Mary wouldn't believe that telegram. Mary knew Nancy had no family in New York. Not one of the 63,000,000 people living there was a relative of Nancy's.

The gang had deactivated the burglar-alarm system of the museum. They had also cut through a lot of the chains and ropes that were meant to keep visitors from touching anything of value. There was no mystery as to who and what had done the cutting. One of the men was armed with brutal lopping shears.

They marched Nancy into a servant's bedroom upstairs. The man with the shears cut the ropes that fenced off the narrow bed. They put Nancy into the bed and two men held Nancy while a woman gave her a knock-out shot.

Billy the Poet had disappeared.

As Nancy was going under, the woman who had given her the shot asked her how old she was.

Nancy was determined not to answer, but discovered that the drug had made her powerless not to answer. "Sixty-three," she murmured.

"How does it feel to be a virgin at sixty-three?"

Nancy heard her own answer through a velvet fog. She was amazed by the answer, wanted to protest that it couldn't possibly be hers. "Pointless," she'd said.

Moments later, she asked the woman thickly, "What was in that needle?"

"What was in the needle, honey bunch? Why, honey bunch, they call that 'truth serum.'"

The moon was down when Nancy woke up—but the night was still out there. The shades were drawn and there was candlelight. Nancy had never seen a lit candle before.

What awakened Nancy was a dream of mosquitoes and bees. Mosquitoes and bees were extinct. So were birds. But Nancy dreamed that millions of insects were swarming about her from the waist down. They didn't sting. They fanned her. Nancy was a nothinghead.

She went to sleep again. When she awoke next time, she was being led into a bathroom by three women, still with stockings over their heads. The bathroom was already filled with the steam from somebody else's bath. There were somebody else's wet footprints crisscrossing the floor and the air reeked of pine-needle perfume.

Her will and intelligence returned as she was bathed and perfumed and dressed in a white nightgown. When the women stepped back to admire her, she said to them quietly, "I may be a nothinghead now. But that doesn't mean I have to think like one or act like one."

Nobody argued with her.

Nancy was taken downstairs and out of the house. She fully expected to be sent down a manhole again. It would be the perfect setting for her violation by Billy, she was thinking—down in a sewer.

But they took her across the green cement, where the grass used to be, and then across the yellow cement, where the beach used to be, and then out onto the blue cement, where the harbor used to be. There were twenty-six yachts that had belonged to various Kennedys, sunk up to their water lines in blue cement. It was to the most ancient of these yachts, the Marlin, once the property of Joseph P. Kennedy, that they delivered Nancy.

It was dawn. Because of the high-rise apartments all around the Kennedy Museum, it would be an hour before any direct sunlight would reach the microcosm under the geodesic dome.

Nancy was escorted as far as the companionway to the forward cabin of the Marlin. The women pantomimed that she was expected to go down the five steps alone.

Nancy froze for the moment and so did the women. And there were two actual statues in the tableau on the bridge. Standing at the wheel was a statue of Frank Wirtanen, once skipper of the Marlin. And next to him was his son and first mate, Carly. They weren't paying any attention to poor Nancy. They were staring out through the windshield at the blue cement.

Nancy, barefoot and wearing a thin white nightgown, descended bravely into the forward cabin, which was a pool of candlelight and pine-needle perfume. The companionway hatch was closed and locked behind her.

Nancy's emotions and the antique furnishings of the cabin were so complex that Nancy could not at first separate Billy the Poet from his surroundings, from all the mahogany and leaded glass. And then she saw him at the far end of the cabin, with his back against the door to the forward cockpit. He was wearing purple silk pajamas with a Russian collar. They were piped in red, and writhing across Billy's silken breast was a golden dragon. It was belching fire.

Anticlimactically, Billy was wearing glasses. He was holding a book.

Nancy poised herself on the next-to-the-bottom step, took a firm grip on the handholds in the companionway. She bared her teeth, calculated that it would take ten men Billy's size to dislodge her.

Between them was a great table. Nancy had expected the cabin to be dominated by a bed, possibly in the shape of a swan, but the Marlin was a day boat. The cabin was anything but a seraglio. It was about as voluptuous as a lower-middle-class dining room in Akron, Ohio, around 1910.

A candle was on the table. So were an ice bucket and two glasses and a quart of champagne. Champagne was as illegal as heroin.

Billy took off his glasses, gave her a shy, embarrassed smile, said, "Welcome."

"This is as far as I come."

He accepted that. "You're very beautiful there."

"And what am I supposed to say—that you're stunningly handsome? That I feel an overwhelming desire to throw myself into your manly arms?"

"If you wanted to make me happy, that would certainly be the way to do it." He said that humbly.

"And what about *my* happiness?"

The question seemed to puzzle him. "Nancy—that's what this is all about."

"What if my idea of happiness doesn't coincide with yours?"

"And what do you think my idea of happiness is?"

"I'm not going to throw myself into your arms, and I'm not going to drink that poison, and I'm not going to budge from here unless somebody makes me," said Nancy. "So I think your idea of happiness is going to turn out to be eight people holding me down on that table, while you bravely hold a cocked pistol to my head—and do what you want. That's the way it's going to have to be, so call your friends and get it over with!"

Which he did.

He didn't hurt her. He deflowered her with a clinical skill she found ghastly. When it was all over, he didn't seem cocky or proud. On the contrary, he was terribly depressed, and he said to Nancy, "Believe me, if there'd been any other way—"

Her reply to this was a face like stone—and silent tears of humiliation.

His helpers let down a folding bunk from the wall. It was scarcely wider than a bookshelf and hung on chains. Nancy allowed herself to be put to bed in it, and she was left alone with Billy the Poet again. Big as she was, like a double bass wedged on that narrow shelf, she felt like a pitiful little thing. A scratchy, war-surplus blanket had been tucked in around her. It was her own idea to pull up a corner of the blanket to hide her face.

Nancy sensed from sounds what Billy was doing, which wasn't much. He was sitting at the table, sighing occasionally, sniffing occasionally, turning the pages of a book. He lit a cigar and the stink of it seeped under the blanket. Billy inhaled the cigar, then coughed and coughed and coughed.

When the coughing died down, Nancy said loathingly through the blanket, "You're so strong, so masterful, so healthy. It must be wonderful to be so manly."

Billy only sighed at this.

"I'm not a very typical nothinghead," she said. "I hated it—hated everything about it."

Billy sniffed, turned a page.

"I suppose all the other women just loved it—couldn't get enough of it."

"Nope."

She uncovered her face. "What do you mean, 'Nope'?"

"They've all been like you."

This was enough to make Nancy sit up and stare at him. "The women who helped you tonight——"

"What about them?"

"You've done to them what you did to me?"

He didn't look up from his book. "That's right."

"Then why don't they kill you instead of helping you?"

"Because they understand." And then he added mildly, "They're *grateful.*"

Nancy got out of bed, came to the table, gripped the edge of the table, leaned close to him. And she said to him tautly, "I am not grateful."

"You will be."

"And what could possibly bring about that miracle?"

"Time," said Billy.

Billy closed his book, stood up. Nancy was confused by his magnetism. Somehow he was very much in charge again.

"What you've been through, Nancy," he said, "is a typical wedding night for a strait-laced girl of a hundred years ago, when everybody was a nothinghead. The groom did without helpers, because the bride wasn't customarily ready to kill him. Otherwise, the spirit of the occasion was much the same. These are the pajamas my great-great-grandfather wore on his wedding night in Niagara Falls.

"According to his diary, his bride cried all that night, and threw up twice. But, with the passage of time, she became a sexual enthusiast."

It was Nancy's turn to reply by not replying. She understood the tale. It frightened her to understand so easily that, from gruesome beginnings, sexual enthusiasm could grow and grow.

"You're a very typical nothinghead," said Billy. "If you dare to think about it now, you'll realize that you're angry because I'm such a bad lover, and a funny-looking shrimp besides. And what you can't help dreaming about from now on is a really suitable mate for a Juno like yourself.

"You'll find him, too—tall and strong and gentle. The nothinghead movement is growing by leaps and bounds."

"But——" said Nancy, and she stopped there. She looked out a porthole at the rising sun.

"But what?"

"The world is in the mess it is today because of the nothingheadedness of olden times. Don't you see?" She was pleading weakly. "The world can't afford sex anymore."

"Of course it can afford sex," said Billy. "All it can't afford anymore is reproduction."

"Then why the laws?"

"They're bad laws," said Billy. "If you go back through history, you'll find that the people who have been most eager to rule, to make the laws, to enforce the laws and to tell everybody exactly how God Almighty wants things here on Earth—those people have forgiven themselves and their friends for anything and everything. But they have been absolutely disgusted and terrified by the natural sexuality of common men and women.

"Why this is, I do not know. That is one of the many questions I wish somebody would ask the machines. I do know this: The triumph of that sort of disgust and terror is now complete. Almost every man and woman looks and feels like something the cat dragged in. The only sexual beauty that an ordinary human being can see today is in the woman who will kill him. Sex is death. There's a short and nasty equation for you: 'Sex is death. Q. E. D.'

"So you see, Nancy," said Billy, "I have spent this night, and many others like it, attempting to restore a certain amount of innocent pleasure to the world, which is poorer in pleasure than it needs to be."

Nancy sat down quietly and bowed her head.

"I'll tell you what my grandfather did on the dawn of his wedding night," said Billy.

"I don't think I want to hear it."

"It isn't violent. It's—it's meant to be tender."

"Maybe that's why I don't want to hear it."

"He read his bride a poem." Billy took the book from the table, opened it. "His diary tells which poem it was. While we aren't bride and groom, and while we may not meet again for many years, I'd like to read this poem to you, to have you know I've loved you."

"Please—no. I couldn't stand it."

"All right, I'll leave the book here, with the place marked, in case you want to read it later. It's the poem beginning:

How do I love thee? Let me count the ways.
I love thee to the depth and breadth and height
My soul can reach, when feeling out of sight
For the ends of Being and ideal Grace."

Billy put a small bottle on top of the book. "I am also leaving you these pills. If you take one a month, you will never have children. And still you'll be a nothinghead."

And he left. And they all left but Nancy.

When Nancy raised her eyes at last to the book and bottle, she saw that there was a label on the bottle. What the label said was this: WELCOME TO THE MONKEY HOUSE.

Happy Families

A. C. HOFFMANN

(1923–   )

If Mama hadn't been so afraid of sex. Brother and sister sit companionably eating chocolates and playing their favorite game. It is seldom now that they find moments to be together. The long afternoons of childhood which they shared have retreated into memory, a flickering image of the ornately patterned rug startles Maude once in a while as she is falling asleep. But why does she remember only part of the pattern—Hal is sitting on the other part absorbed in a game of jacks, his nimble fingers controlling the game, dropping and catching the small rubber ball, humming the score to himself. But even as she asks herself the question, the pattern vanishes and she falls into deeper sleep shaken by more terrible images and voices than that faded pattern in Grandmother's living room rug.

If her brother Hal dreams, and certainly he has never confessed this to Maude, his dreams are probably filled with all the things they missed as children—cousins whose arrival was imminent but who never appeared to play with them, family unavoidably detained by disasters of catastrophic proportions while on their way to the house. He can still taste on his tongue the contents of those enormous boxes of chocolates which Aunt Constance would bring on her infrequent visits—chocolates wrapped in gold and silver paper and filled with whole nuts and cherries floating in pink syrup that ran down his chin and lay in heavy blots on his shirt.

Aunt Constance appeared and disappeared, a happy phantom tripping down the stairs on the way to supper as if she were their younger sister and not their father's. Constance's name appears next to their father's on the family tree and below the name the dates of her birth and death. She had been very young when she died and no one in the family talks about her. Hal turning over in sleep tastes over and over again those fat chocolates filled with syrup and cherries. He is no longer sure if he knows Constance among the faces in the photographs that crowd the shelves in the cabinet, but he has never forgotten the boxes tied in wide red ribbon that she would bring the children. The chocolates he shares with Maude now are poor counterfeits for the real thing.

If Mama had known more about sex, would we be here? They beam affectionately at each other, looking out over the garden and lawn. Like everything in their grandmother's house it is now unkempt but charming. The trees planted when the house was newly built have grown and now overshadow the house and lawn. The perennials in the garden have long ago spread, riotously fighting each other for precious space. The phlox and daisies have reverted back to their original bloodline. The roses unpruned have grown into thickets across the wall. But the peonies bravely bloom, their heads heavy and succulent. Old-fashioned colors, Maude's friends tell her, but she will not touch the hundred-year roots.

Whoever buys the house when I'm gone can worry about that. I won't separate the peony roots. She brings the blooms into the house filling the vases. Even as she and Hal talk, the heavy flowers shed slowly and quietly over the magazines and books that sprawl across the library table. A studio portrait of their parents gazes discreetly at the littered table. If there are any secrets, they never shared them with their children. Mama sits, her eyes enormous in a peaked face. Father has placed his hand heavily on her shoulder as if he is supporting himself. He is considerably older—his face lined, the eyes tired. Both of them seem to be leaning forward, to have achieved a precarious balance, attempting to keep their distance from the urns and palms the photographer has arranged behind them.

Gazing now at the photograph Maude realizes that it has slipped in the frame and is hanging crooked. "Let's straighten out Mama and Papa," she says to Hal and they laugh uproariously. They have begun to drink the sherry now and it is beginnning to affect them. Hal strides over to deal with the frame while Maude pours more wine into Grandma's ruby glasses and nibbles on another biscuit from the tin.

Probably Papa taught her, he had much more experience. The endless mystery of procreation. As children they stood in awe of that massive bed, with brass columns joining together to create a temple pediment larger at the head than at the foot, not unlike the ornate iron fencing that enclosed the family plot at Briarwood. Maude was fond of visiting cemeteries for no other reason than she found them pleasant gardens in which to stroll looking at the epitaphs. She had learned to read by walking among the gravestones with Grandmother, a woman dressed completely in black. She was eternally in mourning for someone—family, or friend, or neighbor, it made no difference to her. And she enjoyed their afternoons in the cemetery, raising her parasol against the sun and strolling with Maude, her long skirts wavering across the granite curbstones. She had trouble bending, her girth was enormous, and so Maude would spell out the letters for her in a bright prattling voice. "C–R–A. I don't know the next letter, Grandmother."

"Go on, go on, don't stop. Skip the ones you don't know."

"F–O–I–D."

"You got another one wrong. You forfeit, you forfeit."

She rocked back and forth on her heels. "The Crawfords. I should have remembered they were stuck back here, the back of beyond. Bucky Crawford thought he was getting a bargain. Like all the Crawfords, he was crass. Your grandpapa kept pointing out that this section would never attract the best families and as always Grandpapa was right, though conceited as he was, I would never tell him so. Now child, here's a sweet, you did very well."

Grandmother pulls a sticky lemon drop out of her pocket, fuzzy with lint, but tasting the more exotic for it. Oh bliss, sucking on a lemon drop, hopping on and off the graves, reading the names and dates for Grandmother, who strides purposefully toward the family plot, surrounded by an ornate fence, stamped in iron with a weeping willow and a woolly sheep alternating around the square.

"I told him, don't waste money on a real fence. Said, Richard, you want to give pride to the relatives looking in, they want to feel that we belong here, made our mark in the world. What counts is what people see. Why should the dead care what's on their side?" So Grandpapa had bargained for a stamped iron enclosure with a real gate. There was a latch that opened and shut the mourner inside with the dead. Grandmother enjoyed standing at some distance away so that she could enjoy the view of the enclosure. In the bright sunlight the fence looked handsome and substantial.

Grandmother was right. Walking around it, Maude felt impressed belonging to the family buried there. Stumbling over the small gravestones embedded in the ground at odd angles around the family plot, she felt a confidence and security much like going to sleep in her mother's massive bed after Mama and Papa were dead and she took the room for herself.

The dead looking out at the world do not care if the stamped iron is hollow and unprepossessing on their side of the wall. They sleep in solitude, in silence, and they do not hear the faint footsteps walking over them, spelling out their names. "C–O–N–. I can't make out this name, Grandmother. T–A–."

"Never mind, Maude, home now. I've had enough walking for one day. Close the gate tight. Don't want dogs fouling the ground in there. Shoo, shoo," she is waving her parasol toward a bush where a dog may or may not be fouling the graves.

Grandmother was always good at changing the subject.

"Where did I come from, Grandmother?"

"God," she said firmly, and the subject was closed.

Well, there was never a breath of scandal attached to them. The only untypical gesture was that their parents owned an open touring car at a time when everyone else bragged about the snugness of riding in a closed automobile—you could take a drive in all kinds of weather without first having to check the barometer to see if it was rising or falling. Papa liked the feeling of being able to look out and practically touch the scenery and besides, if the thunder rumbled and the rain threatened, the car's occupants could always get out and earn their keep putting up the isinglass panels. But that hardly ever happened to them—sunny weather on their expeditions always. Mama raised her eyebrows and pretended to be inspecting the sleeve of her jacket for lint. It was better to acquiesce to Papa's weaknesses—his vices were an open book.

Where Hal got his wildness was anybody's guess—looking at the family tree gave no clue except for the empty spaces under Aunt Constance and their names, which suggested that it might still be possible that they would each send out new growth. But Constance had died young, never marrying though she had plenty of offers, being a pretty, popular girl, well liked, but never wild like some of her contemporaries.

Maude had even been engaged once. The details are blurred in her head now. It is best to erase heartbreak by saying it had never happened. Her only memento was a trip with Hal to Europe to forget it all but Hal was no solace, particularly since he disappeared into the ship's bar even before the ship sailed, leaving her alone in the cabin to go over and over again the steps by which she tricked herself into believing that she really and truly wanted to get married and go to bed with a man and bear his children.

She still chokes at the thought of her escape though at the time she had no way of knowing that the heavy weight on her heart was not grief but guilt over what she had almost done to herself and the hapless young man who had asked her to marry him. She slept at ease in her parents' marriage bed, untroubled by the ghosts of unborn children or the energy, passionate or passive, from which she and Hal were conceived.

There were two grandmothers—that had been confusing to the children, particularly Maude. The tall grim figure who walked the cemetery lanes with Maude is suddenly replaced by a different grandmother, who belonged to Mama and who arrived to keep the children company while the will was probated and the estate divided. Poor Papa was not his father's son when it came to making wills and disposing of property. Grandmother would have turned spiteful and called him a Crawford but as she herself pointed out the dead did not look at the back of a stamped iron fence and she could not comment on her son's ineptness while on her back four feet under, having been thriftily buried on top of Grandpapa so as to leave more room in the plot for the rest of them.

The other grandmother was a slight figure, in her dotage when the children knew her. She wore black satin slippers on her swollen feet, tottering about and whispering. Her deafness was crushing and she had no way of gauging the loudness of her voice. In her other life when she was the bustling happy mother of many children, she had always been meticulously groomed—smart from head to toe, forever bending down to pick up minute particles from the polished floors, to brush the reluctant shoulders of her husband and children already through the door when she calls them back for a final brushing.

"I want you to look your best." Her smile was warm and friendly. And who could grow angry when she finished the inspection with a quick hug and wet kiss on a departing cheek.

But by the time she moved into her daughter's house to supervise the orphaned children she had given up wearing stays and soon gave up wearing her dentures which had always been a torment. Her husband had grudgingly paid the bill, claiming that the dentist overcharged, he had never heard of such foolishness. They did not fit well, but she said nothing, enduring until the night she removed them for the last time and deliberately dropped them into the marble sink where they broke into many pieces.

She kept tins of pound cake under her bed, gifts from the other children who seldom visited. This was not a misfortune since her memory, never very strong, began to slacken and there were days when she thought Maude and Hal were her two youngest children, still in the nursery and needing great care and devotion after a lenghty bout of scarlet fever. She exerted great pressure to keep them in the house consuming hot soup and nourishing custards. "I must fatten you two." She poked Hal in the ribs. "You need more fat there, can't have you sick again."

School was still in term, the weather had turned sulky, moving out of February into March, days of cold drizzly rain which turned the garden into a sea of mud followed by frost and heavy snow. The children discovered a bound set of *National Geographic*—nothing was discarded in either of the two families. The name of the owner on the bookplate was unknown to them and it was never clear who had possessed and relinquished such a treasure. Contentedly they put away their schoolbooks. They were repeating a great deal of work that year because of a change in headmasters and both of them were thoroughly bored. There was nothing more refreshing, they discovered, than to sit cozily in the living room, feet tucked on the fireplace fender, thermostat turned high and heat roaring around the corners of the room, reading about the Orinoco and consuming another creamy custard Grandma brought fresh from the oven on an old tray advertising a soft drink they had never tasted and whose name sounded just as foreign as the tributaries of the Amazon.

Later when Grandma decided that they had recovered from their illness, she would come down, dreamily carrying a tin of pound cake to share a slice with Maude or Hal, starting at her end and picking off tiny pieces with trembling fingers, always surprised that the child at the other end was as voracious and quick-fingered as she, both nibbling the cake like small animals.

Maude and Hal were Papa's children by a second marriage. He had children from that first marriage, but they were enigmas to them—names on the family tree to which twigs were attached bearing more names. There were also cousins who belonged to both sides of the family, but they seldom saw them and whenever one was sent to visit them the afternoon was an occasion. The cousins were never very interesting, the girls eager to show Maude that her tea set was not as expensive or extensive as theirs, that her dolls did not wet their diapers while crying mama. They were not interested in the bound set of the magazines nor in walking in the garden to catch toads after a rain storm.

Hal had less trouble with guests since he and the boys could run races up and down the long staircase, trying to push each other down a flight so as to race ahead. Grandma's deafness was considered a great asset by the boys who could tear away to their heart's content, stopping red-faced only when she came out of her room to ask, "Would you like a bracing cup of cocoa," and then herding them before her on the descent to the kitchen where sheepishly they would help her find the tin of cocoa and the sugar bowl, pour the milk into the saucepan for her, strike the match to pop the gas ring. She kept them busy working around her and when the steaming cups were set before them, she said, laughing like a mischievous child, "I have the loveliest surprise," and floated in each cup a huge dollop of whipped cream that refused to sink and through which they drank the cocoa, a sticky white rime forming around the lips which they licked for a long time after the cup was drained and the games on the stairs resumed.

Once Maude and Hal had been sent down to play with a yellow-faced boy whose name they have forgotten but who suggested to Hal that they undress Maude so that he could show him something. After Maude fled in tears to Grandma who assumed it was some rough boy's game and comforted her with a tiny piece of pound cake and a game of dominos, the boys took down their pants and inspected each other critically. But that boy had never returned nor did they ever glimpse him at the occasional family gathering to which they put in an appearance. They never learned who he was or how he was related to them. Hal had enjoyed the time spent with him, learning once and for all that he was different from Maude, whom he had surreptitiously observed taking a bath, having learned how to construct a periscope from the encyclopedia and poking it up the open transom of the bathroom. He worried that he was different from Maude because there was something wrong with him. In the hazy days before they both came down with scarlet fever he may or may not have been a boy, and the visit and inspection were comforting and the true start of his career as a young man about town who loved them possessively and dearly but who also left them quickly when they responded and began to make demands of him.

"Oh Hal," Maude wept, "I don't know why you are so cruel to Cora." Cora had only just departed, wrung in tears and full of hot tea and sticky buns. The confidences lay heavy on Maude's shoulders which even then were beginning to slope so that Grandma despite her opposition to stays decreed that she should be measured for a surgical brace to keep her posture under control.

Maude inadvertently caught the bride's bouquet which Cora threw spitefully toward the two of them as she stood on the staircase radiant and submissively leaning against her beaming groom. Hal had ducked, realizing what Cora meant to do, but Maude put her arms up to stop the projectile and became the center of much banter and laughter for catching the bride's bouquet.

The family tree was intricate, filled with many lateral branches; they were part of a large enterprise. A fourth cousin spent years compiling it and proudly arrived with a framed copy for them to inspect and hang over the mantel in place of the grim-visaged ancestral photographs that had occupied the space. Cousin Beth pulled the library steps close to the gaping mouth of the fireplace and handed the framed photographs to the children who put them face down on the floor. Proudly she pointed out their names to them. There was just a little space below their names. It was as if the cousin knew instinctively that this branch of the tree was going to stop growing. Lying on the rug Maude would squint her eyes and look up at the tree hanging above her.

"You'll ruin your eyes, my dear." Grandma worries ineffectually about their teeth, their hearts, their livers, their digestions. She has a small hoard of bottles in the bathroom cabinet. No pills are thrown away even after the malady has disappeared. No drops poured down the sink. Her memory is unclear about the illness and remedy prescribed, but medicine paid for is medicine to be used. She doses Maude and Hal, sweetening the dose with a peppermint. Like the other grandmother she believes strongly in the efficacy of camphor to ward off infection, castor oil for constipation, and honey and lemon for coughs. Despite all her doctoring Maude and Hal survive.

Maude and Hal in dim euphoria play their weekly game of dominos. Grandma taught them and Hal spent many happy afternoons playing with Grandma and concentrating on how to cheat. This had always proved impossible since Grandma herself cheated and besides she had altered the rules to suit her style of play without telling the children when she taught them the game. Over the years each player has developed a strategy so that if one of them wins this Friday, the other will inevitably take the game the next time they meet.

"Do you remember our other grandmother?" Hal asks.

"A little." Maude is trying to hold off his attack and even though it is his time to win she will not give him an easy victory.

"That was her picture wasn't it that used to hang over the mantel?"

Maude looks puzzled, staring at the family tree.

"Cousin Beth took them down to put up the tree," he says.

"Right. Now I remember. I think those photographs are still up in the attic."

"We ought to go up there some time and look at them."

"Where would you put them?"

Hal lives in a poky apartment oppressively crowded with his share of the massive furniture that looks sparse in this enormous old house. "I didn't say I wanted them. I just wondered about them. Put names to faces is all I meant."

"Oh." Maude concentrates, willing him to turn around, to go to the tray for more sherry. She is working out a possible trick to defeat him but it will mean some extra maneuvering.

"I know what you're going to try," Hal warns.

"What?"

"Even if you pull it off, which I don't think you will, because I'm watching you, you still won't be able to win the game."

"Damn," says Maude, foiled again.

"Goodbye, love," Hal leans over and brushes her cheek. Tears spring from behind her eyelids. He will return next week. He comes every Friday to visit her. The two of them can never admit that there is no one else who cares for them. Hal's girls seem to grow younger with the years. Each year a new one, though now they arrive and depart more quickly, some only lasting a month. Hal's practiced lechery is contracting into smaller time spans and he is already undressing the girl even as he makes his first cool advance. There is so little time and gratification comes harder.

Maude looks at his thickening body, the face drawn and pouchy. She turns away in alarm. This is a trick her failing eyes are playing on her. She must stop being vain and begin to wear her glasses. Oh she is so weary of trying to move gracefully, to ignore the crepey skin under her chin, the bulging muscles covered by slack skin on her arms.

An athletic Hal smiles at her from the corner of the room, looking over the net, a tennis racket swinging nonchalantly from his hand. It had been fun to play together, the ball rhythmically dropping first on one side of the net and then the other. They could volley for minutes at a time, the ball imperceptibly creeping closer to the top of the net until touching the cord it drops abruptly at Maude's feet.

"Oh, Hal, you dog, you planned that shot on purpose."

Hal modestly disclaims any expertise. "Come on, Maude, your serve, stop grousing."

She slams a serve accurately into the corner. No matter how quickly he runs, how swiftly he lifts the racket to return, the ball puffs the chalk and bounces away from him.

With Hal's departure, the light in the garden extinguishes and the night shadows crawl the wall as she prepares for bed. No need for supper, the biscuits nibbled with the sherry have filled her. How can her body expand when she feeds it reluctantly and erratically? She has inherited the family corpulence. Hal seen from behind is still slim. Before he turns his ravished face, he might be a young man in flannels chasing tennis balls.

Her stocky frame has always promised that her figure would be full, the breasts voluptuous, the abdomen protruding like a woman in the first stages of pregnancy.

She turns on few lights. She has lived in this house a long time, knowing all the creaks on the staircase as she climbs toward bed. She gropes toward the door which leads to her parents' room. Mama is a soft breathy voice in the dark, a faint presence who has no substance in her memory. Maude looks, as she does every night, at her mother's face. A beautiful woman if her photograph is trusted; in the dimness surrounding the table beside the bed she maintains her neutrality. Before Maude switches off the light and gropes her way in the soft darkness toward the bed, she tries to recall both of them—the small-boned woman and the graying, corpulent man. But before her eyes there is only a void into which she prepares to fall, exhausted and spent.

"Oh," Maude laughs softly, stepping on the family tree laid out like a rug. And suddenly under foot the mysterious pattern that haunts her dreams is made visible. This is the section of the family tree which contains the names of her grandparents, their daughter Constance, her father, and his two wives. Over in the right hand corner, barely discernible, are their names. Nothing stems from them. The rug ends there.

"Hal, don't you want to have children?"

Unwillingly, she remembers Cathy's bloated face, looking down at Hal on that long ago picnic. "I can't give you anything but love," her rough awkward voice entreats, and Hal looks up and says, "Pass the pickles, Maude."

No one asks, "Why didn't you have children, Maude?"

Competent efficient sarcastic witty Maude, self-contained and self-centered, having solved once more the mystery of that pattern, submerges like a diver gliding through the smoky water toward the clear light at the bottom of the sea. And she dreams as always of holding a sleeping child hard against her budding breasts.

After the accident, the terrified onlookers pulled the children from the crackling wreck and sat them by the side of the road. Maude, blood running from a cut over her ear, cradles a sobbing Hal to sleep so that he does not hear the ambulance arrive or see the stretcher crew take away their bloody and mangled booty. In every happy family there are such moments when two lives are irrevocably entwined and the family tree ends with their names placed side by side as if already planted in the spaces allotted to them in the family plot.

Sonny's Blues

JAMES BALDWIN

(1924–)

I read about it in the paper, in the subway, on my way to work. I read it, and I couldn't believe it, and I read it again. Then perhaps I just stared at it, at the newsprint spelling out his name, spelling out the story. I stared at it in the swinging lights of the subway car, and in the faces and bodies of the people, and in my own face, trapped in the darkness which roared outside.

It was not to be believed and I kept telling myself that as I walked from the subway station to the high school. And at the same time I couldn't doubt it. I was scared, scared for Sonny. He became real to me again. A great block of ice got settled in my belly and kept melting there slowly all day long, while I taught my classes algebra. It was a special kind of ice. It kept melting, sending trickles of ice water all up and down my veins, but it never got less. Sometimes it hardened and seemed to expand until I felt my guts were going to come spilling out or that I was going to choke or scream. This would always be at a moment when I was remembering some specific thing Sonny had once said or done.

When he was about as old as the boys in my classes his face had been bright and open, there was a lot of copper in it; and he'd had wonderfully direct brown eyes, and great gentleness and privacy. I wondered what he looked like now. He had been picked up, the evening before, in a raid on an apartment downtown, for peddling and using heroin.

I couldn't believe it: but what I mean by that is that I couldn't find any room for it anywhere inside me. I had kept it outside me for a long time. I hadn't wanted to know. I had had suspicions, but I didn't name them, I kept putting them away. I told myself that Sonny was wild, but he wasn't crazy. And he'd always been a good boy, he hadn't ever turned hard or evil or disrespectful, the way kids can, so quick, so quick, especially in Harlem. I didn't want to believe that I'd ever see my brother going down, coming to nothing, all that light in his face gone out, in the condition I'd already seen so many others. Yet it had happened and here I was, talking about algebra to a lot of boys who might, every one of them for all I knew, be popping off needles every time they went to the head. Maybe it did more for them than algebra could.

I was sure that the first time Sonny had ever had horse, he couldn't have been much older than these boys were now. These boys, now, were living as we'd been living then, they were growing up with a rush and their heads bumped abruptly against the low ceiling of their actual possibilities. They were filled with rage. All they really knew were two darknesses, the darkness of their lives, which was now closing in on them, and the darkness of the movies, which had blinded them to that other darkness, and in which they now, vindictively, dreamed, at once more together than they were at any other time, and more alone.

When the last bell rang, the last class ended, I let out my breath. It seemed I'd been holding it for all that time. My clothes were wet—I may have looked as though I'd been sitting in a steam bath, all dressed up, all afternoon. I sat alone in the classroom a long time. I listened to the boys outside, downstairs, shouting and cursing and laughing. Their laughter struck me for perhaps the first time. It was not the joyous laughter which —God knows why—one associates with children. It was mocking and insular, its intent was to denigrate. It was disenchanted, and in this, also, lay the authority of their curses. Perhaps I was listening to them because I was thinking about my brother and in them I heard my brother. And myself.

One boy was whistling a tune, at once very complicated and very simple, it seemed to be pouring out of him as though he were a bird, and it sounded very cool and moving through all that harsh, bright air, only just holding its own through all those other sounds.

I stood up and walked over to the window and looked down into the courtyard. It was the beginning of the spring and the sap was rising in the boys. A teacher passed through them every now and again, quickly, as though he or she couldn't wait to get out of that courtyard, to get those boys out of their sight and off their minds. I started collecting my stuff. I thought I'd better get home and talk to Isabel.

The courtyard was almost deserted by the time I got downstairs. I saw this boy standing in the shadow of a doorway, looking just like Sonny. I almost called his name. Then I saw that it wasn't Sonny, but somebody we used to know, a boy from around our block. He'd been Sonny's friend. He'd never been mine, having been too young for me, and, anyway, I'd never liked him. And now, even though he was a grown-up man, he still hung around that block, still spent hours on the street corner, was always high and raggy. I used to run into him from time to time and he'd often work around to asking me for a quarter or fifty cents. He always had some real good excuse, too, and I always gave it to him, I don't know why.

But now, abruptly, I hated him. I couldn't stand the way he looked at me, partly like a dog, partly like a cunning child. I wanted to ask him what the hell he was doing in the school courtyard.

He sort of shuffled over to me, and he said, "I see you got the papers. So you already know about it."

"You mean about Sonny? Yes, I already know about it. How come they didn't get you?"

He grinned. It made him repulsive and it also brought to mind what he'd looked like as a kid. "I wasn't there. I stay away from them people."

"Good for you." I offered him a cigarette and I watched him through the smoke. "You come all the way down here just to tell me about Sonny?"

"That's right." He was sort of shaking his head and his eyes looked strange, as though they were about to cross. The bright sun deadened his damp dark brown skin and it made his eyes look yellow and showed up the dirt in his conked hair. He smelled funky. I moved a little away from him and I said, "Well, thanks. But I already know about it and I got to get home."

"I'll walk you a little ways," he said. We started walking. There were a couple of kids still loitering in the courtyard and one of them said good night to me and looked strangely at the boy beside me.

"What're you going to do?" he asked me. "I mean, about Sonny?"

"Look. I haven't seen Sonny for over a year, I'm not sure I'm going to do anything. Anyway, what the hell *can* I do?"

"That's right," he said quickly, "ain't nothing you can do. Can't much help old Sonny no more, I guess."

It was what I was thinking and so it seemed to me he had no right to say it.

"I'm surprised at Sonny, though," he went on—he had a funny way of talking, he looked straight ahead as though he were talking to himself—"I thought Sonny was a smart boy, I thought he was too smart to get hung."

"I guess he thought so too," I said sharply, "and that's how he got hung. And how about you? You're pretty goddamn smart, I bet."

Then he looked directly at me, just for a minute. "I ain't smart," he said. "If I was smart, I'd have reached for a pistol a long time ago."

"Look. Don't tell *me* your sad story, if it was up to me, I'd give you one." Then I felt guilty—guilty, probably, for never having supposed that the poor bastard *had* a story of his own, much less a sad one, and I asked, quickly, "What's going to happen to him now?"

He didn't answer this. He was off by himself some place. "Funny thing," he said, and from his tone we might have been discussing the quickest way to get to Brooklyn, "when I saw the papers this morning, the first thing I asked myself was if I had anything to do with it. I felt sort of responsible."

I began to listen more carefully. The subway station was on the corner, just before us, and I stopped. He stopped, too. We were in front of a bar and he ducked slightly, peering in, but whoever he was looking for didn't seem to be there. The juke box was blasting away with something black and bouncy and I half watched the barmaid as she danced her way from the juke box to her place behind the bar. And I watched her face as she laughingly responded to something someone said to her, still keeping time to the music. When she smiled one saw the little girl, one sensed the doomed, still-struggling woman beneath the battered face of the semi-whore.

"I never *give* Sonny nothing," the boy said finally, "but a long time ago I come to school high and Sonny asked me how it felt." He paused, I couldn't bear to watch him, I watched the barmaid, and I listened to the music which seemed to be causing the pavement to shake. "I told him it felt great." The music stopped, the barmaid paused and watched the juke box until the music began again. "It did."

All this was carrying me some place I didn't want to go. I certainly didn't want to know how it felt. It filled everything, the people, the houses, the music, the dark, quicksilver barmaid, with menace; and this menace was their reality.

"What's going to happen to him now?" I asked again.

"They'll send him away some place and they'll try to cure him." He shook his head. "Maybe he'll even think he's kicked the habit. Then they'll let him loose"—he gestured, throwing his cigarette into the gutter. "That's all."

"What do you mean, that's *all?*"

But I knew what he meant.

"I *mean,* that's *all.*" He turned his head and looked at me, pulling down the corners of his mouth. "Don't you know what I mean?" he asked softly.

"How the hell *would* I know what you mean?" I almost whispered it, I don't know why.

"That's right," he said to the air, "how would *he* know what I mean?" He turned toward me again, patient and calm, and yet I somehow felt him shaking, shaking as though he were going to fall apart. I felt that ice in my guts again, the dread I'd felt all afternoon; and again I watched the barmaid, moving about the bar, washing glasses, and singing. "Listen. They'll let him out and then it'll just start all over again. That's what I mean."

"You mean—they'll let him out. And then he'll just start working his way back in again. You mean he'll never kick the habit. Is that what you mean?"

"That's right," he said, cheerfully. "*You* see what I mean."

"Tell me," I said at last, "why does he want to die? He must want to die, he's killing himself, why does he want to die?"

He looked at me in surprise. He licked his lips. "He don't want to die. He wants to live. Don't nobody want to die, ever."

Then I wanted to ask him—too many things. He could not have answered, or if he had, I could not have borne the answers. I started walking. "Well, I guess it's none of my business."

"It's going to be rough on old Sonny," he said. We reached the subway station. "This is your station?" he asked. I nodded. I took one step down. "Damn!" he said, suddenly. I looked up at him. He grinned again. "Damn if I didn't leave all my money home. You ain't got a dollar on you, have you? Just for a couple of days, is all."

All at once something inside gave and threatened to come pouring out of me. I didn't hate him any more. I felt that in another moment I'd start crying like a child.

"Sure," I said. "Don't sweat." I looked in my wallet and didn't have a dollar, I only had a five. "Here," I said. "That hold you?"

He didn't look at it—he didn't want to look at it. A terrible, closed look came over his face, as though he were keeping the number on the bill a secret from him and me. "Thanks," he said, and now he was dying to see me go. "Don't worry about Sonny. Maybe I'll write him or something."

"Sure," I said. "You do that. So long."

"Be seeing you," he said. I went on down the steps.

And I didn't write Sonny or send him anything for a long time. When I finally did, it was just after my little girl died, he wrote me back a letter which made me feel like a bastard.

Here's what he said:

DEAR BROTHER,

You don't know how much I needed to hear from you. I wanted to write you many a time but I dug how much I must have hurt you and so I didn't write. But now I feel like a man who's been trying to climb up out of some deep, real deep and funky hole and just saw the sun up there, outside. I got to get outside.

I can't tell you much about how I got here. I mean I don't know how to tell you. I guess I was afraid of something or I was trying to escape from something and you know I have never been very strong in the head (smile). I'm glad Mama and Daddy are dead and can't see what's happened to their son and I swear if I'd known what I was doing I would never have hurt you so, you and a lot of other fine people who were nice to me and who believed in me.

I don't want you to think it had anything to do with me being a musician. It's more than that. Or maybe less than that. I can't get anything straight in my head down here and I try not to think about what's going to happen to me when I get outside again. Sometime I think I'm going to flip and *never* get outside and sometime I think I'll come straight back. I tell you one thing, though, I'd rather blow my brains out than go through this again. But that's what they all say, so they tell me. If I tell you when I'm coming to New York and if you could meet me, I sure would appreciate it. Give my love to Isabel and the kids and I was sorry to hear about little Gracie. I wish I could be like Mama and say the Lord's will be done, but I don't know it seems to me that trouble is the one thing that never does get stopped and I don't know what good it does to blame it on the Lord. But maybe it does some good if you believe it.

Your brother,
SONNY

Then I kept in constant touch with him and I sent him whatever I could and I went to meet him when he came back to New York. When I saw him many things I thought I had forgotten came flooding back to me. This was because I had begun, finally, to wonder about Sonny, about the life that Sonny lived inside. This life, whatever it was, had made him older and thinner and it had deepened the distant stillness in which he had always moved. He looked very unlike my baby brother. Yet, when he smiled, when we shook hands, the baby brother I'd never known looked out from the depths of his private life, like an animal waiting to be coaxed into the light.

"How you been keeping?" he asked me.

"All right. And you?"

"Just fine." He was smiling all over his face. "It's good to see you again."

"It's good to see you."

The seven years' difference in our ages lay between us like a chasm: I wondered if these years would ever operate between us as a bridge. I was remembering, and it made it hard to catch my breath, that I had been there when he was born; and I had heard the first words he had ever spoken. When he started to walk, he walked from our mother straight to me. I caught him just before he fell when he took the first steps he ever took in this world.

"How's Isabel?"

"Just fine. She's dying to see you."

"And the boys?"

"They're fine, too. They're anxious to see their uncle."

"Oh, come on. You know they don't remember me."

"Are you kidding? Of course they remember you."

He grinned again. We got into a taxi. We had a lot to say to each other, far too much to know how to begin.

As the taxi began to move, I asked, "You still want to go to India?"

He laughed. "You still remember that. Hell, no. This place is Indian enough for me."

"It used to belong to them," I said.

And he laughed again. "They damn sure knew what they were doing when they got rid of it."

Years ago, when he was around fourteen, he'd been all hipped on the idea of going to India. He read books about people sitting on rocks, naked, in all kinds of weather, but mostly bad, naturally, and walking barefoot through hot coals and arriving at wisdom. I used to say that it sounded to me as though they were getting away from wisdom as fast as they could. I think he sort of looked down on me for that.

"Do you mind," he asked, "if we have the driver drive alongside the park? On the west side—I haven't seen the city in so long."

"Of course not," I said. I was afraid that I might sound as though I were humoring him, but I hoped he wouldn't take it that way.

So we drove along, between the green of the park and the stony, lifeless elegance of hotels and apartment buildings, toward the vivid, killing streets of our childhood. These streets hadn't changed, though housing projects jutted up out of them now like rocks in the middle of a boiling sea. Most of the houses in which we had grown up had vanished, as had the stores from which we had stolen, the basements in which we had first tried sex, the rooftops from which we had hurled tin cans and bricks. But houses exactly like the houses of our past yet dominated the landscape, boys exactly like the boys we once had been found themselves smothering in these houses, came down into the streets for light and air and found themselves encircled by disaster. Some escaped the trap, most didn't. Those who got out always left something of themselves behind, as some animals amputate a leg and leave it in the trap. It might be said, perhaps, that I had escaped, after all, I was a school teacher; or that Sonny had, he hadn't lived in Harlem for years. Yet, as the cab moved uptown through streets which seemed, with a rush, to darken with dark people, and as I covertly studied Sonny's face, it came to me that what we both were seeking through our separate cab windows was that part of ourselves which had been left behind. It's always at the hour of trouble and confrontation that the missing member aches.

We hit 110th Street and started rolling up Lenox Avenue. And I'd known this avenue all my life, but it seemed to me again, as it had seemed on the day I'd first heard about Sonny's trouble, filled with a hidden menace which was its very breath of life.

"We almost there," said Sonny.

"Almost." We were both too nervous to say anything more.

We live in a housing project. It hasn't been up long. A few days after it was up it seemed uninhabitably new, now, of course, it's already rundown. It looks like a parody of the good, clean, faceless life—God knows the people who live in it do their best to make it a parody. The beat-looking grass lying around isn't enough to make their lives green, the hedges will never hold out the streets, and they know it. The big windows fool no one, they aren't big enough to make space out of no space. They don't bother with the windows, they watch the TV screen instead. The playground is most popular with the children who don't play at jacks, or skip rope, or roller skate, or swing, and they can be found in it after dark. We moved in partly because it's not too far from where I teach, and partly for the kids; but it's really just like the houses in which Sonny and I grew up. The same things happen, they'll have the same things to remember. The moment Sonny and I started into the house I had the feeling that I was simply bringing him back into the danger he had almost died trying to escape.

Sonny has never been talkative. So I don't know why I was sure he'd be dying to talk to me when supper was over the first night. Everything went fine, the oldest boy remembered him, and the youngest boy liked him, and Sonny had remembered to bring something for each of them; and Isabel, who is really much nicer than I am, more open and giving, had gone to a lot of trouble about dinner and was genuinely glad to see him. And she's always been able to tease Sonny in a way that I haven't. It was nice to see her face so vivid again and to hear her laugh and watch her make Sonny laugh. She wasn't, or, anyway, she didn't seem to be, at all uneasy or embarrassed. She chatted as though there were no subject which had to be avoided and she got Sonny past his first, faint stiffness. And thank God she was there, for I was filled with that icy dread again. Everything I did seemed awkward to me, and everything I said sounded freighted with hidden meaning. I was trying to remember everything I'd heard about dope addiction and I couln't help watching Sonny for signs. I wasn't doing it out of malice. I was trying to find out something about my brother. I was dying to hear him tell me he was safe.

"Safe!" my father grunted, whenever Mama suggested trying to move to a neighborhood which might be safer for children. "Safe, hell! Ain't no place safe for kids, nor nobody."

He always went on like this, but he wasn't, ever, really as bad as he sounded, not even on weekends, when he got drunk. As a matter of fact, he was always on the lookout for "something a little better," but he died before he found it. He died suddenly, during a drunken weekend in the middle of the war, when Sonny was fifteen. He and Sonny hadn't ever got on too well. And this was partly because Sonny was the apple of his father's eye. It was because he loved Sonny so much and was frightened for him, that he was always fighting with him. It doesn't do any good to fight with Sonny. Sonny just moves back, inside himself, where he can't be reached. But the principal reason that they never hit it off is that they were so much alike. Daddy was big and rough and loud-talking, just the opposite of Sonny, but they both had—that same privacy.

Mama tried to tell me something about this, just after Daddy died. I was home on leave from the army.

This was the last time I ever saw my mother alive. Just the same, this picture gets all mixed up in my mind with pictures I had of her when she was younger. The way I always see her is the way she used to be on a Sunday afternoon, say, when the old folks were talking after the big Sunday dinner. I always see her wearing pale blue. She'd be sitting on the sofa. And my father would be sitting in the easy chair, not far from her. And the living room would be full of church folks and relatives. There they sit, in chairs all around the living room, and the night is creeping up outside, but nobody knows it yet. You can see the darkness growing against the window-panes and you hear the street noises every now and again, or maybe the jangling beat of a tambourine from one of the churches close by, but it's real quiet in the room. For a moment nobody's talking, but every face looks darkening, like the sky outside. And my mother rocks a little from the waist, and my father's eyes are closed. Everyone is looking at something a child can't see. For a minute they've forgotten the children. Maybe a kid is lying on the rug half asleep. Maybe somebody's got a kid on his lap and is absent-mindedly stroking the kid's head. Maybe there's a kid, quiet and big-eyed, curled up in a big chair in the corner. The silence, the darkness coming, and the darkness in the faces frightens the child obscurely. He hopes that the hand which strokes his forehead will never stop—will never die. He hopes that there will never come a time when the old folks won't be sitting around the living room, talking about where they've come from, and what they've seen, and what's happened to them and their kinfolk.

But something deep and watchful in the child knows that this is bound to end, is already ending. In a moment someone will get up and turn on the light. Then the old folks will remember the children and they won't talk any more that day. And when light fills the room, the child is filled with darkness. He knows that every time this happens he's moved just a little closer to that darkness outside. The darkness outside is what the old folks have been talking about. It's what they've come from. It's what they endure. The child knows that they won't talk any more because if he knows too much about what's happened to *them,* he'll know too much too soon, about what's going to happen to *him.*

The last time I talked to my mother, I remember I was restless. I wanted to get out and see Isabel. We weren't married then and we had a lot to straighten out between us.

There Mama sat, in black, by the window. She was humming an old church song, *Lord, you brought me from a long ways off.* Sonny was out somewhere. Mama kept watching the streets.

"I don't know," she said, "if I'll ever see you again, after you go off from here. But I hope you'll remember the things I tried to teach you."

"Don't talk like that," I said, and smiled. "You'll be here a long time yet."

She smiled, too, but she said nothing. She was quiet for a long time. And I said, "Mama, don't you worry about nothing. I'll be writing all the time, and you be getting the checks. . . ."

"I want to talk to you about your brother," she said, suddenly. "If anything happens to me he ain't going to have nobody to look out for him."

"Mama," I said, "ain't nothing going to happen to you *or* Sonny. Sonny's all right. He's a good boy and he's got good sense."

"It ain't a question of his being a good boy," Mama said, "nor of his having good sense. It ain't only the bad ones, nor yet the dumb ones that gets sucked under." She stopped, looking at me. "Your Daddy once had a brother," she said, and she smiled in a way that made me feel she was in pain. "You didn't never know that, did you?"

"No," I said, "I never knew that," and I watched her face.

"Oh, yes," she said, "your Daddy had a brother." She looked out of the window again. "I know you never saw your Daddy cry. But *I* did—many a time, through all these years."

I asked her, "What happened to his brother? How come nobody's ever talked about him?"

This was the first time I ever saw my mother look old.

"His brother got killed," she said, "when he was just a little younger than you are now. I knew him. He was a fine boy. He was maybe a little full of the devil, but he didn't mean nobody no harm."

Then she stopped and the room was silent, exactly as it had sometimes been on those Sunday afternoons. Mama kept looking out into the streets.

"He used to have a job in the mill," she said, "and, like all young folks, he just liked to perform on Saturday nights. Saturday nights, him and your father would drift around to different places, go to dances and things like that, or just sit around with people they knew, and your father's brother would sing, he had a fine voice, and play along with himself on his guitar. Well, this particular Saturday night, him and your father was coming home from some place, and they were both a little drunk and there was a moon that night, it was bright like day. Your father's brother was feeling kind of good, and he was whistling to himself, and he had his guitar slung over his shoulder. They was coming down a hill and beneath them was a road that turned off from the highway. Well, your father's brother, being always kind of frisky, decided to run down this hill, and he did, with that guitar banging and clanging behind him, and he ran across the road, and he was making water behind a tree. And your father was sort of amused at him and he was still coming down the hill, kind of slow. The he heard a car motor and that same minute his brother stepped from behind the tree, into the road, in the moonlight. And he started to cross the road. And your father started to run down the hill, he says he don't know why. This car was full of white men. They was all drunk, and when they seen your father's brother they let out a great whoop and holler and they aimed the car straight at him. They was having fun, they just wanted to scare him, the way they do sometimes, you know. But they was drunk. And I guess the boy, being drunk, too, and scared, kind of lost his head. By the time he jumped it was too late. Your father says he heard his brother scream when the car rolled over him, and he heard the wood of that guitar when it give, and he heard them strings go flying, and he heard them white men shouting, and the car kept on a-going and it ain't stopped till this day. And, time your father got down the hill, his brother weren't nothing but blood and pulp."

Tears were gleaming on my mother's face. There wasn't anything I could say.

"He never mentioned it," she said, "because I never let him mention it before you children. Your Daddy was like a crazy man that night and for many a night thereafter. He says he never in his life seen anything as dark as that road after the lights of that car had gone away. Weren't nothing, weren't nobody on that road, just your Daddy and his brother and that busted guitar. Oh, yes. Your Daddy never did really get right again.

Till the day he died he weren't sure but that every white man he saw was the man that killed his brother."

She stopped and took out her handkerchief and dried her eyes and looked at me.

"I ain't telling you all this," she said, "to make you scared or bitter or to make you hate nobody. I'm telling you this because you got a brother. And the world ain't changed."

I guess I didn't want to believe this. I guess she saw this in my face. She turned away from me, toward the window again, searching those streets.

"But I praise my Redeemer," she said at last, "that He called your Daddy home before me. I ain't saying it to throw no flowers at myself, but, I declare, it keeps me from feeling too cast down to know I helped your father get safely through this world. Your father always acted like he was the roughest, strongest man on earth. And everybody took him to be like that. But if he hadn't had *me* there—to see his tears!"

She was crying again. Still, I couldn't move. I said, "Lord, Lord, Mama, I didn't know it was like that."

"Oh, honey," she said, "there's a lot that you don't know. But you are going to find it out." She stood up from the window and came over to me. "You got to hold on to your brother," she said, "and don't let him fall, no matter what it looks like is happening to him and no matter how evil you gets with him. You going to be evil with him many a time. But don't you forget what I told you, you hear?"

"I won't forget," I said. "Don't you worry, I won't forget. I won't let nothing happen to Sonny."

My mother smiled as though she were amused at something she saw in my face. Then, "You may not be able to stop nothing from happening. But you got to let him know you's *there.*"

Two days later I was married, and then I was gone. And I had a lot of things on my mind and I pretty well forgot my promise to Mama until I got shipped home on a special furlough for her funeral.

And, after the funeral, with just Sonny and me alone in the empty kitchen, I tried to find out something about him.

"What do you want to do?" I asked him.

"I'm going to be a musician," he said.

For he had graduated, in the time I had been away, from dancing to the juke box to finding out who was playing what, and what they were doing with it, and he had bought himself a set of drums.

"You mean, you want to be a drummer?" I somehow had the feeling that being a drummer might be all right for other people but not for my brother Sonny.

"I don't think," he said, looking at me very gravely, "that I'll ever be a good drummer. But I think I can play a piano."

I frowned. I'd never played the role of the older brother quite so seriously before, had scarcely ever, in fact, *asked* Sonny a damn thing. I sensed myself in the presence of something I didn't really know how to handle, didn't understand. So I made my frown a little deeper as I asked: "What kind of musician do you want to be?"

He grinned. "How many kinds do you think there are?"

"Be *serious,*" I said.

He laughed, throwing his head back, and then looked at me. "I *am* serious."

"Well, then, for Christ's sake, stop kidding around and answer a serious question. I mean, do you want to be a concert pianist, you want to play classical music and all that, or—or what?" Long before I finished he was laughing again. "For Christ's *sake,* Sonny!"

He sobered, but with difficulty. "I'm sorry. But you sound so—*scared!*" and he was off again.

"Well, you may think it's funny now, baby, but it's not going to be so funny when you have to make your living at it, let me tell you *that.*" I was furious because I knew he was laughing at me and I didn't know why.

"No," he said, very sober now, and afraid, perhaps, that he'd hurt me, "I don't want to be a classical pianist. That isn't what interests me. I mean"—he paused, looking hard at me, as though his eyes would help me to understand, and then gestured helplessly, as though perhaps his hand would help—"I mean, I'll have a lot of studying to do, and I'll have to study *everything,* but I mean, I want to play *with*—jazz musicians." He stopped. "I want to play jazz," he said.

Well, the word had never before sounded as heavy, as real, as it sounded that afternoon in Sonny's mouth. I just looked at him and I was probably frowning a real frown by this time. I simply couldn't see why on earth he'd want to spend his time hanging around night clubs, clowning around on bandstands, while people pushed each other around a dance floor. It seemed—beneath him, somehow. I had never thought about it before, had never been forced to, but I suppose I had always put jazz musicians in a class with what Daddy called "good-time people."

"Are you *serious?*"

"Hell, *yes,* I'm serious."

He looked more helpless than ever, and annoyed, and deeply hurt.

I suggested, helpfully: "You mean—like Louis Armstrong?"

His face closed as though I'd struck him. "No. I'm not talking about none of that old-time, down home crap."

"Well, look, Sonny, I'm sorry, don't get mad. I just don't altogether get it, that's all. Name somebody—you know, a jazz musician you admire."

"Bird."

"Who?"

"Bird! Charlie Parker! Don't they teach you nothing in the goddamn army?"

I lit a cigarette. I was surprised and then a little amused to discover that I was trembling. "I've been out of touch," I said. "You'll have to be patient with me. Now. Who's this Parker character?"

"He's just one of the greatest jazz musicians alive," said Sonny, sullenly, his hands in his pockets, his back to me. "Maybe *the* greatest," he added, bitterly, "that's probably why *you* never heard of him."

"All right," I said, "I'm ignorant. I'm sorry. I'll go out and buy all the cat's records right away, all right?"

"It don't," said Sonny, with dignity, "make any difference to me. I don't care what you listen to. Don't do me no favors."

I was beginning to realize that I'd never seen him so upset before. With another part of my mind I was thinking that this would probably turn out to be one of those things kids go through and that I shouldn't make it seem important by pushing it too hard. Still, I didn't think it would do any harm to ask: "Doesn't all this take a lot of time? Can you make a living at it?"

He turned back to me and half leaned, half sat, on the kitchen table. "Everything takes time," he said, "and—well, yes, sure, I can make a living at it. But what I don't seem to be able to make you understand is that it's the only thing I want to do."

"Well Sonny," I said, gently, "you know people can't always do exactly what they *want* to do—"

"*No*, I don't know that," said Sonny, surprising me. "I think people *ought* to do what they want to do, what else are they alive for?"

"You getting to be a big boy," I said desperately, "it's time you started thinking about your future."

"I'm thinking about my future," said Sonny, grimly. "I think about it all the time."

I gave up. I decided, if he didn't change his mind, that we could always talk about it later. "In the meantime," I said, "you got to finish school." We had already decided that he'd have to move in with Isabel and her folks. I knew this wasn't the ideal arrangement because Isabel's folks are inclined to be dicty and they hadn't especially wanted Isabel to marry me. But I didn't know what else to do. "And we have to get you fixed up at Isabel's."

There was a long silence. He moved from the kitchen table to the window. "That's a terrible idea. You know it yourself."

"Do you have a *better* idea?"

He just walked up and down the kitchen for a minute. He was as tall as I was. He had started to shave. I suddenly had the feeling that I didn't know him at all.

He stopped at the kitchen table and picked up my cigarettes. Looking at me with a kind of mocking, amused defiance, he put one between his lips. "You mind?"

"You smoking already?"

He lit the cigarette and nodded, watching me through the smoke. "I just wanted to see if I'd have the courage to smoke in front of you." He grinned and blew a great cloud of smoke to the ceiling. "It was easy." He looked at my face. "Come on, now. I bet you was smoking at my age, tell the truth."

I didn't say anything but the truth was on my face, and he laughed. But now there was something very strained in his laugh. "Sure. And I bet that ain't all you was doing."

He was frightening me a little. "Cut the crap," I said. "We already decided that you was going to go and live at Isabel's. Now what's got into you all of a sudden?"

"*You* decided it," he pointed out. *I* didn't decide nothing." He stopped in front of me, leaning against the stove, arms loosely folded. "Look, brother. I don't want to stay in Harlem no more, I really don't." He was very earnest. He looked at me, then over toward the kitchen window. There was something in his eyes I'd never seen before, some thoughtfulness, some worry all his own. He rubbed the muscle of one arm. "It's time I was getting out of here."

"Where do you want to *go*, Sonny?"

"I want to join the army. Or the navy, I don't care. If I say I'm old enough they'll believe me."

Then I got mad. It was because I was so scared. "You must be crazy. You goddamn fool, what the hell do you want to go and join the *army* for?"

"I just told you. To get out of Harlem."

"Sonny, you haven't even finished *school*. And if you really want to be a musician, how do you expect to study if you're in the *army?*"

He looked at me, trapped, and in anguish. "There's ways. I might be able to work out some kind of deal. Anyway, I'll have the G.I. Bill when I come out."

"*If* you come out." We stared at each other. "Sonny, please. Be reasonable. I know the setup is far from perfect. But we got to do the best we can."

"I ain't learning nothing in school," he said. "Even when I go." He turned away from me and opened the window and threw his cigarette out into the narrow alley. I watched his back. "At least, I ain't learning nothing you'd want me to learn." He slammed the window so hard I thought the glass would fly out, and turned back to me. "And I'm sick of the stink of these garbage cans!"

"Sonny," I said, "I know how you feel. But if you don't finish school now, you're going to be sorry later that you didn't." I grabbed him by the shoulders. "And you only got another year. It ain't so bad. And I'll come back and I swear I'll help you do *whatever* you want to do. Just try to put up with it till I come back. Will you please do that? For me?"

He didn't answer and he wouldn't look at me.

"Sonny. You hear me?"

He pulled away. "I hear you. But you never hear anything *I* say."

I didn't know what to say to that. He looked out of the window and then back at me. "OK," he said, and sighed. "I'll try."

Then I said, trying to cheer him up a little, "They got a piano at Isabel's. You can practice on it."

And as a matter of fact, it did cheer him up for a minute. "That's right," he said to himself. "I forgot that." His face relaxed a little. But the worry, the thoughtfulness, played on it still, the way shadows play on a face which is staring into the fire.

But I thought I'd never hear the end of that piano. At first, Isabel would write me, saying how nice it was that Sonny was so serious about his music and how, as soon as he came in from school, or wherever he had been when he was supposed to be at school, he went straight to that piano and stayed there until suppertime. And, after supper, he went back to that piano and stayed there until everybody went to bed. He was at the piano all day Saturday and all day Sunday. Then he bought a record player and started playing records. He'd play one record over and over again, all day long sometimes, and he'd improvise along with it on the piano. Or he'd play one section of the record, one chord, one change, one progression, then he'd do it on the piano. Then back to the record. Then back to the piano.

Well, I really don't know how they stood it. Isabel finally confessed that it wasn't like living with a person at all, it was like living with sound. And the sound didn't make any sense to her, didn't make any sense to any of them—naturally. They began, in a way, to be afflicted by this presence that was living in their home. It was as though Sonny were some sort of god, or monster. He moved in an atmosphere which wasn't like theirs at all. They fed him and he ate, he washed himself, he walked in and out of their door; he certainly wasn't nasty or unpleasant or rude, Sonny isn't any of those things; but it was as though he were all wrapped up in some cloud, some fire, some vision all his own; and there wasn't any way to reach him.

At the same time, he wasn't really a man yet, he was still a child, and they had to watch out for him in all kinds of ways. They certainly couldn't throw him out. Neither did they dare to make a great scene about that piano because even they dimly sensed, as I sensed, from so many thousands of miles away, that Sonny was at that piano playing for his life.

But he hadn't been going to school. One day a letter came from the school board and Isabel's mother got it—there had, apparently, been other letters but Sonny had torn them up. This day, when Sonny came in, Isabel's mother showed him the letter and asked where he'd been spending his time. And she finally got it out of him that he'd been down in Greenwich Village, with musicians and other characters, in a white girl's apartment. And this scared her and she started to scream at him and what came up, once she began—though she denies it to this day—was what sacrifices they were making to give Sonny a decent home and how little he appreciated it.

Sonny didn't play the piano that day. By evening, Isabel's mother had calmed down but then there was the old man to deal with, and Isabel herself. Isabel says she did her best to be calm but she broke down and started crying. She says she just watched Sonny's face. She could tell, by watching him, what was happening with him. And what was happening was that they penetrated his cloud, they had reached him. Even if their fingers had been a thousand times more gentle than human fingers ever are, he could hardly help feeling that they had stripped him naked and were spitting on that nakedness. For he also had to see that his presence, that music, which was life or death to him, had been torture for them and that they had endured it, not at all for his sake, but only for mine. And Sonny couldn't take that. He can take it a little better today than he could then but he's still not very good at it and, frankly, I don't know anybody who is.

The silence of the next few days must have been louder than the sound of all the music ever played since time began. One morning, before she went to work, Isabel was in his room for something and she suddenly realized that all of his records were gone. And she knew for certain that he was gone. And he was. He went as far as the navy would carry him. He finally sent me a postcard from some place in Greece and that was the first I knew that Sonny was still alive. I didn't see him any more until we were both back in New York and the war had long been over.

He was a man by then, of course, but I wasn't willing to see it. He came by the house from time to time, but we fought almost every time we met. I didn't like the way he carried himself, loose and dreamlike all the time, and I didn't like his friends, and his music seemed to be merely an excuse for the life he led. It sounded just that weird and disordered.

Then we had a fight, a pretty awful fight, and I didn't see him for months. By and by I looked him up, where he was living, in a furnished room in the Village, and I tried to make it up. But there were lots of other people in the room and Sonny just lay on his bed, and he wouldn't come downstairs with me, and he treated these other people as though they were his family and I weren't. So I got mad and then he got mad, and then I told him that he might just as well be dead as live the way he was living. Then he stood up and he told me not to worry about him any more in life, that he *was* dead as far as I was concerned. Then he pushed me to the door and the other people looked on as though nothing were happening, and he slammed the door behind me. I stood in the hallway, staring at the door. I heard somebody laugh in the room and then the tears came to my eyes. I started down the steps, whistling to keep from crying, I kept whistling to myself, *You going to need me, baby, one of these cold, rainy days.*

I read about Sonny's trouble in the spring. Little Grace died in the fall. She was a beautiful little girl. But she only lived a little over two years. She died of polio and she suffered. She had a slight fever for a couple of days, but it didn't seem like anything and we just kept her in bed. And we would certainly have called the doctor, but the fever dropped, she seemed to be all right. So we thought it had just been a cold. Then, one day, she was up, playing, Isabel was in the kitchen fixing lunch for the two boys when they'd come in from school, and she heard Grace fall down in the living room. When you have a lot of children you don't always start running when one of them falls, unless they start screaming or something. And, this time, Grace was quiet. Yet, Isabel says that when she heard that *thump* and then that silence, something happened in her to make her afraid. And she ran to the living room and there was little Grace on the floor, all twisted up and the reason she hadn't screamed was that she couldn't get her breath. And when she did scream, it was the worst sound, Isabel says, that she'd ever heard in all her life, and she still hears it sometimes in her dreams. Isabel will sometimes wake me up with a low, moaning, strangled sound and I have to be quick to awaken her and hold her to me and where Isabel is weeping against me seems a mortal wound.

I think I may have written Sonny the very day that little Grace was buried. I was sitting in the living room in the dark, by myself, and I suddenly thought of Sonny. My trouble made his real.

One Saturday afternoon, when Sonny had been living with us, or, anyway, been in our house, for nearly two weeks, I found myself wandering aimlessly about the living room, drinking from a can of beer, and trying to work up the courage to search Sonny's room. He was out, he was usually out whenever I was home, and Isabel had taken the children to see their grandparents. Suddenly I was standing still in front of the living room window, watching Seventh Avenue. The idea of searching Sonny's room made me still. I scarcely dared to admit to myself what I'd be searching for. I didn't know what I'd do if I found it. Or if I didn't.

On the sidewalk across from me, near the entrance to a barbecue joint, some people were holding an old-fashioned revival meeting. The barbecue cook, wearing a dirty white apron, his conked hair reddish and metallic in the pale sun, and a cigarette between his lips, stood in the doorway, watching them. Kids and older people paused in their errands and stood there, along with some older men and a couple of very tough-looking women who watched everything that happened on the avenue, as though they owned it, or were maybe owned by it. Well, they were watching this, too. The revival was being carried on by three sisters in black, and a brother. All they had were their voices and their Bibles and a tambourine. The brother was testifying and while he testified two of the sisters stood together, seeming to say, Amen, and the third sister walked around with the tambourine outstretched and a couple of people dropped coins into it. Then the brother's testimony ended and the sister who had been taking up the collection dumped the coins into her palm and transferred them to the pocket of her long black robe. Then she raised both hands, striking the tambourine against the air, and then against one hand, and she started to sing. And the two other sisters and the brother joined in.

It was strange, suddenly, to watch, though I had been seeing these street meetings all my life. So, of course, had everybody else down there. Yet, they paused and watched and listened and I stood still at the window. *"Tis the old ship of Zion,"* they sang, and the sister with the tambourine kept a steady, jangling beat, *"It has rescued many a thousand!"* Not a soul under the sound of their voices was hearing this song for the first time, not one of them had been rescued. Nor had they seen much in the way of rescue work being done around them. Neither did they especially believe in the holiness of the three sisters and the brother, they knew too much about them, knew where they lived, and how. The woman with the tambourine, whose voice dominated the air, whose face was bright with joy, was divided by very little from the woman who stood watching her, a cigarette between her heavy, chapped lips, her hair a cuckoo's nest, her face scarred and swollen from many beatings, and her black eyes glittering like coal. Perhaps they both knew this, which was why, when, as rarely, they addressed each other, they addressed each other as Sister. As the singing filled the air the watching, listening faces underwent a change, the eyes focusing on something within; the music seemed to soothe a poison out of them; and time seemed, nearly, to fall away from the sullen, belligerent, battered faces, as though they were fleeing back to their first condition, while dreaming of their last. The barbecue cook half shook his head and smiled, and dropped his cigarette and disappeared into his joint. A man fumbled in his pockets for change and stood holding it in his hand impatiently, as though he had just remembered a pressing appointment further up the avenue. He looked furious. Then I saw Sonny, standing on the edge of the crowd. He was carrying a wide, flat notebook with a green cover, and it made him look, from where I was standing, almost like a schoolboy. The coppery sun brought out the copper in his skin, he was very faintly smiling, standing very still. Then the singing stopped, the tambourine turned into a collection plate again. The furious man dropped in his coins and vanished, so did a couple of the women, and Sonny dropped some change in the plate, looking directly at the woman with a little smile. He started across the avenue, toward the house. He has a slow, loping walk, something like the way Harlem hipsters walk, only he's imposed on this his own halfbeat. I had never really noticed it before.

I stayed at the window, both relieved and apprehensive. As Sonny disappeared from my sight, they began singing again. And they were still singing when his key turned in the lock.

"Hey," he said.

"Hey, yourself. You want some beer?"

"No. Well, maybe." But he came up to the window and stood beside me, looking out. "What a warm voice," he said.

They were singing *If I could only hear my mother pray again!*

"Yes," I said, "and she can sure beat that tambourine."

"But what a terrible song," he said, and laughed. He dropped his notebook on the sofa and disappeared into the kitchen. "Where's Isabel and the kids?"

"I think they went to see their grandparents. You hungry?"

"No." He came back into the living room with his can of beer. "You want to come some place with me tonight?"

I sensed, I don't know how, that I couldn't possibly say No. "Sure. Where?"

He sat down on the sofa and picked up his notebook and started leafing through it. "I'm going to sit in with some fellows in a joint in the Village."

"You mean, you're going to play, tonight?"

"That's right." He took a swallow of his beer and moved back to the window. He gave me a sidelong look. "If you can stand it."

"I'll try," I said.

He smiled to himself and we both watched as the meeting across the way broke up. The three sisters and the brother, heads bowed, were singing *God be with you till we meet again.* The faces around them were very quiet. Then the song ended. The small crowd dispersed. We watched the three women and the lone man walk slowly up the avenue.

"When she was singing before," said Sonny, abruptly, "her voice reminded me for a minute of what heroin feels like sometimes—when it's in your veins. It makes you feel sort of warm and cool at the same time. And distant. And—and sure." He sipped his beer, very deliberately not looking at me. I watched his face. "It makes you feel—in control. Sometimes you've got to have that feeling."

"Do you?" I sat down slowly in the easy chair.

"Sometimes." He went to the sofa and picked up his notebook again. "Some people do."

"In order," I asked, "to play?" And my voice was very ugly, full of contempt and anger.

"Well"—he looked at me with great, troubled eyes, as though, in fact, he hoped his eyes would tell me things he could never otherwise say—"they *think* so. And *if* they think so—!"

"And what do *you* think?" I asked.

He sat on the sofa and put his can of beer on the floor. "I don't know," he said, and I couldn't be sure if he were answering my question or pursuing his thoughts. His face didn't tell me. "It's not so much to *play*. It's to *stand* it, to be able to make it at all. On any level." He frowned and smiled: "In order to keep from shaking to pieces."

"But these friends of yours," I said, "they seem to shake themselves to pieces pretty goddamn fast."

"Maybe." He played with the notebook. And something told me that I should curb my tongue, that Sonny was doing his best to talk, that I should listen. "But of course you only know the ones that've gone to pieces. Some don't—or at least they haven't *yet* and that's just about all *any* of us can say." He paused. "And then there are some who just live, really, in hell, and they know it and they see what's happening and they go right on. I don't know." He sighed, dropped the notebook, folded his arms. "Some guys, you can tell from the way they play, they on something *all* the time. And you can see that, well, it makes something real for them. But of course," he picked up his beer from the floor and sipped it and put the can down again, "they *want* to, too, you've got to see that. Even some of them that say they don't—*some,* not all."

"And what about you?" I asked—I couldn't help it. "What about you? Do *you* want to?"

He stood up and walked to the window and remained silent for a long time. Then he sighed. "Me," he said. Then: "While I was downstairs before, on my way here, listening to that woman sing, it struck me all of a sudden how much suffering she must have had to go through—to sing like that. It's *repulsive* to think you have to suffer that much."

I said: "But there's no way not to suffer—is there, Sonny?"

"I believe not," he said, and smiled, "but that's never stopped anyone from trying." He looked at me. "Has it?" I realized, with this mocking look, that there stood between us, forever, beyond the power of time or forgiveness, the fact that I had held silence—so long!—when he had needed human speech to help him. He turned back to the window. "No, there's no way not to suffer. But you try all kinds of ways to keep from drowning in it, to keep on top of it, and to make it seem—well, like *you.* Like you did something, all right, and now you're suffering for it. You know?" I said nothing. "Well you know," he said, impatiently, "why *do* people suffer? Maybe it's better to do something to give it a reason, *any* reason."

"But we just agreed," I said, "that there's no way not to suffer. Isn't it better, then, just to—take it?"

"But nobody just takes it," Sonny cried, "that's what I'm telling you! *Everybody* tries not to. You're just hung up on the *way* some people try—it's not *your* way!"

The hair on my face began to itch, my face felt wet. "That's not true," I said, "that's not true. I don't give a damn what other people do, I don't even care how they suffer. I just care how *you* suffer." And he looked at me. "Please believe me," I said, "I don't want to see you—die—trying not to suffer."

"I won't," he said, flatly, "die trying not to suffer. At least, not any faster than anybody else."

"But there's no need," I said, trying to laugh, "is there? in killing yourself."

I wanted to say more, but I couldn't. I wanted to talk about will power and how life could be—well, beautiful. I wanted to say that it was all within; but was it? or, rather, wasn't that exactly the trouble? And I wanted to promise that I would never fail him again. But it would all have sounded—empty words and lies.

So I made the promise to myself and prayed that I would keep it.

"It's terrible sometimes, inside," he said, "that's what's the trouble. You walk these streets, black and funky and cold, and there's not really a living ass to talk to, and there's nothing shaking, and there's no way of getting it out—that storm inside. You can't talk it and you can't make love with it, and when you finally try to get with it and play it, you realize *nobody's* listening. So *you've* got to listen. You got to find a way to listen."

And then he walked away from the window and sat on the sofa again, as though all the wind had suddenly been knocked out of him. "Sometimes you'll do *anything* to play, even cut your mother's throat." He laughed and looked at me. "Or your brother's." Then he sobered. "Or your own." Then: "Don't worry. I'm all right now and I think I'll *be* all right. But I can't forget—where I've been. I don't mean just the physical place I've been, I mean where I've *been*. And *what* I've been."

"What have you been, Sonny?" I asked.

He smiled—but sat sideways on the sofa, his elbow resting on the back, his fingers playing with his mouth and chin, not looking at me. "I've been something I didn't recognize, didn't know I could be. Didn't know anybody could be." He stopped, looking inward, looking helplessly young, looking old. "I'm not talking about it now because I feel *guilty* or anything like that—maybe it would be better if I did, I don't know. Anyway, I can't really talk about it. Not to you, not to anybody," and now he turned and faced me. "Sometimes, you know, and it was actually when I was most *out* of the world, I felt that I was in it, and that I was *with* it, really, and I could play or I didn't really have to *play*, it just came out of me, it was there. And I don't know how I played, thinking about it now, but I know I did awful things, those times, sometimes, to people. Or it wasn't that I *did* anything to them—it was that they weren't real." He picked up the beer can; it was empty; he rolled it between his palms: "And other times—well, I needed a fix, I needed to find a place to lean, I needed to clear a space to *listen*—and I couldn't find it, and I—went crazy, I did terrible things to *me*, I was terrible *for* me." He began pressing the beer can between his hands, I watched the metal begin to give. It glittered, as he played with it, like a knife, and I was afraid he would cut himself, but I said nothing. "Oh well. I can never tell you. I was all by myself at the bottom of something, stinking and sweating and crying and shaking, and I smelled it, you know? *my* stink, and I thought I'd die if I couldn't get away from it and yet, all the same, I knew that everything I was doing was just locking me in with it. And I didn't know," he paused, still flattening the beer can, "I didn't know, I still *don't* know, something kept telling me that maybe it was good to smell your own stink, but I didn't think that *that* was what I'd been trying to do—and—who can stand it?" and he abruptly dropped the ruined beer can, looking at me with a small, still smile, and then rose, walking to the window as though it were the lodestone rock. I watched his face, he watched the avenue. "I couldn't tell you when Mama died—but the reason I wanted to leave Harlem so bad was to get away from drugs. And then, when I ran away, that's what I was running from—really. When I came back, nothing had changed, *I* hadn't changed, I was just—older." And he stopped, drumming with his fingers on the windowpane. The sun had vanished, soon darkness would fall. I watched his face. "It can come again," he said, almost as though speaking to himself. Then he turned to me. "It can come again," he repeated. "I just want you to know that."

"All right," I said, at last. "So it can come again. All right."

He smiled, but the smile was sorrowful. "I had to try to tell you," he said.

"Yes," I said. "I understand that."

"You're my brother," he said, looking straight at me, and not smiling at all.

"Yes," I repeated, "yes. I understand that."

He turned back to the window, looking out. "All that hatred down there," he said, "all that hatred and misery and love. It's a wonder it doesn't blow the avenue apart."

We went to the only night club on a short, dark street, downtown. We squeezed through the narrow, chattering, jam-packed bar to the entrance of the big room, where the bandstand was. And we stood there for a moment, for the lights were very dim in this room and we couldn't see. Then, "Hello, boy," said a voice and an enormous black man, much older than Sonny or myself, erupted out of all that atmospheric lighting and put an arm around Sonny's shoulder. "I been sitting right here," he said, "waiting for you."

He had a big voice, too, and heads in the darkness turned toward us.

Sonny grinned and pulled a little away, and said, "Creole, this is my brother. I told you about him."

Creole shook my hand. "I'm glad to meet you, son," he said, and it was clear that he was glad to meet me *there*, for Sonny's sake. And he smiled, "You got a real musician in *your* family," and he took his arm from Sonny's shoulder and slapped him, lightly, affectionately, with the back of his hand.

"Well. Now I've heard it all," said a voice behind us. This was another musician, and a friend of Sonny's, a coal-black, cheerful-looking man, built close to the ground. He immediately began confiding to me, at the top of his lungs, the most terrible things about Sonny, his teeth gleaming like a lighthouse and his laugh coming up out of him like the beginning of an earthquake. And it turned out that everyone at the bar knew Sonny, or almost everyone; some were musicians, working there, or nearby, or not working, some were simply hangers-on, and some were there to hear Sonny play. I was introduced to all of them and they were all very polite to me. Yet, it was clear that, for them, I was only Sonny's brother. Here, I was in Sonny's world. Or, rather: his kingdom. Here, it was not even a question that his veins bore royal blood.

They were going to play soon and Creole installed me, by myself, at a table in a dark corner. Then I watched them, Creole, and the little black man, and Sonny, and the others, while they horsed around, standing just below the bandstand. The light from the bandstand spilled just a little short of them and, watching them laughing and gesturing and moving about, I had the feeling that they, nevertheless, were being most careful not to step into that circle of light too suddenly: that if they moved into the light too suddenly, without thinking, they would perish in flame. Then, while I watched, one of them, the small, black man, moved into the light and crossed the bandstand and started fooling around with his drums. Then—being funny and being, also, extremely ceremonious—Creole took Sonny by the arm and led him to the piano. A woman's voice called Sonny's name and a few hands started clapping. And Sonny, also being funny and being ceremonious, and so touched, I think, that he could have cried, but neither hiding it nor showing it, riding it like a man, grinned, and put both hands to his heart and bowed from the waist.

Creole then went to the bass fiddle and a lean, very bright-skinned brown man jumped up on the bandstand and picked up his horn. So there they were, and the atmosphere on the bandstand and in the room began to change and tighten. Someone stepped up to the microphone and announced them. Then there were all kinds of murmurs. Some people at the bar shushed others. The waitress ran around, frantically getting in the last orders, guys and chicks got closer to each other, and the lights on the bandstand, on the quartet, turned to a kind of indigo. Then they all looked different there. Creole looked about him for the last time, as though he were making certain that all his chickens were in the coop, and then he—jumped and struck the fiddle. And there they were.

All I know about music is that not many people ever really hear it. And even then, on the rare occasions when something opens within, and the music enters, what we mainly hear, or hear corroborated, are personal private, vanishing evocations. But the man who creates the music is hearing something else, is dealing with the roar rising from the void and imposing order on it as it hits the air. What is evoked in him, then, is of another order, more terrible because it has no words, and triumphant, too, for that same reason. And his triumph, when he triumphs, is ours. I just watched Sonny's face. His face was troubled, he was working hard, but he wasn't with it. And I had the feeling that, in a way, everyone on the bandstand was waiting for him, both waiting for him and pushing him along. But as I began to watch Creole, I realized that it was Creole who held them all back. He had them on a short rein. Up there, keeping the beat with his whole body, wailing on the fiddle, with his eyes half closed, he was listening to everything, but he was listening to Sonny. He was having a dialogue with Sonny. He wanted Sonny to leave the shore line and strike out for the deep water. He was Sonny's witness that deep water and drowning were not the same thing—he had been there, and he knew. And he wanted Sonny to know. He was waiting for Sonny to do the things on the keys which would let Creole know that Sonny was in the water.

And, while Creole listened, Sonny moved, deep within, exactly like someone in torment. I had never before thought of how awful the relationship must be between the musician and his instrument. He has to fill it, this instrument, with the breath of life, his own. He has to make it do what he wants it to do. And a piano is just a piano. It's made out of so much wood and wires and little hammers and big ones, and ivory. While there's only so much you can do with it, the only way to find this out is to try and make it do everything.

And Sonny hadn't been near a piano for over a year. And he wasn't on much better terms with his life, not the life that stretched before him now. He and the piano stammered, started one way, got scared, stopped; started another way, panicked, marked time, started again; then seemed to have found a direction, panicked again, got stuck. And the face I saw on Sonny I'd never seen before. Everything had been burned out of it, and, at the same time, things usually hidden were being burned in, by the fire and fury of the battle which was occurring in him up there.

Yet, watching Creole's face as they neared the end of the first set, I had the feeling that something had happened, something I hadn't heard. Then they finished, there was scattered applause, and then, without an instant's warning, Creole started into something else, it was almost sardonic, it was *Am I Blue*. And, as though he commanded, Sonny began to play. Something began to happen. And Creole let out the reins. The dry, low, black man said something awful on the drums, Creole answered, and the drums talked back. Then the horn insisted, sweet and high, slightly detached perhaps, and Creole listened, commenting now and then, dry, and driving, beautiful and calm and old. Then they all came together again, and Sonny was part of the family again. I could tell this from his face. He seemed to have found, right there beneath his fingers, a damn brand-new piano. It seemed that he couldn't get over it. Then, for awhile, just being happy with Sonny, they seemed to be agreeing with him that brand-new pianos certainly were a gas.

Then Creole stepped forward to remind them that what they were playing was the blues. He hit something in all of them, he hit something in me, myself, and the music tightened and deepened, apprehension began to beat the air. Creole began to tell us what the blues were all about. They were not about anything very new. He and his boys up there were keeping it new, at the risk of ruin, destruction, madness, and death, in order to find new ways to make us listen. For, while the tale of how we suffer, and how we are delighted, and how we may triumph is never new, it always must be heard. There isn't any other tale to tell, it's the only light we've got in all this darkness.

And this tale, according to that face, that body, those strong hands on those strings, has another aspect in every country, and a new depth in every generation. Listen, Creole seemed to be saying, listen. Now these are Sonny's blues. He made the little black man on the drums know it, and the bright, brown man on the horn. Creole wasn't trying any longer to get Sonny in the water. He was wishing him Godspeed. Then he stepped back, very slowly, filling the air with the immense suggestion that Sonny speak for himself.

Then they all gathered around Sonny and Sonny played. Every now and again one of them seemed to say, Amen. Sonny's fingers filled the air with life, his life. But that life contained so many others. And Sonny went all the way back, he really began with the spare, flat statement of the opening phrase of the song. Then he began to make it his. It was very beautiful because it wasn't hurried and it was no longer a lament. I seemed to hear with what burning he had made it his, with what burning we had yet to make it ours, how we could cease lamenting. Freedom lurked around us and I understood, at last, that he could help us to be free if we would listen, that he would never be free until we did. Yet, there was no battle in his face now. I heard what he had gone through, and would continue to go through until he came to rest in earth. He had made it his: that long line, of which we knew only Mama and Daddy. And he was giving it back, as everything must be given back, so that, passing through death, it can live forever. I saw my mother's face again, and felt, for the first time, how the stones of the road she had walked on must have bruised her feet. I saw the moonlit road where my father's brother died. And it brought something else back to me, and carried me past it, I saw my little girl again and felt Isabel's tears again, and I felt my own tears begin to rise. And I was yet aware that this was only a moment, that the world waited outside, as hungry as a tiger, and that trouble stretched above us, longer than the sky.

Then it was over. Creole and Sonny let out their breath, both soaking wet, and grinning. There was a lot of applause and some of it was real. In the dark, the girl came by and I asked her to take drinks to the bandstand. There was a long pause, while they talked up there in the indigo light and after awhile I saw the girl put a Scotch and milk on top of the piano for Sonny. He didn't seem to notice it, but just before they started playing again, he sipped from it and looked toward me, and nodded. Then he put it back on top of the piano. For me, then, as they began to play again, it glowed and shook above my brother's head like the very cup of trembling.

Children on Their Birthdays

TRUMAN CAPOTE

(1924–   )

Yesterday afternoon the six-o'clock bus ran over Miss Bobbit. I'm not sure what there is to be said about it; after all, she was only ten years old, still I know no one of us in this town will forget her. For one thing, nothing she ever did was ordinary, not from the first time that we saw her, and that was a year ago. Miss Bobbit and her mother, they arrived on that same six-o'clock bus, the one that comes through from Mobile. It happened to be my cousin Billy Bob's birthday, and so most of the children in town were here at our house. We were sprawled on the front porch having tutti-frutti and devil cake when the bus stormed around Deadman's Curve. It was the summer that never rained; rusted dryness coated everything; sometimes when a car passed on the road, raised dust would hang in the still air an hour or more. Aunt El said if they didn't pave the highway soon she was going to move down to the seacoast; but she'd said that for such a long time. Anyway, we were sitting on the porch, tutti-frutti melting on our plates, when suddenly, just as we were wishing that something would happen, something did, for out of the red road dust appeared Miss Bobbit. A wiry little girl in a starched, lemon-colored party dress, she sassed along with a grownup mince, one hand on her hip, the other supporting a spinsterish umbrella. Her mother, lugging two cardboard valises and a wind-up victrola, trailed in the background. She was a gaunt shaggy woman with silent eyes and a hungry smile.

All the children on the porch had grown so still that when a cone of wasps started humming the girls did not set up their usual holler. Their attention was too fixed upon the approach of Miss Bobbit and her mother, who had by now reached the gate. "Begging your pardon," called Miss Bobbit in a voice that was at once silky and childlike, like a pretty piece of ribbon, and immaculately exact, like a movie-star or a schoolmarm, "but might we speak with the grownup persons of the house?" This, of course, meant Aunt El; and, at least to some degree, myself. But Billy Bob and all the other boys, no one of whom was over thirteen, followed down to the gate after us. From their faces you would have thought they'd never seen a girl before. Certainly not like Miss Bobbit. As Aunt El said, whoever heard tell of a child wearing make-up? Tangee gave her lips an orange glow, her hair, rather like a costume wig, was a mass of rosy curls, and her eyes had a knowing, penciled tilt; even so, she had a skinny dignity, she was a lady, and, what is more, she looked you in the eye with manlike directness. "I'm Miss Lily Jane Bobbit, Miss Bobbit from Memphis, Tennessee," she said solemnly. The boys looked down at their toes, and, on the porch, Cora McCall, who Billy Bob was courting at the time, led the girls into a fanfare of giggles. "*Country* children," said Miss Bobbit with an understanding smile, and gave her parasol a saucy whirl. "My mother," and this homely woman allowed an abrupt nod to acknowledge herself, "my mother and I have taken rooms here. Would you be so kind as to point out the house? It belongs to a Mrs. Sawyer." Why, sure, said Aunt El, that's Mrs. Sawyer's, right there across the street. The only boarding house around here, it is an old tall dark place with about two dozen lightning rods scattered on the roof: Mrs. Sawyer is scared to death in a thunderstorm.

Coloring like an apple, Billy Bob said, please ma'am, it being such a hot day and all, wouldn't they rest a spell and have some tutti-frutti? and Aunt El said yes, by all means, but Miss Bobbit shook her head. "Very fattening, tutti-frutti; but *merci* you kindly," and they started across the road, the mother half-dragging her parcels in the dust. Then, and with an earnest expression, Miss Bobbit turned back; the sunflower yellow of her eyes darkened, and she rolled them slightly sideways, as if trying to remember a poem. "My mother has a disorder of the tongue, so it is necessary that I speak for her," she announced rapidly and heaved a sigh. "My mother is a very fine seamstress; she has made dresses for the society of many cities and towns, including Memphis and Tallahassee. No doubt you have noticed and admired the dress I am wearing. Every stitch of it was hand-sewn by my mother. My mother can copy any pattern, and just recently she won a twenty-five-dollar prize from the *Ladies' Home Journal*. My mother can also crochet, knit and embroider. If you want any kind of sewing done, please come to my mother. Please advise your friends and family. Thank you." And then, with a rustle and a swish, she was gone.

Cora McCall and the girls pulled their hair-ribbons nervously, suspiciously, and looked very put out and prune-faced. I'm *Miss* Bobbit, said Cora, twisting her face into an evil imitation, and I'm Princess Elizabeth, that's who I am, ha, ha, ha. Furthermore, said Cora, that dress was just as tacky as could be; personally, Cora said, all my clothes come from Atlanta; plus a pair of shoes from New York, which is not even to mention my silver turquoise ring all the way from Mexico City, Mexico. Aunt El said they ought not to behave that way about a fellow child, a stranger in the town, but the girls went on like a huddle of witches, and certain boys, the sillier ones that liked to be with the girls, joined in and said things that made Aunt El go red and declare she was going to send them all home and tell their daddies, to boot. But before she could carry forward this threat Miss Bobbit herself intervened by traipsing across the Sawyer porch, costumed in a new and startling manner.

The older boys, like Billy Bob and Preacher Star, who had sat quiet while the girls razzed Miss Bobbit, and who had watched the house into which she'd disappeared with misty, ambitious faces, they now straightened up and ambled down to the gate. Cora McCall sniffed and poked out her lower lip, but the rest of us went and sat on the steps. Miss Bobbit paid us no mind whatever. The Sawyer yard is dark with mulberry trees and it is planted with grass and sweet shrub. Sometimes after a rain you can smell the sweet shrub all the way into our house; and in the center of this yard there is a sundial which Mrs. Sawyer installed in 1912 as a memorial to her Boston bull, Sunny, who died after having lapped up a bucket of paint. Miss Bobbit pranced into the yard toting the victrola, which she put on the sundial; she wound it up, and started a record playing, and it played the Count of Luxemborg. By now it was almost nightfall, a firefly hour, blue as milkglass; and birds like arrows swooped together and swept into the folds of trees. Before storms, leaves and flowers appear to burn with a private light, color, and Miss Bobbit, got up in a little white skirt like a powderpuff and with strips of gold-glittering tinsel ribboning her hair, seemed, set against the darkening all around, to contain this illuminated quality. She held her arms arched over her head, her hands lily-limp, and stood straight up on the tips of her toes. She stood that way for a good long while, and Aunt El said it was right smart of her. Then she began to waltz around and around, and around and around she went until Aunt El said, why, she was plain dizzy from the sight. She stopped only when it was time to re-wind the victrola; and when the moon came rolling down the ridge, and the last supper bell had sounded, and all the children had gone home, and the night iris was beginning to bloom, Miss Bobbit was still there in the dark turning like a top.

We did not see her again for some time. Preacher Star came every morning to our house and stayed straight through to supper. Preacher is a rail-thin boy with a butchy shock of red hair; he has eleven brothers and sisters, and even they are afraid of him, for he has a terrible temper, and is famous in these parts for his green-eyed meanness: last fourth of July he whipped Ollie Overton so bad that Ollie's family had to send him to the hospital in Pensacola; and there was another time he bit off half a mule's ear, chewed it and spit it on the ground. Before Billy Bob got his growth, Preacher played the devil with him, too. He used to drop cockleburrs down his collar, and rub pepper in his eyes, and tear up his homework. But now they are the biggest friends in town: talk alike, walk alike; and occasionally they disappear together for whole days, Lord knows where to. But during these days when Miss Bobbit did not appear they stayed close to the house. They would stand around in the yard trying to slingshot sparrows off telephone poles; or sometimes Billy Bob would play his ukulele, and they would sing so loud Uncle Billy Bob, who is Judge for this county, claimed he could hear them all the way to the courthouse: *send me a letter, send it by mail, send it in care of the Birming-ham jail.* Miss Bobbit did not hear them; at least she never poked her head out the door. Then one day Mrs. Sawyer, coming over to borrow a cup of sugar, rattled on a good deal about her new boarders. You know, she said, squinting her chicken-bright eyes, the husband was a crook, uh huh, the child told me herself. Hasn't an ounce of shame, not a mite. Said her daddy was the dearest daddy and the sweetest singing man in the whole of Tennessee. . . . And I said, honey, where is he? and just as offhand as you please she says, Oh, he's in the penitentiary and we don't hear from him no more. Say, now, does that make your blood run cold? Uh huh, and I been thinking, her mama, I been thinking she's some kinda foreigner: never says a word, and sometimes it looks like she don't understand what nobody says to her. And you know, they eat everything *raw. Raw* eggs, *raw* turnips, carrots—no meat whatsoever. For reasons of health, the child says, but ho! she's been straight out on the bed running a fever since last Tuesday.

That same afternoon Aunt El went out to water her roses, only to discover them gone. These were special roses, ones she'd planned to send to the flower show in Mobile, and so naturally she got a little hysterical. She rang up the Sheriff, and said, listen here, Sheriff, you come over here right fast. I mean somebody's got off with all my Lady Annes that I've devoted myself to heart and soul since early spring. When the Sheriff's car pulled up outside our house, all the neighbors along the street came out on their porches, and Mrs. Sawyer, layers of cold cream whitening her face, trotted across the road. Oh shoot, she said, very disappointed to find no one had been murdered, oh shoot, she said, nobody's stole them roses. Your Billy Bob brought them roses over and left them for little Bobbit. Aunt El did not say one word. She just marched over to the peach tree, and cut herself a switch. Ohhh, Billy Bob, she stalked along the street calling his name, and then she found him down at Speedy's garage where he and Preacher were watching Speedy take a motor apart. She simply lifted him by the hair and, switching blueblazes, towed him home. But she couldn't make him say he was sorry and she couldn't make him cry. And when she was finished with him he ran into the backyard and climbed high into the tower of a pecan tree and swore he wasn't ever going to come down. Then his daddy came home, and it was time to have supper. His daddy stood at the window and called to him: Son, we aren't mad with you, so come down and eat your supper. But Billy Bob wouldn't budge. Aunt El went and leaned against the tree. She spoke in a voice soft as the gathering light. I'm sorry, son, she said, I didn't mean whipping you so hard like that. I've fixed a nice supper, son, potato salad and boiled ham and deviled eggs. Go away, said Billy Bob, I don't want no supper, and I hate you like all-fire. His daddy said he ought not to talk like that to his mother, and she began to cry. She stood there under the tree and cried, raising the hem of her skirt to dab at her eyes. I don't hate you, son. . . . If I didn't love you I wouldn't whip you. The pecan leaves began to rattle; Billy Bob slid slowly to the ground, and Aunt El, rushing her fingers through his hair, pulled him against her. Aw, Ma, he said, Aw, Ma.

After supper Billy Bob came and flung himself on the foot of my bed. He smelled all sour and sweet, the way boys do, and I felt very sorry for him, especially because he looked so worried. His eyes were almost shut with worry. You're s'posed to send sick folks flowers, he said righteously. About this time we heard the victrola, a lilting faraway sound, and a night moth flew through the window, drifting in the air delicate as the music. But it was dark now, and we couldn't tell if Miss Bobbit was dancing. Billy Bob, as though he were in pain, doubled up on the bed like a jackknife; but his face was suddenly clear, his grubby boy-eyes twitching like candles. She's so cute, he whispered, she's the cutest dickens I ever saw, gee, to hell with it, I don't care, I'd pick all the roses in China.

Preacher would have picked all the roses in China, too. He was as crazy about her as Billy Bob. But Miss Bobbit did not notice them. The sole communication we had with her was a note to Aunt El thanking her for the flowers. Day after day she sat on her porch, always dressed to beat the band, and doing a piece of embroidery, or combing curls in her hair, or reading a Webster's dictionary—formal, but friendly enough; if you said good-day to her she said good-day to you. Even so, the boys never could seem to get up the nerve to go over and talk with her, and most of the time she simply looked through them, even when they tomcatted up and down the street trying to get her eye. They wrestled, played Tarzan, did foolheaded bicycle tricks. It was a sorry business. A great many girls in town strolled by the Sawyer house two and three times within an hour just on the chance of getting a look. Some of the girls who did this were: Cora McCall, Mary Murphy Jones, Janice Ackerman. Miss Bobbit did not show any interest in them either. Cora would not speak to Billy Bob any more. The same was true with Janice and Preacher. As a matter of fact, Janice wrote Preacher a letter in red ink on lace-trimmed paper in which she told him he was vile beyond all human beings and words, that she considered their engagement broken, that he could have back the stuffed squirrel he'd given her. Preacher, saying he wanted to act nice, stopped her the next time she passed our house, and said, well, hell, she could keep that old squirrel if she wanted to. Afterwards, he couldn't understand why Janice ran away bawling the way she did.

Then one day the boys were being crazier than usual; Billy Bob was sagging around in his daddy's World War khakis, and Preacher, stripped to the waist, had a naked woman drawn on his chest with one of Aunt El's old lipsticks. They looked like perfect fools, but Miss Bobbit, reclining in a swing, merely yawned. It was noon, and there was no one passing in the street, except a colored girl, baby-fat and sugar-plum shaped, who hummed along carrying a pail of blackberries. But the boys, teasing at her like gnats, joined hands and wouldn't let her go by, not until she paid a tariff. I ain't studyin' no tariff, she said, what kinda tariff you talkin' about, mister? A party in the barn, said Preacher, between clenched teeth, mighty nice party in the barn. And she, with a sulky shrug, said, huh, she intended studyin' no barn parties. Whereupon Billy Bob capsized her berry pail, and when she, with despairing, piglike shrieks, bent down in futile gestures of rescue, Preacher, who can be mean as the devil, gave her behind a kick which sent her sprawling jellylike among the blackberries and the dust. Miss Bobbit came tearing across the road, her finger wagging like a metronome; like a schoolteacher she clapped her hands, stamped her foot, said: "It is a well-known fact that gentlemen are put on the face of this earth for the protection of ladies. Do you suppose boys behave this way in towns like Memphis, New York, London, Hollywood or Paris?" The boys hung back, and shoved their hands in their pockets. Miss Bobbit helped the colored girl to her feet; she dusted her off, dried her eyes, held out a handkerchief and told her to blow. "A pretty pass," she said, "a fine situation when a lady can't walk safely in the public daylight."

Then the two of them went back and sat on Mrs. Sawyer's porch; and for the next year they were never far apart, Miss Bobbit and this baby elephant, whose name was Rosalba Cat. At first, Mrs. Sawyer raised a fuss about Rosalba being so much at her house. She told Aunt El that it went against the grain to have a nigger lolling smack there in plain sight on her front porch. But Miss Bobbit had a certain magic, whatever she did she did it with completeness, and so directly, so solemnly, that there was nothing to do but accept it. For instance, the tradespeople in town used to snicker when they called her *Miss* Bobbit; but by and by she was Miss Bobbit, and they gave her stiff little bows as she whirled by spinning her parasol. Miss Bobbit told everyone that Rosalba was her sister, which caused a good many jokes; but like most of her ideas, it gradually seemed natural, and when we would overhear them calling each other Sister Rosalba and Sister Bobbit none of us cracked a smile. But Sister Rosalba and Sister Bobbit did some queer things. There was the business about the dogs. Now there are a great many dogs in this town, rat-terriers, bird-dogs, bloodhounds; they trail along the forlorn noon-hot streets in sleepy herds of six to a dozen, all waiting only for dark and the moon, when straight through the lonesome hours you can hear them howling: someone is dying, someone is dead. Miss Bobbit complained to the Sheriff; she said that certain of the dogs always planted themselves under her window, and that she was a light sleeper to begin with; what is more, and as Sister Rosalba said, she did not believe they were dogs at all, but some kind of devil. Naturally the Sheriff did nothing; and so she took the matter into her own hands. One morning, after an especially loud night, she was seen stalking through the town with Rosalba at her side, Rosalba carrying a flower basket filled with rocks; whenever they saw a dog they paused while Miss Bobbit scrutinized him. Sometimes she would shake her head, but more often she said, "Yes, that's one of them, Sister Rosalba," and Sister Rosalba, with ferocious aim, would take a rock from her basket and crack the dog between the eyes.

Another thing that happened concerns Mr. Henderson. Mr. Henderson has a back room in the Sawyer house; a tough runt of a man who formerly was a wildcat oil prospector in Oklahoma, he is about seventy years old and, like a lot of old men, obsessed by functions of the body. Also, he is a terrible drunk. One time he had been drunk for two weeks; whenever he heard Miss Bobbit and Sister Rosalba moving around the house, he would charge to the top of the stairs and bellow down to Mrs. Sawyer that there were midgets in the walls trying to get at his supply of toilet paper. They've already stolen fifteen cents' worth, he said. One evening, when the two girls were sitting under a tree in the yard, Mr. Henderson, sporting nothing more than a nightshirt, stamped out after them. Steal all my toilet paper, will you? he hollered, I'll show you midgets. . . . Somebody come help me, else these midget bitches are liable to make off with every sheet in town. It was Billy Bob and Preacher who caught Mr. Henderson and held him until some grown men arrived and began to tie him up. Miss Bobbit, who had behaved with admirable calm, told the men they did not know how to tie a proper knot, and undertook to do so herself. She did such a good job that all the circulation stopped in Mr. Henderson's hands and feet and it was a month before he could walk again.

It was shortly afterwards that Miss Bobbit paid us a call. She came on Sunday and I was there alone, the family having gone to church. "The odors of a church are so offensive," she said, leaning forward and with her hands folded primly before her. "I don't want you to think I'm a heathen, Mr. C.; I've had enough experience to know that there is a God and that there is a Devil. But the way to tame the Devil is not to go down there to church and listen to what a sinful mean fool he is. No, love the Devil like you love Jesus: because he is a powerful man, and will do you a good turn if he knows you trust him. He has frequently done me good turns, like at dancing school in Memphis. . . . I always called in the Devil to help me get the biggest part in our annual show. That is common sense; you see, I knew Jesus wouldn't have any truck with dancing. Now, as a matter of fact, I have called in the Devil just recently. He is the only one who can help me get out of this town. Not that I live here, not exactly. I think always about somewhere else, somewhere else where everything is dancing, like people dancing in the streets, and everything is pretty, like children on their birthdays. My precious papa said I live in the sky, but if he'd lived more in the sky he'd be rich like he wanted to be. The trouble with my papa was he did not love the Devil, he let the Devil love him. But I am very smart in that respect; I know the next best thing is very often the best. It was the next best thing for us to move to this town; and since I can't pursue my career here, the next best thing for me is to start a little business on the side. Which is what I have done. I am sole subscription agent in this county for an impressive list of magazines, including *Reader's Digest, Popular Mechanics, Dime Detective* and *Child's*

Life. To be sure, Mr. C., I'm not here to sell you anything. But I have a thought in mind. I was thinking those two boys that are always hanging around here, it occurred to me that they are men, after all. Do you suppose they would make a pair of likely assistants?"

Billy Bob and Preacher worked hard for Miss Bobbit, and for Sister Rosalba, too. Sister Rosalba carried a line of cosmetics called Dewdrop, and it was part of the boys' job to deliver purchases to her customers. Billy Bob used to be so tired in the evening he could hardly chew his supper. Aunt El said it was a shame and a pity, and finally one day when Billy Bob came down with a touch of sunstroke she said, all right, that settled it, Billy Bob would just have to quit Miss Bobbit. But Billy Bob cussed her out until his daddy had to lock him in his room; whereupon he said he was going to kill himself. Some cook we'd had told him once that if you ate a mess of collards all slopped over with molasses it would kill you sure as shooting; and so that is what he did. I'm dying, he said, rolling back and forth on his bed, I'm dying and nobody cares.

Miss Bobbit came over and told him to hush up. "There's nothing wrong with you, boy," she said. "All you've got is a stomach ache." Then she did something that shocked Aunt El very much: she stripped the covers off Billy Bob and rubbed him down with alcohol from head to toe. When Aunt El told her she did not think that was a nice thing for a little girl to do, Miss Bobbit replied: "I don't know whether it's nice or not, but it's certainly very refreshing." After which Aunt El did all she could to keep Billy Bob from going back to work for her, but his daddy said to leave him alone, they would have to let the boy lead his own life.

Miss Bobbit was very honest about money. She paid Billy Bob and Preacher their exact commission, and she would never let them treat her, as they often tried to do, at the drugstore or to the picture-show. "You'd better save your money," she told them. "That is, if you want to go to college. Because neither one of you has got the brains to win a scholarship, not even a football scholarship." But it was over money that Billy Bob and Preacher had a big falling out; that was not the real reason, of course: the real reason was that they had grown cross-eyed jealous over Miss Bobbit. So one day, and he had the gall to do this right in front of Billy Bob, Preacher said to Miss Bobbit that she'd better check her accounts carefully because he had more than a suspicion that Billy Bob wasn't turning over to her *all* the money he collected. That's a damned lie, said Billy Bob, and with a clean left hook he knocked Preacher off the Sawyer porch and jumped after him into a bed of nasturtiums. But once Preacher *got* a hold on him, Billy Bob didn't stand a chance. Preacher even rubbed dirt in his eyes. During all this, Mrs. Sawyer, leaning out an upper-story window, screamed like an eagle, and Sister Rosalba, fatly cheerful, ambiguously shouted, Kill him! Kill him! Kill him! Only Miss Bobbit seemed to know what she was doing. She plugged in the lawn hose, and gave the boys a closeup, blinding bath. Gasping, Preacher staggered to his feet. Oh, honey, he said, shaking himself like a wet dog, honey, you've got to decide. "Decide *what?*" said Miss Bobbit, right away in a huff. Oh, honey, wheezed Preacher, you don't want us boys killing each other. You got to decide who is your real true sweetheart. "Sweetheart, my eye," said Miss Bobbit. "I should've known better than to get myself involved with a lot of country children. What sort of businessman are you going to make? Now, you listen here, Preacher Star: I don't want a sweetheart, and if I did, it wouldn't be you. As a matter of fact, you don't even get up when a lady enters the room."

Preacher spit on the ground and swaggered over to Billy Bob. Come on, he said, just as though nothing had happened, she's a hard one, she is, she don't want nothing but to make trouble between two good friends. For a moment it looked as if Billy Bob was going to join him in a peaceful togetherness; but suddenly, coming to his senses, he drew back and made a gesture. The boys regarded each other a full minute, all the closeness between them turning an ugly color: you can't hate so much unless you love, too. And Preacher's face showed all of this. But there was nothing for him to do except go away. Oh, yes, Preacher, you looked so lost that day that for the first time I really liked you, so skinny and mean and lost going down the road all by yourself.

They did not make it up, Preacher and Billy Bob; and it was not because they didn't want to, it was only that there did not seem to be any straight way for their friendship to happen again. But they couldn't get rid of this friendship: each was always aware of what the other was up to; and when Preacher found himself a new buddy, Billy Bob moped around for days, picking things up, dropping them again, or doing sudden wild things, like purposely poking his finger in the electric fan. Sometimes in the evenings Preacher would pause by the gate and talk with Aunt El. It was only to torment Billy Bob, I suppose, but he stayed friendly with all of us, and at Christmas time he gave us a huge box of shelled peanuts. He left a present for Billy Bob, too. It turned out to be a book of Sherlock Holmes; and on the flyleaf there was scribbled, "Friends Like Ivy On The Wall Must Fall." That's the corniest thing I ever saw, Billy Bob said. Jesus, what a dope he is! But then, and though it was a cold winter day, he went in the backyard and climbed up into the pecan tree, crouching there all afternoon in the blue December branches.

But most of the time he was happy, because Miss Bobbit was there, and she was always sweet to him now. She and Sister Rosalba treated him like a man; that is to say, they allowed him to do everything for them. On the other hand, they let him win at three-handed bridge, they never questioned his lies, nor discouraged his ambitions. It was a happy while. However, trouble started again when school began. Miss Bobbit refused to go. "It's ridiculous," she said, when one day the principal, Mr. Copland, came around to investigate, "really ridiculous; I can read and write and there are *some* people in this town who have every reason to know that I can count money. No, Mr. Copland, consider for a moment and you will see neither of us has the time nor energy. After all, it would only be a matter of whose spirit broke first, yours or mine. And besides, what is there for you to teach me? Now, if you knew anything about dancing, that would be another matter; but under the circumstances, yes, Mr. Copland, under the circumstances, I suggest we forget the whole thing." Mr. Copland was perfectly willing to. But the rest of the town thought she ought to be whipped. Horace Deasley wrote a piece in the paper which was titled "A Tragic Situation." It was, in his opinion, a tragic situation when a small girl could defy what he, for some reason, termed the Constitution of the United States. The article ended with a question: *Can she get away with it?* She did; and so did Sister Rosalba. Only she was colored, so no one cared. Billy Bob was not as lucky. It was school for him, all right; but he might as well have stayed home for the good it did him. On his first report card he got three F's, a record of some sort. But he is a smart boy. I guess he just couldn't live through those hours without Miss Bobbit; away from her he always seemed half-asleep. He was always in a fight, too; either his eye was black, or his lip was split, or his walk had a limp. He never talked about these fights, but Miss Bobbit was shrewd enough to guess the reason why. "You are a dear, I know, I know. And I appreciate you, Billy Bob. Only don't fight with people because of me. Of course they say mean things about me. But do you know why that is, Billy Bob? It's a compliment, kind of. Because deep down they think I'm absolutely wonderful."

And she was right: if you are not admired no one will take the trouble to disapprove. But actually we had no idea of how wonderful she was until there appeared the man known as Manny Fox. This happened late in February. The first news we had of Manny Fox was a series of jovial placards posted up in the stores around town: Manny Fox Presents the Fan Dancer Without the Fan; then, in smaller print: Also, Sensational Amateur Program Featuring Your Own Neighbors—First Prize, A Genuine Hollywood Screen Test. All this was to take place the following Thursday. The tickets were priced at one dollar each, which around here is a lot of money; but it is not often that we get any kind of flesh entertainment, so everybody shelled out their money and made a great todo over the whole thing. The drugstore cowboys talked dirty all week, mostly about the fan dancer without the fan, who turned out to be Mrs. Manny Fox. They stayed down the highway at the Chucklewood Tourist Camp; but they were in town all day, driving around in an old Packard which had Manny Fox's full name stenciled on all four doors. His wife was a deadpan pimento-tongued redhead with wet lips and moist eyelids; she was quite large actually, but compared to Manny Fox she seemed rather frail, for he was a fat cigar of a man.

They made the pool hall their headquarters, and every afternoon you could find them there, drinking beer and joking with the town loafs. As it developed, Manny Fox's business affairs were not restricted to theatrics. He also ran a kind of employment bureau: slowly he let it be known that for a fee of $150 he could get for any adventurous boys in the county high-class jobs working on fruit ships sailing from New Orleans to South America. The chance of a lifetime, he called it. There are not two boys around here who readily lay their hands on so much as five dollars; nevertheless, a good dozen managed to raise the money. Ada Willingham took all she'd saved to buy an angel tombstone for her husband and gave it to her son, and Acey Trump's papa sold an option on his cotton crop.

But the night of the show! That was a night when all was forgotten: mortgages, and the dishes in the kitchen sink. Aunt El said you'd think we were going to the opera, everybody so dressed up, so pink and sweet-smelling. The Odeon had not been so full since the night they gave away the matched set of sterling silver. Practically everybody had a relative in the show, so there was a lot of nervousness to contend with. Miss Bobbit was the only contestant we knew real well. Billy Bob couldn't sit still; he kept telling us over and over that we mustn't applaud for anybody but Miss Bobbit; Aunt El said that would be very rude, which sent Billy Bob off into a state again; and when his father bought us all bags of popcorn he wouldn't touch his because it would make his hands greasy, and please, another thing, we mustn't be noisy and eat ours while Miss Bobbit was performing. That she was to be a contestant had come as a last-minute surprise. It was logical enough, and there were signs that should've told us; the fact, for instance, that she had not set foot outside the Sawyer house in how many days? And the victrola going half the night, her shadow whirling on the windowshade, and the secret, stuffed look on Sister Rosalba's face whenever asked after Sister Bobbit's health. So there was her name on the program, listed second, in fact, though she did not appear for a long while. First came Manny Fox, greased and leering, who told a lot of peculiar jokes, clapping his hands, ha, ha. Aunt El said if he told another joke like that she was going to walk straight out: he did, and she didn't. Before Miss Bobbit came on there were eleven contestants, including Eustacia Bernstein, who imitated movie stars so that they all sounded like Eustacia, and there was an extraordinary Mr. Buster Riley, a jug-eared old wool-hat from way in the back country who played "Waltzing Matilda" on a saw. Up to that point, he was the hit of the show; not that there was any marked difference in the various receptions, for everybody applauded generously, everybody, that is, except Preacher Star. He was sitting two rows ahead of us, greeting each act with a donkey-loud boo. Aunt El said she was never going to speak to him again. The only person he ever applauded was Miss Bobbit. No doubt the Devil was on her side, but she deserved it. Out she came, tossing her hips, her curls, rolling her eyes. You could tell right away it wasn't going to be one of her classical numbers. She tapped across the stage, daintily holding up the sides of a cloud-blue skirt. That's the cutest thing I ever saw, said Billy Bob, smacking his thigh, and Aunt El had to agree that Miss Bobbit looked real sweet. When she started to twirl the whole audience broke into spontaneous applause; so she did it all over again, hissing, "Faster, faster," at poor Miss Adelaide, who was at the piano doing her Sunday-school best. "I was born in China, and raised in Jay-pan . . ." We had never heard her sing before, and she had a rowdy sandpaper voice. ". . . if you don't like my peaches, stay away from my can, o-ho o-ho!" Aunt El gasped; she gasped again when Miss Bobbit, with a bump, up-ended her skirt to display blue-lace underwear, thereby collecting most of the whistles the boys had been saving for the fan dancer without the fan, which was just as well, as it later turned out, for that lady, to the tune of "An Apple for the Teacher" and cries of gyp gyp, did her routine attired in a bathing suit. But showing off her bottom was not Miss Bobbit's final triumph. Miss Adelaide commenced an ominous thundering in the darker keys, at which point Sister Rosalba, carrying a lighted Roman candle, rushed onstage and handed it to Miss Bobbit, who was in the midst of a full split; she made it, too, and just as she did the Roman candle burst into fiery balls of red, white and blue, and we all had to stand up because she was singing "The Star Spangled Banner" at the top of her lungs. Aunt El said afterwards that it was one of the most gorgeous things she'd ever seen on the American stage.

Well, she surely did deserve a Hollywood screen test and, inasmuch as she won the contest, it looked as though she were going to get it. Manny Fox said she was: honey, he said, you're real star stuff. Only he skipped town the next day, leaving nothing but hearty promises. Watch the mails, my friends, you'll all be hearing from me. That is what he said to the boys whose money he'd taken, and that is what he said to Miss Bobbit. There are three deliveries daily, and this sizable group gathered at the post office for all of them, a jolly crowd growing gradually joyless. How their hands trembled when a letter slid into their mailbox. A terrible hush came over them as the days passed. They all knew what the other was thinking, but no one could bring himself to say it, not even Miss Bobbit. Postmistress Patterson said it plainly, however: the man's a crook, she said, I knew he was a crook to begin with, and if I have to look at your faces one more day I'll shoot myself.

Finally, at the end of two weeks, it was Miss Bobbit who broke the spell. Her eyes had grown more vacant than anyone had ever supposed they might, but one day, after the last mail was up, all her old sizzle came back. "O.k., boys, it's lynch law now," she said, and proceeded to herd the whole troupe home with her. This was the first meeting of the Manny Fox Hangman's Club, an organization which, in a more social form, endures to this day, though Manny Fox has long since been caught and, so to say, hung. Credit for this went quite properly to Miss Bobbit. Within a week she'd written over three hundred descriptions of Manny Fox and dispatched them to Sheriffs throughout the South; she also wrote letters to papers in the larger cities, and these attracted wide attention. As a result, four of the robbed boys were offered good-paying jobs by the United Fruit Company, and late this spring, when Manny Fox was arrested in Uphigh, Arkansas, where he was pulling the same old dodge, Miss Bobbit was presented with a Good Deed Merit award from the Sunbeam Girls of America. For some reason, she made a point of letting the world know that this did not exactly thrill her. "I do not approve of the organization," she said. "All that rowdy bugle blowing. It's neither good-hearted nor truly feminine. And anyway, what is a good deed? Don't let anybody fool you, a good deed is something you do because you want something in return." It would be reassuring to report she was wrong, and that her just reward, when at last it came, was given out of kindness and love. However, this is not the case. About a week ago the boys involved in the swindle all received from Manny Fox checks covering their losses, and Miss Bobbit, with clodhopping determination, stalked into a meeting of the Hangman's Club, which is now an excuse for drinking beer and playing poker every Thursday night. "Look, boys," she said, laying it on the line, "none of you ever thought to see that money again, but now that you have, you ought to invest it in something practical—like me." The proposition was that they should pool their money and finance her trip to Hollywood; in return, they would get ten percent of her life's earnings which, after she was a star, and that would not be very long, would make them all rich men. "At least," as she said, "in this part of the country." Not one of the boys wanted to do it: but when Miss Bobbit looked at you, what was there to say?

Since Monday, it has been raining buoyant summer rain shot through with sun, but dark at night and full of sound, full of dripping leaves, watery chimings, sleepless scuttlings. Billy Bob is wide-awake, dry-eyed, though everything he does is a little frozen and his tongue is as stiff as a bell tongue. It has not been easy for him, Miss Bobbit's going. Because she'd meant more than that. Than what? Than being thirteen years old and crazy in love. She was the queer things in him, like the pecan tree and liking books and caring enough about people to let them hurt him. She was the things he was afraid to show anyone else. And in the dark the music trickled through the rain: won't there be nights when we will hear it just as though it were really there? And afternoons when the shadows will be all at once confused, and she will pass before us, unfurling across the lawn like a pretty piece of ribbon? She laughed to Billy Bob; she held his hand, she even kissed him. "I'm not going to die," she said. "You'll come out there, and we'll climb a mountain, and we'll all live there together, you and me and Sister Rosalba." But Billy Bob knew it would never happen that way, and so when the music came through the dark he would stuff the pillow over his head.

Only there was a strange smile about yesterday, and that was the day she was leaving. Around noon the sun came out, bringing with it into the air all the sweetness of wisteria. Aunt El's yellow Lady Annes were blooming again, and she did something wonderful, she told Billy Bob he could pick them and give them to Miss Bobbit for good-bye. All afternoon Miss Bobbit sat on the porch surrounded by people who stopped by to wish her well. She looked as though she were going to Communion, dressed in white and with a white parasol. Sister Rosalba had given her a handkerchief, but she had to borrow it back because she couldn't stop blubbering. Another little girl brought a baked chicken, presumably to be eaten on the bus; the only trouble was she'd forgotten to take out the insides before cooking it. Miss Bobbit's mother said that was all right by her, chicken was chicken; which is memorable because it is the single opinion she ever voiced. There was only one sour note. For hours Preacher Star had been hanging around down at the corner, sometimes standing at the curb tossing a coin, and sometimes hiding behind a tree, as if he didn't want anyone to see him. It made everybody nervous. About twenty minutes before bus time he sauntered up and leaned against our gate. Billy Bob was still in the garden picking roses; by now he had enough for a bonfire, and their smell was as heavy as wind. Preacher stared at him until he lifted his head. As they looked at each other the rain began again, falling fine as sea spray and colored by a rainbow. Without a word, Preacher went over and started helping Billy Bob separate the roses into two giant bouquets: together they carried them to the curb. Across the street there were bumblebees of talk, but when Miss Bobbit saw them, two boys whose flower-masked faces were like yellow moons, she rushed down the steps, her arms outstretched. You could see what was going to happen; and we called out, our voices like lightning in the rain, but Miss Bobbit, running toward those moons of roses, did not seem to hear. That is when the six-o'clock bus ran over her.

The Last Voyage

TOM FILER

(1925–)

The first time, she lost her grip and he slid down the ladder to the deck below, where he lay spread-eagled, eyes wide and staring, mouth parted, as if he were about to cry out in protest.

She tried again. It was no use. She was strong but she was no match for the passive stubbornness of death. Finally she decided to use the winch. There seemed no way of doing it that did not outrage her senses, for this limp bundle had once been her husband. "They couldn't wait!" she cried. "Couldn't let us be!"

With a sudden impatience that verged on anger she roughly tied the line about his waist. She raised him, jackknifed, arms waving as though with a new life in the unlife, and set him down beside the gear box on the conn deck. Now she had to empty the box.

It contained a lot of fishing tackle, mostly new, but she came upon some moth-eaten lures that had been buried there and forgotten. Among them was one her husband had made. "Must of had some kind of magic, May," Ed often said, grinning. "Fish always hit it first, every time." And then May would remind him of her contribution to the lure: a red feather from the hat she had worn on their honeymoon. The joke grew old with them, never tired of, for it reminded them of that first voyage twenty-six years ago. The fish had chewed up most of their lures, and Ed, fresh out of "makin's," impulsively removed the feather without telling her, intending to replace it when they reached port. The next afternoon as May pulled in an albacore the barbless lure didn't snap loose and she had to remove it by hand. Instantly she recognized the feather. Ed had pleaded with her to start chumming the sardines before the school sounded, but May responded with an icy stare and went into the cabin.

Later when he tried to talk to her she retired silently to the chain locker, where she spent the night despite his repeated vows that he would buy her a dozen hats when they returned to San Diego. In the morning, her only problem was how to emerge without losing face.

Ed had solved this dilemma by shouting down to her that they were into a big school. She suspected a trick, but scrambled out of the locker when she heard the unmistakable thrashing of a fish on the deck above. Ed had grabbed her before she realized the "school" was a lone dolphin. With a cry of anger she fought him, but Ed held her so tightly the strength drained from her fists and thrusting knees, and the fool was laughing. His hard body, the pulsing engines and the soft rush of the parting sea, all seemed to envelop her as they tumbled to the deck. And then, with a fury that made her anger seem pale, she met him with a fierce joy.

There had been a son and she had been told there would be no more. And in her most secret self she was glad, for after that first voyage she had felt a need to be more than a mother, more than a wife to a man. There were four lonely years at home, and then Ed's partner walked out and May returned to the *Gull*. The child, Sonny, was left with Ed's parents during the school year, and the rest of the time he spent on the boat. And soon he was fishing with them and he had stayed with the *Gull* until he was twenty, until Ed sailed without him one July night. May had known the truth, of course. So had Sonny. Ed felt the *Gull* was too old and too slow to amount to much anymore, and while this no longer mattered much to him, Sonny was young.

Ed didn't fit very well in the box, but she found by raising his knees and lifting his head she could manage. She went below for ice.

His face, almost level with the rim of the box, could not be covered completely. The ice was neatly packed about him and the job was done except for this. She fought an almost uncontrollable urge to force the gaping face down, down into the blue whiteness of the ice. She lowered the lid, knowing she must return within the hour with more ice.

May switched on the radio transmitter in the cabin below. "Hello, *Sarah*. Hello, *Sarah* . . . this is the *Gull*, WCT3, calling. Hello, *Sarah* . . ."

She turned on the receiver. There was no reply. She tried again, until a voice came through.

"Hello, Ma. This is Sonny. Start talking so we can get another bearing on you. You may have drifted. Out."

"I did what they told me, Sonny," she said. "I've got to get back to packing the fish, so I don't have much time. Is there anything else I should do? Out."

"Okay, Ma, got a line on you. You better call every hour. Keep the engine idling so long as you got fuel or the radio'll poop out . . ." He seemed to hesitate. "Need it for the refrigeration too. Out."

"I turned the engine off after . . . after it happened," May replied. What could she tell him? There seemed to be some explanation due for this action, but she could think of nothing that would satisfy her son. "I'll start it again, Sonny. Out."

"Okay. Just sit tight now, Ma. We figure you're about thirty hours away from us. Coast Guard's on the way down from Dago but we should get there first. Take it easy. Everything'll be all right. Keep calling. The *Sarah* signing off."

May took off the earphones. She found herself listening, though she didn't know what for. Almost in a panic she climbed up the ladder to the open conn deck and started the engine. The muffler had gone out earlier in the season, and although the noise was almost unbearable at the wheel they had been too broke to replace it. Now she found herself grateful for the ear-shattering din. What had she been afraid of? Was it only the silence? She looked at her watch. In forty-five minutes she must get more ice. It was nearly dusk. The sun was a child's balloon floating, red, in the sea; a few stars flickered tentatively in the eastern sky.

On the fishing boat *Sarah* a young man was cursing. "I told him!" he cried. "Every goddamn year I told him, cut it out! I knew something'd happen sooner or later. What for? I asked him. The old bastard just grinned at me! They been in the red for five years. Couldn't even afford a lousy muffler this June. Stay home, I said! Then *she* put in her oar. I bought them a cottage out in Del Rio last winter. They spent two weeks in the goddamn place! I gave him money . . . Who the hell did he think he was!"

"Now take it easy, laddie," the old man who was captain said. "It's done. There's nothing you . . ."

"Nothing," Sonny said. "Damn you, I know that."

The captain walked away, leaving the young man alone.

II

There was so little time. She must go below and finish packing the fish. It was then, as she started for the ladder, that she noticed a white cloud of steam rising from the exhaust.

Even as she turned off the ignition switch May knew she was too late. The engine had been running for almost a half hour with no water to cool it. Only this morning Ed had mentioned that the impeller pump was out of kilter. But Ed had said so many things and she couldn't remember them all, not now, not all at once. She climbed down to the engine room and repacked the gland in the pump with grease as she should have done earlier. Now, if she was lucky, it would draw water into the cooling system. She returned to the conn with another load of ice and started up the engine once more.

The sharp tapping sound grew louder. Steam rose from the exhaust again. Metal struck metal in a cruel staccato that rattled up from the heart of the old boat with the erratic urgency of a dying pulse beat. May winced as if her own body were being pummeled by the steel. She knew what had happened or was about to happen but went below and called the *Sarah* anyway; this was the beginning of many things, things she must face, and even the poor comfort of a distant voice would help.

Sonny switched off the receiver. The captain and two of the crew stood near by. When the young man did not turn, the captain approached him.

"No chance of keepin' her going, Sonny?"

The young man shook his head. "Rod gone." The words stood apart, wrenched from his throat.

May wondered how long her radio batteries would last without the generator. And the ice. There was the ice to consider. Thirty hours he had said. Thirty hours she must wait. Time . . .

Eight months of every year for twenty-six years. South every January to the cannery at Cabo San Lucas where they took on a Mexican crew and worked the tuna as a bait boat. Five months up and down lower Baja, into the Gulf, then south to the Tres Marías and the sea of the great turtles. North in June for quick repairs in San Diego and the months that followed were the hard ones, for they fished the albacore alone, using only eight jig lines: south to San Quintín and Ballenas where the gray whales bore their young; west to the Benitos, Guadalupe and beyond. Home with a load and back down again. And always farther south it had been, farther west where others seldom fished, for as the years passed it became impossible for older boats like theirs to compete with the speedy clippers and purse seiners that swept the sea with nets so vast entire herds of porpoises were caught within them too.

This year they had sailed 350 miles southwest of Guadalupe Island while the rest of the fleet was still working the coastal waters. When a storm surprised them there was no time to beat for Guadalupe, nothing to do but ride it out. The storm had pushed them even farther westward, and two of their fuel tanks sprang leaks, until on the third day when the weather lifted they were forced to head directly for the island. And though they never spoke of such things, both had known they might not make it.

Now of course this was no longer important. There was no engine to burn the fuel. There was no Ed. The situation almost seemed logical to May. Now she could do nothing about it, about anything. She must wait here for her son, and all that would inevitably follow—things she and Ed had avoided through the years, never comfortable perhaps, never quite safe, but independent and proud of the life they had made together. Ed had always said he would rather dig his own grave than live "well" like other people. And May too—really she too felt the same way. She could be certain of that at last. No more need to be loyal, to hide anything from the man she had spent these years with, who had given her this life, so different from that of other women. Yes, looking back, May knew it had been best their way; and if this life had finally killed Ed the way Sonny had always said it would, that was all right too.

III

They had been heading toward Guadalupe for several hours. Ed was at the wheel. The afternoon sun glared down from clear, storm-washed skies. There was no wind and the sea was glazed and steamy.

May dozed beneath the canvas awning on the afterdeck, lazily checking the jig lines from time to time through half-opened lids. She had taken off her boots because the albacore rarely struck in mid-afternoon. Then Ed was howling down at her from the conn, and she saw one of the jig poles bending back at an angle that made the stay lines creak. A moment later there was a second strike and then another and another. Silver knives slashed across the mirrored sea. They were into something big.

She cried out when she saw the first one. The line sang as he fought the bite of the hook, lunging and cutting through the water with a power that racked her muscles. She braced herself as she brought him up to the stern. An instant off guard and she could be dragged into the sea. A moment of carelessness, a slack line, and he would throw the hook. There was no pulling him in; he weighed forty pounds at least. She waited for the time when, responding to the strain on the line, he leaped clear of the water in an orgasm of pain and fury, almost standing on his tail, and then she snapped him over the side. All the strength in her body and arms went into this quick movement, yet it would have seemed effortless to an observer. The barbless hook broke loose when the fish hit the deck, and she sent out the line again, seeing that it slid under the others so there would be no fouling. She called up to Ed as she went for the next line. "Lunkers! They're lunkers!" These were a variety of Japanese albacore rarely caught in these waters; they sometimes weighed as much as eighty pounds. Ed stood at the wheel, laughing, holding the boat in a circle course. "Chum 'em! Don't lose 'em, honey! Be right there!" And he started tying down the wheel.

May climbed up on the bait tank and scooped up the squirming sardines. She tossed them out by the handful. Many landed on the deck, but there was no time to be careful; the school which surrounded them could sound and be gone in an instant. She hurried back to the lines. As she hauled them in she could hear Ed talking to himself, cursing as he untangled some rope, chuckling. She didn't need to see him to know his face was flushed, that his hands were trembling as he tied down the wheel. She didn't need to look to know that his eyes were as bright as they had been on their first voyage. She too felt the same ecstasy when the sea spewed forth its harvest with such abandon. It had never occurred to May to wonder why each time was the first time for them, or to marvel that each day could hold the promise of moments like this, no matter how rare they might be.

She chummed again. All eight of the lines were taut now, and both jig poles were bent nearly double. The water boiled wherever she tossed the bait. Then Ed was beside her, a line in his hands too, crying that there would be money in the bank this year and a new engine for the *Gull* and they could look all those mother-huggin' clipper men in the eye again with their fancy women and their goddamn Cadillacs.

He had one of the albacore nearly up to the stern when he clutched his side. May saw his face go white, watched as he resisted the pain and tried to bring in the fish. Then he released the line. And she knew. He staggered toward the cabin, stumbled, and fell. She ran to him. He looked up at her, his face twisted grotesquely with the effort of speaking.

"The lines!" he gasped. "Goddamn it, get the lines, May!"

An hour later when the school finally sounded she went to him. He seemed lost in some dream, but though his body remained limp and still, his eyes met hers as she approached. There was a question in them.

"Four tons," she said. "We've got a load, Ed." She managed to smile. Then she dragged him into the cabin and somehow got him up on the bunk. He lay there, only his eyes alive.

Suddenly it was too much for her. "What'll I do?" she cried. "Oh Ed, tell me what to do!"

His eyes seemed to look beyond her for an instant. She turned, but saw only a patch of blue sky outside the cabin door. "The *Gull* . . ." he said. There was no sound. Only his lips moved. And then he was dead. And she was alone. Terribly alone, for his last words had been the name of their boat. She had hoped for something more.

"The *Gull* . . ." she murmured. Was there something she had missed, some significance here she could not grasp? But her brain was numb with the one awful, bald fact: he was dead. She couldn't think about it now. She had to think of the things she must do.

May would never understand why she had turned off the ignition then. She found herself on the conn deck, the engine dead. There is no stillness more oppressive and profound than that of the open sea when it is calm. The few times the engine had gone out before there had always been Ed, and even if the sea had been at peace as it now was, there were always words to fill the void. May became aware of this stillness for the first time in her life. She was overcome by a stunning lethargy. She stared unseeing into the blue vastness which surrounded her.

A familiar sound had roused her. One of the albacore was beating its tail against the bloody deck in sullen fury, as though trying to deny death in this last violent display of life. Its mouth opened and closed in yawning, hopeless gasps. Then, like a shadow passing over its shining scales, silver faded to gray and the huge fish lay still. May climbed down from the conn. The sun was hot, and there were four tons of fish waiting to be packed.

The task before her was staggering; even with Ed it would have taken half the night. Usually Ed climbed into the freezing compartment first, stacked and covered the fish with finely ground snow ice as she handed them down to him. Then, when the cold became too much for him, they changed jobs. Ed wasn't here. She was alone. And of course there was something she must do before she packed the fish.

She had been unable to reach the *Sarah* for a while. Someone had hit a big school east of Guadalupe and the air was jammed; there wasn't a chance of getting through with her weak set. She began packing the fish, returning to the radio every few minutes. When she finally established contact, Sonny had confirmed her position with his radio direction finder. And then, of course, the authorities in San Diego were notified, for when a man dies anywhere—at sea, in the street, in his bed—everything must go through the proper channels. May kept the radio tuned in loud so that she could hear it, and returned to packing the fish. Working made things easier, except when she caught herself talking to him or when she turned expecting to find him beside her.

A half hour later she had received a radio call from the health authorities in San Diego: they wanted to warn her that if she felt obliged to put the body of the man, her husband, in the ice hold, they must condemn the fish. And so the man had been packed in the gear box on the conn deck, and the *Sarah* was on its way and the fish were saved.

IV

The darkness surprised her. There was no moon tonight. May lit a kerosene lantern and set it by the hatch to the ice hold. She picked up an albacore and lowered it into the compartment, kneeling, for then she only had to drop it a few feet and the impact was slight. She rose, picked up another fish. May had guessed the average weight to be thirty-five or forty pounds. About two hundred fish. Two hundred times she must do this.

When she went into the hold, the difference in temperature was immediately noticeable though the refrigeration unit had been out less than an hour. Little drops of moisture had formed on the freezing pipes, white with encrusted ice, and they glowed yellow in the light of the lantern like a million tiny cat eyes, watching, as she worked. May climbed up on the deck again. Her fingers were numb and she chafed them, but they remained thick and clumsy. Sometimes she dropped a fish and it fell with a thump into the hold and she groaned and beat her fists against her thighs because she knew a bruise had formed, marring the precious white flesh of the albacore. Too many of these and the cannery would reject the fish. She put on some canvas gloves, but before long they were as wet and slippery as her hands. And then it was time to go into the hold again. Soon she must call the *Sarah*.

At two o'clock she had trouble hearing the *Sarah*. She tuned up the volume as far as she could, but it didn't help. When they had taken a bearing she signed off. The battery . . . And now there was the other thing to do. The night was warm.

It almost seemed that the pale, waxen skin of the dead man was generating some special heat, that some life force within it was still at work. She had to return to the hold and fill the pail again. As she scooped up the ice she noticed that it stuck to the shovel, gray now instead of white and dry. Wearily she climbed back to the conn and went on with her grim task.

His eyes glittered darkly in his white face. Strange that it should seem so white. It had been a ruddy, deeply tanned face. May remembered then that the eyes of the dead were supposed to be closed. She tried to accomplish this and was immediately sorry, for the right lid remained half open. Whichever way she forced it, whether open or shut, it kept returning to the same position. The effect was a leering wink so grotesque, such a perversion of the man she knew, that May cried out.

"Oh! Oh! Please!" She threw down the cover of the box. She leaned on it with all the weight of her body.

She must open it again. She must pack the ice firmly about him and then get back to loading the fish. May shuddered. She felt as if the ice, the melting ice, were in her bones. The lantern on the deck below paled, then brightened. In the still darkness the first tentative, chill-soft tongues of an approaching fog bank were sliding over the *Gull*. Heartened by this, she clenched her teeth and opened the cover of the box once more.

May was glad of the fog at first. Fog was cool, and heat was her enemy. Perhaps it would last through the following day. That wouldn't be unusual in these waters. Then she remembered the dying radio. Without a direction finder to guide the *Sarah*, the fog had another meaning. Instead of heat there would be time to contend with. She must live in this new time, think in the gray void enveloping her, grope for meanings that otherwise there might have been no time for.

Kneeling beside the hold again, May stared into the dimming lantern and she saw herself alone: a woman not old, who had worn the clothes of a man for most of her adult life, unwomanlike in the eyes of other women who remained ashore, yet woman enough to have loved a man and borne his son. Old enough to accept what had happened this day, young enough to remember with hunger the feel of the man she had buried in ice, preserving him and . . . yes, herself too, unseparate in the final numbing embrace, for what must be done when they returned to land. Young enough to wonder what lay ahead of her, and knowing it would only be time to be measured, time to forget the feel and the smell and the strength of this man; and of course—strange to know this—when that time came, she too would be dead.

May lowered the last fish into the hold. She didn't straighten up but remained kneeling there, resting her head on the sharp edge of the hatch. Her back was one great, dull ache. The muscle, the substance of her arms, might have dissolved into the chill fog except for the muted pain. The lantern had gone out, but that no longer mattered. It was dawn. There was a sun somewhere.

She tried the radio again, but all she could hear was the faint echoes of voices. She took off the earphones and sat down on the bunk. There was a faint depression in the pillow where his head had rested. How long had it been? She was tired, so tired. She would lie down for a while, a little while, rest. She put her cheek on the pillow.

When May awoke the cabin was stifling. She rushed outside to find a hot sun burning down on the *Gull*. Still there was no wind. This seemed strange to her. How could the fog be gone, if there was no wind?

The hour startled her: eleven o'clock. She opened the hatch and entered the hold. She filled the pail with ice; this time she had to make three trips to the gear box. Then she returned below to pack the last of the albacore. The reserve supply of ice was exhausted, and she had to chop what she could from corners and the freezing pipes. Even during the night there had been melting; now great drops fell upon the deck in an erratic yet insistent rhythm, like some insane clock of water. When she was finished May stood there for a while watching, listening, trying to measure the time granted to her here. She noticed that one of the floor boards was out of place, and discovered as she righted it that the bilge water had risen alarmingly.

The engine room was flooding too. Of course. May accepted this without emotion, like any natural event. Their little *Gull* was an old lady. With the pumps gone, her seams, calked and recalked a thousand times over the years, weren't enough to resist the sea.

It was then, as she looked about her, that May wondered for the first time if she too might die. But no. There was the hand pump. And if worse came to worst she could always load the dinghy with supplies and wait. Still, she found it necessary to think about this possibility. There was so little between her and the blue oblivion under the *Gull*—nothing if one turned a valve and the sea cock were opened . . .

May climbed quickly out of the engine room and went on deck. The sea was smooth and the sky was clear. She was alone. The horizon was a naked ring of nothingness neatly encircling a woman and death.

V

Sonny stood at the wheel, the captain beside him. "Should get there about eleven tonight," the old man said.

"Get where?" the young man replied bitterly. Twelve hours had passed since they'd been able to get a fix on the *Gull*.

"We'll find her," the captain said.

May hardly knew how she had gotten in the engine room. She found herself staring at the valve to the sea cock. Not thinking of anything in particular, not thinking . . . that. No, just *there*. The water had risen almost a foot in two hours. Soon the sea cock would be covered and there would be no reaching it. But of course she didn't want to reach it.

The sun would be setting by now. If the *Sarah* didn't arrive before dusk, she might have to wait another night. May considered loading the dinghy with supplies. She was too weary to move.

Poor Ed. It wasn't right somehow. Going back to San Diego. Going back to the earth, the ground, the *dirt*. It would be more fitting for him to sink down into this blueness, become a part of what his life had been. His life and his death would be one thing then. Yes, that would be fitting. Well, maybe he'd get his wish if the *Sarah* didn't hurry.

The ice in the gear box had melted almost completely. Though she had thrown a canvas tarpaulin over the box and wet it down constantly all afternoon, the sun was too hot on the exposed upper deck. The only ice left in the hold was packed about the fish. And if she moved him there, the fish would be condemned.

May closed the cover to the gear box. "I don't know, I don't know," she groaned, and scanned the empty, shimmering stillness of the sea, searching not for an answer, but for the intrusion of a decision. She wrung her hands. Kneeling, she opened the box again, looked into it, closed it. Ed wouldn't want things that way. The fish were a payload and something more, something she would never be able to explain, but she had a frightening conviction that it would be in the nature of a mortal sin to destroy them deliberately. In a sense Ed had died for them.

And what if she did what she knew he would want? What if she took him and sent him down into the sea? But of course she couldn't do that. For she must think of what people would say. She had his memory to consider. She rebelled at the idea of sniffling into this decision because people might think she prized a load of fish over her husband—or worse—but there it was. What if she left him in the gear box? But in the heat . . . the thought was unbearable. One thing she could not do was leave him where he was.

At dusk there was no sign of the *Sarah*. She filled the kerosene lantern and hung it above the conn, but she knew there was little chance of them finding her before morning. Now she must decide. She could wait no longer. There seemed to be some tremendous moral issue at stake that May didn't quite grasp, but it tortured her all the same. And it was complicated again by the sense of watchful eyes—the eyes of those who waited on land, of those who would be her neighbors in the new life ahead, of her son. But even at the thought of them she knew they had nothing to do with Ed and her. They had always lived apart, and now at the end she must think apart from all the rest, alone now. May discovered then that she was not alone, even while staring full face into his deadness and the melted ice and the first hint of the ugliness of dirt graves. The decision belonged to him.

It was done. And now there would be no smell of death on this boat. May felt clean in a way she would never wish or be able to define for anyone living. Now there would be the smell of the sea on this boat and there would only be the good memories of this man. *Memories*—what poor things they were, fit for gray, shorebound people, afraid to reach out for life any longer. It was done now and there was no time for remembering. She must work to live. And she must live because . . . She would find a reason. That would come to her.

Six o'clock . . . morning . . . second morning . . . third day . . . May wondered how long she had slept this time. The water level hadn't risen much; not more than an hour. It had been like this all through the night. She worked until exhaustion, an old friend now, swept her into unconsciousness and her hands slid from the pump handle and she slept a broken, troubled sleep, always awakening with a start, working again, and then the awakeness fading into dreams once more. But she wouldn't fall asleep now, because it was morning and the *Sarah* would be here soon. She knew that. It was a thing that sang in her bones as did the thought of what she would tell Sonny when he arrived. She had found her reason. No cottage in Del Rio for her! She would keep on fishing. Maybe Sonny would go in with her. Or if he was stubborn she would find someone else. Sonny and Ed's family wouldn't like it. They would tell her she must rest awhile. May knew all the dodges they'd use. That didn't worry her. And the wonderful part was, she didn't need them. There was a little money in the bank, and at $400 a ton this load would bring in close to $1,600, enough to put a new engine in the *Gull*. She was free!

VI

The crew of the *Sarah* were listless. They mended net, made lures, read comic books, sprawled about the deck or lying in their bunks. Occasionally some cast halfhearted looks toward the horizon, but they had reached an unspoken decision and just made this effort for the sake of the intense young man at the wheel.

Only the old man who was captain seemed not to have given up hope. He had climbed up on the conn mast as soon as it was light. The cook tried to press some breakfast on him, but he shook his head and muttered, "No time." Though his perch was precarious, he felt no fatigue. His stubby-fingered, thick-veined hands and short, corded arms were like steel and leather, and time had only tempered them. His brown, seamed face was impassive, but his eyes were never still. He knew the sea too well to turn his back on her. She was a moody old woman and she never did what you expected her to.

"Sonny . . . Sonny . . ." he called softly. "Hand me up the glasses."

The young man at the wheel watched as the captain looked through the binoculars, then slowly lifted his arm and pointed. Sonny could see nothing.

"Here. Give it here," he said, reaching out as the old man descended from the conn mast. He moved the binoculars across the horizon; they wavered, stopped. The young man seemed to be choking. He handed the glasses to the captain, face averted, climbed down from the conn, and rushed into the darkness of the cabin.

She had noticed the difference for some time but had attributed it to any number of natural phenomena. A kelp bed was drifting near by and she knew this brown weed had a pungent odor and often bore the corpses of birds and fish. Later in the morning a breeze sprang up, and she was able to ignore it for a while. She returned to the engine room, but still the memory of it troubled her. In ten minutes she was back on deck again. She made some coffee, forced herself to drink the hot fluid; a moment later she was violently ill. This didn't last, for there was nothing in her stomach, but the nausea persisted. She had heard of such things happening to people who hadn't eaten for several days. She would try some bread when she felt better—something easy to digest, to coat her stomach. That was what was needed. She struggled to her feet, nearly fainted, leaned against the bulkhead. Perhaps she would wait a few minutes before returning to the pump. She breathed deeply, hoping this would make the dizziness go away. And suddenly she could elude it no longer. She went to the ice hold, removed the tarpaulin and raised the hatch. She didn't have to look. She knew immediately. The ice had melted, and the sea and the heat had done the rest. The fish were lost.

Ed's last cry, "Get the lines, May!" was a mockery in her ears now, and each moment she had lost with him seemed weighted to a raw string tightening about her heart. How often in their life it had been like this. Always working, always fighting the sea, never quite winning. So many years, good years and bad years, the sea giving and taking in its own secret ways—all for nothing. Though she had given him to the sea—all for nothing. And so the last voyage was a failure.

VII

The *Sarah* plowed northward, sluggish with its new burden. The sun and the sky were dulled by the thickening mesh of an ominous mackerel sky. Sonny put an arm around his mother. "Tough luck, Ma. If we'd of located you sooner we might have saved 'em."

"Yes," May said. She was looking back toward the *Gull,* which they were towing to Guadalupe Island. Two men were unloading the doomed catch of fish.

"Hope there's no trouble about . . . well, you know . . ."

May looked at her son with a curious, remote expression that made him flush. "He was my husband," she said.

"Yeah, but people are funny. Get funny ideas. You know that."

"Yes."

"I guess we better just tell them the truth though. I guess that's the only thing to do."

May moved a little away from her son. His arm fell to his side. There was an uncomfortable silence.

"Well, we'll have you home in a few days," Sonny said. "Coast Guard cutter's going to meet us at Guadalupe and they'll take you north. I'll have to stay with the *Sarah* till we get a load."

"What about the *Gull?*"

"Engine's shot. I may be able to sell her for you though, get someone else to tow her to Dago."

"I won't sell her."

"Ma, she's dead, finished. It'd cost more'n you got in the bank to fix up that engine again, and *then* she wouldn't be worth a damn! Anyway, you can't fish alone."

"I was thinking maybe you and I could go in together . . ." She spoke slowly, as if she were reciting half-forgotten words memorized long ago.

"Yeah. Well, the thing is old Larson'll be retiring next season, and when he does I'll be skipper. I couldn't pass that up, Ma."

"Maybe someone else."

Sonny's voice grew querulous. "Well, I don't see what we can do, Ma. The boat's a dead loss unless you get it towed to port, and that'd cost a fortune. *We* can't take the time. Gotta get in there fast with a load and get right back down here while they're running."

"I won't sell her," May said. Her voice was mechanical and the words had no meaning. She turned and walked away from her son. She leaned against the rail and looked into the sea.

A boy emerged from the galley and eyed this strange, brooding woman curiously as he dumped a load of garbage over the side. A lone gull had been following the boat; it swooped toward the debris with a shriek. Although she hardly knew why, May found herself watching the bird.

"The gull . . ." he had said. And May remembered.

There had been a day soon after they were married. Ed had just bought the boat and they had gone to Pacific Amusement Park to celebrate. Later in the afternoon they walked down to the beach. The air was still warm, though already foghorns were beginning to moan at the entrance to the harbor. They were trying to think of a name for the boat, which had been called the *Chela;* they wanted something special, something for themselves. Sitting there on the sand, chatting idly, they began to watch a sea gull. The bird had found a mussel among the rocks and was flying high into the air, then dropping it, trying to break the shell in order to reach the rich, orange flesh. The bird tried this again and again, but the shell was too tough. Finally it gave up and flew away. May had smiled at Ed and said she was glad she didn't have to work *that* hard for a living. Ed had frowned slightly. "Fishing's no picnic, you know, honey."

"Oh, I know," she had said, but of course she didn't, not yet.

A slight gasp made her look at Ed in concern. He was smiling now, and his voice was trembling with excitement when he spoke. "They really have to grub, May, but they can fly, too. Look! Look up there!"

The gull had returned for some reason and was circling above them. The fog was rolling in, and the sun had paled to a moonstone in the thickening mists. There was a sudden chill in the air. But the gull was high above all this where the sun was still shining, and it soared through the bright sky with a wild, heartbreaking abandon, a glorious white-golden thing free of the gray world below.

And May had understood what Ed was trying to tell her, and she had turned to him and said, "Let's call her the *Gull.*"

Ed had said nothing, but he took her hand in both of his in a funny, formal way; and though there had been a ceremony weeks before, May knew that now, in this instant, they were married.

And standing on the stern of the great clipper *Sarah,* May found peace. They had grubbed. They had flown. They had been together. It was enough. It was all. The last voyage had not been a failure. It was only the end.

The Grandmother

JOHN HAWKES

(1925–)

"Lebrecht! I'm here, I'm here, Lebrecht!"

It was with all the old impatience that I cried to them, with all the old affection that I announced myself, and my hands were outstretched. A window slammed in the back of the house. How little it had changed; yet I seemed to bring with me the dust and aching of long travel and separation. At that moment, looking up the path, beating my jacket, waiting, I felt the wanderer come home.

"Why, look, Mauschel, it is your Uncle Justus!"

The door opened a crack, then it was wide, and suddenly the four of us intermingled in our confused and unexpected embrace. I shook my brother Lebrecht by the arm, bumped against Metze, his wife, and felt them gather about me.

"And do I smell the stove, Metze?" I threw my chin high, laughing.

"No," she replied in a low flat voice, "you do not. The stove is cold."

With clouds above us and a slight wind ballooning our trousers and sweeping away the summer, I caught hold of Lebrecht Kümmerlich. He was not so much younger than his brother Justus now.

"Lebrecht, Lebrecht, it is so, nicht wahr?"

"Ja, ja, ja, Justus."

Our hands were on each other's shoulders, we faced each other and I cared nothing for the rest.

"Well, then," I whispered, "laugh, Lebrecht, laugh . . ."

And he did so.

The grass was long, the wind blew coldly among us. We all shook hands again, and I noticed that Metze had many wrinkles on her throat. Suddenly I pushed between them and ran back to the car. I pried loose the wooden box I had brought with me, and, though I was hardly able, carried it to them before the house.

"Lebrecht—for you, Lebrecht!"

Metze insisted that we put the box down immediately, there on the path, and open it. She scraped away the ice until they could see the white of fat and the redness of cold meat. Lebrecht began to thank me, he was serious and turned his face from side to side, but he was whispering so softly that I could not hear.

"Mauschel," said Metze, holding tightly to the edge of the box, "bring some coal, bitte."

"Metze," I smiled quickly, sure she would understand, "the lamb is for tomorrow's Mittagessen . . ."

"We will eat it tonight. And tomorrow also."

The three of them hurried inside with the box. I followed.

"Metze," I called, "the meat must season, it must hang in the open air!"

But she disappeared into the kitchen and began washing the pots.

We were silent a moment. Mauschel had climbed down into the darkened cellar, we heard him through the thin floor, moving slowly beneath us; suddenly there came from below, amid barrels and coal dust, a distinct and vituperative profanity as from the other side of Berlin. We sat still. What sort of boy was Mauschel now, shaking the coal scuttle by the throat? He grunted and drove the shovel deep again into the bin. Lebrecht walked softly to the door.

"Mauschel. Will Papa help you with the coal?"

The boy, man-sized, immeasurable, suddenly big in his shadow, emerged from the little stairwell and swung the sack of coal into view. Lebrecht stepped away quickly as Mauschel crashed his burden against the walls and to the kitchen. We could hear the two of them, mother and son, whispering.

"He is so big."

"Bigger than I," said Lebrecht softly.

"That is the way with you family men," I laughed, feeling my forehead, "you have your taxes, your dedication, the satisfaction of your big sons to wrestle with."

"Only one son, Justus."

"Ja. Remember how he needed a beating once, Lebrecht? He was always my favorite. Ah, he knows the character of his Uncle Justus." I smiled in the dark.

We began to smell the smoke of the roasting meat. And Mauschel was sharpening the knives. I noticed Lebrecht's slippers under the window, I was light-headed and content, sitting there, waiting for the meal to be served.

"And Metze, Lebrecht, has she overcome her grief for der Blumenstrauss?"

He lifted his eyes slowly. "Ja," he said.

I nodded.

"She talks to her mother some nights, Justus, but without grief, I assure you."

"So?"

"Ja. She talks. But there is Herr Popanz and the lady from Augenstrasse, neighbors in grief. And God forgives such things, Justus."

I did not answer. I was hungry and would eat a good meal.

"I have been ill, Lebrecht."

"Ill?"

"Ja, Lebrecht, seriously. Perhaps as sick as Papa when he died . . ."

But as soon as our father's name was mentioned, Metze called out that the lamb was done.

"Give the knives to your Uncle Justus, Liebling," said Metze as we entered the dining room, and Mauschel thrust the blades at me.

"In my brother's house . . ." I murmured and extended the knives to Lebrecht, and he was quick enough to take them. Pushing his arms out of his coat sleeves, he worked to free his shoulders.

There was a heavy, gasping, uncontainable sigh at the head of the table as Lebrecht raised his two hands—in one was the great carving fork, in the other a knife—and held them above the smoking lamb as in some kind of feverish dying benediction. His eyes looked straight down at the crackling skin, peering, taking aim at the roast which had been rushed to the table. Lebrecht's head became wet, and still the fork and still the knife hovered powerfully as if he could not bring himself to begin. But his nose was over the meat and he was sniffing it. And with the very smell of the fat and the meat, the juices were already filling his mouth and the acids seeping into his stomach's pit. He seemed so to be smelling that he could not bring his knife down, could not drive the point into the leg of the lamb. Then suddenly he sank back and half turned away, lowering his arms until the steel rested helplessly against the wood. He licked his lips and smiled.

"Ach, Metze, I've forgotten how . . ."

For answer, unable to wait longer, she reached out piercingly through the tumblers and from the platter snatched up a small potato which she immediately began to smash in the bottom of her plate.

"Pardon," he said softly and once more took up knife and fork.

"I'm not hungry," I said cheerfully, smoothing the napkin, "I'll take just a little of the skin, if you please, Lebrecht."

"Not hungry!" Mauschel pushed back his chair and rose menacingly on his big haunches. "Not hungry, Uncle!" He looked as if a fish had been smacked against his eyes. His hands clutched the empty plate. "Ah," he began to sit down again, "you are fooling me, Uncle Justus." Then, he put a large dirty finger into each corner of his mouth and pulled wide. After which he said, "Empty, you see, Uncle, hungry as all that!"

I smoothed my napkin. A shrill tinkle rang from one of the crystal glasses; at last it had been barely touched, nicked by Lebrecht's knife large as a scimitar. Lebrecht pushed his chair to one side of the table.

"Potato. Plenty of potato for me," said Mauschel loudly, peering at the carver. With a black finger he rubbed the bottom of the plate.

Lebrecht nodded, he had heard his son. Then, whispering, holding the knife up to the aging chandelier, "Mauschel. Give me a hair, Knabe."

"I'll give you my whole scalp if you'll cut us some meat . . ."

"Only a hair, Mauschel."

The coal carrier, the only child, pulled a hair from his head and Lebrecht, taking it, began testing the edge of the blade against it, cutting and swinging emptily in the air.

We watched. He leaned down and immersed himself in the delicate clutter of the table, and faced the lamb; obviously he wanted nothing more than to carve and eat.

"If you cannot do it," came the woman's hissing, "then give the knife to Justus."

So he began, as his wife coaxed him and his son leaned toward him salivating like a street dog. Lebrecht carved. But in the last pitiful instant he was unable to wield the fork—the knife alone was quite enough for him—and now one hand was clasped upon the lamb. That hand lay embedded in the fat, the fingers curled down the sides of the meat, squeezing their prints into the golden skin. He perspired, bit his lip, and with the very palm of his hand, and with the fingers—on one was a gold ring—pushed the roast firmly into its platter, despite the hot juice that trickled across the knuckles, the grease that splattered his white cuff. He began triumphantly to smile.

"Metze, you'll forgive me if I serve my brother Justus first . . ." And the plate was passed to me, heaped high.

Then Lebrecht sat and looked at the last filled dish, his own. But as he swung the knife down from its striking position, giving hardly a thought to the blood-covered blade, he brought another tinkling from a goblet, and now, after all his care and watchfulness, it fell over and emptied into his lap.

"Mauschel," said the boy's mother, "bring a cloth."

"Later. After we eat," came Mauschel's voice out of the deep and rattling plate.

"It's all right, Metze," whispered my brother, "eat your food, meine Herzliebste."

"Well," I said when the meal was half-done, at last spreading a piece of bread with preserves from a little pot, "well, I was sick."

"Ah," Lebrecht roused himself, "you were sick, Justus!"

"I was."

"Mama has been sick too, haven't you?" said Mauschel. He grinned at his mother, but Metze's eyes were toward me. Arching her brows and without thinking, she sat holding herself, the ache, under one breast. Her jaws chewed irrevocably and silently behind those pale lips.

"I have been nearly dead. Sick, yes, but worse, Mauschel, your Uncle Justus, mein Neffe, nearly died."

"Ah, Justus," Lebrecht apologized, pushing back his chair, "you had not made it clear. Ah, ah, was it bad as that?" He walked around the table, behind his wife, still carrying the full fork in one hand, and then returned quickly to the head of the table, smiling for their luck in having me that night, then frowning and shaking his shoulders.

"Yes, it was that bad," I said and tasted the jam which was quite sweet. "Yes. I did not think I would come out of it. But other than that I had my holiday . . ."

"Holiday?" Metze stopped chewing.

I nodded. "I stayed at the Gasthof. There was the beach, real sea water. All that."

"How then," her hard yet almost tearful eyes turned sharp like the sights on the end of a gun, and from the twisting of her hand beneath the heart, the pain must have been growing. "How, then, did you nearly die?"

"Sunstroke," I said calmly. "Lebrecht," raising my voice, "I was nearly burned to death by the sun down there."

"Were you, Justus!" he exclaimed, plunging the fork into his mouth and looking from his wife to his son and back again to his plate. "Scheusslich, scheusslich!" he faltered and banged his knife handle on the table.

I took a mouthful of potato. Then I pushed the dinner away.

"There is nothing worse than sunstroke!" exclaimed Lebrecht, wiping his mouth thoroughly.

"Ja. Nothing so bad, Lebrecht, I could actually hear the hoarse cries of the angels, my brother."

"Is that true?" he asked.

"True, Lebrecht. True indeed. And the blisters were big as pullet eggs. It is true: near death, near death."

I glanced at Metze. She was lifting the breast now to probe at her pain. All of a woman's hurt collects there, all of the nerves seem to end there under the breast.

"Did you," turning the wrinkles of her forehead into a cold smile, "did you enjoy swimming in the ocean, Justus?"

"It was perfect," I said briefly.

"Poor Justus, poor Justus," sighed my brother, clacking again at his food, pausing again to stare at me as at a man in his coffin. "How many days did you lie there, Justus?"

"Well taken, Lebrecht. I don't know. It was long enough for that burned body of mine to cool off, long enough for it to cool down like a comet that plunges into the shore and steams in agony for weeks, until the night air and sea breezes cool it a little, and the fires die out. Then, my skin turned to water. And, of course, there was the odor, Lebrecht."

"But you should have called me, Justus. You should have communicated. Metze," turning suddenly upon his wife, "didn't you dream, didn't you get a message? Didn't you know that Justus was slipping from us? Metze never fails, Justus, she is a receiver of the sparks from beyond. We rely on her, Mauschel and I, to interpret for us, to tell us . . . Didn't you know, Metze?"

"I did not," she said.

"You must not have been listening for me, Metze!" I laughed. "Yes," I went on, leaning back to pluck off the end of my cigar as they poked in the debris of gristle and cutlery, "I was red as the lamb's tongue. Red and rather yellow too, I believe. Metze," I held out my glass, "may I have some more water? Sunstroke leaves a man dehydrated, leaves him with a thirst in every cell of the flesh. May I have some water, bitte?"

Mauschel watched his mother. She said nothing and did not move. She simply remained white and perhaps trembling, as if that mechanism inside her bosom had missed a revolution or two.

"How restful it must have been for your Uncle Justus on the beach, Mauschel," she murmured at last.

Mauschel looked at her a moment more, then drew back his elbows, relinquished his massive guard over his plate, got to his feet and fetched the water pitcher from the kitchen.

"Ja, Justus," his mother began, without looking at me, "I have been ill."

"What, Metze! You, too?"

"Ja, Justus. We shall accompany each other," and she touched my hand with one of her frozen fingers.

"Ah, too bad," I answered. "But then, Lebrecht," I looked down the table, "Metze had no blisters after all!" We laughed. "Here, Mauschel," I said, holding out a cigar, "give this to your father."

"Thank you, Justus," my brother said softly and felt in his pockets for a match. I thought that he was going to eat more, but no, he could not and began instead to smoke.

Metze suddenly pulled her fingers away from the breast—gone the pain!—and laughed like a charming mother.

"Mauschel," leaning forward, "Mauschel, my son, go put on your swimming suit. Let us see you in it, Mauschel."

"What? Has Mauschel a swimming suit also?"

"Ja," said Metze proudly. "Hurry, Mauschel!"

It was as if she had asked him to play a piece on the flute or to recite Goethe. His head hung like a sheep dog. He kicked the legs of the table a moment, then left us.

We remained waiting around the drafty and ruined table. Metze smiled. But her eyes were blank and white as the knucklebones of an old woman. Lebrecht Kümmerlich was no longer hungry, he held the burning cigar in his teeth and sent the smoke up into the blue of the ceiling.

"Tell me, Lebrecht," I said out of the silence, pushing back from the table and crossing my knees, "how is the old wireless?"

He did not answer. His mouth made only a small, violent puffing gesture, like a noiseless engine. I watched my cigar ash grow, and sat with them in this room suddenly cold for summer, filled with shadow and plaster, this world full of family dinners and Mauschel's growing pains, far from the sea.

"Come in, Liebling," said Metze toward the dark door, "don't be shy." Then I saw one of Mauschel's bare feet dangling, showing itself just over the edge of the jamb, feeling its way timidly as if into a pool of cold water.

"Gut, gut," exclaimed his mother and smiled upon him.

Mauschel was naked except for a pair of bright black trunks which fit his loins tight as the skin of a melon. They were cut high on the buttocks. He was white, grinning, and came around the table to stand beside Metze. He had large legs and enormous arms; and every section of arm, of leg, was nipped tightly at the joint where it ended, but was otherwise fat. I noticed a few babyish freckles on the white slopes of his shoulders.

"Is he quite fully grown yet, Lebrecht?" I asked.

"Oh, indeed yes. We can get no more out of him. You're not going to grow any bigger, are you, Mauschel."

The boy shook his head. He grinned and slapped his arms loudly.

"Next year," Metze pronounced, trying to twist about to see him, "we're going to take Mauschel to the beach."

"Fine, fine," I answered.

"And you won't get sunstroke, will you, Mauschel?"

"No," he said, "not me." Then, taking courage from the laughter: "This is the way I shall dive!" he exclaimed and suddenly thrust his arms above his head and shook his very gelatinous soul into the swimmer's fishlike form.

"Ah," Metze reached and touched his flesh.

"Mauschel," I spoke softly and drew out my purse. "Come here, Mauschel." Feeling him close by, suddenly obedient, I gave him the bank note. "Don't spend it, Mauschel. It is to bring you good luck."

I heard the earliest sounds of birds outside and, louder than the birds, a woman's sharp voice. I pulled on my trousers, went into the bathroom, carefully raised the green glass window, thrust my head through the opening and looked down. Metze was standing below on the stoop talking loudly. A market boy, leaning on an iron cart filled with food, watched her, grinned, but made no move to unload his packages.

Against the fence that bordered the yard stood Lebrecht's row of birdhouses, and the sun lighted the houses while the birds hopped in and out, quickly, noisily, fluttering and ill-prepared for the morning.

"Put the food in the kitchen," Metze commanded. The boy laughed and scraped one of his muddy boots on the iron spokes. He had only one eye and wore no patch to hide the withered empty bed of the other. His fingers were red from handling wet carrots and sides of beef, his leather apron was splashed from the road; he pulled a green stalk from a bundle in the cart and began to eat, scratched his blood-stained cheek, under the skin his jaws moved sideways back and forth. He looked at Metze. The birds sang loudly.

"No, Frau Kümmerlich. I might leave you this little bag, but no more."

"The kitchen!" Her voice rose to my window. "The whole wagon load goes into my kitchen!"

"No, Frau Kümmerlich," eating more of the green, "why only yesterday the butcher said, 'The Kümmerlichs have stopped eating meat. And they eat no garden produce either. When Herr Kümmerlich's wife grows thin,' he told me, 'leave them a box of meal.' You don't look thin to me, Frau Kümmerlich."

Still leaning on the cart, he began slowly to push his weight on it, swinging and moving it in Metze's direction, and the iron wheels ground slowly with a muddy, metallic noise, slipping, clanging, the cart turning as if to run her down. The boy's bent uncombed shape—I could see that he had brushed against dead fowl and smoked half-cigarettes in the butcher's meat locker—sidled close to Metze. He lifted up a package, shook loose the paper exposing a large beef heart and dropped it again into the wagon.

"Have you a good fire, Frau Kümmerlich?" he whispered and, reaching out stubby fingers, tweaked her arm.

"I want the food," she said, "all of it!"

He stood straight up and with both hands took hold of the cart's push-bar, wheeled the iron-walled vehicle around and ran off, laughing and bouncing the wagon so that a few soft oranges flew from it and fell to the roadside. I shut the window and washed myself.

Downstairs Metze was trying to build a fire in the kitchen stove. The shades were pulled tight in the living room. During the day we ate in the kitchen and there was a plate—a sausage, a piece of bread—for each of us. Metze kept Mauschel's meal on the stove in a large double pot with a black lid.

"Where is the boy?" asked Lebrecht after a long silence.

"He is not late," said Metze. "Mauschel is never late."

Then I saw my nephew's face at the kitchen window: only the head, the face, staring at me over his father's shoulder. He had taken a bit of yellow leaf and wadded it into one eye socket. He winked his visible eye and raised one hand. Satisfied that we were already at the table, he must have walked around the house, for we heard him tramping near the front entrance and the door banged. Lebrecht nodded and smiled. We waited. The forks lingered in the broken skin of our sausages.

"Come in, Mauschel," his mother called, "we've only been eating a moment!" Lebrecht stood up and took the pot off the flame, filled the dish at Mauschel's place and blew lightly on it. Lebrecht sat down. Our heads—Lebrecht's contented, Metze's starched, mine massive—turned toward the door.

Mauschel was leaning there. His belly swayed sleepily, his shoulders massed themselves against the wood, a jacket hung over one arm, the seeds of his eyes were black.

"Welcome, Mauschel," murmured Lebrecht. "Monday's greeting, Mauschel." Lebrecht lowered his eyes and began spreading a piece of bread for his son. The boy said nothing. At the top of his shirt I could see the broad expanse of thick flesh white and damp as a drake's breast.

"Wouldn't you like to eat just a spoonful or two?" his mother asked him.

"You had better join us," I agreed quickly, laughing, "or I will eat your portion, Mauschel!"

Mauschel then started forward. He was fat, he seemed more ready to burst a clod of earth than to rest at the table. His hair was wild and his shirt wet, his bulk cut off the sunlight from the window.

Mauschel walked around the table and stood for a moment beside Metze, letting the jacket slide off his arm. He put his arm like a dead reptile across her shoulders and pushed his face into her hair; his free hand crept to a pocket in the tight trousers and, while Lebrecht and I watched, the fat fingers produced a single bank note and stealthily placed it in the middle of his mother's plate, draped it over the two split sausages.

When he moved, the sun danced thoughtlessly across the kitchen tiles and poured itself into the empty potato bin, swam in the empty sink, cast our four shadows on the white wall. The morning seemed to flow forward and backward, flooding the day with its light and the smell of hungry children, as if all our lives had come here to rest, to stop, and our fortunes were to be found in Mauschel's untouched plate. I heard the sound of a far-off dog, heard the bark that bites into life itself. We sat still and straight.

Then Metze saw the bank note, there on her plate and already soaking up the sausage fat. How she looked! How wide the eyes! To be kissed, yes, but then to find this tender money on the tip of her fork! Metze at that very moment must have felt this bit of paper safe in her bosom, finding a meager breakfast flowered to a fortune. A strand of hair came loose and scraped at her neck, the blue veins sang on the backs of her hands and she reached out, trying to pick up the bill with calm, trying to take it at last between icy fingers.

But Mauschel was quicker than Metze. He snatched the bank note from under her eyes, caught it, leaned and turned in front of her. And then, clicking his teeth in a moment of joy, he stretched the bank note wide, pulled it suddenly until it measured a good foot, elongating the rubber bill wide as his smile, and let one end go, snapped it in Metze's face.

"What shall we buy, Mamma?" he cried. "Look, it is bigger than that even!" And he stretched the hundred marks again. "What do you want, Mamma? A leg of lamb?" He laughed and stuffed the piece of rubber counterfeit into his hip pocket. "It is a good joke," he said flatly as if to himself and walked from the room, leaving his coat on the floor.

"Ach, Mauschel," whispered Lebrecht, hanging his head, "ach, my dangerous son," and slowly emptied the plate into the waiting pot.

With a cold gliding motion Metze went straight to the living-room couch, still tumbled and stale as it was when Mauschel roused himself at dawn. She lay down but did not close her eyes. I saw her ear, a kind of muscular shell, quite separate from the head: I saw the mole on her throat; I saw the line where the hair grew upon the scalp. I watched her, making no sound, and waited to see what she would do. Her wedding hand hung down forgotten. Then, like die Leichenfrau who cares for the dead, her lips moved, her eyelids narrowed, and she began to talk to her dead mother.

"Mamma?"

"Metze?"

"Shall we speak to him, Mamma?"

"Natürlich, Metze!"

"Mamma, we must be firm with him."

"Bring him to me, Metze. Bring him to his Grossmutter . . ."

"Oh, he loves you, Mamma!"

"He is a good boy baby, Metze. Bring him to me . . ."

"Mamma?"

"Ja, Metze?"

"Talk to him, Mamma, talk to him . . ."

When Mauschel stood in the doorway, his mother groaned from the couch. I pushed past him and up the stairs.

Parker's Back

FLANNERY O'CONNOR

(1925–1964)

Parker's wife was sitting on the front porch floor, snapping beans. Parker was sitting on the step, some distance away, watching her sullenly. She was plain, plain. The skin on her face was thin and drawn as tight as the skin on an onion and her eyes were gray and sharp like the points of two icepicks. Parker understood why he had married her—he couldn't have got her any other way—but he couldn't understand why he stayed with her now. She was pregnant and pregnant women were not his favorite kind. Nevertheless, he stayed as if she had him conjured. He was puzzled and ashamed of himself.

The house they rented sat alone save for a single tall pecan tree on a high embankment overlooking a highway. At intervals a car would shoot past below and his wife's eyes would swerve suspiciously after the sound of it and then come back to rest on the newspaper full of beans in her lap. One of the things she did not approve of was automobiles. In addition to her other bad qualities, she was forever sniffing up sin. She did not smoke or dip, drink whiskey, use bad language or paint her face, and God knew some paint would have improved it, Parker thought. Her being against color, it was the more remarkable she had married him. Sometimes he supposed that she had married him because she meant to save him. At other times he had a suspicion that she actually liked everything she said she didn't. He could account for her one way or another; it was himself he could not understand.

She turned her head in his direction and said, "It's no reason you can't work for a man. It don't have to be a woman."

"Aw shut your mouth for a change," Parker muttered.

If he had been certain she was jealous of the woman he worked for he would have been pleased but more likely she was concerned with the sin that would result if he and the woman took a liking to each other. He had told her that the woman was a hefty young blonde; in fact she was nearly seventy years old and too dried up to have an interest in anything except getting as much work out of him as she could. Not that an old woman didn't sometimes get an interest in a young man, particularly if he was as attractive as Parker felt he was, but this old woman looked at him the same way she looked at her old tractor—as if she had to put up with it because it was all she had. The tractor had broken down the second day Parker was on it and she had set him at once to cutting bushes, saying out of the side of her mouth to the nigger, "Everything he touches, he breaks." She also asked him to wear his shirt when he worked; Parker had removed it even though the day was not sultry; he put it back on reluctantly.

This ugly woman Parker married was his first wife. He had had other women but he had planned never to get himself tied up legally. He had first seen her one morning when his truck broke down on the highway. He had managed to pull it off the road into a neatly swept yard on which sat a peeling two-room house. He got out and opened the hood of the truck and began to study the motor. Parker had an extra sense that told him when there was a woman nearby watching him. After he had leaned over the motor a few minutes, his neck began to prickle. He cast his eye over the empty yard and porch of the house. A woman he could not see was either nearby beyond a clump of honeysuckle or in the house, watching him out the window.

Suddenly Parker began to jump up and down and fling his hand about as if he had mashed it in the machinery. He doubled over and held his hand close to his chest. "God dammit!" he hollered, "Jesus Christ in hell! Jesus God Almighty damm! God dammit to hell!" he went on, flinging out the same few oaths over and over as loud as he could.

Without warning a terrible bristly claw slammed the side of his face and he fell backwards on the hood of the truck. "You don't talk no filth here!" a voice close to him shrilled.

Parker's vision was so blurred that for an instant he thought he had been attacked by some creature from above, a giant hawk-eyed angel wielding a hoary weapon. As his sight cleared, he saw before him a tall raw-boned girl with a broom.

"I hurt my hand," he said. "I HURT my hand." He was so incensed that he forgot that he hadn't hurt his hand. "My hand may be broke," he growled although his voice was still unsteady.

"Lemme see it," the girl demanded.

Parker stuck out his hand and she came closer and looked at it. There was no mark on the palm and she took the hand and turned it over. Her own hand was dry and hot and rough and Parker felt himself jolted back to life by her touch. He looked more closely at her. I don't want nothing to do with this one, he thought.

The girl's sharp eyes peered at the back of the stubby reddish hand she held. There emblazoned in red and blue was a tattooed eagle perched on a cannon. Parker's sleeve was rolled to the elbow. Above the eagle a serpent was coiled about a shield and in the spaces between the eagle and the serpent there were hearts, some with arrows through them. Above the serpent there was a spread hand of cards. Every space on the skin of Parker's arm, from wrist to elbow, was covered in some loud design. The girl gazed at this with an almost stupefied smile of shock, as if she had accidentally grasped a poisonous snake; she dropped the hand.

"I got most of my other ones in foreign parts," Parker said. "These here I mostly got in the United States. I got my first one when I was only fifteen year old."

"Don't tell me," the girl said, "I don't like it. I ain't got any use for it."

"You ought to see the ones you can't see," Parker said and winked.

Two circles of red appeared like apples on the girl's cheeks and softened her appearance. Parker was intrigued. He did not for a minute think that she didn't like the tattoos. He had never yet met a woman who was not attracted to them.

Parker was fourteen when he saw a man in a fair, tattooed from head to foot. Except for his loins which were girded with a panther hide, the man's skin was patterned in what seemed from Parker's distance—he was near the back of the tent, standing on a bench—a single intricate design of brilliant color. The man, who was small and sturdy, moved about on the platform, flexing his muscles so that the arabesque of men and beasts and flowers on his skin appeared to have a subtle motion of its own. Parker was filled with emotion, lifted up as some people are when the flag passes. He was a boy whose mouth habitually hung open. He was heavy and earnest, as ordinary as a loaf of bread. When the show was over, he had remained standing on the bench, staring where the tattooed man had been, until the tent was almost empty.

Parker had never before felt the least motion of wonder in himself.

Until he saw the man at the fair, it did not enter his head that there was anything out of the ordinary about the fact that he existed. Even then it did not enter his head, but a peculiar unease settled in him. It was as if a blind boy had been turned so gently in a different direction that he did not know his destination had been changed.

He had his first tattoo some time after—the eagle perched on the cannon. It was done by a local artist. It hurt very little, just enough to make it appear to Parker to be worth doing. This was peculiar too for before he had thought that only what did not hurt was worth doing. The next year he quit school because he was sixteen and could. He went to the trade school for a while, then he quit the trade school and worked for six months in a garage. The only reason he worked at all was to pay for more tattoos. His mother worked in a laundry and could support him, but she would not pay for any tattoo except her name on a heart, which he had put on, grumbling. However, her name was Betty Jean and nobody had to know it was his mother. He found out that the tattoos were attractive to the kind of girls he liked but who had never liked him before. He began to drink beer and get in fights. His mother wept over what was becoming of him. One night she dragged him off to a revival with her, not telling him where they were going. When he saw the big lighted church, he jerked out of her grasp and ran. The next day he lied about his age and joined the navy.

Parker was large for the tight sailor's pants but the silly white cap, sitting low on his forehead, made his face by contrast look thoughtful and almost intense. After a month or two in the navy, his mouth ceased to hang open. His features hardened into the features of a man. He stayed in the navy five years and seemed a natural part of the gray mechanical ship, except for his eyes, which were the same pale slate-color as the ocean and reflected the immense spaces around him as if they were a microcosm of the mysterious sea. In port Parker wandered about comparing the rundown places he was in to Birmingham, Alabama. Everywhere he went he picked up more tattoos.

He had stopped having lifeless ones like anchors and crossed rifles. He had a tiger and a panther on each shoulder, a cobra coiled about a torch on his chest, hawks on his thighs, Elizabeth II and Philip over where his stomach and liver were respectively. He did not care much what the subject was so long as it was colorful; on his abdomen he had a few obscenities but only because that seemed the proper place for them. Parker would be satisfied with each tattoo about a month, then something about it that had attracted him would wear off. Whenever a decent-sized mirror was available, he would get in front of it and study his overall look. The effect was not of one intricate arabesque of colors but of something haphazard and botched. A huge dissatisfaction would come over him and he would go off and find another tattooist and have another space filled up. The front of Parker was almost completely covered but there were no tattoos on his back. He had no desire for one anywhere he could not readily see it himself. As the space on the front of him for tattoos decreased, his dissatisfaction grew and became general.

After one of his furloughs, he didn't go back to the navy but remained away without official leave, drunk, in a rooming house in a city he did not know. His dissatisfaction, from being chronic and latent, had suddenly become acute and raged in him. It was as if the panther and the lion and the serpents and the eagles and the hawks had penetrated his skin and lived inside him in a raging warfare. The navy caught up with him, put him in the brig for nine months and then gave him a dishonorable discharge.

After that Parker decided that country air was the only kind fit to breathe. He rented the shack on the embankment and bought the old truck and took various jobs which he kept as long as it suited him. At the time he met his future wife, he was buying apples by the bushel and selling them for the same price by the pound to isolated homesteaders on back country roads.

"All that there," the woman said, pointing to his arm, "is no better than what a fool Indian would do. It's a heap of vanity." She seemed to have found the word she wanted. "Vanity of vanities," she said.

Well what the hell do I care what she thinks of it? Parker asked himself, but he was plainly bewildered. "I reckon you like one of these better than another anyway," he said, dallying until he thought of something that would impress her. He thrust the arm back at her. "Which you like best?"

"None of them," she said, "but the chicken is not as bad as the rest."

"What chicken?" Parker almost yelled.

She pointed to the eagle.

"That's an eagle," Parker said. "What fool would waste their time having a chicken put on themself?"

"What fool would have any of it?" the girl said and turned away. She went slowly back to the house and left him there to get going. Parker remained for almost five minutes, looking agape at the dark door she had entered.

The next day he returned with a bushel of apples. He was not one to be outdone by anything that looked like her. He liked women with meat on them, so you didn't feel their muscles, much less their old bones. When he arrived, she was sitting on the top step and the yard was full of children, all as thin and poor as herself; Parker remembered it was Saturday. He hated to be making up to a woman when there were children around, but it was fortunate he had brought the bushel of apples off the truck. As the children approached him to see what he carried, he gave each child an apple and told it to get lost; in that way he cleared out the whole crowd.

The girl did nothing to acknowledge his presence. He might have been a stray pig or goat that had wandered into the yard and she too tired to take up the broom and send it off. He set the bushel of apples down next to her on the step. He sat down on a lower step.

"Hep yourself," he said, nodding at the basket; then he lapsed into silence.

She took an apple quickly as if the basket might disappear if she didn't make haste. Hungry people made Parker nervous. He had always had plenty to eat himself. He grew very uncomfortable. He reasoned he had nothing to say so why should he say it? He could not think now why he had come or why he didn't go before he wasted another bushel of apples on the crowd of children. He supposed they were her brothers and sisters.

She chewed the apple slowly but with a kind of relish of concentration, bent slightly but looking out ahead. The view from the porch stretched off across a long incline studded with iron weed and across the highway to a vast vista of hills and one small mountain. Long views depressed Parker. You look out into space like that and you begin to feel as if someone were after you, the navy or the government or religion.

"Who them children belong to, you?" he said at length.

"I ain't married yet," she said. "They belong to momma." She said it as if it were only a matter of time before she would be married.

Who in God's name would marry her? Parker thought.

A large barefooted woman with a wide gap-toothed face appeared in the door behind Parker. She had apparently been there for several minutes.

"Good evening," Parker said.

The woman crossed the porch and picked up what was left of the bushel of apples. "We thank you," she said and returned with it into the house.

"That your old woman?" Parker muttered.

The girl nodded. Parker knew a lot of sharp things he could have said like "You got my sympathy," but he was gloomily silent. He just sat there, looking at the view. He thought he must be coming down with something.

"If I pick up some peaches tomorrow I'll bring you some," he said.

"I'll be much obliged to you," the girl said.

Parker had no intention of taking any basket of peaches back there but the next day he found himself doing it. He and the girl had almost nothing to say to each other. One thing he did say was, "I ain't got any tattoo on my back."

"What you got on it?" the girl said.

"My shirt," Parker said. "Haw."

"Haw, haw," the girl said politely.

Parker thought he was losing his mind. He could not believe for a minute that he was attracted to a woman like this. She showed not the least interest in anything but what he brought until he appeared the third time with two cantaloups. "What's your name?" she asked.

"O. E. Parker," he said.

"What does the O. E. stand for?"

"You can just call me O. E.," Parker said. "Or Parker. Don't nobody call me by my name."

"What's it stand for?" she persisted.

"Never mind," Parker said. "What's yours?"

"I'll tell you when you tell me what them letters are the short of," she said. There was just a hint of flirtatiousness in her tone and it went rapidly to Parker's head. He had never revealed the name to any man or woman, only to the files of the navy and the government, and it was on his baptismal record which he got at the age of a month; his mother was a Methodist. When the name leaked out of the navy files, Parker narrowly missed killing the man who used it.

"You'll go blab it around," he said.

"I'll swear I'll never tell nobody," she said. "On God's holy word I swear it."

Parker sat for a few minutes in silence. Then he reached for the girl's neck, drew her ear close to his mouth and revealed the name in low voice.

"Obadiah," she whispered. Her face slowly brightened as if the name came as a sign to her. "Obadiah," she said.

The name still stank in Parker's estimation.

"Obadiah Elihue," she said in a reverent voice.

"If you call me that aloud, I'll bust your head open," Parker said. "What's yours?"

"Sarah Ruth Cates," she said.

"Glad to meet you, Sarah Ruth," Parker said.

Sarah Ruth's father was a Straight Gospel preacher but he was away, spreading it in Florida. Her mother did not seem to mind his attention to the girl so long as he brought a basket of something with him when he came. As for Sarah Ruth herself, it was plain to Parker after he had visited three times that she was crazy about him. She liked him even though she insisted that pictures on the skin were vanity of vanities and even after hearing him curse, and even after she had asked him if he was saved and he had replied that he didn't see it was anything in particular to save him from. After that, inspired, Parker had said, "I'd be saved enough if you was to kiss me."

She scowled. "That ain't being saved," she said.

Not long after that she agreed to take a ride in his truck. Parker parked it on a deserted road and suggested to her that they lie down together in the back of it.

"Not until after we're married," she said—just like that.

"Oh that ain't necessary," Parker said and as he reached for her, she thrust him away with such force that the door of the truck came off and he found himself flat on his back on the ground. He made up his mind then and there to have nothing further to do with her.

They were married in the County Ordinary's office because Sarah Ruth thought churches were idolatrous. Parker had no opinion about that one way or the other. The Ordinary's office was lined with cardboard file boxes and record books with dusty yellow slips of paper hanging on out of them. The Ordinary was an old woman with red hair who had held office for forty years and looked as dusty as her books. She married them from behind the iron-grill of a stand-up desk and when she finished, she said with a flourish, "Three dollars and fifty cents and till death do you part!" and yanked some forms out of a machine.

Marriage did not change Sarah Ruth a jot and it made Parker gloomier than ever. Every morning he decided he had had enough and would not return that night; every night he returned. Whenever Parker couldn't stand the way he felt, he would have another tattoo, but the only surface left on him now was his back. To see a tattoo on his own back he would have to get two mirrors and stand between them in just the correct position and this seemed to Parker a good way to make an idiot of himself. Sarah Ruth who, if she had had better sense, could have enjoyed a tattoo on his back, would not even look at the ones he had elsewhere. When he attempted to point out especial details of them, she would shut her eyes tight and turn her back as well. Except in total darkness, she preferred Parker dressed and with his sleeves rolled down.

"At the judgement seat of God, Jesus is going to say to you, 'What you been doing all your life besides have pictures drawn all over you?'" she said.

"You don't fool me none," Parker said, "you're just afraid that hefty girl I work for'll like me so much she'll say, 'Come on, Mr. Parker, let's you and me . . .'"

"You're tempting sin," she said, "and at the judgement seat of God you'll have to answer for that too. You ought to go back to selling the fruits of the earth."

Parker did nothing much when he was at home but listen to what the judgement seat of God would be like for him if he didn't change his ways. When he could, he broke in with tales of the hefty girl he worked for. " 'Mr. Parker,' " he said she said, 'I hired you for your brains.' " (She had added, "So why don't you use them?")

"And you should have seen her face the first time she saw me without my shirt," he said. " 'Mr. Parker,' she said, 'you're a walking panner-rammer!' " This had, in fact, been her remark but it had been delivered out of one side of her mouth.

Dissatisfaction began to grow so great in Parker that there was no containing it outside of a tattoo. It had to be his back. There was no help for it. A dim half-formed inspiration began to work in his mind. He visualized having a tattoo put there that Sarah Ruth would not be able to resist—a religious subject. He thought of an open book with HOLY BIBLE tattooed under it and an actual verse printed on the page. This seemed just the thing for a while; then he began to hear her say, "Ain't I already got a real Bible? What you think I want to read the same verse over and over for when I can read it all?" He needed something better even than the Bible! He thought about it so much that he began to lose sleep. He was already losing flesh—Sarah Ruth just threw food in the pot and let it boil. Not knowing for certain why he continued to stay with a woman who was both ugly and pregnant and no cook made him generally nervous and irritable, and he developed a little tic in the side of his face.

Once or twice he found himself turning around abruptly as if someone were trailing him. He had had a granddaddy who had ended in the state mental hospital, although not until he was seventy-five, but as urgent as it might be for him to get a tattoo, it was just as urgent that he get exactly the right one to bring Sarah Ruth to heel. As he continued to worry over it, his eyes took on a hollow preoccupied expression. The old woman he worked for told him that if he couldn't keep his mind on what he was doing, she knew where she could find a fourteen-year-old colored boy who could. Parker was too preoccupied even to be offended. At any time previous, he would have left her then and there, saying drily, "Well, you go ahead on and get him then."

Two or three mornings later he was baling hay with the old woman's sorry baler and her broken down tractor in a large field, cleared save for one enormous old tree standing in the middle of it. The old woman was the kind who would not cut down a large old tree because it was a large old tree. She had pointed it out to Parker as if he didn't have eyes and told him to be careful not to hit it as the machine picked up hay near it. Parker began at the outside of the field and made circles inward toward it. He had to get off the tractor every now and then and untangle the baling cord or kick a rock out of the way. The old woman had told him to carry the rocks to the edge of the field, which he did when she was there watching. When he thought he could make it, he ran over them. As he circled the field his mind was on a suitable design for his back. The sun, the size of a golf ball, began to switch regularly from in front to behind him, but he appeared to see it both places as if he had eyes in the back of his head. All at once he saw the tree reaching out to grasp him. A ferocious thud propelled him into the air, and he heard himself yelling in an unbelievably loud voice, "GOD ABOVE!"

He landed on his back while the tractor crashed upside down into the tree and burst into flame. The first thing Parker saw were his shoes, quickly being eaten by the fire; one was caught under the tractor, the other was some distance away, burning by itself. He was not in them. He could feel the hot breath of the burning tree on his face. He scrambled backwards, still sitting, his eyes cavernous, and if he had known how to cross himself he would have done it.

His truck was on a dirt road at the edge of the field. He moved toward it, still sitting, still backwards, but faster and faster; halfway to it he got up and began a kind of forward-bent run from which he collapsed on his knees twice. His legs felt like two old rusted rain gutters. He reached the truck finally and took off in it, zigzagging up the road. He drove past his house on the embankment and straight for the city, fifty miles distant.

Parker did not allow himself to think on the way to the city. He only knew that there had been a great change in his life, a leap forward into a worse unknown, and that there was nothing he could do about it. It was for all intents accomplished.

The artist had two large cluttered rooms over a chiropodist's office on a back street. Parker, still barefooted, burst silently in on him at a little after three in the afternoon. The artist, who was about Parker's own age—twenty-eight—but thin and bald, was behind a small drawing table, tracing a design in green ink. He looked up with an annoyed glance and did not seem to recognize Parker in the hollow-eyed creature before him.

"Let me see the book you got with all the pictures of God in it," Parker said breathlessly. "The religious one."

The artist continued to look at him with his intellectual, superior stare. "I don't put tattoos on drunks," he said.

"You know me!" Parker cried indignantly. "I'm O. E. Parker! You done work for me before and I always paid!"

The artist looked at him another moment as if he were not altogether sure. "You've fallen off some," he said. "You must have been in jail."

"Married," Parker said.

"Oh," said the artist. With the aid of mirrors the artist had tattooed on the top of his head a miniature owl, perfect in every detail. It was about the size of a half-dollar and served him as a show piece. There were cheaper artists in town but Parker had never wanted anything but the best. The artist went over to a cabinet at the back of the room and began to look over some art books. "Who are you interested in?" he said, "saints, angels, Christs or what?"

"God," Parker said.

"Father, Son or Spirit?"

"Just God," Parker said impatiently. "Christ. I don't care. Just so it's God."

The artist returned with a book. He moved some papers off another table and put the book down on it and told Parker to sit down and see what he liked. "The up-t-date ones are in the back," he said.

Parker sat down with the book and wet his thumb. He began to go through it, beginning at the back where the up-to-date pictures were. Some of them he recognized—The Good Shepherd, Forbid Them Not, The Smiling Jesus, Jesus the Physician's Friend, but he kept turning rapidly backwards and the pictures became less and less reassuring. One showed a gaunt green dead face streaked with blood. One was yellow with sagging purple eyes. Parker's heart began to beat faster and faster until it appeared to be roaring inside him like a great generator. He flipped the pages quickly, feeling that when he reached the one ordained, a sign would come. He continued to flip through until he had almost reached the front of the book. On one of the pages a pair of eyes glanced at him swiftly. Parker sped on, then stopped. His heart too appeared to cut off; there was absolute silence. It said as plainly as if silence were a language itself, GO BACK.

Parker returned to the picture—the haloed head of a flat stern Byzantine Christ with all-demanding eyes. He sat there trembling; his heart began slowly to beat again as if it were being brought to life by a subtle power.

"You found what you want?" the artist asked.

Parker's throat was too dry to speak. He got up and thrust the book at the artist, opened at the picture.

"That'll cost you plenty," the artist said. "You don't want all those little blocks though, just the outline and some better features."

"Just like it is," Parker said, "just like it is or nothing."

"It's your funeral," the artist said, "but I don't do that kind of work for nothing."

"How much?" Parker asked.

"It'll take maybe two days work."

"How much?" Parker said.

"On time or cash?" the artist asked. Parker's other jobs had been on time, but he had paid.

"Ten down and ten for every day it takes," the artist said.

Parker drew ten dollar bills out of his wallet; he had three left in.

"You come back in the morning," the artist said, putting the money in his own pocket. "First I'll have to trace that out of the book."

"No no!" Parker said. "Trace it now or gimme my money back," and his eyes blared as if he were ready for a fight.

The artist agreed. Any one stupid enough to want a Christ on his back, he reasoned, would be just as likely as not to change his mind the next minute, but once the work was begun he could hardly do so.

While he worked on the tracing, he told Parker to go wash his back at the sink with the special soap he used there. Parker did it and returned to pace back and forth across the room, nervously flexing his shoulders. He wanted to go look at the picture again but at the same time he did not want to. The artist got up finally and had Parker lie down on the table. He swabbed his back with ethyl chloride and then began to outline the head on it with his iodine pencil. Another hour passed before he took up his electric instrument. Parker felt no particular pain. In Japan he had had a tattoo of the Buddha done on his upper arm with ivory needles; in Burma, a little brown root of a man had made a peacock on each of his knees using thin pointed sticks, two feet long; amateurs had worked on him with pins and soot. Parker was usually so relaxed and easy under the hand of the artist that he often went to sleep, but this time he remained awake, every muscle taut.

At midnight the artist said he was ready to quit. He propped one mirror, four feet square, on a table by the wall and took a smaller mirror off the lavatory wall and put it in Parker's hands. Parker stood with his back to the one on the table and moved the other until he saw a flashing burst of color reflected from his back. It was almost completely covered with little red and blue and ivory and saffron squares; from them he made out the lineaments of the face—a mouth, the beginning of heavy brows, a straight nose, but the face was empty; the eyes had not yet been put in. The impression for the moment was almost as if the artist had tricked him and done the Physician's Friend.

"It don't have eyes," Parker cried out.

"That'll come," the artist said, "in due time. We have another day to go on it yet."

Parker spent the night on a cot at the Haven of Light Christian Mission. He found these the best places to stay in the city because they were free and included a meal of sorts. He got the last available cot and because he was still barefooted, he accepted a pair of second-hand shoes which, in his confusion, he put on to go to bed; he was still shocked from all that had happened to him. All night he lay awake in the long dormitory of cots with lumpy figures on them. The only light was from a phosphorescent cross glowing at the end of the room. The tree reached out to grasp him again, then burst into flame; the shoe burned quietly by itself; the eyes in the book said to him distinctly GO BACK and at the same time did not utter a sound. He wished that he were not in this city, not in this Haven of Light Mission, not in a bed by himself. He longed miserably for Sarah Ruth. Her sharp tongue and icepick eyes were the only comfort he could bring to mind. He decided he was losing it. Her eyes appeared soft and dilatory compared with the eyes in the book, for even though he could not summon up the exact look of those eyes, he could still feel their penetration. He felt as though, under their gaze, he was as transparent as the wing of a fly.

The tattooist had told him not to come until ten in the morning, but when he arrived at that hour, Parker was sitting in the dark hallway on the floor, waiting for him. He had decided upon getting up that, once the tattoo was on him, he would not look at it, that all his sensations of the day and night before were those of a crazy man and that he would return to doing things according to his own sound judgement.

The artist began where he left off. "One thing I want to know," he said presently as he worked over Parker's back, "why do you want this on you? Have you gone and got religion? Are you saved?" he asked in a mocking voice.

Parker's throat felt salty and dry. "Naw," he said, "I ain't got no use for none of that. A man can't save his self from whatever it is he don't deserve none of my sympathy." These words seemed to leave his mouth like wraiths and to evaporate at once as if he had never uttered them.

"Then why . . ."

"I married this woman that's saved," Parker said. "I never should have done it. I ought to leave her. She's done gone and got pregnant."

"That's too bad," the artist said. "Then it's her making you have this tattoo."

"Naw," Parker said, "she don't know nothing about it. It's a surprise for her."

"You think she'll like it and lay off you a while?"

"She can't hep herself," Parker said. "She can't say she don't like the looks of God." He decided he had told the artist enough of his business. Artists were all right in their place but he didn't like them poking their noses into the affairs of regular people. "I didn't get no sleep last night," he said. "I think I'll get some now."

That closed the mouth of the artist but it did not bring him any sleep. He lay there, imagining how Sarah Ruth would be struck speechless by the face on his back and every now and then this would be interrupted by a vision of the tree of fire and his empty shoe burning beneath it.

The artist worked steadily until nearly four o'clock, not stopping to have lunch, hardly pausing with the electric instrument except to wipe the dripping dye off Parker's back as he went along. Finally he finished. "You can get up and look at it now," he said.

Parker sat up but he remained on the edge of the table.

The artist was pleased with his work and wanted Parker to look at it at once. Instead Parker continued to sit on the edge of the table, bent forward slightly but with a vacant look. "What ails you?" the artist said. "Go look at it."

"Ain't nothing ail me," Parker said in a sudden belligerent voice. "That tattoo ain't going nowhere. It'll be there when I get there." He reached for his shirt and began gingerly to put it on.

The artist took him roughly by the arm and propelled him between the two mirrors. "Now *look,*" he said, angry at having his work ignored.

Parker looked, turned white and moved away. The eyes in the reflected face continued to look at him—still, straight, all-demanding, enclosed in silence.

"It was your idea, remember," the artist said. "I would have advised something else."

Parker said nothing. He put on his shirt and went out the door while the artist shouted, "I'll expect all of my money!"

Parker headed toward a package shop on the corner. He bought a pint of whiskey and took it into a nearby alley and drank it all in five minutes. Then he moved on to a pool hall nearby which he frequented when he came to the city. It was a well-lighted barnlike place with a bar up one side and gambling machines on the other and pool tables in the back. As soon as Parker entered, a large man in a red and black checkered shirt hailed him by slapping him on the back and yelling, "Yeyyyyyy boy! O. E. Parker!"

Parker was not yet ready to be struck on the back. "Lay off," he said, "I got a fresh tattoo there."

"What you got this time?" the man asked and then yelled to a few at the machines. "O.E.'s got him another tattoo."

"Nothing special this time," Parker said and slunk over to a machine that was not being used.

"Come on," the big man said, "let's have a look at O.E.'s tattoo," and while Parker squirmed in their hands, they pulled up his shirt. Parker felt all the hands drop away instantly and his shirt fell again like a veil over the face. There was a silence in the pool room which seemed to Parker to grow from the circle around him until it extended to the foundations under the building and upward through the beams in the roof.

Finally someone said, "Christ!" Then they all broke into noise at once. Parker turned around, an uncertain grin on his face.

"Leave it to O.E.!" the man in the checkered shirt said. "That boy's a real card!"

"Maybe he's gone and got religion," someone yelled.

"Not on your life," Parker said.

"O.E.'s got religion and is witnessing for Jesus, ain't you, O.E.?" a little man with a piece of cigar in his mouth said wryly. "An o-riginal way to do it if I ever saw one."

"Leave it to Parker to think of a new one!" the fat man said.

"Yyeeeeeeyyyyyyy boy!" someone yelled and they all began to whistle and curse in compliment until Parker said, "Aaa shut up."

"What'd you do it for?" somebody asked.

"For laughs," Parker said. "What's it to you?"

"Why ain't you laughing then?" somebody yelled. Parker lunged into the midst of them and like a whirlwind on a summer's day there began a fight that raged amid overturned tables and swinging fists until two of them grabbed him and ran to the door with him and threw him out. Then a calm descended on the pool hall as nerve shattering as if the long barnlike room were the ship from which Jonah had been cast into the sea.

Parker sat for a long time on the ground in the alley behind the pool hall, examining his soul. He saw it as a spider web of facts and lies that was not at all important to him but which appeared to be necessary in spite of his opinion. The eyes that were now forever on his back were eyes to be obeyed. He was as certain of it as he had ever been of anything. Throughout his life, grumbling and sometimes cursing, often afraid, once in rapture, Parker had obeyed whatever instinct of this kind had come to him—in rapture when his spirit had lifted at the sight of the tattooed man at the fair, afraid when he had joined the navy, grumbling when he had married Sarah Ruth.

The thought of her brought him slowly to his feet. She would know what he had to do. She would clear up the rest of it, and she would at least be pleased. It seemed to him that, all along, that was what he wanted, to please her. His truck was still parked in front of the building where the artist had his place, but it was not far away. He got in it and drove out of the city and into the country night. His head was almost clear of liquor and he observed that his dissatisfaction was gone, but he felt not quite like himself. It was as if he were himself but a stranger to himself, driving into a new country though everything he saw was familiar to him, even at night.

He arrived finally at the house on the embankment, pulled the truck under the pecan tree and got out. He made as much noise as possible to assert that he was still in charge here, that his leaving her for a night without word meant nothing except it was the way he did things. He slammed the car door, stamped up the two steps and across the porch and rattled the door knob. It did not respond to his touch. "Sarah Ruth!" he yelled, "let me in."

There was no lock on the door and she had evidently placed the back of a chair against the knob. He began to beat on the door and rattle the knob at the same time.

He heard the bed springs screak and bent down and put his head to the keyhole, but it was stopped up with paper. "Let me in!" he hollered, bamming on the door again. "What you got me locked out for?"

A sharp voice close to the door said, "Who's there?"

"Me," Parker said, "O.E."

He waited a moment.

"Me," he said impatiently, "O.E."

Still no sound from inside.

He tried once more. "O.E.," he said, bamming the door two or three more times. "O. E. Parker. You know me."

There was a silence. Then the voice said slowly, "I don't know no O.E."

"Quit fooling," Parker pleaded. "You ain't got any business doing me this way. It's me, old O.E., I'm back. You ain't afraid of me."

"Who's there?" the same unfeeling voice said.

Parker turned his head as if he expected someone behind him to give him the answer. The sky had lightened slightly and there were two or three streaks of yellow floating above the horizon. Then as he stood there, a tree of light burst over the skyline.

Parker fell back against the door as if he had been pinned there by a lance.

"Who's there?" the voice from inside said and there was a quality about it now that seemed final. The knob rattled and the voice said peremptorily, "Who's there, I ast you?"

Parker bent down and put his mouth near the stuffed keyhole. "Obadiah," he whispered and all at once he felt the light pouring through him, turning his spider web soul into a perfect arabesque of colors, a garden of trees and birds and beasts.

"Obadiah Elihue!" he whispered.

The door opened and he stumbled in. Sarah Ruth loomed there, hands on her hips. She began at once, "That was no hefty blonde woman you was working for and you'll have to pay her every penny on her tractor you busted up. She don't keep insurance on it. She came here and her and me had us a long talk and I . . ."

Trembling, Parker set about lighting the kerosene lamp.

"What's the matter with you, wasting that kerosene this near daylight?" she demanded. "I ain't got to look at you."

A yellow glow enveloped them. Parker put the match down and began to unbutton his shirt.

"And you ain't going to have none of me this near morning," she said.

"Shut your mouth," he said quietly. "Look at this and then I don't want to hear no more out of you." He removed the shirt and turned his back to her.

"Another picture," Sarah Ruth growled. "I might have known you was off after putting some more trash on yourself."

Parker's knees went hollow under him. He wheeled around and cried, "Look at it! Don't just say that! *Look* at it!"

"I done looked," she said.

"Don't you know who it is?" he cried in anguish.

"No, who is it?" Sarah Ruth said. "It ain't anybody I know."

"It's him," Parker said.

"Him who?"

"God!" Parker cried.

"God? God don't look like that!"

"What do you know how he looks?" Parker moaned. "You ain't seen him."

"He don't *look*," Sarah Ruth said. "He's a spirit. No man shall see his face."

"Aw listen," Parker groaned, "this is just a picture of him."

"Idolatry!" Sarah Ruth screamed. "Idolatry! Enflaming yourself with idols under every green tree! I can put up with lies and vanity but I don't want no idolator in this house!" and she grabbed up the broom and began to thrash him across the shoulders with it.

Parker was too stunned to resist. He sat there and let her beat him until she had nearly knocked him senseless and large welts had formed on the face of the tattooed Christ. Then he staggered up and made for the door.

She stamped the broom two or three times on the floor and went to the window and shook it out to get the taint of him off it. Still gripping it, she looked toward the pecan tree and her eyes hardened still more. There he was—who called himself Obadiah Elihue—leaning against the tree, crying like a baby.

Light Timber

NANCY POTTER

(1926–)

My Uncle Jude was a throwback, everyone agreed. He would have liked to have been in the mainstream, but lost his way. Jude was my mother's brother, only son in the family, which, I suppose, was part of the problem. My using his first name, by the way, shows no disrespect. He was fond of saying that he was a simple sort, which in some ways was true. He disliked the rain and the calls of doves or pigeons, but he was something of a crape hanger and liked to read the obituaries or visit the old in nursing homes and he always teared up when he heard "O Promise Me" or "Panis Angelicus."

He was my godfather, and until I was about ten, he was my favorite person. His pockets held gifts to be searched for—tin whistles, measuring tape, yo-yos, barrettes, thimbles, once even a compass. For me he furnished a whole doll's house piece by piece and before that a tiny farm with wooden animals and barns and fuzzy hedges and little fences. But when I got into junior high, he faded considerably from my life. Oh, he took all of us, Mother and Dad and the aunts and married uncles, cousins and my closest friends to dinner in the Show Boat Restaurant after my Confirmation and always remembered my birthday with crisp bills, even when I was working after college in New York.

He probably made a list of anniversaries and birthdates and had the bills all ready for sending with a carefully addressed card. Of course, the mail was an important part of his life. After the service he became a mail carrier and, when his legs gave out, he was promoted to sorting in the main post office. Something had happened to his feet, frostbite probably, during the war. For a long time after the war, my mother kept all the letters and cards he had sent her, although they said little. "Paris is like any other big town. Can't find anything to eat here. Six months more before I see God's country. Yours in haste." Then she must have thrown them out. I was searching yesterday for a scrap of his handwriting, but couldn't find any. Because as an adult I always found conversation in person or on paper with him awkward, I flinched guiltily when I saw again his black scrawls on the birthday cards and heard his voice sometimes during Thanksgiving or Christmas telephone calls. As with those who are usually only heard in choruses, it is hard to recall his voice, and we made no tapes and took few pictures in my family. Those pictures in which he can be seen only show his head in the back row behind his sisters and their families. There was something about him that even Kodacolor never caught. His shyness turned then to frown or squint.

As a child, I was puzzled by grown-up men in civilian uniforms, working as elevator operators, doormen, or train conductors. However, Jude's drab clothes on the job and his weather-darkened mailbag looked very unofficial. When you saw him at a distance, he seemed very much shorter than up close. He stooped, probably a little embarrassed at being six feet tall in a house of small women, and his feet bothered him.

Like most mail carriers, he was full of cheery patter along his route. "Oh, don't call me Mr. McNamarra. Jude's the name. Not Judas. Jude. For the patron saint of lost causes. My mother must have thought I needed all the help I could get. A hardship case. Now you take it easy."

Another reason Jude stumbled a lot was that he was always looking up, not at the sky, but at trees. Nobody in our family was interested in gardening, except to keep grass in its place. And in Jude's generation they were still congratulating themselves on having escaped being farmers in County Clare. Jude went over on an Aer Lingus flight from Boston to Shannon to help the cousins hay in July. "We're well out of that," he used to tell me.

It was trees that he cared about. "I don't know why. They try so hard. They give a lot and don't ask much. All that ice and smog and cutting back from the wires. And all the different shapes they grow into. You never know. It's all inside, telling them but not letting you know until it happens." In passing, he sometimes touched the trunks of the trees along his route—the last of the sickly elms, some old maples, ailanthus coming sturdily along through cracks in the pavement. First he set out a couple of dwarf fruit trees in the back of my grandmother's three-decker. "They give a good harvest with little space." Then he put in a row of poplars, over my father's protest that they would be dead in thirty years. "Time enough for me," Jude answered. Whenever we saw him reading, it seemed to be about trees, their leaves and bark and root systems. The few times in recent years that I was in that gloomy parlor for grandmother's birthday parties, Jude would be going out onto the back porch to stare at the branches of the fruit trees. He would make detours on the way to the garage or incinerator to look some more.

When I was growing up, the family would have described themselves as close. They saw each other on Sundays and in between called on the phone. They all lived within about a twenty-five mile radius and when they said "The Family" we all knew what they meant. They didn't go in for elaborate explanations but instead seemed to operate by subtle signaling like flocks of birds. They shared a prejudice against extreme behavior; my mother maintained that you didn't need to wear a Miraculous Medal to prove that you were a Catholic or display a dozen family photographs on the piano to show that you cared about the subjects. Excesses of religious piety like putting up Holy Thursday altars at home or Fátima statues in the front yard were frowned on. My parents generally regretted the noisy social confusion resulting from the English Mass, the handshakes, the unmelodic hymns, all the strange moving around. They missed the dreamy quiet of the Latin Mass, although neither of them knew Latin.

Like Jude's devotion to trees, his religious enthusiasm was a respected mystery to us. We assumed that it took the place of wife and children for him. At forty-five after Vatican II, he seemed to have come into his own. He was elected to the newly formed Parish Council. He passed the basket at any early Sunday Mass and, finally, he became a lector. He used to practice the reading up in his room so that he wouldn't stumble over the difficult place names in the Epistles. "Your uncle," my father muttered, glancing toward the ceiling from which Jude's voice was solemnly describing Paul's travels, "your uncle should have been born a church mouse."

It was about this time that he began to notice Sister Stanislas Kostka who was often on reception duty at the parish convent. Probably, the first time he rang the bell with a special delivery letter and flustered in her immediate presence, he blundered into his usual chatter about the wet spring good for saplings, mold, and the infield grass at Fenway. It was always safe to talk with nuns about baseball. This was before the modifications began, and she was in the old habit, an impressive eighteenth-century widow's costume.

It was also considered, in those days, that it was all right to joke a lot with the sisters and even outside of the classroom to call them by familiar nicknames. Of course, she was Sister Stash. She had come from a Polish family in another part of the state and was the first religious in generations. Once they got over the shock, they canonized her, driving up to the convent on Sundays in their big Buicks to cart her off with another sister for an expensive dinner in some fancy restaurant. They would dance around her, laughing and smiling. She was their talisman. New babies were brought to sit on her lap, her nephews made her hand-tooled missal covers at camp, her father provided Styrofoam hampers of kielbasa, and her brother told her frequently how lucky she really was.

At the end of the summer of 1967, I came home from waitressing to get ready for another year at college. It was Labor Day, when the big parish fair is always held. It grows bigger every year. They raffle off a new Mercury, which is the central attraction, import through a concessionaire several fairly dull rides on which no one can get hurt, offer free blood pressure tests, provide a different band every night, and serve two sittings of a cheap shore dinner of chowder, clam cakes, and watermelon. And, of course, there are the tables of fancy work and white elephants. Jude led me toward the jewelry table behind which Sister Stash was installed. That year the jewelry was particularly ugly; the table featured bead necklaces, name bracelets, little animals painted on shells and ceramic pansies. Sister Stash was sitting on a folding chair behind the table, looking out in a dazed, indifferent way. She was in the newly modified habit, which added ten years and several pounds to all the wearers. It included a midcalf skirt, high-necked blouse, and a little cotton head scarf.

I was not surprised that Jude stopped at the table. He was a compulsive buyer of books of chances and lottery tickets. "Never know when our ship will come in." He was a pushover for any Sunday solicitors for causes or kids unloading giant candy bars for Little League or holding canisters for band uniforms.

"I want you to pick out some earrings," he said, "anything you want." He seemed quite nervous. "This is my niece, Molly, Sister Stash. I want her to have something nice. Remember, I told you she's the one up at State. She could become a lawyer some day."

I was surprised that he had mentioned me to her at all. We stood uncomfortably in front of the card table looking at shells awkwardly glued to earrings and sea horses stuck in plastic. I couldn't see one possibility in the whole lot. Looking across into Sister Stash's eyes, I thought she recognized my dilemma, but her expression never revealed. Her face was like a doll's, perfect without being beautiful or memorable. Because her lips were often parted, she looked about to say something. The white blouse and kerchief gave her the look of a sturdy peasant in a costume movie.

Jude must have had a beer or two at the Rathskeller tent (they were featuring a German theme at the fair that year). He had a low tolerance for drinking; it made him silly and sleepy. He held up a pair of tiered sparkling earrings to his own ear lobes, against his large flushed face.

Sister Stash looked confused and was rather abrupt: "You'll take these?"

"What a saleswoman you make," he said. "Come on, Molly, don't you want to buy some Christmas gifts for your chums?"

I asked Sister Stash what grade she would be teaching next year, and she said, "Who knows? They never tell you until the day school opens. I guess it doesn't matter."

"They'll be lucky kids, whichever ones they are," Jude said. And as we walked away, he was still holding the earrings which he fortunately forgot to give me. "What a wonderful spirit she has," he said.

A few weeks before the Christmas after that fair, I had a strange telephone call from my mother. She always waited for cheaper rates, and she never called in the morning. I thought that grandmother had gone when I heard her strained voice.

"No, it's worse than that, if you can imagine."

"What?" I asked, shivering in the ugly dorm phone booth, trying to keep my voice calm.

"It's Jude. He wants to get married. To Sister Stash. That is, Rose, whatever her real name is."

"Maybe he's in love," I said.

"How could he be? Jude? Why, he hardly knows her. She's coming out, though."

"Well, that's lucky. They couldn't very well live in the convent," I said.

"Don't be smart," she said. "There's nothing funny about this. I wanted you to know so that you can plan to go somewhere else for Christmas if you want. It's going to be terrible around here. The embarrassment. The bad luck. What did we ever do to deserve this?"

"I don't see that he's done anything wrong," I said. "He's a good man. A lot better than most."

"That's just it. Your father says it's like a cow that gives a fine pail of milk and then kicks it over."

It was impossible to discover where my father picked up these comparisons. "Where is Jude now?" I asked. "Shouldn't I congratulate him?"

"He's upstairs fixing his breakfast," my mother replied.

"Well, he won't have to do that any more," I said.

My mother ignored that comment. Jude's making his own breakfast had always seemed the ultimate loneliness. He was meticulous about the details, setting out the coffee cup and plate the night before with the knife and spoon and one paper napkin.

About the wedding, we were torn between confusion and curiosity. By now I was so absorbed in college life that what I was seeing at home was distanced, as in a movie.

So many religious were then leaving the orders that Sister Stash's request for release from vows was processed rapidly, and the simple document arrived back from Rome in no time. Rose (we had to remember to call her that) was waiting at the Motherhouse to be fetched. On the first day of my Christmas vacation, my mother and I, somewhat like chaperons, drove up there with Jude. I didn't see them greet each other. He rang the doorbell and went inside, returning quickly with her and a small suitcase. She may have gone shopping earlier or perhaps they gave her the navy blue polo coat, which was too long and a few sizes too big. We had the car radio on and sang along with the Christmas carols, then stopped at a Friendly's for hamburgers and shakes. Rose pushed the food around her plate, while Jude ate heartily.

She stayed in my parents' apartment since her family was still so scandalized by her coming out that no one among them could be mustered to communicate, let alone participate in the ceremony. Therefore, there was no point in delaying the wedding, and the holidays ran together in confusion. Jude was a changed man, laughing, touching things, waving his hands in the air, but I never saw him embrace her.

Rose and I went shopping once before the wedding. Used to the company of women, she talked more with me than in the house with Jude. She went busily through the crowded shopping mall, feeling fabrics, picking over the bargain tables, and finally selected a marked-down street-length blue wool dress that she could wear later. Although the order had become much less strict, she had ten years to make up for. I wasn't used to seeing her in bright colors, and she tended to buy everything a size too large. Since they were taking a package tour to Acapulco, she also bought a bathing suit. The whole idea of their honeymoon seemed indiscreet to me.

We tried to make the wedding as festive as we could, but it was clear that we were all on edge, bumping into each other and talking too loudly. They were married at a ten o'clock Mass on the day after Christmas. Our timing was off. The ceremony was very brief, and we got to the Mona Lisa Lounge too early. They hadn't set up the tables for lunch, and even the bar wasn't open. Rose observed that this wedding had been a good deal shorter than the other one. That was the only funny thing anyone said.

After the drinks and food arrived, matters improved. Then, as so often, my father surprised me. He had stood up for Jude, and as best man was expected to offer the toast. He must have searched through the Biblical glossary for the one he gave. He made some reference to Jude as a tree planter and then he quoted Isaiah, "As the days of a tree are the days of my people, and the works of their hands shall be of long continuance." My father has a lovely voice and he spoke with real conviction as if making up for years of slighting Jude. The tension broke for a while, and we noisily got into our cars and congregated on the observation deck of our shabby little state airport to see them off. Rose was wearing her polo coat to which she had pinned the orchid corsage. She seemed not to walk with Jude as much as to run ahead with a bunch of strangers. He stood behind, waving repeatedly at us.

Then we drove back home, uneasy and not wanting to separate. Over the old-fashioneds my father said that it was the oddest Christmas he ever wanted to spend.

Family gatherings after that time maintained the tension. It took some getting used to, thinking of Jude as married, and he was busy creating a cult for her. She was often absent in her sewing room or shopping, when he talked about her. When she did appear, she was as elusive as a breeze. She looked different from the rest of us. We are swarthy Irish like big shade trees. She was light and supple as a birch, the leaves glistening like ghosts. Jude was totally absorbed by her, plying her continually with questions. Should he wear the black necktie with the green suit? Should they cash in the matured savings bonds? Should they take up line dancing? Could she explain existentionalism simply to him? All the while she seemed to be looking sideways to escape his scrutiny. Or perhaps she was dreaming with her eyes open. Her answers were minimal.

Once he said to me, "She's so quiet she scares me. I don't know what's going on in her mind. Remembering, I suppose. She's been through so much."

And sometimes when we were all sitting around after dinner, he would try to lead her into the conversation. "Rose, tell them about almost setting the novitiate on fire when you were scrambling eggs after lights out." She would protest, "It wasn't that funny. They wouldn't be interested." And quite lamely she would begin the story. We felt constrained to laugh far more than it deserved, which may have convinced Jude that she was witty. But anyone loking carefully at her impassive face and twisting hands knew otherwise. Occasionally she would interrupt the stories with a sigh as if the weight of the words troubled her tongue, and Jude would finish them.

They had been married two years when she left him, apparently not for anyone else. Simply for herself. Not that we ever really got the whole story. Maybe there was no one episode, probably no great disagreement, and there was no divorce. So quiet were they that the rest of the family did not discover the loss until she had been gone a few days. It was certainly inconceivable that they would have shouted or cried out or thrown things at each other or slammed doors. She may have figured out finally that he had married her for what she represented or he thought she represented.

To everyone but Jude her departure caused little dislocation. They had continued to live in the top floor apartment of my grandmother's three-decker. So there Jude stayed, among all his things, having, one might say, the run of the house, looking in on the other relatives and out at his trees.

"You were right to plant those poplars. They'll be here long after us. That's for sure," my father repeatedly told him.

My cousins and I were busy with our lives, falling in and out of love, marrying and unmarrying, preferring to believe that all of our old life was waiting for us, back there, capable of being taken up, though we seldom tested it.

Jude's was the first death in the family I remember. He was rushed to the hospital by his buddies when he slumped over the sorting desk one afternoon, and then suffered two massive coronaries, almost too grand an ailment for his modesty.

Until then, our family had escaped death and, summoned with no preparation, we all stood around Grady's Funeral Home in unfamiliar dark clothes, wrong for the season. It was July and humid. While gardens were heavy with zinnias and marigolds, mid-July is not a good time for floral sprays: too late for roses and carnations, too early for mums.

Over the whir of the air conditioner, we tried to cheer each other up, to get used to the circumstance. We had not realized that our ceremonies had always been happy—weddings, graduations, christenings. I suppose Jude had attended a lot of wakes and funerals. He would have been in his element. What struck me all over again is how reduced so much of modern living is, not just the fancy "Quality of Life" about which my erudite friends worry but the simple routines that people like Jude hanker for. For instance, wakes aren't what they used to be or parades or family picnics, or Sunday dinner. Maybe they never were what they were supposed to be. Even summers aren't as good any more.

Naturally, we were all thinking about Rose who now lives on the West Coast under mysterious circumstances in something like a commune. There was a pay phone in the place and all sorts of background noises, children, shouts, and barking dogs, according to my cousin who was given the responsibility of informing her of Jude's death without encouraging her to attend the funeral. There had been no danger of that. She expressed sympathy to everyone, thanked him for calling, and said goodbye.

"Can you imagine," my mother said, "she didn't even send a flower. Ashamed, I suppose."

"Light timber," my father said in an uncontrolled voice. He was more shaken than any of us, perhaps because he was close to Jude in age. I had never seen him cry before and great untidy tears rained over his face. "That girl was light timber."

Voice of the Town

CURTIS HARNACK

(1927–)

Theodore Rueff took on his life as if it held no mystery he couldn't solve. He tithed his income and served as elder in the Protestant church, sang the gaunt, sad hymns from his usual spot on the aisle in the fifth pew—even God seemed taken care of. But behind this amiable show of certitude we saw the looming figure of his youngest son, Danny, who by age fifteen was seven feet two inches tall.

As he began to sprout, Clara Rueff joshed with her friends about what a big boy she had produced. They squinted behind their smiles and let her think what she wanted. Theodore was put to the trouble of buying special shoes and clothes in the city, but all he talked about was what a swell basketball player Danny would become. Years later Danny's surprising marriage to LaVonne seemed to fulfill his father's hopes of a normal life for his son—hopes which we of the town knew Danny could never possibly realize. All the time Danny and LaVonne lived and worked together, we saw their alliance with our own eyes but groped for an important truth lurking somewhere in their privacy. Who would tell of it? Theodore never cracked. He was Kaleburg's leading banker, keeper of the public confidence, and no one ever knew what torments of doubt or unease afflicted him. Finally he was to go to the grave clean and fast with a heart attack, before any audible whimpers could begin, or any revelations. Because of men like Ted Rueff the general faith is held—or deeply doubted. One wonders why anybody'd like to see himself in such a dubious role, and why we always expect someone to play it.

The Rueffs' was the third house in from the highway as you entered town, green clapboard with steeply pitched eaves and one hundred running feet of porch, all of it screened. There, on card-party evenings, Ted Rueff was the smiling host clearly visible through the windows to passers-by in automobiles, as if he were on display. At the party everyone talked a great deal—but mostly about the tricks just taken and who should have trumped but hadn't. The four Rueff children, according to custom, were kept out of the way. But Danny the giant, dazzled by the company, would climb like Jack-and-the-beanstalk up into those rooms of people from the basement playroom. "What were you doing in the cellar, big fellow?" a guest might call. "Lifting the house?"

"Hey, how's the weather up there?" (This from one of Clara's twinkly friends.)

He never answered. Even his face was peculiarly unresponsive; his round jowls simply hung there like a peeled eggplant. "Danny, you get your sleep," Clara said, in her soft-sigh way. "Go on now—you're the youngest," an excuse she used to hide the fact that sometimes he got so tired he fell asleep standing up or sitting in a chair and had to be caught before he hit the floor and broke his flesh open. He couldn't bear the cold in winter like the others; he fainted from the heat if he went out in August without his blue baseball cap. Germs found a haven in his huge interior, and nothing could stop their proliferation—as if inside, not all the caverns had yet been accounted for.

Clara was like the hen that sat on a duck egg along with her own and she refused to see a difference among her offspring. She was very bosomy, such an enormous pillow that it seemed ample not only for the Rueff family to cushion its fears upon but also for anyone who might need this reassurance. In winter she draped herself in a fox-collared coat, soft as a dog's shank. Her creamy pearls—a double strand, for years the only real pearls in town—stood for the things which were not of flesh, and she believed in them.

While he was young, Danny moved along from grade to grade, but at the start of high school the principal had a closed-door talk with Ted Rueff. Soon Danny showed up as clerk in his father's bank. "Hey there, big boy," customers called, "got your hands on the money yet?"

Cheerful as always and now even somewhat handsome in a blown-up way, he'd grin and wave his baseball-mitt hand. But he never said much. "He understands real good," said the teller. "He's taking it all in," said the cashier. "He'll be a banker yet," said Ted Rueff, thinking he was among friends, but it soon got around town.

Danny performed simple clerical errands such as going into the vault with a customer's safe-deposit key. He swept the floor and kept the cooler filled with water. Try as he might, he couldn't learn to work with figures. He found it hard to concentrate, sitting at a desk, his spine curved like a wishbone. Ted had new furniture built, but Danny still couldn't remember the multiplication table. "What do they teach in that school!" Theodore shouted one day, and a farmer at the grilled window overheard and passed it along. "What do they *teach?* What do they *teach?*" was savored in taverns and stores all week. To think, Ted Rueff hadn't been taught the difference between a soft-head and a normal person!

Danny was dismissed on orders from "someone higher up" and for a time not even the family seemed to pay much attention to him. The two older boys were busy suiting-up for basketball after school; they dribbled down the glistening floor with the cocky good feeling of being loose in the joints. Girl friends tumbled to them quickly. They had no time to look after Danny, and even his sister ran out on the old tender responsibility. She became a cheerleader.

"Luckily, Danny's found something he likes to do," Clara announced, smiling, imperturbable. "He just *loves* cars!" Although Danny couldn't pass the written driver's test, he knew how to operate them. He'd take the wheel whenever it was offered and barrel through the curves of the nearest winding road. Each hairpin turn and two-wheeled squealing corner seemed to thrill him into a skin-close consciousness otherwise unattainable. A couple of no-goods around town got a kick out of letting Danny loose on the highway. As he laughed aloud at the nearness of death, for a few vital seconds he did not feel buried alive in his body. The result was, however, he rolled a car over and was in the hospital half a year.

"He's not the same," Clara said, when Danny got out. "He's been affected," she told her card-playing cronies, shaking her head, and they let her talk. At last she'd been given a respectable excuse.

"He's got to learn a simple trade," said Ted, urging a farmer who was heavily in debt to the bank to take Danny on as a harvest worker. But it didn't work out. "The lummox," said the farmer, "he's always on the ground under the bundle-wagons, sucking on a lemonade jug."

In no time Danny was drifting around the pool halls and one saw him drunk in the middle of the afternoon. Sometimes Theodore Rueff in his neatly pressed blue suit, gold-flecked tie, shiny shoes, and snap-brim hat walked right down the sidewalk past his sprawled, half-unconscious son, who was loafing on the bench in front of the bank. They wouldn't look at each other or speak.

When the Korean War broke out, the two Rueff brothers, who were graduating from college, arrived home in their uniforms and made their last romantic impact upon the town: the one in Air Force blue with silver buttons, the other in ROTC Army officer's twill. One on each side of Clara, with Ted Rueff following behind, they walked down the church aisle under the eyes of God and the town. In the excitement they forgot to include Danny, who awoke from a late sleep to find the house empty, the church bells ringing for the world but not for him. He wept, and he was still weeping when the Rueffs gaily tromped back into the house. "Danny—Danny! Don't be such a big baby!" called Clara, one arm still around Army, the other looped to Air Force.

"Hey there—" both brothers cried out and leaped to Danny's side to pick up the easy old romp of their childhood.

"Don't punch him," called Clara, "you know how easy he bruises."

"Leave me alone! Just leave me alone!" Face still shiny with tears, he loomed up and entered the stairwell, mounting the steps carefully to his room, a giant on business. The family was stunned, almost offended by the discovery that Danny felt he had a right to his own emotions—which might not be theirs. He would not come down to dinner, nor could he be persuaded to tag along as the Rueffs bid farewell to their patriotic sons, later that afternoon. "If they don't come back," Clara said finally, taking leave of him, the horn honking, "just *think* how bad you'll feel then!"

He looked at her angrily, stirring his huge limbs, and for the first time she felt afraid of him—and fled the house. She didn't tell her husband what had made Danny so furious, only that "he looked about to hit me!"

"If it gets any worse," said Army, "you know what you'll have to do."

"But we always said, your Dad and I" (Ted sitting right beside her in the backseat), "why have him put away when he's so harmless?"

"Some of the women in town are starting to worry," said Air Force, who'd spent most of his leave getting reacquainted with high school loves. Both boys had already confided to their father that Danny was actually no threat on that score, since he was impotent. They were certain of it. Some years back, in an attempt to explain sex to him, they'd sat on a pasture gate and watched a pony stud in action. Much to their surprise, Danny wasn't the least interested. Now the rumors of his threat to the local girls was just the dirty country gossip one might expect, given his outsize proportions in that department, too. Every time he was caught taking a leak there were guffaws and comments. But neither Rueff boy could bear to inform their father of the indecent nature of his talk—yet they felt some little warning should be voiced.

The following week Danny insisted he be allowed to enlist in the Navy. Theodore Rueff went through it all: helped Danny pack his bag, watched him bid farewell to his Mom, and drove him to the Navy recruiting office above the city post office. He and Danny walked up the steps as if they truly expected to get somewhere. "My son here wants—" Ted began, apologetically, while the petty chief on duty, red-faced from sea-winds, widened his eyes, pushed back his chair. "My son—"

"I come to enlist in the Navy," said Danny, his deep, half-muffled voice seeping out of the tower of himself. "I'm of age." A blush suffused his neck and lower cheeks, as if the blood of his life were coming forth, once he proclaimed himself a man.

The five-foot-three petty chief grinned and leaped to his feet. With a side wink to Rueff he reached up and thumped Danny on the back. "More fellas like you and we'd win this war in no time!"

"Where do I go?" Danny twirled his little satchel nervously, while Rueff blinked, looked embarrassed, and turned to gaze out the window.

"Trouble is—you're so big you'd put the fleet to shame."

"I'm too big?"

"No, *they're* too small!" He marched Danny into the examination room, laughing to leeward all the way. It was a slack day, and the medical officer was waiting. "Look what I've brought you!"

They took great pains to describe the narrow, stacked seamen's bunks on a typical U. S. Navy vessel. They showed him skivvies and bell-bottoms so that he could see that none of them fit him. When the interview was over they shook hands with Danny, called him a fine American, urged him to stop in and see them whenever he liked.

"Well, son?" said Theodore. "Ready to go home now?"

Danny nodded agreeably but with a new independence. At last he'd gone beyond his father—and the family's network in Kaleburg. He'd been seriously discussing his life with representatives of the United States Government. All the way home he couldn't keep the grin from his face.

Then, through a pool-hall friend, Danny got a job with a pinball machine company, Idle Hour Games. They helped him pass his driver's license exam and loaned him a car. His chief duty was to collect revenue from pinball machines and punchboards. Although they were illegal, most bars had several kinds of punchboards for the customers' amusement. You could buy a punch for a dime or a quarter, the whole card bringing the company ten times the cash value of the prize for the lucky-punch winner.

Danny took a room in a small hotel in the city, where he could receive messages that came while he was on the road. He collected coins from the pinball machines and learned to fix broken ones. Without his father close at his side, he managed to keep his accounts straight. After three months he was courier for half a dozen shady operations, including a numbers pool, ball-game pools, and a system whereby servicemen met girls. He was known and hailed as he made his rounds. Men would clap him on the shoulder and pump his soft hand, and Danny would bray with pleasure, showing his long-toothed, horsy grin.

But suddenly Theodore Rueff received a call to bail Danny out of jail. He and the Idle Hour Games people had been arrested and charged with racketeering and procurement for the purposes of prostitution. An understanding judge commuted Danny's sentence, sending him home in the custody of his parents, who were henceforth to keep an eye on him.

"We've been all alone here, Danny," Clara whimpered. "This big house and all the children gone but you." However, she couldn't make him her baby any more. Before a week was out he fled. They didn't know where he'd gone and were afraid to ask the authorities to hunt him up, since surely then he'd have to be "put away." Both Rueffs became highly guarded on the subject: and while the addresses of the two boys in uniform and the girl in Los Angeles studying fashion were printed in the church bulletin, Danny was left out.

Soon everyone read of Danny's marriage—to LaVonne Zimmer—before a justice of the peace in a town forty miles away, one of those many villages where Danny had become known as a traveling man. Clara said it was wonderful "to have somebody taking care of Danny." The Rueffs helped settle the newlyweds in a Kaleburg house available for twenty-five dollars a month, provided Danny and LaVonne "look in" on the eighty-year-old lady who lived alone next door, their landlady. Wedding presents arrived, but Clara gave no tea to introduce her daughter-in-law, and suggestions of a bridal shower were quashed for no reason, unless it was that Clara and Ted didn't want to pretend they expected grandchildren from this alliance.

The old rumors about Danny's sexual abnormality began to surface—*he* wasn't interested in girls, everybody knew. So, what was going on? LaVonne was tall and squarely built, as strong as Danny was weak. Her dark brown hair, the color of flaxseed, was done up in a coil over each ear and flat spit-curls just above her forehead were held in place by hairpins that seemed to staple her crown. She had deeply recessed, small blue eyes and run-together eyebrows. Her mouth was a neat, thin line, and except for her nose, which projected a modest distance, she seemed almost bereft of the usual features that distinguish one of us from another. Everyone thought she was up to no good and had probably married the village idiot in order to cash in eventually on the Rueff money. Clara made a point of telling her friends that LaVonne had nursed her father through a long illness, that she was a good, shy, devoted soul—hard to get to know, but in every way worthy of her son.

LaVonne didn't entertain in her home nor did she accept any of the invitations to join women's clubs. "He's being looked after," said Clara joyously, "that's what counts." The life of the elder Rueffs separated easily and decisively from that of their son and his wife. Soon nobody thought to remark that it was odd Danny and LaVonne were never seen in the big green house on Main Street. It was increasingly hard to remember he was a Rueff at all.

When the old drunk who ran the dray service got run over and killed by his own cart, Danny and LaVonne took over his business. They acquired a sorrel gelding used to plowing and corn-planting and shod him for service on town streets. LaVonne showed the horse where to graze on the strips of pasture along the railroad embankment, and in the evenings he cleaned up the spilled oats and corn around the spouts of the Farmer's Elevator. The wagon was an ancient, heavy box on four thick wheels; panels slid into place making a rectangle four feet deep—or the wagon could be stripped down like a railroad flatcar. Originally there'd been a pair of horses for the outfit, but something had happened to one of them. Since the old man couldn't afford a new horse, he'd adjusted the rig; the load could be pulled from the whiffletrees, by a single brute in harness.

You may wonder what need there is for a dray service in a town as small as Kaleburg, since most citizens have cars and could make periodic trips to the dump with tin cans, glass, and junk that won't go into the backyard compost pile. But some people hate to run the risk of having their tires cut by broken glass or nails. They detest the sight of rats among the refuse, should they go out there in daylight—or the bright little rat-headlights gleaming all over the place at night. They called Danny's Dray. Customers also phoned to have salvaged bricks hauled to the site of a foundation for a new house; or to carry lumber in a hurry, when the normal delivery couldn't be made. Even the stores employed Danny and LaVonne to transport heavy merchandise. The price for service wasn't high, and thanks to LaVonne the job was always done neatly and in good time, without much fuss.

In going about their business, Danny and LaVonne wore overalls and heavy work shoes, the leather so thick it didn't much matter what dropped on their toes. The only way to tell it was a man and a woman on the cart, not two men, was that LaVonne wore a babushka, except in summer, when she was forced by the intense sun to wear a farmer's straw hat. Unlike junk carriers the world over, they never seemed interested in their burdens or considered their freight in any light except that it was something to be disposed of. No little trinket was ever filched and kept in secret at home. When something of possible value was included in the load, LaVonne would speak about it to the person employing her. "That hairbrush?" the woman might reply, "*Ach*, its bristles are mostly broken. No, it ain't good for nothing but curryin' your horsie." And then LaVonne would use it for that, as long as it lasted. She seemed to understand the dangers that might develop if she ever wised up to the business she was in. She was, in short, incorruptible; but the town believed nothing of the sort. *They* thought she ignored salvageable items because she was waiting for the Rueff fortune itself, when the old folks died off.

Meanwhile, Danny's Dray made money, though they never seemed to spend any. Now and then they'd go to a movie, settle themselves in the front row where Danny had always sat, share a nickel bag of popcorn, and watch the cowboys galloping across the screen. They put a dime or two in the collection plate when they attended church, which was infrequently. They didn't drink liquor or even beer because LaVonne said (what everybody knew), it didn't agree with Danny. Their car was a beat-up 1939 Chevrolet. Every morning LaVonne was first at the bakery for day-old bread. She kept a sizable garden and canned all summer. She knew what farmers could be approached about picking the tart plums in a forgotten lane, to be made into preserves. The grocery supplies LaVonne bought were of the austere, pioneer sort: flour, sugar, salt. Even the meat supply was arranged for privately, during the country butchering time in February. The town speculated that perhaps Danny preferred the safety of his mattress or the sugar bowl for his hoard, rather than his father's bank.

Years later the true tale leaked out, in the surprising, appropriate way these revelations occur. In the prosecution of one of Danny's pinball-machine buddies, who'd been released after serving his term only to return to his rackets, the district attorney discovered that Danny Rueff had been paying hush-money sometimes amounting to two hundred a month. The convict had terrorized him into believing he could be re-arrested at any moment, and even LaVonne was convinced. Nowadays some blame Theodore and Clara for not inquiring into the reason why Danny and LaVonne's back-breaking drudgery showed so little profit. But misery is often obscured because of the pride everyone takes in hard labor, the virtue it entails—the fact that "work never hurt anybody."

But it broke Danny—or rather the strain did. He was such a big, calm, plodding creature no one thought he might be a mass of anguish inside. One day he got into the Chevy and drove to the state insane asylum twenty-five miles away "to turn in." LaVonne was summoned for interview, and the authorities talked to Clara and Ted, each of them separately. Danny planned to remain safe inside the walls, LaVonne reported; "He's real happy there." She spoke without bitterness or even resignation. "Now I got to carry on with the Dray alone, I guess."

The town would have speculated at length about Danny's surprising action had not Clara succumbed to a stroke the same week. Her right side was paralyzed from top to bottom. She could only speak disjointedly with half a tongue, smile with half a mouth, and think with half a brain. It happened because of her grief over Danny's collapse—that's what people said. LaVonne immediately began to nurse her. In the morning she'd go over to the house on Main and fix Theodore's breakfast before he walked to the bank, then lift Clara from her bed, carry her to the bathroom, wash her and dress her and put her in the wheelchair. After a ramp was built over the front steps, Clara's trips in the mobile chair could be down the block or even to the stores, LaVonne always in attendance. The dray service dwindled, but she still maintained the business. She continued to live in the little house next to the very old lady (now in her nineties) and checked each morning to see if the woman was alive.

Clara was expected to regain use of her arm and leg; there seemed to be improvement for several months. But Clara enjoyed being taken care of by LaVonne and wasn't much interested in using the doctor's spring-contraption to exercise her hand, biceps, and calf. She had no reason in particular to want to get up and walk again. "I've got it pretty easy, wheeling along," she'd say with a laugh. "I don't know's you folks have it so good." She would never be quite right in the head again, that was the trouble. There were no devices to fix that lesion. The doctor told Theodore that the end would most likely come suddenly, one of these years, with another series of strokes. Hard to tell just when.

During this time the three other Rueff children didn't come back. They had youngsters of their own, of course, which was fair excuse, but it seemed odd that in those four years none of them was able to make the trip home. Mostly it was thought the reason was guilt over Danny—and shame that he was where he was, when the Rueffs could certainly afford a private sanitarium. But who would start doing something? Theodore washed his hands of it—he had enough to think about with Clara; his face in profile was pewter gray and stern, the look of George Washington on twenty-five-cent pieces. The letters between the Rueff children flew back and forth, from New York to California and Washington, guardedly speculating on what should be done about the home situation. But the last word was always, "Thank God for LaVonne!"

When Theodore died of a heart attack, all of them came back. What a strange procession they made: the children in their well-tailored dark clothes walking behind the coffin, along with dotty Clara, who was weeping, snuffling, and carrying on aloud; and sober, lean-faced LaVonne, pushing the wheelchair down the church aisle, looking no more grim than usual—in fact, she was "just the same's ever!" She was about as tough as a mortal could be, in the best sense of the word, for no matter what was dished out, she took it without a whimper.

She was not entirely of iron, however. A few weeks after Theodore's burial, when she moved into the house on Main Street in order to be closer at hand in ministering to Clara, she put her horse in the barn out back, which had been used as a garage. The city fathers said there was an ordinance against it. She received an official letter from the mayor, warning her that she'd be fined if she didn't remove the animal. But she *had* to have him close by, not in the shed giving onto a pasture (outside the city limits) where she'd formerly kept him. She was wildly attached to the beast who'd been her companion all these years. She wouldn't give in—no, she'd pay the fine.

But the penalty, it was explained, would be levied again next month and each succeeding month until she did something about complying with the city ordinance. Ladies who came to visit Clara got a full, emotional report from the invalid, slightly off-key, a peculiar wheezing screech, as if a half-melted phonograph record were being played on a faulty machine. "She got Theodore's pistol out—oh yes, she found that! And she cleaned it up real good, and dug up some bullets, too. Just you wait—anybody comes trying to move her horse—you'll see some shooting, you will. Our property, ain't it? They can't do this to us. And after all we've done for this town!"

That kind of talk, bruited about the village, was just the sort of thing the high school hoodlums liked to take up. They deviled LaVonne as she walked the streets or drove her dray cart in the alleys. They cackled and hooted and even threw firecrackers, daring her to shoot the pistol. She never gave them the satisfaction of paying any attention.

A special dispensation for the horse was finally granted "in respect to the memory of Theodore Rueff." Everybody knew LaVonne had won because of her strange, fierce love for that animal. In farm country you seldom hear of anyone getting affectionate over a cow or a pig or a workhorse because that sort of thing upsets the system. These beasts are in bondage to man; it's not the other way around. If only LaVonne had had the sense not to put that straw hat of Danny's on the creature, cutting out holes for his ears. If only the horse hadn't had such big blue eyes which did indeed resemble Danny's; if the animal had been given some name like Nick or Dobbin. But he had no name, and so the high school kids began calling him Danny. Then you began to see other connections:

the fact that he was a gelding; his lumbering gait and size; his sad, half-witted look. The effort LaVonne made protecting the horse got her into closer alliance, really a companionship. Cart, horse, and woman roamed the alleys even when there was nothing to be hauled, the cart empty.

Some village gossip must have written to the Rueff daughter in California, describing the situation and saying that Clara was being neglected because of LaVonne's infatuation with the horse. A practical nurse was suddenly engaged to come and live in the house. LaVonne was no longer to attend the invalid. The stranger, sent by a city agency, was a hearty, gray-haired, meat-and-potatoes sort. She was righteously indignant over the filthy condition of the house, which apparently hadn't been cleaned for a couple of years. Moths had infested the clothes, mice and rats had the run of the basement and attic, and even poor dear Clara Rueff herself was so dirty on the back of the neck that she had to be scrubbed hard with a rough washcloth and strong laundry soap. Purveyor of all this juicy news, the practical nurse was welcomed into every household on the block.

She told more than she should have. Or rather, she kept repeating everything Clara said, and these ravings were increasingly unreliable and not to be listened to. For one thing, apparently LaVonne had been in the habit of caressing the old woman in those regions where one would imagine only the young feel intense pleasure. Clara liked to be handled gently, dreamily, and for a good long time, until she went off to sleep. LaVonne, questioned about this by the practical nurse, who was shocked by such manipulations, was reported to have answered: "She'd smile and feel so good, I never had to give her no sleeping pills. That's more than *you've* done for her!"

The remark, coupled with Clara's own peculiar notion about LaVonne, began to spread. The nurse quoted Clara as having said: "LaVonne's got whiskers like a man. A girl ain't supposed to have a chin like that. No, I don't think she's a girl at all." Actually, LaVonne had always carefully shaved the stubble she'd been afflicted with on her upper lip and chin. As these growths flourished in later years, she'd tried to cover them up with talcum powder. But one time Clara's hand had happened to reach out, in a moment that might have been ecstasy, in the evening when the light was dimming in the bedroom, and LaVonne was soothing the old lady for the night. She touched LaVonne's face—her eyes widening—suddenly she thought she understood the mystery of this creature who'd come so accidentally into the Rueff household and now was such an indispensable part of it. "Always in overalls, she is. Works like a man. No wonder my poor Danny sent himself away!"

So when Clara died, and after the funeral and the dutiful visits from the far-off children, when the practical nurse lost her job and had to return to the city, in the settlement of the estate the clapboard house on Main went to LaVonne, plus a small income from farm property—largely because the Rueff children realized that she'd forever make those twice-a-month visits to the state hospital, keeping an eye on Danny. She lived alone and never went out in the streets or alleys with the cart anymore. The horse was too old, and nobody phoned to have LaVonne do a job. They knew her circumstances had changed. By now LaVonne's hair was streaked with gray, and she wore it severely back in a bun and looked like some prairie sod-house woman of the nineteenth century. You might guess that she'd be left alone to live out her years in peace, with whatever private hells she experienced, and wherever she found her heavens. But you don't know our town, if you think that.

The kids kept talking about the rumor that LaVonne was really a man dressed up in woman's clothing. One night in late spring a bunch of the graduating seniors, out drinking and celebrating, sneaked through the backyard and walked right into the Rueff kitchen—because nobody, not even widows and old maids, locks their doors. Maybe she knew why they'd come and what they meant to do to her. She did not shriek or run for the telephone. They tried to corner her in the front parlor, but she escaped up the stairs. Yelling like animals, they were hot after her. They thought she was merely fleeing—and she was in part—but she was also trying to remember where she'd put Theodore's Colt .45. Finally they pinned her down on a musty bed in a back room and ripped every shred of clothing from her body. She fought so wildly that the young athlete astride her got aroused—a local football hero I shan't name, for he later joined the Marines and died in Vietnam. With his teammates co-operating, as they used to do on the playing fields, he made the full discovery of her womanhood, something no man had ever done before—not even her husband Danny. They saw the deep stain on the bedspread and knew her secret, a different one from what they'd come to find. She writhed free of their grasp in the moment her assailants saw the blood. The pistol lay on the washstand next to the only window with a clear view of the barn door. She grabbed the gun and, naked in the starlight, flung herself through the window, shattering the glass as she flew.

Aghast and suddenly sober, they raced downstairs and out the front door, got into their cars and spurted away. They didn't even have the decency to go round back to see what might be done to help her. They just wanted to get away and not be caught. A neighbor heard the crash but couldn't figure out for a long time what had caused it. Then he saw the pale, nude figure on the lawn, slowly moving through the grass, long hair down her back. He'd have gone over at once if he hadn't also noticed that she was entirely naked, her breasts flat and loose. There seemed to be some dark stuff like paint here and there on her body. He figured that whatever she was up to, she wanted to do it alone. She squirmed across the long backyard lawn, hung awhile on the picket gate till she worked the latch open, then slumped down again to wiggle through the hollyhocks. It took nearly twenty minutes for her to get to the barn—the horse whinnying and trampling the earth as she came. She reached him at last and somehow managed to pull herself upright in the stall—so that she could explain to the horse and to herself what she was about to do—in a voice none of us ever heard give utterance to anything that mattered.

You can be sure she spoke. She got very close to his wall-eye, we know from the wound, and pulled the trigger. Then she shot herself, left hand clutching the mane, a fistful of sorrel hair. Her head lay near his furry ear, as if she'd just stopped speaking. Those who came up after the pistol fired and saw the naked woman sprawled across the horse's body said, later, that Lady Godiva herself had not been more beautiful. Isn't it just like them to say something like that? Her leg had been broken, the doctor reported—*her* leg, not the horse's.

Sand

W. S. MERWIN

(1927–)

An ant was born in an hourglass. Before it hatched out there was nothing to notice—and who would have looked, who would have suspected that one instant in each measure of time was an egg? And after the ant had emerged, it was too late to ask whether the birth was a mistake. Anyway, there was no one to ask, except those nameless hosts, his brothers, at once much older and much younger than he was, who nudged and ground past him, rustling toward the neck of the glass, and fell, and lay blind, deaf, and dreamless in the mountain made of each other, and would never hatch, though the mountain itself turned over again and again and sent them smoking down from its tip like souls into time. Besides, it never occurred to him that there was a question to ask. He did not know that things ever had been or ever could be any different, and whatever capacity for speech he may have been born with slept on inside him like a grain of sand.

There was nothing to eat. But he had never been told about hunger, and ants, particularly those of his species, can subsist for long periods, sometimes for generations, without consuming other life of any kind. The same was true of thirst, dry though that place surely was, made of nothing but those rocks his family. Whatever discomfort he may have become aware of, arising from either hunger or thirst, seemed to him to be like something that we would no doubt call a memory, returning inexplicably to trouble him in a new life, and certain to fade. It stirred in him like some ghost from his days as a grain of sand, but he could not remember what use it had been to him then. And he would hold it to him and save it for a while, as though there was a danger of losing it. He would hold it, trying to understand it, not knowing that it was pain. Something of the kind was true also of breathing. He was breathing. But he knew nothing of breath. What, after all, reached him through the glass? The light. The darkness. Sounds. Gravity. The desire to climb. What reached the grains of sand? Light. Darkness. Vibrations. Gravity. No one knows what else.

His brothers tried to crush him. He tried to count them. He could see that they were not infinite. But he could never start at the beginning. He would count them as they edged past him faster and faster. He had no names for numbers, but he tried to count the brothers even so, as he was borne along with them, as he climbed on their shoulders, as he swam on their heads, falling with them. He tried to count them as they fell on him and rolled after him to the foot of the next mountain, to the glass. He would start to the top again at once, trying to count them as they slipped under his feet. He would climb, counting, till the mountain turned over, and then he would begin again. Each time the mountain flowed out from under him he delayed the falling for an instant, and a measure of time paused while he clung to the neck of the glass, climbing on sand. Then everything went on just the same.

No one had told him about time. He did not know why he was trying to count. He did not know what a number, a final sum, would tell him, what use it would be to him, what he would call it, where he would put it. He did not know that they were not his real brothers. He thought he was a grain of sand.

He did not know that he was alone.

Lost in the Funhouse

JOHN BARTH
(1930–)

For whom is the funhouse fun? Perhaps for lovers. For Ambrose it is *a place of fear and confusion.* He has come to the seashore with his family for the holiday, *the occasion of their visit is Independence Day, the most important secular holiday of the United States of America.* A single straight underline is the manuscript mark for italic type, *which in turn* is the printed equivalent to oral emphasis of words and phrases as well as the customary type for titles of complete works, not to mention. Italics are also employed, in fiction stories especially, for "outside," intrusive, or artificial voices, such as radio announcements, the texts of telegrams and newspaper articles, et cetera. They should be used *sparingly*. If passages originally in roman type are italicized by someone repeating them, it's customary to acknowledge the fact. *Italics mine.*

Ambrose was "at that awkward age." His voice came out high-pitched as a child's if he let himself get carried away; to be on the safe side, therefore, he moved and spoke with *deliberate calm* and *adult gravity*. Talking soberly of unimportant or irrelevant matters and listening consciously to the sound of your own voice are useful habits for maintaining control in this difficult interval. *En route* to Ocean City he sat in the back seat of the family car with his brother Peter, age fifteen, and Magda G——, age fourteen, a pretty girl, an exquisite young lady, who lived not far from them on B—— Street in the town of D——, Maryland. Initials, blanks, or both were often substituted for proper names in nineteenth-century fiction to enhance the illusion of reality. It is as if the author felt it necessary to delete the names for reasons of tact or legal liability. Interestingly, as with other aspects of realism, it is an *illusion* that is being enhanced, by purely artificial means. Is it likely, does it violate the principle of verisimilitude, that a thirteen-year-old boy could make such a sophisticated observation? A girl of fourteen is *the psychological coeval* of a boy of fifteen or sixteen; a thirteen-year-old boy, therefore, even one precocious in some other respects, might be three years *her emotional junior*.

Thrice a year—on Memorial, Independence, and Labor Days—the family visits Ocean City for the afternoon and evening. When Ambrose and Peter's father was their age, the excursion was made by train, as mentioned in the novel *The 42nd Parallel* by John Dos Passos. Many families from the same neighborhood used to travel together, with dependent relatives and often with Negro servants; schoolfuls of children swarmed through the railway cars; everyone shared everyone else's Maryland fried chicken, Virginia ham, deviled eggs, potato salad, beaten biscuits, iced tea. Nowadays (that is in 19—, the year of our story) the journey is made by automobile—more comfortably and quickly though without the extra fun though without the *camaraderie* of a general excursion. It's all part of the deterioration of American life, their father declares; Uncle Karl supposes that when the boys take *their* families to Ocean City for the holidays they'll fly in Autogiros. Their mother, sitting in the middle of the front seat like Magda in the second, only with her arms on the seat-back behind the men's shoulders, wouldn't want the good old days back again, the steaming trains and stuffy long dresses; on the other hand she can do without Autogiros, too, if she has to become a grandmother to fly in them.

Description of physical appearance and mannerisms is one of several standard methods of characterization used by writers of fiction. It is also important to "keep the senses operating"; when a detail from one of the five senses, say visual, is "crossed" with a detail from another, say auditory, the reader's imagination is oriented to the scene, perhaps unconsciously. This procedure may be compared to the way surveyors and navigators determine their positions by two or more compass bearings, a process known as triangulation. The brown hair on Ambrose's mother's forearms gleamed in the sun like. Though right-handed, she took her left arm from the seat-back to press the dashboard cigar lighter for Uncle Karl. When the glass bead in its handle glowed red, the lighter was ready for use. The smell of Uncle Karl's cigar smoke reminded one of. The fragrance of the ocean came strong to the picnic ground where they always stopped for lunch, two miles inland from Ocean City. Having to pause for a full hour almost within sound of the breakers was difficult for Peter and Ambrose when they were younger; even at their present age it was not easy to keep their anticipation, *stimulated by the briny spume,* from turning into short temper. The Irish author James Joyce, in his unusual novel entitled *Ulysses,* now available in this country, uses the adjectives *snot-green* and *scrotum-tightening* to describe the sea. Visual, auditory, tactile, olfactory, gustatory. Peter and Ambrose's father, while steering their black 1936 LaSalle sedan with one hand, could with the other remove the first cigarette from a white pack of Lucky Strikes and, more remarkably, light it with a match forefingered from its book and thumbed against the flint paper without being detached. The matchbook cover merely advertised U.S. War Bonds and Stamps. A fine metaphor, simile, or other figure of speech, in addition to its obvious "first-order" relevance to the thing it describes, will be seen upon reflection to have a second order of significance: it may be drawn from the *milieu* of the action, for example, or be particularly appropriate to the sensibility of the narrator, even hinting to the reader things of which the narrator is unaware; or it may cast further and subtler lights upon the thing it describes, sometimes ironically qualifying the more evident sense of the comparison.

To say that Ambrose's and Peter's mother was *pretty* is to accomplish nothing; the reader may acknowledge the proposition, but his imagination is not engaged. Besides, Magda was also pretty, yet in an altogether different way. Although she lived on B—— Street she had very good manners and did better than average in school. Her figure was very well developed for her age. Her right hand lay casually on the plush upholstery of the seat, very near Ambrose's left leg, on which his own hand rested. The space between their legs, between her right and his left leg, was out of the line of sight of anyone sitting on the other side of Magda, as well as anyone glancing into the rearview mirror. Uncle Karl's face resembled Peter's—rather, vice versa. Both had dark hair and eyes, short husky statures, deep voices. Magda's left hand was probably in a similar position on her left side. The boy's father is difficult to describe; no particular feature of his appearance or manner stood out. He wore glasses and was principal of a T—— County grade school. Uncle Karl was a masonry contractor.

Although Peter must have known as well as Ambrose that the latter, because of his position in the car, would be the first to see the electrical towers of the power plant at V——, the halfway point of their trip, he leaned forward and slightly toward the center of the car and pretended to be looking for them through the flat pinewoods and tuckahoe creeks along the highway. For as long as the boys could remember, "looking for the Towers" had been a feature of the first half of their excursions to Ocean City, "looking for the standpipe" of the second. Though the game was childish, their mother preserved the tradition of rewarding the first to see the Towers with a candybar or piece of fruit. She insisted now that Magda play the game; the prize, she said, was "something hard to get nowadays." Ambrose decided not to join in; he sat far back in his seat. Magda, like Peter, leaned forward. Two sets of straps were discernible through the shoulders of her sun dress; the inside right one, a brassiere-strap, was fastened or shortened with a small safety pin. The right armpit of her dress, presumably the left as well, was damp with perspiration. The simple strategy for being first to espy the Towers, which Ambrose had understood by the age of four, was to sit on the right-hand side of the car. Whoever sat there, however, had also to put up with the worst of the sun, and so Ambrose, without mentioning the matter, chose sometimes the one and sometimes the other. Not impossibly Peter had never caught on to the trick, or thought that his brother hadn't simply because Ambrose on occasion preferred shade to a Baby Ruth or tangerine.

The shade-sun situation didn't apply to the front seat, owing to the windshield; if anything the driver got more sun, since the person on the passenger side not only was shaded below by the door and dashboard but might swing down his sunvisor all the way too.

"Is that them?" Magda asked. Ambrose's mother teased the boys for letting Magda win, insinuating that "somebody [had] a girlfriend." Peter and Ambrose's father reached a long thin arm across their mother to butt his cigarette in the dashboard ashtray, under the lighter. The prize this time for seeing the Towers first was a banana. Their mother bestowed it after chiding their father for wasting a half-smoked cigarette when everything was so scarce. Magda, to take the prize, moved her hand from so near Ambrose's that he could have touched it as though accidentally. She offered to share the prize, things like that were so hard to find; but everyone insisted it was hers alone. Ambrose's mother sang an iambic trimeter couplet from a popular song, femininely rhymed:

"What's good is in the Army;
What's left will never harm me."

Uncle Karl tapped his cigar ash out the ventilator window; some particles were sucked by the slipstream back into the car through the rear window on the passenger side. Magda demonstrated her ability to hold a banana in one hand and peel it with her teeth. She still sat forward; Ambrose pushed his glasses back onto the bridge of his nose with his left hand, which he then negligently let fall to the seat cushion immediately behind her. He even permitted the single hair, gold, on the second joint of his thumb to brush the fabric of her skirt. Should she have sat back at that instant, his hand would have been caught under her.

Plush upholstery prickles uncomfortably through gabardine slacks in the July sun. The function of the *beginning* of a story is to introduce the principal characters, establish their initial relationships, set the scene for the main action, expose the background of the situation if necessary, plant motifs and foreshadowings where appropriate and initiate the first complication or whatever of the "rising action." Actually, if one imagines a story called "The Funhouse," or "Lost in the Funhouse," the details of the drive to Ocean City don't seem especially relevant. The *beginning* should recount the events between Ambrose's first sight of the funhouse early in the afternoon and his entering it with Magda and Peter in the evening. The *middle* would narrate all relevant events from the time he goes in to the time he loses his way; middles have the double and contradictory function of delaying the climax while at the same time preparing the reader for it and fetching him to it. Then the *ending* would tell what Ambrose does while he's lost, how he finally finds his way out, and what everybody makes of the experience. So far there's been no real dialogue, very little sensory detail, and nothing in the way of a *theme*. And a long time has gone by already without anything happening; it makes a person wonder. We haven't even reached Ocean City yet: we will never get out of the funhouse.

The more closely an author identifies with the narrator, literally or metaphorically, the less advisable it is, as a rule, to use the first-person narrative viewpoint. Once three years previously the young people *aforementioned* played Niggers and Masters in the backyard; when it was Ambrose's turn to be Master and theirs to be Niggers Peter had to go serve his evening papers; Ambrose was afraid to punish Magda alone, but she led him to the whitewashed Torture Chamber between the woodshed and the privy in the Slaves Quarters; there she knelt sweating among bamboo rakes and dusty Mason jars, pleadingly embraced his knees, and while bees droned in the lattice as if on an ordinary summer afternoon, purchased clemency at a surprising price set by herself. Doubtless she remembered nothing of this event; Ambrose on the other hand seemed unable to forget the least detail of his life. He even recalled how, standing beside himself with awed impersonality in the reeky heat, he'd stared the while at an empty cigar box in which Uncle Karl kept stone-cutting chisels: beneath the words *El Producto,* a laureled, loose-taga'd lady regarded the sea from a marble bench; beside her, forgotten or not yet turned to, was a five-stringed lyre. Her chin reposed on the back of her right hand; her left depended negligently from the bench-arm. The lower half of scene and lady was peeled away; the words EXAMINED BY — were inked there into the wood. Nowadays cigar boxes are made of pasteboard. Ambrose wondered what Magdo would have done, Ambrose wondered what Magda would do when she sat back on his hand as he resolved she should. Be angry. Make a teasing joke of it. Give no sign at all. For a long time she leaned forward, playing cow-poker with Peter against Uncle Karl and Mother and watching for the first sign of Ocean City. At nearly the same instant, picnic ground and Ocean City standpipe hove into view; an Amoco filling station on their side of the road cost Mother and Uncle Karl fifty cows and the game; Magda bounced back, clapping her right hand on Mother's right arm; Ambrose moved clear "in the nick of time."

At this rate our hero, at this rate our protagonist will remain in the funhouse forever. Narrative ordinarily consists of alternating dramatization and summarization. One symptom of nervous tension, paradoxically, is repeated and violent yawning; neither Peter nor Magda nor Uncle Karl nor Mother reacted in this manner. Although they were no longer small children, Peter and Ambrose were each given a dollar to spend on boardwalk amusements in addition to what money of their own they'd brought along. Magda too, though she protested she had ample spending money. The boys' mother made a little scene out of distributing the bills; she pretended that her sons and Magda were small children and cautioned them not to spend the sum too quickly or in one place. Magda promised with a merry laugh and, having both hands free, took the bill with her left. Peter laughed also and pledged in a falsetto to be a good boy. His imitation of a child was not clever. The boys' father was tall and thin, balding, fair-complexioned. Assertions of that sort are not effective; the reader may acknowledge the proposition, but. We should be much farther along than we are; something has gone wrong; not much of this preliminary rambling seems relevant. Yet everyone begins in the same place; how is it that most go along without difficulty but a few lose their way?

"Stay out from under the boardwalk," Uncle Karl growled from the side of his mouth. The boys' mother pushed his shoulder *in mock annoyance.* They were all standing before Fat May the Laughing Lady who advertised the funhouse. Larger than life, Fat May mechanically shook, rocked on her heels, slapped her thighs while recorded laughter—uproarious, female—came amplified from a hidden loudspeaker. It chuckled, wheezed, wept; tried in vain to catch its breath; tittered, groaned, exploded raucous and anew. You couldn't hear it without laughing yourself, no matter how you felt. Father came back from talking to a Coast-Guardsman on duty and reported that the surf was spoiled with crude oil from tankers recently torpedoed offshore. Lumps of it, difficult to remove, made tarry tidelines on the beach and stuck on swimmers. Many bathed in the surf nevertheless and came out speckled; others paid to use a municipal pool and only sunbathed on the beach. We would do the latter. We would do the latter. We would do the latter.

Under the boardwalk, matchbook covers, grainy other things. What is the story's theme? Ambrose is ill. He perspires in the dark passages; candied apples-on-a-stick, delicious-looking, disappointing to eat. Funhouses need men's and ladies' room at intervals. Others perhaps have also vomited in corners and corridors; may even have had bowel movements liable to be stepped in in the dark. The word *fuck* suggests suction and/or and/or flatulence. Mother and Father; grandmothers and grandfathers on both sides; great-grandmothers and great-grandfathers on four sides, et cetera. Count a generation as thirty years: in approximately the year when Lord Baltimore was granted charter to the province of Maryland by Charles I, five hundred twelve women—English, Welsh, Bavarian, Swiss—of every class and character, received into themselves the penises the intromittent organs of five hundred twelve men, ditto, in every circumstance and posture, to conceive the five hundred twelve ancestors of the two hundred fifty-six ancestors of the et cetera et cetera et cetera et cetera et cetera et cetera et cetera et cetera of the author, of the narrator, of this story, *Lost in the Funhouse.* In alleyways, ditches, canopy beds, pinewoods, bridal suites, ship's cabins, coach-and-fours, coaches-and-four, sultry toolsheds; on the cold sand under boardwalks, littered with *El Producto* cigar butts, treasured with Lucky Strike cigarette stubs, Coca-Cola caps, gritty turds, cardboard lollipop sticks, matchbook covers warning that A Slip of the Lip Can Sink a Ship. The shluppish whisper, continuous as seawash round the globe, tidelike falls and rises with the circuit of dawn and dusk.

Magda's teeth. She *was* left-handed. Perspiration. They've gone all the way, through, Magda and Peter, they've been waiting for hours with Mother and Uncle Karl while Father searches for his lost son; they draw french-fried potatoes from a paper cup and shake their heads. They've named the children they'll one day have and bring to Ocean City on holidays. Can spermatozoa properly be thought of as male animalcules when there are no female spermatozoa? They grope through hot, dark windings, past Love's Tunnel's fearsome obstacles. Some perhaps lose their way.

Peter suggested then and there that they do the funhouse; he had been through it before, so had Magda, Ambrose hadn't and suggested, his voice cracking on account of Fat May's laughter, that they swim first. All were chuckling, couldn't help it; Ambrose's father, Ambrose's and Peter's father came up grinning like a lunatic with two boxes of syrup-coated popcorn, one for Mother, one for Magda; the men were to help themselves. Ambrose walked on Magda's right; being by nature left-handed, she carried the box in her left hand. Up front the situation was reversed.

"What are you limping for?" Magda inquired of Ambrose. He supposed in a husky tone that his foot had gone to sleep in the car. Her teeth flashed. "Pins and needles?" It was the honeysuckle on the lattice of the former privy that drew the bees. Imagine being stung there. How long is this going to take?

The adults decided to forgo the pool; but Uncle Karl insisted they change into swimsuits and do the beach. "He wants to watch the pretty girls," Peter teased, and ducked behind Magda from Uncle Karl's pretended wrath. "You've got all the pretty girls you need right here," Magda declared, and Mother said: "Now that's the gospel truth." Magda scolded Peter, who reached over her shoulder to sneak some popcorn. "Your brother and father aren't getting any." Uncle Karl wondered if they were going to have fireworks that night, what with the shortages. It wasn't the shortages, Mr. M—— replied: Ocean City had fireworks from pre-war. But it was too risky on account of the enemy submarines, some people thought.

"Don't seem like Fourth of July without fireworks," said Uncle Karl. The inverted tag in dialogue writing is still considered permissible with proper names or epithets, but sounds old-fashioned with personal pronouns. "We'll have 'em again soon enough," predicted the boys' father. Their mother declared she could do without fireworks: they reminded her too much of the real thing. Their father said all the more reason to shoot off a few now and again. Uncle Karl asked *rhetorically* who needed reminding, just look at people's hair and skin.

"The oil, yes," said Mrs. M——.

Ambrose had a pain in his stomach and so didn't swim but enjoyed watching the others. He and his father burned red easily. Magda's figure was exceedingly well developed for her age. She too declined to swim, and got mad, and became angry when Peter attempted to drag her into the pool. She always swam, he insisted; what did she mean not swim? Why did a person come to Ocean City?

"Maybe I want to lay here with Ambrose," Magda teased.

Nobody likes a pedant.

"Aha," said Mother. Peter grabbed Magda by one ankle and ordered Ambrose to grab the other. She squealed and rolled over on the beach blanket. Ambrose pretended to help hold her back. Her tan was darker than even Mother's and Peter's. "Help out, Uncle Karl!" Peter cried. Uncle Karl went to seize the other ankle. Inside the top of her swimsuit, however, you could see the line where the sunburn ended and, when she hunched her shoulders and squealed again, one nipple's auburn edge. Mother made them behave themselves. "*You* should certainly know," she said to Uncle Karl. Archly. "That when a lady says she doesn't feel like swimming, a gentleman doesn't ask questions." Uncle Karl said excuse *him;* Mother winked at Magda; Ambrose blushed; stupid Peter kept saying "Phooey on *feel like!*" and tugging at Magda's ankle; then even he got the point, and cannonballed with a holler into the pool.

"I swear," Magda said, in mock *in feigned* exasperation.

The diving would make a suitable literary symbol. To go off the high board you had to wait in a line along the poolside and up the ladder. Fellows tickled girls and goosed one another and shouted to the ones at the top to hurry up, or razzed them for bellyfloppers. Once on the springboard some took a great while posing or clowning or deciding on a dive or getting up their nerve; others ran off. Especially among the younger fellows the idea was to strike the funniest pose or do the craziest stunt as you fell, a thing that got harder to do as you kept on and kept on. But whether you hollered *Geronimo!* or *Sieg heil!*, held your nose or "rode a bicycle," pretended to be shot or did a perfect jacknife or changed your mind halfway down and ended up with nothing, it was over in two seconds, after all that wait. Spring, pose, splash. Spring, neat-o, splash. Spring, aw fooey, splash.

The grown-ups had gone on; Ambrose wanted to converse with Magda; she was remarkably well developed for her age; it was said that that came from rubbing with a turkish towel, and there were other theories. Ambrose could think of nothing to say except how good a diver Peter was, who was showing off for her benefit. You could pretty well tell by looking at their bathing suits and arm muscles how far along the different fellows were. Ambrose was glad he hadn't gone in swimming, the cold water shrank you up so. Magda pretended to be uninterested in the diving; she probably weighed as much as he did. If you knew your way around in the funhouse like your own bedroom, you could wait until a girl came along and then slip away without ever getting caught, even if her boyfriend was right with her. She'd think *he* did it! It would be better to be the boyfriend, and act outraged, and tear the funhouse apart.

Not act; *be*.

"He's a master diver," Ambrose said. In feigned admiration. "You really have to slave away at it to get that good." What would it matter anyhow if he asked her right out whether she remembered, even teased her with it as Peter would have?

There's no point in going farther; this isn't getting anybody anywhere; they haven't even come to the funhouse yet. Ambrose is off the track, in some new or old part of the place that's not supposed to be used; he strayed into it by some one-in-a-million chance, like the time the roller-coaster car left the tracks in the nineteen-teens against all the laws of physics and sailed over the boardwalk in the dark. And they can't locate him because they don't know where to look. Even the designer and operator have forgotten this other part, that winds around on itself like a whelk shell. That winds around the right part like the snakes on Mercury's caduceus. Some people, perhaps, don't "hit their stride" until their twenties, when the growing-up business is over and women appreciate other things besides wisecracks and teasing and strutting. Peter didn't have one-tenth the imagination *he* had, not one-tenth. Peter did this naming-their-children thing as a joke, making up names like Aloysius and Murgatroyd, but Ambrose knew *exactly* how it would feel to be married and have children of your own, and be a loving husband and father, and go comfortably to work in the morning and to bed with your wife at night, and wake up with her there. With a breeze coming through the sash and birds and mockingbirds singing in the Chinese-cigar trees. His eyes watered, there aren't enough ways to say that. He would be quite famous in his line of work. Whether Magda was his wife or not, one evening when he was wise-lined and gray at the temples he'd smile gravely, at a fashionable dinner party, and remind her of his youthful passion. The time they went with his family to Ocean City; the *erotic fantasies* he used to have about her. How long ago it seemed, and childish! Yet tender, too, *n'est-ce pas?* Would she have imagined that the world famous whatever remembered how many strings were on the lyre on the bench beside the girl on the label of the cigar box he'd stared at in the toolshed at age ten while she, age eleven. Even then he had felt *wise beyond his years;* he'd stroked her hair and said in his deepest voice and correctest English, as to a dear child: "I shall never forget this moment."

But though he had breathed heavily, groaned as if ecstatic, what he'd really felt throughout was an odd detachment, as though someone else were Master. Strive as he might to be transported, he heard his mind take notes upon the scene: *This is what they call* passion. *I am experiencing it.* Many of the digger machines were out of order in the penny arcades and could not be repaired or replaced for the duration. Moreover the prizes, made now in USA, were less interesting than formerly, pasteboard items for the most part, and some of the machines wouldn't work on white pennies. The gypsy fortune-teller machine might have provided a foreshadowing of the climax of this story if Ambrose had operated it. It was even dilapidateder than most: the silver coating was worn off the brown metal handles, the glass windows around the dummy were cracked and taped, her kerchiefs and silks long-faded. If a man lived by himself, he could take a department-store mannequin with flexible joints and modify her in certain ways. *However:* by the time he was that old he'd have a real woman. There was a machine that stamped your name around a white-metal coin with a star in the middle: *A*——. His son would be the second, and when the lad reached thirteen or so he would put a strong arm around his shoulder and tell him calmly: "It is perfectly normal. We have all been through it. It will not last forever." Nobody knew how to be what they were right. He'd smoke a pipe, teach his son how to fish and softcrab, assure him he needn't worry about himself. Magda would certainly give, Magda would certainly yield a great deal of milk, although guilty of occasional solecisms. It don't taste so bad. Suppose the lights came on now!

The day wore on. You think you're yourself, but there are other persons in you. Ambrose gets hard when Ambrose doesn't want to, *and obversely*. Ambrose watches them disagree; Ambrose watches him watch. In the funhouse mirror room you can't see yourself go on forever, because no matter how you stand, your head gets in the way. Even if you had a glass periscope, the image of your eye would cover up the thing you really wanted to see. The police will come; there'll be a story in the papers. That must be where it happened. Unless he can find a surprise exit, an unofficial backdoor or escape hatch opening on an alley, say, and then stroll up to the family in front of the funhouse and ask where everybody's been; *he's* been out of the place for ages. That's just where it happened, in that last lighted room: Peter and Magda found the right exit; he found one that you weren't supposed to find and strayed off into the works somewhere. In a perfect funhouse you'd be able to go only one way, like the divers off the highboard; getting lost would be impossible; the doors and halls would work like minnow traps or the valves in veins.

On account of German U-boats, Ocean City was "browned out": streetlights were shaded on the seaward side; shop-windows and boardwalk amusement places were kept dim, not to silhouette tankers and Liberty-ships for torpedoing. In a short story about Ocean City, Maryland, during World War II, the author could make use of the image of sailors on leave in the penny arcades and shooting galleries, sighting through the crosshairs of toy machine guns at swastika'd subs, while out in the black Atlantic a U-boat skipper squints through his periscope at real ships outlined by the glow of penny arcades. After dinner the family strolled back to the amusement end of the boardwalk. The boys' father had burnt red as always and was masked with Noxzema, a minstrel in reverse. The grown-ups stood at the end of the boardwalk where the Hurricane of '33 had cut an inlet from the ocean to Assawoman Bay.

"Pronounced with a long *o*," Uncle Karl reminded Magda with a wink. His shirt sleeves were rolled up; Mother punched his brown biceps with the arrowed heart on it and said his mind was naughty. Fat May's laugh came suddenly from the funhouse, as if she'd just got the joke; the family laughed too at the coincidence. Ambrose went under the boardwalk to search for out-of-town matchbook covers with the aid of his pocket flashlight; he looked out from the edge of the North American continent and wondered how far their laughter carried over the water. Spies in rubber rafts; survivors in lifeboats. If the joke had been beyond his understanding, he could have said: *"The laughter was over his head."* And let the reader see the serious wordplay on second reading.

He turned the flashlight on and then off at once even before the woman whooped. He sprang away, heart athud, dropping the light. What had the man grunted? Perspiration drenched and chilled him by the time he scrambled up to the family. "See anything?" his father asked. His voice wouldn't come; he shrugged and violently brushed sand from his pants legs.

"Let's ride the old flying horses!" Magda cried. I'll never be an author. It's been forever already, everybody's gone home, Ocean City's deserted, the ghost-crabs are tickling across the beach and down the littered cold streets. And the empty halls of clapboard hotels and abandoned funhouses. A tidal wave; an enemy air raid; a monster-crab swelling like an island from the sea. *The inhabitants fled in terror.* Magda clung to his trouser leg; he alone knew the maze's secret. "He gave his life that we might live," said Uncle Karl with a scowl of pain, as he. The fellow's hands had been tattooed; the woman's legs, the woman's fat white legs had. *An astonishing coincidence.* He yearned to tell Peter. He wanted to throw up for excitement. They hadn't even chased him. He wished he were dead.

One possible ending would be to have Ambrose come across another lost person in the dark. They'd match their wits together against the funhouse, struggle like Ulysses past obstacle after obstacle, help and encourage each other. Or a girl. By the time they found the exit they'd be closest friends, sweethearts if it were a girl; they'd know each other's inmost souls, be bound together *by the cement of shared adventure;* then they'd emerge into the light and it would turn out that his friend was a Negro. A blind girl. President Roosevelt's son. Ambrose's former archenemy.

Shortly after the mirror room he'd groped along a musty corridor, his heart already misgiving him at the absence of phosphorescent arrows and other signs. He'd found a crack of light—nor a door, it turned out, but a seam between the plyboard wall panels—and squinting up to it, espied a small old man, *in appearance not unlike* the photographs at home of Ambrose's late grandfather, nodding upon a stool beneath a bare, speckled bulb. A crude panel of toggle- and knife-switches hung beside the open fuse box near his head; elsewhere in the little room were wooden levers and ropes belayed to boat cleats. At the time, Ambrose wasn't lost enough to rap or call; later he couldn't find that crack. Now it seemed to him that he'd possibly dozed off for a few minutes somewhere along the way; certainly he was exhausted from the afternoon's sunshine and the evening's problems; he couldn't be sure he hadn't dreamed part or all of the sight. Had an old black wall fan droned like bees and shimmied two flypaper streamers? Had the funhouse operator—gentle, somewhat sad and tired-appearing, in expression not unlike the photographs at home of Ambrose's late Uncle Konrad—murmured in his sleep? Is there really such a person as Ambrose, or is he a figment of the author's imagination? Was it Assawoman Bay or Sinepuxent? Are there other errors of fact in this fiction? Was there another sound besides the little slap slap of thigh on ham, like water sucking at the chine-boards of a skiff?

When you're lost, the smartest thing to do is stay put till you're found, hollering if necessary. But to holler guarantees humiliation as well as rescue; keeping silent permits some saving of face—you can act surprised at the fuss when your rescuers find you and swear you weren't lost, if they do. What's more you might find your own way yet, *however belatedly*.

"Don't tell me your foot's still asleep!" Magda exclaimed as the three young people walked from the inlet to the area set aside for ferris wheels, carrousels, and other carnival rides, they having decided in favor of the vast and ancient merry-go-round instead of the funhouse. What a sentence, everything was wrong from the outset. People don't know what to make of him, he doesn't know what to make of himself, he's only thirteen, *athletically and socially inept,* not astonishingly bright, but there are antennae; he has . . . some sort of receivers in his head; things speak to him, he understands more than he should, the world winks at him through its objects, grabs grinning at his coat. Everybody else is in on some secret he doesn't know; they've forgotten to tell him. Through simple *procrastination* his mother put off his baptism until this year. Everyone else had it done as a baby; he'd assumed the same of himself, as had his mother, so she claimed, until it was time for him to join Grace Methodist-Protestant and the oversight came out. He was mortified, but pitched sleepless through his private catechizing, intimidated by the ancient mysteries, a thirteen year old would never say that, resolved to experience conversion like St. Augustine. When the water touched his brow and Adam's sin left him, he contrived by a strain like defecation to bring tears into his eyes—but felt nothing. There was some simple, radical difference about him; he hoped it was genius, feared it was madness, devoted himself to amiability and inconspicuousness. Alone on the seawall near his house he was seized by the terrifying transports he'd thought to find in toolshed, in Communion-cup. The grass was alive! The town, the river, himself, were not imaginary; time roared in his ears like wind; the world was *going on!* This part ought to be dramatized. The Irish author James Joyce once wrote. Ambrose M—— is going to scream.

There is no *texture of rendered sensory detail,* for one thing. The faded distorting mirrors beside Fat May; the impossibility of choosing a mount when one had but a single ride on the great carrousel; the *vertigo attendant on his recognition* that Ocean City was worn out, the place of fathers and grandfathers, straw-boatered men and parasoled ladies survived by their amusements. Money spent, the three paused at Peter's insistence beside Fat May to watch the girls get their skirts blown up. The object was to tease Magda, who said: "I swear, Peter M——, you've got a one-track mind! Amby and me aren't *interested* in such things." In the tumbling-barrel, too, just inside the Devil's-mouth entrance to the funhouse, the girls were upended and their boyfriends and others could see up their dresses if they cared to. Which was the whole point, Ambrose realized. Of the entire funhouse! If you looked around, you noticed that almost all the people on the boardwalk were paired off into couples except the small children; in a way, that was the whole point of Ocean City! If you had X-ray eyes and could see everything going on at that instant under the boardwalk and in all the hotel rooms and cars and alleyways, you'd realize that all the normally *showed*, like restaurants and dance halls and clothing and test-your-strength machines, was merely preparation and intermission. Fat May screamed.

Because he watched the goings-on from the corner of his eye, it was Ambrose who spied the half-dollar on the boardwalk near the tumbling-barrel. Losers weepers. The first time he'd heard some people moving through a corridor not far away, just after he'd lost sight of the crack of light, he'd decided not to call to them, for fear they'd guess he was scared and poke fun; it sounded like roughnecks; he'd hoped they'd come by and he could follow in the dark without their knowing. Another time he'd heard just one person, unless he imagined it, bumping along as if on the other side of the plywood; perhaps Peter coming back for him, or Father, or Magda lost too. Or the owner and operator of the funhouse. He'd called out once as though merrily: "Anybody know where the heck we are?" But the query was too stiff, his voice cracked, when the sounds stopped he was terrified: maybe it was a queer who waited for fellows to get lost, or a longhaired filthy monster that lived in some cranny of the funhouse. He stood rigid for hours it seemed like, scarcely respiring. His future was shockingly clear, in outline. He tried holding his breath to the point of unconsciousness. There ought to be a button you could push to end your life absolutely without pain; disappear in a flick, like turning out a light. He would push it instantly! He despised Uncle Karl. But he despised his father too, for not being what he was supposed to be. Perhaps his father hated *his* father, and so on, and his son would hate him, and so on. Instantly!

Naturally he didn't have nerve enough to ask Magda to go through the funhouse with him. With incredible nerve and to everyone's surprise he invited Magda, quietly and politely, to go through the funhouse with him. "I warn you, I've never been through it before," he added, *laughing easily*; "but I reckon we can manage somehow. The important thing to remember, after all, is that it's meant to be a *fun*house; that is, a place of amusement. If people really got lost or injured or too badly frightened in it, the owner'd go out of business. There'd even be lawsuits. No character in a work of fiction can make a speech this long without interruption or acknowledgment from the other characters."

Mother teased Uncle Karl: "Three's a crowd, I always heard." But actually Ambrose was relieved that Peter now had a quarter too. Nothing was what it looked like. Every instant, under the surface of the Atlantic Ocean, millions of living animals devoured one another. Pilots were falling in flames over Europe; women were being forcibly raped in the South Pacific. His father should have taken him aside and said: "There is a simple secret to getting through the funhouse, as simple as being first to see the Towers. Here it is. Peter does not know it; neither does your Uncle Karl. You and I are different. Not surprisingly, you've often wished you weren't. Don't think I haven't noticed how unhappy your childhood has been! But you'll understand, when I tell you, why it had to be kept secret until now. And you won't regret not being like your brother and your uncle. *On the contrary!*" If you knew all the stories behind all the people on the boardwalk, you'd see that *nothing* was what it looked like. Husbands and wives often hated each other; parents didn't necessarily love their children; et cetera. A child took things for granted because he had nothing to compare his life to and everybody acted as if things were as they should be. Therefore each saw himself as the hero of the story, when the truth might turn out to be that he's the villain, or the coward. And there wasn't one thing you could do about it!

Hunchbacks, fat ladies, fools—that no one chose what he was was unbearable. In the movies he'd meet a beautiful young girl in the funhouse; they'd have hairs-breadth escapes from real dangers; he'd do and say the right things; she also; in the end they'd be lovers; their dialogue lines would match up; he'd be perfectly at ease; she'd not only like him well enough, she'd think he was *marvelous;* she'd lie awake thinking about *him*, instead of vice versa—the way *his* face looked in different lights and how he stood and exactly what he'd said—and yet that would be only one small episode in his wonderful life, among many many others. Not a *turning point* at all. What had happened in the toolshed was nothing. He hated, he loathed his parents! One reason for not writing a lost-in-the-funhouse story is that either everybody's felt what Ambrose feels, in which case it goes without saying, or else no normal person feels such things, in which case Ambrose is a freak. "Is anything more tiresome, in fiction, than the problems of sensitive adolescents?" And it's all too long and rambling, as if the author. For all a person knows the first time through, the end could be just around any corner; perhaps, *not impossibly* it's been within reach any number of times. On the other hand he may be scarcely past the start, with everything yet to get through, an intolerable idea.

Fill in: His father's raised eyebrows when he announced his decision to do the funhouse with Magda. Ambrose understands now, but didn't then, that his father was wondering whether he knew what the funhouse was *for*—especially since he didn't object, as he should have, when Peter decided to come along too. The ticket-woman, witchlike, mortifying him when inadvertently he gave her his name-coin instead of the half-dollar, then unkindly calling Magda's attention to the birthmark on his temple: "Watch out for him, girlie, he's a marked man!" She wasn't even cruel, he understood, only vulgar and insensitive. Somewhere in the world there was a young woman with such splendid understanding that she'd see him entire, like a poem or story, and find his words so valuable after all that when he confessed his apprehensions she would explain why they were in fact the very things that made him precious to her . . . and to Western Civilization! There was no such girl, the simple truth being. Violent yawns as they approached the mouth. Whispered advice from an old-timer on a bench near the barrel: "Go crabwise and ye'll get an eyeful without upsetting!" Composure vanished at the first pitch: Peter hollered joyously, Magda tumbled, shrieked, clutched her skirt; Ambrose scrambled crabwise, tight-lipped with terror, was soon out, watched his dropped name-coin slide among the couples. Shamefaced he saw that to get through expeditiously was not the point; Peter feigned assistance in order to trip Magda up, shouted "I see Christmas!" when her legs went flying. The old man, his latest betrayer, cacked approval. A dim hall then of black-thread cobwebs and recorded gibber: he took Magda's elbow to steady her against revolving discs set in the slanted floor to throw your feet out from under, and explained to her in a calm, deep voice his theory that each phase of the funhouse was triggered either automatically, by a series of photoelectric devices, or else manually by operators stationed at peepholes. But he lost his voice thrice as the discs unbalanced him; Magda was anyhow squealing; but at one point she clutched him about the waist to keep from falling, and her right cheek pressed for a moment against his belt-buckle. Heroically he drew her up, it was his chance to clutch her close as if for support and say: "I love you." He even put an arm lightly about the small of her back before a sailor-and-girl pitched into them from behind, sorely treading his left big toe and knocking Magda asprawl with them. The sailor's girl was a string-haired hussy with a loud laugh and light blue drawers; Ambrose realized that he wouldn't have said "I love you" anyhow, and was smitten with self-contempt. How much better it would be to be that common sailor! A wiry little Seaman 3rd, the fellow squeezed a girl to each side and stumbled hilarious into the mirror room, closer to Magda in thirty seconds than Ambrose had got in thirteen years. She giggled at something the fellow said to Peter; she drew her hair from her eyes with a movement so womanly it struck Ambrose's heart; Peter's smacking her backside then seemed particularly coarse. But Magda made a pleased indignant face and cried, "All right for *you,* mister!" and pursued Peter into the maze without a backward glance. The sailor followed after, leisurely, drawing his girl against his hip; Ambrose understood not only that they were all so relieved to be rid of his burdensome company that they didn't even notice his absence, but that he himself shared their relief. Stepping from the treacherous passage at last into the mirror-maze, he saw once again, more clearly than ever, how readily he deceived himself into supposing he was a person. He even foresaw, wincing at his dreadful self-knowledge, that he would repeat the deception, at ever-rarer intervals, all his wretched life, so fearful were the alternatives. Fame, madness, suicide; perhaps all three. It's not believable that so young a boy could articulate that reflection, and in fiction the merely true must always yield to the plausible. Moreover, the symbolism is in places heavy-footed. Yet Ambrose M—— understood, as few adults do, that the famous loneliness of the great was no popular myth but a general truth—furthermore, that it was as much cause as effect.

All the preceding except the last few sentences is exposition that should've been done earlier or interspersed with the present action instead of lumped together. No reader would put up with so much with such *prolixity*. It's interesting that Ambrose's father, though presumably an intelligent man (as indicated by his role as grade-school principal), neither encouraged nor discouraged his sons at all in any way—as if he either didn't care about them or cared all right but didn't know how to act. If this fact should contribute to one of them's becoming a celebrated but wretchedly unhappy scientist, was it a good thing or not? He too might someday face the question; it would be useful to know whether it had tortured his father for years, for example, or never once crossed his mind.

In the maze two important things happened. First, our hero found a name-coin someone else had lost or discarded: *AMBROSE,* suggestive of the famous lightship and of his late grandfather's favorite dessert, which his mother used to prepare on special occasions out of coconut, oranges, grapes, and what else. Second, as he wondered at the endless replication of his image in the mirrors, second, as he *lost himself in the reflection* that the necessity for an observer makes perfect observation impossible, better make him eighteen at least, yet that would render other things unlikely, he heard Peter and Magda chuckling somewhere together in the maze.

"Here!" "No, here!" they shouted to each other; Peter said, "Where's Amby?" Magda murmured. "Amb?" Peter called. In a pleased, friendly voice. He didn't reply. The truth was, his brother was a *happy-go-lucky youngster* who'd've been better off with a regular brother of his own, but who seldom complained of his lot and was generally cordial. Ambrose's throat ached; there aren't enough different ways to say that. He stood quietly while the two young people giggled and thumped through the glittering maze, hurrah'd their discovery of its exit, cried out in joyful alarm at what next beset them. Then he set his mouth and followed after, as he supposed, took a wrong turn, strayed into the pass *wherein he lingers yet.*

The action of conventional dramatic narrative may be represented by a diagram called Freitag's Triangle:

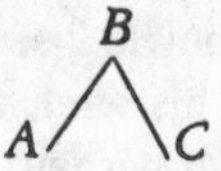

or more accurately by a variant of that diagram:

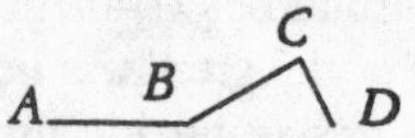

in which *AB* represents the exposition, *B* the introduction of conflict, *BC* the "rising action," complication, or development of the conflict, *C* the climax, or turn of the action, *CD* the dénouement, or resolution of the conflict. While there is no reason to regard this pattern as an absolute necessity, like many other conventions it became conventional because great numbers of people over many years learned by trial and error that it was effective; one ought not to forsake it, therefore, unless one wishes to forsake as well the effect of drama or has clear cause to feel that deliberate violation of the "normal" pattern can better can better effect that effect. This can't go on much longer; it can go on forever. He died telling stories to himself in the dark; years later, when that vast unsuspected area of the funhouse came to light, the first expedition found his skeleton in one of its labyrinthine corridors and mistook it for part of the entertainment. He died of starvation telling himself stories in the dark; but unbeknownst unbeknownst to him, an assistant operator of the funhouse, happening to overhear him, crouched just behind the plyboard partition and wrote down his every word. The operator's daughter, an exquisite young woman with a figure unusually well developed for her age, crouched just behind the partition and transcribed his every word. Though she had never laid eyes on him, she recognized that here was one of Western Culture's truly great imaginations, the eloquence of whose suffering would be an inspiration to unnumbered. And her heart was torn between her love for the misfortunate young man (yes, she loved him, though she had never laid though she knew him only—but how well!—through his words, and the deep, calm voice in which he spoke them) between her love et cetera and her womanly intuition that only in suffering and isolation could he give voice et cetera. Lone dark dying. Quietly she kissed the rough plyboard, and a tear fell upon the page. Where she had written in shorthand *Where she had written in shorthand* Where she had written in shorthand *Where she* et cetera. A long time ago we should have passed the apex of Freitag's Triangle and made brief work of the *dénouement;* the plot doesn't rise by meaningful steps but winds upon itself, digresses, retreats, hesitates, sighs, collapses, expires. The climax of the story must be its protagonist's discovery of a way to get through the funhouse. But he has found none, may have ceased to search.

What relevance does the war have to the story? Should there be fireworks outside or not?

Ambrose wandered, languished, dozed. Now and then he fell into his habit of rehearsing to himself the unadventurous story of his life, narrated from the third-person point of view, from his earliest memory parenthesis of maple leaves stirring in the summer breath of tidewater Maryland end of parenthesis to the present moment. Its principal events, on this telling, would appear to have been *A, B, C,* and *D.*

He imagined himself years hence, successful, married, at ease in the world, the trials of his adolescence far behind him. He has come to the seashore with his family for the holiday: how Ocean City has changed! But at one seldom at one ill-frequented end of the boardwalk a few derelict amusements survive from times gone by: the great carrousel from the turn of the century, with its monstrous griffins and mechanical concert band; the roller coaster rumored since 1916 to have been condemned; the mechanical shooting gallery in which only the image of our enemies changed. His own son laughs with Fat May and wants to know what a funhouse is; Ambrose hugs the sturdy lad close and smiles around his pipestem at his wife.

The family's going home. Mother sits between Father and Uncle Karl, who teases him good-naturedly who chuckles over the fact that the comrade with whom he'd fought his way shoulder to shoulder through the funhouse had turned out to be a blind Negro girl—to their mutual discomfort, as they'd opened their souls. But such are the walls of custom, which even. Whose arm is where? How must it feel. He dreams of a funhouse vaster by far than any yet constructed; but by then they may be out of fashion, like steamboats and excursion trains. Already quaint and seedy: the draperied ladies on the frieze of the carrousel are his father's father's mooncheeked dreams; if he thinks of it more he will vomit his apple-on-a-stick.

He wonders: will he become a regular person? Something has gone wrong; his vaccination didn't take; at the Boy-Scout initiation campfire he only pretended to be deeply moved, as he pretends to this hour that it is not so bad after all in the funhouse, and that he has a little limp. How long will it last? He envisions a truly astonishing funhouse, incredibly complex yet utterly controlled from a great central switchboard like the console of a pipe organ. Nobody had enough imagination. He could design such a place himself, wiring and all, and he's only thirteen years old. He would be its operator: panel lights would show what was up in every cranny of its cunning of its multifarious vastness; a switch-flick would ease this fellow's way, complicate that's, to balance things out; if anyone seemed lost or frightened, all the operator had to do was.

He wishes he had never entered the funhouse. But he has. Then he wishes he were dead. But he's not. Therefore he will construct funhouses for others and be their secret operator—though he would rather be among the lovers for whom funhouses are designed.

Concerning the Bodyguard

DONALD BARTHELME

(1931–)

Does the bodyguard scream at the woman who irons his shirts? Who has inflicted a brown burn on his yellow shirt purchased expensively from Yves St. Laurent? A great brown burn just over the heart?

Does the bodyguard's principal make conversation with the bodyguard, as they wait for the light to change, in the dull gray Citroën? With the second bodyguard, who is driving? What is the tone? Does the bodyguard's principal comment on the brown young women who flock along the boulevard? On the young men? On the traffic? Has the bodyguard ever enjoyed a serious political discussion with his principal?

Is the bodyguard frightened by the initials D.I.T.?

Is the bodyguard frightened by the initials C.N.D.?

Will the bodyguard be relieved, today, in time to see the film he has in mind—*Emmanuelle Around the World*? If the bodyguard is relieved in time to see *Emmanuelle Around the World*, will there be a queue for tickets? Will there be students in the queue?

Is the bodyguard frightened by the slogan *Remember 17 June*? Is the bodyguard frightened by black spray paint, tall letters ghostly at the edges, on this wall, on this wall? At what level of education did the bodyguard leave school?

Is the bodyguard sufficiently well-paid? Is he paid as well as a machinist? As well as a foreman? As well as an army sergeant? As well as a lieutenant? Is the Citroën armored? Is the Mercedes armored? What is the best speed of the Mercedes? Can it equal that of a BMW? A BMW motorcycle? Several BMW motorcycles?

Does the bodyguard gauge the importance of his principal in terms of the number of bodyguards he requires? Should there not be other cars leading and following his principal's car, these also filled with bodyguards? Are there sometimes such additional precautions, and does the bodyguard, at these times, feel himself part of an ocean of bodyguards? Is he exalted at these times? Does he wish for even more bodyguards, possibly flanking cars to the right and left and a point car far, far ahead?

After leaving technical school, in what sort of enterprises did the bodyguard engage before accepting his present post? Has he ever been in jail? For what sort of offense? Has the bodyguard acquired a fondness for his principal? Is there mutual respect? Is there mutual contempt? When his principal takes tea, is the bodyguard offered tea? Beer? Who pays?

Can the bodyguard adduce instances of professional success?

Had he a previous client?

Is there a new bodyguard in the group of bodyguards? Why?

How much does pleasing matter? What services does the bodyguard provide for his principal other than the primary one? Are there services he should not be asked to perform? Is he nevertheless asked from time to time to perform such services? Does he refuse? Can he refuse? Are there, in addition to the bodyguard's agreed-upon compensation, tips? Of what size? On what occasions?

In the restaurant, a good table for his principal and the distinguished gray man with whom he is conferring. Before it (between the table with the two principals and the door), a table for the four bodyguards. What is the quality of the conversation between the two sets of bodyguards? What do they talk about? Soccer, perhaps, Holland vs. Peru, a match which they have all seen. Do they rehearse the savaging of the Dutch goalkeeper Piet Schrijvers by the bastard Peruvian? Do they discuss Schrijver's replacement by the brave Jan Jongbloed, and what happened next? Has the bodyguard noted the difference in quality between his suit and that of his principal? Between his shoes and those of his principal?

In every part of the country, large cities and small towns, bottles of champagne have been iced, put away, reserved for a celebration, reserved for a special day. Is the bodyguard aware of this?

Is the bodyguard tired of waking in his small room on the Calle Caspe, smoking a Royale Filtre, then getting out of bed and throwing wide the curtains to discover, again, eight people standing at the bus stop across the street in postures of depression? Is there on the wall of the bodyguard's small room a poster showing Bruce Lee in a white robe with his feet positioned in such-and-such a way, his fingers outstretched in such-and-such a way? Is there a rosary made of apple beads hanging from a nail? Is there a mirror whose edges have begun to craze and flake, and are there small blurrish Polaroids stuck along the left edge of the mirror, Polaroids of a woman in a dark-blue scarf and two lean children in red pants? Is there a pair of dark-blue trousers plus a long-sleeved white shirt (worn once already) hanging in the dark-brown wardrobe? Is there a color foldout of a naked young woman torn from the magazine VIR taped inside the wardrobe door? Is there a bottle of Long John Scotch atop the cheese-colored mini-refrigerator? Two-burner hotplate? Dull-green ceramic pot on the windowsill containing an unhealthy plant? A copy of *Explication du Tai Chi,* by Bruce Tegner? Does the bodyguard read the newspaper of his principal's party? Is he persuaded by what he reads there? Does the bodyguard know which of the great blocs his country aligned itself with during the Second World War? During the First World War? Does the bodyguard know which countries are the preeminent trading partners of his own country, at the present time?

Seated in a restaurant with his principal, the bodyguard is served, involuntarily, turtle soup. Does he recoil, as the other eats? Why is this near-skeleton, his principal, of such importance to the world that he deserves six bodyguards, two to a shift with the shifts changing every eight hours, six bodyguards of the first competence plus supplementals on occasion, two armored cars, stun grenades ready to hand under the front seat? What has he meant to the world? What are his plans?

Is the retirement age for bodyguards calculated as it is for other citizens? Is it earlier, fifty-five, forty-five? Is there a pension? In what amount? Those young men with dark beards staring at the Mercedes, or staring at the Citroën, who are they? Does the bodyguard pay heed to the complaints of his fellow bodyguards about the hours spent waiting outside this or that Ministry, this or that Headquarters, hours spent propped against the fenders of the Mercedes while their principal is within the (secure) walls? Is the thick glass of these specially prepared vehicles thick enough? Are his fellow bodyguards reliable? Is the new one reliable?

Is the bodyguard frightened by young women of good family? Young women of good family whose handbags contain God knows what? Does the bodyguard feel that the situation is *unfair*? Will the son of the bodyguard, living with his mother in a city far away, himself become a bodyguard? When the bodyguard delivers the son of his principal to the school where all of the children are delivered by bodyguards, does he stop at a grocer's on the way and buy the child a peach? Does he buy himself a peach?

Will the bodyguard, if tested, be equal to his task? Does the bodyguard know which foreign concern was the successful bidder for the construction of his country's nuclear reprocessing plant? Does the bodyguard know which sections of the National Bank's yearly report on debt service have been falsified? Does the bodyguard know that the general amnesty of April coincided with the rearrest of sixty persons? Does the bodyguard know that the new, liberalized press laws of May were a provocation? Does the bodyguard patronize a restaurant called the Crocodile? A place packed with young, loud, fat Communists? Does he spill a drink, to disclose his spite? Is his gesture understood?

Are the streets full of stilt-walkers? Stilt-walkers weaving ten feet above the crowd in great papier-mâché bird heads, black and red costumes, whipping thirty feet of colored cloth above the heads of the crowd, miming the rape of a young female personage symbolizing his country? In the Mercedes, the bodyguard and his colleague stare at the hundreds, men and women, young and old, who move around the Mercedes, stopped for a light, as if it were a rock in a river. In the rear seat, the patron is speaking into a telephone. He looks up, puts down the telephone. The people pressing around the car cannot be counted, there are too many of them; they cannot be known, there are too many of them; they cannot be predicted, they have volition. Then, an opening. The car accelerates.

Is it the case that, on a certain morning, the garbage cans of the city, the garbage cans of the entire country, are over-flowing with empty champagne bottles? Which bodyguard is at fault?

The Bulgarian Poetess

JOHN UPDIKE
(1932–)

"Your poems. Are they difficult?"

She smiled and, unaccustomed to speaking English, answered carefully, drawing a line in the air with two delicately pinched fingers holding an imaginary pen. "They are difficult—to write."

He laughed, startled and charmed. "But not to read?"

She seemed puzzled by his laugh, but did not withdraw her smile, though its corners deepened in a defensive, feminine way. "I think," she said, "not so very."

"Good." Brainlessly he repeated "Good," disarmed by her unexpected quality of truth. He was, himself, a writer, this fortyish young man, Henry Bech, with his thinning curly hair and melancholy Jewish nose, the author of one good book and three others, the good one having come first. By a kind of oversight, he had never married. His reputation had grown while his powers declined. As he felt himself sink, in his fiction, deeper and deeper into eclectic sexuality and bravura narcissism, as his search for plain truth carried him further and further into treacherous realms of fantasy and, lately, of silence, he was more and more thickly hounded by homage, by flat-footed exegetes, by arrogantly worshipful undergraduates who had hitchhiked a thousand miles to touch his hand, by querulous translators, by election to honorary societies, by invitations to lecture, to "speak," to "read," to participate in symposia trumped up by ambitious girlie magazines in shameless conjunction with venerable universities. His very government, in airily unstamped envelopes from Washington, invited him to travel, as an ambassador of the arts, to the other half of the world, the hostile, mysterious half. Rather automatically, but with some faint hope of shaking himself loose from the burden of himself, he consented, and found himself floating, with a passport so stapled with visas it fluttered when pulled from his pocket, down into the dim airports of Communist cities.

He arrived in Sofia the day after a mixture of Bulgarian and African students had smashed the windows of the American legation and ignited an overturned Chevrolet. The cultural officer, pale from a sleepless night of guard duty, tamping his pipe with trembling fingers, advised Bech to stay out of crowds and escorted him to his hotel. The lobby was swarming with Negroes in black wool fezzes and pointed European shoes. Insecurely disguised, he felt, by an astrakhan hat purchased in Moscow, Bech passed through to the elevator, whose operator addressed him in German. "*Ja, vier,*" Bech answered, "*danke,*" and telephoned, in his bad French, for dinner to be brought up to his room. He remained there all night, behind a locked door, reading Hawthorne. He had lifted a paperback collection of short stories from a legation window sill littered with broken glass. A few curved bright crumbs fell from between the pages onto his blanket. The image of Roger Malvin lying alone, dying, in the forest—"Death would come like the slow approach of a corpse, stealing gradually towards him through the forest, and showing its ghastly and motionless features from behind a nearer and yet a nearer tree"—frightened him. Bech fell asleep early and suffered from swollen, homesick dreams. It had been Thanksgiving Day.

In the morning, venturing downstairs for breakfast, he was surprised to find the restaurant open, the waiters affable, the eggs actual, the coffee hot, though syrupy. Outside, Sofia was sunny and (except for a few dark glances at his big American shoes) amenable to his passage along the streets. Lozenge-patterns of pansies, looking flat and brittle as pressed flowers, had been set in the public beds. Women with a touch of Western chic walked hatless in the park behind the mausoleum of Georgi Dimitrov. There was a mosque, and an assortment of trolley cars salvaged from the remotest corner of Bech's childhood, and a tree that talked—that is, it was so full of birds that it swayed under their weight and emitted volumes of chirping sound like a great leafy loudspeaker. It was the inverse of his hotel, whose silent walls presumably contained listening microphones. Electricity was somewhat enchanted in the Socialist world. Lights flickered off untouched and radios turned themselves on. Telephones rang in the dead of the night and breathed wordlessly in his ear. Six weeks ago, flying from New York City, Bech had expected Moscow to be a blazing counterpart and instead saw, through the plane window, a skein of hoarded lights no brighter, on that vast black plain, than a girl's body in a dark room.

Past the talking tree was the American legation. The sidewalk, heaped with broken glass, was roped off, so that pedestrians had to detour into the gutter. Bech detached himself from the stream, crossed the little barren of pavement, smiled at the Bulgarian militiamen who were sullenly guarding the jewel-bright heaps of shards, and pulled open the bronze door. The cultural officer was crisper after a normal night's sleep. He clenched his pipe in his teeth and handed Bech a small list. "You're to meet with the Writer's Union at eleven. These are writers you might ask to see. As far as we can tell, they're among the more progressive."

Words like "progressive" and "liberal" had a somewhat reversed sense in this world. At times, indeed, Bech felt he had passed through a mirror, a dingy flecked mirror that reflected feebly the capitalist world; in its dim depths everything was similar but left-handed. One of the names ended in "-ova." Bech said, "A woman."

"A poetess," the cultural officer said, sucking and tamping in a fury of bogus efficiency. "Very popular, apparently. Her books are impossible to buy."

"Have you read anything by these people?"

"I'll be frank with you. I can just about make my way through a newspaper."

"But you always know what a newspaper will say anyway."

"I'm sorry, I don't get your meaning."

"There isn't any." Bech didn't quite know why the Americans he met irritated him—whether because they garishly refused to blend into this shadow-world or because they were always so solemnly sending him on ridiculous errands.

At the Writer's Union, he handed the secretary the list as it had been handed to him, on U.S. legation stationery. The secretary, a large stooped man with the hands of a stonemason, grimaced and shook his head but obligingly reached for the telephone. Bech's meeting was already waiting in another room. It was the usual one, the one that, with small differences, he had already attended in Moscow and Kiev, Yerevan and Alma-Ata, Bucharest and Prague: the polished oval table, the bowl of fruit, the morning light, the gleaming glasses of brandy and mineral water, the lurking portrait of Lenin, the six or eight patiently sitting men who would leap to their feet with quick blank smiles. These men would include a few literary officials, termed "critics," high in the Party, loquacious and witty and destined to propose a toast to international understanding; a few selected novelists and poets, mustachioed, smoking, sulking at this invasion of their time; a university professor, the head of the Anglo-American Literature department, speaking in a beautiful withered English of Mark Twain and Sinclair Lewis; a young interpreter with a moist handshake; a shaggy old journalist obsequiously scribbling notes; and, on the rim of the group, in chairs placed to suggest that they had invited themselves, one or two gentlemen of ill-defined status, fidgety and tieless, maverick translators who would turn out to be the only ones present who had ever read a word by Henry Bech.

Here this type was represented by a stout man in a tweed coat leather-patched at the elbows in the British style. The whites of his eyes were distinctly red. He shook Bech's hand eagerly, made of it almost an embrace of reunion, bending his face so close that Bech could distinguish the smells of tobacco, garlic, cheese, and alcohol. Even as they were seating themselves around the table, and the Writer's Union chairman, a man elegantly bald, with very pale eyelashes, was touching his brandy glass as if to lift it, this anxious red-eyed interloper blurted at Bech, "Your *Travel Light* was so marvellous a book. The motels, the highways, the young girls with their lovers who were motorcyclists, so marvellous, so American, the youth, the adoration for space and speed, the barbarity of the advertisements in neon lighting, the very poetry. It takes us truly into another dimension."

Travel Light was the first novel, the famous one. Bech disliked discussing it. "At home," he said, "it was criticized as despairing."

The man's hands, stained orange with tobacco, lifted in amazement and plopped noisily to his knees. "No, no a thousand times. Truth, wonder, terror even, vulgarity, yes. But despair, no, not at all, not one iota. Your critics are dead wrong."

"Thank you."

The chairman softly cleared his throat and lifted his glass an inch from the table, so that it formed with its reflection a kind of playing card.

Bech's admirer excitedly persisted. "You are not a *wet* writer, no. You are a dry writer, yes? You have the expressions, am I wrong in English, dry, hard?"

"More or less."

"I want to translate you!"

It was the agonized cry of a condemned man, for the chairman coldly lifted his glass to the height of his eyes, and like a firing squad the others followed suit. Blinking his white lashes, the chairman gazed mistily in the direction of the sudden silence, and spoke in Bulgarian.

The young interpreter murmured in Bech's ear. "I wish to propose now, ah, a very brief toast. I know it will seem doubly brief to our honored American guest, who has so recently enjoyed the, ah, hospitality of our Soviet comrades." There must have been a joke here, for the rest of the table laughed. "But in seriousness permit me to say that in our country we have seen in years past too few Americans, ah, of Mr. Bech's progressive and sympathetic stripe. We hope in the next hour to learn from him much that is interesting and, ah, socially useful about the literature of his large country, and perhaps we may in turn inform him of our own proud literature, of which perhaps he knows regrettably little. Ah, so let me finally, then, since there is a saying that too long a courtship spoils the marriage, offer to drink, in our native plum brandy *slivovica,* ah, firstly to the success of his visit and, in the second place, to the mutual increase of international understanding."

"Thank you," Bech said and, as a courtesy, drained his glass. It was wrong; the others, having merely sipped, stared. The purple burning revolved in Bech's stomach and a severe distaste for himself, for his role, for this entire artificial and futile process, focused into a small brown spot on a pear in the bowl so shiningly posed before his eyes.

The red-eyed fool smelling of cheese was ornamenting the toast. "It is a personal honor for me to meet the man who, in *Travel Light,* truly added a new dimension to American prose."

"The book was written," Bech said, "twelve years ago."

"And since?" A slumping, mustached man sat up and sprang into English. "Since, you have written what?"

Bech had been asked that question often in these weeks and his answer had grown curt. "A second novel called *Brother Pig,* which is St. Bernard's expression for the body."

"Good. Yes, and?"

"A collection of essays and sketches called *When the Saints.*"

"I like the title less well."

"It's the beginning of a famous Negro song."

"We know the song," another man said, a smaller man, with the tense, dented mouth of a hare. He lightly sang, "Lordy, I just want to be in that number."

"And the last book," Bech said, "was a long novel called *The Chosen* that took six years to write and that nobody liked."

"I have read reviews," the red-eyed man said. "I have not read the book. Copies are difficult here."

"I'll give you one," Bech said.

The promise seemed, somehow, to make the recipient unfortunately conspicuous; wringing his stained hands, he appeared to swell in size, to intrude grotesquely upon the inner ring, so that the interpreter took it upon himself to whisper, with the haste of an apology, into Bech's ear, "This gentleman is well known as the translator into our language of *Erewhon.*"

"A marvellous book," the translator said, deflating in relief, pulling at his pockets for a cigarette. "It truly takes us into another dimension. Something that must be done. We live in a new cosmos."

The chairman spoke in Bulgarian, musically, at length. There was polite laughter. Nobody translated for Bech. The professorial type, his hair like a flaxen toupee, jerked forward. "Tell me, is it true, as I have read"—his phrases whistled slightly, like rusty machinery—"that the stock of Sinclair Lewis has plummeted under the Salinger wave?"

And so it went, here as in Kiev, Prague, and Alma-Ata, the same questions, more or less predictable, and his own answers, terribly familiar to him by now, mechanical, stale, irrelevant, untrue, claustrophobic. The door opened. In came, with the rosy air of a woman fresh from a bath, a little breathless, having hurried, hatless, a woman in a blond coat, her hair also blond. The secretary, entering behind her, seemed to make a cherishing space around her with his large curved hands. He introduced her to Bech as Vera Something-ova, the poetess he had asked to meet. None of the others on the list, he explained, answered their telephones.

"Aren't you kind to come?" As Bech asked it, it was a genuine question, to which he expected some sort of an answer.

She spoke to the interpreter in Bulgarian. "She says," the interpreter told Bech, "she is sorry she is so late."

"But she was just called!" In the warmth of his confusion and pleasure Bech turned to speak directly to her, forgetting he would not be understood. "I'm terribly sorry to have interrupted your morning."

"I am pleased," she said, "to meet you. I heard of you spoken in France."

"You speak English!"

"No. Very little amount."

"But you *do*."

A chair was brought for her from a corner of the room. She yielded her coat, revealing herself in a suit also blond, as if her clothes were an aspect of a total consistency. She sat down opposite Bech, crossing her legs. Her legs were very good; her face was perceptibly broad. Lowering her lids, she tugged her skirt to the curve of her knee. It was his sense of her having hurried, hurried to him, and of being, still, graciously flustered, that most touched him.

He spoke to her very clearly, across the fruit, fearful of abusing and breaking the fragile bridge of her English. "You are a poetess. When I was young, I also wrote poems."

She was silent so long he thought she would never answer; but then she smiled and pronounced, "You are not old now."

"Your poems. Are they difficult?"

"They are difficult—to write."

"But not to read?"

"I think—not so very."

"Good. Good."

Despite the decay of his career, Bech had retained an absolute faith in his instincts; he never doubted that somewhere an ideal course was open to him and that his intuitions were pre-dealt clues to his destiny. He had loved, briefly or long, with or without consummation, perhaps a dozen women; yet all of them, he now saw, shared the trait of approximation, of narrowly missing an undisclosed prototype. The surprise he felt did not have to do with the appearance, at last, of this central woman; he had always expected her to appear. What he had not expected was her appearance here, in this remote and abused nation, in this room of morning light, where he discovered a small knife in his fingers and on the table before him, golden and moist, a precisely divided pear.

Men travelling alone develop a romantic vertigo. Bech had already fallen in love with a freckled Embassy wife in Prague, a buck-toothed chanteuse in Rumania, a stolid Mongolian sculptress in Kazakhstan. In the Tretyakov Gallery he had fallen in love with a recumbent statue, and at the Moscow Ballet School with an entire roomful of girls. Entering the room, he had been struck by the aroma, tenderly acrid, of young female sweat. Sixteen and seventeen, wearing patchy practice suits, the girls were twirling so strenuously their slippers were unravelling. Demure student faces crowned the unconscious insolence of their bodies. The room was doubled in depth by a floor-to-ceiling mirror. Bech was seated on a bench at its base. Staring above his head, each girl watched herself with frowning eyes frozen, for an instant in the turn, by the imperious delay and snap of her head. Bech tried to remember the lines of Rilke that expressed it, this snap and delay: *did not the drawing remain/that the dark stroke of your eyebrow/swiftly wrote on the wall of its own turning?* At one point the teacher, a shapeless old Ukrainian lady with gold canines, a *prima* of the thirties, had arisen and cried something translated to Bech as, "No, no, the arms free, *free!*" And in demonstration she had executed a rapid series of pirouettes with such proud effortlessness that all the girls, standing this way and that like deer along the wall, had applauded. Bech had loved them for that. In all his loves, there was an urge to rescue—to rescue the girls from the slavery of their exertions, the statue from the cold grip of its own marble, the Embassy wife from her boring and unctuous husband, the chanteuse from her nightly humiliation (she could not sing), the Mongolian from her stolid race. But the Bulgarian poetess presented herself to him as needing nothing, as being complete, poised, satisfied, achieved. He was aroused and curious and, the next day, inquired about her of the man with the vaguely contemptuous mouth of a hare—a novelist turned playwright and scenarist, who accompanied him to the Rila Monastery. "She lives to write," the playwright said. "I do not think it is healthy."

Bech said, "But she seems so healthy." They stood beside a small church with whitewashed walls. From the outside it looked like a hovel, a shelter for pigs or chickens. For five centuries the Turks had ruled Bulgaria, and the Christian churches, however richly adorned within, had humble exteriors. A peasant woman with wildly snarled hair unlocked the door for them. Though the church could hardly ever have held more than thirty worshippers, it was divided into three parts, and every inch of wall was covered with eighteenth-century frescoes. Those in the narthex depicted a Hell where the devils wielded scimitars. Passing through the tiny nave, Bech peeked through the iconostasis into the screened area that, in the symbolism of Orthodox architecture, represented the next, the hidden world—Paradise—and glimpsed a row of books, an easy chair, a pair of ancient oval spectacles. Outdoors again, he felt released from the unpleasantly tight atmosphere of a children's book. They were on the side of a hill. Above them was a stand of pines whose trunks glistened with ice. Below them sprawled the monastery, a citadel of Bulgarian national feeling during the years of the Turkish Yoke. The last monks had been moved out in 1961. An aimless soft rain was falling in these mountains, and there were not many German tourists today. Across the valley, whose little silver river still turned a water wheel, a motionless white horse stood silhouetted against a green meadow, pinned there like a brooch.

"I am an old friend of hers," the playwright said. "I worry about her."

"Are the poems good?"

"It is difficult for me to judge. They are very feminine. Perhaps shallow."

"Shallowness can be a kind of honesty."

"Yes. She is very honest in her work."

"And in her life?"

"As well."

"What does her husband do?"

The other man looked at him with parted lips and touched his arm, a strange Slavic gesture, communicating an underlying racial urgency, that Bech no longer shied from. "But she has no husband. As I say, she is too much for poetry to have married."

"But her name ends in '-ova.'"

"I see. You are mistaken. It is not a matter of marriage; I am Petrov, my unmarried sister is Petrova. All females."

"How stupid of me. But I think it's such a pity, she's so charming."

"In America, only the uncharming fail to marry?"

"Yes, you must be very uncharming not to marry."

"It is not so here. The government indeed is alarmed; our birth rate is one of the lowest in Europe. It is a problem for economists."

Bech gestured at the monastery. "Too many monks?"

"Not enough, perhaps. With too few of monks, something of the monk enters everybody."

The peasant woman, who seemed old to Bech but who was probably younger than he, saw them to the edge of her domain. She huskily chattered in what Petrov said was very amusing rural slang. Behind her, now hiding in her skirts and now darting away, was her child, a boy not more than three. He was faithfully chased, back and forth, by a small white pig, who moved, as pigs do, on tiptoe, with remarkably abrupt changes of direction. Something in the scene, in the open glee of the woman's parting smile and the unself-conscious way her hair thrust out from her head, something in the mountain mist and spongy rutted turf into which frost had begun to break at night, evoked for Bech a nameless absence to which was attached, like a horse to a meadow, the image of the poetess, with her broad face, her good legs, her Parisian clothes, and her sleekly brushed hair. Petrov, in whom he was beginning to sense, through the wraps of foreignness, a clever and kindred mind, seemed to have overheard his thoughts, for he said, "If you would like, we could have dinner. It would be easy for me to arrange."

"With her?"

"Yes, she is my friend, she would be glad."

"But I have nothing to say to her. I'm just curious about such an intense conjunction of good looks and brains. I mean, what does a soul do with it all?"

"You may ask her. Tomorrow night?"

"I'm sorry, I can't. I'm scheduled to go to the ballet, and the next night the legation is giving a cocktail party for me, and then I fly home."

"Home? So soon?"

"It does not feel soon to me. I must try to work again."

"A drink, then. Tomorrow evening before the ballet? It is possible? It is not possible."

Petrov looked puzzled, and Bech realized that it was his fault, for he was nodding to say Yes, but in Bulgaria nodding meant No, and a shake of the head meant Yes. "Yes," he said. "Gladly."

The ballet was entitled *Silver Slippers*. As Bech watched it, the word "ethnic" kept coming to his mind. He had grown accustomed, during his trip, to this sort of artistic evasion, the retreat from the difficult and disappointing present into folk dance, folk tale, folk song, with always the implication that, beneath the embroidered peasant costume, the folk was really one's heart's own darling, the proletariat.

"Do you like fairy tales?" It was the moist-palmed interpreter who accompanied him to the theatre.

"I *love* them," Bech said, with a fervor and gaiety lingering from the previous hour. The interpreter looked at him anxiously, as when Bech had swallowed the brandy in one swig, and throughout the ballet kept murmuring explanations of self-evident events on the stage. Each night, a princess would put on silver slippers and dance through her mirror to tryst with a wizard, who possessed a magic stick that she coveted, for with it the world could be ruled. The wizard, as a dancer, was inept, and once almost dropped her, so that anger flashed from her eyes. She was, the princess, a little redhead with a high round bottom and a frozen pout and beautiful free arm motions, and Bech found it oddly estatic when, preparatory to her leap, she would dance toward the mirror, an empty oval, and another girl, identically dressed in pink, would emerge from the wings and perform as her reflection. And when the princess, haughtily adjusting her cape of invisibility, leaped through the oval of gold wire, Bech's heart leaped backward into the enchanted hour he had spent with the poetess.

Though the appointment had been established, she came into the restaurant as if, again, she had been suddenly summoned and had hurried. She sat down between Bech and Petrov slightly breathless and fussed, but exuding, again, that impalpable warmth of intelligence and virtue.

"Vera, Vera," Petrov said.

"You hurry too much," Bech told her.

"Not so very much," she said.

Petrov ordered her a cognac and continued with Bech their discussion of the newer French novelists. "It is tricks," Petrov said. "Good tricks, but tricks. It does not have enough to do with life, it is too much verbal nervousness. Is that sense?"

"It's an epigram," Bech said.

"There are just two of their number with whom I do not feel this: Claude Simon and Samuel Beckett. You have no relation, Bech, Beckett?"

"None."

Vera said, "Nathalie Sarraute is a very modest woman. She felt motherly to me."

"You have met her?"

"In Paris I heard her speak. Afterward there was the coffee. I liked her theories, of the, oh, *what?* Of the *little* movements within the heart." She delicately measured a pinch of space and smiled, through Bech, back at herself.

"Tricks," Petrov said. "I do not feel this with Beckett; there, in a low form, believe it or not, one has human content."

Bech felt duty-bound to pursue this, to ask about the theatre of the absurd in Bulgaria, about abstract painting (these were the touchstones of "progressiveness"; Russia had none, Rumania some, Czechoslovakia plenty), to subvert Petrov. Instead, he asked the poetess, "Motherly?"

Vera explained, her hands delicately modelling the air, rounding into nuance, as it were, the square corners of her words. "After her talk, we—talked."

"In French?"

"And in Russian."

"She knows Russian?"

"She was born Russian."

"How is her Russian?"

"Very pure but—old-fashioned. Like a book. As she talked, I felt in a book, safe."

"You do not always feel safe?"

"Not always."

"Do you find it difficult to be a woman poet?"

"We have a tradition of woman poets. We have Elisaveta Bagriana, who is very great."

Petrov leaned toward Bech as if to nibble him. "Your own works? Are they influenced by the *nouvelle vague?* Do you consider yourself to write anti-*romans?*"

Bech kept himself turned toward the woman. "Do you want to hear about how I write? You don't, do you?"

"Very much yes," she said.

He told them, told them shamelessly, in a voice that surprised him with its steadiness, its limpid urgency, how once he had written, how in *Travel Light* he had sought to show people skimming the surface of things with their lives, taking tints from things the way that objects in a still life color one another, and how later he had attempted to place beneath the melody of plot a countermelody of imagery, interlocking images which had risen to the top and drowned his story, and how in *The Chosen* he had sought to make of this confusion the theme itself, an epic theme, by showing a population of characters whose actions were all determined, at the deepest level, by nostalgia, by a desire to get back, to dive, each, into the springs of their private imagery. The book probably failed; at least, it was badly received. Bech apologized for telling all this. His voice tasted flat in his mouth; he felt a secret intoxication and a secret guilt, for he had contrived to give a grand air, as of an impossibly noble and quixotically complex experiment, to his failure when at bottom, he suspected, a certain simple laziness was the cause.

Petrov said, "Fiction so formally sentimental could not be composed in Bulgaria. We do not have a happy history."

It was the first time Petrov had sounded like a Communist. If there was one thing that irked Bech about these people behind the mirror, it was their assumption that, however second-rate elsewhere, in suffering they were supreme. He said, "Believe it or not, neither do we."

Vera calmly intruded. "Your personae are not moved by love?"

"Yes, very much. But as a form of nostalgia. We fall in love, I tried to say in the book, with women who remind us of our first landscape. A silly idea. I used to be interested in love. I once wrote an essay on the orgasm—you know the word?—"

She shook her head. He remembered that it meant Yes.

"—on the orgasm as perfect memory. The one mystery is, what are we remembering?"

She shook her head again, and he noticed that her eyes were gray, and that in their depths his image (which he could not see) was searching for the thing remembered. She composed her fingertips around the brandy glass and said, "There is a French poet, a young one, who has written of this. He says that never else do we, do we so gather up, collect into ourselves, oh—" Vexed, she spoke to Petrov in rapid Bulgarian.

He shrugged and said, "Concentrate our attention."

"—concentrate our attention," she repeated to Bech, as if the words, to be believed, had to come from her. "I say it foolish—foolishly—but in French it is very well put and—*correct*."

Petrov smiled neatly and said, "This is an enjoyable subject for discussion, love."

"It remains," Bech said, picking his words as if the language were not native even to him, "one of the few things that still deserve meditation."

"I think it is good," she said.

"Love?" he asked, startled.

She shook her head and tapped the stem of her glass with a fingernail, so that Bech had an inaudible sense of ringing, and she bent as if to study the liquor, so that her entire body borrowed a rosiness from the brandy and burned itself into Bech's memory—the silver gloss of her nail, the sheen of her hair, the symmetry of her arms relaxed on the white tablecloth, everything except the expression on her face.

Petrov asked aloud Bech's opinion of Dürrenmatt.

Actuality is a running impoverishment of possibility. Though he had looked forward to seeing her again at the cocktail party and had made sure that she was invited, when it occurred, though she came, he could not get to her. He saw her enter, with Petrov, but he was fenced in by an attaché of the Yugoslav Embassy and his burnished Tunisian wife; and, later, when he was worming his way toward her diagonally, a steely hand closed on his arm and a rasping American female told him that her fifteen-year-old nephew had decided to be a writer and desperately needed advice. Not the standard crap, but real brass-knuckles advice. Bech found himself balked. He was surrounded by America: the voices, the narrow suits, the watery drinks, the clatter, the glitter. The mirror had gone opaque and gave him back only himself. He managed, in the end, as the officials were thinning out, to break through and confront her in a corner. Her coat, blond, with a rabbit collar, was already on; from its side pocket she pulled a pale volume of poems in the Cyrillic alphabet. "Please," she said. On the flyleaf she had written, "to H. Beck, sincerelly, with bad spellings but much"—the last word looked like "leave" but must have been "love."

"Wait," he begged, and went back to where his ravaged pile of presentation books had been and, unable to find the one he wanted, stole the legation library's jacketless copy of *The Chosen.* Placing it in her expectant hands, he told her, "Don't look," for inside he had written, with a drunk's stylistic confidence,

Dear Vera Glavanakova—

It is a matter of earnest regret for me that you and I must live on opposite sides of the world.

"I Always Wanted You to Admire My Fasting"; or, Looking at Kafka

PHILIP ROTH
(1933–)

To the students of English 275,
University of Pennsylvania,
Fall 1972

"I always wanted you to admire my fasting," said the hunger artist. "We do admire it," said the overseer, affably. "But you shouldn't admire it," said the hunger artist. "Well then we don't admire it," said the overseer, "but why shouldn't we admire it?" "Because I have to fast, I can't help it," said the hunger artist. "What a fellow you are," said the overseer, "and why can't you help it?" "Because," said the hunger artist, lifting his head a little and speaking, with his lips pursed, as if for a kiss, right into the overseer's ear, so that no syllable might be lost, "because I couldn't find the food I liked. If I had found it, believe me, I should have made no fuss and stuffed myself like you or anyone else." These were his last words, but in his dimming eyes remained the firm though no longer proud persuasion that he was still continuing to fast.

—*"A Hunger Artist,"* Franz Kafka

I

I am looking, as I write of Kafka, at the photograph taken of him at the age of forty (my age)—it is 1924, as sweet and hopeful a year as he may ever have known as a man, and the year of his death. His face is sharp and skeletal, a burrower's face: pronounced cheekbones made even more conspicuous by the absence of sideburns; the ears shaped and angled on his head like angel wings; an intense, creaturely gaze of startled composure—enormous fears, enormous control; a black towel of Levantine hair pulled close around the skull the only sensuous feature; there is a familiar Jewish flare in the bridge of the nose, the nose itself is long and weighted slightly at the tip—the nose of half the Jewish boys who were my friends in high school. Skulls chiseled like this one were shoveled by the thousands from the ovens; had he lived, his would have been among them, along with the skulls of his three younger sisters. Of course it is no more horrifying to think of Franz Kafka in Auschwitz than to think of anyone in Auschwitz—to paraphrase Tolstoy, it is just horrifying in its own way. But he died too soon for the holocaust. Had he lived, perhaps he would have escaped with his good friend and great advocate Max Brod, who eventually found refuge in Palestine, a citizen of Israel until his death there in 1970. But *Kafka* escaping? It seems unlikely for one so fascinated by entrapment and careers that culminate in anguished death. Still, there is Karl Rossman, his American greenhorn. Having imagined Karl's escape to America and his mixed luck here, could not Kafka have found a way to execute an escape for himself? The New School for Social Research in New York becoming *his* Great Nature Theater of Oklahoma? Or perhaps through the influence of Thomas Mann, a position in the German department at Princeton . . . But then had Kafka lived it is not at all certain that the books of his which Mann celebrated from *his* refuge in New Jersey would ever have been published; eventually Kafka might either have destroyed those manuscripts that he had once bid Max Brod to dispose of at his death, or, at the least, continued to keep them his secret. The Jewish refugee arriving in America in 1938 would not then have been Mann's "religious humorist," but a frail and bookish fifty-five-year-old bachelor, formerly a lawyer for a government insurance firm in Prague, retired on a pension in Berlin at the time of Hitler's rise to power—an author, yes, but of a few eccentric stories, mostly about animals, stories no one in America had ever heard of and only a handful in Europe had read; a homeless K., but without K.'s willfulness and purpose, a homeless Karl, but without Karl's youthful spirit and resilience; just a Jew lucky enough to have escaped with his life, in his possession a suitcase containing some clothes, some family photos, some Prague mementos, and the manuscripts, still unpublished and in pieces, of *Amerika, The Trial, The Castle,* and (stranger things happen) three more fragmented novels, no less remarkable than the bizarre masterworks that he keeps to himself out of Oepidal timidity, perfectionist madness, and insatiable longings for solitude and spiritual purity.

July, 1923: Eleven months before he will die in a Vienna sanatorium, Kafka somehow finds the resolve to leave Prague and his father's home for good. Never before has he even remotely succeeded in living apart, independent of his mother, his sisters and his father, nor has he been a writer other than in those few hours when he is not working in the legal department of the Workers' Accident Insurance Office in Prague; since taking his law degree at the university, he has been by all reports the most dutiful and scrupulous of employees, though he finds the work tedious and enervating. But in June of 1923—having some months earlier been pensioned from his job because of his illness—he meets a young Jewish girl of nineteen at a seaside resort in Germany, Dora Dymant, an employee at the vacation camp of the Jewish People's Home of Berlin. Dora has left her Orthodox Polish family to make a life of her own (at half Kafka's age); she and Kafka—who has just turned forty—fall in love . . . Kafka has by now been engaged to two somewhat more conventional Jewish girls—twice to one of them—hectic, anguished engagements wrecked largely by his fears. "I am mentally incapable of marrying," he writes his father in the forty-five-page letter he gave to his mother to deliver, " . . . the moment I make up my mind to marry I can no longer sleep, my head burns day and night, life can no longer be called life." He explains why. "Marrying is barred to me," he tells his father, "because it is your domain. Sometimes I imagine the map of the world spread out and you stretched diagonally across it. And I feel as if I could consider living in only those regions that either are not covered by you or are not within your reach. And in keeping with the conception I have of your magnitude, these are not many and not very comforting regions—and marriage is not among them." The letter explaining what is wrong between this father and this son is dated November, 1919; the mother thought it best not even to deliver it, perhaps for lack of courage, probably, like the son, for lack of hope.

During the following two years Kafka attempts to wage an affair with Milena Jesenská-Pollak, an intense young woman of twenty-four who has translated a few of his stories into Czech and is most unhappily married in Vienna; his affair with Milena, conducted feverishly, but by and large through the mails, is even more demoralizing to Kafka than the fearsome engagements to the nice Jewish girls. They aroused only the paterfamilias longings that he dared not indulge, longings inhibited by his exaggerated awe of his father—"spellbound," says Brod, "in the family circle"—and the hypnotic spell of his own solitude; but the Czech Milena, impetuous, frenetic, indifferent to conventional restraints, a woman of appetite and anger, arouses more elemental yearnings and more elemental fears. According to a Prague critic, Rio Preisner, Milena was "psychopathic"; according to Margaret Buber-Neumann, who lived two years beside her in the German concentration camp where Milena died following a kidney operation in 1944, she was powerfully sane, extraordinarily humane and courageous. Milena's obituary for Kafka was the only one of consequence to appear in the Prague press; the prose is strong, so are the claims she makes for Kafka's accomplishment. She is still only in her twenties, the dead man is hardly known as a writer beyond his small circle of friends—yet Milena writes, "His knowledge of the world was exceptional and deep, and he was a deep and exceptional world in himself . . . [He had] a delicacy of feeling bordering on the miraculous and a mental clarity that was terrifyingly uncompromising, and in turn he loaded on to his illness the whole burden of his mental fear of life . . . He wrote the most important books in recent German literature." One can imagine this vibrant young woman stretched diagonally across the bed, as awesome to Kafka as his own father spread out across the map of the world. His letters to her are disjointed, unlike anything else of his in print; the word fear, frequently emphasized, appears on page after page. "We are both married, you in Vienna, I to my Fear in Prague." He yearns to lay his head upon her breast; he calls her "Mother Milena"; during at least one of their two brief rendezvous, he is hopelessly impotent. At last he has to tell her to leave him be, an edict that Milena honors though it leaves her hollow with grief. "Do not write," Kafka tells her, "and let us not see each other; I ask you only to quietly fulfill this request of mine; only on those conditions is survival possible for me; everything else continues the process of destruction."

Then in the early summer of 1923, during a visit to his sister who is vacationing with her children by the Baltic Sea, he finds young Dora Dymant, and within a month Franz Kafka has gone off to live with her in two rooms in a suburb of Berlin, out of reach at last of the "claws" of Prague and home. How can it be? How can he, in his illness, have accomplished so swiftly and decisively the leave-taking that was so beyond him in his healthiest days? The impassioned letter-writer who could equivocate interminably about which train to catch to Vienna to meet with Milena (if he should meet with her for the weekend at all); the bourgeois suitor in the high collar, who, during his drawn-out agony of an engagement with the proper Fräulein Bauer, secretly draws up a memorandum for himself, countering the arguments "for" marriage with the arguments "against"; the poet of the ungraspable and the unresolved, whose belief in the immovable barrier separating the wish from its realization is at the heart of his excruciating visions of defeat, the Kafka whose fictions refute every easy, touching, humanish daydream of salvation and justice and fulfillment with densely imagined counter-dreams that mock all solutions and escapes—this Kafka, escapes! Overnight! K. penetrates the Castle walls—Joseph K. evades his indictment—"a breaking away from it altogether, a mode of living completely outside the jurisdiction of the court." Yes, the possibility of which Joseph K. has just a glimmering in the Cathedral, but can neither fathom nor effectuate—"not . . . some influential manipulation of the case, but . . . a circumvention of it"—Kafka realizes in the last year of his life.

Was it Dora Dymant or was it death that pointed the new way? Perhaps it could not have been one without the other. We know that the "illusory emptiness" at which K. gazed upon first entering the village and looking up through the mist and the darkness to the Castle was no more vast and incomprehensible than was the idea of himself as husband and father to the young Kafka; but now it seems the prospect of a Dora forever, of a wife, home, and children everlasting, is no longer the terrifying, bewildering prospect it would once have been, for now "everlasting" is undoubtedly not much more than a matter of months. Yes, the dying Kafka is determined to marry, and writes to Dora's Orthodox father for his daughter's hand. But the imminent death that has resolved all contradictions and uncertainties in Kafka is the very obstacle placed in his path by the young girl's father. The request of Franz Kafka, a dying man, to bind to him in his invalidism Dora Dymant, a healthy young girl, is—denied!

If there is not one father standing in Kafka's way, there is another—and, to be sure, another beyond him. Dora's father, writes Max Brod in his biography of Kafka, "set off with [Kafka's] letter to consult the man he honored most, whose authority counted more than anything else for him, the 'Gerer Rebbe.' The rabbi read the letter, put it to one side, and said nothing more than the single syllable, 'No.'" *No.* Klamm himself could have been no more abrupt—or any more removed from the petitioner. *No.* In its harsh finality, as telling and inescapable as the curselike threat delivered by his father to Georg Bendemann, that thwarted fiancé: "Just take your bride on your arm and try getting in my way. I'll sweep her from your very side, you don't know how!" *No.* Thou shalt not have, say the fathers, and Kafka agrees that he shall not. The habit of obedience and renunciation; also his own distaste for the diseased and reverence for strength, appetite, and health. "'Well, clear this out now!' said the overseer, and they buried the hunger artist, straw and all. Into the cage they put a young panther. Even the most insensitive felt it refreshing to see this wild creature leaping around the cage that had so long been dreary. The panther was all right. The food he liked was brought him without hesitation by the attendants; he seemed not even to miss his freedom; his noble body, furnished almost to the bursting point with all that it needed, seemed to carry freedom around with it too; somewhere in his jaws it seemed to lurk; and the joy of life streamed with such ardent passion from his throat that for the onlookers it was not easy to stand the shock of it. But they braced themselves, crowded around the cage, and did not want ever to move away." So no is no; he knew as much himself. A healthy young girl of nineteen cannot, *should* not, be given in matrimony to a sickly man twice her age, who spits up blood ("I sentence you," cries Georg Bendemann's father, "to death by drowning!") and shakes in his bed with fevers and chills. What sort of un-Kafka-like dream had Kafka been dreaming?

And those nine months spent with Dora have still other "Kafkaesque" elements: a fierce winter in quarters inadequately heated; the inflation that makes a pittance of his own meager pension, and sends into the streets of Berlin the hungry and needy whose sufferings, says Dora, turn Kafka "ash-gray"; and his tubercular lungs, flesh transformed and punished. Dora cares as devotedly and tenderly for the diseased writer as does Gregor Samsa's sister for her brother, the bug. Gregor's sister plays the violin so beautifully that Gregor "felt as if the way were opening before him to the unknown nourishment he craved"; he dreams, in his condition, of sending his gifted sister to the Conservatory! Dora's music is Hebrew, which she reads aloud to Kafka, and with such skill that, according to Brod, "Franz recognized her dramatic talent; on his advice and under his direction she later educated herself in the art . . ."

Only Kafka is hardly vermin to Dora Dymant, *or to himself*. Away from Prague and his father's home, Kafka, in his fortieth year, seems at last to have been delivered from the self-loathing, the self-doubt, and those guilt-ridden impulses to dependence and self-effacement that had nearly driven him mad throughout his twenties and thirties; all at once he seems to have shed the pervasive sense of hopeless despair that informs the great punitive fantasies of *The Trial*, "The Penal Colony," and "The Metamorphosis." Years earlier, in Prague, he had directed Max Brod to destroy all his papers, including three unpublished novels, upon his death; now, in Berlin, when Brod introduces him to a German publisher interested in his work, Kafka consents to the publication of a volume of four stories, and consents, says Brod, "without much need of long arguments to persuade him." With Dora to help, he diligently resumes his study of Hebrew; despite his illness and the harsh winter, he travels to the Berlin Academy for Jewish Studies to attend a series of lectures on the Talmud—a very different Kafka from the estranged melancholic who once wrote in his diary, "What have I in common with the Jews? I have hardly anything in common with myself and should stand very quietly in a corner, content that I can breathe." And to further mark the change, there is ease and happiness with a woman: with this young and adoring companion, he is playful, he is pedagogical, and one would guess, in light of his illness (*and* his happiness), he is chaste. If not a husband (such as he had striven to be to the conventional Fräulein Bauer), if not a lover (as he struggled hopelessly to be with Milena), he would seem to have become something no less miraculous in his scheme of things: a father, a kind of father to this sisterly, mothering daughter. *As Franz Kafka awoke one morning from uneasy dreams he found himself transformed in his bed into a father, a writer, and a Jew.*

"I have completed the construction of my burrow," begins the long, exquisite, and tedious story that he wrote that winter in Berlin, "and it seems to be successful. . . . Just the place where, according to my calculations, the Castle Keep should be, the soil was very loose and sandy and had literally to be hammered and pounded into a firm state to serve as a wall for the beautifully vaulted chamber. But for such tasks the only tool I possess is my forehead. So I had to run with my forehead thousands and thousands of times, for whole days and nights, against the ground, and I was glad when the blood came, for that was proof that the walls were beginning to harden; in that way, as everybody must admit, I richly paid for my Castle Keep." "The Burrow" is the story of an animal with a keen sense of peril whose life is organized around the principle of defense, and whose deepest longings are for security and serenity; with teeth and claws —*and* forehead—the burrower constructs an elaborate and ingeniously intricate system of underground chambers and corridors that are designed to afford it some peace of mind; however, while this burrow does succeed in reducing the sense of danger from without, its maintenance and protection are equally fraught with anxiety: "these anxieties are different from ordinary ones, prouder, richer in content, often long repressed, but in their destructive effects they are perhaps much the same as the anxieties that existence in the outer world gives rise to." The story (whose ending is lost) terminates with the burrower fixated upon distant subterranean noises that cause it "to assume the existence of a great beast," itself burrowing in the direction of the Castle Keep.

Another grim tale of entrapment, and of obsession so absolute that no distinction is possible between character and predicament. Yet this fiction imagined in the last "happy" months of his life is touched with a spirit of personal reconciliation and sardonic self-acceptance, with a tolerance for one's own brand of madness, that is not apparent in "The Metamorphosis"; the piercing masochistic irony of the early animal story—as of "The Judgment" and *The Trial*—has given way here to a critique of the self and its preoccupations that, though bordering on mockery, no longer seeks to resolve itself in images of the uttermost humiliation and defeat

. . . But there is more here than a metaphor for the insanely defended ego, whose striving for invulnerability produces a defensive system that must in its turn become the object of perpetual concern—there is also a very unromantic and hard-headed fable about how and why art is made, a portrait of the artist in all his ingenuity, anxiety, isolation, dissatisfaction, relentlessness, obsessiveness, secretiveness, paranoia, and self-addiction, a portrait of the magical thinker at the end of his tether, Kafka's Prospero . . . It is an infinitely suggestive story, this story of life in a hole. For, finally, remember the proximity of Dora Dymant during the months that Kafka was at work on "The Burrow" in the two underheated rooms that was their illicit home. Certainly a dreamer like Kafka need never have entered the young girl's body for her tender presence to kindle in him a fantasy of a hidden orifice that promises "satisfied desire," "achieved ambition," and "profound slumber," but that once penetrated and in one's possession, arouses the most terrifying and heartbreaking fears of retribution and loss. "For the rest I try to unriddle the beast's plans. Is it on its wanderings, or is it working on its own burrow? If it is on its wanderings then perhaps an understanding with it might be possible. If it should really break through to the burrow I shall give it some of my stores and it will go on its way again. It will go on its way again, a fine story! Lying in my heap of earth I can naturally dream of all sorts of things, even of an understanding with the beast, though I know well enough that no such thing can happen, and that at the instant when we see each other, more, at the moment when we merely guess at each other's presence, we shall blindly bare our claws and teeth . . ."

He died of tuberculosis of the lungs and the larynx a month short of his forty-first birthday, June 3, 1924. Dora, inconsolable, whispers for days afterward, "My love, my love, my good one . . ."

II

1942. I am nine; my Hebrew school teacher, Dr. Kafka, is fifty-nine. To the little boys who must attend his "four to five" class each afternoon, he is known—in part because of his remote and melancholy foreignness, but largely because we vent on him our resentment at having to learn an ancient calligraphy at the very hour we should be out screaming our heads off on the ballfield—he is known as Dr. Kishka. Named, I confess, by me. His sour breath, spiced with intestinal juices by five in the afternoon, makes the Yiddish word for "insides" particularly telling, I think. Cruel, yes, but in truth I would have cut out my tongue had I ever imagined the name would become legend. A coddled child, I do not yet think of myself as persuasive, nor, quite yet, as a literary force in the world. My jokes don't hurt, how could they, I'm so adorable. And if you don't believe me, just ask my family and the teachers in school. Already at nine, one foot in Harvard, the other in the Catskills. Little Borscht Belt comic that I am outside the classroom, I amuse my friends Schlossman and Ratner on the dark walk home from Hebrew school with an imitation of Kishka, his precise and finicky professorial manner, his German accent, his cough, his gloom. "Doctor *Kishka!*" cries Schlossman, and hurls himself savagely against the newsstand that belongs to the candy store owner whom Schlossman drives just a little crazier each night. "Doctor Franz—Doctor Franz—Doctor Franz—*Kishka!*" screams Ratner, and my chubby little friend who lives upstairs from me on nothing but chocolate milk and Mallomars does not stop laughing until, as is his wont (his mother has asked me "to keep an eye on him" for just this reason), he wets his pants. Schlossman takes the occasion of Ratner's humiliation to pull the little boy's paper out of his notebook and wave it in the air—it is the assignment Dr. Kafka has just returned to us, graded; we were told to make up an alphabet of our own, out of straight lines and curved lines and dots. "That is all an alphabet is," he had explained. "That is all Hebrew is. That is all English is. Straight lines and curved lines and dots." Ratner's alphabet, for which he received a C, looks like twenty-six skulls strung in a row. I received my A for a curlicued alphabet inspired largely (as Dr. Kafka would seem to have surmised from his comment at the top of the page) by the number eight. Schlossman received an F for forgetting even to do it—and a lot he seems to care, too. He is content—he is *overjoyed*—with things as they are. Just waving a piece of paper in the air, and screaming, *"Kishka! Kishka!"* makes him deliriously happy. We should all be so lucky.

At home, alone in the glow of my goose-necked "desk" lamp (plugged after dinner into an outlet in the kitchen, my study) the vision of our refugee teacher, sticklike in a fraying three-piece blue suit, is no longer very funny—particularly after the entire beginner's Hebrew class, of which I am the most studious member, takes the name "Kishka" to its heart. My guilt awakens redemptive fantasies of heroism. I have them often about "the Jews in Europe." I must save him. If not me, who? The demonic Schlossman? The babyish Ratner? And if not now, when? For I have learned in the ensuing weeks that Dr. Kafka lives in "a room" in the house of an elderly Jewish lady on the shabby lower stretch of Avon Avenue, where the trolley still runs, and the poorest of Newark's Negroes shuffle meekly up and down the street, for all they seem to know still back in Mississippi. A *room.* And *there!* My family's apartment is no palace, but it is ours at least, so long as we pay the thirty-eight-fifty a month in rent; and though our neighbors are not rich, they refuse to be poor and they refuse to be meek. Tears of shame and sorrow in my eyes, I rush into the living room to tell my parents what I have heard (though not that I heard it during a quick game of "aces up" played a minute before class against the synagogue's rear wall—worse, played directly beneath a stained glass window embossed with the names of the dead): "My Hebrew teacher lives in a *room.*"

My parents go much further than I could imagine anybody going in the real world. Invite him to dinner, my mother says. *Here?* Of course here—Friday night; I'm sure he can stand a home-cooked meal and a little pleasant company. Meanwhile my father gets on the phone to call my Aunt Rhoda, who lives with my grandmother and tends her and her potted plants in the apartment house at the corner of our street. For nearly two decades now my father has been introducing my mother's forty-year-old "baby" sister to the Jewish bachelors and widowers of New Jersey. No luck so far. Aunt Rhoda, an "interior decorator" in the dry goods department of "The Big Bear," a mammoth merchandise and produce market in industrial Elizabeth, wears falsies (this information by way of my older brother) and sheer frilly blouses, and family lore has it that she spends hours in the bathroom every day applying powders and sweeping her stiffish hair up into a dramatic pile on her head; but despite all this dash and display, she is, in my father's words, "still afraid of the facts of life." He, however, is undaunted, and administers therapy regularly and gratis: "Let 'em squeeze ya, Rhoda—it *feels* good!" I am his flesh and blood, I can reconcile myself to such scandalous talk in our kitchen—*but what will Dr. Kafka think?* Oh, but it's too late to do anything now. The massive machinery of matchmaking has been set in motion by my undiscourageable father, and the smooth engines of my proud homemaking mother's hospitality are already purring away. To throw my body into the works in an attempt to bring it all to a halt—well, I might as well try to bring down the New Jersey Bell Telephone Company by leaving our receiver off the hook. Only Dr. Kafka can save me now. But to my muttered invitation, he replies, with a formal bow that turns me scarlet—who has ever seen a person do such a thing outside of a movie house?—he replies that he would be *honored* to be my family's dinner guest. "My aunt," I rush to tell him, "will be there too." It appears that I have just said something mildly humorous; odd to see Dr. Kafka smile. Sighing, he says, "I will be delighted to meet her." Meet her? He's supposed to *marry* her. How do I warn him? And how do I warn Aunt Rhoda (a very great admirer of me and my marks) about his sour breath, his roomer's pallor, his Old World ways, so at odds with her up-to-dateness? My face feels as if it will ignite of its own—and spark the fire that will engulf the synagogue, Torah and all—when I see Dr. Kafka scrawl our address in his notebook, and beneath it, some words *in German.* "Good night, Dr. Kafka!" "Good night, and thank you, thank you." I turn to run, I go, but not fast enough: out on the street I hear Schlossman—that fiend!—announcing to my classmates who are punching one another under the lamplight down from the synagogue steps (where a card game is also in progress, organized by the Bar Mitzvah boys): "Roth invited Kishka to his *house!* To *eat!*"

Does my father do a job on Kafka! Does he make a sales pitch for familial bliss! What it means to a man to have two fine boys and a wonderful wife! Can Dr. Kafka imagine what that's like? The thrill? The satisfaction? The pride? He tells our visitor of the network of relatives on his mother's side that are joined in a "family association" of over two hundred and fifty people located in seven states, including the state of Washington! Yes, relatives even in the Far West: here are their photographs, Dr. Kafka; this is a beautiful book we published entirely on our own for five dollars a copy, pictures of every member of the family, including infants, and a family history by "Uncle" Lichtblau, the eighty-five-year-old patriarch of the clan. This is our family newsletter that is published twice a year and distributed nationwide to all the relatives. This, in the frame, is the menu from the banquet of the family association, held last year in a ballroom of the "Y" in Newark, in honor of my father's mother on her seventy-fifth birthday. My mother, Dr. Kafka learns, has served *six consecutive years* as the secretary-treasurer of the family association. My father has served a two-year term as president, as have each of his three brothers. We now have fourteen boys in the family in uniform. Philip writes a letter on V-mail stationery to five of his cousins in the Army every single month. "Religiously," my mother puts in, smoothing my hair. "I firmly believe," says my father, "that the family is the cornerstone of everything." Dr. Kafka, who has listened with close attention to my father's *spiel,* handling the various documents that have been passed to him with great delicacy and poring over them with a kind of rapt absorption that reminds me of myself over the watermarks of my stamps, now for the first time expresses himself on the subject of family; softly he says, "I agree," and inspects again the pages of our family book. "Alone," says my father, in conclusion, "alone, Dr. Kafka, is a stone." Dr. Kafka, setting the book gently upon my mother's gleaming coffee table, allows with a nod how that is so. My mother's fingers are now turning in the curls behind my ears; not that I even know it at the time, or that she does. Being stroked is my life; stroking me, my father, and my brother is hers.

My brother goes off to a Boy Scout "council" meeting, but only after my father has him stand in his neckerchief before Dr. Kafka and describe to him the skills he has mastered to earn each of his badges. I am invited to bring my stamp album into the living room and show Dr. Kafka my set of triangular stamps from Zanzibar. "Zanzibar!" says my father rapturously, as though I, not even ten, have already been there and back. My father accompanies Dr. Kafka and myself into the "sun parlor," where my tropical fish swim in the aerated, heated, and hygienic paradise I have made for them with my weekly allowance and my Hanukah *gelt*. I am encouraged to tell Dr. Kafka what I know about the temperament of the angelfish, the function of the catfish, and the family life of the black molly. I know quite a bit. "All on his own he does that," my father says to Kafka. "He gives me a lecture on one of those fish, it's seventh heaven, Dr. Kafka." "I can imagine," Kafka replies.

Back in the living room my Aunt Rhoda suddenly launches into a rather recondite monologue on "scotch plaids," designed, it would appear, only for the edification of my mother. At least she looks fixedly at my mother while she delivers it. I have not yet seen her look directly at Dr. Kafka; she did not even turn his way at dinner when he asked how many employees there were at "The Big Bear." "How would I know?" she replies, and continues conversing with my mother, something about a grocer or a butcher who would take care of her "under the counter" if she could find him nylons for his wife. It never occurs to me that she will not look at Dr. Kafka because she is shy—nobody that dolled up could, in my estimation, be shy—I can only think that she is outraged. *It's his breath. It's his accent. It's his age.* I'm wrong—it turns out to be what Aunt Rhoda calls his "superiority complex." "Sitting there, sneering at us like that," says my aunt, somewhat superior now herself. "Sneering?" repeats my father, incredulous. "Sneering and laughing, yes!" says Aunt Rhoda. My mother shrugs: "*I* didn't think he was laughing." "Oh, don't worry, by himself there he was having a very good time—*at our expense*. I know the European-type man. Underneath they all think they're lords of the manor," Rhoda says. "You know something, Rhoda?" says my father, tilting his head and pointing a finger, "I think you fell in love." "With *him*? Are you *crazy*?" "He's too quiet for Rhoda," my mother says, "I think maybe he's a little bit of a wallflower. Rhoda is a lively person, she needs lively people around her." "Wallflower? He's not a wallflower! He's a gentleman, that's all. And he's lonely," my father says assertively, glaring at my mother for coming in over his head like this *against* Kafka. My Aunt Rhoda is forty years old—it is not exactly a shipment of brand-new goods that he is trying to move. "He's a gentleman, he's an educated man, and I'll tell you something, he'd give his eye teeth to have a nice home and a wife." "Well," says my Aunt Rhoda, "let him find one then, if he's so educated. Somebody who's his equal, who he doesn't have to look down his nose at with his big sad refugee eyes!" "Yep, she's in love," my father announces, squeezing Rhoda's knee in triumph. "With him?" she cries, jumping to her feet, taffeta crackling around her like a bonfire. "With *Kafka?*" she snorts, "I wouldn't give an old man like him the time of day!"

Dr. Kafka calls and takes my Aunt Rhoda to a movie. I am astonished, both that he calls and that she goes; it seems there is more desperation in life than I have come across yet in my fish tank. Dr. Kafka takes my Aunt Rhoda to a play performed at the "Y." Dr. Kafka eats Sunday dinner with my grandmother and my Aunt Rhoda, and at the end of the afternoon, accepts with that formal bow of his the Mason jar of barley soup that my grandmother presses him to carry back to his room with him on the No. 8 bus. Apparently he was very taken with my grandmother's jungle of potted plants—and she, as a result, with him. Together they spoke in Yiddish about gardening. One Wednesday morning, only an hour after the store has opened for the day, Dr. Kafka shows up at the dry goods department of "The Big Bear"; he tells Aunt Rhoda that he just wanted to see where she worked. That night he writes in his diary, "With the customers she is forthright and cheery, and so managerial about 'taste' that when I hear her explain to a chubby young bride why green and blue do not 'go,' I am myself ready to believe that Nature is in error and R. is correct."

One night, at ten, Dr. Kafka and Aunt Rhoda come by unexpectedly, and a small impromptu party is held in the kitchen—coffee and cake, even a thimbleful of whiskey all around, to celebrate the resumption of Aunt Rhoda's career on the stage. I have only heard tell of my aunt's theatrical ambitions. My brother says that when I was small she used to come to entertain the two of us on Sundays with her puppets—she was at that time employed by the W.P.A. to travel around New Jersey and put on puppet shows in schools and even in churches; Aunt Rhoda did all the voices, male and female, and with the help of another young girl, manipulated the manikins on their strings. Simultaneously she had been a member of the "Newark Collective Theater," a troupe organized primarily to go around to strike groups to perform *Waiting for Lefty;* everybody in Newark (as I understood it) had had high hopes that Rhoda Pilchik would go on to Broadway—everybody except my grandmother. To me this period of history is as difficult to believe in as the era of the lake-dwellers that I am studying in school; of course, people say it was once so, so I believe them, but nonetheless it is hard to grant such stories the status of the real, given the life I see around me.

Yet my father, a very avid realist, is in the kitchen, *schnapps* glass in hand, toasting Aunt Rhoda's success. She has been awarded one of the starring roles in the Russian masterpiece, *The Three Sisters,* to be performed six weeks hence by the amateur group at the Newark "Y." Everything, announces Aunt Rhoda, everything she owes to Franz, and his encouragement. One conversation—"One!" she cries gaily—and Dr. Kafka had apparently talked my grandmother out of her lifelong belief that actors are not serious human beings. And what an actor *he* is, in his own right, says Aunt Rhoda. How he had opened her eyes to the meaning of things, by reading her the famous Chekhov play—yes, read it to her from the opening line to the final curtain, all the parts, and actually left her in tears. Here Aunt Rhoda says, "Listen, listen—this is the first line of the play—it's the key to everything. Listen—I just think about what it was like that night Pop passed away, how I thought and thought what would happen, what would we all do—and, and, listen—"

"We're listening," laughs my father.

Pause; she must have walked to the center of the kitchen linoleum. She says, sounding a little surprised, " 'It's just a year ago today that father died.' "

"Shhh," warns my mother, "you'll give the little one nightmares."

I am not alone in finding my aunt "a changed person" during the ensuing weeks of rehearsal. My mother says this is just what she was like as a little girl. "Red cheeks, always those hot, red cheeks—and everything exciting, even taking a bath." "She'll calm down, don't worry," says my father, "and then he'll pop the question." "Knock on wood," says my mother. "Come on," says my father, "he knows what side his bread is buttered on—he sets foot in this house, he sees what a family is all about, and believe me, he's licking his chops. Just look at him when he sits in that club chair. This is his dream come true." "Rhoda says that in Berlin, before Hitler, he had a young girlfriend, years and years it went on, and then she left him. For somebody else. She got tired of waiting." "Don't worry," says my father, "when the time comes I'll give him a little nudge. He ain't going to live forever, either, and he knows it."

Then one weekend, as a respite from the "strain" of nightly rehearsals—which Dr. Kafka regularly visits, watching in his hat and coat from a seat at the back of the auditorium until it is time to accompany Aunt Rhoda home—they take a trip to Atlantic City. Ever since he arrived on these shores Dr. Kafka has wanted to see the famous boardwalk and the horse that dives from the high board. But in Atlantic City something happens that I am not allowed to know about; any discussion of the subject conducted in my presence is in Yiddish. Dr. Kafka sends Aunt Rhoda four letters in three days. She comes to us for dinner and sits till midnight crying in our kitchen; she calls the "Y" on our phone to tell them (weeping) that her mother is still ill and she cannot come to rehearsal again—she may even have to drop out of the play—no, she can't, she can't, her mother is too ill, she herself is too upset! Good-bye! Then back to the kitchen table to cry; she wears no pink powder and no red lipstick, and her stiff brown hair, down, is thick and spiky as a new broom.

My brother and I listen from our bedroom, through the door that silently he has pushed ajar.

"Have you ever?" says Aunt Rhoda, weeping. "Have you *ever?*"

"Poor soul," says my mother.

"Who?" I whisper to my brother. "Aunt Rhoda or—"

"Shhhh!" he says. "Shut *up!*"

In the kitchen my father grunts. "Hmm. Hmm." I hear him getting up and walking around and sitting down again—and then grunting. I am listening so hard that I can hear the letters being folded and unfolded, stuck back into their envelopes and then removed to be puzzled over one more time.

"Well?" demands Aunt Rhoda. *"Well?"*

"Well what?" answers my father.

"Well what do you want to say now?"

"He's *meshugeh,"* admits my father. "Something is wrong with him all right."

"But," sobs Aunt Rhoda, "no one would believe me when *I* said it!"

"Rhody, Rhody," croons my mother in that voice I know from those times that I have had to have stitches taken, or when I awaken in tears, somehow on the floor beside my bed. "Rhody, don't be hysterical, darling. It's over, kitten, it's all over."

I reach across to my brother's "twin" bed and tug on the blanket. I don't think I've ever been so confused in my life, not even by death. The speed of things! Everything good undone in a moment! By what? *"What?"* I whisper. *"What is it?"*

My brother, the Boy Scout, smiles leeringly and with fierce hiss that is no answer and enough answer, addresses my bewilderment: "Sex!"

Years later, a junior at college, I receive an envelope from home containing Dr. Kafka's obituary, clipped from the *Jewish News,* the tabloid of Jewish affairs that is mailed each week to the homes of the Jews of Essex County. It is summer, the semester is over, but I have stayed on at school, alone in my room in the town, trying to write short stories; I am fed by a young English professor and his wife in exchange for babysitting; I tell the sympathetic couple, who are also loaning me the money for my rent, why it is I can't go home. My tearful fights with my father are all I can talk about at their dinner table. "Keep him away from me!" I scream at my mother. "But, darling," she asks me, "what is going on? What is this all about?"—the very same question with which I used to plague my older brother, asked of me now out of the same bewilderment and innocence.

"He *loves* you," she explains. But that, of all things, seems to me to be precisely what is blocking my way. Others are crushed by paternal criticism—I find myself oppressed by his high opinion of me! Can it possibly be true (and can I possibly admit) that I am coming to hate him for loving me so? praising me so? But that makes no sense—the ingratitude! the stupidity! the contrariness! Being loved is so obviously a blessing, *the* blessing, praise such a rare bequest; only listen late at night to my closest friends on the literary magazine and in the drama society—they tell horror stories of family life to rival *The Way of All Flesh*, they return shell-shocked from vacations, drift back to school as though from the wars. What they would give to be in my golden slippers! "What's going on?" my mother begs me to tell her; but how can I, when I can neither fully believe that this is happening to us, nor that I am the one who is making it happen. That they, who together cleared all obstructions from my path, should seem now to be my final obstruction! No wonder my rage must filter through a child's tears of shame, confusion, and loss. All that we have constructed together over the course of two century-long decades, and look how I must bring it down—in the name of this tyrannical need that I call my "independence"! Born, I am told, with the umbilical cord around my neck, it seems I will always come close to strangulation trying to deliver myself from my past into my future. . . . My mother, keeping the lines of communication open, sends a note to me at school: "We miss you"—and encloses the very brief obituary notice. Across the margin at the bottom of the clipping, she has written (in the same hand that she wrote notes to my teachers and signed my report cards, in the very same handwriting that once eased my way in the world), "Remember poor Kafka, Aunt Rhoda's beau?"

"Dr. Franz Kafka," the notice reads, "a Hebrew teacher at the Talmud Torah of the Schley Street Synagogue from 1939 to 1948, died on June 3 in the Deborah Tuberculosis Sanitorium in Browns Mills, New Jersey. Dr. Kafka had been a patient there since 1950. He was 70 years old. Dr. Kafka was born in Prague, Czechoslovakia, and was a refugee from the Nazis. He leaves no survivors."

He also leaves no books: no *Trial*, no *Castle*, no "Diaries." The dead man's papers are claimed by no one, and disappear—all except those four "*meshugeneh*" letters that are, to this day as far as I know, still somewhere in amongst the memorabilia accumulated in her dresser drawers by my spinster aunt, along with a collection of Broadway "Playbills," sales citations from "The Big Bear," and transatlantic steamship stickers.

Thus all trace of Dr. Kafka disappears. Destiny being destiny, how could it be otherwise? Does the Land Surveyor reach the Castle? Does K. escape the judgment of the Court, or Georg Bendemann the judgment of his father? "'Well, clear this out now!' said the overseer, and they buried the hunger artist, straw and all." No, it simply is not in the cards for Kafka ever to become *the* Kafka—why, that would be stranger even than a man turning into an insect. No one would believe it, Kafka least of all.

The Screamers

LeROI JONES
(1934–   )

Lynn Hope adjusts his turban under the swishing red green yellow shadow lights. Dots. Suede heaven raining, windows yawning cool summer air, and his musicians watch him grinning, quietly, or high with wine blotches on four dollar shirts. A yellow girl will not dance with me, nor will Teddy's people, in line to the left of the stage, readying their *Routines*. Haroldeen, the most beautiful, in her pitiful dead sweater. Make it yellow, wish it whole. Lights. Teddy, Sonny Boy, Kenney & Calvin, Scram, a few of Nat's boys jamming long washed handkerchiefs in breast pockets, pushing shirts into homemade cummerbunds, shuffling lightly for any audience.

"The Cross-Over," Deen laughing at us all. And they perform in solemn unison a social tract of love. (With no music till Lynn finishes "macking" with any big-lipped Esther screws across the stage.) White and green plaid jackets his men wear, and that twisted badge, black turban/on red string conked hair. (OPPRESSORS!) A greasy hipness, down-ness, nobody in our camp believed (having social worker mothers and postman fathers; or living squeezed in light skinned projects with adulterers and proud skinny ladies with soft voices). The theory, the spectrum, this sound baked inside their heads, and still rub sweaty against those lesser lights. Those niggers. Laundromat workers, beauticians, pregnant short haired jail bait separated all ways from "us," but in this vat we sweated gladly for each other. And rubbed. And Lynn could be a common hero, from whatever side we saw him. Knowing that energy, and its response. That drained silence we had to make with our hands, leaving actual love to Nat or Al or Scram.

He stomped his foot, and waved one hand. The other hung loosely on his horn. And their turbans wove in among those shadows. Lynn's tighter, neater, and bright gorgeous yellow stuck with a green stone. Also, those green sparkling cubes dancing off his pinkies. A-boomp bahba bahba, A-boomp bahba bahba, A-Boomp bahba bahba, A-boomp bahba bahba, the turbans sway behind him. And he grins before he lifts the horn, at deen or drunk becky, and we search the dark for girls.

Who would I get? (Not anyone who would understand this.) Some light girl who had fallen into bad times and ill-repute for dating Bubbles. And he fixed her later with his child, now she walks Orange St. wiping chocolate from its face. A disgraced white girl who learned to calypso in vocational school. Hence, behind halting speech, a humanity as paltry as her cotton dress. (And the big hats made a line behind her, stroking their erections, hoping for photographs to take down south.) Lynn would oblige. He would make the most perverted hopes sensual and possible. Chanting at that dark crowd. Or some girl, a wino's daughter, with carefully vaselined bow legs would drape her filthy angora against the cardboard corinthian, eyeing past any greediness a white man knows, my soft tyrolean hat, pressed corduroy suit, and "B" sweater. Whatever they meant, finally to her, valuable shadows barely visible. Some stuck-up boy with "good" hair. And as a naked display of America, for I meant to her that same oppression. A stunted head of greased glass feathers, orange lips, brown pasted edge to the collar of her dying blouse. The secret perfume of poverty and ignorant desire. Arrogant too, at my disorder, which calls her smile mysterious. Turning to be eaten by the crowd. That mingled foliage of sweat and shadows: *Night Train* was what they swayed to. And smelled each other in The Grind, The Rub, The Slow Drag. From side to side, slow or jerked staccato as their wedding dictated. Big hats bent tight skirts, and some light girls' hair swept the resin on the floor. Respectable ladies put stiff arms on your waist to keep some light between, looking nervously at an ugly friend forever at the music's edge.

I wanted girls like Erselle, whose father sang on television, but my hair was not straight enough, and my father never learned how to drink. Our house sat lonely and large on a half-Italian street, filled with important Negroes. (Though it is rumored they had a son, thin with big eyes, they killed because he was crazy.) Surrounded by the haughty daughters of depressed economic groups. They plotted in their projects for mediocrity, and the neighborhood smelled of their despair. And only the wild or the very poor thrived in Graham's or could be roused by Lynn's histories and rhythms. America had choked the rest, who could sit still for hours under popular songs, or be readied for citizenship by slightly bohemian social workers. They rivaled pure emotion with wind-up record players that pumped Jo Stafford into Home Economics rooms. And these carefully scrubbed children of my parents' friends fattened on their rhythms until they could join the Urban League or Household Finance and hound the poor for their honesty.

I was too quiet to become a murderer, and too used to extravagance for their skinny lyrics. They mentioned neither cocaine nor Bach, which was my reading, and the flaw of that society. I disappeared into the slums, and fell in love with violence, and invented for myself a mysterious economy of need. Hence, I shambled anonymously thru Lloyd's, The Nitecap, The Hi-Spot, and Graham's desiring everything I felt. In a new English overcoat and green hat, scouring that town for my peers. And they were old pinch faced whores full of snuff and weak dope, celebrity fags with radio programs, mute bass players who loved me, and built the myth of my intelligence. You see, I left America on the first fast boat.

This was Sunday night, and the Baptists were still praying in their "faboulous" churches. Though my father sat listening to the radio, or reading pulp cowboy magazines, which I take in part to be the truest legacy of my spirit. God never had a chance. And I would be walking slowly towards The Graham, not even knowing how to smoke. Willing for any experience, any image, any further separation from where my good grades were sure to lead. Frightened of post offices, lawyer's offices, doctor's cars, the deaths of clean politicians. Or of the imaginary fat man, advertising cemeteries to his "good colored friends." Lynn's screams erased them all, and I thought myself intrepid white commando from the West. Plunged into noise and flesh, and their form become an ethic.

Now Lynn wheeled and hunched himself for another tune. Fast dancers fanned themselves. Couples who practiced during the week talked over their steps. Deen and her dancing clubs readied avant-garde routines. Now it was *Harlem Nocturne,* which I whistled loudly one Saturday in a laundromat, and the girl who stuffed in my khakis and stiff underwear asked was I a musician. I met her at Graham's that night and we waved, and I suppose she knew I loved her.

Nocturne was slow and heavy and the serious dancers loosened their ties. The slowly twisting lights made specks of human shadows, the darkness seemed to float around the hall. Any meat you clung to was yours those few minutes without interruption. The length of the music was the only form. And the idea was to press against each other hard, to rub, to shove the hips tight, and gasp at whatever passion. Professionals wore jocks against embarrassment. Amateurs, like myself, after the music stopped, put our hands quickly into our pockets, and retreated into the shadows. It was as meaningful as anything else we knew.

All extremes were popular with that crowd. The singers shouted, the musicians stomped and howled. The dancers ground each other past passion or moved so fast it blurred intelligence. We hated the popular song, and any freedman could tell you if you asked that white people danced jerkily, and were slower than our champions. One style, which developed as Italians showed up with pegs, and our own grace moved towards bell-bottom pants to further complicate the cipher, was the honk. The repeated rhythmic figure, a screamed riff, pushed in its insistence past music. It was hatred and frustration, secrecy and despair. It spurted out of the diphthong culture, and reinforced the black cults of emotion. There was no compromise, no dreary sophistication, only the elegance of something that is too ugly to be described, and is diluted only at the agent's peril. All the saxophonists of that world were honkers, Illinois, Gator, Big Jay, Jug, the great sounds of our day. Ethnic historians, actors, priests of the unconscious. That stance spread like fire thru the cabarets and joints of the black cities, so that the sound itself became a basis for thought, and the innovators searched for uglier modes. Illinois would leap and twist his head, scream when he wasn't playing. Gator would strut up and down the stage, dancing for emphasis, shaking his long gassed hair in his face and coolly mopping it back. Jug, the beautiful horn, would wave back and forth so high we all envied him his connection, or he'd stomp softly to the edge of the stage whispering those raucous threats. Jay first turned the mark around, opened the way further for the completely nihilistic act. McNeeley, the first Dada coon of the age, jumped and stomped and yowled and finally sensed the only other space that form allowed. He fell first on his knees, never releasing the horn, and walked that way across the stage. We hunched together drowning any sound, relying on Jay's contorted face for evidence that there was still music, though none of us needed it now. And then he fell backwards, flat on his back, with both feet stuck up high in the air, and he kicked and thrashed and the horn spat enraged sociologies.

That was the night Hip Charlie, the Baxter Terrace Romeo, got wasted right in front of the place. Snake and four friends mashed him up and left him for the ofays to identify. Also the night I had the grey bells and sat in the Chinese restaurant all night to show them off. Jay had set a social form for the poor, just as Bird and Dizzy proposed it for the middle class. On his back screaming was the Mona Lisa with the mustache, as crude and simple. Jo Stafford could not do it. Bird took the language, and we woke up one Saturday whispering Ornithology. Blank verse.

And Newark always had a bad reputation, I mean, everybody could pop their fingers. Was hip. Had walks. Knew all about The Apple. So I suppose when the word got to Lynn what Big Jay had done, he knew all the little down cats were waiting to see him in this town. He knew he had to cook. And he blasted all night, crawled and leaped, then stood at the side of the stand, and watched us while he fixed his sky, wiped his face. Watched us to see how far he'd gone, but he was tired and we weren't, which was not where it was. The girls rocked slowly against the silence of the horns, and big hats pushed each other or made plans for murder. We had not completely come. All sufficiently eaten by Jay's memory, "on his back, kicking his feet in the air, Ga-ud Dam!" So he moved cautiously to the edge of the stage, and the gritty muslims he played with gathered close. It was some mean honking blues, and he made no attempt to hide his intentions. He was breaking bad. "Okay, baby," we all thought, "Go for yourself." I was standing at the back of the hall with one arm behind my back, so the overcoat could hang over in that casual gesture of fashion. Lynn was moving, and the camel walkers were moving in the corners. The fast dancers and practicers making the whole hall dangerous. "Off my suedes, motherfucker." Lynn was trying to move us, and even I did the one step I knew, safe at the back of the hall. The hippies ran for girls. Ugly girls danced with each other. Skippy, who ran the lights, made them move faster in that circle on the ceiling, and darkness raced around the hall. Then Lynn got his riff, that rhythmic figure we knew he would repeat, the honked note that would be his personal evaluation of the world. And he screamed it so the veins in his face stood out like neon. "Uhh, yeh, Uhh, yeh, Uhh, yeh," we all screamed to push him further. So he opened his eyes for a second, and really made his move. He looked over his shoulder at the other turbans, then marched in time with his riff, on his toes across the stage. They followed; he marched across to the other side, repeated, then finally he descended, still screaming, into the crowd, and as the sidemen followed, we made a path for them around the hall. They were strutting, and all their horns held very high, and they were only playing that one scary note. They moved near the back of the hall, chanting and swaying, and passed right in front of me. I had a little cup full of wine a murderer friend of mine made me drink, so I drank it and tossed the cup in the air, then fell in line behind the last wild horn man, strutting like the rest of them. Bubbles and Rogie followed me, and four eyed Moselle Boyd. And we strutted back and forth pumping our arms, repeating with Lynn Hope, "Yeh, Uhh, Yeh, Uhh." Then everybody fell in behind us, yelling still. There was confusion and stumbling, but there were no real fights. The thing they wanted was right there and easily accessible. No one could stop you from getting in that line. "It's too crowded. It's too many people on the line!" some people yelled. So Lynn thought further, and made to destroy the ghetto. We went out into the lobby and in perfect rhythm down the marble steps. Some musicians laughed, but Lynn and some others kept the note, till the others fell back in. Five or six hundred hopped up woogies tumbled out into Belmont Avenue. Lynn marched right in the center of the street. Sunday night traffic stopped, and honked. Big Red yelled at a bus driver, "Hey, baby, honk that horn in time or shut it off!" The bus driver cooled it. We screamed and screamed at the clear image of ourselves as we should always be. Ecstatic, completed, involved in a secret communal expression. It would be the form of the sweetest revolution, to hucklebuck into the fallen capitol, and let the oppressors lindy hop out. We marched all the way to Spruce, weaving among the stalled cars, laughing at the dazed white men who sat behind the wheels. Then Lynn turned and we strutted back towards the hall. The late show at the National was turning out, and all the big hats there jumped right in our line.

Then the Nabs came, and with them, the fire engines. What was it, a labor riot? Anarchists? A nigger strike? The paddy wagons and cruisers pulled in from both sides, and sticks and billies started flying, heavy streams of water splattering the marchers up and down the street. America's responsible immigrants were doing her light work again. The knives came out, the razors, all the Biggers who would not be bent counterattacked or came up behind the civil servants, smashing at them with coke bottles and aerials. Belmont writhed under the dead economy and splivs floated in the gutters, disappearing under cars. But for awhile, before the war had reached its peak, Lynn and his musicians, a few other fools, and I, still marched, screaming thru the maddened crowd. Onto the sidewalk, into the lobby, half-way up the stairs, then we all broke our different ways, to save whatever it was each of us thought we loved.

The Kugelmass Episode

WOODY ALLEN

(1935–)

Kugelmass, a professor of humanities at City College, was unhappily married for the second time. Daphne Kugelmass was an oaf. He also had two dull sons by his first wife, Flo, and was up to his neck in alimony and child support.

"Did I know it would turn out so badly?" Kugelmass whined to his analyst one day. "Daphne had promise. Who suspected she'd let herself go and swell up like a beach ball? Plus she had a few bucks, which is not in itself a healthy reason to marry a person, but it doesn't hurt, with the kind of operating nut I have. You see my point?"

Kugelmass was bald and as hairy as a bear, but he had soul.

"I need to meet a new woman," he went on. "I need to have an affair. I may not look the part, but I'm a man who needs romance. I need softness, I need flirtation. I'm not getting younger, so before it's too late I want to make love in Venice, trade quips at '21,' and exchange coy glances over red wine and candlelight. You see what I'm saying?"

Dr. Mandel shifted in his chair and said, "An affair will solve nothing. You're so unrealistic. Your problems run much deeper."

"And also this affair must be discreet," Kugelmass continued. "I can't afford a second divorce. Daphne would really sock it to me."

"Mr. Kugelmass—"

"But it can't be anyone at City College, because Daphne also works there. Not that anyone on the faculty at C.C.N.Y. is any great shakes, but some of those coeds . . ."

"Mr. Kugelmass—"

"Help me. I had a dream last night. I was skipping through a meadow holding a picnic basket and the basket was marked 'Options.' And then I saw there was a hole in the basket."

"Mr. Kugelmass, the worst thing you could do is act out. You must simply express your feelings here, and together we'll analyze them. You have been in treatment long enough to know there is no overnight cure. After all, I'm an analyst, not a magician."

"Then perhaps what I need is a magician," Kugelmass said, rising from his chair. And with that he terminated his therapy.

A couple of weeks later, while Kugelmass and Daphne were moping around in their apartment one night like two pieces of old furniture, the phone rang.

"I'll get it," Kugelmass said. "Hello."

"Kugelmass?" a voice said. "Kugelmass, this is Persky."

"Who?"

"Persky. Or should I say The Great Persky?"

"Pardon me?"

"I hear you're looking all over town for a magician to bring a little exotica into your life? Yes or no?"

"Sh-h-h," Kugelmass whispered. "Don't hang up. Where are you calling from, Persky?"

Early the following afternoon, Kugelmass climbed three flights of stairs in a broken-down apartment house in the Bushwick section of Brooklyn. Peering through the darkness of the hall, he found the door he was looking for and pressed the bell. I'm going to regret this, he thought to himself.

Seconds later, he was greeted by a short, thin, waxy-looking man.

"*You're* Persky the Great?" Kugelmass said.

"The Great Persky. You want a tea?"

"No, I want romance. I want music. I want love and beauty."

"But not tea, eh? Amazing. O.K., sit down."

Persky went to the back room, and Kugelmass heard the sounds of boxes and furniture being moved around. Persky reappeared, pushing before him a large object on squeaky roller-skate wheels. He removed some old silk handkerchiefs that were lying on its top and blew away a bit of dust. It was a cheap-looking Chinese cabinet, badly lacquered.

"Persky," Kugelmass said, "what's your scam?"

"Pay attention," Persky said. "This is some beautiful effect. I developed it for a Knights of Pythias date last year, but the booking fell through. Get into the cabinet."

"Why, so you can stick it full of swords or something?"

"You see any swords?"

Kugelmass made a face and, grunting, climbed into the cabinet. He couldn't help noticing a couple of ugly rhinestones glued onto the raw plywood just in front of his face. "If this is a joke," he said.

"Some joke. Now, here's the point. If I throw any novel into this cabinet with you, shut the doors, and tap it three times, you will find yourself projected into that book."

Kugelmass made a grimace of disbelief.

"It's the emess," Persky said. "My hand to God. Not just a novel, either. A short story, a play, a poem. You can meet any of the women created by the world's best writers. Whoever you dreamed of. You could carry on all you like with a real winner. Then when you've had enough you give a yell, and I'll see you're back here in a split second."

"Persky, are you some kind of outpatient?"

"I'm telling you it's on the level," Persky said.

Kugelmass remained skeptical. "What are you telling me—that this cheesy homemade box can take me on a ride like you're describing?"

"For a double sawbuck."

Kugelmass reached for his wallet. "I'll believe this when I see it," he said.

Persky tucked the bills in his pants pocket and turned toward his bookcase. "So who do you want to meet? Sister Carrie? Hester Prynne?

Ophelia? Maybe someone by Saul Bellow? Hey, what about Temple Drake? Although for a man your age she'd be a workout."

"French. I want to have an affair with a French lover."

"Nana?"

"I don't want to have to pay for it."

"What about Natasha in 'War and Peace'?"

"I said French. I know! What about Emma Bovary? That sounds to me perfect."

"You got it, Kugelmass. Give me a holler when you've had enough." Persky tossed in a paperback copy of Flaubert's novel.

"You sure this is safe?" Kugelmass asked as Persky began shutting the cabinet doors.

"Safe. Is anything safe in this crazy world?" Persky rapped three times on the cabinet and then flung open the doors.

Kugelmass was gone. At the same moment, he appeared in the bedroom of Charles and Emma Bovary's house at Yonville. Before him was a beautiful woman, standing alone with her back turned to him as she folded some linen. I can't believe this, thought Kugelmass, staring at the doctor's ravishing wife. This is uncanny. I'm here. It's her.

Emma turned in surprise. "Goodness, you startled me," she said. "Who are you?" She spoke in the same fine English translation as the paperback.

It's simply devastating, he thought. Then, realizing that it was he whom she had addressed, he said, "Excuse me. I'm Sidney Kugelmass. I'm from City College. A professor of humanities. C.C.N.Y.? Uptown. I—oh, boy!"

Emma Bovary smiled flirtatiously and said, "Would you like a drink? A glass of wine, perhaps?"

She is beautiful, Kugelmass thought. What a contrast with the troglodyte who shared his bed! He felt a sudden impulse to take this vision into his arms and tell her she was the kind of woman he had dreamed of all his life.

"Yes, some wine," he said hoarsely. "White. No, red. No, white. Make it white."

"Charles is out for the day," Emma said, her voice full of playful implication.

After the wine, they went for a stroll in the lovely French countryside. "I've always dreamed that some mysterious stranger would appear and rescue me from the monotony of this crass rural existence," Emma said, clasping his hand. They passed a small church. "I love what you have on," she murmured. "I've never seen anything like it around here. It's so . . . so modern."

"It's called a leisure suit," he said romantically. "It was marked down."

Suddenly he kissed her. For the next hour they reclined under a tree and whispered together and told each other deeply meaningful things with their eyes. Then Kugelmass sat up. He had just remembered he had to meet Daphne at Bloomingdale's. "I must go," he told her. "But don't worry, I'll be back."

"I hope so," Emma said.

He embraced her passionately, and the two walked back to the house. He held Emma's face cupped in his palms, kissed her again, and yelled, "O.K., Persky! I got to be at Bloomingdale's by three-thirty."

There was an audible pop, and Kugelmass was back in Brooklyn.

"So? Did I lie?" Persky asked triumphantly.

"Look, Persky, I'm right now late to meet the ball and chain at Lexington Avenue, but when can I go again? Tomorrow?"

"My pleasure. Just bring a twenty. And don't mention this to anybody."

"Yeah. I'm going to call Rupert Murdoch."

Kugelmass hailed a cab and sped off to the city. His heart danced on point. I am in love, he thought, I am the possessor of a wonderful secret. What he didn't realize was that at this very moment students in various classrooms across the country were saying to their teachers, "Who is this character on page 100? A bald Jew is kissing Madame Bovary?" A teacher in Sioux Falls, South Dakota, sighed and thought, Jesus, these kids, with their pot and acid. What goes through their minds!

Daphne Kugelmass was in the bathroom-accessories department at Bloomingdale's when Kugelmass arrived breathlessly. "Where've you been?" she snapped. "It's four-thirty."

"I got held up in traffic," Kugelmass said.

Kugelmass visited Persky the next day, and in a few minutes was again passed magically to Yonville. Emma couldn't hide her excitement at seeing him. The two spent hours together, laughing and talking about their different backgrounds. Before Kugelmass left, they made love. "My God, I'm doing it with Madame Bovary!" Kugelmass whispered to himself. "Me, who failed freshman English."

As the months passed, Kugelmass saw Persky many times and developed a close and passionate relationship with Emma Bovary. "Make sure and always get me into the book before page 120," Kugelmass said to the magician one day. "I always have to meet her before she hooks up with this Rodolphe character."

"Why?" Persky asked. "You can't beat his time?"

"Beat his time. He's landed gentry. Those guys have nothing better to do than flirt and ride horses. To me, he's one of those faces you see in the pages of *Women's Wear Daily*. With the Helmut Berger hairdo. But to her he's hot stuff."

"And her husband suspects nothing?"

"He's out of his depth. He's a lacklustre little paramedic who's thrown in his lot with a jitterbug. He's ready to go to sleep by ten, and she's putting on her dancing shoes. Oh, well . . . See you later."

And once again Kugelmass entered the cabinet and passed instantly to the Bovary estate at Yonville. "How you doing, cupcake?" he said to Emma.

"Oh, Kugelmass," Emma sighed. "What I have to put up with. Last night at dinner, Mr. Personality dropped off to sleep in the middle of the dessert course. I'm pouring my heart out about Maxim's and the ballet, and out of the blue I hear snoring."

"It's O.K., darling. I'm here now," Kugelmass said, embracing her. I've earned this, he thought, smelling Emma's French perfume and burying his nose in her hair. I've suffered enough. I've paid enough analysts. I've searched till I'm weary. She's young and nubile, and I'm here a few pages after Léon and just before Rodolphe. By showing up during the correct chapters, I've got the situation knocked.

Emma, to be sure, was just as happy as Kugelmass. She had been starved for excitement, and his tales of Broadway night life, of fast cars and Hollywood and TV stars, enthralled the young French beauty.

"Tell me again about O.J. Simpson," she implored that evening, as she and Kugelmass strolled past Abbé Bournisien's church.

"What can I say? The man is great. He sets all kinds of rushing records. Such moves. They can't touch him."

"And the Academy Awards?" Emma said wistfully. "I'd give anything to win one."

"First you've got to be nominated."

"I know. You explained it. But I'm convinced I can act. Of course, I'd want to take a class or two. With Strasberg maybe. Then, if I had the right agent—"

"We'll see, we'll see. I'll speak to Persky."

That night, safely returned to Persky's flat, Kugelmass brought up the idea of having Emma visit him in the big city.

"Let me think about it," Persky said. "Maybe I could work it. Stranger things have happened." Of course, neither of them could think of one.

"Where the hell do you go all the time?" Daphne Kugelmass barked at her husband as he returned home late that evening. "You got a chippie stashed somewhere?"

"Yeah, sure, I'm just the type," Kugelmass said wearily. "I was with Leonard Popkin. We were discussing Socialist agriculture in Poland. You know Popkin. He's a freak on the subject."

"Well, you've been very odd lately," Daphne said. "Distant. Just don't forget about my father's birthday. On Saturday?"

"Oh, sure, sure," Kugelmass said, heading for the bathroom.

"My whole family will be there. We can see the twins. And Cousin Hamish. You should be more polite to Cousin Hamish—he likes you."

"Right, the twins," Kugelmass said, closing the bathroom door and shutting out the sound of his wife's voice. He leaned against it and took a deep breath. In a few hours, he told himself, he would be back in Yonville again, back with his beloved. And this time, if all went well, he would bring Emma back with him.

At three-fifteen the following afternoon, Persky worked his wizardry again. Kugelmass appeared before Emma, smiling and eager. The two spent a few hours at Yonville with Binet and then remounted the Bovary carriage. Following Persky's instructions, they held each other tightly, closed their eyes, and counted to ten. When they opened them, the carriage was just drawing up at the side door of the Plaza Hotel, where Kugelmass had optimistically reserved a suite earlier in the day.

"I love it! It's everything I dreamed it would be," Emma said as she swirled joyously around the bedroom, surveying the city from their window. "There's F.A.O. Schwarz. And there's Central Park, and the Sherry is which one? Oh, there—I see. It's too divine."

On the bed there were boxes from Halston and Saint Laurent. Emma unwrapped a package and held up a pair of black velvet pants against her perfect body.

"The slacks suit is by Ralph Lauren," Kugelmass said. "You'll look like a million bucks in it. Come on, sugar, give us a kiss."

"I've never been so happy!" Emma squealed as she stood before the mirror. "Let's go out on the town. I want to see 'Chorus Line' and the Guggenheim and this Jack Nicholson character you always talk about. Are any of his flicks showing?"

"I cannot get my mind around this," a Stanford professor said. "First a strange character named Kugelmass, and now she's gone from the book. Well, I guess the mark of a classic is that you can reread it a thousand times and always find something new."

The lovers passed a blissful weekend. Kugelmass had told Daphne he would be away at a symposium in Boston and would return Monday. Savoring each moment, he and Emma went to the movies, had dinner in

Chinatown, passed two hours at a discothèque, and went to bed with a TV movie. They slept till noon on Sunday, visited SoHo, and ogled celebrities at Elaine's. They had caviar and champagne in their suite on Sunday night and talked until dawn. That morning, in the cab taking them to Persky's apartment, Kugelmass thought, It was hectic, but worth it. I can't bring her here too often, but now and then it will be a charming contrast with Yonville.

At Persky's, Emma climbed into the cabinet, arranged her new boxes of clothes neatly around her, and kissed Kugelmass fondly. "My place next time," she said with a wink. Persky rapped three times on the cabinet. Nothing happened.

"Hmm," Persky said, scratching his head. He rapped again, but still no magic. "Something must be wrong," he mumbled.

"Persky, you're joking!" Kugelmass cried. "How can it not work?"

"Relax, relax. Are you still in the box, Emma?"

"Yes."

Persky rapped again—harder this time.

"I'm still here, Persky."

"I know, darling. Sit tight."

"Persky, we *have* to get her back," Kugelmass whispered. "I'm a married man, and I have a class in three hours. I'm not prepared for anything more than a cautious affair at this point."

"I can't understand it," Persky muttered. "It's such a reliable little trick."

But he could do nothing. "It's going to take a little while," he said to Kugelmass. "I'm going to have to strip it down. I'll call you later."

Kugelmass bundled Emma into a cab and took her back to the Plaza. He barely made it to his class on time. He was on the phone all day, to Persky and to his mistress. The magician told him it might be several days before he got to the bottom of the trouble.

"How was the symposium?" Daphne asked him that night.

"Fine, fine," he said, lighting the filter end of a cigarette.

"What's wrong? You're as tense as a cat."

"Me? Ha, that's a laugh. I'm as calm as a summer night. I'm just going to take a walk." He eased out the door, hailed a cab, and flew to the Plaza.

"This is no good," Emma said. "Charles will miss me."

"Bear with me, sugar," Kugelmass said. He was pale and sweaty. He kissed her again, raced to the elevators, yelled at Persky over a pay phone in the Plaza lobby, and just made it home before midnight.

"According to Popkin, barley prices in Kraków have not been this stable since 1971," he said to Daphne, and smiled wanly as he climbed into bed.

The whole week went by like that. On Friday night, Kugelmass told Daphne there was another symposium he had to catch, this one in Syracuse. He hurried back to the Plaza, but the second weekend there was nothing like the first. "Get me back into the novel or marry me," Emma told Kugelmass. "Meanwhile, I want to get a job or go to class, because watching TV all day is the pits."

"Fine. We can use the money," Kugelmass said. "You consume twice your weight in room service."

"I met an Off Broadway producer in Central Park yesterday, and he said I might be right for a project he's doing," Emma said.

"Who is this clown?" Kugelmass asked.

"He's not a clown. He's sensitive and kind and cute. His name's Jeff Something-or-Other, and he's up for a Tony."

Later that afternoon, Kugelmass showed up at Persky's drunk.

"Relax," Persky told him. "You'll get a coronary."

"Relax. The man says relax. I've got a fictional character stashed in a hotel room, and I think my wife is having me tailed by a private shamus."

"O.K., O.K. We know there's a problem." Persky crawled under the cabinet and started banging on something with a large wrench.

"I'm like a wild animal," Kugelmass went on. "I'm sneaking around town, and Emma and I have had it up to here with each other. Not to mention a hotel tab that reads like the defense budget."

"So what should I do? This is the world of magic," Persky said. "It's all nuance."

"Nuance, my foot. I'm pouring Dom Pérignon and black eggs into this little mouse, plus her wardrobe, plus she's enrolled at the Neighborhood Playhouse and suddenly needs professional photos. Also, Persky, Professor Fivish Kopkind, who teaches Comp Lit and who has always been jealous of me, has identified me as the sporadically appearing character in the Flaubert book. He's threatened to go to Daphne. I see ruin and alimony jail. For adultery with Madame Bovary, my wife will reduce me to beggary."

"What do you want me to say? I'm working on it night and day. As far as your personal anxiety goes, that I can't help you with. I'm a magician, not an analyst."

By Sunday afternoon, Emma had locked herself in the bathroom and refused to respond to Kugelmass's entreaties. Kugelmass stared out the window at the Wollman Rink and contemplated suicide. Too bad this is a low floor, he thought, or I'd do it right now. Maybe if I ran away to Europe and started life over . . . Maybe I could sell the *International Herald Tribune,* like those young girls used to.

The phone rang. Kugelmass lifted it to his ear mechanically.

"Bring her over," Persky said. "I think I got the bugs out of it."

Kugelmass's heart leaped. "You're serious?" he said. "You got it licked?"

"It was something in the transmission. Go figure."

"Persky, you're a genius. We'll be there in a minute. Less than a minute."

Again the lovers hurried to the magician's apartment, and again Emma Bovary climbed into the cabinet with her boxes. This time there was no kiss. Persky shut the doors, took a deep breath, and tapped the box three times. There was the reassuring popping noise, and when Persky peered inside, the box was empty. Madame Bovary was back in her novel. Kugelmass heaved a great sigh of relief and pumped the magician's hand.

"It's over," he said. "I learned my lesson. I'll never cheat again, I swear it." He pumped Persky's hand again and made a mental note to send him a necktie.

Three weeks later, at the end of a beautiful spring afternoon, Persky answered his doorbell. It was Kugelmass, with a sheepish expression on his face.

"O.K., Kugelmass," the magician said. "Where to this time?"

"It's just this once," Kugelmass said. "The weather is so lovely, and I'm not getting any younger. Listen, you've read 'Portnoy's Complaint'? Remember The Monkey?"

"The price is now twenty-five dollars, because the cost of living is up, but I'll start you off with one freebie, due to all the trouble I caused you."

"You're good people," Kugelmass said, combing his few remaining hairs as he climbed into the cabinet again. "This'll work all right?"

"I hope. But I haven't tried it much since all that unpleasantness."

"Sex and romance," Kugelmass said from inside the box. "What we go through for a pretty face."

Persky tossed in a copy of "Portnoy's Complaint" and rapped three times on the box. This time, instead of a popping noise there was a dull explosion, followed by a series of crackling noises and a shower of sparks. Persky leaped back, was seized by a heart attack, and dropped dead. The cabinet burst into flames, and eventually the entire house burned down.

Kugelmass, unaware of this catastrophe, had his own problems. He had not been thrust into "Portnoy's Complaint," or into any other novel, for that matter. He had been projected into an old textbook, "Remedial Spanish," and was running for his life over a barren, rocky terrain as the word *"tener"* ("to have")—a large and hairy irregular verb—raced after him on its spindly legs.

A Man Who Writes

RUSSELL EDSON

(1935–)

A man had written *head* on his forehead, and *hand* on each hand, and *foot* on each foot.

His father said, stop stop stop, because the redundancy is like having two sons, which is two sons too many, as in the first instance which is one son too many.

The man said, may I write *father* on father?

Yes, said father, because one father is tired of bearing it all alone.

Mother said, I'm leaving if all these people come to dinner.

But the man wrote *dinner* all over the dinner.

When dinner was over father said to his son, will you write *belch* on my belch?

The man said, I will write *God bless everyone* on God.

In the Region of Ice

JOYCE CAROL OATES

(1938–)

Sister Irene was a tall, deft woman in her early thirties. What one could see of her face made a striking impression—serious, hard gray eyes, a long slender nose, a face waxen with thought. Seen at the right time, from the right angle, she was almost handsome. In her past teaching positions she had drawn a little upon the fact of her being young and brilliant and also a nun, but she was beginning to grow out of that.

This was a new university and an entirely new world. She had heard—of course it was true—that the Jesuit administration of this school had hired her at the last moment to save money and to head off the appointment of a man of dubious religious commitment. She had prayed for the necessary energy to get her through this first semester. She had no trouble with teaching itself; once she stood before a classroom she felt herself capable of anything. It was the world immediately outside the classroom that confused and alarmed her, though she let none of this show—the cynicism of her colleagues, the indifference of many of the students, and, above all, the looks she got that told her nothing much would be expected of her because she was a nun. This took energy, strength. At times she had the idea that she was on trial and that the excuses she made to herself about her discomfort were only the common excuses made by guilty people. But in front of a class she had no time to worry about herself or the conflicts in her mind. She became, once and for all, a figure existing only for the benefit of others, an instrument by which facts were communicated.

About two weeks after the semester began, Sister Irene noticed a new student in her class. He was slight and fair-haired, and his face was blank, but not blank by accident, blank on purpose, suppressed and restricted into a dumbness that looked hysterical. She was prepared for him before he raised his hand, and when she saw his arm jerk, as if he had at last lost control of it, she nodded to him without hesitation.

"Sister, how can this be reconciled with Shakespeare's vision in *Hamlet?* How can these opposing views be in the same mind?"

Students glanced at him, mildly surprised. He did not belong in the class, and this was mysterious, but his manner was urgent and blind.

"There is no need to reconcile opposing views," Sister Irene said, leaning forward against the podium. "In one play Shakespeare suggests one vision, in another play another; the plays are not simultaneous creations, and even if they were, we never demand a logical—"

"We must demand a logical consistency," the young man said. "The idea of education is itself predicated upon consistency, order, sanity—"

He had interrupted her, and she hardened her face against him—for his sake, not her own, since she did not really care. But he noticed nothing. "Please see me after class," she said.

After class the young man hurried up to her.

"Sister Irene, I hope you didn't mind my visiting today. I'd heard some things, interesting things," he said. He stared at her, and something in her face allowed him to smile. "I . . . could we talk in your office? Do you have time?"

They walked down to her office. Sister Irene sat at her desk, and the young man sat facing her; for a moment they were self-conscious and silent.

"Well, I suppose you know—I'm a Jew," he said.

Sister Irene stared at him. "Yes?" she said.

"What am I doing at a Catholic university, huh?" He grinned. "That's what you want to know."

She made a vague movement of her hand to show that she had no thoughts on this, nothing at all, but he seemed not to catch it. He was sitting on the edge of the straight-backed chair. She saw that he was young but did not really look young. There were harsh lines on either side of his mouth, as if he had misused that youthful mouth somehow. His skin was almost as pale as hers, his eyes were dark and not quite in focus. He looked at her and through her and around her, as his voice surrounded them both. His voice was a little shrill at times.

"Listen, I did the right thing today—visiting your class! God, what a lucky accident it was; some jerk mentioned you, said you were a good teacher—I thought, what a laugh! These people know about good teachers here? But yes, listen, yes, I'm not kidding—you are good. I mean that."

Sister Irene frowned. "I don't quite understand what all this means."

He smiled and waved aside her formality, as if he knew better. "Listen, I got my B.A. at Columbia, then I came back here to this crappy city. I mean, I did it on purpose, I wanted to come back. I wanted to. I have my reasons for doing things. I'm on a three-thousand-dollar fellowship," he said, and waited for that to impress her. "You know, I could have gone almost anywhere with that fellowship, and I came back home here—my home's in the city—and enrolled here. This was last year. This is my second year. I'm working on a thesis, I mean I was, my master's thesis—but the hell with that. What I want to ask you is this: Can I enroll in your class, is it too late? We have to get special permission if we're late."

Sister Irene felt something nudging her, some uneasiness in him that was pleading with her not to be offended by his abrupt, familiar manner. He seemed to be promising another self, a better self, as if his fair, childish, almost cherubic face were doing tricks to distract her from what his words said.

"Are you in English studies?" she asked.

"I was in history. Listen," he said, and his mouth did something odd, drawing itself down into a smile that made the lines about it deepen like knives, "listen, they kicked me out."

He sat back, watching her. He crossed his legs. He took out a package of cigarettes and offered her one. Sister Irene shook her head, staring at his hands. They were small and stubby and might have belonged to a ten-year-old, and the nails were a strange near-violet color. It took him awhile to extract a cigarette.

"Yeah, kicked me out. What do you think of that?"

"I don't understand."

"My master's thesis was coming along beautifully, and then this bastard—I mean, excuse me, this professor, I won't pollute your office with his name—he started making criticisms, he said some things were unacceptable, he—" The boy leaned forward and hunched his narrow shoulders in a parody of secrecy. "We had an argument. I told him some frank things, things only a broad-minded person could hear about himself. That takes courage, right? He didn't have it! He kicked me out of the master's program, so now I'm coming into English. Literature is greater than history; European history is one big pile of garbage. Sky-high. Filth and rotting corpses, right? Aristotle says that poetry is higher than history; he's right; in your class today I suddenly realized that this is my field, Shakespeare, only Shakespeare is—"

Sister Irene guessed that he was going to say that only Shakespeare was equal to him, and she caught the moment of recognition and hesitation, the half-raised arm, the keen, frowning forehead, the narrowed eyes; then he thought better of it and did not end the sentence. "The students in your class are mainly negligible, I can tell you that. You're new here, and I've been here a year—I would have finished my studies last year but my father got sick, he was hospitalized, I couldn't take exams and it was a mess—but I'll make it through English in one year or drop dead. I can do it, I can do anything. I'll take six courses at once—" He broke off, breathless. Sister Irene tried to smile. "All right then, it's settled? You'll let me in? Have I missed anything so far?"

He had no idea of the rudeness of his question. Sister Irene, feeling suddenly exhausted, said, "I'll give you a syllabus of the course."

"Fine! Wonderful!"

He got to his feet eagerly. He looked through the schedule, muttering to himself, making favorable noises. It struck Sister Irene that she was making a mistake to let him in. There were these moments when one had to make an intelligent decision. . . . But she was sympathetic with him, yes. She was sympathetic with something about him.

She found out his name the next day: Allen Weinstein.

After this she came to her Shakespeare class with a sense of excitement. It became clear to her at once that Weinstein was the most intelligent student in the class. Until he had enrolled, she had not understood what was lacking, a mind that could appreciate her own. Within a week his jagged, protean mind had alienated the other students, and though he sat in the center of the class, he seemed totally alone, encased by a miniature world of his own. When he spoke of the "frenetic humanism of the High Renaissance," Sister Irene dreaded the raised eyebrows and mocking smiles of the other students, who no longer bothered to look at Weinstein. She wanted to defend him, but she never did, because there was something rude and dismal about his knowledge; he used it like a weapon, talking passionately of Nietzsche and Goethe and Freud until Sister Irene would be forced to close discussion.

In meditation, alone, she often thought of him. When she tried to talk about him to a young nun, Sister Carlotta, everything sounded gross. "But no, he's an excellent student," she insisted. "I'm very grateful to have him in class. It's just that . . . he thinks ideas are real." Sister Carlotta, who loved literature also, had been forced to teach grade-school arithmetic for the last four years. That might have been why she said, a little sharply, "You don't think ideas are real?"

Sister Irene acquiesced with a smile, but of course she did not think so: only reality is real.

When Weinstein did not show up for class on the day the first paper was due, Sister Irene's heart sank, and the sensation was somehow a familiar one. She began her lecture and kept waiting for the door to open and for him to hurry noisily back to his seat, grinning an apology toward her—but nothing happened.

If she had been deceived by him, she made herself think angrily, it was as a teacher and not as a woman. He had promised her nothing.

Weinstein appeared the next day near the steps of the liberal arts building. She heard someone running behind her, a breathless exclamation: "Sister Irene!" She turned and saw him, panting and grinning in embarrassment. He wore a dark-blue suit with a necktie, and he looked, despite his childish face, like a little old man; there was something oddly precarious and fragile about him. "Sister Irene, I owe you an apology, right?" He raised his eyebrows and smiled a sad, forlorn, yet irritatingly conspiratorial smile. "The first paper—not in on time, and I know what your rules are. . . . You won't accept late papers, I know—that's good discipline, I'll do that when I teach too. But, unavoidably, I was unable to come to school yesterday. There are many—many—" He gulped for breath, and Sister Irene had the startling sense of seeing the real Weinstein stare out at her, a terrified prisoner behind the confident voice. "There are many complications in family life. Perhaps you are unaware—I mean—"

She did not like him, but she felt this sympathy, something tugging and nagging at her the way her parents had competed for her love so many years before. They had been whining, weak people, and out of their wet need for affection, the girl she had been (her name was Yvonne) had emerged stronger than either of them, contemptuous of tears because she had seen so many. But Weinstein was different; he was not simply weak—perhaps he was not weak at all—but his strength was confused and hysterical. She felt her customary rigidity as a teacher begin to falter. "You may turn your paper in today if you have it," she said, frowning.

Weinstein's mouth jerked into an incredulous grin. "Wonderful! Marvelous!" he said. "You are very understanding, Sister Irene, I must say. I must say . . . I didn't expect, really . . ." He was fumbling in a shabby old briefcase for the paper. Sister Irene waited. She was prepared for another of his excuses, certain that he did not have the paper, when he suddenly straightened up and handed her something. "Here! I took the liberty of writing thirty pages instead of just fifteen," he said. He was obviously quite excited; his cheeks were mottled pink and white. "You may disagree violently with my interpretation—I expect you to, in fact I'm counting on it—but let me warn you, I have the exact proof, right here in the play itself!" He was thumping at a book, his voice growing louder and shriller. Sister Irene, startled, wanted to put her hand over his mouth and soothe him.

"Look," he said breathlessly, "may I talk with you? I have a class now I hate, I loathe, I can't bear to sit through! Can I talk with you instead?"

Because she was nervous, she stared at the title page of the paper: " 'Erotic Melodies in *Romeo and Juliet*' by Allen Weinstein, Jr."

"All right?" he said. "Can we walk around here? Is it all right? I've been anxious to talk with you about some things you said in class."

She was reluctant, but he seemed not to notice. They walked slowly along the shaded campus paths. Weinstein did all the talking, of course, and Sister Irene recognized nothing in his cascade of words that she had mentioned in class. "The humanist must be committed to the totality of life," he said passionately. "This is the failing one finds everywhere in the academic world! I found it in New York and I found it here and I'm no ingénu, I don't go around with my mouth hanging open—I'm experienced, look, I've been to Europe, I've lived in Rome! I went everywhere in Europe except Germany, I don't talk about Germany . . . Sister Irene, think of the significant men in the last century, the men who've changed the world! Jews, right? Marx, Freud, Einstein! Not that I believe Marx, Marx is a madman . . . and Freud, no, my sympathies are with spiritual humanism. I believe that the Jewish race is the exclusive . . . the exclusive, what's the word, the exclusive means by which humanism will be extended. . . . Humanism begins by excluding the Jew, and now," he said with a high, surprised laugh, "the Jew will perfect it. After the Nazis, only the Jew is authorized to understand humanism, its limitations and its possibilities. So, I say that the humanist is committed to life in its totality and not just to his profession! The religious person is totally religious, he is his religion! What else? I recognize in you a humanist and a religious person—"

But he did not seem to be talking to her or even looking at her.

"Here, read this," he said. "I wrote it last night." It was a long free-verse poem, typed on a typewriter whose ribbon was worn out.

"There's this trouble with my father, a wonderful man, a lovely man, but his health—his strength is fading, do you see? What must it be to him to see his son growing up? I mean, I'm a man now, he's getting old, weak, his health is bad—it's hell, right? I sympathize with him. I'd do anything for him, I'd cut open my veins, anything for a father—right? That's why I wasn't in school yesterday," he said, and his voice dropped for the last sentence, as if he had been dragged back to earth by a fact.

Sister Irene tried to read the poem, then pretended to read it. A jumble of words dealing with "life" and "death" and "darkness" and "love." "What do you think?" Weinstein said nervously, trying to read it over her shoulder and crowding against her.

"It's very . . . passionate," Sister Irene said.

This was the right comment; he took the poem back from her in silence, his face flushed with excitement. "Here, at this school, I have few people to talk with. I haven't shown anyone else that poem." He looked at her with his dark, intense eyes, and Sister Irene felt them focus upon her. She was terrified at what he was trying to do—he was trying to force her into a human relationship.

"Thank you for your paper," she said, turning away.

When he came the next day, ten minutes late, he was haughty and disdainful. He had nothing to say and sat with his arms folded. Sister Irene took back with her to the convent a feeling of betrayal and confusion. She had been hurt. It was absurd, and yet— She spent too much time thinking about him, as if he were somehow a kind of crystallization of her own loneliness; but she had no right to think so much of him. She did not want to think of him or of her loneliness. But Weinstein did so much more than think of his predicament: he embodied it, he acted it out, and that was perhaps why he fascinated her. It was as if he were doing a dance for her, a dance of shame and agony and delight, and so long as he did it, she was safe. She felt embarrassment for him, but also anxiety; she wanted to protect him. When the dean of the graduate school questioned her about Weinstein's work, she insisted that he was an "excellent" student, though she knew the dean had not wanted to hear that.

She prayed for guidance, she spent hours on her devotions, she was closer to her vocation than she had been for some years. Life at the convent became tinged with unreality, a misty distortion that took its tone from the glowering skies of the city at night, identical smokestacks ranged against the clouds and giving to the sky the excrement of the populated and successful earth. This city was not her city, this world was not her world. She felt no pride in knowing this, it was a fact. The little convent was not like an island in the center of this noisy world, but rather a kind of hole or crevice the world did not bother with, something of no interest. The convent's rhythm of life had nothing to do with the world's rhythm, it did not violate or alarm it in any way. Sister Irene tried to draw together the fragments of her life and synthesize them somehow in her vocation as a nun: she was a nun, she was recognized as a nun and had given herself happily to that life, she had a name, a place, she had dedicated her superior intelligence to the Church, she worked without pay and without expecting gratitude, she had given up pride, she did not think of herself but only of her work and her vocation, she did not think of anything external to these, she saturated herself daily in the knowledge that she was involved in the mystery of Christianity.

A daily terror attended this knowledge, however, for she sensed herself being drawn by that student, that Jewish boy, into a relationship she was not ready for. She wanted to cry out in fear that she was being forced into the role of a Christian, and what did that mean? What could her studies tell her? What could the other nuns tell her? She was alone, no one could help; he was making her into a Christian, and to her that was a mystery, a thing of terror, something others slipped on the way they slipped on their clothes, casually and thoughtlessly, but to her a magnificent and terrifying wonder.

For days she carried Weinstein's paper, marked A, around with her; he did not come to class. One day she checked with the graduate office and was told that Weinstein had called in to say his father was ill and that he would not be able to attend classes for a while. "He's strange, I remember him," the secretary said. "He missed all his exams last spring and made a lot of trouble. He was in and out of here every day."

So there was no more of Weinstein for a while, and Sister Irene stopped expecting him to hurry into class. Then, one morning, she found a letter from him in her mailbox.

He had printed it in black ink, very carefully, as if he had not trusted handwriting. The return address was in bold letters that, like his voice, tried to grab onto her: Birchcrest Manor. Somewhere north of the city. "Dear Sister Irene," the block letters said, "I am doing well here and have time for reading and relaxing. The Manor is delightful. My doctor here is an excellent, intelligent man who has time for me, unlike my former doctor. If you have time, you might drop in on my father, who worries about me too much, I think, and explain to him what my condition is. He doesn't seem to understand. I feel about this new life the way that boy, what's his name, in *Measure for Measure,* feels about the prospects of a different life; you remember what he says to his sister when she visits him in prison, how he is looking forward to an escape into another world. Perhaps you could *explain* this to my father and he would stop worrying." The letter ended with the father's name and address, in letters that were just a little too big. Sister Irene, walking slowly down the corridor as she read the letter, felt her eyes cloud over with tears. She was cold with fear, it was something she had never experienced before. She knew what Weinstein was trying to tell her, and the desperation of his attempt made it all the more pathetic; he did not deserve this, why did God allow him to suffer so?

She read through Claudio's speech to his sister, in *Measure for Measure:*

Ay, but to die, and go we know not where;
To lie in cold obstruction and to rot;
This sensible warm motion to become
A kneaded clod; and the delighted spirit
To bathe in fiery floods, or to reside
In thrilling region of thick-ribbed ice,

To be imprison'd in the viewless winds
And blown with restless violence round about
The pendent world; or to be worse than worst
Of those that lawless and incertain thought
Imagines howling! 'Tis too horrible!
The weariest and most loathed worldly life
That age, ache, penury, and imprisonment
Can lay on nature is a paradise
To what we fear of death.

Sister Irene called the father's number that day. "Allen Weinstein residence, who may I say is calling?" a woman said, bored. "May I speak to Mr. Weinstein? It's urgent—about his son," Sister Irene said. There was a pause at the other end. "You want to talk to his mother, maybe?" the woman said. "His mother? Yes, his mother, then. Please. It's very important."

She talked with this strange, unsuspected woman, a disembodied voice that suggested absolutely no face, and insisted upon going over that afternoon. The woman was nervous, but Sister Irene, who was a university professor, after all, knew enough to hide her own nervousness. She kept waiting for the woman to say, "Yes, Allen has mentioned you . . ." but nothing happened.

She persuaded Sister Carlotta to ride over with her. This urgency of hers was something they were all amazed by. They hadn't suspected that the set of her gray eyes could change to this blurred, distracted alarm, this sense of mission that seemed to have come to her from nowhere. Sister Irene drove across the city in the late afternoon traffic, with the high whining noises from residential streets where trees were being sawed down in pieces. She understood now the secret, sweet wildness that Christ must have felt, giving himself for man, dying for the billions of men who would never know of him and never understand the sacrifice. For the first time she approached the realization of that great act. In her troubled mind the city traffic was jumbled and yet oddly coherent, an image of the world that was always out of joint with what was happening in it, its inner history struggling with its external spectacle. This sacrifice of Christ's, so mysterious and legendary now, almost lost in time—it was that by which Christ transcended both God and man at one moment, more than man because of his fate to do what no other man could do, and more than God because no god could suffer as he did. She felt a flicker of something close to madness.

She drove nervously, uncertainly, afraid of missing the street and afraid of finding it too, for while one part of her rushed forward to confront these people who had betrayed their son, another part of her would have liked nothing so much as to be waiting as usual for the summons to dinner, safe in her room. . . . When she found the street and turned onto it, she was in a state of breathless excitement. Here lawns were bright green and marred with only a few leaves, magically clean, and the houses were enormous and pompous, a mixture of styles: ranch houses, colonial houses, French country houses, white-bricked wonders with curving glass and clumps of birch trees somehow encircled by white concrete. Sister Irene stared as if she had blundered into another world. This was a kind of heaven, and she was too shabby for it.

The Weinstein's house was the strangest one of all: it looked like a small Alpine lodge, with an inverted-V-shaped front entrance. Sister Irene drove up the black-topped driveway and let the car slow to a stop; she told Sister Carlotta she would not be long.

At the door she was met by Weinstein's mother, a small, nervous woman with hands like her son's. "Come in, come in," the woman said. She had once been beautiful, that was clear, but now in missing beauty she was not handsome or even attractive but looked ruined and perplexed, the misshapen swelling of her white-blond professionally set hair like a cap lifting up from her surprised face. "He'll be right in. Allen?" she called, "our visitor is here." They went into the living room. There was a grand piano at one end and an organ at the other. In between were scatterings of brilliant modern furniture in conversational groups, and several puffed-up white rugs on the polished floor. Sister Irene could not stop shivering.

"Professor, it's so strange, but let me say when the phone rang I had a feeling—I had a feeling," the woman said, with damp eyes. Sister Irene sat, and the woman hovered about her. "Should I call you Professor? We don't . . . you know . . . we don't understand the technicalities that go with—Allen, my son, wanted to go here to the Catholic school; I told my husband why not? Why fight? It's the thing these days, they do anything they want for knowledge. And he had to come home, you know. He couldn't take care of himself in New York, that was the beginning of the trouble. . . . Should I call you Professor?"

"You can call me Sister Irene."

"Sister Irene?" the woman said, touching her throat in awe, as if something intimate and unexpected had happened.

Then Weinstein's father appeared, hurrying. He took long, impatient strides. Sister Irene stared at him and in that instant doubted everything—he was in his fifties, a tall, sharply handsome man, heavy but not fat, holding his shoulders back with what looked like an effort, but holding them back just the same. He wore a dark suit and his face was flushed, as if he had run a long distance.

"Now," he said, coming to Sister Irene and with a precise wave of his hand motioning his wife off, "now, let's straighten this out. A lot of confusion over that kid, eh?" He pulled a chair over, scraping it across a rug and pulling one corner over, so that its brown underside was exposed. "I came home early just for this, Libby phoned me. Sister, you got a letter from him, right?"

The wife looked at Sister Irene over her husband's head as if trying somehow to coach her, knowing that this man was so loud and impatient that no one could remember anything in his presence.

"A letter—yes—today—"

"He says what in it? You got the letter, eh? Can I see it?"

She gave it to him and wanted to explain, but he silenced her with a flick of his hand. He read through the letter so quickly that Sister Irene thought perhaps he was trying to impress her with his skill at reading. "So?" he said, raising his eyes, smiling, "so what is this? He's happy out there, he says. He doesn't communicate with us any more, but he writes to you and says he's happy—what's that? I mean, what the hell is that?"

"But he isn't happy. He wants to come home," Sister Irene said. It was so important that she make him understand that she could not trust her voice; goaded by this man, it might suddenly turn shrill, as his son's did. "Someone must read their letters before they're mailed, so he tried to tell me something by making an allusion to—"

"What?"

"—an allusion to a play, so that I would know. He may be thinking suicide, he must be very unhappy—"

She ran out of breath. Weinstein's mother had begun to cry, but the father was shaking his head jerkily back and forth. "Forgive me, Sister, but it's a lot of crap, he needs the hospital, he needs help—right? It costs me fifty a day out there, and they've got the best place in the state, I figure it's worth it. He needs help, that kid, what do I care if he's unhappy? He's unbalanced!" he said angrily. "You want us to get him out again? We argued with the judge for two hours to get him in, an acquaintance of mine. Look, he can't control himself—he was smashing things here, he was hysterical. They need help, lady, and you do something about it fast! You do something! We made up our minds to do something and we did it! This letter—what the hell is this letter? He never talked like that to us!"

"But he means the opposite of what he says—"

"Then he's crazy! I'm the first to admit it." He was perspiring, and his face had darkened. "I've got no pride left this late. He's a little bastard, you want to know? He calls me names, he's filthy, got a filthy mouth—that's being smart, huh? They give him a big scholarship for his filthy mouth? I went to college too, and I got out and knew something, and I for Christ's sake did something with it; my wife is an intelligent woman, a learned woman, would you guess she does book reviews for the little newspaper out here? Intelligent isn't crazy—crazy isn't intelligent. Maybe for you at the school he writes nice papers and gets an A, but out here, around the house, he can't control himself, and we got him committed!"

"But—"

"We're fixing him up, don't worry about it!" He turned to his wife. "Libby, get out of here, I mean it. I'm sorry, but get out of here, you're making a fool of yourself, go stand in the kitchen or something, you and the goddamn maid can cry on each other's shoulders. That one in the kitchen is nuts too, they're all nuts. Sister," he said, his voice lowering, "I thank you immensely for coming out here. This is wonderful, your interest in my son. And I see he admires you—that letter there. But what about that letter? If he did want to get out, which I don't admit—he was willing to be committed, in the end he said okay himself—if he wanted out I wouldn't do it. Why? So what if he wants to come back? The next day he wants something else, what then? He's a sick kid, and I'm the first to admit it."

Sister Irene felt that sickness spread to her. She stood. The room was so big it seemed it must be a public place; there had been nothing personal or private about their conversation. Weinstein's mother was standing by the fireplace, sobbing. The father jumped to his feet and wiped his forehead in a gesture that was meant to help Sister Irene on her way out. "God, what a day," he said, his eyes snatching at hers for understanding, "you know—one of those days all day long? Sister, I thank you a lot. There should be more people in the world who care about others, like you. I mean that."

On the way back to the convent, the man's words returned to her, and she could not get control of them; she could not even feel anger. She had been pressed down, forced back, what could she do? Weinstein might have been watching her somehow from a barred window, and he surely would have understood. The strange idea she had had on the way over, something about understanding Christ, came back to her now and sickened her. But the sickness was small. It could be contained.

About a month after her visit to his father, Weinstein himself showed up. He was dressed in a suit as before, even the necktie was the same. He came right into her office as if he had been pushed and could not stop.

"Sister," he said, and shook her hand. He must have seen fear in her because he smiled ironically. "Look, I'm released. I'm let out of the nut house. Can I sit down?"

He sat. Sister Irene was breathing quickly, as if in the presence of an enemy who does not know he is an enemy.

"So, they finally let me out. I heard what you did. You talked with him, that was all I wanted. You're the only one who gave a damn. Because you're a humanist and a religious person, you respect . . . the individual. Listen," he said, whispering, "it was hell out there! Hell Birchcrest Manor! All fixed up with fancy chairs and *Life* magazines lying around—and what do they do to you? They locked me up, they gave me shock treatments! Shock treatments, how do you like that, it's discredited by everybody now—they're crazy out there themselves, sadists. They locked me up, they gave me hypodermic shots, they didn't treat me like a human being! Do you know what that is," Weinstein demanded savagely, "not to be treated like a human being? They made me an animal—for fifty dollars a day! Dirty filthy swine! Now I'm an outpatient because I stopped swearing at them. I found somebody's bobby pin, and when I wanted to scream I pressed it under my fingernail and it stopped me—the screaming went inside and not out—so they gave me good reports, those sick bastards. Now I'm an outpatient and I can walk along the street and breathe in the same filthy exhaust from the buses like all you normal people! Christ," he said, and threw himself back against the chair.

Sister Irene stared at him. She wanted to take his hand, to make some gesture that would close the aching distance between them. "Mr. Weinstein—"

"Call me Allen!" he said sharply.

"I'm very sorry—I'm terribly sorry—"

"My own parents committed me, but of course they didn't know what it was like. It was hell," he said thickly, "and there isn't any hell except what other people do to you. The psychiatrist out there, the main shrink, he hates Jews too, some of us were positive of that, and he's got a bigger nose than I do, a real beak." He made a noise of disgust. "A dirty bastard, a sick, dirty, pathetic bastard—all of them. Anyway, I'm getting out of here, and I came to ask you a favor."

"What do you mean?"

"I'm getting out. I'm leaving. I'm going up to Canada and lose myself. I'll get a job, I'll forget everything, I'll kill myself maybe—what's the difference? Look, can you lend me some money?"

"Money?"

"Just a little! I have to get to the border, I'm going to take a bus."

"But I don't have any money—"

"No money?" He stared at her. "You mean—you don't have any? Sure you have some!"

She stared at him as if he had asked her to do something obscene. Everything was splotched and uncertain before her eyes.

"You must . . . you must go back," she said, "you're making a—"

"I'll pay it back. Look, I'll pay it back, can you go to where you live or something and get it? I'm in a hurry. My friends are sons of bitches: one of them pretended he didn't see me yesterday—I stood right in the middle of the sidewalk and yelled at him, I called him some appropriate names! So he didn't see me, huh? You're the only one who understands me, you understand me like a poet, you—"

"I can't help you, I'm sorry—I . . ."

He looked to one side of her and flashed his gaze back, as if he could control it. He seemed to be trying to clear his vision.

"You have the soul of a poet," he whispered, "you're the only one. Everybody else is rotten! Can't you lend me some money, ten dollars maybe? I have three thousand in the bank, and I can't touch it! They take everything away from me, they make me into an animal. . . . You know I'm not an animal, don't you? Don't you?"

"Of course," Sister Irene whispered.

"You could get money. Help me. Give me your hand or something, touch me, help me—please. . . ." He reached for her hand and she drew back. He stared at her and his face seemed about to crumble, like a child's. "I want something from you, but I don't know what—I want something!" he cried. "Something real! I want you to look at me like I was a human being, is that too much to ask? I have a brain, I'm alive, I'm suffering—what does that mean? Does that mean nothing? I want something real and not this phony Christian love garbage—it's all in the books, it isn't personal—I want something real—look. . . ."

He tried to take her hand again, and this time she jerked away. She got to her feet. "Mr. Weinstein," she said, "please—"

"You! You nun!" he said scornfully, his mouth twisted into a mock grin. "You nun! There's nothing under that ugly outfit, right? And you're not particularly smart even though you think you are; my father has more brains in his foot than you—"

He got to his feet and kicked the chair.

"You bitch!" he cried.

She shrank back against her desk as if she thought he might hit her, but he only ran out of the office.

Weinstein: the name was to become disembodied from the figure, as time went on. The semester passed, the autumn drizzle turned into snow,

Sister Irene rode to school in the morning and left in the afternoon, four days a week, anonymous in her black winter cloak, quiet and stunned. University teaching was an anonymous task, each day dissociated from the rest, with no necessary sense of unity among the teachers: they came and went separately and might for a year just miss a colleague who left his office five minutes before they arrived, and it did not matter.

She heard of Weinstein's death, his suicide by drowning, from the English Department secretary, a handsome white-haired woman who kept a transistor radio on her desk. Sister Irene was not surprised; she had been thinking of him as dead for months. "They identified him by some special television way they have now," the secretary said. "They're shipping the body back. It was up in Quebec. . . ."

Sister Irene could feel a part of herself drifting off, lured by the plains of white snow to the north, the quiet, the emptiness, the sweep of the Great Lakes up to the silence of Canada. But she called that part of herself back. She could only be one person in her lifetime. That was the ugly truth, she thought, that she could not really regret Weinstein's suffering and death; she had only one life and had already given it to someone else. He had come too late to her. Fifteen years ago, perhaps, but not now.

She was only one person, she thought, walking down the corridor in a dream. Was she safe in this single person, or was she trapped? She had only one identity. She could make only one choice. What she had done or hadn't done was the result of that choice, and how was she guilty? If she could have felt guilt, she thought, she might at least have been able to feel something.

A Matter of Vocabulary

JAMES ALAN McPHERSON

(1943–)

Thomas Brown stopped going to church at thirteen after one Sunday morning when he had been caught playing behind the minister's pulpit by several deacons who had come up into the room early to count the money they had collected in the Sunday School downstairs. Thomas had seen them putting some of the change in their pockets, and they had seen him trying to hide behind the big worn brown pulpit with the several black Bibles and the pitcher of iced water and the glass used by the minister in the more passionate parts of his sermons. It was a Southern Baptist Church.

"Come on down off of that, little Brother Brown," one of the fat black-suited deacons had told him. "We see you tryin' to hide. Ain't no use tryin' to hide in God's House."

Thomas had stood up and looked at them; all three of them, big-bellied, severe, and religiously righteous. "I wasn't tryin' to hide," he said in a low voice.

"Then what was you doin' behind Reverend Stone's pulpit?"

"I was praying," Thomas had said.

After that he did not like to go to church. Still, his mother would make him go every Sunday morning; and being only thirteen and very obedient, he could find no excuse not to leave the house. But after leaving the house with his brother, Edward, he would not go all the way to church. He would make Edward, who was a year younger, leave him at a certain corner a few blocks away from the church where Saturday-night drunks were sleeping or waiting for the bars to open on Monday morning. His own father had been that way, and Thomas knew that the waiting was very hard. He felt good toward the men, being almost one of them, and liked to listen to them curse and threaten each other lazily in the hot Georgia sun. He liked to look into their faces and wonder what was in them that made them not care about anything except the bars opening on Monday morning. He liked to try to distinguish the different shades of black in their hands and arms and faces. And he liked the smell of them. But most of all he liked it when they talked to him and gave him an excuse for not walking down the street two blocks to the Baptist Church.

"Don't you ever get married, boy," Arthur, one of the meaner drunks with a missing eye, told him on several occasions.

The first time he had said it the boy had asked: "Why not?"

"'Cause a bitch ain't shit, man. You mind you don' get married now, hear? A bitch'll take all yo money and then throw you out *in the street!*"

"Damn straight!" Leroy, another drunk much darker than Arthur and a longshoreman, said. "That's all they fit for, takin' a man's money and runnin' around."

Thomas would sit on the stoop of an old deserted house with the men lying on the ground below him, too lazy to brush away the flies that came at them from the urine-soaked dirt on the hot Sunday mornings, and he would look and listen and consider. And after a few weeks of this he found himself very afraid of girls.

Things about life had always come to him by listening and being quiet.

He remembered how he had learned about being black, and about how some other people were not. And the difference it made. He felt at home sitting with the waiting drunks because they were black, and he knew that they liked him because for months before he had stopped going to church, he had spoken to them while passing, and they had returned his greeting. His mother had always taught him to speak to people in the streets because Southern blacks do not know how to live without neighbors who exchange greetings. He had noted, however, when he was seven or eight, that certain people did not return his greetings. At first he had thought that their silence was due to his own low voice: he had gone to a Catholic school for four years where the black-caped nuns put an academic premium on silence. He had learned that in complete silence lay his safety from being slapped or hit on the flat of the hand with a wooden ruler. And he had been a model student. But even when he raised his voice, intentionally, to certain people in the street they still did not respond. Then he had noticed that while they had different faces, like the nuns, whom he never thought of as real people, these nonspeakers were completely different in dress and color from the people he knew. But still, he wondered why they would not speak.

He never asked his mother or anyone else about it; ever since those four years with the nuns he did not like to talk much. And he began to consider certain things about his own person as possible reasons for these slights. He began to consider why it was necessary for one to go to the bathroom. He began to wonder whether only people like him had to go to the toilet and whether or not this thing was the cause of his complexion; and whether the other people could know about the bathroom merely by looking at his skin and did not speak because they knew he did it. This bothered him a lot, but he never asked anyone about it. Not even his brother, Edward, with whom he shared a bed and with whom, in the night and dark closeness of the bed, there should have been no secret thoughts. Nor did he speak of it to Leroy, the most talkative drunk, who wet the dirt behind the old house where they sat with no shame in his face, and always shook himself in the direction of the Baptist Church, two blocks down the street.

"You better go to church," his mother told him when he was finally discovered. "If you don' go, you going to hell for sure."

"I don' think I wanna go back," he said.

"You'll be a Sinner if you don' go," she said, pointing her finger at him with great gravity. "You'll go to hell, sure enough."

Thomas felt doomed already. He had told the worst lie in the world in the worst place in the world, and he knew that going back to church would not save him now. He knew that there was a hell because the nuns had told him about it, and he knew that he would end up in one of the little rooms in that place. But he still hoped for some time in purgatory, with a chance to move into a better room later, if he could be very good for a while before he died. He wanted to be very good, and he tried very hard all the time not to have to go to the bathroom. But when his mother talked about hell, he thought again that perhaps he would have to spend all his time, after death, in that great fiery-hot burning room she talked about. She had been raised in the Southern Baptist Church, and had gone to church, to the same minister, all her life, up until the time she had to start working on Sundays. But she still maintained her faith and never talked, in her conception of hell and how it would be for Sinners, about the separate rooms for certain people. Listening to his mother in the kitchen talk about hell while she cooked supper and sweated, Thomas thought that perhaps she knew more than the nuns because there were so many people who believed like her, including the bald Reverend Stone in their church, in that one great burning room and the Judgment Day.

"The hour's gonna come when the Horn will blow," his mother told him while he cowered in the corner behind the stove, feeling the heat from it on his face. "The Horn's gonna blow all through the world on that Great Morning, and all them in the graves will hear it and be raised up," she would continue.

"Even Daddy?"

His mother paused, and let the spoon stand still in the pot on the stove. "Everybody," she said, "both the Quick and the Dead and everybody that's alive. Then the stars are gonna fall, and all the Sinners will be cryin' and tryin' to hide in the corners and under houses. But it won't do no good to hide. You can't hide from God. Then they gonna call the roll with everybody's name on it, and the sheeps are gonna be divided from the goats, the Good on the Right and the Bad on the Left. And then the ground's gonna open up, and all of them on the Left are gonna fall right into a burnin' pool of fire and brimstone, and they're gonna be cryin' and screamin' for mercy, but there won't be none because it will be too late. Especially for those who don't repent and go to church."

Now his mother stood over him, her eyes almost red with emotion, her face wet from the stove and shining black, and very close to tears.

Thomas felt the heat from the stove where he sat in the corner next to the broom. He was scared. He thought about being on the Left with Leroy and Arthur, and all the men who sat on the corner two blocks away from the Baptist Church. He did not think it was at all fair.

"Won't there be rooms for different people?" he asked her.

"What kind of rooms?" his mother said.

"Rooms for people who ain't done too much wrong."

"There ain't gonna be no separate rooms for any Sinners on the *Left!* Everybody on the Left is gonna fall right into the same fiery pit, and the ones on the Right will be raised up into glory. Where do you want to be, Tommy?"

He could think of nothing to say.

"You want to be on the Right or on the Left?"

"I don't know."

"What do you mean?" she said. "You still got time, son."

"I don't know if I can ever get over on the Right," Thomas said.

His mother looked down at him. She was a very warm person, and sometimes she hugged him or touched him on the face when he least expected it. But sometimes she was severe.

"You can still get on the Right side, Tommy, if you go to church."

"I don't see how I can," he said again.

"Go on back to church, son," his mother said.

"I'll go," Tommy said. But he was not sure whether he could ever go back again after what he had done right behind the pulpit. But to please her, and to make her know that he was really sorry and that he would really try to go back to church, and to make certain in her mind that he genuinely wanted to have a place on the Right on Judgment Day, he helped her cook dinner and then washed the dishes afterward.

They lived on the top floor of a gray wooden house next to a funeral parlor. Thomas and his brother could look out the kitchen window and down into the rear door of the funeral parlor, which was always open, and watch George Herbs, the mortician, working on the bodies. Sometimes George Herbs would come to the back door of the embalming room in his white coat and look up at them, and laugh, and wave for them to come down. They never went down. And after a few minutes of getting fresh air, George Herbs would look at them again and go back to his work.

Down the street, almost at the corner, was a police station. There were always fat, white-faced, red-nosed, blue-suited policemen who never seemed to go anywhere sitting in the small room. Also, these two men had never spoken to Thomas except on one occasion when he had been doing some hard thinking about getting on the Right Side on Judgment Day.

He had been on his way home from school in the afternoon. It was fall, and he was kicking leaves. His eyes fell upon a green five-dollar bill on the black-sand sidewalk, just a few steps away from the station. At first he did not know what to do; he had never found money before. But finding money on the ground was a good feeling. He had picked up the bill and carried it home, to a house that needed it, to his mother. It was not a great amount of money to lose, but theirs was a very poor street; and his mother had directed him, without any hesitation, to turn in the lost five dollars at the police station. And he had done this, going to the station himself and telling the men, in a scared voice, how he had found the money, where he had found it, and how his mother had directed him to bring it to the station in case the loser should come in looking for it. The men had listened and then had spoken to him for the first time. They even eventually smiled at him and then at each other, and a man with a long red nose with gray spots on it had assured him, still smiling, that if the owner did not call for the five dollars in a week, they would bring the money to his house and it would be his. But the money never came to his house, and when he saw the red-nosed policeman coming out of the station more than a week later, the man did not even look at him, and Thomas had known that he should not ask what had happened to the money. Instead, in his mind, he credited it against that Judgment Time when, perhaps, there would be some uncertainty about whether he should stand on the Right Side, or whether he should cry with Leroy and Arthur and the other sinners on the Left.

There was another interesting place on that street. It was across from his house, next to the Michelob Bar on the corner. It was an old brown house, and an old woman, Mrs. Quick, lived there. Every morning on his way to school, Thomas would see her washing her porch with potash and water in a steel tub and a little stiff broom. The boards on her porch were very white from so much washing, and he could see no reason why she should have to wash it every morning. She never had any visitors to track it except the Crab Lady, who, even though she stopped to talk with Mrs. Quick every morning on her route, never went up on the porch. Sometimes the Crab Lady's call would waken Thomas and his brother in the big bed they shared. *"Crabs! Buy my crabs!"* she would sing, like a big, loud bird because the words all ran together in her song, and it sounded to them like *"Crabbonniee crabs!"* They both would race to the window in their underwear and watch her walking on the other side of the street, an old wicker basket balanced on her head and covered with a bright red cloth that moved up and down with the bouncing of the crabs under it as she walked. She was a big, dull-black woman and wore a checkered apron over her dress, and she always held one hand up to the basket on her head as she swayed down the black-dirt sidewalk. She did not sell many crabs on that street; they were too plentiful in the town. But still she came, every morning, with her song: *"Crabbonniee crabs!"*

"Wonder why she comes every morning," Thomas said to his brother once. "She oughta come at night when the guys are over at Michelob."

"Maybe she just comes by to talk to Mrs. Quick," Edward said.

And that was true enough. For every morning the Crab Lady would stop and talk to Mrs. Quick while Mrs. Quick washed down her porch. She would never set the basket on the ground while she talked, but stood all the time with one hand on her wide hip and the other balancing the basket on her head, talking. And Mrs. Quick would continue to scrub her porch. Both Thomas and his brother would watch them until their mother came in to make them wash and dress for school. Leaving the window, Thomas would try to get a last look at Mrs. Quick, her head covered by a white bandanna, her old back bent in scrubbing, still talking to the Crab Lady. He would wonder what they talked about every morning. Not knowing this bothered him, and he began to imagine their morning conversations. Mrs. Quick was West Indian and knew all about roots and voodoo, and Thomas was afraid of her. He suspected that they talked about voodoo and who in the neighborhood had been fixed. Roots were like voodoo, and knowing about them made Mrs. Quick something to be feared. Thomas thought that she must know everything about him and everyone in the world because once he and Edward and Luke, a fat boy who worked in the fish market around the corner, had put some salt and pepper and brown sand in a small tobacco pouch, and had thrown it on her white-wood porch, next to the screen door. They had done it as a joke and had run away afterward, into an alley between his house and the funeral parlor across the street, and waited for her to come out and discover the pouch. They had waited for almost fifteen minutes, and still she did not come out; and after all that time waiting it was not such a good joke anymore, and so they had gone off to the graveyard to gather green berries for their slingshots. But the next morning, on his way to school, Mrs. Quick had looked up from scrubbing her porch and called him over, across the dirt street. "You better watch yourself, boy," she had said. "You hear me?"

"Why?" Thomas had asked, frightened and eager to be running away to join his brother.

Mrs. Quick had looked at him, very intensely. Her face was black and wrinkled, and her hair was white where it was not covered by the white bandanna. Her mouth was small and tight and deliberate, and her eyes were dark and red where they should have been white. "You left-handed, ain't you?"

"Yes ma'am."

"Then watch yourself. Watch yourself good, less you get fixed."

"I ain't done nothin'," he said. But he knew that she was aware that he was lying.

"You left-handed, ain't you?"

He nodded.

"Then you owe the Devil a day's work, and you better keep watch on yourself less you get fixed." Upon the last word in this pronouncement she had locked her eyes on his and seemed to look right into his soul. It was as if she knew that he was doomed to stand on the Left Side on that Day, no matter what good he still might do in life. He looked away, and far up the street he could see the Crab Lady swaying along in the dirt. Then he had run.

Late in the night there was another sound Thomas could hear in his bed, next to his brother. This sound did not come every night, but it was a steady sound, and it made him shiver when it did come. He would be lying close and warm against his brother's back, and the sound would bring him away from sleep.

"Mr. Jones! I love you, Mr. Jones!"

This was the horrible night sound of the Barefoot Lady, who came whenever she was drunk to rummage through the neighborhood garbage cans for scraps of food, and to stand before the locked door of the Herbert A. Jones Funeral Parlor and wake the neighborhood with her cry: *"Mr. Jones! I love you, Mr. Jones!"*

"Eddie, wake up!" He would push his brother's back. "It's the Barefoot Lady again."

Fully awake, they would listen to her pitiful moans, like a lonely dog at midnight or the faraway low whistle of a night train pushing along the edge of the town, heading north.

"She scares me," he would say to his brother.

"Yeah, Tommy," his brother would say.

There were certain creaking sounds about the old house that were only audible on the nights when she screamed.

"Why does she love Mr. Jones? He's a undertaker," he would ask his brother. But there would be no answer because his brother was younger than him and still knew how to be very quiet when he was afraid.

"Mr. Jones! I love you, Mr. Jones!"

"It's nighttime," Thomas would go on, talking to himself. "She ought to be scared by all the bodies he keeps in the back room. But maybe it ain't the bodies. Maybe Mr. Jones buried somebody for her a long time ago for free, and she likes him for it. Maybe she never gets no chance to see him in the daytime so she comes at night. I bet she remembers that person Mr. Jones buried for her for free and gets drunk and comes in the night to thank him."

"Shut up, Tommy, please," Eddie said in the dark. "I'm scared." Eddie moved closer to him in the bed and then lay very quiet. But he still made the covers move with his trembling.

"Mr. Jones! I love you, Mr. Jones!"

Thomas thought about the back room of the Herbert A. Jones Funeral Parlor and with the blue-and-white neon sign above its door and the Barefoot Lady, with feet caked with dirt and layers of skin and long yellow-and-black toenails, standing under that neon light. He had only seen her once in the day, but that once had been enough. She wore rags and an old black hat, and her nose and lips were huge and pink, and her hair was long and thick and hanging far below her shoulders, and she had been drooling at the mouth. He had come across her one morning digging into their garbage can for scraps. He had felt sorry for her because he and his brother and his mother threw out very few scraps, and had gone back up the stairs to ask his mother for something to give her. His mother had sent down some fresh biscuits and fried bacon, and watching her eat with her dirty hands with their long black fingernails had made him sick. Now, in his bed, he could still see her eating the biscuits, flakes of the dough sticking to the bacon grease around her mouth. It was a bad picture to see above his bed in the shadows on the ceiling. And it did not help to close his eyes, because then he could see her more vividly, with all the horrible dirty colors of her rags and face and feet made sharper in his mind. He could see her the way he could see the bad man and monsters from *The Shadow* and *Suspense* and *Gangbusters* and *The Six Shooter* every night after his mother had made him turn off the big brown radio in the living room. He could see these figures, men with long faces and humps in their backs, and old women with streaming hair dressed all in black, and cats with yellow eyes, and huge rats, on the walls in the living room when it was dark there; and when he got into bed and closed his eyes, they really came alive and frightened him, the way the present picture in his mind of the Barefoot Lady, her long toenails scratching on the thirty-two stairs as she came up to make him give her more biscuits and bacon, was frightening him. He did not know what to do, and so he moved closer to his brother, who was asleep now. And downstairs, from below the blue-and-white neon sign above the locked door to the funeral parlor, he heard her scream again; a painful sound, lonely, desperate, threatening, impatient, angry, hungry, he had no word to place it.

"Mr. Jones! I love you, Mr. Jones!"

Both Thomas and his brother worked at the F & F Supermarket, owned by Milton and Sarah Feinburg. Between the two of them they made a good third of a man's salary. Thomas had worked himself up from carry-out boy and was now in the Produce Department, while his brother, who was still new, remained a carry-out boy. Thomas enjoyed the status he had over the other boys. He enjoyed not having to be put outside on the street like the boys up front whenever business was slow and Milton Feinburg wanted to save money. He enjoyed being able to work all week after school while the boys up front had to wait for weekends when there would be sales and a lot of shoppers. He especially liked becoming a regular boy because then he had to help mop and wax the floors of the store every Sunday morning and could not go to church. He knew that his mother was not pleased when he had been taken into the mopping crew because now he had an excuse not to attend church. But being on the crew meant making an extra three dollars, and he knew that she was pleased with the money. Still, she made him pray at night, and especially on Sunday.

His job was bagging potatoes. Every day after school and all day Saturday he would come into the air-conditioned produce room, put on a blue smock, take a fifty-pound sack of potatoes off a huge stack of sacks, slit open the sack and let the potatoes fall into a shopping cart next to a scale, and proceed to put them into five- and ten-pound plastic bags. It was very simple; he could do it in his sleep. Then he would spend the rest of the day bagging potatoes and looking out the big window, which separated the produce room from the rest of the store, at the customers. They were mostly white, and after almost a year of this type of work, he began to realize why they did not speak to him in the street. And then he did not mind going to the bathroom, knowing, when he did go, that all of them had to go, just as he did, in the secret places they called home. Some of them had been speaking to him for a long time now, on this business level, and he had formed some small friendship grounded in this.

He knew Richard Burke, the vet who had a war injury in his back and who walked funny. Richard Burke was the butcher's helper, who made hamburger from scraps of fat and useless meat cuttings and red powder in the back of the produce room, where the customers could not see. He liked to laugh when he mixed the red powder into the ground white substance, holding gobs of the soft stuff up over the big tub and letting it drip, and then dunking his hands down into the tub again. Sometimes he threw some of it at Thomas, in fun, and Thomas had to duck. But it was all in fun, and he did not mind it except when the red-and-white meat splattered the window and Thomas had to clean it off so that his view of the customers, as he bagged potatoes, would not be obstructed.

He thought of the window as a one-way mirror which allowed him to examine the people who frequented the store without being noticed himself. His line of vision covered the entire produce aisle, and he could see everyone who entered the store making their way down that aisle, pushing their carts and stopping, selectively, first at the produce racks, then at the meat counter, then off to the side, beyond his view, to the canned goods and frozen foods and toilet items to the unseen right of him. He began to invent names for certain of the regular customers, the ones who came at a special time each week. One man, a gross fat person with a huge belly and the rough red neck and face of a farmer, who wheeled one shopping cart before him while he pulled another behind, Thomas called Big Funk because, he thought, no one could be that fat and wear the same faded dungaree suit each week without smelling bad. Another face he called the Rich Old Lady, because she was old and pushed her cart along slowly, with a dignity shown by none of the other shoppers. She always bought parsley, and once, when Thomas was wheeling a big cart of bagged potatoes out to the racks, he passed her and for just an instant smelled a perfume that was light and very fine to smell. It did not linger in the air like most other perfumes he had smelled. And it seemed to him that she must have had it made just for her and that it was so expensive that it stayed with her body and would never linger behind her when she had passed a place. He liked that about her. Also, he had heard from the boys up front that she would never carry her own groceries to her house, no more than half a block from the store, and that no matter how small her purchases were, she would require a boy to carry them for her and would always tip a quarter. Thomas knew that there was always a general fight among the carry-out boys whenever she checked out. Such a fight seemed worthy of her. And after a while of watching her, he would make a special point of wheeling a cart of newly bagged potatoes out to the racks when he saw her come in the store, just to smell the perfume. But she never noticed him either.

"You make sure you don't go over on them scales now," Miss Hester, the Produce manager, would remind him whenever she saw him looking for too long a time out the window. "Mr. Milton would git mad if you went over ten pounds."

Thomas always knew when she was watching him and just when she would speak. He had developed an instinct for this from being around her. He knew, even at that age, that he was brighter than she was; and he thought that she must know it too because he could sense her getting uncomfortable when she stood in back of him in her blue smock, watching him lift the potatoes to the plastic bag until it was almost full, and then the plastic bag up to the gray metal scale, and then watching the red arrow fly across to ten. Somehow it almost always stopped wavering at exactly ten pounds. Filling the bags was automatic with him, a conditioned reflex, and he could do it quite easily, without breaking his concentration on things beyond the window. And he knew that this bothered her a great deal; so much so, in fact, that she continually asked him questions, standing by the counter or the sink behind him, to make him aware that she was in the room. She was always nervous when he did not say anything for a long time, and he knew this too, and was sometimes silent, even when he had something to say, so that she could hear the thud and swish of the potatoes going into the bag, rhythmically, and the sound of the bags coming down on the scale, and after a second, the sound, sputtering and silken, of the tops of the bags being twisted and sealed in the tape machine. Thomas liked to produce these sounds for her because he knew she wanted something more.

Miss Hester had toes like the Barefoot Lady, except that her nails were shorter and cleaner, and she was white. She always wore sandals, was hefty like a man, and had hair under her arms. Whenever she smiled he could not think of her face or smile as that of a woman. It was too tight. And her laugh was too loud and came from too far away inside her. And the huge crates of lettuce or cantaloupes or celery she could lift very easily made her even less a woman. She had short red-brown hair, and whenever he got very close to her it smelled funny, unlike the Rich Old Lady's smell.

"What you daydreamin' about so much all the time?" she asked him once.

"I was just thinking," he had said.

"What about?"

"School and things."

He could sense her standing behind him at the sink, letting her hands pause on the knife and the celery she was trimming.

"You gonna finish high school?"

"I guess so."

"You must be pretty smart, huh, Tommy?"

"No. I ain't so smart," he said.

"But you sure do think a lot."

"Maybe I just daydream," Thomas told her.

Her knife had started cutting into the celery branches again. He kept up his bagging.

"Well, anyway, you a good worker. You a good boy, Tommy."

Thomas did not say anything.

"Your brother, he's a good worker too. But he ain't like you though."

"I know," he said.

"He talks a lot up front. All the cashiers like him."

"Eddie likes to talk," Thomas said.

"Yeah," said Miss Hester. "Maybe he talks too much. Mr. Milton and Miss Sarah are watchin' him."

"What for?"

She stopped cutting the celery again. "I dunno," she said. "I reckon it's just that he talks a lot."

On Saturday nights Thomas and his brother would buy the family groceries in the F & F Supermarket. Checking the list made out by his mother gave Thomas a feeling of responsibility that he liked. He was free to buy things not even on the list, and he liked this too. They paid for the groceries out of their own money, and doing this, with some of the employees watching, made an especially good feeling for Thomas. Sometimes they bought ice cream or a pie or something special for their mother. This made them exceptional. The other black employees, the carry-out boys, the stock clerks, the bag boys, would have no immediate purpose in mind for their money beyond eating a big meal on Saturday nights or buying whiskey from a bootlegger because they were minors, or buying a new pair of brightly colored pants or pointed shoes to wear into the store on their days off, as if to make all the other employees see that they were above being, at least on this one day, what they were all the rest of the week.

Thomas and Edward did not have days off; they worked straight through the week, after school, and they worked all days on Saturdays. But Edward did not mop on Sunday mornings, and he still went to church. Thomas felt relieved that his brother was almost certain to be on the Right Side on That Day because he had stayed in the church and would never be exposed to all the stealing the mopping crew did when they were alone in the store on Sunday mornings with Lloyd Bailey, the manager, who looked the other way when they took packages of meat and soda and cartons of cigarettes. Thomas suspected that Mr. Bailey was stealing bigger things himself, and that Milton Feinburg, a big-boned Jew who wore custom-made shoes and smoked very expensive, bad-smelling green cigars, knew just what everyone was stealing and was only waiting for a convenient time to catch certain people. Thomas could see it in the way he smiled and rolled the cigar around in his mouth whenever he talked to certain of the bigger stealers; and seeing this, Thomas never stole. At first he thought it was because he was afraid of Milton Feinburg, who had green eyes that could look as deep as Mrs. Quick's; and then he thought that he could not do it because the opportunity only came on Sunday mornings when, if he had never told that first lie, he should have been in church.

Both Milton and Sarah Feinburg liked him. He could tell it by the way Sarah Feinburg always called him up to her office to clean. There were always rolls of coins on her desk, and scattered small change on the floor when he swept. But he never touched any of it. Instead, he would gather what was on the floor and stack the coins very neatly on her desk. And when she came back into the office after he had swept and mopped and waxed and dusted and emptied her wastebaskets, Miss Sarah Feinburg would smile at Thomas and say: "You're a good boy, Tommy."

He could tell that Milton Feinburg liked him because whenever he went to the bank for money he would always ask Thomas to come out to the car to help him bring the heavy white sacks into the store, and sometimes up to his office. On one occasion, he had picked Thomas up on the street, after school, when Thomas was running in order to get to work on time. Milton Feinburg had driven him to the store.

"I like you," Milton Feinburg told Thomas. "You're a good worker."

Thomas could think of nothing to say.

"When you quit school, there'll be a place in the store for you."

"I ain't gonna quit school," Thomas had said.

Milton Feinburg smiled and chewed on his green cigar. "Well, when you finish high school, you can come on to work full time. Miss Hester says you're a good worker."

"Bagging potatoes is easy," said Thomas.

Milton Feinburg smiled again as he drove the car. "Well, we can get you in the stock room, if you can handle it. Think you can handle it?"

"Sure," said Thomas. But he was not thinking of the stock room and unloading trucks and stacking cases of canned goods and soap in the big, musty, upstairs storeroom. He was thinking of how far away he was from finishing high school and how little that long time seemed to matter to Milton Feinburg.

Thomas was examining a very ugly man from behind his window one afternoon when Miss Hester came into the produce room from the front of the store. As usual, she stood behind him. And Thomas went on with his work and watching the very ugly man. This man was bald and had a long thin red nose that twisted down unnaturally, almost to the level of his lower lip. The man had no chin, only three layers of skin that lapped down onto his neck like a necklace. Barney Benns, one of the stock clerks who occasionally passed through the produce room to steal an apple or a banana, had christened the very ugly man "Do-funny," just as he had christened Thomas "Little Brother" soon after he had come to the job. Looking at Do-funny made Thomas sad; he wondered how the man had lost his chin. Perhaps, he thought, Do had lost it in the war, or perhaps in a car accident. He was trying to picture just how Do-funny would look after the accident when he realized that his chin was gone forever, when Miss Hester spoke from behind him.

"Your brother's in a lotta trouble up front," she said.

Thomas turned to look at her. "What's the matter?"

Miss Hester smiled at him in that way she had, like a man. "He put a order in the wrong car."

"Did the people bring it back?"

"Yeah," she said. "But some folks is still missin' their groceries. They're out there now mad as hell."

"Was it Eddie lost them?"

"Yeah. Miss Sarah is mad as hell. Everybody's standin' round up there."

He looked through the glass window and up the produce aisle and saw his brother coming toward him from the front of the store. His brother was untying the knot in his blue smock when he came in the swinging door of the air-conditioned produce room. His brother did not speak to him but walked directly over to the sink next to Miss Hester and began to suck water from the black hose. He looked very hot, but only his nose was sweating. Thomas turned completely away from the window and stood facing his brother.

"What's the matter up front, Eddie?" he said.

"Nothing," his brother replied, his jaws tight.

"I heard you put a order in the wrong car and the folks cain't git it back," said Miss Hester.

"Yeah," said Eddie.

"Why you tryin' to hide back here?" she said.

"I ain't tryin' to hide," said Eddie.

Thomas watched them and said nothing.

"You best go on back up front there," Miss Hester said.

At that moment Miss Sarah Feinburg pushed through the door. She had her hands in the pockets of her blue sweater and she walked to the middle of the small, cool room and glared at Edward Brown. "Why are you back here?" Miss Sarah Feinburg asked Edward.

"I come back for some water."

"You know you lost twenty-seven dollars' worth of groceries up there?"

"It wasn't my fault," said Eddie.

"If you kept your mind on what you're supposed to do this wouldn't have happened. But no. You're always talking, always smiling around, always running your mouth with everybody."

"The people who got the wrong bags might bring them back," Eddie said. His nose was still sweating in the cool room. "Evidently somebody took my cart by mistake."

"*Evidently! Evidently!*" said Sarah Feinburg. "Miss Hester, you should please listen to *that! Evidently*. You let them go to school, and they think they know everything. *Evidently*, you say?"

"Yeah," said Eddie. Thomas saw that he was about to cry.

Miss Hester was still smiling like a man.

Sarah Feinburg stood with her hands in her sweater pockets and braced on her hips, looking Eddie in the face. Eddie did not hold his eyes down, and Thomas felt really good but sad that he did not.

"You get back up front," said Sarah Feinburg. And she shoved her way through the door again and out of the cool produce room.

"Evidently, evidently, that sure was funny," said Miss Hester when the fat woman was halfway down the produce aisle, "Lord, was she mad. I ain't never seen her git so mad."

Neither Thomas nor Eddie said anything.

Then Miss Hester stopped smiling. "You best git on back up front, Eddie."

"No," said Eddie. "I'm goin' home."

"You ain't quittin'?" said Miss Hester.

"Yeah."

"What for?"

"I dunno, I just gotta go home."

"But don't your folk need the money?"

"No," Eddie said.

He took off his blue smock and laid it on the big pile of fifty-pound potato sacks. "I'm goin' home," he said again. He did not look at his brother. He walked through the door, and slowly down the produce aisle and then out the front door, without looking at anything at all.

Then Thomas went over to the stack of unbagged potatoes and pushed the blue smock off the top sack and into a basket on the floor next to the stack. He picked up a fifty-pound sack and lugged it over to the cart and tore it open with his fingers, spilling its contents of big and small dirty brown potatoes into the cart. He could feel Miss Hester's eyes on him, on his arms and shoulders and hands as they moved. He worked very quickly and looked out the window into the store. Big Funk was supposed to come this afternoon. He had finished seven five-pound bags before Miss Hester moved from where she had been standing behind him, and he knew she was about to speak.

"You going to quit too, Tommy?"

"No," he said.

"I guess your folk *do* need the money now, huh?"

"No," he said. "We don't need the money."

She did not say anything else. Thomas was thinking about Big Funk and what could be done with the time if he did not come. He did not want to think about his brother or his mother or the money, or even the good feeling he got when Milton Feinburg saw them buying the Saturday-night groceries. If Big Funk did not come, then perhaps he could catch another glimpse of Do-funny before he left the store. The Rich Old

Lady would not come again until next week. He decided that it would be necessary to record the faces and bodies of new people as they wandered, selectively, with their shopping carts beyond the big window glass. He liked it very much now that none of them ever looked up and saw him watching. That way he did not have to feel embarrassed or guilty. That way he would never have to feel compelled to nod his head or move his mouth or eyes, or make any indication of a greeting to them. That way he would never have to feel bad when they did not speak back.

In his bed that night, lying very close to his brother's back, Thomas thought again very seriously about the Judgment Day and the Left Side. Now, there were certain people he would like to have with him on the Left Side on That Day. He thought about church and how he could never go back because of the place where the deacons had made him tell his first great lie. He wondered whether it was because he did not want to have to go back to church on Sunday mornings that he had not quit. He wondered if it was because of the money or going to church or because of the window that he had not walked out of the store with his brother. That would have been good: the two of them, walking out together. But he had not done it, and now he could not make himself know why. Suddenly, in the night, he heard the Barefoot Lady under the blue-and-white Herbert A. Jones neon light, screaming.

"Mr. Jones! I love you, Mr. Jones!"

But the sound did not frighten him now. He pushed against his brother's back.

"Eddie? *Eddie.*"

"Yeah?"

"Wonder why she does it?"

"I dunno."

"I wonder why," he said again.

Eddie did not answer. But after the sound of the woman came again, his brother turned over in the bed and said to Thomas:

"You gonna quit?"

"No."

"Why not? We could always carry papers."

"I dunno, I just ain't gonna quit. Not now."

"Well *I* ain't goin' back. I'll go back in there one day when I'm rich. I'm gonna go in and buy everything but hamburger."

"Yeah," said Thomas. But he was not listening to his brother.

"Mr. Jones! I love you, Mr. Jones!"

"And I'm gonna learn all the big words in the world too," his brother went on. "When I go back in there I'm gonna be talking so big that fat old Miss Sarah won't even be able to understand me."

"That'll be good," said Thomas. But he was thinking to himself now.

"You'll see," said Eddie. "I'll do it too."

But Thomas did not answer him. He was waiting for the sound to come again.

"Mr. Jones! I love you, Mr. Jones!"

And then he knew why the Barefoot Lady came to that place almost every night to cry when there was no one alive in the building to hear or care about her sound. He felt what she must feel. And he knew now why the causes of the sound had bothered him and would always bother him. There was a word in his mind now, a big word, that made good sense of her sound and the burning, feeling thing he felt inside himself. It was all very clear, and now he understood that the Barefoot Lady came in the night, not because she really loved Mr. Jones, or because he had once buried someone for her for free, or even because she liked the blue-and-white neon light. She came in the night to scream because she, like himself, was in misery, and did not know what else to do.

The Farm

JOY WILLIAMS

(1944–)

It was a dark night in August. Sarah and Tommy were going to their third party that night, the party where they would actually sit down to dinner. They were driving down Mixtuxet Avenue, a long black avenue of trees that led out of the village, away from the shore and the coastal homes into the country. Tommy had been drinking only soda that night. Every other weekend, Tommy wouldn't drink. He did it, he said, to keep trim. He did it because he could.

Sarah was telling a long story as she drove. She kept asking Tommy if she had told it to him before, but he was noncommittal. When Tommy didn't drink, Sarah talked and talked. She was telling him a terrible story that she had read in the newspaper about an alligator at a jungle farm attraction in Florida. The alligator had eaten a child who had crawled into its pen. The alligator's name was Cookie. Its owner had shot it immediately. The owner was sad about everything, the child, the parents' grief,

Cookie. He was quoted in the paper as saying that shooting Cookie was not an act of revenge.

When Tommy didn't drink, Sarah felt cold. She was shivering in the car. There were goosepimples on her tanned, thin arms. Tommy sat beside her smoking, saying nothing.

There had been words between them earlier. The parties here had an undercurrent of sexuality. Sarah could almost hear it, flowing around them all, carrying them all along. In the car, on the night of the accident, Sarah was at that point in the evening when she felt guilty. She wanted to make things better, make things nice. She had gone through her elated stage, her jealous stage, her stubbornly resigned stage and now she felt guilty. Had they talked about divorce that night, or had that been before, on other evenings? There was a flavor she remembered in their talks about divorce, a scent. It was hot, as Italy had been hot when they had been there. Dust, bread, sun, a burning at the back of the throat from too much drinking.

They hadn't been talking about divorce that night. The parties had been crowded. Sarah had hardly seen Tommy. Then, on her way to the bathroom, she had seen him sitting with a girl on a bed in one of the back rooms. He was telling the girl about condors, about hunting for condors in small, light planes.

"Oh, but you didn't hurt them, did you?" the girl asked. She was someone's daughter, a little overweight but with beautiful skin and large green eyes.

"Oh no," Tommy assured her, "we weren't hunting to hurt."

Condors. Sarah looked at them sitting on the bed. When they noticed her, the girl blushed. Tommy smiled. Sarah imagined what she looked like, standing in the doorway. She wished that they had shut the door.

That had been at the Steadmans'. The first party had been at the Perrys'. The Perrys never served food. Sarah had had two or three drinks there. The bar had been set up beneath the grape arbor and everyone stood outside. It had still been light at the Perrys' but at the Steadmans' it was dark and people drank inside. Everyone spoke about the end of summer as though it were a bewildering and unnatural event.

They had stayed at the Steadmans' longer than they should have and they were going to be late for dinner. Nevertheless, they were driving at a moderate speed, through a familiar landscape, passing houses that they had been entertained in many times. There were the Salts and the Hollands and the Greys and the Dodsons. The Dodsons kept their gin in the freezer and owned two large and dappled crotch-sniffing dogs. The Greys imported Southerners for their parties. The women all had lovely voices and knew how to make spoon bread and pickled tomatoes and artillery punch. The men had smiles when they'd say to Sarah, "Why, let me get you another. You don't have a thing in that glass, ah swear." The Hollands gave the kind of dinner party where the shot was still in the duck and the silver should have been in a vault. Little whiskey was served but there was always excellent wine. The Salts were a high-strung couple who often quarreled. Jenny Salt was on some type of medication for tension and often dropped the canapés she attempted to serve. Jenny and her husband, Pete, had a room in which there was nothing but a large doll house where witty mâché figures carried on assignations beneath tiny clocks and crystal chandeliers. Once, when Sarah was examining the doll house's library where two figures were hunched over a chess game which was just about to be won, Pete had always said, on the twenty-second move, Pete told Sarah that she had pretty eyes. She had moved away from him immediately. She had closed her eyes. In another room, with the other guests, she had talked about the end of summer.

On that night, at the end of summer, the night of the accident, Sarah was still talking as they passed the Salts' house. She was talking about Venice. She and Tommy had been there once. They had drunk in the Plaza and listened to the orchestras. Sarah quoted D. H. Lawrence on Venice . . . "Abhorrent green and slippery city . . ." But she and Tommy had liked Venice. They drank standing up at little bars. Sarah had had a cold and she drank grappa and the cold had disappeared for the rest of her life.

After the Salts' house, the road swerved north and became very dark. There were no lights, no houses for several miles. There were stone walls, an orchard of sickly peach trees, a cider mill. There was St. James Episcopal Church where Tommy took their daughter, Martha, to Sunday School. The Sunday School was highly fundamental. There were many arguments among the children and their teachers as to the correct interpretation of Bible Story favorites. For example, when Lazarus rose from the dead, was he still sick? Martha liked the fervor at St. James. Each week, her dinner graces were becoming more impassioned and fantastic. Martha was seven.

Each Sunday, Tommy takes Martha to her little classes at St. James. Sarah can imagine the child sitting there at a low table with her jars of colors. Tommy doesn't go to church himself and Martha's classes are two hours long. Sarah doesn't know where Tommy goes. She suspects he is seeing someone. When they come home on Sundays, Tommy is sleek, exhilarated. The three of them sit down to the dinner Sarah has prepared.

Over the years, Sarah suspects, Tommy has floated to the surface of her. They are swimmers now, far apart, on the top of the sea.

Sarah at last fell silent. The road seemed endless as in a dream. They seemed to be slowing down. She could not feel her foot on the accelerator. She could not feel her hands on the wheel. Her mind was an untidy cupboard filled with shining bottles. The road was dark and silvery and straight. In the space ahead of her, there seemed to be something. It beckoned, glittering. Sarah's mind cleared a little. She saw Martha with her hair cut oddly short, Sarah gently nibbled on the inside of her mouth to keep alert. She saw Tommy choosing a succession of houses, examining the plaster, the floorboards, the fireplaces, deciding where windows should be placed, walls knocked down. She saw herself taking curtains down from a window so that there would be a better view of the sea. The curtains knocked her glass from the sill and it shattered. The sea was white and flat. It did not command her to change her life. It demanded of her, nothing. She saw Martha sleeping, her paint-smudged fingers curled. She saw Tommy in the city with a woman, riding in a cab. The woman wore a short fur jacket and Tommy stroked it as he spoke. She saw a figure in the road ahead, its arms raised before its face as though to block out the sight of her. The figure was a boy who wore dark clothing, but his hair was bright, his face was shining. She saw her car leap forward and run him down where he stood.

Tommy had taken responsibility for the accident. He had told the police he was driving. The boy apparently had been hitchhiking and had stepped out into the road. At the autopsy, traces of a hallucinogen were found in the boy's system. The boy was fifteen years old and his name was Stevie Bettencourt. No charges were filed.

"My wife," Tommy told the police, "was not feeling well. My wife," Tommy said, "was in the passenger seat."

Sarah stopped drinking immediately after the accident. She felt nauseous much of the time. She slept poorly. Her hands hurt her. The bones in her hands ached. She remembered that this was the way she felt the last time she had stopped drinking. It had been two years before. She remembered why she had stopped and she remembered why she had started again. She had stopped because she had done a cruel thing to her little Martha. It was spring and she and Tommy were giving a dinner party. Sarah had two martinis in the late afternoon when she was preparing dinner and then she had two more martinis with her guests. Martha had come downstairs to say a polite good-night to everyone as she had been taught. She had put on her nightie and brushed her teeth. Sarah poured a little more gin in her glass and went upstairs with her to brush out her hair and put her to bed. Martha had long, thick blonde hair of which she was very proud. On that night she wore it in a pony tail secured by an elasticized holder with two small colored balls on the end.

Sarah's fingers were clumsy and she could not get it off without pulling Martha's hair and making her cry. She got a pair of scissors and carefully began snipping at the stubborn elastic. The scissors were large, like shears, and they had been difficult to handle. A foot of Martha's gathered hair had abruptly fallen to the floor. Sarah remembered trying to pat it back into place on the child's head.

So Sarah had stopped drinking the first time. She did not feel renewed. She felt exhausted and wary. She read and cooked. She realized how little she and Tommy had to talk about. Tommy drank Scotch when he talked to her at night. Sometimes Sarah would silently count as he spoke to see how long the words took. When he was away and he telephoned her, she could hear the ice tinkling in the glass. She loved him.

Tommy was in the city four days a week. He often changed hotels. He would bring Martha little bars of soap wrapped in the different colored papers of the hotels. Martha's drawers were full of the soaps scenting her clothes. When Tommy came home on the weekends he would work on the house and they would give parties at which Tommy was charming. Tommy had a talent for holding his liquor and for buying old houses, restoring them and selling them for three times what he had paid for them. Tommy and Sarah had moved six times in eleven years. All their homes had been fine old houses in excellent locations two or three hours from New York. Sarah would stay in the country while Tommy worked in the city. Sarah did not know her way around New York.

For three weeks, Sarah did not drink. Then it was her birthday. Tommy gave her a slim gold necklace and fastened it around her neck. He wanted her to come to New York with him, to have dinner, see a play, spend the night with him in the fine suite the company had given him at the hotel. They had got a baby-sitter for Martha, a marvelous woman who polished the silver in the afternoon when Martha napped. Sarah drove. Tommy had never cared for driving. His hand rested on her thigh. Occasionally, he would slip his hand beneath her skirt. Sarah was sick with the thought that this was the way he touched other women.

By the time they were in Manhattan, they were arguing. They had been married for eleven years. Both had had brief marriages before. They could argue about anything. In midtown, Tommy stormed out of the car as Sarah braked for a light. He took his suitcase and disappeared.

Sarah drove carefully for many blocks. When she had the opportunity, she would pull to the curb and ask someone how to get to Connecticut. No one seemed to know. Sarah thought she was probably phrasing the question poorly but she didn't know how else to present it. After half an hour, she made her way back to the hotel where Tommy was staying. The doorman parked the car and she went into the lobby. She looked into the hotel bar and saw Tommy in the dimness, sitting at a small table. He jumped up and kissed her passionately. He rubbed his hands up and down her sides. "Darling, darling," he said, "I want you to have a happy birthday."

Tommy ordered drinks for both of them. Sarah sipped hers slowly at first but then she drank it and he ordered others. The bar was subdued. There was a piano player who sang about the lord of the dance. The words seemed like those of a hymn. The hymn made her sad but she laughed. Tommy spoke to her urgently and gaily about little things. They laughed together like they had when they were first married. They had always drunk a lot together then and fallen asleep, comfortably and lovingly entwined on white sheets.

They went to their room to change for the theater. The maid had turned back the beds. There was a fresh rose in a bud vase on the writing desk. They had another drink in the room and got undressed. Sarah awoke the next morning curled up on the floor with the bedspread tangled around her. Her mouth was sore. There was a bruise on her leg. The television set was on with no sound. The room was a mess although Sarah could see that nothing had been really damaged. She stared at the television where black-backed gulls were dive-bombing on terrified and doomed cygnets in a documentary about swans. Sarah crept into the bathroom and turned on the shower. She sat in the tub while the water beat upon her. Pinned to the outside of the shower curtain was a note from Tommy who had gone to work. "Darling," the note said, "we had a *good* time on your birthday. I can't say I'm sorry we never got out. I'll call you for lunch. Love."

Sarah turned the note inward until the water made the writing illegible. When the phone rang just before noon, she did not answer it.

There is a certain type of conversation one hears only when one is drunk and it is like a dream, full of humor and threat and significance, deep significance. And the way one witnesses things when one is drunk is different as well. It is like putting a face mask against the surface of the sea and looking into things, into their baffled and guileless hearts.

When Sarah had been a drinker, she felt that she had a fundamental and inventive grasp of situations, but now that she drank no longer, she found herself in the midst of a great and impenetrable silence which she could in no way interpret.

It was a small village. Many of the people who lived there did not even own cars. The demands of life were easily met in the village and it was pretty there besides. It was divided between those who always lived there and who owned fishing boats and restaurants and the city people who had more recently discovered the area as a summer place and winter weekend investment. On the weekends, the New Yorkers would come up with their houseguests and their pâté and cheeses and build fires and go cross-country skiing. Tommy came home to Sarah on weekends. They did things together. They agreed on where to go. During the week she was on her own.

Once, alone, she saw a helicopter carrying a tree in a sling across the sound. The wealthy could afford to leave nothing behind.

Once, with the rest of the town, she saw five boats burning in their storage shrouds. Each summer resort has its winter pyromaniac.

Sarah did not read any more. Her eyes hurt when she read and her hands ached all the time. During the week, she marketed and walked and cared for Martha.

It was three months after Stevie Bettencourt was killed when his mother visited Sarah. She came to the door and knocked on it and Sarah let her in.

Genevieve Bettencourt was a woman Sarah's age although she looked rather younger. She had been divorced almost from the day that Stevie was born. She had another son named Bruce who lived with his father in Nova Scotia. She had an old powder-blue Buick parked on the street before Sarah's house. The Buick had one white door.

The two women sat in Sarah's handsome, sunny living room. It was very calm, very peculiar, almost thrilling. Genevieve looked all around the room. Off the living room were the bedrooms. The door to Sarah's and Tommy's was closed but Martha's door was open. She had a little hanging garden against the window. She had a hamster in a cage. She had an enormous bookcase filled with dolls and books.

Genevieve said to Sarah, "That room wasn't there before. This used to be a lobster pound. I know a great deal about this town. People like you have nothing to do with what I know about this town. Do you remember the way things were, ever?"

"No," Sarah said.

Genevieve sighed. "Does your daughter look like you or your husband?"

"No one's ever told me she looked like me," Sarah said quietly.

On the glass-topped table before them there was a little wooden sculpture cutout that Tommy had bought. A man and woman sat on a park bench. Each wore a startled and ambiguous expression. Each had a terrier on the end of a string. The dogs were a puzzle. One fit on top of the other. Sarah was embarrassed about it being there. Tommy had put it on the table during the weekend and Sarah hadn't moved it. Genevieve didn't touch it.

"I did not want my life to know you," Genevieve said. She removed a hair from the front of her white blouse and dropped it to the floor. She looked out the window at the sun. The floor was of a very light and varnished pine. Sarah could see the hair upon it.

"I'm so sorry," Sarah said. "I'm so very, very sorry." She stretched her neck and put her head back. She looked as though she were choking.

"Stevie was a mixed-up boy," Genevieve said. "They threw him off the basketball team. He took pills. He had bad friends. He didn't study and he got a D in geometry and they wouldn't let him play basketball."

She got up and wandered around the room. She wore green rubber boots, dirty jeans and a beautiful, hand-knit sweater. "I once bought all my fish here," she said. "The O'Malleys owned it. There were practically no windows. Just narrow high ones over the tanks. Now it's all windows, isn't it? Don't you feel exposed?"

"No, I . . ." Sarah began. "There are drapes," she said.

"Off to the side, where you have your garden, there are whale bones if you dig deep enough. I can tell you a lot about this town."

"My husband wants to move," Sarah said.

"I can understand that, but you're the real drinker, after all, aren't you, not him."

"I don't drink any more," Sarah said. She looked at the woman dizzily.

Genevieve was not pretty but she had a clear, strong face. She sat down on the opposite side of the room. "I guess I would like something," she said. "A glass of water." Sarah went to the kitchen and poured a glass of Vichy for them both. Her hands shook.

"We are not strangers to one another," Genevieve said. "We could be friends."

"My first husband always wanted to be friends with my second husband," Sarah said after a moment. "I could never understand it." This had somehow seemed analogous when she was saying it but now it did not. "It is not appropriate that we be friends," she said.

Genevieve continued to sit and talk. Sarah found herself concentrating desperately on her articulate, one-sided conversation. She suspected that the words Genevieve was using were codes for other words, terrible words. Genevieve spoke thoughtlessly, dispassionately, with erratic flourishes of language. Sarah couldn't believe that they were chatting about food, men, the red clouds massed above the sea.

"I have a friend who is a designer," Genevieve said. "She hopes to make a great deal of money someday. Her work has completely altered her perceptions. Every time she looks at a view, she thinks of sheets. 'Take out those mountains,' she will say, 'lighten that cloud a bit and it would make a great sheet.' When she looks at the sky, she thinks of lingerie. Now when I look at the sky, I think of earlier times, happier times when I looked at the sky. I have never been in love, have you?"

"Yes," Sarah said, "I'm in love."

"It's not a lucky thing, you know, to be in love."

There was a soft scuffling at the door and Martha came in. "Hello," she said. "School was good today. I'm hungry."

"Hello, dear," Genevieve said. To Sarah, she said, "Perhaps we can have lunch sometime."

"Who is that?" Martha asked Sarah after Genevieve had left.

"A neighbor," Sarah said, "one of Mommy's friends."

When Sarah told Tommy about Genevieve coming to visit her, he said, "It's harassment. It can be stopped."

It was Sunday morning. They had just finished breakfast and Tommy and Martha were drying the silver and putting it away. Martha was wearing her church-school clothes and she was singing a song she had learned the Sunday before.

". . . I'm going to the Mansion on the Happy Days' Express . . ." she sang.

Tommy squeezed Martha's shoulders. "Go get your coat, sweetie," he said. When the child had gone, he said to Sarah, "Don't speak to this woman. Don't allow it to happen again."

"We didn't talk about that."

"What else could you talk about? It's weird."

"No one talks about that. No one, ever."

Tommy was wearing a corduroy suit and a tie Sarah had never seen before. Sarah looked at the pattern in the tie. It was random and bright.

"Are you having an affair?" Sarah asked.

"No," he said easily. "I don't understand you, Sarah. I've done everything I could to protect you, to help you straighten yourself out. It was a terrible thing but it's over. You have to get over it. Now, just don't see her again. There's no way that she can cause trouble if you don't speak to her."

Sarah stopped looking at Tommy's tie. She moved her eyes to the potatoes she had peeled and put in a bowl of water.

Martha came into the kitchen and held on to her father's leg. Her hair was long and thick, but it was getting darker. It was as though it had never been cut.

After they left, Sarah put the roast in the oven and went into the living room. The large window was full of the day, a colorless windy day without birds. Sarah sat on the floor and ran her fingers across the smooth, varnished wood. Beneath the expensive flooring was cold cement. Tanks had once lined the walls. Lobsters had crept back and forth across the mossy glass. The phone rang. Sarah didn't look at it, suspecting it was Genevieve. Then she picked it up.

"Hello," said Genevieve, "I thought I might drop by. It's a bleak day, isn't it. Cold. Is your family at home?"

"They go out on Sunday," Sarah said. "It gives me time to think. They go to church."

"What do you think about?" The woman's voice seemed far away. Sarah strained to hear her.

"I'm supposed to cook dinner. When they come back we eat dinner."

"I can prepare clams in forty-three different ways," Genevieve said.

"This is a roast. A roast pork."

"Well, may I come over?"

"All right," Sarah said.

She continued to sit on the floor, waiting for Genevieve, looking at the water beneath the sky. The water on the horizon was a wide, satin ribbon. She wished that she had the courage to swim on such a bitter, winter day. To swim far out and rest, to hesitate and then to return. Her life was dark, unexplored. Her abstinence had drained her. She felt sluggish, robbed. Her body had no freedom.

She sat, seeing nothing, the terrible calm light of the day around her. The things she remembered were so far away, bathed in a different light. Her life seemed so remote to her. She had sought happiness in someone, knowing she could not find it in herself and now her heart was strangely hard. She rubbed her head with her hands.

Her life with Tommy was broken, irreparable. Her life with him was over. His infidelities kept getting mixed up in her mind with the death of the boy, with Tommy's false admission that he had been driving when the boy died. Sarah couldn't understand anything. Her life seemed so random, so needlessly constructed and now threatened in a way which did not interest her.

"Hello," Genevieve called. She had opened the front door and was standing in the hall. "You didn't hear my knock."

Sarah got up. She was to entertain this woman. She felt anxious, adulterous. The cold rose from Genevieve's skin and hair. Sarah took her coat and hung it in the closet. The fresh cold smell lingered on her hands. She found herself staring at her hands as though they were predatory animals.

Sarah moved into the kitchen. She took a package of rolls out of the freezer.

"Does your little girl like church?" Genevieve asked.

"Yes, very much."

"It's a stage," said Genevieve. "I'm Catholic myself. As a child, I used to be fascinated by the martyrs. I remember a picture of St. Lucy, carrying her eyes like a plate of eggs, and St. Agatha. She carried her breasts on a plate."

Sarah said, "I don't understand what we're talking about. I know you're just using these words, that they mean other words, I . . ."

"Perhaps we could take your little girl to a movie sometime, a matinee, after she gets out of school."

"Her name is Martha," Sarah said. She saw Martha grown up, her hair cut short once more, taking rolls out of the freezer, waiting.

"Martha, yes," Genevieve said. "Have you wanted more children?"

"No," Sarah said. Their conversation was illegal, unspeakable. Sarah couldn't imagine it ever ending. Her fingers tapped against the ice-cube trays. "Would you care for a drink?"

"A very tall glass of vermouth," Genevieve said. She was looking at a little picture Martha had made, that Sarah had tacked to the wall. It was a very badly drawn horse. "I wanted children. I wanted to fulfill myself. One can never fulfill oneself. I think it is an impossibility."

Sarah made Genevieve's drink very slowly. She did not make one for herself.

"When Stevie was Martha's age, he knew everything about whales. He kept notebooks. Once, on his birthday, I took him to the whaling museum in New Bedford." She sipped her drink. "It all goes wrong somewhere," she said. She turned her back on Sarah and went into the other room. Sarah followed her.

"There are so many phrases for 'dead,' you know," Genevieve was saying. "The kids think them up. Or they come out of wars. There was one Stevie would use for dead animals and rock stars. He'd say they'd 'bought the farm.'"

Sarah nodded. She was pulling and peeling at the nails of her hands.

"I think it's pretty creepy. A dark farm, you know. Weedy. Run-down. Broken machinery everywhere. A real job."

Sarah raised her head. "You want us to share Martha, don't you," she said. "It's only right, isn't it?"

". . . the paint blown away, acres and acres of tangled, black land, a broken shutter over the well."

Sarah lowered her head again. Her heart was cold, horrified. The reality of the two women, placed by hazard in this room, this bright functional tasteful room that Tommy had created, was being tested. Reality would resist, for days, perhaps weeks, but then it would yield. It would yield to this guest, this visitor, for whom Sarah had made room.

"Would you join me in another drink?" Genevieve asked. "Then I'll go."

"I mustn't drink," Sarah said.

"You don't forget," Genevieve said, "that's just an old saw." She went into the kitchen and poured more vermouth for herself. Sarah could smell the meat cooking. From another room, the clock chimed.

"You must come to my home soon," Genevieve said. She did not sit down. Sarah looked at the pale green liquid in the glass.

"Yes," Sarah said, "soon."

"We must not greet one another on the street, however. People are quick to gossip."

"Yes," Sarah said. "They would condemn us." She looked heavily at Genevieve, full of misery and submission.

There was knocking on the door. "Sarah," Tommy's voice called, "why is the door locked?" She could see his dark head at the window.

"I must have thrown the bolt," Genevieve said. "It's best to lock your house in winter, you know. It's the kids mostly. They get bored. Stevie was a robber once or twice, I'm sure." She put down her glass, took her coat from the closet and went out. Sarah heard Martha say, "That's Mommy's friend."

Tommy stood in the doorway and stared at Sarah. "Why did you lock the door?" he asked again.

Sarah imagined seeing herself, naked. She said, "There are robbers."

Tommy said, "If you don't feel safe here, we'll move. I've been looking at a wonderful place about twenty miles from here, on a cove. It only needs a little work. It will give us more room. There's a barn, some fence. Martha could have a horse."

Sarah looked at him with an intent, halted expression, as though she were listening to a dialogue no one present was engaged in. Finally, she said, "There are robbers. Everything has changed."

A Reasonable Man

ANN BEATTIE

(1947–)

She is waiting for the telephone to ring. It has not rung for at least six days, which is most unusual. Usually there would be a wrong number, or some sort of salesman trying to sell something she has never considered buying or that she did not know existed. In fact, it might be more than six days. At first she may not have been conscious that the phone was not ringing. You don't notice something being absent for a day or two: a mislaid pen, clouds. It may well not have rung for quite some time.

She tells the man this at dinner, remarking on how unusual it is. The man likes to know exactly why she mentions things because he often cannot follow her. So she is in the habit, now, of mentioning something and commenting on it, explaining why she mentioned it at all. Of course, this is often more trouble than it's worth, so their dinners are sometimes silent from beginning to end. They are good dinners. She is competent in that area. A home economics major, she fixes dinners that are not only good to eat, but balanced and nutritious. They rarely have colds. They have never had a major illness. Tonight they eat cream of asparagus soup, a salad of beans and pears on chopped lettuce, broiled chicken with mushrooms, a glass of white wine and baked custard.

"For heaven's sake," the man says. "It might have rung when you were out getting groceries. If you had been downstairs, it might have rung and you wouldn't have heard it." He raises a single green bean to his lips. She smiles at him. He chews swallows and smiles. Everything he says is logical. She follows perfectly. She does not believe that the phone rang when she was out buying groceries, and anyway, she bought groceries three days ago. She was not downstairs today, or yesterday. She frowns. Did she go down there yesterday? He lifts another piece of food to his mouth. He notices that she is frowning. "You see that, don't you?" he says. Of course. She understands everything the man says.

The phone has not rung for seven days—assuming that it will not ring tonight. In a novel she is very fond of the main character tries to bring on her period by sleeping in white, on fresh bed sheets. She tries to think what she could do to make the phone ring. Perhaps make love to the man. That may be a little difficult, though, because he is still at a meeting and will be tired and hungry when he comes home. She will feed him and then seduce him. Another thing she might try, if this doesn't work, is showering.

The man comes home. He looks as though he has been in a windstorm. He confirms that it is very windy out. "Look," he says, pointing her toward the kitchen window. Leaves that they did not rake up during the winter blow across the yard. She is so glad! Usually her procrastination results in nothing good, but there are the leaves, blowing through the air and across the grass, which is already turning green.

"Didn't you go out today?" the man asks.

"No. I didn't go anywhere. I didn't have anywhere to go."

"But you went out yesterday, I presume."

"Yesterday?" (She is not a good liar.)

He nods again.

"I don't think I went out yesterday. No."

He sighs heavily. Seducing him will not be easy.

He brightens a bit at the table when she serves him marinated herring. He likes fish very much. The main course is beef stew, which he also seems to enjoy. They have oranges for dessert, coffee with milk.

"Tomorrow I guess you'll be going out to do some errands," he says. "Would you take my gray suit to the cleaners, please?"

"Certainly," she says. She will tell him that she forgot. That will work for one day. But the day after tomorrow she will have to go to the cleaners. That might not be so bad: the phone might ring tomorrow, and then the next day she would have no reason to wait home because the phone would have rung recently. She smiles.

"Aren't you going to answer me?" he says.

"I did answer. I said I would."

He looks at her blankly. His eyes are blank, but his mouth is a little tight.

"I didn't hear you," he says, with syrupy graciousness.

She thinks that she, too, might have a hearing problem. After dinner, alone in the kitchen, she puts down the dish-towel and goes to the phone, puts her ear against it. Shouldn't it hum like the refrigerator when it isn't ringing? There is always some slight noise, isn't there? She's had insomnia in the past and felt as though there were a war going on in the house, it was so noisy. The faint hum of electrical appliances, the glow in the little box in back of the television when it's not on. There must be something wrong with her hearing, or with the phone.

The next day she goes to the cleaners. There's a way to make the phone ring! Go out and leave it and surely it will ring in the empty house. She is not as happy as she might be about this, though, for the obvious reason that she will not have the satisfaction of hearing the phone. Driving home, she tries to remember the last phone conversation she had. She can't. It might have been with her neighbor, or with some salesman . . . a relative? If she kept a journal, she could check on this. Maybe now is the time to keep a journal. That way she could just flip back through the pages and check on details she has forgotten. She parks the car and goes into a drugstore and buys a blue tablet—actually it is called a theme book—and a special pen to write with: a black fountain pen, and a bottle of ink. She has to go back for the ink. She has never thought things through. At vacation time the man would stand at the front door saying, "Do you have beach shoes? Did you bring our toothbrushes? What about a hat for the sun? I know you brought suntan lotion, but what about Solarcaine?" She would run to her closet, to the bathroom, take down hat-boxes, reopen her suitcase. "And Robby's raft—did you put that in the trunk?" Yes. She always thought a lot about Robby. He always had the correct clothes packed, his favorite toys included, comics to read in the car. She took very good care of Robby. She does not quite understand why he must live with his grandmother. Of all of them, she took the best care of Robby. She *does* understand why he is with the man's mother, but she does not like it, or want to accept it. She has been very honest with the man, has told him her feelings about this, and has not been converted to his way of thinking. She never did anything to Robby. He agrees with this. And she does not see why she can't have him. There they disagree. They disagree, and the man has not made love to her for months—as long as the disagreement has gone on.

She is so frustrated. Filling the pen is harder than she thought—to do it carefully, making sure not to spill the ink or put too much in. And what details, exactly, should she write down? What if she wanted to remember the times she went to the bathroom the day before? Should she include everything? It would take too long. And it would seem silly to write down the times she went to the bathroom. The journal is to make her feel better. What would be the point of flipping back through her journal and seeing things that would embarrass her? There are enough things that embarrass her around the house. All the bowls that the man likes so much are a tiny bit lopsided. He agrees with her there, but says no value should be placed on a perfect bowl. Once he became very excited and told her there was no such thing as perfection—it was all in the eye of the beholder. He went on to talk about molecules; fast, constantly moving molecules that exist in all things. She is afraid of the bowls now, and doesn't dust them. He wants her to dust them—to take pride in them. He talks and talks about the negative value of "perfection." He put the word in quotes. This, he explained, was because he, himself, did not think in those terms, but it was a convenient word. He left the note on the door one morning before leaving for work, and she found it when she went into the kitchen. She asked about it. It is established that they can ask about anything. Anything at all. And that the other has to answer. She would like to ask him if he has had the phone disconnected. She can ask, but she is frightened to.

The man's mother pays for her to take the crafts classes. In the summer, June through August, they spun the bowls (they could have made vases, plates, but she stuck with bowls); September through November they learned macramé, and for Christmas she gave all of it away—a useless tangle of knots. She had no plants to hang in them, and she did not want them hung on her walls. She likes plain walls. The one Seurat is enough. She likes to look at the walls and think. For the past four months they have been making silver jewelry. She is getting worse at things instead of better. Fatigue at having been at it so long, perhaps, or perhaps what she said to her teacher, which her teacher denied: that she is just too old, that her imagination is insufficient, that her touch is not delicate enough. She is used to handling large things: plates, vacuums. She has no feel for the delicate fibers of silver. Her teacher told her that she certainly *did*. He wears one of the rings she made—bought it from her and wears it to every class. She is flattered, although she has no way of knowing whether he is wearing it out of class. Like the garish orange pin Robby selected for her in the dime store, his gift to her for her birthday. He was four years old, and naturally the bright orange pin caught his eye. She wore it to the PTA meeting, on her coat, to show him how much she liked it. She took it off in the car and put it back on before coming in the house—just in case the baby-sitter had failed and he was still awake. Now, however, she would never consider taking off the pin. She wears it every day. It's as automatic as combing her hair. She's as used to seeing it on her blouse or dress as she is to waiting for the phone to ring.

The man says it is remarkable that they always have such good meals when she shops so seldom. She went out two days ago to the cleaners, and she showed him the stub, so he knows this, but he is still subtly criticizing her failure to go out every day. She gets tired of going out. She has to go to crafts classes Thursday, Friday and Saturday nights, and on Sunday she has to go to his mother's house. She says this to him by way of argument, but actually she *loves* to go to his mother's house. It is the best day of the week. She does not love, or even like, his mother, but she can be with Robby from afternoon until his bedtime. They can throw the ball back and forth on the front lawn (who cares if they spy on them through the window?), and she can brush his hair (she cuts it too short! Just a little longer. He's so beautiful that the short hair doesn't make him ugly, but he would be even more beautiful if it could grow an inch on the sides, on the top). He gives her pictures he has colored. He thinks that kindergarten should be more sophisticated and is a little embarrassed about the pictures, but he explains that he has to do what the teacher says. She nods. If he were older, she could explain that she *had* to make the bowls. He rebels by drawing sloppily, sometimes. "I didn't even try on that one," he says. She knows what he means. She says—as the man says to her about the bowls, as the crafts instructor says—that they are still beautiful. He likes that. He gives them all to her. There is not even one tacked up in his grandmother's kitchen. There are none on her walls, either, but she looks through the pile on the coffee table every day. She prefers the walls blank. When he comes with Grandma to visit, which hardly ever happens, she puts them up if she knows he's coming or points to the pile to show him that she has them close-by to examine. She never did anything to Robby, not one single thing. She argues and argues with the man about this. He goes to business meetings at night and comes home late. He does not fully enjoy the meals she prepares because he is so tired. This he denies. He says he does fully enjoy them. What can she say? How can you prove that someone is not savoring sweet-potato soufflé?

"How *do* you cook such delicious things when you shop so seldom?" he asks.

"I don't shop that infrequently," she says.

"Don't vegetables . . . I mean, aren't they very perishable?"

"No," she says. She smiles sweetly.

"You always have fresh vegetables, don't you?"

"Sometimes I buy them fresh and parboil them myself. Later I steam them."

"Ah," he says. He does not know exactly what she is talking about.

"Today I was out for a walk," she says. No way he can prove she wasn't.

"It's a late spring," he says. "But today it was very nice, actually."

They are having a civilized discussion. Perhaps she can lure him into bed. Perhaps if that works, the phone will also ring. Hasn't he noticed that it doesn't ring at night, that it hasn't for nights? That's unusual, too. She would ask what he makes of this, but talking about the phone makes him angry, and if he's angry, he'll never get into bed. She fingers her pin. He sees her do it. A mistake. It reminds him of Robby.

She sips her wine and thinks about their summer vacation—the one they already took. She can remember so little about the summer. She will not remember the spring if she doesn't get busy and write in her book. What, exactly, should she write? She thinks the book should contain feelings instead of just facts. Surely that would be less boring to do. Well, she was going to write something during the afternoon, but she was feeling blue, and worried—about the telephone—and it wouldn't cheer her up to go back and read about feeling blue and being worried. Her crafts teacher had given her a book of poetry to read: *Winter Trees* by Sylvia Plath. It was interesting. She was certainly interested in it, but it depressed her. She didn't go out of the house for days. Finally—she is glad she can remember clearly some details—he asked her to go to the cleaners and she went out. She did several errands that day. What was the weather like, though? Or does it really matter? She corrects herself: it does matter. It matters very much what season it is, whether the weather is typical or unusual. If you have something to say about the weather, you will always be able to make conversation with people, and communicating is very important. Even for yourself: you should know that you feel blue because the weather is cold or rainy, happy because it's a sunny day with high clouds. Tonight she feels blue. Probably it is cold out. She would ask, but she has already lied that she was out. It might have turned cold, however.

"I was out quite early," she says. "What was the weather like when you came home?"

"Ah," he says. "I called this morning."

She looks up at him, suddenly. He sees her surprise, knows she wasn't out.

"Just to say that I loved you," he says.

He smiles. It is not worth seducing him to make the phone ring. She will shower, wash her hair, stand there a long time, hoping, but she won't make love to the man. He is a rotten liar.

In the morning, when he is gone, she finds that she remembers her feelings of the night before exactly, and writes them down, at length, in the book.

On Friday night he no longer picks her up after crafts class. He has joined a stock club, and he has a meeting that night. The bus stop is only a block from where the class meets; it lets her off five minutes from where she lives. It is unnecessary for the man ever to pick her up. But he says that the streets are dangerous at night, and that she must be tired. She says that the bus ride refreshes her. She likes riding buses, looking at the people. There is good bus service. He smiles. But it is not necessary to ride them; and the streets are dangerous at night.

Tonight her instructor asks to speak to her when the class has ended. She has no interest in the thin silver filaments she is working with and says he can talk to her now. "No," he says. "Later is fine."

She remains when the others have left. The others are all younger than she, with one exception: a busty grandmother who is learning crafts hoping to ease her arthritis. The others are in their teens or early twenties. They have long hair and wear Earth shoes and are unfriendly. They are intense. Perhaps that's what it is. They don't talk because they're intense. They walk (so the ads for these shoes say) feeling clouds beneath them, their spines perfectly and comfortably straight, totally relaxed and enjoying their intensity. Their intensity results in delicate necklaces, highly glazed bowls—some with deer and trees, others with Mister Moon smiling. All but three are women.

When they have all left, he opens a door to a room at the back of the classroom. It opens into a tiny room, where there is a mattress on the floor, covered with a plaid blanket, two pairs of tennis shoes aligned with it, and a high, narrow bookcase between the pipe and window. He wants to know what she thought of the Sylvia Plath book. She says that it depressed her. That seems to be the right response, the one that gets his head nodding—he always nods when he looks over her shoulder. He told her in November that he admired her wanting to perfect her bowls—her not moving on just to move on to something else. They nod at each other. In the classroom they whisper so as not to disturb anyone's intensity. It is strange now to speak to him in a normal tone of voice. When she sees her son, now, she also whispers. That annoys the man and his mother. What does she have to say to him that they can't all hear? They are noisy when they play, but when they are in the house—in his room, or when she is pouring him some juice from the refrigerator—she will kneel and whisper. A gentle sound, like deer in the woods. She made the bowl with the deer on it, gave it to the instructor because he was so delighted with it. He was very appreciative. He said that he meant for her to keep the book. But he would lend her another. Or two: *The Death Notebooks* and *A Vision.* The instructor puts his foot on the edge of the second shelf to get one of the books down from the top. She is afraid he will fall, stands closer to him, behind him, in case he does. She has a notion of softening his fall. He does not fall. He hands her the books. The instructor knows all about her, she is sure. The man's mother visited his studio before she suggested, firmly, that she enroll. The man's mother was charmed by the instructor. Imagine what she must have said to him about her. From the first, he was kind to her. When he gave her *Winter Trees,* he somehow got across the idea to her that many women felt enraged—sad and enraged. He said a few things to her that impressed her at the time. If only she had had the notebook then, she could have written them down, reread them.

He boils water in a pan for tea. She admires the blue jar he spoons the tea out of. He made it. Similarly, he admires her work. She sees that her bowl holds some oranges and bananas. She would like to ask what false or unfair things the man's mother said about her. That would cast a pall over things, though. The instructor would feel uncomfortable. It is not right to blurt out everything you feel like saying. People don't live like that in society. Talk about something neutral. Talk about the weather. She says to the instructor what the man always says to her: it is a late spring. She says more: she is keeping a journal. He asks again—the third time?—whether she writes poetry. She says, truthfully, that she does not. He shows her a box full of papers that he doodled on, wrote on, the semester he dropped out of Stanford. The doodles are very complex, heavily inked. The writing is sloppy, in big letters that were written with a heavy black pen. She understands from reading a little that he was unhappy when he dropped out of Stanford. He says that writing things down helps. Expressing yourself helps. Her attention drifts. When she concentrates again, he is saying the opposite: she must feel these classes are unpleasant, having been sentenced to them; all those books—he gestures to the bookcase—were written by unhappy people, and it's doubtful if writing them made them any happier. Not Sylvia Plath, certainly. He tells her that she should not feel obliged to act nicely, feel happy. He thumps his hand on the books he has just given her.

She tells him that the phone never rings anymore. She tells him that last, after the story about the summer vacation, how she and Robby set out to race through the surf, and Robby lagged behind, and she felt such incredible energy, she ran and ran. They got separated. She ran all the way to the end of the sand, to the rocks, and then back—walked back—and couldn't find Robby or the man anywhere. All the beach umbrellas looked the same, and so did the people. What exactly did Robby look like? Or the man? The man looked furious. He found her, came back for her in his slacks and shirt, having taken Robby back to the motel. His shoes were caked with wet sand, his face was furious. She is not sure how to connect this to what she really wants to talk about, the inexplicably silent telephone.

AUTHOR INDEX

TITLE INDEX